Susan Sallis is now firmly established as one of the most successful writers of engaging family sagas. Her novels include the Rising family sequence, *Summer Visitors, By Sun and Candlelight, An Ordinary Woman, Daughters of the Moon, Sweeter Than Wine, Water Under the Bridge, Touched by Angels, Choices, Come Rain or Shine, The Keys to the Garden* and *The Apple Barrel*. She lives in Clevedon, Somerset.

T0316378

www.booksattransworld.co.uk

Also by Susan Sallis

RISING SEQUENCE:
A SCATTERING OF DAISIES
THE DAFFODILS OF NEWENT
BLUEBELL WINDOWS
ROSEMARY FOR REMEMBRANCE

SUMMER VISITORS
BY SUN AND CANDLELIGHT
AN ORDINARY WOMAN
DAUGHTERS OF THE MOON
SWEETER THAN WINE
WATER UNDER THE BRIDGE
TOUCHED BY ANGELS
CHOICES
COME RAIN OR SHINE
THEY KEYS TO THE GARDEN
THE APPLE BARREL

and published by Corgi books

A SCATTERING
OF DAISIES

and

THE DAFFODILS
OF NEWENT

Susan Sallis

CORGI BOOKS

A SCATTERING OF DAISIES and THE DAFFODILS OF NEWENT
A CORGI BOOK : 0 552 14981 0

This edition first published by Corgi Books 2002
Copyright © Susan Sallis 2001

3 5 7 9 10 8 6 4 2

including

A SCATTERING OF DAISIES
Originally published in Great Britain by Corgi,
a division of Transworld Publishers
Copyright © Susan Sallis 1984

THE DAFFODILS OF NEWENT
Originally published in Great Britain by Corgi,
a division of Transworld Publishers
Copyright © Susan Sallis 1985

The right of Susan Sallis to be identified as author of
this work has been asserted in accordance with sections 77
and 78 of the Copyright Designs and Patents Act 1988.

Set in Linotype Sabon by
Phoenix Typesetting, Ilkley, West Yorkshire.

Corgi Books are published by Transworld Publishers,
61–63 Uxbridge Road, London W5 5SA,
a division of The Random House Group Ltd,
in Australia by Random House Australia (Pty) Ltd,
20 Alfred Street, Milsons Point, Sydney, NSW 2061, Australia,
in New Zealand by Random House New Zealand Ltd,
18 Poland Road, Glenfield, Auckland 10, New Zealand
and in South Africa by Random House (Pty) Ltd,
Endulini, 5a Jubilee Road, Parktown 2193, South Africa.

The Random House Group Limited supports The Forest Stewardship
Council (FSC®), the leading international forest certification organisation.
Our books carrying the FSC label are printed on FSC® certified paper.
FSC is the only forest certification scheme endorsed by the leading
environmental organisations, including Greenpeace. Our
paper procurement policy can be found at
www.randomhouse.co.uk/environment

Printed and bound in Great Britain by Clays Ltd, St Ives PLC

A SCATTERING
OF DAISIES

1

April Rising was born in 1902, well into the twentieth century, the first of Florence's children to be born into the new era. Yet Florence still dated her letters 18 . . . and then deleted the digits and started again. She wondered whether she herself should have been born sooner. There was something about writing a one and a nine at the top of her correspondence that frightened her.

The room in which April first saw the evening light, was newly oilclothed for the occasion. The wash-stand and giant clothes closet both leaned slightly outward with the sagging ceiling joists; the heavy Nottingham lace curtains, donated by Florence's Aunt Lizzie, smelled of must in spite of Florence's efforts; the ceiling flaked gently — one large whitewash petal floated in the ready chamber-pot, another in the china ewer of water on the floor beneath the matching basin above.

The rest of the house echoed the same paradox; a mixture of 'nice things' in a gently decaying setting. Number thirty-three, Chichester Street, Gloucester, amounted to a home that was just a bit more comfortable than its neighbours. All the houses in Chichester Street were rented by people who could ill afford new decorations. If their fortunes improved they would be likely to move into another house where the paint and paper might be newer. Or, just as probably, older.

Chichester Street was typical of Gloucester of that

time. The Romans had taken the city over and bridged the narrow Severn to push into Wales and their work could still be seen everywhere. The first William had recognised its strategic position and had taken the decaying monastery in hand, compiled his Domesday Book in its chapter house and set the pattern for the inland port for the next thousand years. Roman fortifications and Elizabethan dwellings crumbled together. The Parliamentary headquarters of the Civil War was hemmed in by a warehouse, and where Bishop Hooper had burned and burned and refused to die, slums festered into gypsy encampments, and every spring the Severn floods cleared the rubbish anew with its brown waters.

Chichester Street was an offshoot of one of the four roads sprouting from the Cross, the Northgate. It had been the drive and grounds of Chichester House, but that too was now owned by one of the rich merchants and let out to an impoverished cleric. The old carriageway was lined with two rows of pseudo-Regency houses, erected when the city had tried to be a spa to keep up with nearby Cheltenham. The Gloucester Coal and Coke Company had a slice of land there too, and dominated the houses with their gas container. At the top of the street, Goodrich's Dairy and the Lamb and Flag eyed each other with their bright windows. Mr. Goodrich kept bees in his garden and apple trees spread their branches over his wall. Otherwise there was little greenery. Two steps led up to each front door, flanked by a boot-scraper and a metal lid covering the entry to the coal chute and cellar. Window boxes were considered foreign. Some houses kept the privacy of their front room with a withered pot plant. The Risings used their front room for their work: Will Rising was a tailor.

The local midwife, nicknamed by Albert and March as Snotty Lottie because her year-long cold was never attended to during a lying-in, rolled April in a threadbare towel and laid her in the prepared drawer.

Satisfied with her strugglings and puny cries, she returned to Florence, holding a large meat dish, and sat on the bed to await the afterbirth.

Florence lay back exhausted, the relief from the pain and the pushing and the lump inside her making her feel so light she might have been floating above the bed. She remembered Lottie telling her it was a girl, and for that she was glad too. Her first-born had been a boy and for the first two or three years there had been certain indelicacies to be seen to. In the end he had been circumcised and Florence had wondered why it couldn't have been done immediately. She was prudish to a degree and the whole business of childbirth was a mental as well as a physical agony for her.

When she had her daily all-over wash, she dressed each part of her body before commencing on the next. Once she had caught sight of herself in the dark kitchen window, rigidly stayed from an eighteen-inch waist up, but minus drawers, petticoats and stockings as she prepared the wash cloth to deal with her lower parts. The sight had appalled her; this was surely how scarlet women must appear. She had made certain that in future she donned a petticoat and lifted it chastely on each side to wash from the hips down. To make assurance doubly sure, she got Will to fix one of the new-fangled blinds to the kitchen window though it looked out on to the high blank wall guarding the gas company's cylinder. She could not risk another reflection, which might well reveal the moment when, lower half petticoated, she scrubbed vigorously from the waist up.

She had undergone this physical and mental torture of childbirth four times now, and as she studied the ceiling, seeing in its patchiness a map of the Scandinavian peninsula, she felt not only relief at expelling the kicking lump that was April, but more relief still that surely she had done her duty and no-one would expect more of her. Four children: Albert, March and May within three short and terrible years; now April after an

9

interval of eight years. This last birth would prove she was still a dutiful wife; there would be no need for further evidence.

She felt a flutter inside her and shrank against an inexplicable return of pain. Lottie said, 'Just another little push Mrs. Rising, just one more . . .' and dragged the sleeve of her black dress across her nose before thrusting the meat dish hard beneath Florence's buttocks.

'Good. Good. Everything there?' She poked searchingly and her nose dripped. 'Think so. Couldn't be better.'

Florence sighed. 'No need of a doctor then?'

Lottie fetched paper and rolled up the contents of the meat dish.

'Five bob!' she commented scornfully. 'Five bob to stand around and do nowt. And all the hot water — he's for ever washing!'

Florence adjusted the sheet. 'Our March will see to that, Mrs. Jenner. There's a good fire down below. I told her to keep it stoked up and the two kettles on the hob.'

'Right. Righty-oh.' Lottie spoke with the same familiarity which labour and childbirth made just permissible. But that time was over. Florence tucked the sheet firmly around her waist and tightened her mouth. Lottie went to the door and bawled for March.

'And bring up the hot water now my maid!' she ordered. 'You'mgot another sister and she en't even washed yet!'

There were no sounds of jubilation. Nine-year-old March disapproved of the whole situation as much as Florence did herself, and Albert had wanted — demanded — another boy. Will had wanted a son too, but he wouldn't mind over-much because girls were helpful in the workroom. He was busy there now and hadn't even opened the door to enquire of the children what was happening. Florence sighed; she did not blame him, indeed did not want him. A local landowner

10

had recently died and Will had to alter the funeral suits of half a dozen tenant farmers. They all wanted letting out so farming couldn't be that bad. Will himself had come from Kempley just outside the city — that was how he had got the work — and had said, 'Never a farthing in their pockets, but plenty in their bellies. That's our farmers!' Florence had ignored the coarseness of this comment and asked, 'Is the work worth doing then? Shall we get paid?' And he had twinkled at her in the way that had won her heart so long ago: 'Our bellies will all be as full as yours is now my dear,' he had said. And then as she turned her head down to the button-hole she was sewing, he had pecked at her forehead remorsefully. 'Ah, Flo, you should be used to my country talk by now. And let me add, there will be plenty of goose-grease next winter for May's chest. That will please you, I'll be bound!'

They all accepted that May was her favourite. None of them minded — or so Florence thought. May, as fair as Florence was dark, but with Florence's own fragile, delicate, yet patrician beauty. May, sweet-tempered as March was sharp; as loving as Albert but without his demanding ways; with her father's easy-going nature combined with her mother's fastidiousness. May was a flaxen angel, and like an angel could disappear into another world at any time. May went into flannel drawers and petticoats in mid-September and did not come out of them until the first of June. May was rubbed with goose-grease every winter and dosed with glycerine and lemon at the first husky whisper of a cough. Where March would have protested furiously, she accepted it all with her sunny smile. Florence had overheard March once — at six years old mind you — inciting May to rebellion. 'Why don't you go upstairs — quietly — and change into your cotton cover-up? It's in the summer chest in the bandy room. I've been wearing mine since my birthday!'

'No you haven't,' May replied peaceably, skipping the issue as always.

11

Everyone would always know when March, May and April had been born, so March said angrily, 'Well, your birthday then! Go on cowardy custard. Do something for once.'

May obviously thought about it, then said, surprised, 'They only makes me wear my winter things cos' they loves me.'

'I know *that*! But if it makes you hot and stuffy, it's a pity they do love you isn't it?'

Florence waited for May's reply; she knew it would be something special as it always was. When it came she crept away and felt for her handkerchief.

'But . . .' May's voice had been ultra reasonable. 'But March . . . I loves *them*!'

Now, as Florence let Lottie wash and bind her, she took her mind away from her present circumstances, by imagining May downstairs. May would be pleased it was a girl. May would become, on the instant, the little mother. April would have a sympathetic ear always from May. In fact Florence would have to guard against the child doing too much for her new sister. Of course, March, strong and capable March, would do her share too. She could push the baby carriage which might well strain May's chest; she could also fetch the bath water and change the napkins when she was home.

The thought brought Florence back to her surroundings.

'You need not bother with the baby Mrs. Jenner,' she said, fastening her nightgown firmly over the calico breast-binding. 'March is quite capable. I've been sending her down to young Mrs. Goodrich this past month for her to help out with the new baby.'

'So I did hear. An' guessed why.' Hard work now over, Lottie fished for her handkerchief and dealt with a drip. She never actually blew into a handkerchief, merely sniffed and wiped. 'Well, you can do with all the help you can get now Mrs. Rising. Some years since you had to see to a baby and you're getting on yourself too. I did begin to wonder ... Mrs. Luker started same time as you and what was young Gladys? The eighth or ninth?'

Florence flushed. 'I haven't been in good health since May's birth.'

'No.' Lottie picked up her bag of tricks and prepared to leave, knowing she would get no confidences out of Mrs. Rising. But perhaps it was worth a last try. 'Of course Mr. Rising is a considerate man, en't he? I well remember when he arrived from the country to be prenticed to old Mr. Daker down the Barton — he was only a young shaver of thirteen then, but I allus said ... I said, That young Will, I said, That young Will Rising — he's *consid'rate*.' She liked the word. It had a ring to it. 'Consid'rate,' she repeated.

'Thank you Mrs. Jenner. Mr. Rising will pay you on the way down, if you will just knock at the workroom door —'

'Not one to pester a woman, I'd say. And not one for the public either. Mind you — ' she was in full spate so used her sleeve this time. 'Mind you, I'm not saying he don't like a glass with his neighbours. Many's the time he's bought me ...' she snuffled a laugh and sniffed vigorously, 'a cup of tea!' She winked and her head jerked sideways as if pulled by the eyelid. 'But what I mean is, he en't one to come home roaring drunk and want —'

Florence said firmly, 'Tell March to come up straightaway with more hot water for the baby, will you Mrs. Jenner?' She was longing with all her soul for a drink of tea, but if she mentioned it she would have to offer one to Lottie too. 'And again thank you. You have been so kind.'

Lottie went to the door, disappointed. She thoroughly enjoyed discussing her patients' husbands, and immediately after a lying-in was the accepted time for many intimacies.

She said, 'Well, it were a sight easier this time than last. I thought young May 'ud never come. An' if that doctor had had his way she'd have been scarred for life.'

Lottie never failed to remind Florence, and May herself, that it was her expertise that had ensured May's beauty. The doctor had actually taken the forceps from his bag when Lottie, dripping freely, had got her clawing fingers beneath May's armpit and started the spiral action of removal for which she was locally famous.

She closed the door behind her, leaving Florence shuddering at the memory. The next instant, March's clatter could be heard on the stairs. There was a metallic thump as she put the enamel pail on the step above her, doubtless splashing it over her pinafore, Florence thought with a sigh. Then the scuff of her boots as she caught it up. The stair drugget, again donated by Aunt Lizzie, was as unresilient as the old oilcloth had been and never absorbed any sound louder than the tread of the mice. And there were plenty of those. Florence sighed again; they'd have to get another cat. When the last one had died horribly from the poison put down by the Lukers, she had sworn they would never have another. But the mice were on the increase and they carried germs which might well infect delicate May. Or, of course, the new baby.

It seemed March, or some other member of the family, had forestalled her.

'Mother —' The door flew open and the bucket swung after it, followed — as if pulled by its handle — by the lanky figure of March. She plonked the bucket between her spread feet. 'Mother, guess what. We've got a kitten. She's black — all black, not a bit of white anywhere — and she's got the greenest, glassiest eyes you ever saw!'

Florence felt, for the fourth time, complete surprise that the life of the little household in Chichester Street had gone on normally, even excitingly it seemed, while she had been fighting a battle up here with only Lottie Jenner for company. Just for a second she forgot Lottie's undoubted commonness and felt a genuine closeness to her.

She said to March, 'And the kitten is far more interesting than your new baby sister I suppose?'

March glanced sideways at the drawer. There were a

14

great many nasty-looking cloths and sheets in the corner which she quickly did not look at.

'It's going to be called April I suppose?'

'She is going to be called April don't you mean?'

'Well. Is she?'

'Yes. Don't you like it?'

'It's the prettiest of all. March is just silly, nobody is called March.'

It was a perennial complaint. Florence smiled amiably, not realising how infuriatingly like May she looked.

'Then it's unusual, which is good. Distinguished. You will be the distinguished member of the family.' She put her head back, exhausted with the effort of talking. 'Now go and look at the baby, then you can wash her and bind her.' The baby must come first; she would ask for some tea afterwards.

March stared down at her sister. April was quiet now, disliking the rough towel but recognising that she had been handled and wrapped by someone who knew her business.

March said slowly, 'She isn't a bit pretty. And her hair's ginger. Like Albert's. What would you have done if she'd been born in October?'

'Called her October,' Florence said weakly but seriously. It was her whim that all her girls should be called after their birth months. It seemed to make them special, regal.

March prepared the wash-stand efficiently and lifted the baby on to it. She wished it had been called October. Then, what between its ginger hair and its ugliness, she could have loved it whole-heartedly. As it was, the musical name April must come between them.

There was a tap at the door and in came May bearing a tray beautifully laid with Mother's best china tea-cup, milk jug and teapot. Florence sat up with a cry of sheer gladness, made room for the tray, took May in her arms and wept. Dark hair mingled with gold. May said, 'Don't cry, my beautiful little mamma . . . don't cry . . .' and Florence sobbed. 'I'm crying with happiness darling. Oh I do love you.' She looked up and saw March through her tears, sleeves rolled up, nine-year-old hands red with washing, auburn-brown eyes watchful. She added, 'I do love you all — so much.'

March turned back to the baby, slid a penny into the little lint pocket she had sewn ages ago, and bound it carefully over the hideous, protruding navel. May would be the beautiful one. March would be clever; distinguished and very clever. And this one, April, what would she be? March glanced again at the pile of laundry in the corner and tried not to think how much soaking and boiling and bleaching and blue-bagging it would need. She compressed her lips. April could be the worker. April could help Father do the button-holes in the workroom, help Mother in the steamy wash-house and over the hot cooking range. April would be . . . *useful*.

Downstairs, Will Rising finished sewing the last braces button on to the last pair of expanded trousers and put them on the pile. He flexed his shoulders, dropped his neatly bearded chin on to his chest, then pointed it at the newly-lit gas lamp. He clenched his hands then stretched them, the fingers cracking and bending back slightly. 'Flexible fingers,' old Mr. Daker had said when he had looked him over in the dark little shop down the Barton. 'Flexible fingers. Necessary for a pianist. Even more necessary for a tailor!'

Will grinned at the memory, then stretched his grin into a grimace and relaxed. Another of Mr. Daker's maxims: take time to relax after a day's work. Old man Daker had stitched by hand, sitting crosslegged in the midst of his table like a tailor in a fairy story. Will had never done that. Around his cutting table there were tall stools and a comfortable chair before the treadle sewing machine. He remembered once, creeping out from beneath the Daker table where he slept, finding Mr.

Daker above him, standing on his head. 'Put yourself to extremes lad,' he had said on descending. 'Tension makes relaxing easier. To stand on the head ensures that the simplicity of standing on the feet is blissful. Sometimes even pain is worthwhile because its ending is so very good.' Will had thought of that very hard when he attended the barber's the following week to have a tooth pulled. It had worked. He wondered now whether poor Florence might have found comfort from such a simple philosophy if he'd passed it on to her. But Florence was stoical at all times. Will had quickly learned that — in a strange way — life itself meant suffering to Florence. Yet she bore it. Sometimes she almost seemed to enjoy the suffering.

He picked up the pile of trousers and carried them into the kitchen where March would help him press them tomorrow morning. By the ashy range sat Albert, clutching the new kitten. The unshaded gas mantel in the bracket above the mantelpiece spluttered. Flo would have changed that for a new one and ground the old one into silver cleaner by now. It had been a day and a half and no mistake.

Albert said, 'There's some milk left Dad. Shall we have bread and milk for supper? Or are you going to the public?'

'Might. Might not.' Will did not like committing himself. Daker had said that too. 'Don't give a customer a completion date. Not definite. Never. Never commit yourself lad.' He put the trousers on a corner of the table. 'If it's bread and milk, keep it away from these. I want to deliver them tomorrow.' He wouldn't mind popping along to the Lamb and Flag for an hour. It would be a nice change. And if Snotty Lottie was there she'd tell him more about the birth than Flo ever would. But Flo wouldn't like it. Flo didn't believe in the custom of wetting the baby's head.

'Will you be hiring a trap Dad?' Albert tried to encourage the kitten to settle around his neck like a

17

scarf. 'Can I come? I could help you take in the suits and hold the horse. And I don't mind not going to school.' He remembered a grievance. 'March didn't go today.'

'Because she had to help here. You know that. May went.'

'I could have helped here.'

'Button-holing?'

'Well . . .' he flinched as the kitten's claws dug in. Bright spots of blood appeared on his collar. 'Can I come Dad? The daffs will be out round Newent way. And the apple blossom.'

'We'll see. You'd better get that shirt off and soak it in cold water. The blood will stain.'

'March will do it,' Albert said carelessly as he nestled the kitten back into his elbow. 'She's got a load of stuff in the copper already.'

'Oh . . .' Will swallowed a curse. He had forgotten March would be fully occupied tomorrow morning with the maternity washing. 'All right,' he capitulated. 'You can come with me tomorrow. On condition you help me with the pressing first.' He cut short the boy's ecstasy. 'Can we go upstairs now? Since May came and told me it was another girl I haven't heard a thing.'

'Oh you have!' Albert looked for a twinkle in his father's blue eyes. 'Snotty Lottie came into your work-room, I heard her. She was talking for ages.'

'She wanted her florin, that was all.' Will looked disapproving. 'And what has your mother told you about using that name?' He really wouldn't mind popping in to the Lamb and Flag before closing time. From a sense of loyalty he had cut Lottie short once she'd assured him that Flo was all right and the new baby perfect; if he bought her a gin there would be no stopping her.

Albert was grinning, they both knew it was Will who had originally coined Lottie's name. 'Lottie's gottie an awful lottie snottie,' he said experimentally. The twinkle came at last. It transformed Will from a round-faced, straw-haired nonentity, into a replica of the King as seen on their Coronation tea caddy. Albert laughed raucously just as March clattered down the stairs almost hidden by the pile of linen she was carrying.

'You can go up now,' she said tersely, bundling past them on her way to the wash-house. The copper was already full of the week's normal laundry soaking in soda and ammonia before having the fire lit beneath it tomorrow morning. What she could do with this lot, she did not know. Wearily she began spreading each layer in the shallow sink, letting the cold water run through the stains. Her mother had taught her long ago the main tenet of wash day: hot water for grease, cold water for blood. She turned the mottled brass tap on full so that the water splashed her pinafore. She didn't care. If only she had thought of taking up a tray of tea . . . if only Florence had wept into her mouse-brown hair . . . if only April had been born in October.

The scene that met Will's eyes as he went into the front bedroom delighted him. For the whole of his lifetime the institution of the family had been revered, the old Queen had made certain of that. In any case Will was a natural family man; the sight of his wife, flushed, beautiful, and still, after everything she had been through, refined, was enough to stir his heart. But when she was flanked, on one side by their exquisite daughter May, and on the other by the bundle of new life, and when the whole was lit by the soft yellow glow of gas, like a scene in the Theatre Royal, then it made Will stop in the doorway, it made tears start to his eyes, it made him eventually stumble forward and kneel down by the bed to take Florence's hand and press it to his lips.

'My darling. My beautiful darling,' he mumbled, keeping his head down.

Albert said, 'I thought you said it would be a boy? It's not very pretty is it?'

May said tremulously, 'Mamma . . . Daddy's crying. He's crying!'

19

'Like me. Because he is so happy.' Florence leaned over Will's head, kissing the silky hair and pressing the sheet to his eyes with her free hand.

'I suppose you'll want to call it April?' Albert queried, embarrassed and irritable with this show of emotion. He hated tears. It was the reason he could never feel close to May; she was for ever in tears about something. Now March . . . March never cried. She had a fiery temper, but she never cried.

'Her name will be April. Yes my darling.' Florence lifted her head slightly and smiled into her son's eyes. Strange that none of her children took after her. Albert was ginger, his eyes pale blue; March a little darker with strange, transparent, tea-coloured eyes; May heavenly blonde; and now this new one, ginger again. It did not occur to her that they had all inherited her long thin frame and sharp, defined bone-structure. But she saw that in his way Albert was going to be beautiful.

Will mumbled, 'I worship you Florrie. I worship you.'

He was like another child; she could love him freely now, just like another child. There would be no more . . . indignities. He lifted his head to smile wetly at her, and, unthinkingly, she pressed him to her swollen bound bosom.

'Dear heart,' she murmured. 'Dearest heart.'

May moved around the bed and put an arm across Albert's shoulders. 'Are you crying, Albert?' she asked hopefully.

Albert shrugged, more irritable than ever. 'No. I was thinking that if this one had been before you, it would have been much more sensible.'

'Why?' she asked, surprised.

'You would have been in proper order then,' he explained. 'March, April and May.'

May thought about it and then giggled deliciously. Albert, irritability gone in the face of such appreciation, said, 'Mother should have twelve girls really, shouldn't she? January, February, March —'

'She's *got* March,' laughed May. 'And April, and May. So the next would be —'

'June,' he supplied. 'Then July —' they gabbled through the year laughing inordinately. Will said in a low voice, 'You're all right Flo? You're really all right?'

'Of course.'

'I'll have to check on that. With Snotty Lottie.'

'Oh *Will* —' but she could not resist a smile. Then the smile went. 'Does that mean you're going to the public this evening?'

'Well . . . I must make sure you're really all right before I slide in beside you tonight my darling.'

She withdrew slightly. 'I made up the other bed in Albert's room dear. For tonight.'

'It'll be all right Flo —'

'The baby will disturb you Will. And you're so busy with the suits.'

'I've finished them dearest. Albert and I will be hiring a trap from Luker tomorrow and taking the lot of them out to Newent.'

'Will — you can't keep Albert away from school —'

'Just for once Flo! Good grief, May is always away for one reason or another.'

'You know I want him to go to the King's next year. He deserves to be a chorister with his voice.'

'And go to the King's he shall. Don't worry sweetheart. Albert will be a credit to you, March will be clever, May beautiful. And I . . .' he pressed himself ardently against the calico binding. 'I will always worship you.'

'What about April?' Albert asked loudly and cockily. He had been listening to the exchange in between May's idiotic comments, and knew that he would be able to go to Newent tomorrow. 'What will April be good at?'

Florence leaned away from Will and over the sleeping baby.

'She does not need to be good at anything,' she said

21

fondly. 'She will be the youngest. The baby of the family.'

Will stood up. She was giving in about Albert so that she could win over having her bed to herself.

'I'm going to the Lamb and Flag then,' he announced. 'Take care of your mother, Albert. Some of the bread and milk might not come amiss.'

Luker was in the public bar as he had known he would be; Lottie in the snug. He fixed to hire a trap for tomorrow and answered Luker's not-very-interested enquiries for Florrie and the new baby.

'Lottie —' Luker jerked his head in the direction of the snug. 'Lottie said it was normal. I did wonder after so long. And your wife being a bit on the delicate side. Now my Hettie, you see, she's kept going Mr. Rising. She's into the swing of things as you might say.' He lowered his voice, 'Expecting again you know. December. Not everyone knows — told Lottie of course.'

Will wiped froth from his moustache. 'But the last one — Gladys wasn't it — she was only born last month surely?'

'Well, February. But, yes, this is the best yet. Ten months between them. Bit of a record, eh?'

'I should say,' Will propped his mug on the brass rail around the bar. ''Course, only eleven months between our March and May. Calls for a drink. You on stout?'

'How about a drop of whisky? For the two of them. Yours just been borned. Mine just been made.'

Will felt like a giant refreshed after the unaccustomed spirit. He borrowed Sidney Goodrich's last edition of the Citizen and scanned it knowledgeably. Since the end of the war in Africa there wasn't much news outside the county boundary that interested him. He saw that some treaty was being signed with Japan and wondered why. Presumably Mr. Balfour knew what he was doing. He turned to the Hatches, Matches and Despatches. He'd have to send Albert along to the

22

Citizen office in Saint John's Lane early tomorrow with an announcement of April's birth. He could probably make it an advertisement in part: 'Mr. William Rising, well-known tailor, and his wife, are proud to announce. . . .'

Lottie's voice spoke in his ear. 'Wetting the baby's head then Will Rising? Reckon I should have some share in the celebrations. Reckon I did my bit. Not as well as you did your bit — I'll grant you that —' her cackle broke above the general hum of conversation and he ordered quickly and hustled her back to the snug.

'I want to thank you Lottie. . . .' She put her mouth one side of her gin glass and her nose the other, and swigged. When she emerged the usual dewdrop had disappeared. Will grinned. He must remember to tell Albert that tomorrow.

'Nothing to it. Not with your wife. Not with Florence Rising. She were a Davies afore she married you.' She swigged again. 'Welsh stock. Strong as Welsh ponies. Anyway, she wouldn't scream and fight like Hettie Luker. Not if you put the thumb screws on her.'

'No. No, she wouldn't scream. But strong . . . is she really strong?'

'Don't you believe me?' She was suddenly drink-belligerent. She thrust her head at him and there was another dewdrop. 'She could have a baby a year and not notice it. She'll outlive you Will Rising!' She sucked the dregs from the gin glass and wiped nose and mouth together on her silvery sleeve. 'Just like you've outlived poor old Daker. D'you see that? You was looking at the paper just now wasn't you? D'you see poor ole Daker's gone?'

'No!' He felt the news like a hammer blow on his chest. Mr. Daker who had apprenticed him because of his flexible fingers and thereby saved him from being a ploughboy. Mr. Daker who had stood on his head on his cutting table and told him to bear pain gladly because

23

its eventual absence was then doubly wonderful. Mr. Daker was part of Will's life. When Will had started up on his own, Mr. Daker had sent along many a customer besides letting Will have all his alterations.

He said weakly, 'Are you sure? He's not sixty yet surely?'

'Don't believe me again?' She slid cumbrously around the table then back, holding the *Citizen*. 'Here's proof. Doubting Thomas.'

He read the small black-framed notice. 'Dearly beloved father of Hester and David.' He saw his name was Emmanuel. He had never imagined Mr. Daker to have a forename.

'I must get home,' he said. 'Florrie will want to know about this. I must get home.'

'Now don't you go telling her no upsetting news now mind. Not until tomorrow at the earliest.' Lottie put a restraining hand on his arm but he shook it off and stood up. 'Now Will Rising —' she stood up too, oddly like a bedraggled Queen Victoria in her rusty black. 'Just you remember. As one comes into this world, so another goes out. It's the law of nature and there's nothing we can do about it.'

Her words rang in his ears as he made his way back to Chichester Street with the April breeze suddenly keen and chilling searching through his waistcoat buttons for his very soul. As his new child had fought her way into the world, so Daker had gone out. Somehow it made Daker's death his responsibility. He wished he had gone to see him since his brief call for work last month. But there had been Sir Henry's death and the funeral and all the alterations to do. He had worked till three am for the past two nights, and Florrie had sewn button-holes till her fingers were raw.

He found he was crying again. It was the whisky. He knew that. But Daker . . . maybe if he hadn't rolled over on to Florrie that night nine months ago, Daker would be alive now. He broke into a shambling trot. He must

24

tell Florrie, shock or no shock. He must get into bed beside her and weep on her shoulder and let her smooth his hair and kiss his wet eyes and.... He wanted Florrie.

Albert went downstairs and got the milk jug off the stone floor of the larder, fetched a saucepan and tipped it in. He used a taper for the gas, hating the way it popped at him, then went out to the wash-house. It was quite dark now but the stars made the sky pale. He sniffed ecstatically, smelling frost. No school tomorrow. Kempley instead, and the daffodils and the red stone of Kempley Church and the wide shallow River Leadon, crystal clear and as cold as iron. Dad might let him paddle.

'March!' He opened the wash-house door and saw her leaning on her elbows on the sink, water pouring on to a pile of sheets. She was soaked from the waist down. 'March, come on. Leave that now. We're going to have bread and milk with Mother and she'll tell us a story. Come on.' He hesitated. She had lit a candle in a saucer on the shelf above her head where Mother kept the bar soap. He was almost sure she was crying, except that March never cried. 'Are you coming?' he repeated tentatively.

She turned off the tap and blew out the candle in one movement. They went back to the house and she put four bowls on to a tray and began to break bread into them without enthusiasm. Albert hovered over the milk saucepan.

'Put plenty of sugar on mine,' he ordered. 'Shall we take the kitten up? What are we going to call her?'

She made no reply and he added carelessly, 'She dug her fingers into my neck and made my shirt collar bloody. You'll have to wash it for me March. But it's all right, I'm not going to school tomorrow'cos Dad's taking me to Kempley with him and the next day is Saturday, so —'

March screamed.

He spun round from the steaming saucepan just in time to catch her open hand on his face. She came up with her other hand, then again with the first, screaming and spitting all the time worse than the kitten. He thrust her from him and she fell in a heap against the table leg and there she stayed, hanging on to it, sobbing wildly, banging her head deliberately every now and then, completely hysterical.

The milk boiled over and put out the gas, and immediately the kitchen was filled with its stink. Albert flicked at the tap and left the milk to crust hard on the stove top. He did not feel his usual irritability at the sight of female tears. This was something quite different. This was a thunderstorm. He was reminded of Fred Luker in the playground at school, bawling all the awful words he could think of at the top of his voice before the Headmistress caned him. When asked for explanations he'd said, 'You got to get it out your system. That's what me mam says. Get it out your system. She has a go now and then. But 'course she don't have to put up with a caning for it.'

Neither did March. He knelt by her and watched her bang her head. Maybe she was caning herself.

'What's the matter?' he asked as soon as she stopped.

She spurted snot and spit worse than Lottie. 'Everyone. Everyone is the matter. All that washing. And now you with your shirt. I haven't had time to look at the kitten — got to wash the baby instead. And now you . . . going to Kempley . . . you *swine*! You spoilt brat!' She choked and he passed her his handkerchief. She used it and threw it on the floor. 'Nobody thinks I've got any feelings do they?' She picked up the handkerchief and tried to tear it but the good linen resisted her. 'All that fuss over May because she takes up tea! *Tea!* When the baby's lying there covered in the most awful slimy muck you ever saw!'

'I should have thought Snotty Lottie would have seen to all that.'

'That would have cost money you fool! Don't you understand anything?' She gave up the handkerchief and banged her head furiously. 'And now you've messed up your shirt —'

'I'll wash my shirt March.'

'And you're going to Kempley. You're leaving me here all by myself —'

'Mother and the new baby are —'

'It's you I want.' She stared at him malevolently and crashed her head against the table leg. 'Nobody loves me. Nobody cares whether I'm happy or not. Nobody loves —'

'I love you March.'

'No you don't. You're going to Kempley —'

'You can go in my place March —' Albert had never felt so fine in his life. The pale stars and the frost and Kempley . . . he would sacrifice them for his sister. 'I'll do the washing, don't worry. I —'

'You can't. You don't know how to.' But she did not bang her head and there was no anger in her voice. Her sobs died down slowly. 'Do you really love me Albert?'

'Yes.'

'How much?'

'I don't know . . . I. . . .'

'More than May?'

'Oh yes. And more than the new baby of course. And more than the kitten and —'

'More than Mother?'

He hesitated. 'I think so. I can't tell Mother things can I? Or say some words. I can tell you anything. Anything in the world. Like I told you when I fell down in Mrs. Luker's yard and looked up her skirt and saw she didn't wear drawers. Like I told you about my sore John Thomas and you got some of Mother's vaseline —'

'I love you too Albert.' She weighed her words carefully. 'I would die for you Albert.'

He said happily, 'I would die for you too March.'

'I'm happy you're going to Kempley. I don't want you

to stay at home. I want you to have good times. Even if I can't have them too.' She stood up and began sprinkling sugar on the bowls. In the pale green bowl, which was Albert's, she sprinkled a double helping. He brought over the skinny milk and poured it carefully. They went upstairs. They both felt the holy joy of renunciation.

Will stumbled into the bedroom feeling slightly sick at the heavy smell of sweet, burned milk. The room was dim, the gas turned down to a bead. On the heaped pillows of the double bed were three heads. The brown one raised itself.

'Hush Daddy,' March put a finger to her lips. 'Mother and May are fast asleep and the baby has just dropped off.'

Will felt frustration boil deep inside him.

'What's all this?' He did not lower his voice and he was quite certain Florrie was awake.

'We had bread and milk and Mother told us a story, then she said to get our night clothes on. She needs me here to see to the baby and that meant May had to stay too!' March sounded patronising and smug. She whispered a giggle. 'We used all the milk and Mother says she can't do any feeding herself for a while, so we put some of Mrs. Goodrich's honey on to a dummy and April just *loved* it!'

Will stared at Florence as if the intensity of his gaze could wake her up. She did not stir. He turned and blundered out. 'There's other nights, my girl,' he muttered as he felt his way to Albert's room and began to undress in the dark. 'There's other nights. And you're as strong as a Welsh pony remember.' He flung back the ice-cold sheets and got into the spare bed. On the other side of the room, Albert grunted and muttered March's name. Will remembered old Daker. He whispered, 'You could have stayed awake to hear about him. That's all I wanted. Just to share that. After all, we're meant to comfort each other aren't we? That's what marriage is for isn't it?'

No-one answered his question. He turned his head into the pillow. 'More like a nun than a Welsh pony.' It came to him suddenly that Florence would have made a good nun. Living with suffering. No screaming.

He slept at last.

2

Will and Albert were late leaving for Kempley. The girls, all four of them in the big bedroom, slept late, exhausted after a disturbed night. April simply would not believe there was no milk to be had and woke again at eight-thirty to demand her rights. March could spare her no more time; May had to be bullied to school and there was all that washing and no sound at all from Albert's room. She banged on the door as she scurried down the landing, lifting her skirt high above her bare feet, terrified of mice. May followed sleepily and took her time about setting out five cups and saucers on the part of the table not already occupied by the funeral trousers. She then sat in a chair cuddling the kitten and making no attempt to dress or fetch newspaper and sticks for the fire. March washed in cold water in the scullery, dressed hurriedly, discovering her clothes still damp from last night's swilling in the wash-house, and took the jug down to Mrs. Goodrich for milk.

Snotty Lottie was coming out of her door.

'Bab all right?' she called wheezily.

March, like her mother, did not believe in encouraging Mrs. Jenner. She raised the milk jug by way of reply. A breeze, funnelled into a near gale by the tunnel that was Chichester Street, almost took it from her; and Lottie gave up dealing with her nose and clutched her shawl.

'That's no good,' she grumbled. 'Bab's too little for that. I'll go on down and —'

'We're managing thank you Mrs. Jenner,' March said politely, terrified of incurring another florin fee. 'And — and my father isn't about yet, so —'

Lottie laughed horribly. 'Won't be the first time I've seen a man in his nightshirt — or without it! Won't be the last let's hope!'

There was nothing March could do. She watched Lottie go down the street, head bent, just a bundle of old clothes flapping in the wind.

Young Mrs. Goodrich was freshly aproned and bustling around the dairy laying out butter pats and cheeses for the day's business.

'I've heard,' she beamed at March. 'So I've lost my little nurse-maid.'

March smiled back. Young Mrs. Goodrich made her feel grown up, yet a cherished child at the same time. She watched her put the half-pint dipper in the churn and pour the contents carefully into Mother's china jug.

'I'd like to come still, and see little Charlotte. When there's more time,' she said shyly.

The dipper went in again and again. And again. 'You know you're welcome March.' Mrs. Goodrich dipped a fifth time. 'And if Granny or me can help you like you've helped us, then we'd be very pleased to do so.'

March knew that her occasional ministrations to baby Charlotte had been by way of practice for April and, in fact, a privilege. So she did not mention the washing. Instead she said huskily and gratefully, 'Just the quart Mrs. Goodrich. The jug won't hold any more.'

Mrs. Goodrich smiled. 'I think it will. Just a little drop more. Enough for a new baby at any rate.' She put the lace fly cover, weighted with beads, carefully in place. 'And she will be called April I daresay?'

March took the brimming jug with great concentration and nodded.

'And Mrs. Rising is well? And the baby strong?'

'Mother is fine. But the baby is crying a lot.'

'You take her that milk then. And tell your mother I will visit just as soon as we close this evening.' She came from behind the counter and held the door open. 'Now is there something I can bring? A pound of butter perhaps? Or a wedge of cheese?'

May and Albert would finish the butter between them, and Daddy would eat the cheese. March lifted her eyes from the jug and said, 'Mother is very fond of your honey Mrs. Goodrich. And so is April.'

'Then honey it shall be.' Young Mrs. Goodrich suddenly rested her hand on March's brown head. 'What a good girl you are March. I hope Charlotte grows up like you. You're a proper little Martha.'

'Martha, Mrs. Goodrich?'

'Never mind dear. Now mind the step. And walk as quickly as you can. You shouldn't have come out without your coat you know. The weather is very deceptive.'

March wasn't absolutely certain about the word deceptive, but she had a feeling it was what she was. She remembered how she had screamed and wept last night. Would young Mrs. Goodrich think she was so good if she knew about last night? But then, March was certain she would never behave like that again. The declaration of love between Albert and herself was sufficient to buoy her above her fierce temper and perpetual simmering resentment. She loved Mother and April of course, and — to a much lesser degree — May and Daddy; but her love for Albert was different. It was completely absorbing.

Will came into the bedroom barefooted, nightshirted.

'Why the devil didn't March wake me? Where is she? Where's May? What's the matter with the dratted baby?'

Florence was unperturbed. She had won her night and the day stretched endlessly ahead, all hers, even if April cried incessantly. She observed Will with detachment and felt amused affection; he looked so funny with his pale gingery hair on end and his rounded calves emerging from the shirt. Usually a compact, well-made man, mild and pleasant of face, he looked this morning like a small bull pawing the oilcloth.

'March has gone for milk I expect. May is downstairs getting breakfast. Make sure she wears her muffler to school Will, the wind looks cruel this morning.'

He softened immediately at the sound of her gentle voice. She had brushed out her long dark hair and it lay like a shawl around her shoulders. How beautiful she was and how completely inaccessible.

'How did you sleep my darling?' he asked, the endearment only a slight afterthought. 'Did the baby keep you awake?'

'No. March was very good.' She smiled. 'They're good children Will.' She held out a hand. 'Four now,' she added softly. 'A regular family.'

He remembered she had said last night that April would be the youngest.

He walked over to the drawer and looked down on the squalling child. He said jovially and loudly, 'My mother had seven. But how she put up with this seven times over I don't know!'

Before Florence had time to reply to this comment or statement or whatever it was Will intended, there was a very perfunctory tap on the bedroom door and Lottie surged in, suddenly capable in her role as midwife. Will moved hastily around to the other side of the bed, making a jocular remark that would nevertheless show Lottie that as William Rising, tailor, he was outraged at being discovered in his nightshirt. Florence sat up very straight and emanated the same outrage. April yelled.

Lottie ignored the two adults and swooped on the baby.

'Did they starve you my little precious?'

She was different when she handled the baby; Will was amazed. Expertly she cupped the sagging head, unwound the sheet, lifted the long robe and examined March's work with the penny. She grunted satisfaction then changed the soggy napkin. Will managed to drape himself modestly — as he thought — in one of Florence's many shawls, and edge to the door, but there he stopped in spite of Florence's urgent dismissive gestures, to watch, fascinated by Lottie's expertise. Who would have thought, observing the old girl with her gin glass last night, that she had such a shining place in the scheme of things? Will had long known about her reputation: most of the women in the district would prefer Lottie to the doctor, and would have done if their fees had been reversed, but he had imagined a dark and sordid mystery at which she merely presided. It wasn't like that. He backed onto the landing — where Albert, on his way downstairs to find March, was much affected by the sight of the shawl-swathed rear of his father — but kept the door ajar so that he could see without being seen.

In any case, Lottie was only interested in April. The child was still crying but now, it seemed, in answer to Lottie's enquiries.

'Did they give you a nasty sticky dummy then?' she said through a mouthful of pins. April grizzled acquiescence and Lottie sniffed vigorously just in time. 'Never mind my beauty. Lottie's here now. Lottie will see to it.' She laid the baby on the bottom of the bed and approached Florence.

Florence said firmly, 'March has gone for milk Mrs. Jenner. She'll be another two or three minutes —'

'I saw her. Cow's milk!' Lottie sniffed then used her sleeve. 'And you with enough for two or three babies —' she unbuttoned Florence's nightgown so efficiently that Florence's flapping protesting hands were brushed aside like butterflies. 'And no good telling me there's nothing there yet. Your milk might not be in until tomorrow but there's something there for your baby. Nature provides, my girl. Nature always provides.'

Will watched with all his eyes as the calico was deftly unpinned and a huge breast exposed. Florence was weeping. Incredibly, after fighting her way tearlessly through childbirth, she was weeping at the sight of her fecund body.

'There's nothing Mrs. Jenner! And it hurts!'

'Then it must hurt!' Lottie was inexorable. 'I remember we had this with baby March. Not with May though!' She seized a handful of flesh and with a brutality that made Will gasp, squeezed until her ancient purple knuckles showed white. Florence turned her head, covering her eyes with her hands.

'Don't — oh don't —'

A bead of clear fluid collected on the distended nipple, and then another. Lottie gave another grunt of satisfaction and reached for the baby. Will watched until April was sucking hungrily, then withdrew. He was breathing quickly. He went back into Albert's room and began to dress. There were coppers in his pocket kept handily for the gas. He counted out six of them. It was an expensive start to the morning, but worth every penny. When he got the money for the funeral suits he'd treat Lottie to another gin.

The trap made a reassuring rattle as it turned right at the Cross and began the long clatter down Westgate Street. Albert relished the trip even more than he would have done normally, because it was a gift from March. He clutched the springboard and lifted himself to see over the crowding houses to the cathedral spire. He knew that his mother wanted him to sing there one day. It meant going to the King's School and wearing that uniform and playing rugby football on Westgate fields, and first of all passing a scholarship. He must do it somehow. He was the eldest; he had to set a good

35

example. He was the only boy too. He sat down suddenly, overwhelmed by the abrupt realisation of responsibility. They came to the Causeway and the water meadows stretched either side of them, still soggy from the winter floods. The breeze was keener and began at last to wash away the clinging smell of steamy cloth which had filled the whole kitchen as they had pressed the funeral suits an hour before.

Albert said, 'May will be late for school.'

Dad let the reins go loose on Luker's pony and he trotted along busily, obviously enjoying the empty road and the river smells and the strong breeze. 'She won't mind. Nothing worries May.'

Albert thought about this. May cried a lot certainly, but it was not because anything affected her personally. It was because something was sad, or beautiful, or sweet.

He pulled the peak of his cap over his forehead and said gloomily, 'The trouble with May is, she's always happy.'

Dad put his head back and laughed loudly at this in a way Mother would disapprove strongly. But no-one was about. 'What's the trouble with that then my son? And what's so unusual? You're happy too aren't you?'

'Yes.' Albert was surprised about it. 'Yes, I am.' He looked up at his father, amazed. 'I'm quite like May, aren't I Dad? I'm a boy and I'm older and more sensible — May is so *silly* sometimes — but we're quite similar.' He was pleased with the mature word that proved his seriousness. 'Yes. We're quite similar,' he repeated triumphantly.

Dad was in a good mood. He laughed again, his small pale beard pointing to the sky. Albert loved him like this. Loved having him alone and forming a male alliance with him. He bounced on the seat and the trap swayed and the pony's rhythm changed hastily as the shafts leapt at his sides.

'Steady on!' Dad flipped the reins gently to reassure

the pony and guide him into the middle of the road which had narrowed now. It was crowded with fresh hawthorn hedges springing over the ditches and threatening to take their caps at any minute. The pony slowed and they both ducked under an apple tree, blushing pink with blossom, and drove past an orchard. Dad laughed again. 'D'you know, I used to walk this road every Sunday morning to see your mother? Ten miles there and ten miles back.'

Albert found himself reacting as May would have done. It made him feel guilty; his likeness to May made him feel guilty altogether, as if he were being disloyal to March. He made himself remember March's temper last night, her pain, her resentment.

He said, 'That must have been hard work Dad.'

'It was. I was only fourteen. I was thankful to get my apprenticeship with Mr. Daker. It meant I could see your mother most days. It meant . . . a lot.'

Dad's happiness seemed suddenly to fade. Albert said quickly, 'Look over there Dad. The blossom is all full on those trees. But not the other side of the road.' He jabbed with his finger.

Dad nodded, pleased with such keen observation. 'South side,' he said briefly. 'Lambournes — good apple that. They'll be ready a month before the others. Catch the market when the prices are up. Good bit of farming that, Albert. Good bit of business too. Always remember, catch the market in your favour. Whether it's buying or selling. Mr. Daker used to say that.'

'Tell me about when Mr. Daker used to stand on his head Dad.'

Albert grasped obscurely that his father wanted to talk about the old days and thought to please him, but Will's buoyancy continued to evaporate.

'Put yourself to extremes. That's what he said. That's what Mr. Daker used to say.'

Albert couldn't make head nor tail of this. 'What did he mean Dad?'

'If you stand on your head for five minutes, life seems rosy when you get back on your feet. Even if it isn't.'

This made sense because of March and her head-banging last night. She had been quietly happy ever since. He had told her about Dad wearing Mother's shawl like a skirt and she had giggled delightfully, her tea-brown eyes holding depths of amusement into which he had felt drawn and warmed. May had only smiled and continued to cuddle the kitten and invent names for it.

Dad said abruptly, 'Mr. Daker died. Yesterday morning. I can hardly believe it.'

Albert was undismayed, though he now saw the reason for his father's sudden unhappiness. Death featured frequently in playground gossip, but more often than not as a release from the workhouse. That was the real bogey, the real terror. Many old people from the city ended up in the workhouse. There was a workhouse at Westbury-on-Severn, and Albert had surveyed its grim high walls once while on a picnic to Newnham with the Sunday School. 'Solid stone,' the Sunday School superintendent had remarked with pride and doom. Albert imagined the beds, tables, even plates and cups, carved from solid stone.

'He wasn't in the workhouse though Dad,' he offered now as consolation.

It worked. Dad laughed, though without throwing back his head.

'That would be the final extreme, I should think,' he said appreciatively. Then, relapsing into moroseness, added, 'Though maybe that is what life is all about. It's so awful generally. It makes death more acceptable.' He looked down at Albert and let go the reins with one hand to hit him companionably on the shoulder. 'Why did I say that? When it's spring and the blossom is out and we've just decided our natural state is happiness?'

Albert spoke up with innocent, yet logical, wisdom. 'Well Dad . . . I suppose . . . if you're miserable sometimes, then you know you're happy other times.'

Will didn't laugh but he looked ahead and smiled as he caught a first glimpse of the little River Leadon where he had fished as a boy. How Mr. Daker would enjoy hearing Albert say that. And how true it was. If Will himself didn't occasionally feel out of sorts with Florence, would he know with such certainty how much he loved her in between? He remembered with horror how he had watched this morning. Watched and gloated. Yes, he had so nearly gloated because Florence was being forced to accept the physical realities of Nature itself. When he had always known that she was above Nature. All sensitivity and delicate manufacture, like a piece of porcelain, that was his Florence. He had known it when he met her first; known it in his twelve-year-old bones. She had stayed with the vicar at Kempley, pale and ill and dying — so the village children had said. When she talked to him among the gravestones where he helped his father with the weeding, it seemed her grandparents had sent her out of Gloucester while smallpox raged. Because she was so precious. Her own parents were dead, and only through her would the blood, if not the name, of Rhys-Davies live on. She was the last frail pennant of a line that went back to King Arthur. Will had stared at the thin white face beneath the shovel bonnet, and worshipped.

Albert, worried by the long silence, said in a small voice, 'I suppose, if it hadn't been for Mr. Daker, you'd never have been a tailor Dad?'

Will smiled down at his son, his world right again, Florence back on her plinth.

'It goes back before that, son. If it hadn't been for your mother I wouldn't have been a tailor. I'd have been a ploughboy. And you wouldn't be going to the King's. You'd be a ploughboy too.' He remembered a lewd jibe the village schoolchildren had made to him years ago in the school privy, and used it in a different context. 'The Risings are rising, Albert me lad! The Risings are rising!'

They rounded a bend, and stretching before them was

a golden sea of daffodils. Facing south, sheltered, cupped, held by a crescent of elms, the small trumpets of blossom seemed to be lifted by the breeze to make a silent fanfare for their arrival. In a corner of the field three gypsy women picked rhythmically, their baskets, high up one arm, already full. In two hours they would be on Gloucester Cross crying their wares. Albert voiced the sentiments of many of the townspeople.

'Newent daffs . . .' he sounded awestruck. 'It's really spring.'

Will slapped the reins on the pony's fat back and the trap lurched forward with new impetus.

'And we've got a new baby. With a voice like a bugle and yellow hair.' He laughed again, loudly. 'Not unlike a daffodil, eh?'

Albert laughed too, delighted that the shadow on the festivity had been lifted. Will had given two of his children the gift for happiness; and the need for it too.

May and Sybil Luker talked about babies during the dinner hour. The weather was fine and the yard sheltered from the stiff breeze; the boys had been banned from playing on the coal heap, so the two girls settled themselves comfortably on upturned buckets and opened their dinner tins. May's had originally held chocolates from the model village at Bourneville near Birmingham; Sybil's had held tobacco.

Sybil said knowledgeably, 'What you got to do is, give 'em something to suck on. All the time. Stands to reason don't it? If they're sucking they can't be screaming.'

'That was all right at first,' May agreed. 'March stuck the dummy into some of Mrs. Goodrich's honey and April loved it. But then she spat it out and cried again.' She picked up a square of bread, liberally spread with beef dripping and salted. She held it carefully on the crust so that her fingers would not get greasy, then she nibbled at it with her front teeth, chewing quickly like a rabbit. Sybil's meal was exactly the same, yet when she picked up the bread and fitted it as far into her mouth as possible, it looked much less delicious.

'Didn't your mam give her some titty?' Sybil giggled at May's expression. 'You didn't know, did you May Rising? You didn't know babies had to have titties?'

May was incapable of being shocked for long; curiosity quickly overcame her distaste for the coarse word.

'What do you mean Sybil?'

Sybil chewed enjoyably and explained. May nibbled right down to her crusts and listened, intrigued at first, then, as usual, touched.

'How *sweet* . . . oh Sibbie, how sweet. When we went to collect our kitten he was feeding like that. No wonder he has such a job to drink his milk out of a saucer. Oh Sibbie, how *sweet*!'

For an instant, there flashed into eight-year-old Sybil's consciousness that she almost loved May Rising. She said ardently. 'I'm ever so glad, ever and ever so glad, you've had a baby too. Perhaps Gladys and April will be best friends like us.'

'Oh they will. Of course they will.' May was sunnily certain, although in fact March had nothing to do with the Lukers, and Albert and Fred met only over a football and had none of the easy companionship she shared with Sybil.

'And I hope your mam will fall for another pretty quick too,' went on Sybil. 'Then our next will have someone to play with.' She stared at the high walls of Chichester Street Elementary and sighed ecstatically. 'Our families will be bound together for all eternity,' she concluded grandly, using the dialogue from a play seen by her father at the Theatre Royal.

May was gloriously impressed. 'How lovely!' Her enormous blue eyes watered. 'Oh Sybil how lovely.' She was just going to beg Sybil to tell her yet again about the play, when something else struck her. 'But . . . what do you mean? Are you going to have another baby? *Again*?'

'Not for ages,' Sybil said carelessly. 'I'm not supposed

to know. But I heard them going on about it the other night.' Sides, when Mam's expecting, she lets Dad do it any time. An' I can hear them night after night bouncing about in their bed.'

'Do what?' asked May.

Sybil was suddenly baffled. 'I don't know. Just bounce in bed I suppose. It makes them happy though. They laugh a lot.'

'That's nice.' May thought about it. 'That's lovely Sibbie. Bouncing in bed and laughing. Mother won't let us bounce on our beds because of the springs. Oh Sibbie, isn't it lovely having babies?'

Sybil giggled. 'Because you can be late at school and Miss Pettinger will let you stand up and tell everyone about your new baby and why it's called April?' She peered into May's chocolate tin. 'Can I have your crusts if you don't want them? They might make my hair curl like yours.'

The washing took all of a very long morning and March couldn't turn the handle of the mangle on some of the big sheets, so they hung dripping sadly in the yard. But they were clean. Damp and happy she went into the kitchen to take some food up to her mother. The kitten was on the table and she picked him up and held him to her face.

'Not allowed,' she told him and put him down by his milk. He lapped inexpertly then staggered to his tray where he began to paw at the sand. March watched, entranced. It was all so sweet and funny. If only April would behave like that.

She spread dripping carefully on to two slices of jaggedly-cut bread, dipping deep into the basin to bring up the lovely brown bits and streaking them in diagonal patterns across the bread. Then she swilled out the teapot, still half-full of tea from this morning, and rinsed the cups to go with it. It all looked as nice as when May had done it yesterday. She made the tea and carried the tray carefully up the stairs, glad when the kitten scampered after her because where he was, surely no mouse would dare to be.

Florence was sleeping but she roused immediately the door opened.

'March. Darling. Oh what a treat! My dearest girl.'

March glowed. She poured the tea and she and her mother ate together.

'Has April been good like this all the time?' she asked, peering into the drawer at the sleeping baby.

'Yes. I've been sleeping since Mrs. Jenner left.'

'Oh yes. Mrs. Jenner.' March recalled Snotty Lottie's unstoppable interference this morning. 'Dad gave her sixpence when she came downstairs.'

'Did he? I wonder whether that was wise. It might encourage her to come again.' Florence nibbled at her bread like May. 'However . . . she is excellent with the baby, I have to admit.' She smiled warmly at March. 'After tomorrow I shall get up, March. Your father will bring home some meat from the country this evening I daresay. Put it on the stone in the larder dear, and I will get up on Sunday and cook it. Then on Monday you can go back to school.'

March hesitated, on the verge of protesting. She enjoyed the importance of staying at home and taking over the household. On the other hand, there would be washing every day from now on; she knew that because of young Mrs. Goodrich's Charlotte. Even in the Goodrichs' well-ordered household the smell of washing permeated through to the shop.

She said, 'Mrs. Goodrich was in bed for more than a week. And she's stronger than you, Mamma.'

Florence smiled again. 'She has Granny Goodrich to see to things. And I don't want my little March getting old and bent like Granny Goodrich, do I?'

Florence rarely teased her children and when she did it was in moments of great tenderness. March felt joy blossom inside her like an explosion, not the deep

43

pleasure that had flowed after Albert's declaration of love, but a flowering that was pure and unalloyed. Nevertheless it called again for personal sacrifice.

'I don't mind! I don't mind being old and bent for you Mamma!'

And Florence actually laughed; another rare occurrence.

'I can't imagine your back bending. Ever.' She stared down into her teacup as if reading the leaves. 'You have my pride March. It will keep your back straight even when it is breaking.' She looked up, discovering something with pleasure. 'Yes, you have my pride dear child. How interesting.' She was suddenly solemn. 'It can help you a great deal March. With your temper. You can control your temper by using your pride.'

March, on the crest of the wave because of her kinship with her mother, was in the trough now. She said, subdued, 'Where does my temper come from Mamma? Have you got one too?'

'No dear. I think you inherit that from Grandpa Rising.' Florence sighed. 'Your father is mild enough. So are Albert and May.'

Comfortingly, there came a sound from the drawer; a rude and unapologetic sound. Then April grizzled and began to cry.

Florence smiled again. 'Perhaps April will share your temper, March. Fetch her for me, will you dear?'

March lifted the baby lovingly. Grandpa Rising was an ugly little man who spoke in grunts, never words. She wanted nothing from him, but if she was forced to accept his unwelcome legacy at least April might share it.

She said, 'Shall I fetch some milk Mother?'

'No dear. Just give me the baby then take the tray downstairs will you? Then change your pinafore in case anyone comes calling — oh March it is wet! What have you been doing?'

'The mangle was dripping and the sheets were dripping —'

'And you are dripping!' Florence turned misfortune
into another opportunity for gentle teasing. Then
spoiled everything. 'And you must wash china in hot
water with a knob of soda dear. Polish it well with a
clean cloth. Then there will be no more smears like
this.' She indicated her teacup and March saw that she
had drunk only half a cup of tea. She carried the tray
back down with less care. The kitten waited for her
halfway down, and suddenly, before she could stop
herself or even remember her pride, she put out a toe
and shoved it hard. It rolled bonelessly to the bottom,
picked itself up and galloped into the kitchen ahead of
her. She followed it, placed the tray on the table, put
the back of her wrist to her mouth and bit hard.

The visit to Kempley was everything Albert had
expected. The tiny tied cottage where Grandma Rising
had raised her huge family was even more ramshackle
than usual and seemed full of babies; all rolling on the
stone floor 'happy as pigs in shit' as Gran so vividly put
it. Gran herself was dealing with a large bucket of
boiling sheep's heads on the range, while Aunty Vi and
Aunty Sylv cleared the recent dinner table and washed
up at a sort of trough in the corner, where Albert well
remembered having a bath with March when they had
stayed here while May arrived. It was his earliest
memory and set the pattern for all his future visits to
his grandmother's cottage.

Shouting; you always shouted when you went to
Kempley. It was the only way to be heard for one thing,
for another it expressed the life force in you. Laughing;
you laughed a lot even when there was nothing much to
laugh at. And you laughed without discrimination.
When Aunty Vi had tripped over the latest baby and
broken her leg, everyone had laughed till their sides
ached. Through Vi's cursing and bawling, through the

arrival of the doctor and the subsequent splinting and Vi's attempts to get about on crutches — through it all — the laughter had rung loud and clear. Even now Aunty Vi walked with a nautical roll and Uncle Wallie still clapped her on the shoulder and shouted, 'Anyone 'ud think you'd broke y'r leg our Vi!' And the shrieks of mirth went up anew.

'Got to that fancy singing school yet 'ave you my 'andsome?' Gran asked as she stirred and prodded and skimmed indescribable mess from the top of the bucket. 'Wun't speak to your ole gran will you? Not when you gets to that fancy school?'

'Not yet Gran,' he shouted. 'September. If I pass the scholarship.' He had to shout because Aunty Sylv was singing.

'You'll pass. You'll pass.' Gran threw the skimmings on to the back of the fire where they hissed furiously. She put down the spoon and turned to him. 'You'll be the pride of the Risings. You see lad.'

Aunty Sylv repeated 'The pride of the Risings,' and laughed loudly, and Aunty Vi, clattering away in the trough, joined her.

Dad came in from pipe smoking with Grampa and straddled a stool and they had to start on the stew. Albert found if he didn't look too closely at his plate and stoppered his nose, it tasted all right.

'Look at our Albert!' shouted Aunty Vi. 'He's got his nose all a-twisted round — what you doing that for, our Albert?' And they swayed about laughing so that Albert laughed too and smelled the sheep's head like a tanner's yard and twisted his nose frantically and had to be thumped on the back by Dad. Everyone managed to listen while Dad told them about April, and they were momentarily sober to hear of Mr. Daker's death. Then Albert told them through his gravy that they'd got a new kitten to keep down the mice, and they burst forth again.

All too soon it was time to deliver the suits. Grandma

promised them strong tea and stronger cheese on their return. 'Jack and Austin will be in then. And you'll catch your pa again in between the cows and the new grave.' This joke was much appreciated, though Albert knew that it meant quite simply his grandfather was digging another grave after he'd done the evening's milking. He watched them until the little red church at Kempley blocked them from view, then straightened with a sigh of repletion. The long winter had come between him and his country memories; he had been stupid to think Dad could stay in an unhappy mood for long. Not when he was going to Kempley.

He said, 'I wish you had been a ploughboy Dad. And me a ploughboy too.'

Will was amazed. He said, 'You couldn't stand it boy. Not all the time. It's like living on rough cider! And what about Mother? You wouldn't have had her. Not down here.'

Albert considered this. 'I'd have had March.'

'How? You wouldn't have had March without Mother.' Will laughed down at him. 'I couldn't be a ploughboy Albert. I love 'em — don't make any mistake about that. But they — they —' he searched for words to explain their tough insensitivity.

Albert used Gran's phrase. 'They're as happy as pigs in shit.'

Will looked alarmed. 'Don't ever let Mother hear you say that Albert. Else it'll be the last time you come to Kempley Cottage!' But then he grinned. Then laughed uproariously, sounding exactly like Aunt Sylv.

Albert said nothing. He could not find the words to explain that pigs living that way did not have to go to the King's School nor be responsible for so many women. They just revelled all the time in that unthinking happiness.

After school May was permitted in to the Luker kitchen to view Gladys being breast-fed. Hettie blushed slightly under the astonished blue gaze, but was reassuring when she heard the whole story.

'Don't you worry your pretty golden head about your new sister dearie.' Hettie joggled Gladys to get her going again; she was always falling asleep in the middle of her feeds, and Hettie had to get tea with her still in position. 'I'll be over to see your mam just as soon as I've got this little terror to bed. A nice bottle of milk stout, that's what she needs. Our Fred can pop to the jug and bottle and get one for me. I'll bring it over and we'll have a chat. Everything will be fine and dandy. But you sleep in your own bed tonight, remember.'

'I'll remember Mrs. Luker. Thank you Mrs. Luker.' May continued to gaze as she backed towards the door. 'Oh Mrs. Luker, I think it's lovely. It's like our new kitten. It's so sweet!' She left the house still jabbering to Sibbie. She did not notice the bare boards in the hall and the bits of paper that always scuffed about underfoot in the Luker house. It was one of her gifts; May did not see unpleasant things.

If it had been anyone else in the world, Florence might have been frigidly angry; with May she was sorrowful.

'Darling. You must never say that word again as long as you live,' she begged, two bright red spots on her face, her hands to her ears.

'What is it really called then Mamma?' May put a knee on the bed and her arms around her mother's shoulders. She could not bear to distress her.

Florence took her hands from her ears where they had flown in self-preservation, and cupped May's face.

'My dear innocent child . . . it is Nature's way of feeding, darling. Nature's way.'

'I see Mamma. That's a very beautiful way of saying it, isn't it? Nature's way. Darling Mamma, you're not angry with me are you?'

'How could I be angry with you May? I could wish

however that you were not so friendly with the little Luker girl.'

'Sibbie?' May was loyal too. 'Oh Mother, she's the best girl in the school. I love Sibbie.'

'I know dearest. I only ask . . . try not to pick up her . . . er — sayings. You would not dream of dressing like her. Or going about unwashed as she does, so —'

'Mamma. I truly and honestly did not know titty was a bad word.'

'May!'

'Oh I'm sorry — I'm sorry Mamma.' May tugged the hands down from the crimson ears. 'Let's talk of something else. Please. What have you been doing all day? And how is my dearest little sister? And has Albert gone with Daddy to Kempley? And has March christened the kitten?'

Florence succumbed and embraced May fondly. They talked. April was admired. May prepared to go and help March get the tea.

'Mother. Mrs. Luker might come over and see you and the baby after tea.' Florence flung up her hands, but teasingly this time. 'Please be kind to her, Mother. Please. She wants to help you. Really and truly.'

Florence looked at the enchanting face framed in the angel-gold hair. She smiled.

'Very well darling. I'll be polite.'

'You're always polite, Mother. Be *friendly*.'

Florence said nothing for a moment. She was not friendly with any of her neighbours and, in fact, could not recall having a friend in her life. She nodded slowly. 'Very well May. I'll try. I promise.'

It had been another very long day. Albert slept intermittently, pillowed on Aunty Sylv's spongy bosom, smelling the natural smells of her that combined now to remind him of a human haystack. The bread, cheese and a huge mound of watercress, fresh picked by Uncle Austin, still took up the centre of the table,

49

the perimeter was crowded with arms, bare or sleeved, hairy or smooth. The babies were in bed. The two chickens, donated by one of the owners of the funeral suits, were packed in the trap and the horse was fresh and ready for the ten-mile trot back to the city.

Grandma said, 'Don't leave it so long next time our Will. We shan't be here for ever you know.' There was laughter at this ridiculous statement and Jack's voice bellowed, 'You didn't speck him to run down every five minutes our mother did you? Not when Flo's childing. God, he wanted to make the most of that I reckon! Eh our Will? Eh?'

Dad's voice, maudlin with cider, said, 'Little do you know our Jack. B'God. Little do you know.' Everyone laughed again. Aunty Sylv said, 'Drink talking. Eh Vi? Better get the lad up to bed praps.'

Aunty Vi gasped through her giggles, 'He's asleep our Sylv.'Sides, he's too young to understand.'

Albert lifted his chin to tell them he was not asleep and Aunty Sylv laughed louder than anyone, then leaned down and kissed him on the nose, then on each of his eyes. He relapsed again and dreamt that they were on the road back to Gloucester and the outline of the cathedral was black against the pale night sky and Dad was singing under his breath, 'I don't want to leave you but I feel I ought to go,' and the smell of the Kempley daffs was in his nose.

It had been a longer day for March. She had opened the door to young Mrs. Goodrich wearing a clean starched pinafore and a welcoming smile. Young Mrs. Goodrich had held on to the stone jar of honey in her one hand but had given March the bunch of golden daffodils from her other.

'Now dear, put them in the kitchen for tonight. Flowers shouldn't be in a bedroom overnight you know, and the family can have the joy of them until tomorrow.

Then take them up on your mother's breakfast tray. The gypsies brought them round this morning, fresh from Kempley, and I thought of your mother straightaway.'

March was overcome. The fact that she and Mother did not wish to be reminded of Kempley did not matter at all. Young Mrs. Goodrich's generosity and gentility did. March arranged the flowers in the Welsh pottery jug and put them in the middle of the table on the dark red plush cloth. When she lit the gas the kitchen looked almost as it did when Mother was about. She fetched May from the back parlour to see it. May came, dangling the scissors and a string of paper dolls from one hand. 'Oooh. They're beautiful March. No wonder Albert wanted to go with Papa. They're beautiful.'

Sometimes May's reactions were intensely satisfying. March kissed the golden head peremptorily. 'Go up and get ready for bed now May. I'll join you as soon as I've let Mrs. Goodrich out.'

'In our own room March?'

March nodded. April seemed to have stopped crying incessantly and she hoped her mother would not need her again tonight. March did not remember ever feeling so tired before.

She was not pleased to see Mrs. Luker.

'I won't keep your dear mother longer than a minute,' said Hettie breathlessly. 'I meant to come earlier but Sibbie fell and cut her leg and Fred was shoeing a horse with his dad . . . now you get on to bed dearie and I'll let myself out. You've got to leave the door for your father haven't you? So that ull be all right . . . and in your own bed I hope.'

What had May been saying over in that dreadful house?

Mrs. Luker actually came in to say goodnight to them on her way out. 'And you're all tucked up neat and nice and cosy. Just as it should be. No need to worry over your mother any more my dears. What some pretty

51

dears ... eh ... eh. ...' March wondered whether Mrs. Luker had been to the Lamb and Flag. She was no better than Snotty Lottie. March smiled against closed lids. Albert had said something this morning about Lottie. 'Snotty Lottie gottie lottie snotty.' Something like that. Albert was clever. Albert was beautiful. Albert loved her.

Florence held out her arms to her husband.

'Oh Will. My dearest husband. Why didn't you tell me about poor Mr. Daker? Mrs. Luker has just brought me last night's *Citizen*. Oh my dear, I am so sorry.'

He gazed at her. After the uproar of Kempley, his terraced house in Chichester Street was a peaceful haven and his wife more beautiful and refined than he had ever remembered. He sank to his knees by the bed and took her in his arms, and she, mellowed by milk stout, bent her dark head and kissed him.

'I didn't want you to know. Not yet. Not after the birth,' he murmured.

She whispered, 'My dearest. We're here to comfort each other in a cruel world.'

He held her gently, drawing comfort from her, until she fell asleep in his arms. Then he laid her head on the pillow and undressed, standing above April and looking down at her fondly as he compared her with the babies at Kempley. He was a lucky man. He must never forget he was a lucky man.

He climbed into bed beside his wife and put his hand on her waist. He thought of Albert. And his mother and sisters and brothers and the family scattered all over the Kempley and Newent area. He thought of the big funeral that would take place on Monday and how his suits would be there. And he slept with a smile on his lips.

3

They called the kitten Rags, and he grew leggily into a wonderful mouser. He spent every night at the top of the cellar steps and some mornings he had as many as half-a-dozen tails to show for his night's vigil. March no longer held her skirts high as she went upstairs; mice were unknown at number thirty-three. Thirty-one and thirty-five borrowed Rags occasionally, but Florence would never let him out of the front door in case he wandered across the road to the Lukers' and swallowed some of their poison.

Albert took the scholarship for the King's School and did not do very well, but he was given a place because of his voice. Mr. Filbert, who trained the choristers, said he had never heard such a true voice. Florence bought some royal blue and golden yellow Melton cloth from the Co-op in Southgate Street, and Will cut his suit. On August the twenty-seventh he left home with trepidation, walked along Northgate Street, cut down Saint John's Lane and through the cathedral close and presented himself at the arched door in the wall. Mr. Filbert gathered the new boys around him and took them into the music room. Albert relaxed immediately; his clear soprano soared easily without accompaniment. Mr. Filbert said, 'Where did you learn to sight-read boy?' And Albert answered literally, 'In the bandy room sir.' That was where Mother's piano was, plus a banjo acquired by his father. Mr. Filbert smiled and did not pursue the subject.

53

At midday Albert sat with the other boys at a long trestle table and unpacked his bread and dripping. The boy next to him had banana sandwiches and seeing Albert's envious eyes, offered to do a swop. He was as retiring as Albert himself, but during that first week they managed to exchange basic information and begin a friendship. His name was Harry Hughes: he had been a choirboy at Longford church: his father worked on the railway and put him on a tram every morning and he got off at Worcester Street. Albert began to wait for him where Alvin Street spewed its tenements into the Westgate. They would walk down to the cathedral together arm-in-arm, feeling a pair of real lads. They read Dumas together and evolved a clarion cry of comradeship. 'We'll live together! We'll die together!' They would proclaim this with exaggerated gestures and then snuffle and grunt their special, repressed laugh. Albert said to March, 'As soon as Mother is better, I want to ask Harry to tea.' March, immediately jealous, blurted, 'You like him better than me, don't you?' Albert said, 'I like Harry Hughes. I love you. You're my sister.' He knew by now the right thing to say to March.

They could all see that Florence was not well and it did not occur to her that she was pregnant again. She was still breast-feeding April and after his long celibacy during that pregnancy, Will was now very demanding. She imagined she was over-tired, nothing more. It was Lottie Jenner who enlightened her.

The Goodriches and the Risings were the only families in the street who sported a baby carriage for their offspring: the other mothers sat in their open doorways and nursed their babies on fine days and kept them indoors otherwise until they could use their own legs. Florence had wheeled April down to Chichester Street school one golden day in September, simply to give March and May the pleasure of wheeling her back home. The two small girls, trailed by an envious Sibbie Luker, walked sedately behind the wooden handle, and April, sitting up now, gurgled at them enchantingly. It was a picture to remember. Florence found it easy to smile at the appreciative Lottie as she lumbered out of the dairy with her morning milk. At four o'clock in the afternoon.

'Lovely girls. All three of them. And the babby looks well enough considerin' she was early weaned.'

Florence regretted the smile which had encouraged Lottie to behave like . . . Lottie. 'She is not weaned yet,' she said against her better judgement. Florence still did not enjoy breast-feeding but she was proud of April's progress.

Lottie drew in her lips disapprovingly. 'Should be. For your sake Mrs. Rising. How far on are you? Three months? Four? Surprised you got any milk, but then, you thin ones are always deceptive.'

Florence stared, her surprise obvious, then she recovered herself with difficulty. 'It — it's early days yet Mrs. Jenner,' she said meaninglessly. She quickened her step to catch up with the girls and leave Lottie behind. It couldn't be. It couldn't. Yet she knew it was.

Doctor Green was blunt.

'Either you rest — lie down for twenty-four hours a day — or you lose this child. It's up to you.'

Florence knew where her duty lay and told Will about it that night. Will did not say a word. Once a pregnancy was confirmed, Florence would not allow him near her; the new baby became her duty before her husband. Will sat on the edge of the bed and stared down at his bare legs and accepted the cold fact of several months' more celibacy without protest. He could have said 'Alf and Hettie Luker make the most of their pregnancies.' But he didn't. Florrie wasn't Hettie Luker. He straightened his shoulders; neither was he Alf Luker. He must remember that.

It was Will who decreed that the children — all of them, even April — must be sent away. He would take the trap again and drive down to Kempley and see if his mother would have them.

'They'll be all right down at Kempley till Christmas,' he said defensively as Florence's horrified face turned towards him. 'And there's no other way you will stay up here in bed, I know that for a fact.'

Florence imagined how it would be: Albert out with Austin and Jack all day, Wallie thinking it amusing to introduce the boy to rough cider: her beautiful May among those coarse voices: April grubbing on the floor with the other babies.

She said, 'I'll write to Aunt Lizzie first.' She glanced at the new curtains. 'She's always been generous. I'll write to her.'

Will looked doubtful. It was one thing to send birthday and Christmas presents, quite another to receive their objects into a quiet, childless home. Especially when one of the objects was only five months old. But Aunt Lizzie was one of the mystical Rhys-Davies clan; and she was married to Edwin Tomms who owned two ironmongeries in Bath and might even be a Freemason.

Aunt Lizzie was overjoyed with the idea of having her nephew and three nieces on a three-month visit. She was not strong and number thirty-three Chichester Street offered little comfort to a semi-invalid, so she had never stayed there. The last time she had come for the day had been when May was christened and as Florence had never been able to afford the journey to Bath, they were virtual strangers to each other.

The children were not told the reason for this unexpected holiday and decided that Aunt Lizzie had summoned them for an inspection. Albert, long ago primed on his aristocratic Welsh blood, commented gloomily, 'I expect she wants me to change my name to Rhys-Davies.' March exclaimed in sudden terror, 'Or adopt you!' May, infuriatingly sensible in spite of her romanticism, said, 'Don't be silly, Mother wouldn't part with a hair of our heads.'

Their chief concern at leaving home was the kitten. But the fact that Mother spent so much time lying down was useful in that respect as Rags very much enjoyed joining her on the feather bed in the big front room. They all went in to kiss Mother and assure her they were going to be good. May had her underwear checked and was given some wintergreen ointment for her chest; March was given last-minute instructions for April; Albert was told to be a little man and look after his sisters. They all stroked Rags, laughing delightedly as he rolled on to his back displaying his knotty curls. Then they were off, March pushing the carriage with one case balanced on it, Dad carrying another, Albert a canvas holdall. 'Like a moonlight flit,' Dad joked as they turned into Northgate Street where the pavement was high above the road and railed off beneath the railway bridge. 'It isn't night time Dad.' 'What do you mean Papa?' asked the children. Will shook his head, already breathing heavily. 'Step it out,' he said instead.

Bristol was the most amazing station in the world. Instead of wooden bridges over the line, it had tunnels beneath, tiled white like the public lavatories and echoing to every murmur. They saw a cattle train trundle slowly through between the platforms: twenty-four open wagons of lowing, terrified cows, heads tossing above each other's flanks, eyes rolling, bodies jerking as the wagons clanked together. May wept, though she was used to seeing herds being driven through the traffic of the Northgate on market days.

Bristol was amazing, Bath just beautiful. They changed to the Great Western line and travelled through a lush, enclosed Somerset. Hills wrapped them gently and the river was next to them, willow-edged and full of reflections, not a bit like their own Severn.

May breathed, 'It's lovely. Just lovely.' And March, holding April to the window, had to agree.

They emerged from the train, almost in awe. In the heart of their own city nothing was visible because it was so flat. Here, standing on the platform surrounded by their luggage, they could see the whole of Bath. The abbey, then the bays of terraces rising to woods; the river below, spanned by arched bridges; the green of parks. And though it was two o'clock of a November afternoon, no trace of fog. There might be a river mist later, but the sooty fog that settled over Gloucester on winter days was not here. And the smell was different too. As the train went on its way to Chippenham and Westbury, the sulphur smell went with it and left dampness. Not the muddy dampness of the canal over-laid with the vinegar of the pickle factory and the pulped wood from the match works, but the dampness of grass and leaves and the smiling, meandering Avon and the deep warm springs that the Romans had found.

March was silent through May's exclamations and Albert's grinning guffaws, but it was only because she could hardly believe her eyes. March did not have May's ability to see beauty through ugliness. Her home town was spoilt for her because of the grime and grimness; the countryside meant the squalor of Kempley Cottage. Bath was quite different. She was to discover ugly parts later, but that first impression remained. Bath was beauty and luxury. She surrendered the pram to May and walked through the booking hall in a trance. Already she knew that quiet, grey days in November would remind her of Bath for the rest of her life.

Aunt Lizzie was a surprise too. March could see she was a Rhys-Davies. There was the dark hair, though very much threaded with greys that were inclined to escape from their bun and frizz up on their own. There were the straight aquiline features and the brown eyes and the tiny, neat feet and long thin hands, but the whole added up differently. Aunt Lizzie had had a sister to share the narrow confines of the Davies household and they had both escaped early to marriage. When Alice had died in childbirth, the baby, Florence, had lived in the gaunt old house in Westgate Street with no company save for a stiff governess, until she was sent to Kempley to escape the smallpox. All the laughter and fun she had known had come from Will Rising and their subsequent children.

Aunt Lizzie loved to talk, and March, the elder girl and the darkest of the three children, became her confidante. Before Will had left them that afternoon to catch the two trains back to Florence, she had set the pattern for their three months with her.

'Now darlings —' she patted Will's arm reassuringly. The fact that he had obviously impregnated Florence five times made him very special — Florence had always reminded Lizzie of a nun — but seeing him separately with his children like this, she could sense his attractions. She recalled her mother telling her in despair how ardent he was, and how poor Florence would never be able to stand against him; how she had wanted to send the girl abroad but Will Rising had threatened to kill himself if she went away. . . . There had been so many things, so many romantic things.

'Now darlings, I've looked out all my old games. Snakes and ladders and ludo and backgammon and . . . oh, ever so many things. You will have to amuse yourselves because I'm far too old to do it for you!' She laughed, obviously expecting them to deny this, but when nobody spoke, she sped on, 'Letty will take you for a walk each afternoon when she has finished in the house. And when I drive into town — or make suitable calls — you may come with me. Otherwise —'

'They're quite used to seeing to themselves Mrs. Jephcott — er — aunt,' Will said, liking the old lady better than before. At first he had hated all the Rhys-Davies because they came between himself and his Flo,

59

but when the old pair died it became evident that Aunt Lizzie had not entirely disapproved of him as a suitor. She had sent them the stair carpet and the curtains for the Chichester Street house, besides remembering all the birthdays. He patted the back of the hand that was patting his arm. She was amazingly like an older Florence.

'Then that's fine,' she beamed at them. 'I was afraid you might feel dull here but perhaps, after all. . . . And this is the new baby? She's going to look like you Albert, isn't she? And what could be nicer?' She left Will's arm and put her hand on March's head. 'And you are the little mother March? Will you mind permitting Letty to see to April now? Because I am so looking forward to talking to you and hearing about your dear mother.'

She made no comment on May's beauty, her smile was entirely for March, and her words gave March place and importance.

'Oh . . . oh so am I Aunt Lizzie,' March breathed delightedly.

'Then we'll ring for Letty now — the bell is by the fire-place dear — and she can bring our tea in here by the fire and then take April downstairs and give her some of that porage stuff and pop her into bed. I've given her a room near Letty dear, on the top floor, so that you can sleep undisturbed.'

'Oh . . . Aunt Lizzie . . .' breathed March.

May suddenly said, 'Daddy, do you have to go back tonight?'

'Of course he does.' Albert, usually masking his fondness for May in front of March, was piqued by March's unaccustomed success. He draped a protective arm across the blonde head. 'Dad has to look after Mother, don't you remember?'

'Please stay for tea at least William.' Aunt Lizzie fluttered above his coat sleeve again. One would expect him to be well turned out as he was a tailor, but not to be quite so much like the dear King when he had been the errant Prince of Wales. 'You cannot return all the way to Gloucester without any refreshment at all.'

March was surprised when her father mentioned nothing about the sandwiches she had so laboriously cut for the journey; even more surprised when he carried Aunt Lizzie's hand to his lips in exactly the same way as he did Mother's. It affected May too and she began to weep silently as always, huge tears threatening to drown her blue eyes.

Albert said fiercely, 'We'd better say cheerio then Dad hadn't we? Tempus fugits and all that.' Albert had been doing Latin for exactly six weeks.

The children were hugged by Will in turn. March knew it nearly made him weep too to leave them, but she felt no reciprocal sentiment. She and Aunt Lizzie were going to talk while May and Albert played silly games and April was looked after, washed, fed and cleaned by poor Letty. But then Letty would be paid for doing it.

On November the fifth there was an enormous bonfire in Green Park and a firework display. The children drove along the Royal Crescent in Uncle Edwin's carriage and watched with all their eyes. March sat in the curve of Aunt Lizzie's arm, May on Uncle Edwin's knee; Albert in a Norfolk jacket and breeches knelt on the seat, his elbows on the folded hood. He thought how much more fun it would be if Dad was there, laughing and pointing his beard to the sky. It was strange; at home Mother was always serious and quiet and Dad full of fun. Here it was quite the other way around. Aunt Lizzie laughed more each day, but Uncle Edwin was more than just serious. He looked solemn even when May smiled up at him and asked whether he was quite sure he was warm enough.

Aunt Lizzie said, 'Are you warm enough kitten? That's the important thing. Your dear mamma will never forgive me if you catch cold while you're staying in Bath.'

March snuggled hard against the inside of Aunt

Lizzie's elbow, not minding a bit that Aunt Lizzie was as concerned as everyone always seemed to be about May. Aunt Lizzie's concern had a kind of indulgence to it; she used the same voice that she used to April. She never used that voice to March. March and Aunt Lizzie were equals in her sight.

A huge spray of sparks glowed against the night sky and gradually changed colour until they became a vase of flowers. March twisted her head to see whether Aunt Lizzie was enjoying it and saw that the dark eyes were not watching the fireworks at all. They were watching her.

'You see March dear. . . .'

After the fireworks, there was cocoa and little sugar biscuits by the fire, and while Uncle Edwin was unwillingly coerced into a game of dominoes with May and Albert, Aunt Lizzie talked to March. It was eight o'clock, when they should have been abed, but November the fifth was special. March watched the sparks collecting on the fire back — black-leaded every morning by Letty's underdog — and thought how pleasant it all was.

'My father — your great-grandfather that was — lost his inheritance because of an entailment. No dear, I do not understand it myself, but sometimes a great estate is entailed to a distant relative so that it will not be left to a woman or perhaps to a son who was not quite — er — regular. Born on the wrong side of the sheets as it were. And though dear Papa was brought up in the house and recognised as my grandfather's son, I rather think . . . however dear, this is mere speculation. All I know is that he was forced to leave Llanfenon when he was sixteen and he never got over it. He was embittered. At that age! What a fate! Guard against bitterness March, it eats at the soul like rust at iron.'

March touched Aunt Lizzie's hand; it was like one of May's stories but it was real. She said in a low voice so that the others could not hear, 'Lemons are bitter too Aunt Lizzie.'

Aunt Lizzie recollected for a moment that she was talking to a nine-year-old child and spoke in the voice reserved for May and April.

'But lemons are clean and fresh dearest. Are they not? Not a bit like rust.'

March was reassured. She might be only nine but she knew she was capable of bitterness. She hoped it was the lemon kind and not the rusty.

'But you're not — em — embittered Aunt Lizzie.'

'I'm a realist, child.' Aunt Lizzie's smile became roguish. 'To pin one's hope on litigation is a dream in this country March. Remember that. I daresay laws and rules can bludgeon people into doing what they want occasionally. I find *persuasion* works better.' She laughed delightfully. 'Did you not take note of the way I persuaded your uncle to play with Albert and May? I kissed him my dear, and told him I was tired and you would soothe my nerves and could he possibly amuse the other two for me!'

March pondered this. Some of it was unwelcome: May got her way with Mother by means of a kiss and a hug. On the other hand she was also a dreamer and Aunt Lizzie obviously had no time for dreamers.

She looked up at Aunt Lizzie and laughed too and Albert said disapprovingly, 'Why are you laughing March?' They'd been at Bath just under a week and though he was making the best of it and nearly enjoying it in spite of himself, he did not expect March to do so. She was the one who wanted to go to school and become clever; she was the one who depended on his attention for her happiness. Yet here she was missing her precious school and Aunt Lizzie seemed set on taking her away from Albert. And she could still laugh.

She said with simple truth, 'I'm laughing because Aunt Lizzie is laughing!'

He was frankly jealous. 'Watch out you don't wake

May,' he said sternly. 'She's exhausted after all the excitement of the fireworks.' He made it sound as though Aunt Lizzie had forced them down to the park.

It was the first time the two gossipers had noticed May's comatose state and Aunt Lizzie pulled the bell while March dusted the crumbs from her pinafore into the glowing fire, suitably subdued. Uncle Edwin protested unexpectedly, 'We haven't finished the game yet my boy. A game must always be finished properly — that's something you should learn as soon as possible.'

Letty arrived and took in the situation at a glance. She bawled over her shoulder, 'Come on Rosie — stir yourself!' and in five minutes a drowsy May was helped upstairs and into her thickest flannel nightgown already thoroughly impregnated with wintergreen. As March followed her into the warmed bed, she felt sorry that Albert could not share her ever-present delight in this new existence. But his reticence did not mar anything. It almost accentuated her pleasure. And she adored Aunt Lizzie. Whatever Aunt Lizzie was and did, March would be and would do.

Teddy was born six weeks early on Christmas Eve. In spite of staying in bed, things did not go well for Florence. Doctor Green attended and Lottie was ousted by a professional nurse in starched white uniform. Ether was used, and the dreaded forceps, and Will, waiting on the landing in an agony of fear, heard the word 'haemorrhaging' and associated it always with the sickly gas smell seeping beneath the bedroom door. Somehow Florence clung to life. Pale and anaemic she would always be now, but she was alive. Teddy, under five pounds but healthy enough, was removed to a foster home known to Doctor Green, where a strong young woman, just delivered of a son herself, had enough milk for two or more.

Teddy thrived quickly, though Florence obstinately refused to believe it and sat white-faced through all the ten days of Christmas, unable to reply to the children's letters or do more than shudder at her daily diet of raw liver. On January the fourth Doctor Green made a bargain with her.

'If I go and fetch your son now and let you hold him for half an hour, will you start eating your liver and drinking your stout?'

Florence shuddered again, but nodded faintly and without much hope.

It was a cold day, the rain falling as sleet on to the thick oily water of the docks. The doctor drove his brougham carefully through the tiny back streets behind Gloucester prison to the house where the wet nurse lived. She had been the doctor's own kitchenmaid, and, in spite of her mean quarters, knew how he liked things done. Teddy and her own baby lay side by side in an upstairs room, well heated by a small fire and well ventilated too. Doctor Green nodded approval and especially so when he examined the children.

'You're doing a good job Kitty. A very good job. My patient will be very grateful to you. As I am. Not much money I'm afraid, but good warm clothing for your young Sir Nib here. The husband's a tailor.'

'Thank you sir.' Kitty was an amiable girl and would have suckled Teddy for the sake of her old employers, but her husband would want to render an account.

The doctor received the swaddled Teddy and pulled the shawl well up around his face. 'Once the mother is on her feet she will visit you until you wean the child, Kitty. We can't have too many of these outings while the weather is so unkind.'

'Certainly not sir. You tell her she's welcome here any old time. And she's not to worry one mite. That baby ent no trouble to no-one down here. An' he's not doing too badly by the looks of things.' She indicated just above her waist line, unashamed, and the doctor patted her shoulder approvingly. How much easier his life would be if all his patients were like Kitty Hall. He recalled Florence Rising's taut embarrassment at each examination and sighed.

But her joy at the sight of Teddy compensated for all the good doctor's trouble. She held out her arms with a little cry and stared down into the tumbled shawl incredulously.

'He's beautiful!'

'What did I say? Now fetch that liver Mr. Rising and —'

'He's so strong! He's stronger than April and she was the strongest of the children!'

'I said that too.'

Will brought the revolting liver, chopped as fine as he could do it on the bread board, with a little parsley added to make it just palatable.

'Oh that does look delicious.' Doctor Green took the dish and spoon, determined that Florence should not welsh on her bargain. 'Now, if you let your husband hold his son for five minutes Mrs. Rising —'

She relinquished the baby unwillingly and began on her liver, hardly noticing it. Her brown eyes, feverishly bright, never left that dark head and her hands shook as if eager to begin living again. She and Will had decided before the baby's birth that if it was a girl it should be named Elizabeth and if a boy, Edwin, in gratitude to her aunt and uncle in Bath. She had been glad not to be forced to stray from her month-names; now for the first time, she called the baby Teddy.

'We'll call him Teddy, Will,' she said, chewing desperately, her eyes watering, her hand held ready for the glass of water offered by Doctor Green. She gulped and gasped. 'Teddy. It suits him, don't you think? He looks so sturdy! And yet — and yet —' she swallowed again, 'he's dark like me. He's the first of the children to look like me!'

Will grinned at the tiny bundle. 'Oh I don't know, Flo. March has your eyes.'

Florence took another spoonful of her mess and chewed again.

'But Teddy — Teddy is a Rhys-Davies!' she said.

Will looked up quickly, his grin fading. 'Teddy he shall be if you like, Flo. But Teddy Rising. And don't you forget it.'

The doctor glanced from one to the other as he scraped the liver dish. He had wanted to say something at the time of the birth, but it had seemed inappropriate. Now he felt the time had come.

'Mrs. Rising . . . well done . . . a short drink will help it down, I think. Now. I have to say — to tell you — an unpleasant — er — fact. No good beating about the bush.' He looked at Will. 'Let Mother hold the baby again Mr. Rising. I think . . . yes . . . it would be best if she held. . . .' The transfer was made and the doctor cleared his throat. 'He's a very good specimen Mrs. Rising — that is to say — he's a lovely baby. As you see of course. All your children . . . lovely. But this one — this one must be the last my dear. I'm sorry. But I cannot be responsible if there are any more pregnancies.' She looked remarkably calm. It doubtless had not penetrated as yet. She was obviously one of Nature's mothers so it would hit her hard. He turned to Will. 'You understand what I am saying Mr. Rising? If your wife has another baby she will — er — forfeit her — er —'

Florence's voice spoke calmly at his side.

'We understand, Doctor. Perfectly. Please don't be anxious. We have five beautiful children, as you so kindly said. We are perfectly satisfied.'

Doctor Green looked at her. She meant it, at least for the moment. Of course in a year or two it would doubtless be a different story, but for now . . . well, she was an amazing little woman. Beautiful in a classic sort of way, and with that black hair folded over her brow she had the look of a nun. He smiled to himself and stood up.

'Time for young Teddy to go back to his meal ticket,'

he said heartily. 'Don't worry too much about it all, Mrs. Rising. As soon as you've had some of that liver and got strength back into your limbs, you can visit him every day. And we'll wean him early. There's a school of thought around these days that says babies can go on to solids as early as eight weeks.' He boomed a laugh. Mrs. Rising did not echo it, indeed she looked hopeful. 'Just eat up that liver,' he concluded quickly. 'As much as you can possibly manage.' He swaddled the baby again, pulling the lapel of his Burberry over the tiny head as he went out into the awful weather. He was pleased with himself. This time, disaster had been averted.

Will sat late over some turn-ups that night. Bitterness was a taste in his mouth and even the snowy rain slurping stickily over the smoked glass of his workroom had the look of gall. For one thing, he was exhausted. Since Mr. Daker's death last April, he had acquired most of his business, on the understanding that he paid ten per cent of his takings to Mrs. Daker as commission. Women. Old Daker had been a Jew, no doubt of that, but he had never struck bargains in quite the same way as his wife. It had seemed fair enough at the time. Florence had been doubtful, but he'd reassured her in his easy-going way. 'She's frightened, Flo. Frightened of being alone and poor. But David is nearly fourteen. Soon old enough to support all three of them.'

He'd been glad of the work at first. Mrs. Daker had put him on to a glazier in Barton Street who had supplied the new smoked glass window with his name let into it: 'W. Rising. Tailor.' Florence said it was in excellent taste and so much better than advertising in the Citizen. It was the nearest she had come to criticising his announcement of April's birth. It seemed to bring more work than ever. Complete strangers, taking their daughters to the new school in Denmark Road through Chichester Street, knocked on his door and enquired whether he tailored ladies' coats — navy-blue cloth, melton, with a half belt, suitable for school wear. He showed them March's, pockets full of moth balls for the summer. They were impressed. If he had more orders for next September, he might write a discreet letter to the headmistress suggesting that he become the school's recommended tailor.

Then there had been the upset over the new baby. He had reconciled himself to a few months' celibacy and had boasted in the Lamb and Flag of his prowess. Florence was his small wiry Welsh pony and as soon as the new baby arrived, she would do her duty again and March would be that much older to help out, and Albert would be singing solo in the cathedral, and May more beautiful than ever . . . he was the luckiest man in the world. Or so he had thought until today.

Angrily he laid the finished trousers on the pressing table, and, not finding the iron holder, picked up the iron from the gas using his handkerchief. Florence would have done the turn-ups for him while he tacked the new smoking jacket for one of Mr. Daker's friends, but he couldn't bring himself to ask her. He couldn't bring himself to speak to her since Doctor Green's departure. Mrs. Goodrich had brought in some fresh lamb's liver and he should have chopped it and taken it in to her while she sat with Mrs. Luker in the back parlour. Hettie Luker came over most evenings with a bottle of stout and bits of laundry, rough-dried and not very clean. He couldn't wait for Florence to be back on her feet so that his collars were decently starched and he didn't have to make do with the same shirt all week. But then, if he wanted Flo on her feet again he should have chopped that liver and taken it in to her.

Angrier than ever, he banged the iron back on to the trivet and folded the trousers into their creases and over a chair. His handkerchief had a large brown scorch mark across it, which meant it couldn't go into his top pocket for callers. He rammed it into the pocket of his trousers and banged down the passage into the kitchen. There was no sign of the liver on the table but Rags sat by his dish washing his face smugly. Will looked at the table, looked at the cat, and some of the temper which his father had passed to March exploded inside him. He leaned down and whacked the soft furry body as hard as he could. Rags sailed into the air with a startled squawk and landed feet first by the gas stove. Panic-stricken, he skidded beneath it then poked his triangular mask apprehensively from beneath the oven door. He couldn't believe his senses. The tall skinny dark one, yes. But not this one.

Will stared back, horrified at his own behaviour. He had never struck an animal or child in anger before. Never bullied his wife. Perhaps it would have been better if he had. He turned and strode into the back parlour. It was in darkness, the guard around the fire, the curtains drawn back ready for the morning. He closed the door on it and took the stairs two at a time. Voices came from behind the front bedroom door. Inside Hettie sat by the bed, recounting a small incident which proved how much Sibbie missed May.

'I'm not one to lie Mrs. Rising,' she concluded. 'Specially about children. Our Sibbie thinks of your May as her sister. More than her sister. They're like that!' She held up her forefingers side by side. 'Peas in a pod. Peas in a pod.' She smiled at Will, a wide self-congratulatory smile. 'And all the liver gone Mr. Rising,' she went on without a pause. 'I did chop it like you does and put in a bit of parsley and down it went as sweet as a nut!'

Hettie stood up and smoothed down her filthy pinafore. She was proud of her figure since her last birth six weeks ago. She moved her smile towards Florence.

'I'd best be going. Christamighty it must be gone ten and Henry wanting his supper I'll be bound.' Henry was the new baby. 'Oh, it's nice we birthed so close Mrs. Rising. Just like Sibbie and May is such friends so will Glad and April be. And now Henry and your little Edwin.'

70

Will said, 'I didn't realise you'd done the liver Hettie. Thank you . . . I've been kept late over some trouser turn-ups.'

Florence was distressed. 'Oh Will, why didn't you bring them in to me? I've been sitting idly talking to Mrs. Luker.' Will knew she didn't approve of him using Hettie's first name. 'Now, lock up quickly dear and come to bed.'

Hettie giggled and went to the door still smoothing her pinafore. Will followed, wishing there was a reason for the giggle, noticing for the first time the voluptuousness of Hettie's still swelling abdomen.

He said, 'Wait a minute Hettie. You'd better take an umbrella. You shouldn't have come over without a coat or anything.'

She laughed more loudly at this and came after him down the passage and into the kitchen. Rags was still beneath the gas stove.

Will said, 'Oh Christ. I thought the cat had eaten the liver and I kicked him there. Look at the poor little devil.' His voice dropped automatically into a slovenly drawl and Hettie's laughter increased accordingly.

'Oh Will Rising, I didn't know you could be . . . oh Will, you *do* make me laugh. Honestly!'

Will turned and saw her open mouth and very white teeth gleaming in the gaslight. The sleet, probably snow by now, brushed sibilantly against the dark kitchen window where the gasometer kept a constant watch for any indiscretions. She reminded him of his sisters, dirty, uncaring, full of senseless laughter that sprang from life; generous to a fault. . . .

He put his hands either side of her waist, leaned forward and kissed the open mouth. Immediately he sprang backwards as if she'd bitten him.

'Hettie I — my God — Hettie, I'm sorry —'

She put a hand to her mouth as if to stop the laughter, but her eyes danced and bubbled with it. They were blue eyes like his own and they were full of knowledge.

'Don't you dare apologise Will Rising! It ud be an insult that would!' She took a deep breath through her fingers. 'I never thought you'd look at me! Don't be sorry for that . . . for doing what you wanted!' She dropped her hand and took a step towards him. 'I'm honoured Will. I'm real honoured. Honest. I wouldn't lie to you Will. Not about something like that.' She was moving closer to him as she spoke those oft-used words. He noticed her neck was dirty and again he was reminded of Sylv and Vi. Pigs in shit. As happy as pigs in shit. 'I've never dared look at you Will. Not *look* at you. You know. Like that. Not till now.' She put her hands behind her back and undid her pinafore then slipped it over her head. Her fingers went to her throat and began on her blouse buttons. 'I've always said you was a handsome man. Like the King. And we all know what he's like, don't we?' She laughed yet again and showed those animal-white teeth and he smelled the comforting smell of stout on her breath. And if it was all right for the King. . . .

He said, 'I durstn't Het. . . .' He sounded like his brother Jack. 'I durstn't. Supposin' . . . supposin'. . . .'

Again she laughed. 'Chrisamighty Will . . . you don't think any harm can come do you? I'm a month gone again a'ready. Cursed Alf last week when I found out, but now . . . it's a blessing in disguise en't it? A real blessing. . . .' Her hands took his and slid them inside her camisole and her laughter seemed to go into his throat so that they shook together and happiness burst inside him again as it always did. He couldn't be unhappy for long. It wasn't in his nature. They lay on the mat before the dead range and Rags came and sniffed at them and was sent flying back to the gas stove for his trouble. Hettie was laughing so much she hardly had the strength to pull down her drawers.

He could not face Florrie. He slept in Albert's bed and wept into the pillow. He had never touched anyone but Florrie, not until tonight. Since he was twelve Florence Davies had been everything to him. He had loved her with his whole being and he knew she had loved him with a tenderness and a selflessness he would not find again. He slept somehow, waking frequently in the hope that the incident with Hettie Luker was a fevered dream, groaning with despair as each time he realised it was not. In the morning he crept downstairs, hardly noticing the snow banked greyly against the windows. He boiled some water and made tea; scraped out the range and lit it; did the same to the fireplace in the back parlour. He boiled an egg for Florence and laid a tray as beautifully as May would have done.

She said, 'Oh Will . . . how kind you are!' and he felt terrible.

Later as he sat in his workroom and heard her moving slowly about, washing and dressing and settling herself in the back parlour, he wondered how they would manage until the children returned. They had to be alone together so often. It would be unbearable. And when Hettie came over this evening with the stout, what could he say? If he went to the Lamb and Flag she would be waiting for him when he got back. What could he do? He felt trapped in his own house.

It was time for him to make some dinner and take it in to her when the bell rang. He peered through the advertisement on the window and could just make out the bulky, well-wrapped figure of a woman. Not Hettie. Snow or no snow, Hettie would have slipped over the road hatless. This one huddled on the top step, level with the boot-scraper, head down and shoulders hunched against the east wind; it was his sister, Sylvia.

'Sylv!' He flung open the door and dragged her in. She was almost hidden in shawls and beneath them she was holding a large bundle tied just as his mother had tied his bundle when he had come to Mr. Daker. Sylvia, with her clothes? 'This is marvellous Sylv! Never been to see us have you? And not for want of an invitation — come in girl, out of that snow — never mind the oilcloth —' She was salvation. He led her into the back parlour, still exclaiming, so that she couldn't begin on any explanations just yet. She could have been about to report a death; it did not matter just so long as she was there between himself and Florrie.

Florence had kept the fire in and it was warm and elegant with the round table covered in a dark plush cloth and Florence sitting with her crochet in her lap. He was proud all over again.

Sylv took off snow-sodden gloves and exposed red-raw hands. Her face was red and raw too as if she'd been crying. Florence tried to get up.

'My dear! Whatever brings you here a day like this? Sit down — yes, I insist. Will — fetch the brandy.'

He pushed Flo back and drew up the other chair for Sylv. Then he hastened to the chiffonier and put sugar in a glass, then a thimbleful of brandy. Florence made distressed noises and Sylv kept saying, 'No need to fuss, Ma's all right. And Pa. Everyone — everyone's quite all right.' Then as the brandy thawed her throat, she added anxiously, 'You, what about you Flo? We heard about the new boy o'course, but the message didn't say nothing about you being ill. Hardly anything of you my dear — hardly anything at all!'

'I'm recovering fast. With the help of your dear brother.' Suddenly and unexpectedly, Florence picked up Will's hand from the back of her chair and put it to her cheek. 'He is goodness itself Sylvia. I cannot begin to tell you —'

Will snatched his hand away, then covered the rebuff with a laugh.

'So kind I leave you alone hour after hour while I'm in the workroom!'

'The work has to be done dearest. And you won't allow me to help.'

He couldn't bear it. He drew up a footstool and squatted between the two women. 'You'll stay for a few nights Sylv?' Hettie could expect nothing this evening if his sister was here. 'You can see we could do with your help. Florence has anaemia and the baby is out to a wet nurse, the other children all at Bath —'

'Why didn't you send and ask for one of us to come, Will?' Sylvia was looking better by the minute. 'Keeping it all to yourself like this. What are families for?'

'Florence wouldn't let me tell you —'

'Then she should!' Sylvia spoke unusually vehemently. 'I coulda come up before Christmas and saved all this fuss and bother.'

'There has been no fuss and bother Sylvia.' Florence spoke quietly but her voice over-rode her sister-in-law's. 'We have managed very well indeed.'

'Fuss and bother for me I meant m'dear.' Sylvia looked directly and appealingly at Florence then back to her brandy glass. Very carefully she placed it on the mantelpiece. 'Father would have taken it far more kindly if I'd been here for a month or two helping you out. As it is. . . .'

Will stared at her. She was all right, but she wasn't laughing.

'Come on. What's happened Sylv?'

She said roughly, 'Silly old bugger's turned me out!' At last she mustered a laugh. 'He reckoned four babies between Vi and me and not one husband, weren't good enough. Turned me out when I told him about the next one. Nearly told me to take the boys with me, but Ma stepped in and put a stop to that.' She met their eyes, defiantly. 'I didn't know what to do. Baby's due come April and the weather being like this —'

Will said in a strangled voice, 'God Sylv — not another one! No wonder Father kicked up this time! Who's the man?'

'Someone who can't do much about it Will. Same as last time and the time before that.' She looked at her red hands. 'Flo . . . I'm sorry. Vi and me . . . we're too old to get married now. And we can't keep saying no all the time —'

'That's enough Sylv!' Will was afraid Florrie would faint. 'Don't try to excuse yourself please!'

Sylvia flushed sullenly. 'Well, it's done. An' it can't be undone. An' there's nowhere else I can go. You going to turn me out too?'

Florence pushed her crochet to the floor as she reached across to take the big hands in her long delicate ones.

'Of course we're not going to turn you out Sylvia! Didn't you hear Will say we could do with your help? My dear, you are Will's sister — your home is here for as long as you need it!'

Sylvia looked up, surprised. She had thought Florence's disapproval would have shown itself in icy withdrawal if not outright dismissal. For a long moment her pale blue eyes stared into liquid brown ones, then she slipped to her knees with completely uncharacteristic humility and put her head in her sister-in-law's lap.

Will stood up and picked up the brandy glass and looked down at the two women. His sister and his wife. He had torn himself from one to reach for the other and had always thought them aeons apart. Perhaps seeing them together, like this, perhaps then he could view the incident of Hettie in perspective.

Meanwhile it was enough that Sylvia was here. Between him and Florence. Between him and Hettie.

He touched her shoulder.

'You're welcome to stay here Sylv,' he said benevolently.

4

Sylvia Rising pulled her weight at the Chichester Street house. For the rest of the month the snow was piled in drifts to the ground floor window sills, and while Will worked and reluctantly let Florrie help him — so long as she did so by the fire in the back parlour — Sylvia dug a way out of the front door and cleared the yard to the wash-house; kept the fires going, fed the cat and prepared huge sloppy meals of wet cabbage and potatoes and tough meat. Incredibly, Florence thrived. She eked out her liver with bread and butter and honey and small pieces of the heavy fruit cake Sylv produced twice weekly; she drank cocoa made entirely with milk, and after a glass of Hettie's stout one night she even shared bread, cheese and onions with her sister-in-law.

The respect which Florence gave to everyone was appreciated by the feckless Sylv and foundations laid for a lifetime of protective devotion. Sylvia washed Florence's smalls in the kitchen and dried them by the range; hers and Will's went into the copper with the linen and froze rigidly on the outside lines. Will's combinations were never the same again, they came halfway up his legs and were yellow ochre in colour instead of pale cream. In other ways Sylv's efforts were more successful. When Mrs. Goodrich and baby Charlotte were taken to the fever hospital near Tewkesbury, she stood over Hettie Luker during her visits in case any word should be dropped to Florence.

Will was not sure whether he liked Sylvia's devotion or not. Just as Albert in Bath was made uncomfortable by an unexpected invasion into his private territory, so was Will back in the sanctuary of Chichester Street.

He came down one morning to find Sylv scraping some mess from Rags off the floor with unaccustomed zeal.

'Don't bother with that Sylv,' he said. 'I'll do it later.' His sister appeared to have doubled in size since her arrival just two weeks ago, and it was all too evident from her heavy breathing that to stoop to scrub the floor was difficult.

'Flo might be down in a minute,' she panted. 'She mustn't see this our Will. It 'ud turn her up.'

He didn't deny it. 'Why doesn't it turn you up then?' he asked as he stepped over her to warm himself at the range.

She laughed. He realised how rarely that laugh sounded now. 'Oh get on with you our Will! I'm used to it'n course.'

He turned his back to the fire and straddled his legs. The warmth seeped inside his trousers and helped to thaw the frozen remembrance of yet another night in Albert's room. He said resentfully, 'She should be used to it too. Five children. She should be used to it.'

'Get on with you!' she said again, standing up, scuffing her shoe over the wiped oilcloth. 'Flo in't like us. We're rough.'

Unaccountably Will recalled watching Snotty Lottie — less than a year ago — squeezing Florence's breast. He said angrily, 'She should be made to do it. You're spoiling her Sylv. Next time, leave it — she's had to do it in the past!'

Sylv looked up, surprised. ''Course she has! An' she'll do it again brother!' She laughed stoutly. 'Not while I'm here though. Flo en't going to clean up cat shit while I'm here!' She wiped her soiled hands on her skirt and took the teapot to the stove. 'And that puts me in mind of what I want to say Will. I mun't stay much longer. Flo wants her babbies back with her. They can't see me like this.'

'Rubbish!' Will moved a step away from the range and rubbed his backside. 'And anyway, what if they do? I'm not having my sister in the workhouse Sylv. And that's that.' He wondered, even as he spoke, whether he would have been so vehement before Doctor Green's dictum three weeks before.

She brought the teapot to the table and left it to brew while she cut bread and butter for Florence.

'It won't come to that Will. Leas-ways, I dun't think so. I hoped — when the snow gives over — I hoped as you'd go and talk to Pa.' She slapped half-inch slices on to a plate next to the sticky honey pot. 'He'll listen to you. 'Specially if you tells him that your kids are coming back from Bath and you dun't want them to see . . . owt.'

'He doesn't know they're in Bath. So that won't cut much ice.'

'Dun't be daft Will. You can explain about Flo nearly dying and having to be fed —'

'I'm not turning my sister away and that is that!' Will seized the tray, slopping the tea over the edge of the cup and not regretting it, nor the doorstep wedges of bread and butter. 'We need you here Sylv, surely you can see that?'

'You wun't need me when the little 'uns get back. You're always on about 'em Will. And Flo is too. I know little May can tempt her mam to eat food like I can't. And March gets the washing that soft. And you miss young Albert . . .' she took a deep breath. 'Chris-amighty. Don't you think I know how you feels? I can't wait to see my babs again. Ma'll treat 'em good, 'course. But I want 'em Will. I *want* my kids!'

He dug the edge of the tray into his waistcoat buttons. He'd never seen Sylv cry.

'Hang on till this lot thaws then —' he jerked his head

at the looming white-coated monster outside. 'I'll go out to Kempley as soon as I can. But if they won't have you back Sylv — you're stopping with us.'

He thought he might have an ally in Florence. It was the first time he had taken up her tray since Sylv arrived, and he surprised her tying the strings of her camisole. The room smelled of the translucent soap sent by Aunt Lizzie for Christmas. She slid into her blouse before she took the tray from him.

'Oh Will, how good to see you! I thought I had not heard the sewing machine.' She put the tray on the bed and lifted her face to him. He kissed her chastely. 'Darling, darling Will. I am so happy.' She smelled sweet. 'Nearly the end of the month and Doctor Green said Teddy could come home in February.'

Her thinness, well disguised by thick flannel petticoats, looked neat and trim. Especially compared with Sylv.

'And I suppose once Teddy comes home, so can the others.' Yes, Sylv was right, he was missing his family badly. Perhaps when they were all in the house again he would forget that he must be impotent.

Florence picked up a wedge of bread, dabbed it with honey and nibbled its edge just as May did.

'Well . . .' she looked up at Will. 'It is a little awkward, dearest. I wondered whether Aunt Lizzie could be prevailed upon to keep them until Easter —'

'Easter! Good Lord Florrie, it was you who was so anxious about Albert's missed schooling!'

'And still am. But . . . they mustn't be here when Sylvia's baby is born, Will. Surely you agree with me that such a situation would be impossible. I would prefer Albert to miss a year's schooling rather than —'

'They're coming home as soon as Doctor Green says they can,' Will maintained stubbornly. He could have told her that Sylv wanted to go back to Kempley, but he did not. Not then. She would know soon enough, and meanwhile she must face up to . . . things. 'Albert has doubtless already realised that there are more babies at Kempley Cottage than fathers to go with them! And if not then this is as good a way as any of learning the facts of life!'

Florence was bright red. She busied herself pouring her slopped tea from saucer to cup. Will left the room, glad to be properly and overtly angry with her. Already he saw that Sylvia must not be at Chichester Street when the children returned, but he was determined that if his father took her back, Florence should think it was at her instigation.

For the first time in her life, March had a cold that kept her in bed. Letty consigned April to her underling, Rosie, and took May and Albert for walks and refused to let them throw snowballs. Aunt Lizzie sat with March for an hour in the morning, and an hour in the afternoon. They played Lexicon and read to each other and talked.

Aunt Lizzie said, 'I felt I deserted your poor little mamma. She must have been lonely in that house with her grandparents. But I was trying very hard to have a family . . . and I missed my dead sister . . . I'm afraid I was very selfish.'

'Oh no Aunt Lizzie!' March said passionately. 'Mother was very happy. She has told us she did not miss her own mother and father because she never knew them. And she met Papa when she was fourteen and though he was only twelve he used to walk into Gloucester to see her every Saturday.' March blew through her blocked nose. 'She said Great Grandmamma felt bound to receive him because he looked so tired!' She had mentioned this before and knew it would make Aunt Lizzie smile sentimentally, which indeed it did.

Aunt Lizzie said, 'Yes. Florence must be a realist also, though she is a dreamer. She knew it was hopeless to wait for a Prince Charming — how could she meet anyone in that old house?' She added hastily, 'Mind you March, your father is a very handsome man. It would be difficult to turn him down.'

March nodded, though she had never considered her parents' courtship seriously. They were the two poles of her planet and that was that.

Encouraged, Aunt Lizzie proceeded. 'My sister made a love match and look where it landed her. Your dear mamma and I, we married where we could. With great affection of course but . . .' she sighed. 'I was lucky because Edwin inherited the business and some money. Yet you see dear March, I did not need it. None of my children were born alive. And your mother, with five of you, married a man with very little money. How odd life is, child.'

March was breathless. This conversation was quite the most interesting she had ever had. So . . . May was wrong, it was possible to marry without falling in love. Obediently she sniffed at the eucalyptus bottle and considered the prospects opening up before her.

Before she was allowed out of her room, Uncle Edwin came to visit her. He was a gloomy man, but May's constant smiling attention had by now had a cheering effect on him. March felt only a small qualm when his head appeared around her door.

'A little present,' he mumbled, standing between the bed and the fire. 'Thought May would be here. A little present for the two of you.'

March smoothed the sheet over her waist with one of the many small mannerisms she had picked up from Aunt Lizzie. 'May was moved in with Albert when I first had my cold, Uncle,' she said primly. 'I can knock on the wall for her if you like.'

'No. No, indeed no. You can show her. . . .' He approached the bed and held out what appeared to be a pair of wooden shears. 'You close the ends . . . so . . . and the monkey leaps . . . so.' A wooden monkey on a string turned frantic somersaults. March smiled.

'He's sweet. Oh, May will like him!'

'He's for you as well. May prefers dolls I imagine.'

'Oh Uncle . . . thank you.'

'He'll turn more slowly. Look —' He sat on the end of the bed and demonstrated. March took the toy from him and began to work it. Her brown eyes shone.

'My goodness child, you are very like your aunt. When I met her first. Just like you.'

March flushed with pleasure. 'I always wanted to look like May,' she confessed suddenly. 'But if I remind you of Aunt Lizzie, I would rather look like myself.'

Uncle Edwin actually smiled, delighted with the result of his compliment. 'May is a sweet little girl. She takes after your father's side perhaps. She is not a Rhys-Davies. You are.'

'Am I?' March was fascinated. Perhaps that was why she did not approve of Lottie or the Lukers.

Uncle Edwin said briskly, 'The toy is for you. I will find May something else. Now give me a kiss for it, child, and say nothing.'

He levered himself up and leaned over her. She lifted her face, smelling his tobacco smell and the frost on his clothes. He parted his lips, put them over her puckered mouth and sucked hard for a long two seconds. March had never been kissed in such a way before and wasn't sure whether she liked it, but when she saw how happy he looked she did not mind too much.

He lifted his head and stared down at her. Then he said hoarsely, 'If you want anything child, ask me. Anything at all.'

'Thank you Uncle,' she murmured.

After he had gone she lay down and played with the monkey, making him turn somersaults at a dizzy rate. She felt very powerful.

Two days later the afternoon post brought a letter from Florence saying that Will would arrive on February the fourth to bring the children back home.

Albert and May were like mad creatures. They went outside and pelted the thawing snowman with hard pellets of ice until he disintegrated entirely. When Aunt Lizzie went downstairs to order the meals, they fell about in front of the fire, giggling and making up songs about going home. Albert said, 'No more dominoes with Awful Uncle Edwin!' May said, 'No more walks with Letty!' Albert said, 'Petty Letty!' May shrieked and threw herself back against March's knees. 'Oh — oh — we'll see darling Rags again!' Albert said with great satisfaction, 'And I'll see old Harry Hughes. Good old Harry!'

March, sitting sedately in Aunt Lizzie's own chair, suddenly kicked out with her legs and sent May flying. May shrieked again but not with laughter. Albert said, aggrieved, 'What did you do that for?'

March clenched her hands into fists. She said tightly, 'She was hurting my legs. I'm not strong enough yet to have people flopping against me like that.'

May rubbed her back. 'I'm sorry March. I didn't know.'

Albert said, 'You cow. You don't want to go back home, do you?'

May said, 'Albert! Don't speak like that to March!'

March said, 'No, I don't. I don't want to go back to cleaning grates and washing smelly sheets and sleeping in the same bed with May and being more of a skivvy than Letty!'

'Shut up!' Albert shouted. 'Shut up! You're not to speak like that — I'll kill you if you —'

March went on as if he hadn't interrupted. 'I want to stay here where I'm warm and looked after and loved properly —'

Albert threw himself at her and dragged her out of the chair. They rolled together on to the floor. May screamed.

'I'm going to fetch Aunt Lizzie! You're not to fight — oh!' They crashed against her and she jumped away

84

and ran out of the door still screaming. Albert knelt on March's stomach.

'Say you're sorry,' he panted. 'Say you're sorry — quickly!'

She sobbed and spat at him. 'I'm not! I'm not!'

'Say you love us better than you love Aunt Lizzie and Uncle Edwin! You've got to say it March! You've got to!'

Aunt Lizzie's voice was outraged above them.

'Get off your sister this minute young man!' She was stronger than she looked and helped him up by the scruff of his neck. 'Now go to your room. Go on. I don't want to see you again this evening!'

She gathered the weeping March into her arms. 'All right my dearest . . . just a quarrel . . . nothing to fret about . . . let Aunt Lizzie take you upstairs —' She sent May for Letty and ordered the bedroom fire to be lit again. 'Come on darling. A nice supper by your very own fire. Don't cry.'

But March could not stop. When Uncle Edwin presented her with a brooch without even suggesting a kiss, she wept again.

'I wanted a hairslide. Like May's,' she sobbed.

'Then you shall have it,' he knelt by her, rubbing her hand ineffectually. 'Tomorrow I will bring you a hairslide.'

She quietened gradually and when Aunt Lizzie came to kiss her goodnight, she was tranquil again. She waited until she heard the downstairs clock chime a quarter past midnight, then she slipped out of bed and crept down the passage to Albert's room where Albert and May slept in another double feather bed. Slowly and carefully she pushed at Albert until he rolled closer to May, then she insinuated herself into his place. The three children slept peacefully together. When Letty came in with their washing water, she gazed at them sentimentally.

'Three little angels,' she breathed to herself. 'Just

three little angels.' Faintly from above came the sound of April's urgent demand for breakfast. Letty sighed. The rumpus last night had been explained to her as a relapse in Miss March's health, but she had no doubt about April's weeping. 'Temper,' she went on as she poured the water carefully into the basin. 'That little one's got a temper and no mistake!'

Will went to Kempley to talk to his father and as the snow had gone, Sylv agreed to lend an arm to her sister-in-law as far as Bearland.

'It's over three weeks since I saw him Sylvia. In fact I've only seen him once. Doctor Green would have brought him again but the weather was so inclement.'

'Better leave him where he is m'dear. He'll be home for good and all very soon now.'

'I know. I know. But it's been a long time.'

They went beneath the railway bridge where melting snow from the ballast above dripped through. Everything was wet and dismal and smelled of soot. Florence said suddenly, 'I'm so lucky Sylvia. The children. Teddy. Dear Will. I'm so very lucky.'

Sylvia laughed. 'Sound a bit more cheerful about it then Flo!'

Florence leaned a little more heavily on the stalwart arm beneath her own. 'I want you to know, when your baby is born, you are welcome to come back to Gloucester.'

They turned into Saint John's Lane past the second-hand book shops and the *Citizen* office.

'You're a good woman Flo,' Sylvia said. 'A real good woman.'

Florence felt guilty as never before. 'I am not a good woman Sylvia,' she replied humbly. 'If I was a good woman, you would be staying at Chichester Street to have your baby and the children would remain at Bath.'

Sylvia glanced sideways, surprised. ''Tis my own

choice to leave your house Flo. You need feel no responsibility for it.'

They crossed Westgate Street and plunged into one of the narrow passages that led to the docks. The whole area was forbidding, yet number sixteen Prison Lane sported a polished brass knocker and the step had been stoned to gleaming whiteness.

''Ten't too bad,' Sylvia said reassuringly. ''Tis better than Kempley Cottage!' She laughed but got no answering smile. Florence was looking suddenly tense and stood aside while Sylvia knocked on the door. She was shaking slightly like a young girl meeting her lover. Sylvia squeezed her arm. ''Tis all right our Flo,' she whispered. 'You knew where it was . . . certainly en't no slum.'

Florence summoned a smile. 'I don't care about the house.' She looked around her as if seeing the street for the first time. 'I'm looking forward so much to seeing Teddy. Oh Sylvia . . . I'm looking forward so very much!'

Sylvia smiled back. She had never seen her sister-in-law so excited before. Always a bit apart, that was Flo. Like a nun.

Kitty Hall made them tea and settled them by the fire in her tiny kitchen before she went upstairs to fetch Teddy. She placed him, round, sleeping and content, in Florence's arms and went back for her own son. Teddy did not open his eyes but his lashes were dark and his wispy hair as black as Florence's own.

'You're right Flo,' Sylvia said, looking down at him. 'He's a beautiful child. Not a Rising though.'

'No.' Florence's hand shook as she adjusted the shawl around Teddy's face. 'No, he's not a Rising.' She forced herself to look away from him as Kitty came back down the bare wooden stairs. 'I must thank you Mrs. Hall. He is looking so strong and well.'

'Not a bit of trouble Mrs. Rising.' Kitty sat back from the other two and kept her baby tucked well into her elbow. 'I shouldn't have brought this one down,' she apologised. 'But he does cry so when little Edwin goes from him.'

Sylvia said in her broad Kempley voice, 'Aye, they'll miss each other when this 'un comes back home Flo. You'll have a job keeping Teddy quiet I reckon.'

Florence smiled down at the baby in her arms. 'He can cry all he wants to,' she said. 'So long as he's well, I shan't mind.'

Kitty, relaxed by Sylvia's country presence, poured more tea and remarked conversationally, 'A pity yours weren't to be borned a bit earlier. Then you could have done my job.'

Sylvia laughed easily. 'I might look big, but I barely have enough for my own generally. Yet Flo here — my goodness, she fed the other four and couldn't stop the milk this time. Could you Flo?'

It had occurred to Florence that Sylvia, doing the laundry, would know only too well the difficulty she had had to staunch her liberal flow of milk. She wished she had not found it necessary to mention it. Not that it mattered when she had Teddy in her arms. This one she would have fed so willingly. The thought of him at Kitty Hall's breast gave her her first pang of jealousy.

Sylvia misinterpreted her flushed cheeks and silence. 'I'm sorry Florence.' She turned back to Kitty. 'He looks a good weight on what you give him Mrs. Hall.'

'The doctor weighed him yesterday and he's nine pound. Considering he was five pound borned the doctor was very pleased.'

'I should think so!' Sylvia waited for Florence's reciprocal gratitude. 'That's very good Flo isn't it? Nine pound!' she prompted.

'Very good.' Florence forced herself to smile at Kitty. Then her joy in the baby excluded any other lesser feeling. He was hers, so completely hers. His conception, whenever it had been, had been a time of horror, when the only way she could stop from crying out, was to hold herself apart. So it seemed as if Will had had nothing to do with it. Certainly, physically, there was no trace of his father in him. Yes, he was hers. Hers. She held him closer, pressing him deliberately into the softness of her breast as if she could absorb him into her being. And as if her feeling echoed in him, he opened his eyes wide and brown and looked up at her. Then he smiled.

'My saints, he's young to be grinning away like that,' Sylvia said, looking over Florence's shoulder.

Kitty laughed. 'He can't see proper yet I don't reckon. 'Tis the wind.'

Florence said nothing. She smiled back at Teddy, then lowered her head and kissed him. His little fists came up and minute nails clawed at her chin. Florence laughed. And at that rare sound, Sylvia laughed too and all three women filled the tiny house with their merriment. Florence looked around her at the leaping firelight, the hard wooden chairs, the scrubbed flagged floor, the rag rug; she knew, surprised, that she had never been so happy before. Not like this. Not so happy that every small detail of the scene was printed on her mind. She thought: I'll never forget it; the smell of soot and baking and warmth and babies; the taste of Teddy overlying the raw liver; the sense of well-being; the three of us with our babies. I'll always remember this and know that I was happy.

Something happened as they were leaving that helped cement the occasion into Florence's very self. The babies were put back in their small cocoons upstairs, the fire banked and guarded, the window opened. Kitty assured them yet again that Teddy was bathed every day and powdered well afterwards, also that his midday feed now consisted of arrowroot spooned into him according to Doctor Green's instructions. He would be fully weaned in another month. They went outside, Kitty and Sylvia shawled, Florence neat in a tight-waisted coat made by Will ten years ago and newly trimmed with left-over braid. The little cottage, hemmed in by the high wall of the prison on this side, was almost in darkness. Suddenly the sound of marching feet echoed from side to side, bouncing up from the cobbles sharply and ominously. Sylvia took Florence's arm.

'What is it?' she asked, looking at Kitty.

'Some of the prisoners.' Kitty opened the door wider. 'Step inside until they pass. It is sad to see.'

They crammed behind Kitty in the passage. The tramping of feet drew nearer, accompanied by another dreadful sound: the clanking of chains. Florence shivered and Kitty said, "Tis only till they reach the new prison. They take them by barge down the river to Bristol. Then they're allowed to work in the fields — oh, all sorts. 'Tis just to transport them.' She turned her head as an order was rapped out and the feet stopped. 'Oh . . . 'tis my husband with a message for me. I'll be only a minute!' She flew outside and the two women left in the passage had a full view of a grim sight. Half a dozen men, shaven and dressed in drab grey uniforms, stood outside the little cottage, chained to each other by their wrists. But it was their attitude that distressed both Florence and Sylvia. It seemed as if all the spirit had left them and they drooped where they stood. Like ancient blinkered horses in the traces, they waited for the next order.

Kitty ignored them and went to the end of the line where a stocky man in smart blue began to talk to her earnestly. She listened then flew back. 'Needs some food,' she gasped. 'He has to go with them to Sharpness —' she disappeared down the passage and Florence and Sylvia, thoroughly uncomfortable now, confronted the man and his charges. He touched his cap, but could not come nearer to introduce himself. Florence murmured, 'Should we go and speak to him?' Sylvia tightened her grip on her sister-in-law's arm. 'No. Will would not like it.' She lowered her voice still further and added, 'Lice.'

As if the single word had penetrated at least one pair of ears, a man looked up. His chain clinked warningly and Kitty's husband growled in his throat like a dog. The man seemed not to notice. His eyes went to the two women and even through the murk of the January afternoon it was possible to see their blueness. He stared. Florence looked away immediately but Sylvia narrowed her own eyes and stared back with the honesty — some said brazenness — which she always gave to men. He focused on her completely. For a very long minute they looked at each other without faltering. Then Kitty rushed past them with a package which she gave to her Barty. An order was rapped out and the men marched clankingly on.

Both women were quiet on the way home. Florence thought how lucky she was. Teddy was so healthy. Will and the children. Sylvia. Teddy. . . .

She said suddenly, 'Did you know that man Sylvia? That convict outside Mrs. Hall's?'

'No.' Sylvia trudged solidly through the darkening afternoon, Flo's arm tucked firmly into hers. 'And then . . . yes.'

'How do you mean dear?'

'I've never clapped eyes on 'im before. But when I looked at 'im, I sort of recognised 'im.' Sylvia shook her head, baffled by her own feelings. 'No. That en't right.' She looked down at the slight figure beside her and said tactfully, 'You wouldn't understand Flo. What I mean is, I reckon if things were a bit different, we could 'a bin friends. 'Im and me.'

'Ah.' Florence thought she understood only too well. It was the side of Sylvia that she tried not to think about. 'Ah.' She turned her mind quickly away, just as she had when she had seen her own reflection in the kitchen window that time. She thought of Teddy again.

And Will and the children. But especially of Teddy.

Old man Rising agreed grudgingly to have Sylv home for her lying-in. Jack and Austin drove in with some crates of poultry the next market day and took her back with them on the wagon. Will and Florence had a week together before he fetched the children. They were awkward together; she was afraid he would not keep to the attic room and did not know that the image of Hettie Luker was still between them. It was a relief when the fourth of February arrived.

'Have you had a lovely time?'

Florence looked at them all as the prisoner had looked at Sylvia. April was fat, her hair a mass of ginger curls. May had new stature; she it was who carried April from the baby carriage and asked Albert to fetch a clean napkin. Albert guffawed constantly and looked uneasily at his sisters.

May said, 'Lovely. Lovely. And Daddy is such a gentleman — you would be proud of him. He kisses Aunt Lizzie's hand and bows — oh she thinks he is marvellous. Doesn't she March? She says how handsome he is and —'

March said, 'Mother, Aunt Lizzie wants me to visit by myself this summer. Could I? D'you think I could?'

Albert said, 'Where's my brother? I thought I had a brother instead of all these girls? Where is he?' He laughed loudly and pushed March and Will frowned.

'It's all right Father ... Mother, may I visit Aunt Lizzie —?'

Albert said, 'Well, we don't want to go if that's what's worrying you March! You and Aunt Lizzie — always talking! May and me having to go for walks with that crazy Letty, and play dominoes with boring old Uncle Edwin!'

'He's not boring!' March looked at Albert without annoyance. 'He's not a bit boring. I love him very much.' She spoke with great deliberation.

Albert flushed darkly and Florence intervened.

'Tea is laid in the kitchen. Boiled eggs and fruit cake. It'll be like Christmas having you all back. And Rags has missed you too. Come along — we've so much to talk about!'

April sat in the high chair for the first time and made them all laugh a great deal. Rags lay on his back in front of the range just as he'd done when they left. May talked about the fireworks and Christmas morning in the abbey. March asked some surprising questions about the Rhys-Davies' inheritance and though Florence answered them prosaically, May's eyes shone with the romance of it and March said, 'So one day, if it's all sorted out, we might be rich?' Florence laughed and shook her head. 'That is the way your poor great grandfather thought, March dearest. Put it out of your head.' Albert laughed shrilly. 'Be a reellist March! I heard Aunt Lizzie say that — be a reellist!' Will chuckled. 'Well, if your Aunt Lizzie is a realist, Flo, she's done very nicely out of it.' Florence shook her head, 'I've done better, Will. A good husband and five beautiful children. I've done very much better.'

Later, as she carried April up to her bed while the girls unpacked their treasures, he followed her into the bedroom.

'Flo. It will be all right now we're all together again, won't it?'

He was like a child asking for reassurance. Of course she knew it would be perfectly all right once Teddy was home. She looked at him, her face unusually bright. 'I hope you are as happy as I am, dear husband,' she said.

He took her in his arms suddenly and held on to her like another child. April lay on the bed and examined her toes. They clung together. Then Will cupped her face and kissed her quietly. At that moment he was quite certain that their love was grander than anything earthly and could transcend the physical.

They had never been so close.

5

The first thing April Rising could remember was watching her sister May in a concert at the Corn Exchange in Southgate Street. Until her family told her the actual facts, she was inclined to confuse it with the more auspicious occasion of Albert's solo at the cathedral when he sang Faure's *Requiem* in honour of a lamented dean. That took place when April was two years old and her memory consisted of huge columns climbing to heaven, a peculiar vibratory note on the organ which put her off organ music for ever, and Albert apparently screaming for help. This had led her to scream also and to be removed.

April's musical ear was much more suited to the sentimental songs with which that period abounded. She was quite certain — at three years old in fact — that May was not screaming when she tripped on to the stage in white crepe paper and told everyone she was a 'dainty, dancing fairy'. She loved both her sisters, but May was her favourite. May never lost her temper, shared all her treats, was beautiful and fun.

The concert was in aid of Blind Babies, and May had suggested to April that they tie scarves over their eyes and spend half an hour each day finding out what it was like to be blind. April hated it until May pushed up the blindfold so that she could see her feet. March scoffed at them both and told them they were 'ludicrous' which was even worse than being ridiculous. But April never forgot what it must be like to be blind and she clapped her tiny palms until they were sore when May curtsied, kissed her hand at her assembled family, and retired reluctantly into the wings.

That evening April announced that when she grew up she would be a misery. She spoke with such exaltation that May questioned her and finally discovered she wanted to be a misery like at Sunday School.

'A missionary!' May said, smiling lovingly. 'Why not indeed?' May had many of her mother's phrases.

Albert sniggered — the loud guffaws of three years ago had long been subdued into the accepted King's School snuffle.

'Let's see Ape ...' Florence was out of the room otherwise this name would not be permitted. 'Old Livingstone was a bit of a misery wasn't he?'

April nodded vigorously, delighted when March and Albert laughed and May hugged her and Daddy slapped his knee. She was encouraged to expand. 'Praps I'll sing like May and give the money to the miseries. 'Cus I don't want to go all the way to foreign parts.'

At that, Will picked her up and sat her on his knee and kissed her ear lobe. Florence, entering with Teddy on her hip though he was a hefty two-year-old, had to know what it was all about. April listened in a dream of content. This was how it had been at the concert. She was Daddy's girl, he was always telling her so. Albert was specially his too. Mother claimed Teddy and May for her own. And March needed to belong to no-one. March was strong. When Gladys Luker pinched April as they sat on the front step once, March had smiled brilliantly, taken a piece of Glady's arm between pointed finger and thumb, lifted it slowly and started to twist. 'Do you enjoy it Gladys dear?' she had asked. Later, May, finding both children weeping copiously, had kissed April's red mark and shown both of them how to spit on their forefingers and massage their wounds. She had then sat between them and told them a story about how little girls must be kind to each other and never pinch.

So April listened to the chatter of her family above her head and watched Teddy eating the bits of coal left in the bucket from last winter and was utterly content. Soon it would be bedtime and she would put on her own nightie and kneel with Teddy to say 'Gentle Jesus meek and mild. . . .' And she knew that to the end of her days she would remember May singing, 'I'm a dainty dancing fairy.' And the awful head-fluttering note of that organ and the hugeness of the place where Albert had screamed. . . .

Teddy too was happy enough; though never content. He had no caution, no decorum whatever. He had recently acquired the knack of holding his water and now performed publicly whenever necessary. If Albert had done this, Florence would have died of mortification. She screened Teddy as best she could with her long, fashionable hobble skirt, but she smiled at him all the same. Already he showed great ingenuity in getting in and out of scrapes. The coal bucket was always his goal, but he had also fallen out of his cot, thrown his wooden horse through the kitchen window and regularly coasted head-first down the druggeted stairs. March was the only one who got cross with him, so he saw no need to mend his ways. Even Hettie, on the few occasions he and April played in the Luker house, kissed him when he knocked Henry over. Henry was older than Teddy by a few weeks, but much smaller so it was hardly a contest. When Teddy discovered he could also send Gladys Luker flying, he felt more confident. Hettie laughed at this too and told him he was a bigger bully than his father. Gladys wiped her nose on the back of her hand like Lottie Jenner and took an early opportunity of pulling April's ginger curls as hard as she could. Again, May was the peacemaker.

*　　*　　*

When Teddy was three and the Christmas holiday finished, Florence reluctantly agreed to both her babies attending a private school in Midland Road. The Misses Midwinter were highly recommended by one of Will's clients. They took a dozen children aged three to seven for a shilling each per week, and taught them refined manners, the three R's, music and dancing. Will was delighted. It was all part of their climb up the social ladder. He and Florence hired Luker's trap and took the children down past Daker's in Barton Street and over the level crossing by Park to Midland Road. They were nervous and Will kept talking. 'It's called California Crossing,' he improvised, 'because a fellow called Clarence built it. They called him Cal for short, then California Cal and —'

Florence laughed to show April that it was a joke but as a train snorted past, reverberating the road like an organ note, the child said fearfully, 'Will we have to go over Cally . . . Cally . . . by ourselves?'

'Certainly not!' Florence forced a reassuring smile. 'March or I will meet you. And we will come through the subway. It's a tunnel and you will love it.'

Miss Midwinter was terrifying. She took them into the back parlour for their 'perticlers' which April thought might be her drawers but turned out to be the catechism. She did not smile when April announced her intention to be a 'misery'. And she asked with great significance whether Teddy could 'behave'. She had grey hair arranged in hundreds of small curls over her forehead like Queen Alexandra. When she finished writing she clipped a pair of pince-nez on to her nose and peered over them.

'When I wear these,' she announced, 'I am about to address a child. When I address a child, that child immediately stands.' She waited. Suddenly April understood and was no longer afraid. She took Teddy's hand in hers and pulled him from Florence's knee. Together they looked over the edge of Miss Midwinter's big desk and received approving smiles. It was so easy. You watched for the glitter of the gold-rimmed glasses . . . you stood . . . you were approved.

A little girl of six appeared as if by magic. Miss Midwinter announced that her name was Bridget Williams and she was the granddaughter of Alderman Williams and she was to be a friend to April and Edwin Rising.

Florence smiled at the solemn pig-tailed child.

'When I was your age, your grandfather used to come to visit my grandfather,' she said encouragingly.

Miss Midwinter thawed on the instant. 'Ah . . . and your family Mrs. Rising? Old Gloucester stock, I knew the minute I set eyes. . . .'

'I was brought up by my grandparents. Next to Bishop Hooper's lodging.' Florence surreptitiously unfastened the buttons on Teddy's new sailor jacket. He was slow with buttons and she had made his trousers so that they would slip over his tiny hips.

Miss Midwinter was delighted. 'Mr. Rhys-Davies? Of course — the scholar! I can see him now, walking the cloisters . . . his white beard and his frock coat — and I can see the likeness. Of course! And especially in little Edwin. My sister and I are delighted — delighted, Mrs. Rising —'

April liked that bit very much indeed. And she liked Bridget Williams too. In fact within three days of starting school, she loved Bridget Williams. And on the strength of that long-ago connection, Mrs. Williams eventually invited April to tea at their house. They lived in the country at Barnwood and got there in a motor car. April could remember March telling her that quite soon she was going to buy a motor car. Now April understood why. When she got home from Barnwood she fetched the sovereign from the locket Aunt Lizzie had given her at Christmas and tried to give it to March.

'What's that for?' March asked ungraciously. She had had a talk with Miss Pettinger that morning and had been told that in that lady's opinion March's disposition was unsuited to the teaching profession.

'For your motor car,' April said. 'Mr. Williams' motor car has a folding-back roof for the summer. Could you get one like that March? And can I have a ride in it if I give you some more money?'

'May I have a ride in it,' March corrected.

'May I have a ride in it please March?'

'No,' said March. 'And if you think a single sovereign will help — it will take a hundred of those to buy a car!'

April said confidently, 'You'll get one March. And you'll have to let me have a ride in it if my sovereign was the first one you had!'

It hadn't occurred to March to save for the motor car bit by bit, she had imagined it would come in one fell swoop. She smiled unwillingly at her small sister then, uncharacteristically, gave her a hug.

'You're my favourite sister,' she said. 'And I'll get a cocoa tin from Mother and we'll save in it for a car. And your sovereign will be the very first!'

April felt guilty. She wished she could tell March that she loved her better than May also, but she could not. The tin was duly labelled and put on the mantelpiece in their bedroom. It grew heavy very quickly but when April peeped inside one rainy Sunday afternoon it seemed to contain nothing but her sovereign and a lot of farthings. Albert was paid three farthings for weddings; they must come from him.

Bridget had to be asked back to Chichester Street for a reciprocal tea. The invitation was given and accepted; March would meet them out of school and walk them home and Will would hire the trap to drive Bridget home in the evening. April was so excited she forgot to stand up when Miss Alicia spoke to her and forfeited her teacher's smile. Teddy made it worse by piping up with an unsolicited excuse.

'Bridget Williams is coming to tea Mishalisha!' It

was the best he could do with the sibilants of the name. 'April's all sited!'

Amazingly Miss Alicia then smiled. It was the first time that April realised Teddy was her favourite.

'Ah I see. So no work will be done properly today.'

The laughter brought in Miss Midwinter, and soon April was chanting with the other four-year-olds, 'Mrs. D., Mrs. I., Mrs. F.F.I., Mrs. C., Mrs. U., Mrs. L.T.Y.' She was top in spelling and tables and Teddy was bottom. But Teddy was still the favourite.

The three of them held hands, Teddy in the middle, and ran down into the subway, then stood directly under the railway line until a train went over their heads. March, walking sedately behind, put her fingers in her ears and went quickly up the other side. April would have preferred to do the same, but Bridget and Teddy thought it was thrilling to be underneath a moving train. Bridget ceased being the quiet girl she was at school and Barnwood, and screamed loudly to produce echoes. Teddy screamed too and March hurried back and grabbed his hand, making him walk with her. Bridget said contentedly, 'I like being friends with a huge family like Queen Victoria's. Papa says it will be good for me to rough and tumble for once.'

They had boiled eggs for tea in the back parlour. Mother had drawn faces on each egg, some smiling, some downcast. When they took their egg cosies off and saw the faces they laughed, and Bridget laughed loudest of all. There was a pot of Mrs. Goodrich's clear golden honey and piles of white bread and butter and a big fruit cake. After tea Bridget wanted to play outside. 'Like a street arab,' she said sunnily. So they joined the Luker children who were giving wheelbarrow rides to the Lamb and Flag and back. April bowled her hoop, Bridget jumped feverishly on to the wheelbarrow and Teddy looked for something else to do. Something which would impress Bridget Williams once and for all.

He staggered down Luker's side way with a heavy rope from the dray.

'Come on! We'll make a swing. Over that branch there!' He pointed to one of the Goodrich apple trees.

April was fearful. 'What about the bees? We mustn't, Teddy. Go and put that rope back and Henry will let you have a ride on —'

But Bridget was bored with the wheelbarrow and the hoop.

'Go on Teddy! I'll lift you up! Come and help me April — you with the dirty face — come on!'

Gladys, thus addressed, pinched April furiously and Bridget was left to lift Teddy as best she could. April couldn't help noticing through her tears of pain how much Bridget enjoyed holding her brother's plump little body aloft. Then the rope was over the branch and Teddy swung away from Bridget, whooping like an Indian. For three glorious seconds he swung in short arcs above the other children while they clamoured for their turn, then there was a hideous groan from the arthritic old apple tree, then a sharp crack, then he descended on to the unyielding pavement. April registered the ghastly sound of a human body, plump and resilient, hitting stone. The next instant Bridget began to scream.

Teddy had a broken arm and mild concussion. Hearing the news Bridget spluttered noisily, 'If God will make Teddy live, I will be his servant for the rest of his life!' And May, romantic realist that she was, said sensibly, 'Don't be silly Bridget, Teddy isn't dead by any means. And he certainly doesn't need a servant!'

Fred Luker drove Bridget back to Barnwood with March for company. Coming back it was almost dark and March was suddenly conscious that though Fred Luker was the same age as Albert, he was grown-up. His short, burly form squatted sideways opposite her, and his silence was patently embarrassed. To relieve that embarrassment she laughed lightly.

'It's good of you to look after us like this Freddy. After all Teddy isn't very popular with Henry and Gladys I understand!' She was glad to hear how cool and adult she sounded. But in the long pause which followed it was obvious Fred Luker was still at a loss. Then at last he cleared his throat, turned and spat over the side of the trap into the road. March tightened her lips.

'I — I . . .' more throat clearing. 'I dunno nothing about the little 'uns Miss . . . er . . . March.' He hawked and spat again. 'No-one called me Freddy for a long time.'

'We used to call you Freddy when we played.' She and Albert, Fred and George had 'played' no oftener than three times. 'And you used to call me Marchy.' She tugged her single brown plait to the front and brushed her chin with its frayed end. 'I hate my name. Marchy is better. But when I'm grown up I shall call myself Marcie.' March would not have dreamed of talking like this to anyone else; with Fred Luker it was rather like confiding in a dog. Or an ox.

He looked at her outline, chin raised against the darkening sky, silky hair brushing it gently. He blurted, 'Your April did tell our Glad that you be saving for a motor car. That right?'

'It is.'

'I got one.' Fred's voice was harsh with triumph.

'You *what?*'

'I got a motor car. In the yard.' He rested on one elbow and flapped the reins on the pony's back. 'Breakdown. Towed 'n back with Jenny and left 'n in our yard for a mechanic to call.' Jenny was the carthorse who pulled the goods dray which earned most of Alf Luker's money.

March was awed. 'What's it like? April says Bridget's has got a folding roof.'

'This one's got everything. An' . . . I got 'er started too.'

'You *what*?' repeated March.

'Got 'er started. Druv 'er down the side and back.'

They passed Barnwood House where all the rich loonies were locked up, clattered under the railway bridge and slowed for the Pitch.

March said, 'I'll never save enough to buy a car. Never.'

Fred spat again, judiciously. 'Reckon you could. You got brains. You could be a secerty. This bloke what's got the car . . . 'e's got a secerty. She's arranging for the mechanic to call . . . she arranges every bloody thing for 'im. You could do that.'

March swallowed at the vicious swear word, but decided to ignore it. 'D'you really think so . . . Freddy?'

''Course you could. . . . An' if you wants to come an' 'ave a drive now . . . tonight . . . you're welcome!'

'Freddy!' March jumped about on the seat like Teddy. 'Freddy! May I really? Oh Freddy!'

She waited in the blackness of the side way while Freddy unharnessed the pony and put away the trap. She felt guilty, knowing she should go straight home to comfort Mother and reassure April about the Williamses. The workroom light was on, so was the front bedroom's; Father working in spite of everything, Mother in bed. No-one would see her if they looked out. As for the Lukers hearing anything, nothing was more unlikely. Through the thickness of the wall she could hear the noise of the eleven children like bees in a hive. She pressed her back against the rough stone, taut with excitement. It crossed her mind that a week ago she had suffered agonies of jealousy when May was given a paintbox for her birthday. It was accepted that May was artistic and March was practical, yet March had wanted that paintbox so much it hurt her. Now . . . now she had something that May would want, yet be frightened to accept. Through the darkness came the astounding roar of an engine followed immediately by a terrible smell. March shrank against the wall and wondered whether her courage was trickling away.

The roar changed note slightly and started to hiccough as it came closer. March peered into the road again expecting a constable or the Goodriches — already alerted to sudden disaster that day — to appear. No-one stirred. Below, on the corner, the lighted door of the Lamb and Flag suddenly opened and someone fell into the gutter. Then the enormous bulk of a two-seater Delage loomed at her side and Fred's voice hissed urgently, 'Come round this side Marchy — come on now — make haste!'

She made haste and was hauled up by his side. The car bounced into the road, the leather seat was slippery, the door much too shallow, she held Fred's arm and her breath squealed in her throat.

'Not frightened Marchy? This en't nothing. She can do thirty or more. Look at that there shine on 'er!'

His words barely made sense but she could see that in the light from the gas lamps the car gleamed richly.

He turned slowly and inexpertly into Northgate Street and pulled out the throttle. They roared to the top of the Pitch in two minutes when it had taken ten to come down in the trap. March kept bouncing and squealing and Fred started to laugh and swung round in a huge circle at the top of the Pitch so that she was thrown about helplessly. They returned jerkily — 'Easier goin' up than down —' panted Fred as he grabbed and released the big brake lever on the running board. 'Yes,' said March, holding the door and the edge of her seat and her breath. Somehow they turned back into Chichester Street and edged up to the yard again.

'Oh Freddy. Oh . . . that was lovely.' March let her breath go ecstatically.

'You sound like your May. Everything is lovely for her.'

'Not for me. But this is.'

She got out and waited for him. The smell of the

exhaust fumes was no longer terrible and she sniffed them sharply like Mr. Goodrich sniffed his snuff. And she remembered Uncle Edwin.

They walked down the side way and into the road and she turned and put her arms around his neck and kissed him.

'Thank you Freddy. Dear Freddy.'

He was aghast. He stood there watching her dart across the road and up the steps of thirty-three. Then, inspired, he called softly, 'G'night Marcie. Sleep tight.'

When Teddy came out of hospital, even Florence's devotion was taxed to the limit. His arm was heavy with plaster and pulled at his tiny shoulder until the pain made him cry. For perhaps an hour each day he would rest it on the table and practise his letters, puzzled and amused at the unexpected difficulty of using his left hand. Then frustration would overtake him and he would demand a story in a petulant voice, or, if Florence was established in the chair with some sewing, he would want a drink of cocoa and a buttered nobby.

Will said, 'What that boy needs is a good thrashing.' He had never touched one of the children in anger and his words shocked Florence.

'Poor Teddy. He's never known a time when he hasn't had companions. When you go to Daker's next, Will, walk on down to Bearland and ask Mrs. Hall if she would like to bring little Tolly up for an afternoon.'

'Bearland is in the opposite direction from the Barton,' Will pointed out. Then seeing the pleading in her beautiful eyes, he inclined his head over his sewing with mock gallantry. 'I am yours to command, my lady Flo. As always.'

Florence was certain they had never been so happy. But there were times when she wished Will's sincere concern for that happiness did not seem . . . slightly ironic.

* * *

106

Kitty, big with her second child, was a port in a storm as usual. The weather was unexpectedly sultry and she did not feel up to the walk through the city to Chichester Street. However if Mr or Mrs Rising could bring little Teddy down to Bearland, she would be delighted to look after him each and every day until his arm healed. Young Bartholomew was looking forward to having his old playmate no end.

So it was that Teddy and Tolly were playing five stone on the scrubbed step of number sixteen Prison Lane, when a man, shabbily dressed, swarthy, with unexpectedly blue eyes, shambled from the docks towards them. Tolly, heeding his mother's instructions for such a situation, retreated down the passage beseeching Teddy to come with him, but Teddy was curious, and, as always, completely unafraid. 'I can smell the sea on him,' he declared. 'Let's ask him where he's been — Tolly — cowardy custard — Tolly —' but Tolly was in the kitchen looking for his mother.

The man took another few steps, his knees buckling under him. He reached out with one hand as if pointing at Teddy, then crashed to the cobbles and lay face down, head sideways on the outstretched arm, rear end pointing to the hot sky.

Teddy galloped towards him, pumping with his one good arm. He crouched by the man, put his plaster near his head and leaned on it. The man's eyes, open and strangely alert, surveyed him.

''Tis the heat boy. Don' be frit. Get me water.'

The words and accent reminded Teddy powerfully of *Treasure Island* which May was reading to him at bedtime. The man definitely smelled of boats and the sea. He scrambled back to his feet and shouted to Kitty and Tolly just emerging from the cottage. Kitty hesitated then turned back for water.

Teddy said confidently, 'Just coming. What's your name mister?'

The man replied automatically, 'Dick Turpin. Four, five, eight, nine.'

Teddy hugged his plaster to his midriff, annoyed. Albert sometimes bammed him along like that and it wasn't particularly funny. Dick Turpin indeed. 'I'm the one who didn't run away,' he reminded the man coldly.

The man closed his eyes. 'Thanks boy. Thanks,' he whispered.

Kitty arrived with her Barty's shaving mug full of water, determined not to contaminate her glasses or cups. Tolly stood back, obviously following further instructions, while she put the mug near the man. He saw it, grinned feebly at the two figures standing well back, felt for the handle and lifted the mug to his mouth. Half of it slurped on to the cobbles, the other half disappeared without the man seeming to swallow. He put down the mug and supported himself on one elbow, straightening his legs painfully.

'You're Mrs. Hall,' he said in a low voice. 'The wife of Bartholomew Hall, warder of Gloucester prison?'

Kitty took a pace backwards; confirmation enough.

'I ain't in no condition to harm you or the children, lady . . . wondered if you could help me in my search for a . . . long-lost relative.'

'Where does he live?' Teddy asked avidly.

'"Tis a lady, boy. Friend o' Mrs. Hall's I b'lieve. Staying 'ere two or three year ago when I passed by. Could not claim kinship then Mrs. Hall . . . you knows why.' The man pushed up his sleeve and Teddy saw some marks there. They meant nothing to him, but Kitty drew back again. The man put up a pleading arm. 'I've paid for what I done — you of all people must know how I've paid!' He lay back and took some deep breaths, then spoke with his eyes closed. 'She's the only one 'ud 'elp me — I know that. Tell me where she lives . . . please.'

Kitty said nothing and Teddy asked, 'How can we? We don't know her name or what she looks like or anything.'

Kitty warned, 'Teddy —'

The man said, 'She was big. Wrapped in shawls — sleet and slush everywhere. Blue eyes, grey bonnet —'

Kitty gasped. 'If it was three years ago it was Mrs. Rising and her sister-in-law.!'

Teddy was full of importance. He took a step forward and stooped down, holding his plastered arm. 'That's my aunty. Aunty Sylv,' he announced. 'I'm Teddy Rising and Aunty Sylv is my father's sister.'

Kitty said, 'Teddy! You don't know . . . and get away dear — germs —'

The man growled, 'I'm not diseased Mrs. Hall. Just starved and done in. Thanks boy.' He opened his eyes and looked, then nodded. 'Yes. I remember the other woman now. She was your mother all right.'

Teddy said cockily, 'And I've got three sisters and a brother and he's a bishop's page now 'cos his voice is breaking and he can't sing for a bit and —'

'Where's she live?' interrupted the man.

Kitty put her hand on Teddy's shoulder. 'Come on dear. We've done what we can —'

'Kempley Cottage —'

'Teddy, you are *not* to speak to this man again!' Kitty propelled him back up Prison Lane. Tolly ran ahead and held the door ready to slam after his mother as if he expected a siege.

'Thank you boy!' called the man.

The door slammed. Teddy said, aggrieved, 'Why did we have to leave him Mrs. Hall? He was interesting!'

'He was a no-good down-and-out,' Kitty scolded. 'And you shouldn't have ought to have told him where your aunty lives! What if he goes there and makes a nuisance of himself?'

Teddy was amazed. 'Everyone's a nuisance at Kempley,' he told her. 'If they get too much of a nuisance, Gramps and Uncle Jack throw them out.'

Kitty was partially reassured. When Florence arrived to collect Teddy she made light of it.

'I think it was someone your sister-in-law knew from the country,' she said deviously. 'I doubt whether he will look her up after all. He is probably at the Salvation Army rescue home by now.'

Teddy was not able to jog his mother's memory by referring to Dick Turpin as an ex-prisoner, and after hearing his garbled account of the incident, Florence dismissed it from her mind. She certainly did not wish to question Prison Lane's suitability for Teddy; not at the moment. The new school in Denmark Road was well established now and Will had twenty-two navy-blue uniform coats to make before September; he needed all the help she could give.

She fully intended to tell him about the mysterious 'Dick Turpin' but that night he scattered all their wits with an announcement. They were to move house. They were sitting in the back parlour, almost afraid to move because of the flashing summer lightning.

'Frightened of a few fireworks in the sky!' he scoffed at the three oldest as they huddled over the Happy Family cards as if it were midwinter. 'And these are the travellers who saw the firework display at Bath if you please!'

April, turning the pages of Teddy's book for him in the empty hearth, glanced fearfully at the uncurtained window. 'Gladys Luker says her cousin was struck by lightning and burnt to a crisp. They only knew it was him 'cos there were just four teeth in the road. And that was all he had. Four teeth.'

Will said, 'Forget about the weather for a moment — you can wallow in your gory stories when I've told you mine. Which isn't a bit gory, but much more exciting.' He had their attention, they stared at him over their cards and books, even Florrie over her eternal button-holes.

Will grinned. 'How would you like to move? Yes, *move*, young Teddy! Not very far. But into a much bigger house where I can have a workroom that will hold two sewing machines and a pressing table as well as a cutting table. Where you can have a bedroom each if you want it.

Where the bandy room can be downstairs so that we can use it in the winter.' Florence leaned forward; she loathed carrying coals to the fireplace in the attic, which meant her piano was not used for six months of the year and grew damp. Will twinkled down at her. 'A house with a garden — plenty of trees and a lawn big enough for tennis. The wash-house on the side so that you don't have to go outside to do the laundry — room for indoor lines when it's wet —' Children jumped and leapt around him and Teddy's plaster caught him painfully on the shin. 'Tell us Dad! Where? When? How can we afford it?'

Will held up a restraining hand and answered the last question first; it was a matter of great pride to him. 'We can afford it because the Risings are rising!' He looked at Albert and they both remembered the old joke. 'We're doing well — your mother is working every minute she can spare to help me, and if I had more room I could afford to employ a sempstress part-time, which would mean —' The children leapt again like a bubbling cauldron. 'Where is the house, Father?' and Will laughed and relented. 'Further up the street. Chichester House, no less.'

The silence was awe-struck and completely satisfactory. A retired vicar lived in Chichester House and had done for the past twenty years. He was a recluse and used the back gate which led into Mews Lane.

May said in a low voice, 'Has the reverend died, Daddy?'

Will shook his head. 'When Mr. Amies came for the rent last week he told me the old man was going into a home for clerics and the house would become vacant, and was I interested? The rent is twenty-two and sixpence a week — twice what we are paying now — but with the increased business —'

'The house will keep us poor, Will,' Florence warned. 'All those rooms to heat. And the garden. . . .'

'The children will do the garden.' He played his trump

card. 'And they will never need to play in the street again Florence.' He looked sternly at Teddy. 'You will play in the old stables at the back and break your limbs in private my lad. D'you hear?'

April breathed, 'Bridget could come to tea again, couldn't she?'

'I think we might just put up with her once more, might we not Florrie?' enquired Will, twinkling again.

'And — and there will be room for my motor car!' March said amid much laughter.

Albert said, 'Can Harry stay a night now?'

'*May* Harry stay a night Albert.'

'Well, may he? There's never been room before but —'

'Yes, he may, my boy.' Will put an arm on Florence's shoulder. 'Perhaps you'd like to have your Aunt Lizzie down too Florrie?'

March forgot about Harry Hughes. 'Oh, I'll always love summer lightning after this! It will remind me of Aunt Lizzie!'

'Everything reminds you of Aunt Lizzie,' grumbled Albert. But for once he smiled as he said it.

6

Florence worked hard to make Chichester House into a home, but though number thirty-three had been too small for them, this new house was too big. They had been there three days when the staggering news of two deaths was brought by Sibbie Luker: Mrs. Goodrich and her daughter Charlotte had been killed by a tram in Worcester Street. Florence could hardly believe it.

'To escape the fever — do you remember they were ill when Teddy was born? And now to be struck down like this! It's too cruel.'

Sibbie said virtuously, 'Mam says all the trams should be taken off the roads. This could never have happened with a coach an' horses —'

'Of course it could,' snapped March, grief making her impatient. Mrs. Goodrich had been the only genteel person in the street and had always shown a preference for March. And Charlotte, little seen, tiny, delicate, had called March 'Aunt' and wanted to sit in her lap.

Florence sighed. 'It was meant to be, Sibbie. And, somehow, they were meant to go together.' She touched Teddy's shoulder unobtrusively. 'They could not manage without each other.'

'That's a lovely thought Mamma,' breathed May. 'Perfectly beautiful.'

Sibbie said, 'Mam says these things always go in threes and she wonders who will be the next.'

'Stuff and nonsense!' Will stood up, spilling French chalk on the newly-swept floor. 'Off you go to school you girls. Albert, you'll be late! April, Teddy, coats and hats and wait for me at the gate!' He spoke in a lower voice to Florence beneath the immediate hubbub. 'I'll see to the little ones. You go and sit with Granny Goodrich. Tell Sid I'll be along later.'

So it was that the three older Rising children went to their first funeral.

It was September the first and the apple and plum trees, neglected for years, were yielding their over-ripe fruit to the children and the wasps, and Florence was trying to make jam, sort out her linen and press finished school coats all at the same time. The weather was warm and golden, and after four weeks' grace school had started again and the big old house was quiet. Will wandered around it before he began the tricky task of cutting a ladies' riding habit; he had gone on a tour of inspection with Mr. Amies, the rent collector, otherwise there had been no time to explore his new domain. For the past month it had been dominated by children and it had been as much as he could do to gather his things around him in the new workroom and make a routine for himself. The bereavement in the Goodrich household had shaken him more than he cared to admit; he imagined it being Flo and April — Flo and any of them. He knew he could not manage alone. At the back of his mind he wondered about a third death. . . .

The house was big; Flo was right, it was too big. But he did not view it as a dwelling. It was a symbol of his success. It had been here long before the twin rows of terraced houses and it still sat in the midst of its own grounds quite separate from them. In fact they belonged to it, tenantry. Yes, the rest of Chichester Street was tenantry to Chichester House. Which made him a bit of a squire. He grinned, well pleased with the image. It was how he felt. A bit of a squire.

He wandered through attics still cluttered with stuff left by the old vicar. Four big rooms with board ceilings smelling of sweet wood. Then down to the middle floor where five bedrooms were grouped around a square landing, and a bathroom led off from one of them. A proper bathroom with a closet and a gas geyser and two steps leading up to the bath. Woodworm in the closet seat; he must tell Flo to get some beeswax down those holes. There were views from all the windows, pleasant leafy views with no glimpse of the gasometer. From the bathroom he could see the four-square cathedral tower. He leaned out and watched Flo lugging in another basket of plums. Maybe it *would* be more expensive living here, but there would be plenty of jam next winter to sweeten the outlay!

He grinned as he went down the wider, shallower stairs into the tiled hall. It impressed clients, did this hall. And the house was double-fronted so that Flo could have her parlour looking out at callers, and he could still have a front room for his work. Mr. Daker had stressed the importance of a front workroom. 'Take them down a dark passage and you've lost them already my son,' he'd always said. But over the road at number thirty-three that had meant the parlour being in the middle room, dark with a view of the wash-house. Will said aloud, 'Yes. It might be pricey but it knocks spots off what we had before!' As if in reply to this remark, the outside bell jangled on its spring and the next minute Sylvia appeared in the garden, bundled up as if it were winter. Will rapped on the parlour window and hurried to the front door.

'Thought you'd come and see the palace, did you?' he welcomed her, grinning broadly. 'You're a one for turning up unexpected our Sylv — but welcome just the same!'

He expected her to remind him that she had visited him only once before, but she bundled into the hall without a word and looked around her vaguely. It was enough to overwhelm anyone, of course.

'Come on,' he encouraged. 'Straight through to the kitchen same as before. Flo's jamming the plums.' He clapped her on the shoulder as if she were another man. She hadn't brought a bundle of clothes with her this time.

Flo looked up from the steaming preserving pan and gave a small cry of pleasure. Her wooden spoon went down, she wiped her hands on the towel nearby and held them out to her sister-in-law. And as before Sylvia lowered her head to them without her Kempley laughter, and it was obvious she was near tears.

Will fussed about behind her, drawing chairs to the plush-covered kitchen table, covering her emotion with enquiries for Jack and Austin and Wallie and his many sisters. 'Mam all right?' he asked sharply when she at last collapsed into a chair and he saw her face.

She nodded slowly. ''Tis Pa. He's gone my dears. Dropped dead in the field next to his shires. Master 'ad him put on a gate and brought 'ome. Ma laid 'im out nice. Austin's gone to Newent for the undertakers. Jack's telling the others. I wanted to come and tell you.'

'Thank you Sylvia.' Florence fetched the teapot automatically.

Will was stunned. 'The third death,' he muttered. 'The third one to go.'

Sylvia said, 'A good way too. In harness. He really were in harness. But Ma. . . .'

'Is she taking it badly?' Florence asked.

'She is that. Master will want the cottage see. Jack and Austin was casual workers and not entitled to the tenancy. It were tied to Pa. So we'll have to get out.'

Florence and Will were silent. They both knew that this was a worse catastrophe than the actual death. But inevitable.

Sylvia went on, 'Vi is taking the boys — mine as well — and going with Wallie.' Wallie had a smallholding

116

along the Dymock road and could always do with extra hands to weed, prick out the seedlings, pick flowers and fruit and sell them wherever they could be sold. 'Jack and Austin are off to Wales. To the mines.' She glanced sideways at Will. 'That leaves Ma. And me.'

Will said nothing. He was unwilling to take his mind away from the shock of losing his father. Surely he could be given a little time for grief before he had to start worrying about the others?

Florence looked at him as she reached again for Sylvia's rough hand. 'You will come here. Of course. You and Daisy. And the boys if you wish. You know that Sylvia.'

'The boys will be happier with Vi and Wallie. And me . . . I shall be all right. But thank you for Ma. Thank you Florrie.'

Will said brusquely to cover his silence: 'What do you mean you'll be all right? You'll come here with Ma. No more to be said.'

Sylvia withdrew her hand from Florence's and stared down at the flagstones. 'I — I shall be getting wed. I think. Quite soon.'

This news created much more of a furore than the previous items. Flo exclaimed with delight and Will opened his eyes wide with astonishment.

'Who?' he asked with uncomplimentary disbelief.

Sylvia kept her eyes to the ground and explained quickly in a low voice. 'I saw 'im first when I were with you before, Will.' She glanced at Flo and away again. 'Down at Kitty Hall's, d'you remember Florrie? He were a prisoner then —'

'A *convict?*'

'Not any more!' Sylvia lifted her head angrily. 'He's been punished and he's out now.' She smiled proudly. 'He came to me.'

Florence put two and two together. 'Dick . . . Turpin? Was it? Teddy told me he collapsed outside Kitty's cottage — back in the spring that was. Is it the same man?'

117

'Yes. Yes. Name you don't forget, eh?' Sylvia looked at her hands this time. 'He was near done when he got to Kempley an' Pa wouldn't 'ave 'im in the cottage, so I kep' 'im in Master's barn. No-one did know.'

There was a short silence. Florence looked uneasy. Will said, 'Where is he now then?'

Sylvia thinned her lips and took a breath. 'He don't know about Pa's dying. He left last month to find work. So we could get married.'

Will followed up remorselessly. 'He asked you to marry him?'

''Twas understood.'

Florence gestured to Will over Sylvia's head. 'Then you can come to us until the wedding day. You can be married from here. Nothing could be nicer.'

Sylvia shook her head. 'No. No Florrie. You don't see what I'm telling you. 'Tis the same now as before — when I was expecting our Daze. And the girls are older now. It would be worse. There's April and young Teddy. And Albert is just at an age when . . . no, I can't come 'ere.'

There was another silence. Florence's face was flaming red. Will said, 'You fool Sylv. Christamighty. Four kids and no husband. You damned *fool*!'

''Tis different this time. Dick will be back. 'E'll be back. You see.'

'And where d'you go meanwhile?'

'We'll go in the workhouse for a while. Me and Daze. Just till — just till —'

Will made an explosive sound of disgust and flung over to the boiling kettle where he made the tea angrily.

Florence said, 'When is the baby due my dear?'

'Roundabout March's birthday I reckon. Now don't you worry your head Flo, we'll be all right. And it's different this time. Dick an' me . . . we think a lot of each other. A lot.'

Florence took the teapot and poured tea, pushing a cup across the table to Sylvia. Then she went to the preserving pan and stirred thoughtfully. Will sat down and humped his shoulders. It was a mess. Bad enough poor old Pa dying, but they couldn't even bury him without trying to think of all these other things.

Florence said from the depths of the steam above the jam: 'You can't go to the workhouse. That's for sure. And Will was talking of taking on a sempstress anyway. And all this food . . . my goodness, we've got work and shelter and food . . . enough for an army.'

'I am not coming here Flo, not in my state. But I thank you —'

'And number thirty-three empty just across the street,' Florence continued, dabbing her wooden spoon on a saucer to see if the mixture jelled. 'Eleven shillings a week. That's all. If we can't find that it will be a poor look-out. Don't you think Will?' She emerged from the steam and gave one of her rare smiles. 'Your — Mr. Turpin — will be able to manage the rent when he comes back Sylvia. Meanwhile if you can help Will in the workroom, I'm sure we can arrange something.'

Will and Sylvia stared at her as if she were an angel. Steam clung to her hair like a nimbus and she did indeed look ethereal. As they applauded her joyously, she smiled again and shook her head. 'My tea will be cold. Will, fetch the bread from the crock, Sylv must be hungry.'

The funeral was as untidy as Walter Rising's whole life had been. The vicar had no-one to take his place as grave-digger, so his sons hurriedly dug a grave the night before, taking it turn and turn about while a big harvest moon saved the use of lanterns. Hubbard the undertaker presented his bill before he brought the coffin. It was twenty-two and sixpence, and each of the eleven children found two shillings towards it and ignored the odd sixpence. Mr. Hubbard, lips tight, wore his second-best topper and walked ahead of the five brothers as if they were not carrying one of his coffins at all. Behind the brothers, Albert supported his grandmother. She and her six girls wore a motley collection of black shawls, muslin veils and bonnets. The other grandchildren ran about even during the service. The rest of the mourners had come straight from the fields and looked it. March, trying hard to think of Grampy Rising, understood why his temper had been so fierce. It was all so . . . messy!

There were no funeral meats. The gaffer wanted his cottage the next day and Will took as much as he could back with him in the trap. The weather seemed set fair, so much of the bedding was removed. Teddy and April sat on rolled-up feather beds in the well of the trap and May held Gran's precious brown teapot on her lap. It began to drizzle as they crossed the Causeway and Florence opened umbrellas and held them in strategic positions. April, thinking of Bridget and her grandfather who was Alderman Williams, suddenly started to cry. 'We haven't got a grandfather at *all*,' she wailed to the skies. 'He wasn't very nice but at least he was some sort of grandfather!' March shushed her quickly but put a sympathetic arm around her neat school coat. She agreed that Grampy Rising had not been very nice, but at least he was now gone and perhaps the whole sad business of Kempley Cottage could be forgotten.

She had not reckoned on the ability of the Risings to bring their environment with them. Wallie borrowed a flat wagon for the rest of their belongings and they arrived the next day like a pack of gypsies. The house, which had always been bare and shabby, was now like a barracks. Florence had left the drugget on the stairs because Chichester House had a polished staircase that needed no covering, but the thin carpet seemed to shred away almost overnight and the wood beneath became splintery in another day or two. The table and chair legs were kicked, there were no curtains — Kempley Cottage had never had any — the brass beds sagged to the floor, the mice came back to wallow in the dirt in spite of frequent visits by Rags. If Sylvia had not been in an unusual state over her new baby, the house might have looked better; after all she had kept it before. But Sylvia wanted this child as she had never wanted her others. So the brass was not polished and the step went unscrubbed, and soon number thirty-three looked a twin to the house opposite where the Lukers lived.

However, Gran, Sylvia and Daisy were well received in the street. Lottie Jenner called often to drink tea with Gran, and on several occasions Gran took on Lottie's layings-out when she was under the weather after a session at the Lamb and Flag. Hettie Luker would have loved them simply because they were Will Rising's relatives, but she liked them for their own sakes too. Their easy-going generosity, their laughter — which returned very soon after the funeral — their feckless-ness with Daisy, made her her sort of people. The more respectable residents of the street admired their ability to work even if this did not extend to keeping house. Gran and Sylvia worked all hours at finishing for Will and Gran went out scrubbing each morning before breakfast. Even little Daisy hawked round chestnuts that winter and shared her earnings with her cousin April.

It was not only Daisy who repaid the generosity from Chichester House. Gran and Sylvia were not too proud to do their week's shopping as late as possible on Saturday afternoons. They would scrimmage around East-gate Market by the light of the naked gas lamps, taking the squashed vegetables from the the fruiterer's stall at a penny a sack, delving through the bloody shambles of the butcher's for one of Gran's favourite sheep heads, buying up stale bread and buns from Fearis'. Gran delighted to take a basin of home-made brawn with her when she carried Will's finished work back to him on a Sunday and Sylvia would take a pot of jam and

121

some goose-grease from Flo with one hand and return a basin of dripping with the other.

Florence was too wise to refuse these gifts although she frequently gave Rags the brawn and used the dripping for frying, saving her own carefully rendered pork and beef fat for toast and sandwiches. An intuitive relationship between the two houses flourished. Albert was the favourite as always; May and April were always welcome; Teddy was a continual surprise and they viewed him warily, as slow-moving cows might watch a playful puppy; March was a visitor treated with respect, Flo a visitor treated with love. Strangely enough, Will — completely at home during his evening calls — was odd man out when they were all together.

Will felt as ambivalent about his family's closeness as he had about Sylvia's visit four years before. Half of him wanted to cut right away from them and the dirt and chaos they brought with them. The other half found it relaxing: a relief. Also, by visiting number thirty-three each day, he felt he was driving a wedge between the alliance of Sylvia and Florence. An alliance which he saw would soon include his mother.

There was another reason for his daily visits. He usually found Hettie Luker there, gossiping in the kitchen. There had never been another touch exchanged between them, nevertheless he had not been unaware of her adoration over the years and it was flattering. Now, in the company of the Other Risings, Hettie would tell a joke, wink and give him a nudge. One filthy November night she followed him into the wind and rain, stumbled on the boot-scraper and was suddenly in his arms. Laughing hysterically she delivered him a smacking kiss. Then, shocking at first, but provocative and amusing as time went on, she grabbed at him, laughed wildly and shouted, 'It's still there then! Standing up for its rights too by the feel of things!' He had watched the darkness of her hurry over the road and knew he ought to think of her as a whore.

But Hettie Luker was no whore, any more than Sylv or Vi were. She made him feel a bit of a devil. Like the King again. He chuckled as he bent his head and fought his way up to Chichester House.

About this time, Fred Luker sold his father's one good horse and bought a car. Uncomplainingly he took Alf's punishment, then went out to clean it, sporting two black eyes and a bleeding mouth. March, coming home from school, was waylaid by Gladys, who led her furtively down the side way to the stables.

March gasped, 'Freddy! What's happened — your eyes —'

Fred said brusquely, 'Nemmind that. Small payment for this, eh?' He took her into the dark interior where she could just see the gleam of metal. 'Tidn't no Deelaje nor nothing,' he cautioned as she grabbed at his arm. ''Tis one of they Austins. One of the first 'e made I reckon. Fifteen year old. One or two things I dun't unnerstand so I be going up to Brum to see 'im and ask a question.'

'Brum?' March hung on his arm as she had done last Whitsun when he'd taken her for that first spin.

'Birmingham. Just near there. Place called Northfield where 'e's got 'is factory.'

'But Freddy, you can't just *go*! I mean . . .' the enormity of his proposal overwhelmed March. For anyone to beard the lion of car manufacture in his own den was bad enough, but for Freddy to do so was incredible. His cap, always worn sideways, his filthy shirt and big misshapen boots . . . . 'Freddy Luker. You're wonderful,' she amended with conviction.

'Aye. I know that,' he wasn't joking. 'But not that wunnerful. I wants you to help me Marchy. If you'll help me I'll teach you how to drive — let you take the wheel.'

'I — I'm not fourteen till March —'

'Dun't you *want* to drive the bloody car? I only got it

123

— got this —' he jabbed a finger towards his eyes ' —
'cos I thought you'd be so bloody pleased!'

She was about to tell him just what to do with his car
and his beastly black eyes, then she paused. To take
Aunt Lizzie for a drive in her own car meant being able
to drive.

She said, 'Of course I want to drive. But would I be
allowed to?'

'No-one need know if you're so bloody bothered!' He
softened suddenly at the thought of himself and March
secretly in his beautiful Austin. 'Be better that way. No
bloody fuss.'

'All right Freddy. And thank you.'

He put his hand on hers to keep her by him. 'Dun't go
yet Marchy. You 'aven't 'eard 'ow you can 'elp me, 'ave
you?'

'Oh. I thought you meant . . . sort of encourage you.'
March was not unaware of how her sudden kiss had
affected the eldest Luker son, and she was not
displeased. She remembered how Uncle Edwin had got
so much pleasure out of his wet kisses when she was a
little girl.

'I wants that, too. En't going to get none of it from my
bloody family, that's for sure.' Freddy led her deeper
into the darkness of the stable and pressed her hospit-
ably down on to the running board of the Austin. He
said nervously, 'I've used Pa's money and me own to get
this, Marchy. Can you get 'old of five bob for me fare to
Brum?'

March found she was enjoying the darkness and
sense of intrigue. There was the car money in the cocoa
tin. Apart from April's sovereign which had started it
last Easter, there wasn't much. Would she be justified
in using that sovereign?

She said, 'I'll bring the money tomorrow. On my way
to school. Will you be here?'

'Thank you Marchy.' Relief made him collapse by her
side. Their legs were pressed tightly together. March

glanced sideways and could see the greasiness of his face shining in the half-light.

'What did you call me Freddy?' she asked softly.

'Marchy . . . I mean, Marcie.'

She leaned forward and put her lips to his. 'That's better,' she whispered. 'And Freddy?'

'Oh Christ. What?'

'I'd much rather you didn't swear any more.'

'Oh Christ . . . Oh Christ I'm sorry Marcie.'

She laughed. She felt light-headed. She kissed him again and felt him tremble all over and smelled his sweat. Then she turned and ran down the side way, past the waiting Gladys, up the street and through the door in the wall of Chichester House. Like her father she felt . . . marvellous.

At Christmas Florence insisted that her in-laws should come and share dinner. She tried to contact Vi, Jack and Austin, but it was hopeless: the short distance between Wallie's smallholding at Dymock and Gloucester defeated the Other Risings, and as for the boys they were as good as gone for ever. Neither Gran nor Sylvia seemed to mind. When Florence suggested to Sylvia that she might be missing Sam and George, Sylvia looked surprised. 'I know they're all right m'dear,' she said as if reassuring Florence. 'Every season comes in its turn. In winter you can't 'ave summer. 'Tis no good 'ankering for it.'

It sounded to Florence as if that could be interpreted as 'out of sight out of mind'. Gran's stoic acceptance of her loss and Sylv's of the absence of her sons and the father of her unborn child, must not be seen as heartless however. Florence was fast learning to accept them as they were.

So they ate their goose and sage stuffing around the big dining-room table, the ten of them, and Rags was allowed to sit on May's lap and lick each of the plates in turn, by which time the fire in the bandy room had taken hold and they retired there to sing carols and doze, drink tea and play dominoes and feel frankly bored.

Florence was playing 'Hark the Herald Angels . . .' when there came the faint tinkle of the garden door. Will stood up with alacrity.

'Probably one of the Lukers to wish us a merry Christmas and collect a mince pie or an orange.' It occurred to him they might well be accompanied by Hettie. No-one would mind if he bussed her beneath the mistletoe Teddy had suspended above the door. He hurried out.

Florence stood up and closed the vicar's heavy old velvet curtains. 'It's completely dark. How can Hettie let the children out at this hour?' she asked. No-one answered. Teddy, thoroughly irritable, knocked down the house April had made with the dominoes; March dragged him away and Albert turned to the bamboo table loaded with old *Citizens*. Not even his fondness for Gran could induce him to be sociable this year.

The door opened again and Sylvia manoeuvred her bulk out of the armchair and stood stock still, staring and clutching her bodice like a heroine in a play. Everyone turned to look. A man stood diffidently in the doorway, dwarfing Will who was just behind him.

Teddy, who had embroidered the incident in his mind many times over, announced, 'Crikey-dikey! It's the escaped convict!'

Florence said, 'Hush Teddy dear. No swearing *please*!'

Sylvia swallowed and spoke steadily. 'My dear. I knewed you'd come.' She walked forward, her abdomen carrying the rest of her with it. The man opened his arms wide and engulfed every last ounce of her. They stood rocking from side to side for so long it became embarrassing. The Rising girls fidgeted, Teddy and Albert exchanged glances, Daze suddenly let out a wail of jealousy, Gran rolled her eyes and made snicking noises of exasperation.

Will made his voice heard. 'This calls for a celebration I reckon — eh? Get by the fire our Sylv . . . warm your . . . er . . . this gentleman. Albert come down and help me with the cider. Newent cider our Mam. From Hayward's farm. Payment for an alteration I did for him.'

They put the poker in the fire and mulled their cider and made a terrible sparky mess roasting chestnuts to go with it. Through it all Dick and Sylvia did not speak. They smiled at each other. Sylv smiled at her family. Dick ducked his head at them. But apparently they had no words for each other or for anyone else.

Florence played more carols and May sang a solo, and in an effort to keep the ball rolling April said ecstatically that May should have proper singing lessons.

'No money for extras like that,' Will said with unusual sharpness, affronted by the arrival of this stranger laying claim to his sister. It was one thing to turn a blind eye to suitors he had never set eyes on, but this was bordering on the brazen. 'We have to earn our money the way we know how with so many mouths to feed.'

The silent Mr. Turpin looked up at that and suddenly smiled, his blue eyes crinkling 'irresistibly' as May told Sibbie later. Then he stuck his hand inside his waistcoat and brought it out clutching a wad of notes.

'I can look after some of 'em from now on,' he announced proudly. 'My own won't want again, and them she'd live with —'

Gran said, 'Where d'you get that money young man? Truth now. We don't want no constables a-knocking on our door! Shabby we might be but honest we definitely is!'

'I earned it old lady.' The face flushed and the eyes were angry. 'An' if I 'ears anyone making out different, they'll be sorry.'

A row sprang up immediately. 'No-one threatens me!' Gran squawked. 'Not even me own 'usband threatened me — 'e knew better! Will, you 'eard what 'e said!

No-one threatens your mam — tell 'im!'

'You called me a thief missis an' —'

'I think it behoves some of us to watch our tongues,' Will said ambiguously. Daisy yelled. And at last Sylvia spoke.

'Be quiet all of you!' she spoke sternly but not very loudly. Everyone was quiet. 'There's bound to be misunderstandings. We expect that, Dick and me. But he's my man and he's come back to look after me and the baby.' She turned to her daughter. 'Daze, you will sleep with Gran from now on and stop that silly blubbering. If you're a good girl Dick might let you call 'im Daddy.' She put her arm through his. 'Come on now my dear. You'm tired and so am I. Goodnight everyone. Good night Flo. I do thank you for a wonderful Christmas. 'Tis the 'appiest in my 'ole life.'

May watched them go out and her father follow them hastily. Then she turned to March and Albert and said breathlessly, 'That was the most romantic thing I've seen. Ever. When I marry, that is how it will be. He will find me out of every girl in the world. And I will cleave to him through thick and thin —'

'Oh shut up May!' Albert said.

'Albert! Mother doesn't like you to say shut up!' May reminded him amazed. March was also surprised.

'I don't care. Just shut up. All that love business . . . it's sickening!'

March said, 'Look, they're all going now. I'll see them out and bring up some bread and milk, shall I? Like before. And May and I can play our duet and April and Teddy can dance —'

'So can Mother and Dad,' said Albert. 'That leaves me. What plans have you got for me March . . . or should I call you Marchy?'

March glanced at him sharply and saw that he knew. She whispered, 'I'll tell you about it . . . it's nothing. Honestly.'

She told him while the others sped the visitors down

128

the street and she heated milk and broke bread into a basin. He did not seem very interested after all. He had seen her standing in the side way with Fred and heard him use that special name.

'It's just that . . . he's beneath you,' he said sulkily. 'All the Lukers are rubbish and you know it. Or you did know it.'

She said, 'Yes, but if they can help you to get what you want, Albert . . . don't you see? When I'm grown up I'm going to buy a car and drive straight down to Bath to take out Aunt Lizzie. You can come, too.'

'Oh . . . rubbish,' he repeated.

It was in the small hours that same night, when she woke to the heavy anti-climax of after-Christmas and heard someone on the landing. Carefully she edged away from May — they had chosen to share a room still — and padded barefoot to the open door. It was Albert mounting the stairs with a glass of water. In the light from the bead of gas, she saw that he was weeping.

'What is it?' She followed him into his room, fully lit, a pile of books tumbled over the bed.

'Nothing. Clear off.'

Stunned, she watched him drink then get into bed kicking the books to the floor. He looked up at her. 'Well? What are you staring at?'

'I thought you loved me.'

'I do. That's why I want you to go away. Go on March. I'm different now. Keep away from me.'

She made a stifled exclamation and went to him. He tried to push her off, but she knelt on the bed above him, her arms in a strangle-hold around his neck. Suddenly he crumpled and began to cry again, pushing his head into her shoulder. She slid to his side, kicked her legs beneath the clothes and, shivering, held him to her. The crying was awful. A blubbering boy's sound that she had never heard before.

His tears soaked through her nightdress and were immediately cold in the freezing night. She pulled him lower in the bed, stroked his strawberry blond hair and kissed his forehead.

'Tell me . . . tell me . . .' she whispered.

He began to talk, unable to hold back any more. His voice came in gasping sobs, husky with shame and disgust. She felt her own body go rigid against his and could not believe what he was saying.

'But the bishop . . . he couldn't . . . he's a man of God . . .'

'He does it to all the pages. Harry told me. He picks the pages for that very reason, March. So there must be something in me!'

'But why? Why does he do it?'

'I don't know. It's like Aunt Sylv tonight. That's how it is March. When he kissed me first I didn't understand . . . realise. And then — and then —' March listened again, believing this time, feeling sick. He told her the same story a dozen or more times. Once the flood-gates were open he could not stop. She went with him through every degrading experience, building from that first kiss which he had thought a blessing, to after last night's Midnight Mass when he had disrobed his master.

At last he whispered, exhausted, 'What can I do March? What can I do?'

'Leave school,' she said promptly. 'Now. Don't go back in January —'

'I thought of that. But what would Mother and Dad say? I'd get no end-of-school report —'

'D'you think they'd care about that? When you tell them what the bishop is really like, they'll — they'll —' March did not know what they would do exactly because a bishop was next to the King, but she knew they would do something.

'I couldn't tell them March . . . I couldn't. And anyway, there was a boy once who made a fuss. He was expelled for lying and his father lost his position . . . no-one believed him.'

March could understand that. Adults frequently disbelieved children for no reason at all.

'Just tell him you won't! You won't let him do anything any more.'

'He laughs. He says I will like it quite soon . . . oh March, shall I? Do you think I shall start to like it? It's a horrible dream . . .'

March dried his eyes on the corner of the pillow case.

'That's all it is. A dream. It won't happen again. I promise you that my dearest brother. I'll think of something. You know I'm the clever one in the family, so I'll think of something.' She kissed his hair. 'And even the dream will go away because I'll be here. I'll be here all the time Albert. All the time.' She put her mouth to his eyes and he closed them obediently. Then she held him close to her until he was asleep. She did not sleep for a long time. It was very cold and she was high in the bed supporting Albert. She did not mind. She wanted to stay awake with a cold brain that could sift facts and this new knowledge very carefully. She made plans and cast them aside. If Albert was powerless to frighten the bishop, so was she. She had to find someone important who would side with her.

Uncle Edwin brought Aunt Lizzie for a New Year visit. They arrived in an old-fashioned hansom from the station, Aunt Lizzie swathed in scarves but noticeably thinner than when March had visited her last year. Uncle Edwin, in spite of the familiarity of March's annual holidays at Bath, was still a shadowy figure, largely ignored by everyone. Except March. He looked better for being older, his hair was now white beneath his curly-brimmed bowler. As soon as she saw the way he handed his coat so casually to May in the hall, she knew he was the one to help.

They were both enchanted with Teddy, who

131

informed Aunt Lizzie she was a 'Christmas apple'. Uncle Edwin pronounced Albert 'a man'. Aunt Lizzie hugged May and patted April on the head. They both smiled at March, including her with themselves, adults for whom little compliments were unnecessary.

They celebrated that first day of 1908 traditionally. Pork and turnips at midday, a sedate walk down Henry Street to view the new high school for girls in Denmark Road, then back along Worcester Street and home for buttered pikelets and fruit cake and carols in the bandy room. There was ginger wine and the Christmas port and gentle reminiscing for the women while Will and Uncle Edwin discussed the cowardly way Campbell Bannerman had given in to the trade unions. As self-employed men they could agree on this one point until the cows came home. March yawned and wondered how she could get Uncle Edwin alone and whether she would be able to tell Albert's story when she did.

It happened the next morning. Her father and Albert were filling the dozen coal buckets for the day, Aunt Lizzie was lying in and Uncle Edwin was permitted the sitting-room in glorious isolation with the morning papers.

March crept in ostentatiously and raked at the glowing firebars. Neither of them spoke, not even to exchange a 'good morning', yet their silence heightened a mutual awareness to the tension of a violin string.

He gave way first.

'Well March?' He lowered his paper and looked at her as she fiddled with the irons in the grate. 'Have you come to talk to your old uncle?'

March smiled and quite deliberately patted her hair with one of Aunt Lizzie's mannerisms. She said quietly, 'I would like to talk, Uncle. To ask your advice. But if you would prefer to be quiet, then I am content just to be with you.'

He drew in an audible breath, let the paper fall to the rug, scrubbed at his eyes with the back of his thumbs. He looked at her again. 'My goodness, you look more like your aunt as each year goes by.'

She settled herself on a low stool; she felt odd; slightly sick and hot from the waist up.

'How are you Uncle Edwin? And how is the business?'

He leaned back, surprised. 'I am tolerably well. Yes, tolerably well I think. And as for the business — that is something ladies do not understand March. Remember that.'

She was deflated and slumped on the stool wondering how she could tell him and what he could do when . . . if . . . he knew.

He misunderstood her dejection. 'That is not to say ladies do not understand how to use the end results of business, March dear.' He leaned forward again and touched her shoulder. 'Do not imagine because Christmas is over, you cannot ask me for another present. Our presents have always been a special joy for me March. A special secret.'

She said in a low voice, not looking at him, 'You told me once, I could ask you . . . anything.'

'I have not forgotten, March.' He sounded hoarse and his grip on her shoulder tightened. She let herself be drawn towards him . . . on to her knees, her head on his lap.

'I do not know how to say it Uncle. First I have to tell you . . . something. Terrible.'

He ran his tongue around his lips. 'Tell me March,' he commanded.

She whispered, 'It's Albert . . .'

'A girl.' He was disappointed. 'He's got some girl into trouble.'

March had no idea what he meant. 'No. It's the bishop. Oh Uncle it's so horrible. What the bishop does to him . . . it's horrible . . .'

He knew what she meant but wanted to hear her say it. He gathered her to his shoulder and she felt his arms

133

tremble. After all, he was an old man.

'Just tell me March dearest. Don't be afraid. I will deal with it for you, but I must know exactly what has passed between Albert and the bishop. Then I can act.'

She sobbed with relief. Her cold midnight vigils were over; it was her turn for reassurance and sympathy. She drew a breath and began to speak in short truncated sentences. When Uncle Edwin showed no sign of shock and continued to stroke her upper arm with his shaking old hand, it became easier. Each time she paused he said softly, 'Go on. Go on dearest.' And gradually the whole sordid story unfolded. March wept with the relief of it and felt quite literally that she had laid a heavy load on Uncle Edwin's lap.

'I've promised to help him and I don't know what to do. I don't know what to do.'

She could feel Uncle Edwin breathing into her hair and when he spoke his voice was muffled by it.

'Poor little March. Dear little March. Uncle Edwin will see to it. Don't worry any more.'

'How? What will you do?' She was frightened that he would do the wrong thing; implicate Albert; or Father.

'I will go to see the man.' He seemed to be kissing her scalp.

She said, 'But he'll think that Albert has told you! He'll blame Albert!'

'Give me another name, my dear. The name of one of the other boys.'

She said without thinking, 'Harry Hughes. Harry Hughes is in the same form as Albert.'

'Then I shall tell him Harry Hughes has confided in me. I shall not give my name. He will assume I am a relative or friend.' His voice became stronger as he lifted his head. 'I shall have to rely on my demeanour and bearing to frighten him. Do you think I can do it March?'

She looked up. Her face was streaked with tears; she was almost unbearably beautiful and vulnerable. She whispered adoringly, 'Oh yes Uncle. Oh yes.'

And then, because she knew it was the proper payment now, she reached up and kissed him.

That night she crept out before supper for a driving lesson with Fred. She was almost dizzy with happiness. Fred wound energetically and the engine jumped under the bonnet. 'Throttle!' he bawled and March throttled obediently. She drove them to the bottom of Westgate Street and on to the waste ground where February floods would come. She did not grind the gears and by the light of the moon and the flickering oil lamps on the car, she manoeuvred successfully around the ruins of old buildings that could have been there when the Romans came to Caer Glow or when the Parliamentary forces had billeted themselves in the city. Fred was cautious with his praise.

'Din't put 'er through it like you usually do,' he said running his hand lovingly over the upholstery. 'You'm getting better Marcie, I'll give you that.'

It was better than a paean coming from Fred. She relinquished the wheel for the run home. She needed no more practice. She could drive. Fred could keep his lessons and his car; Uncle Edwin would buy her a car in the summer. When she went to live with Aunt Lizzie for good.

She ran back down the side way without saying goodbye and he stared after her like a hungry dog. She knew he was there and she did not wave when she reached the street. She thought her brief eighteen-month friendship with Fred Luker was finished.

7

At the end of January 1908, Sylvia Rising was married
to Richard Turpin at Gloucester Registry Office in
Saint John's Lane. Florence, Will and old Mrs. Rising
were there, and afterwards they all went to the
Cadena for a cup of tea and a fancy cake. It was
snowing, big white wet flakes that stuck to eyelashes
and veils and piled beneath shoes and boots, but Sylvia
looked warm and enormous and very happy. Dick
called her 'Mrs. Turpin' and she pretended she did not
know who he meant. 'I din't know you'd brought your
mam along Dick —' and he said dramatically, 'I en't got
no mam any more my child, but I 'ave got me a bran'
new wife!' And they both laughed uproariously.

Florence went home with a headache and Will was
strangely irritable. That night when he went down the
road to see his mother, Sylv and Dick were in bed
already and Hettie and his mother were far gone on the
stout Dick had brought in from the Lamb and Flag. Will
took Hettie's hand and led her up the hall and into his
old workroom now full of junk. In the thick cold darkness, their usual kiss was not enough. Trembling, he
fought his way through her layers of clothing and
pushed her down on the bare boards. Afterwards he
had to dress her again she was so far gone, and even
the snow outside did not revive her. Sibbie Luker
answered his knock and smiled knowingly as she said,
'What you bin doing to 'er Mr. Rising?'

He didn't like that. Sibbie was the same age as his

May. His irritability was still there, so he went on down to the Lamb and Flag to conclude a wedding day as it should be concluded. And there Lottie made everything twice as bad by elbowing him for a drink and saying, 'Hettie not 'llowed out tonight Will?'

As he spat snow on his way back home, he did not feel guilty as he had done that first time; far from it. It was Flo's own fault now. She couldn't expect him to behave like a monk for the rest of his life. But he wished Hettie did not have such a long tongue. Dammit, if it got back to Alf Luker there might well be trouble.

Albert's duties with the bishop were minimal and absolutely straightforward during his remaining time at the King's School. Although he begged March to tell him what she had done, she was obdurate in her silence, and as the weeks passed he was tempted to believe she had done nothing at all and it had just happened. Even, at times, that he had imagined the whole thing.

He was happy again. Mr. Filbert was training Harry and himself with the men's choir, and had asked them both to attend practices after they left school. Harry was to be articled to the cathedral solicitors and Albert was not far away; it was ideal. They had similar natures, unadventurous and content with their lot. Harry's father was a railwayman and Harry would have liked to have joined the G.W.R., but there was no money in it and lawyers were always rich and respected.

On March the third there was a party at Chichester House: it was March's fourteenth birthday. Harry was invited, Sybil Luker, David Daker, Bridget Williams and Tolly Hall. Daze was there, invited or not.

It was the first time David had come to see the Risings. After Mr. Daker's death, Will had made several attempts to encourage a friendship but Mrs. Daker suddenly turned to the faith she and her husband had left before their marriage, and decided that David would not play with non-Jewish children. Frustrated, Will had still taken April and Teddy with him when he made one of his calls. April, usually so friendly, had stared at the sloe-black eyes of David Daker and hidden her face in her father's trouser leg. Teddy, following Albert's example, had said pertly, 'Hello David. Daker the Baker.' Will did not take them again.

Now David, a tall lean man of sixteen, leaned nonchalantly against the piano in the bandy room, letting it be seen by his faintly insolent glance that he had come for the sake of his business only. He was dressed in a suit he had made himself, with the new cut-away jacket and narrow lapels, showing a waistcoat and a drooping watch chain. March and Albert thought him unbearable, May still brimmed with sympathy for him though his father had been dead for five years; April was still vaguely frightened of him, and Teddy did not notice he was there.

They had supper in the dining-room, the table pushed level with the chiffonier to make a proper buffet. There were sandwiches of every kind with tiny labelled flags stuck into them, mince pies, plum trifle, apple turnovers, wedges of Christmas cake, ginger beer served in wine glasses and tea for the ladies.

The younger ones sat on the fender surrounded by plates and glasses and Bridget recounted the terrible tale of Teddy's Accident for the delectation of Daze and Tolly. 'It was all my fault and I said I'd be your servant for ever after, and I have, haven't I Teddy?'

Daze and Tolly, bored stiff by the old story, exchanged glances. Daze said rebelliously, 'How? How have you been Teddy's servant, Bridget Williams?'

Bridget glanced at them in return. 'I help him with his spellings. And I told Miss Midwinter it was my fault when he spilled the ink.'

April gasped. 'That's lying Bridget! And cheating!'

Teddy said swiftly, 'I don't need any help with spellings. And I wouldn't have cared about Miss Midwinter knowing I spilled the ink. Those things are nothing. If you really want to do something for me Bridie ...' he grinned provokingly. 'I want one of those new scooters like in Marshall's toy shop in Eastgate street. I wanted one for my birthday and I didn't get one. And I wanted one for Christmas and I didn't get one. You get me one Bridget. You get me a scooter.'

'She can't,' Daze said flatly.

Tolly commented, 'They're a lot of money. My Pa says it's wicked to charge all that money for two wheels and a bit of tin.'

'I want one all the same,' Teddy said blandly, looking at Bridget.

'She can't get you one,' repeated Daze.

'I can!' Bridget picked up her wine glass defiantly. 'I can Daisy Rising. So there.'

April said, 'You're not to, Bridget. You're not to ... and you're not to do Teddy's spellings any more. You'll lead him into bad ways!'

But Teddy was already smiling with anticipation. He squeezed April's arm painfully. 'We'll share it,' he whispered. 'We'll share the scooter all the time!'

David Daker said, 'Let me fetch you something sweet, Miss May. A mince pie perhaps?'

'That would be nice.' May's face dazzled at him like a flower. 'Sibbie, would you like a mince pie?'

' 'Drather some trifle — stay there May, I'll help David to fetch it.' They passed Bridget carrying a cake. 'Stuck-up little madam,' commented Sibbie, looking at David to see how he would take it.

David had already sensed that Bridget Williams was on a higher social rung than anyone else. He smiled suddenly, and his saturnine face lifted into good looks. Sibbie stood by him while he hovered uncertainly with a plate. Then she loaded it confidently. They both knew where they were.

Will said, 'Flo dearest, shall I go down the road and see how Sylv is getting along? Everyone looks well settled here.'

Florence glanced over her teacup, well satisfied. Granny Goodrich had come out of her shell to help her prepare all the food and she was now sitting back like Flo herself, enjoying its fast disappearance. Of course it must remind her agonisingly of the loss of her daughter-in-law and little Charlotte ... but perhaps it was not all pain.

Will pressed her hand. She was more beautiful than ever tonight in a severe shirt-waist with long tight sleeves fastened with a row of tiny buttons from elbow to wrist. Desire flamed in him. 'I'll go on over to my mother then, Flo. I won't be long.'

Florence looked doubtful. 'Be back for the dancing Will. You must lead off with March.'

'Of course. Don't fuss dear.'

'I'll come to the door with you.' They went into the tiled hall, ice-cold, piled with coats, hats, mufflers, the enormous Goodrich umbrella. Florence found Will's things, wrapping him into them with tender care. She opened the front door and took a deep breath of the frosty night. The sky was high and milky and made the gas lamps beyond the garden wall look sickly yellow. 'Oh Will ... oh Will, we have so much.' She was almost frightened and hung onto his arm. 'We have too much.'

He too was affected by the hugeness of the night and the thought of the warm crowded room behind them in the midst of an empty universe. He held her face and kissed her lips tenderly. He said in a low voice, 'Flo ... dearest Florrie ... you're forty years old, my darling.'

She smiled her slight smile. 'Don't remind me Will. I know it.'

'Surely it would be all right now. . . . No chance of another child.' He kissed her again, smelling her clean fragrance with half-closed eyes.

She drew back. 'Oh Will how can you think of such things now?' He knew she was blushing. After eighteen years of marriage. 'My dear, we're much too old for that sort of thing.'

He straightened and pulled his knitted gloves over already cold hands. He knew with sudden clarity that she would never sleep with him again. The knowledge was a knell in his heart. He shivered.

'Will, you're cold. Come back inside — they will send over when the baby is safely delivered.'

'No. No, I must go.' Hettie would smell of stout and sweat and the meal she had just cooked, but she would be warm and welcoming. He needed her as he had never needed her before. 'I must go. Now.' He was halfway down the path, last year's leaves crackling under foot with frost. Florence watched until the garden door closed after him. Then she too shivered. It really was very cold.

The adults cleared the food into the kitchen and sat around the big table drinking tea while water boiled for washing up. The children — though David Daker could hardly be called a child — played hide-and-seek all over the house. It was noisy, disorganised, and an opportunity for the younger ones to let off steam. Albert chased March with Harry tagging along obediently, then quite suddenly disappeared, leaving March alone with Harry in the bandy room.

March said, 'Pax! Pax now Harry! Where's Albert?' She got behind the upright piano, her rich brown hair already tumbling from its pins. Her flannel blouse was tight and beginning to smell under the arms. She clasped her hands primly on her waistband and repeated on a rising inflexion, 'Where is Albert?'

'Gone to help your mamma —' the King's School snigger bubbled nervously through Harry's nostrils.

141

'He says I am to collect my forfeit. And bring you downstairs and —'

'Forfeit?' March wanted Albert very much indeed.

'When I catch you, you must pay a forfeit before I let you go.' Harry side-stepped to one side of the piano and she to the other. He struck a bass chord that set her nerves on edge.

She said, 'First you have to catch me!' then feinted towards the table and immediately doubled back. Harry played rugger and caught her quite easily. They struggled.

'Let me go!' March was furious. He must surely smell her blouse, flannel was notorious for holding a smell.

He was at a loss, but Albert had spoken of nothing but March and how she must be the belle of the ball. He gasped, 'A kiss! A kiss is all I demand fair maid!' And without giving himself time for second thoughts of what he guessed awaited him, he lowered his head.

The next moment he was sitting with his back clapped against the hot fender and every ounce of wind knocked from his body. March ran out of the bandy room, trying to push her hair back into its pins. As she lifted her arm, the sharp smell of sweat made her eyes water with fury. It was all Albert's fault for leaving her with that — that — lummock!

Every time David Daker looked for May, he found Sibbie, and as May ran off into the darkness, Sibbie stayed right where she was, next to him. The third time it happened, she hung on to his arm when he made to run after May.

'I've found you,' he reminded her. 'You have to go back to the parlour now. That's the game.'

Sibbie pouted. 'And you have to come with me.'

'I've still not caught May however.'

'Well, I'll be off again if you go now. You have to make sure I go back to the parlour, even if you have to drag me there.'

'I'm certainly not going to do that.'

'Don't you like me David? I like you.'

'You're making that obvious.' He lounged against the passage wall, his face a white blur, but his attitude one of boredom. Sibbie played her trump card.

'I'll let you see under my vest David.'

He said, 'Good God little girl. I've seen what you've got and more.'

She was completely enthralled. He had sworn so beautifully. And she guessed he must be telling the truth because he was so matter of fact about it.

'I'm thirteen you know,' she tempted. 'I'm six months older than May. She's a little girl. I'm not.'

He said cruelly, 'She's a lady. And you're not.'

She took a step back and came against the wall. An old nail, driven in for a long-ago picture, scagged at her best blouse, and tears sprang into her eyes. She wasn't a needlewoman like May and her cobbled darn would show dreadfully. David Daker was turning away from her, going after May again. She said sharply, 'She doesn't want you. And I do!'

He laughed carelessly as he disappeared into the darkness. 'What a shame,' he whispered back. 'What a great pity. For you.'

She stayed where she was and deliberately worked the nail head through to her shoulder blade. She hoped it would bleed. She hoped it was a rusty nail and she'd get blood poisoning and lie near death's door in the infirmary and David Daker would visit her and lean over her bed and murmur, 'How can you forgive me Sibyl? Please recover and I will spend my whole life making you happy.'

May was prosaically in the parlour, talking to a subdued Bridget who had fallen down the stairs.

'I thought I was supposed to catch you?' said David, all his mystery and panache gone in the full gaslight.

May laughed up at him. She was exquisite. He'd never seen anything like her. She made him forget the

143

drudgery of working for his mamma in the small shop in the Barton, counting every penny. May was refined in the true sense of the word. All the dross, all the superficiality was gone from her. She was like a candle flame, pure, dancing, coolly yet warmly alive.

'You *were* supposed to catch me,' she agreed. 'But I escaped. And here I am, back home!' She stood up and caught Bridget's hand in hers. 'Come on. Harry and March are helping Mamma in the kitchen. Let's go and see if they're ready to start the dancing.'

She was talking to Bridget — David realised this with a sinking heart. He followed her into the hall and as she turned towards the kitchen, he noticed a glimmer of white at the top of the stairs. He paused. If it was Sibbie still after him, he'd go up and twist her arm behind her back until she cried. It would be some compensation for May's indifference. He waited by the newel post and April came slowly down the stairs until she saw him, then waited herself. Her heart beat uncomfortably. She hadn't really enjoyed the game since Bridget fell down the stairs and she had left Teddy and Daze enjoying a strictly forbidden pillow fight. Now her way was blocked by the dark and terrifying David Daker.

She said in a small voice, 'Excuse me, have you seen May?'

He didn't answer her. The gas mantle popped suddenly and she jumped with it and that made him smile. But it wasn't a friendly smile.

She quavered, 'Teddy's burst one of the pillows I think. And he won't stop and . . .' her voice died away as his foot went on the bottom stair. He was still smiling, his teeth whiter than his pale face. But it was his eyes that were so terrifying. They did not move from her for an instant and they didn't blink. She blinked herself, rapidly, half a dozen times. Then she said, 'I don't think we're playing the game any more. I think I heard March say it was finished.'

He was still silent and his other foot was on the next step.

She retreated and he advanced.

She said, 'Oh dear . . . oh Mr. Daker, I'm frightened. Please don't . . . please . . .'

At last he spoke. In his deep, man's voice, he said, 'I'm coming to get you. April Rising. Youngest of the Rising girls. I'm coming to get you!'

April squeaked a scream like a mouse, turned and ran up the stairs. They seemed endless and very slippery. Mother did not like them clattering up the polished wood in shoes, so their outdoor shoes were kept in the hall flanked by a row of home-made slippers with felt soles. The soles skidded desperately as April pounded up one step at a time on her five-year-old legs. She could hear David Daker laughing quietly behind her as he took the stairs two at a time, and she knew if he caught her she would go mad on the instant. Her reaching arm gripped the landing banisters and she swung on them expertly, just avoiding his grasping fingers on her skirt. The bathroom door was open. She let the impetus of her swing take her through it, slammed the door, turned the key and sagged against the lock, trembling in all her limbs. There was no sound at all from outside.

'You can't get me,' she called tremulously. 'I've locked the door — it's no good trying to get me.'

Nobody replied. She stared in terror all around the tiny room. There was nowhere he could get in. The window opened only at the top and was of frosted glass. There was a ventilator above the pot-bellied gas geyser and another beneath the lavatory cistern. She looked through the geyser vents in case he was in there.

She said, 'You can't get in. No-one can get in.'

There was no reply and after another few moments she sat on the broad mahogany lid of the lavatory and stared at the door. Was he out there or had he gone downstairs immediately she'd got inside? She was cold now, sweat drying on her bare arms and face and chilling her right through. She got up and stood in the bath to pull at the gas chain and light the room thoroughly. Daddy always said the gas light warmed the bathroom; she tried to believe it. She clambered back out of the bath and looked at the door again and thought how silly she was, it was only a game. And then with a slowness that was awful, the door knob began to turn.

She knew that she had turned the key, yet at the first movement of the knob she doubted it and flung herself against the door to block his entry. 'Go away!' she called, hysterical now. 'Go away — or I'll scream for Teddy!'

The door knob twisted back, there was a short silence, then the laughter again. His voice said, 'I'll be out here whenever you open that door April. Just waiting.'

'I won't come out then! I won't come out at all!'

She sat on the lavatory seat again and folded her arms. Teddy would come downstairs in a minute. Dear Teddy who would tackle anyone or anything on her behalf. He'd protect her from Devil Daker. Yes, that was a good name for him. She must tell that to Albert. Devil Daker. She went back to the door and put her mouth to the keyhole. 'Devil Daker!' she called.

Dick and Hettie sat close to the kitchen range. Will sidestepped through the usual mess on the floor.

'What's to do?' His accent slid sideways as it always did with Hettie. 'Nothing happened yet?'

Dick said nothing, just spat into the fire. Hettie lifted one shoulder. 'They'm up there. Lottie and y'r mam. Something en't quite right I shouldn't wonder.'

Will shot a warning glance at Dick. 'Sylv's as strong as a horse,' he said. He'd heard those words before and they had not proved true. 'Young Daisy is enjoying herself over there.' He jerked his head towards the door and looked at Dick.

Dick ignored him and hoisted himself out of his chair.

'If owt 'appens to Sylv, that'll be it. I shall be off like a shot. You wun't see me 'ere no more.'

'Nothing will happen to our Sylv! I told you she's —'

'I dun't care about the babby. That's all she do talk about, the bloody babby!' He lifted his head and stared at the ceiling. 'You can 'ave the babby!' He spoke loudly as if talking to Heaven. 'Take it an' welcome! But not Sylv. Anything . . . not Sylv.'

'Look Dick, sit down.' Dick was taller by a whole head than Will and seemed to fill the small kitchen. 'Sit down and I'll make us all a nice cup o' tea. Christamighty, I coulda brought over some food, there's enough back 'ome to sink a ship!'

'Goin' well, is it?' Hettie asked, smiling up at him, biting her lip, her light blue eyes full of anticipation. 'Good of you to leave it to come and enquire for your sister. Good of 'im, innit Dick?'

'What? Ah. . . .' Dick prowled to the door. 'I'm a-goin' to go up. I'll stop outside the door. Can't wait down 'ere no more.'

They did not try to dissuade him. As soon as his tread rasped on the bare stairs, Will was at the door securing it, Hettie busy with her buttons. Will turned down the gas as Florence had always insisted, then came back to her. Just for a split second he felt a surge of disgust that was almost nausea as he caught sight of her billowing folds, the abdomen stretched and permanently gross after too many babies and too much stout, the breasts pendulous and flaccid. Then her arms went round him and he buried his face in her neck. 'Christamighty Het . . . Christamighty. I want you tonight. It's been awful . . . awful my love.' He forgot the wide night and the frost and the stars and beautiful Florence. Or perhaps he did not forget them at all. Perhaps they were all sublimated in the coarse body of Hettie Luker.

* * *

David Daker bowed low over April's stockinged knees.

'Will you forgive me enough to dance with me, little lady?'

Bridget screamed with delight. 'Go on April . . . go on . . . a proper dance!'

April said, 'I don't know . . .' even as she stood up.

He had been waiting for her outside the bathroom door, just as he'd said. She'd heard Daze giggling and Teddy saying, 'Are you waiting to go in there Mr. Daker? I'll bang on the door shall I?' And she had screamed, 'Teddy! Teddy!' and unlocked the door and hurried out to find David Daker still laughing and telling Teddy that he had trapped April in there so that she couldn't get 'home'. Teddy had laughed as well, then Daze — though Daze did not know what it was all about, but like her mother she would laugh at anything. Then David had looked at her with his sloe eyes and said, 'You weren't a bit frightened were you April? I knew you weren't when you called me that wicked name.' Then he picked her up and carried her to the bandy room where the piano was striking out some commanding chords and Mr. Goodrich was leading March to the middle of the floor. Sibbie and May and Bridget and everyone had looked at them as they came in and David had said, 'Look what I've caught. One Rising. One female Rising. Very pretty. Very, very pretty indeed.' And everything was suddenly wonderful.

It went on being wonderful. He danced with her again and again. He danced with Sibbie too. And with May. But he came to April every time. She wasn't quite comfortable about it because he kept looking at her and laughing even when she didn't say anything very funny. But everyone else laughed too. Mother smiled from the piano and Albert's friend called her 'the belle of the ball'. Only March, in a clean white blouse, frowned disapprovingly.

Sylvia's screams were ringing through number thirty-three as Hettie and Will squirmed on the floor of the kitchen. Will lifted his head. 'Oh God. . . .' He tried to concentrate, but could not.

Hettie said, 'It dun't matter my love. It dun't matter. Another night. Plenty more nights.'

'Oh God. . . .' More screams, and more. Then silence.

Will staggered to his feet. 'What shall we do? What shall we do Het?'

'En't nothin' we can do my love. Surely you knows that after your five.'

He shook his head. 'Florrie never screamed or cried out. Never. Not even when she was bleeding to death after Teddy.'

'Christamighty.' Hettie sat up slowly and began to button herself. Her drawers lay where she had kicked them, beneath the gas stove where Rags had crouched that first time. She listened; there were no more sounds. ''Tis all right now Will. Babby must be borned. Come on back.'

He shook his head again, shoulders hunched. 'Not tonight Het.' He shouldn't have remembered Florrie and her stoicism. He wanted to cry.

Then the door opened. Dick stood there looking at them in the half-light. Hettie sprang up but it was too late, he'd seen her bare legs and open blouse and anyway she spoiled it by diving for the gas stove and her drawers.

Will said, 'Dick — listen — we haven't — not tonight —'

Dick said, 'Babby's borned dead. Sylv's all right but the babby's borned dead.'

Hettie stopped her scrabbling and stared at him, hair round her face.

Will said, 'I'm sorry Dick. But so long as Sylv's all right. Eh?'

Dick said, 'Bloody fool. 'Tis all my fault en't it? I said, din't I? You 'eard me — the two o' you! I said to take the babby — and the babby's took!'

Will said, 'Pull yourself together Dick. She's going to

149

want you any minute now and she en't going to want to see you like this. She'll be quite bad enough herself. Come on, sit down. Any brandy in the house Hettie?'

Hettie went to the dresser, poured and returned. They sat Dick in the chair. By the time Granny came through the door, the whole scene looked normal. In the circumstances.

Will did not know how he went back to the party and danced with March and avoided Florence's reproachful look for being late. But he did. He danced with every one of the ladies present, even Daze. He held her with special tenderness because the small sister she might have had was dead. Then he helped find everyone's coats and wraps and he handed Bridget into the family Daimler as it arrived in Mews Lane, and told April to find Daze a nightie and let her sleep in with her for tonight. He drank the cocoa that March made and kissed his three girls goodnight, clapped Albert and Harry on their shoulders, hoisted Teddy into his arms. It had been a good party, he agreed with them all, a very good party. And there was no reason why May shouldn't have one; April too when she was a little older. No reason at all.

And then, just as had happened before, he found Florence asleep or feigning sleep, and he had to take his grief upstairs with him. Was she really frightened that he might try to climb into bed with her after all this time? He smiled wryly and then began to cry as he remembered Sylv's agony of body and spirit. Little did Florence know. Little did she know.

There was no party for May. The whole family were surprisingly stricken by the loss of Aunt Sylv's baby and May herself spent more time sitting with her grandmother and being a little mother to Daze.

March was relieved that there would be no more socialising in Chichester House for a while. She had tried to be polite to Harry Hughes for Albert's sake, and look where it had got her. And as for that insufferable David Daker making a fool of little April — she had no wish to repeat any of it. The summer would go on very pleasantly now until the annual visit to Bath. Certainly there was the boredom of the Whit-walk and the business of leaving school and receiving her attendance prize, but she was still warm with the knowledge of saving Albert. Moreover she could drive a motor car.

She brought her plait forward and tickled her chin with it, wondering whether she dared ask Uncle Edwin another favour quite soon. Although really, it was she doing him the favour. He probably needed a personal secretary without realising it. And if he bought a motor car she could drive him to the office besides doing his typing for him.

She flipped her plait over her shoulder again and smiled at the bright May sunshine. She had always wanted to live in Bath.

Gladys Luker suddenly popped out of their side way, dirty-faced as usual. March thought it was a pity April and Teddy would be going to Chichester Street school next autumn; Bridget might be dreadful but at least she wasn't common. Sibbie was the only Luker who was presentable and that was May's influence. March could have wished that she had had the same effect on Fred, but he continued to wear his flannelette shirt without a collar and had even taken to using a thick leather belt to anchor it inside his trousers rather than braces. He looked no more than a navvy. Luckily the driving lessons had all taken place during the dark evenings and only Albert knew of them.

Gladys hopped in front of her and walked backwards. 'Our Fred wants you,' she said.

'Is that so?' March replied coolly. She side-stepped Gladys and quickened her step, not only to avoid Fred but because she was passing thirty-three on the other side. Aunty Sylv might be sitting outside for a breath of air. Aunty Sylv did not like sitting indoors any more and she didn't like Granny's company much. She spent part of each day at Chichester House 'being quiet' as Florence explained it. March knew that since the baby had been born dead Aunty Sylv had gone a bit queer.

Gladys leapt in front of her.

'Our Fred says it's important. Real 'portant.' As March did not take any notice of this she added desperately, 'March, please come and see our Fred! 'E'll 'it me else!'

The thought of Gladys Luker being hit did not bother March; Fred had a right to hit his sister just as she hit Teddy when he was more than usually obstreperous. But if it was that important it might well be to her advantage to investigate further.

She said, 'All right. Five minutes.' She turned on her heel and went down the side way. Gladys kept watch.

Fred was shovelling horse's dung into a stiff sack. The ramshackle stables in the sunshine stank to high heaven, as did Fred himself. Nevertheless his grin was wide as he saw her.

'Hello Marcie. You en't stopped by since end of Febr'y.'

March stepped delicately on to the mounting block; there was actually steam coming from the sack. She breathed shallowly.

'No. You're working when I'm home.' It was true yet she felt slightly uncomfortable. She had almost cut Fred since the end of her driving lessons.

Fred shrugged, not offended. 'Well, I suppose the lessons were over when the light nights come along, eh?' he grinned again. 'Didn't want to be seen with Fred Luker, eh Marcie?'

She said defiantly, 'I told Albert about it. About the lessons.'

'An' about the kissing?' He guffawed at her expression. 'No, you never, did you my maid? Never tole 'im about that.'

Wishing she had not mentioned Albert's name, she said quickly, 'Boys are all the same! Always wanting . . . that.'

His grin died as he stared up at her. Standing there on the mounting block she looked like an angel aureoled in light.

'What d'you mean? Who bin kissing you Marcie?'

'You of course.'

''Oo else? You meant someone else — come on —'

She shrugged. 'Oh, just a boy at my party. Nothing.'

'That bloody David Daker — why din't you tell me — I'd bloody well kill 'im —'

'It wasn't David Daker you idiot. Never mind.' She jumped down. 'I must go Freddie. Mother will be waiting tea.'

''Alf a mo. I en't told you. I'm gonna start a cab service. What d'you think of that Marcie? A motor cab. All me own.' He followed her down the side way, taking off his cap and knocking it against the wall so that dust flew. 'I'm gonna make a fortune Marcie. See if I don't. Next thing you know I'll 'ave a char-a-banc.'

She reached the safety of the street and turned to look at him. How on earth she could have kissed him she'd never know.

She said deliberately, 'It was Harry Hughes. The one who kissed me. He's going to be a solicitor you know.'

He said nothing. He watched her all the way down the street and his face was without expression.

Albert was in the fruit enclosure picking gooseberries into his spread handkerchief, head down. She peered at him through the netting.

'Albert, I thought it was your practice night with Mr. Filbert.' She wished with all her heart he would look up and say he preferred to be with her.

'I'm missing it. Don't say anything to Mother.'

'Why? Why are you missing it? Are you ill?'

He turned his face down further. 'Harry's not going.' His head came up and she saw he had been crying. 'Harry's been sacked, March! Sacked from school! Some trumped-up charge about him pinching money from the lockers — you know Harry wouldn't do that!'

She couldn't take it in at first. Jealousy of Harry almost overwhelmed her.

Albert's distress turned to anger. 'You know Harry's not a thief March! And you know why he's been sacked — you're the only one who does know!'

She stared, then said through stiff lips, 'What do you mean?'

He left his handkerchief and the few token gooseberries and pushed his way blindly through the wire gate.

'That — that — swine! Harry won't say anything of course, but the bishop must have — must have — asked him.' He looked at her painfully. 'You know what.' He hung on to her shoulder and turned his face towards the clear blue sky and the fruit trees budding. 'Oh March, if only I'd said no. Like Harry must've done. I'd be proud to be sacked. . . now I feel a miserable coward. And there's nothing to be done about it. Harry. Or me.'

March let out her breath tremblingly, terrified that Albert would sense through his contact with her shoulder that she was the cause of Harry's expulsion. She clenched her fists. It couldn't be that. And even if it was, it was nothing to do with her. Uncle Edwin had taken the matter into his hands.

Albert said, 'I think I'll go up to the attics for a while. Don't say anything to Mother.'

'I won't.'

She watched him go between the laurels towards the house. He was desperately unhappy. He would miss Harry Hughes far more than he would miss her if she was suddenly removed from him.

She clenched her hands harder still. If Harry had been sacked because of anything Uncle Edwin had done, she didn't care. She didn't care.

The rest of the story was sorted out by Whitsun. Some money had been found in Harry's locker which had belonged to an eleven-year-old. It was all hushed up, but there was no question of him being articled to the cathedral solicitors any more. His father used his influence and secured him a position as lamp-boy at Longhope station. He went into digs and rarely came to Gloucester. And Albert seemed to withdraw from everyone, even March. He stuck the rest of that school year, but his spare time was spent in the garden or the attics. And he wanted no company.

8

It was from then — Harry's expulsion — that March felt her life turn sour. Her exclusion from Albert's real presence was a continuing sore that did not heal, even when they both left school that summer and started with Will in the workroom. She chose to find the work boring, though had she known a year ago that she would spend her entire day with Albert she would have been overjoyed. Now she resurrected the old idea of being a personal secretary and used her tiny salary to pay for lessons in writing Mr. Pitman's shorthand.

Her plans for going to Bath were also balked when Aunt Lizzie's continued ill-health was diagnosed as consumption, and she was hurried off to a sanatorium by a frantic Uncle Edwin.

April told May that she thought March was 'simmering'. Neither girl tried to talk more intimately about it. March's temper outbursts were experiences to be avoided at all costs. They knew that after an eruption March would be serene and happy, but still they had no wish to precipitate the eruption. So March continued to 'simmer' and to become resentful; and as bitter as a girl of fourteen can become.

For Albert, this was a time of sanctuary. He was unexpectedly dexterous at transforming written measurements into a French-chalk outline on material and cutting a superbly fitting garment. Rarely were alterations needed. By using identically patterned woollen worsteds for three suits, he saved enough cloth to make

March a winter costume of impeccable line and smartness. She trimmed the collar with fur and borrowed a hat of Florence's that tipped over her eyes. When the tedium of button-holing became unbearable, she would go to the bandy room and parade in front of the big glass in her new clothes, pretending to be a 'secretary'. It became her solace and the height of her ambition.

That winter was marred too by ill-health for April and Teddy. Normally robust, the two of them were plagued by sore throats, each time diagnosed by a terrified Florence as diphtheria. The children, transplanted from the hot-house atmosphere of Midland Road School to Chichester Street Elementary, picked up every germ that was around. They hated the change. They whined and were intractable, and their quarrelling, reaching the ears of March in the workroom, did not endear her family to her.

On Teddy's birthday and Christmas Day, they were confined to bed, only saved from complete misery by visits from Bridget and Tolly. They played Happy Families on a large tray, then Bridget invented a mother-and-father game wherein she and Teddy sat in one bed, while April was a sick child in another, and Tolly a general dogsbody. Bridget and Teddy kept falling out of bed and April kept crying. Tolly was relieved when his father called to take him home.

In January it was decided that the children should have their tonsils removed. It was a mild winter with no frost to kill the germs and the School Inspector had shamed them three times already with enquiries regarding their non-attendance.

Gladys Luker said, 'I know someone 'oo 'ad it done. Spat blood for a fortnight they did. Couldn't eat nothin'. Couldn't speak 'cept for a squeak now and then.'

Teddy said sturdily, 'Don't believe that.'

April enquired, 'Who was it Glad?'

'A girl,' Gladys said unspecifically. ''Er said it was agony. Absolute agony.'

The phrase 'absolute agony' confirmed it for April. She quavered, 'I don't want it done.' Her voice rose. 'Mother! I don't want my tonsils out —' She stood up from the stairs where the three of them were sitting and ran down the passage towards the kitchen. 'Mother . . . Mother . . . I don't want —'

Teddy said, 'I reckon Bridget would faint if I spat blood. I'd like that.'

'What? Seeing her faint?' Gladys asked jealously.

'No, stupid. Spitting blood. I'd wait till dinner was all out on the table then I'd say excuse me and I'd —'

'You won't be able to talk. The girl what I'm tellin' you about, 'er couldn't talk. Just gave a squeak now and then.'

'All right then, stupid. I'd —'

Florence arrived post haste. 'What are you saying Gladys? I wish you wouldn't frighten April. I can assure you Teddy, there is nothing to having your tonsils out.'

'Have you had yours out?' Teddy asked directly.

'No, but . . .' Florence could not help smiling at the trap he had set for her. She put her arms around his delightful stockiness. 'Darling boy, do you think if there was the slightest risk I would permit you —'

Of course Teddy knew she would not. But April, snivelling in the background, knew that adults did things against their wishes sometimes.

'Listen.' Florence gathered them both to her. 'You be good about this and you can have a present. Nothing to do with Christmas or birthdays. An extra present.'

'What?' Teddy pounced.

'Anything. Anything you like. Within reason.'

Teddy looked at April and took a breath. 'A scooter?' he asked.

'Yes. All right.' Florence did some quick reckoning.

The Risings were still rising. 'Yes. I think I can promise you a scooter.'

Teddy smiled beatifically. 'We'll be good.'

April whispered, 'It won't hurt, Mamma?'

'We'll be *good*, April,' Teddy said sternly.

April bit her lip. It was all right for Teddy. He had gone on having accidents in spite of the lesson he had learned on Mr. Goodrich's tree. He simply was never frightened.

She went to Barton Street with her father, and while he had coffee with Mrs. Daker, she stood shyly at the counter staring across it at David. He stared back quizzically, his head on one side.

'Well my Sweet Primrose?'

She looked uncomprehending.

'April brings the primrose sweet —'

She finished triumphantly, 'Scatters daisies at our feet!'

He smiled. 'That's better. You forgot to be shy. Now — what can I do for you?'

She had to disentangle her tongue from her back teeth, then clear her throat. 'Teddy and me . . . Teddy and I . . . have to have our tonsils out. Next week. We have to go to the infirmary and have our tonsils out.'

He looked at her for a long moment with his black eyes blank, then his mouth turned up slightly as if he'd thought of something pleasant. He came around the counter and lifted her on to it.

'You're scared,' he said, with just a touch of scorn.

She flushed. 'I'm not —'

'You're scared like you were when I chased you up the stairs and into the bathroom.'

'I wasn't scared. And afterwards . . . I wasn't scared. I enjoyed it!'

He flung back his head and laughed and she saw the way his Adam's apple bobbed in his throat like a marble in the neck of a ginger-ale bottle.

He said, 'Things that are frightening are also

159

exciting, April. Remember how you faced up to being scared and called me a wicked name? What was it?'

She shook her head.

'All right then, don't say it again. But you must use it inside your head about the tonsils. Do you understand?'

She looked at him. After a while she nodded very slightly.

He said briskly, 'Good. It shouldn't be hard. Look it in the eye. You'll have gas — a face mask I expect. You breathe very deeply and then you sleep. That is all.'

She thought about it doubtfully. Then she came to the important part. 'Afterwards . . . after the bathroom . . . you danced with me. That was what made it so exciting.'

He seemed to consider, though he knew already what he was going to say, she could tell from the smile which still pulled up the long thin mouth.

'You won't feel like dancing. But I'll visit you. Every day I'll call on you if your mamma will permit it.'

April let out a great sigh. 'She will permit it. Oh David. . . .'

He tucked some of the mass of dark gold hair beneath her bonnet and his smile became wide and open.

'Oh April . . . Primrose Sweet.' He lifted her to the floor again and prepared to join the others in the parlour. 'Remember, you can only be brave if you are frightened first.'

April knew this was true because her father had reported similar strange paradoxes from old Mr. Daker's repertoire. And old Mr. Daker was next to a disciple.

They made a detour via Eastgate Street on their way to the infirmary. Marshall's Toys wasn't open at that hour in the morning — they had to present themselves at Outpatients by nine o'clock — but the scooter was still displayed in the window after nearly a year.

'It must be dear if no-one can afford to buy it,' April said apprehensively, looking at her mother, clinging desperately to the thought of dark David who brought ecstasy with him.

'Stupid!' scoffed Teddy. 'They've sold dozens! They send to the factory for more each time they sell one.' He glanced up at Florence. 'Girls are silly sometimes Mamma, aren't they?'

'What would you do without April?' Florence reminded him gently.

Teddy frowned with concentration, then admitted generously, 'I couldn't go to school without April. And nothing is so much fun if she isn't there.' He looked around his mother's skirt at his pale sister. 'I love you,' he said frankly. 'And March and May.' He glanced at the gleaming red scooter. 'And Bridget,' he added.

'What about Albert and Papa?' prompted Florence, urging the children inexorably away from the window and towards the Cross.

'Of course.' He looked surprised that she could ask. 'And you. You more than me,' he concluded matter-of-factly.

Florence swallowed. Her own love did not blind her to the fact that Teddy was innately selfish; his charm lay in the fact that he knew it. So she had to believe him now. She closed her eyes, momentarily dazzled by the grey January morning. The years since Teddy's birth had been filled with such joy and peace that she thanked God for them every day. She thanked him now and added a fervent prayer that the forthcoming operation would not hurt her son. Quickly — hardly an afterthought — she included April in the prayer. The she opened her eyes and looked down at April, bonnet brim tipped towards the pavement.

She said, 'We'll play snakes and ladders this afternoon April, shall we?'

The bonnet brim came up. 'That would be nice Mamma.' April tried to smile. 'I am expecting David to call too.'

Florence squeezed the small hand. 'Gentleman callers already,' she teased.

'Oh David belongs to May,' April said seriously. 'But she won't mind. May never minds sharing anything.'

Florence thanked God again. May, her favourite until Teddy's birth, was not only beautiful, but since her visit to Bath many years ago, was strong too. And with the disposition of an angel as well as the looks. Sometimes Florence wondered whether she was too fortunate. A devoted husband and five lovely children, a beautiful, spacious home and enough money to help others. She turned into Southgate Street, prompting the children to say their good mornings to the old newspaper-seller already ensconced there. From her cramped and sunless childhood had sprung this flowering. And all because of Will. Dear Will.

April was never to forget the ordeal of having her tonsils out. The lights, the indignity of the gag in her mouth, the gas — she never understood why it was called laughing gas — that threatened to suffocate her forever, enclosed as she was in a mask too big for her. But most of all it was the lights, which burned into her as electric light was to do for the rest of her life, and silhouetted the gargantuan figures who bore down upon her and consisted only of eyes . . . eyes . . . eyes . . . then her mother, gently patting her cheeks and saying, 'It's all over and done with, little April. Come back to the big wide world . . . it's all over and done with.' And then the racking sobs came that hurt her throat and made her spit blood just as Gladys had prophesied.

A nurse delivered Teddy into Florence's arms; he was already coming round. She supported the two of them, April one side, Teddy the other. When Teddy lifted a groggy head and whispered hoarsely, 'Can we go and get the scooter now Mamma?' she wept and laughed at the same time. April never forgot that either.

Fred Luker came for them in his Austin. The nurse

gave April a fresh gauze pad and told Teddy not to keep talking. There were other instructions too, about food and drink. Lots of water. April knew she would never swallow again. Fred carried her out to his car where it said 'Ambulances only' and tucked her into the back seat, clucking all the while. April found it a most comforting sound. When Teddy started to speak, Fred stopped clucking long enough to say, 'Tha's enough young 'un. You 'eard what that there nurse told you.'

At last they were back home. April had never been so pleased to see it before and the sight of Will provoked more tears. Albert, who hated 'waterworks' as much as ever, spent an unusually long day in the workroom from where it was almost impossible to hear the distress of his sister. Teddy looked at the group around April's bed, his father holding her while she retched, his mother stroking her sweat-dark hair, his other sisters running back and forth with basins; he had found the lights and the masked men very interesting, and his throat was no sorer now than it had been when he had tonsillitis. If April thought to have a lion's share of the scooter by making so much fuss, she must have another think. Grinning to himself, Teddy curled up in his bed and slept.

David came in the evening. He was not allowed to see April who was sleeping at last, so he sat with March and May in the parlour and talked about the new National Health Insurance Act which Mr. Lloyd George was presenting to Parliament. March was too proud to ask for enlightenment, but May questioned him closely and thought it sounded very fair .

'Not for me. Nor for your father,' David said in his young-cynical voice. 'We're our own employers, so the ninepence for fourpence nonsense won't help us much, will it?'

'No ... but *we* can help ourselves,' said May. 'I expect Mr. Lloyd George is thinking of all the people who are in the *power* of their overseers and such like.'

163

'Or thinking of himself and his own political future.' David said quickly before May's sweetness could bring him to his knees. Her fairness shone like a sun in the gas-lit parlour and made March look plain and prim by contrast. He wished March would go away and wondered whether Florence had commanded her to stay as a chaperone. His heart quickened at the thought; did they take him that seriously? He had loved May for nearly a year and she must guess that his call on April was merely a ploy to see her. Yet she was so young and so innocent . . . innocent as the day she was born. How this could be when her close friend was the Luker girl, he did not know, yet so it was.

March said suddenly, 'Could Father — and you — stick the whole ninepenny stamp on your card? That would be fair, wouldn't it?'

David was at a loss, but would not admit it. He looked at March's clear, light-brown eyes and thoroughly disliked her.

'I can't see anyone agreeing to sticking stamps on a card,' he scoffed. 'The British John Bull is a sight too intelligent for that, I'll be bound!'

'Probably,' said March, losing interest. She and Albert still found David Daker insufferable; it was one of the few topics they could discuss fluently. The way May and Sibbie whispered and giggled about him made her absolutely sick. And April was as bad. She stood up. 'I'll fetch some more coal.' She took her time picking up the bucket, expecting David to be there before her. He made no move and she knew he wanted her gone. She walked stiffly into the hall where Rags met her, mewing to be let out into the frosty night. Deliberately she stumbled into him and sent him yowling ahead of her into the kitchen. 'You nearly sent me flying Rags!' she said loudly, in case Florence was within earshot. But no-one was downstairs, they were with April, or entertaining David Daker or sitting late in the workroom over something quite unnecessary. She opened the kitchen door and watched Rags scutter through it. If only Aunt Lizzie would come home. If only she could get a job as a secretary. If only Uncle Edwin hadn't mentioned Harry Hughes' name to the bishop. If only . . . if only . . . if only Albert really loved her. As she loved him.

David said, 'May. I wish to ask you something. Privately.'

May said comfortably, 'Certainly David.' She smiled encouragingly. This was a potentially romantic situation and she must remember every detail to share with Sibbie at school tomorrow. The glowing fire, the gaslight on David's wiry hair — it was a pity it was so very bushy — his intense dark eyes.

Suddenly he dropped to one knee before her and put his hands on the arms of her chair so that she could not get up.

'May. Dearest, beautiful May. Will you marry me?'

May gasped and sat tight back as far as she could from the intense dark eyes which were now much too serious. She wanted to clutch at the arms of the chair and push herself further away, but that would mean touching his hands. There were dark hairs along the backs of his hands. He must be seventeen now. Seventeen.

He said, 'May, I didn't mean to frighten you. You must know I love you to distraction.'

She said squeakily, 'It's all right. I'm not frightened. But I think you had better sit up again. March will be back and will think it most odd to see you down there.'

'But May . . . I love you!'

'Oh David. Oh David.' She clasped her hands on her lap and gripped hard. 'Oh David . . . I'm only thirteen!'

He lowered his head and there was a sense of respite. 'I'm sorry dearest, I meant to wait. I really did. But I cannot think of anything else but you — all day and all night. Just give me a word — one word and I'll be patient. Say you'll think of marrying me.'

165

Without his eyes on her she could see it all as wonderfully romantic again. Nevetherless she still repeated helplessly, 'I'm only thirteen.'

He looked up and fixed his eyes on her. 'You'll be fourteen in three months, May. Will you give me an answer then? Juliet was fourteen.'

It was the right thing to say. Juliet. Romeo and Juliet. It was so romantic. She wanted desperately to get away and think about it, she also wanted to giggle.

'I don't know what to say. Please sit up David. I'm worried about your trousers and whether March will come in — and all sorts of things! I can't think about it properly.'

He coughed a sort of laugh. 'Oh May. Sweetness — yes, you are truly sweetness itself. I'll sit up if you will tell me you think of me just a little.'

'I think of you often David.'

'And you do not hate me?' he persisted.

'I would hardly visit the shop with Papa if I hated you.'

'Then you must love me a little.'

'I don't know! I talk of you and I think of you and I like you —'

'It is enough! There, I keep my promise.' He stood up, dragged a hassock to her chair and squatted by her, clasping one of her hands in both of his. 'Just go on thinking of me. All the time. Believe that I am thinking of you. We will see each other as often as we can and when you are sixteen — oh God, two whole years — we will be married.'

May was alarmed. 'Oh David. I'm not sure. Really.'

He laughed, his dark face radiant. 'You will be sure by then my darling.' He pressed her hand to his cheek and she felt the heat of his skin. 'Oh May I did not mean to speak so soon. Surely not many girls become engaged when they are thirteen —'

'David, I have not become engaged!'

'Just between us May,' he pleaded. 'A secret. It will be fun.'

May bit her lip. That was true.

He stood up, knowing when to leave.

'Remember when you go to bed tonight my love, David is thinking of you. Every hour of every day he is thinking of you.'

It was so innocuous, no harm in it at all. May put her hands to her face, glad that he had gone, yet regretful too. She went to the mirror and looked at herself. Her hair was wild and her face unbecomingly red. She stared, then began to giggle. She could hardly wait to see Sibbie tomorrow morning.

By the end of the week Teddy was scampering along the landing in his bare feet, playing through the banisters with Rags and even slipping into the freezing bandy room to pick out a tune on the piano's black notes. April stayed where she was, improving daily but unwilling to leave the security of her bed. She wondered too whether David would stop his daily visits once she was up. He came promptly at seven each evening and sat with her until Florence brought up bread and milk at half-past. Then he pretended to eat a spoonful himself and fed her in between. The agony of swallowing was nothing when he was there. Once, when she was particularly fretful and refused to drink water, he seized her wrist and twisted the skin. 'How much of this can you stand, little April?' She bore it gaspingly for several seconds, then he held the glass to her lips. 'Quickly. Drink now. It won't hurt any more.' And with her wrist still burning and smarting, it hardly did. She told her father about it and he laughed his surprise and recounted once again his early experiences with old Mr. Daker. April understood it all. You paid first for happiness. She was happier than she had been for ages because David came to see her every day. And she had paid for it by having her tonsils out.

167

Bridget and Tolly came as usual to play with the invalids. Bridget had a nurse's uniform and donned it with great importance.

'I'm going to look after you,' she announced. 'Tolly, you get into April's bed and I'll take your temperature.' She extracted an enamelled tin thermometer and shook it busily. 'Hurry up Tolly. April, make room for him and lie down. You're at Death's Door.'

'I'll be the doctor,' Tolly said quickly, not liking the look of April's rumpled bed. 'Then I can play snakes and ladders with April and take her mind off her troubles.'

Bridget looked at him scornfully as she jabbed the thermometer into Teddy's mouth. 'Miss Midwinter sent her best wishes to you both and Miss Alicia asked if she might call with some hot-house grapes. I said yes.'

'Oh *yes*,' mumbled Teddy happily. He removed the thermometer. 'Hot-house grapes *and* a scooter.' He looked slyly at Bridget.

Momentarily confused she stared at him. 'Scooter? Oh the scooter. I'm doing my best Teddy dear, you must be patient.'

'No need.' He passed the thermometer across beds to April. 'No need at all is there April?'

'Mmm?'

'No need to be patient about the scooter,' he reminded her significantly. Then giving up all pretence at finesse, he blurted, 'We've got it thank you Bridget Williams. And no thanks to you!' he added contradictorily.

'How do you mean, you've got it?'

'We got it for having our tonsils out bravely!' he informed her triumphantly. 'Our own mother and father bought it for us and it is to be delivered next week when we are 'llowed to go outside.'

Bridget stared for only another instant, then she heaved a gigantic sigh of relief. 'Thank goodness.' She smiled modestly. 'I thought it would take longer than this.' She marched over to April, removed the thermometer, examined it and shook it down vigorously. 'But you're right of course. No need for gratitude.'

Teddy spluttered annoyance and April and Tolly stared. Bridget held up her hands. 'It's my doing. Idiots. You didn't think it just happened did you?'

'How your doing?' Teddy jumped out of bed with frustration. 'How can it be your doing when you didn't even know about it?'

'I knew all right. But not when it would come, nor how it would happen.' Bridget sighed again. 'I prayed for it. Every morning and every night. I prayed to God to send Teddy Rising a scooter from Marshall's Toy shop. And He did.' She spoke quietly, reverently, casting her eyes to the ceiling. Teddy tugged furiously at his nightshirt.

'I told you. Our mother and father bought it!'

'They were instruments.' Bridget had a good repertory of words. It was one of the many things April missed about Midland Road, the session when they 'collected words'. Bridget put away the thermometer and produced a stethoscope. 'Yes. They were instruments of God. And I asked God to send you the scooter.' She fitted the earpieces in position and said thoughtfully, 'I must remember to say thank you in Sunday School.'

Teddy's nightshirt creaked threateningly as he tugged it down as if holding in his temper. 'You don't have to wait till Sunday to say thank you,' was all he could find to say.

'It's better then. God's always in church.' Bridget's smug matter-of-factness was too much for Teddy, he collapsed back on his bed groaning.

'Does it hurt Teddy dear?' Bridget was over him anxiously. 'Now just lie quiet — give me the thermometer April — oh, I've got it in my bag — I'll just wipe this fluff off —' Teddy groaned again because it stopped Bridget talking about God. She devoted all her attention to him, smoothing his forehead, then gently brushing his hair. It was delightful. He might marry her one day then he'd be looked after all the time. He opened his eyes and mumbled through the tin-tasting tube, 'Wanna gla water.'

'A glass of water my darling?' Bridget crooned above him. 'There's none in the jug. Eridget will get it for you.' Apparently she was nurse no longer. She ran off downstairs while Teddy chewed on the tin and April and Tolly climbed ladders and fell down steps and hardly realised time passed.

In the kitchen March said, 'What do you want? I'm supposed to be laying the tea and I certainly don't want you under my feet.'

Bridget was always wary of March. She said, 'I only want some water for poor Teddy. I'm looking after him in my nurse's uniform. D'you like it March? I've got a thermometer and a stethoscope and lots of bottles of pretend medicine and —'

'Get the water and go on upstairs then.' March tried to shoo the child away kindly but she longed with all her soul to shove her hard. Bridget's good background was her only excuse in March's opinion: apart from that she was impossible, encouraging Teddy in his rowdiness and making him think he was so wonderful. March banged down five plates and thought bitterly that it would be she who took a tray for three upstairs. No, a tray for four, Tolly Hall was there too! She began to cut very thin bread, having to spread Goodrich's yellow butter to hold it together.

She bit her lip angrily. Children were all spoiled now; she remembered when she and Albert and May had been little, how they had had to work. When April was born she had done all the washing for weeks until Aunt Lizzie had rescued her from drudgery. She thought of Aunt Lizzie and her anger melted into tears. If only she could be with her, how different it would all be. Then she frowned suddenly at a recent recollection, her thoughts

170

switching unexpectedly to Teddy and April. Was Bridget really putting a toy thermometer in their mouths?

Tolly and April were deep into their game, so as usual, all Bridget's attention was lavished on Teddy. She held him in the crook of her arm while he sipped at the water, then she kissed him and laid him gently back on the pillow. 'Now I have to listen to your chest.'

She fitted the stethoscope into her ears again and lifted his nightshirt. He woke up suddenly and pushed it down, but not before Bridget, only child, had seen what she had seen. Her eyes opened wide.

He said, 'You can get down my neck. Not up there, if you don't mind.' But he was grinning without embarrassment because he shared a bath with April and in any case had never had inhibitions since those early days when he had 'performed' almost anywhere and received nothing but praise.

Bridget's curiosity was thoroughly aroused. 'No, I can't. There isn't room. Besides, I have to examine you. All over.'

'Oh no you don't —'

'I *do*! I'm your nurse and you have to do exactly what I tell you. Besides,' she looked pious again. 'You shouldn't argue with me Teddy. Not after I arranged for you to have that scooter.'

He sighed exasperation but lay back resigned, eyes closed. 'Oh. . . . all right.'

His nightshirt came up and the stethoscope was cold on his chest. But not for long. 'I might have to hurt you a bit,' Bridget said briskly. 'You must try to be brave.'

'I am brave. Always.' But she did hurt. He dared not open his eyes to see what she was doing and was surprised April did not protest. But April and Tolly were deep in their card game and Bridget had her back to them.

And then the door opened.

Bridget had his nightshirt down and the bedclothes

171

up in an instant, but March had seen. She stopped for a moment, affronted and shocked beyond words. Teddy clasped the sheet to his chin and said defiantly, 'Bridget's a nurse. She's got a proper uniform look March, and here's her ther — thermom —'

March recovered herself and walked around the cringing Bridget to place the tray on the bamboo table between the beds. 'Thermometer,' she said smoothly. 'It's called a thermometer Teddy. Now, I've cut this bread and butter very thinly, so I want you two to have a slice each. And there's milk to drink. Bridget, perhaps you will see to things, dear.'

Bridget could hardly believe her ears. She busied herself at the tea tray, eyes down, and after a few moments of plumping April's pillows and looking over her shoulder at her hand of cards, March left them again. Bridget avoided Teddy's eyes as she passed the bread and butter, but Teddy himself seemed not to realise anything was unusual.

March was waiting in the hall when Bridget and Tolly came downstairs.

'You father is here Tolly,' she said, wrapping him in his coat and handing him his cap. 'In the kitchen talking to Albert.' She turned to Bridget. 'Your car isn't here yet Bridget, but you may as well put your coat on ready.' She watched, leaning against the newel, as Bridget struggled into her thick coat alone. The gas hissed and Tolly could be heard laughing in the kitchen. 'Sit on the hall chest to change your shoes,' she instructed in the same detached voice. The small girl obeyed, red-faced and silent. March waited until she was in bonnet and gloves, then she said, 'Bridget, you've been putting that awful tin thermometer in Teddy's and April's mouths, haven't you?'

Bridget looked up for a startled instant, then whispered, relieved, 'Yes March.'

'Do you realise it has probably poisoned them?'

Another startled pause then Bridget gasped, 'Oh no, they use them in hospital! I know!'

'In hospital they are made of glass and they are clean.'

'This one is clean March! Look — I wiped it on my hanky — look —' she began to tug open the little case containing her toys. March held up her hand.

'They have to be boiled, Bridget. To kill the germs.'

'Oh . . . oh March!'

'If Teddy or April should die, it will be your fault,' March continued implacably.

Bridget's eyes looked about to fall out. March went on, 'We will say nothing about that. Nor anything else that happened this afternoon, Bridget. Do you understand me?'

Bridget was a long time understanding, but at last she nodded, terrified.

'On one condition,' March paused. She had not had long to think this out and she did not like confiding in this child even if she did have her in the palm of her hand. But there was nothing else for it. 'I want a job Bridget. I want to be a secretary. Do you know what I mean?'

Bridget stared anew, another long time taking in the change of topic. March prompted impatiently, 'Well? Do you know what I mean by a secretary?'

Bridget nodded again. 'Like Miss Pym is Grandfather's secretary,' she whispered.

March was satisfied. 'Like Miss Pym,' she agreed. 'You are to persuade your father — or your grandfather — to give me a position as a secretary, Bridget. If you will do that we will say nothing about this afternoon.'

Bridget sobbed, but she understood now. These were the tactics used at school. Secrets were kept by a system of barter.

She said, 'Daddy and Grandfather have already got Miss Pym, March! What can I do? They won't listen to me. Not even Mamma is allowed to talk about the business! Oh March — I can't — I can't!'

'I think you can,' March said with more assurance than she actually felt. 'I think Miss Pym has too much work to do for the two of them. I think she would enjoy training me. And I am very efficient and come from a good family . . . you know all this Bridget. Surely you can remember it by yourself?'

Bridget was sobbing rhythmically now, but little hiccoughing sobs that did not interfere with her hearing. She nodded quickly as March paused. Then she said, 'And you promise you won't tell them about Teddy? I couldn't bear it if they knew about — about —'

March smiled. 'There's your father now, isn't it? I think I hear the bell. . . . Of course I won't mention the business of the —' she hesitated deliberately, looking down at Bridget with her transparent eyes. 'Of course I won't even breathe the word thermometer!' She opened the heavy front door and walked to the car. 'Ah Mr. Williams. Will you come in for a few minutes?' She knew he would not. The car throbbed obediently but was difficult to start and Mr. Williams did not have a flair with the handle like Fred. They exchanged pleasantries as Bridget climbed in beside her father. Edward Williams had always been glad of his daughter's friendship with the Risings, believing that the large family must be good for his only child. Besides, Miss Midwinter had assured him of their excellent background.

He said, 'Thank your mother once again for her hospitality Miss Rising, won't you?'

Bridget piped up quickly, 'Oh, it was March who got our tea and carried it up on a tray and looked after us Daddy. March is very official.'

Mr. Williams laughed. 'I think you mean efficient my darling. There's a nice compliment for you Miss Rising. And unsolicited too.'

March, pleased with Bridget's quick wit, sighed,

174

'I've just been confiding my ambitions to your daughter Mr. Williams. She has a sympathetic ear.'

Edward Williams suppressed a smile at this fifteen-year-old's quaint phrases. But he also approved them.

'I've never noticed it myself Miss Rising,' he teased.

Bridget protested and, amid the laughter, they drove away.

March bit her lip again and wondered. Still, even if it came to nothing at all, it had probably scared the girl out of her wits and she'd never touch Teddy again. Horrible little madam. And Teddy deserved a jolly good smacking for permitting her to do such a thing.

Dick thrust his way into the kitchen a week later and announced in his gruff mumble that he was 'off'. Will and Florence were clearing up after a picnic tea eaten half in the kitchen, half in the bedroom with the two invalids. Will was looking forward to his evening visit to his mother with her quota of sewing for the next day. Doubtless he would bump into Hettie somewhere along the way.

He said, 'Don't follow you, Dick old man. If you're off to the Lamb and Flag, that's not news. I'll join you myself later.' He guffawed, but Florence frowned, looking at Dick as he stood huge and uncomfortable by the gas stove.

'I'm off to London,' Dick said briefly. 'Where I went before. There's a living of sorts to be got there — no-one will 'ave me down 'ere with my record. I'll send money back when I can but I want you to keep an eye on Sylv.'

Will was surprised but not displeased. Florence was aghast.

'Dick — you cannot leave Sylvia now! You are all she's got.'

'She's got Daze. An' 'er ma. I can't give 'er nuthin'. Not now.'

Florence was horrified at the hardness of him and the finality of his decision.

'What does she say?'

'I must do what I please.'

Florence looked at Will in distress and could see she would get no help from him. Her mind was overworked with concern for Teddy and April, but she did her best. For ten abortive minutes she argued with the silent adamant Dick. When she gave up at last, standing before him drooping, he said, 'I dun't want her sent away. She en't daft nor nothin'.'

'Dick of course we won't —'

'An' I don't want 'er ma to keep pesterin' 'er to work. She dun't want to do nuthin' except sit. She'll heal 'erself soon enough.'

'She will. I know she will, Dick. But what if she is ill — how can we get in touch with you?'

He shrugged and said nothing. After a few more moments he held out his hand and Florence perforce took it. She remembered how she had seen him first, chained and in uniform. If she had been a different type of woman she might have wished that Sylvia had hever clapped eyes on him: he had brought very little happiness with him.

Will said, 'I'll walk down the street with you.'

Florence said, 'Oh *Dick* — goodbye.'

He barged awkwardly to the door. 'Look after Sylv,' he said again. And followed Will into the night.

Once in the street, he overtook Will and put his foot on the doorstep at thirty-three as if barring Will's way.

'We'll say goodbye 'ere I reckon Will. Dun't want Sylv upset nor nuthin'.' He did not give his hand to his brother-in-law. Will, hoping to see Hettie, murmured something. Dick said, 'I dun't want you seeing Hettie Luker while I be gone. 'Tisn't safe and will get back to Flo one o'these days.'

Will blustered. 'What the devil are you talking about man?'

'I saw you, dun't you recall? I sawed the two of you last year and I've kep' me eye open since. Without me 'ere, Mam's goin' to twig dam quick, then there'll be trouble. So dun't go seein' 'er no more.' There was no condemnation in the level voice.

Will said angrily, 'I don't know what business it is of yours —'

'Sylv loves your Flo,' Dick explained simply. 'I 'ad to tell 'er about Hettie Luker so she can make sure no word gets out.' He paused while Will continued to splutter his outrage, then said, 'Dun't excite yourself Will. Sylv en't goin' to say nuthin' to no-one in case it gets back to Flo. But 'er'll 'ave a word with you mind, if there's any more of it!'

And with these admonitory words — from Dick Turpin of all people — he opened the door of Will's old home, went in and closed it behind him. Will had a glimpse of splintering boards in the hall and a smell of mice, then Chichester Street was his again.

He stood there and swore quietly into the damp February air. It was bad enough Dick knowing, but Sylv! He wouldn't be able to look at her again, he wouldn't be able to face her. His own sister.

Then a deeper sadness took hold of him. He had lost Hettie. He'd have to lose her, he couldn't risk keeping her. And part of him loved Hettie.

Sibbie said, 'I couldn't come round last night. Our mam was that upset! I don't know what's got into her. She sits and cries and rocks herself all the time . . . it's awful May.'

'Perhaps you should have the doctor,' May suggested. 'He's coming round to see Teddy again today. Should I run back and ask Mother to send him to you afterwards?'

'Better not. She'd skin me for running up a bill. Fred says he'll put a drop of brandy in her stout tonight and see if that'll buck her up.' She tucked her hand in her friend's arm. 'Tell me what David said last night. Did he get down on his knees again?'

May giggled. It was a typical February morning and Florence had lent the girls her grey umbrella. May lowered it over their heads, giving them a spurious privacy, and felt with her free hand in her pocket. 'He went down on his knees the moment Mamma took April up to bed,' she said. 'And the next minute, he gave me . . . this!' She opened her gloved hand and there, gleaming, was a ring with a single garnet in a claw setting.

Sibbie stopped in her tracks and drew in a hissing breath. 'May! Is it real? Is it an engagement ring?'

'He didn't say — mind the brolly spoke in your eye Sib — he just asked me to keep it. Then he put it on my finger for size and kissed it! He kissed the ring and my finger! He sealed it there — isn't it the most romantic thing you have ever heard in the whole of your life?'

Sibbie was a-twitter, jumping up and down and jogging the umbrella so that the rain poured down her neck. 'You're engaged May! You're engaged, and you're only thirteen! Oh May!' She threw her arms around her friend's neck and hugged her ecstatically.

At last they reached the school playground, late as usual. Miss Pettinger was counting the heads in each line and they joined their class just in time.

Sibbie hissed, 'Oh May . . . I do love you. We still share everything, don't we?'

'Of course,' hissed back May, one eye on Miss Pettinger. 'I've got blackcurrant jam — from our own bushes. What have you got?'

'Dripping. As usual. But we share everything, don't we May?'

'Of course,' May said again and remembered David and his complete devotion. It was quite worrying in a way. A responsibility. She was glad she had Sibbie to confide in.

It was Doctor Green's fourth visit in four days. He used a

tablespoon to look down Teddy's throat, then he felt all around his neck and took his temperature and pulse. On the landing he frowned and sucked in his lips consideringly.

Florence gripped her hands. 'Is it diphtheria Doctor?' she asked.

'I don't think so Mrs. Rising. If it was diphtheria there would be signs in April. I've also visited Kitty Hall and her little Bartholomew is very healthy. He's been here frequently I understand.'

'Yes.' Florence tried to smile. 'If only it's not diphtheria —'

'It's a very severe infection, Mrs. Rising. He has a nasty throat and a high temperature. I am wondering whether the fever hospital —'

'Oh no! Please Doctor! Surely we can look after him at home?'

'It is not easy. You will need a sheet at the door, soaked in disinfectant. Separate dishes and cutlery — everything sterilised.'

'We can manage Doctor. Teddy must not go away.'

'Very well. Yes. If you're sure. I'll be back this afternoon with some medicine. Meanwhile, if you can get him to drink some milk it will help to sustain him.'

'Yes. Yes of course.' Florence left March to see the doctor out and went back to Teddy. She was anxious, but not frantic by any means. Teddy had survived so much and he had recovered from his operation better than April had done. Now he grinned at her in quite his old way and whispered, 'Has the scooter come Mamma?'

'Yes my darling boy. We've put it in the stables, but you may try it up and down the passage as soon as you get well.'

He murmured, 'Let April have it.'

Florence smiled as she began to sponge his forehead. 'It's for both of you dearest. But April won't want to try it until you are well.'

He frowned and said quite fiercely, 'That's silly. Make

179

her have a go now. Right now.'

He became so fretful about it that Florence went downstairs and asked Albert to fetch her a cabbage, and while he was at it to bring back the new scooter from the stables. Only when Teddy could hear April dabbing her foot frantically up and down the hall, did he smile and close his eyes. Then the sheet was hung at his door and he and Florence were together until his death a week later.

On the day of his funeral it rained unceasingly for twenty-four hours and that evening's *Citizen* was full of news of the floods, not only at the Causeway and Sandhurst, but girdling the city itself as the many streams entering the Severn rose and burst their banks. The black umbrellas clustered around Teddy's grave like an outcrop of mushrooms and the handful of earth thrown on the tiny white coffin was a mud-pat in three seconds flat. Will and Albert supported Florence somehow and her two eldest girls stood close to her, while her sister-in-law was behind her.

Somehow a message had been got to the Rising uncles, and they clustered around their mother. Other members of the family from cottages and in service around Newent who had never seen Teddy, lurked unsheltered by the grim avenue of poplars and bared their heads to the cruel rain as the vicar's voice intoned dust to dust and ashes to ashes.

April, at home with Gran, let out a high wail just at this moment and held out her arms as if she could keep Teddy back from wherever he was going. But no-one had been able to hold Teddy in life, let alone in death. His motivation had always been curiosity unbridled by fear or apprehension. His last words had been 'Don't cry Mamma. I'm not going to cry.' And Florence, true to her character as well as her promise, had not wept again. They all wished she would. Her dark, blank eyes reminded them horribly of Aunty Sylv; her helpless idle hands more so. Three times since his death she had fainted without warning, and Doctor Green asked March to be sure to give her a slice of raw chopped liver every day with her other food. She refused it steadfastly. She had eaten it before to stay alive for Teddy.

The floods receded slowly. In Barnwood the Williams were cut off from their work and school, but their newly-acquired telephone brought them the news of the Risings' loss. They told Bridget as gently as possible and she took it without blinking or speaking. That night, as soon as it was dark, she left the house and walked as far as the Pitch where the water lay dark and deep, guarding Northgate Street like a moat. Carefully she waded into it until she was up to her neck, shivering, weeping and hysterical. Then shrieking, 'Teddy! Teddy!' she threw herself forward and for five terrible minutes of chaos was borne up by her clothes, during which time the boat which ferried people across the floods heard her screams and rescued her unharmed.

Two weeks later when she was taken to school again, she threw herself in front of a tram and would have been killed if her father had not scooped her frantically to him and hurled them both to the ground.

Again she was hysterical and her father took her to his office in King's Lane and held her to him while she sobbed herself quiet. 'My darling girl . . .' his worry and grief made him sob too. 'I know you are terribly sad at losing your little friend, but you must learn to bear these griefs. Teddy is safe in heaven.' They had already told her this a dozen times, but it seemed not to help her at all. He changed his tactics. 'Listen Bridget. Is there anything — anything at all — your mother and I can do to make it better? Would you like April to come and stay with you when you are well enough? Would you like to go away somewhere — with her of course . . . anything, darling.'

Bridget held onto him tightly and her weeping gradually abated.

She whispered frantically, 'I want March to be . . . I want to help March somehow. She wants to be a secretary — I told you Daddy —'

'My dearest girl —'

'I know you laughed, but listen — please listen Daddy. If March could be your secretary I should feel I'd done something to help them all. It's the only thing — the only thing — oh Daddy, Daddy —'

He kissed the top of her head and rocked her until the next paroxysm of grief abated.

Then he said, 'I'll see what I can do. Yes, yes. I promise you, Bridie. All right dearest, don't cry, all right. . . .'

They clustered round Florence protectively, making sure she saw none of the many callers. But Harry Hughes was different. Harry brought the careless happiness of schooldays with him. February had given way to March and the wind howled around the house and bent the trees double.

He paid his respects and presented Florence with a tiny nosegay of snowdrops picked around the railway line at Longhope. They seemed to give her some pleasure.

'And I've got a new job. In the signal box at Churchdown.' He grinned at Albert. 'Still menial, but I can take signalling exams and try for a box of my own one day.'

Albert hit him between the shoulder blades, more animated than he'd been for months. 'That's splendid old man. D'you want lodgings? We can offer you any of the attic rooms I reckon. Can't we Mother?'

Florence smiled blindly and Harry said, 'I'm fixed up at Churchdown thanks old chap. But when my turns work out right, I could come in and we could go to old Filbert's choir practices. What d'you say?'

Albert glanced at March, expecting her to share his happiness.

'That will be marvellous. Won't it March? Won't it just?'

182

March found an excuse to leave the parlour and discovered the afternoon post lying on the hall floor. There was one for her. Typewritten.

She opened it without much interest. It was a letter requesting her to attend for an interview at Charles Williams and Son, Auctioneers of King's Street, on the third of the month. Tomorrow. Her birthday.

She looked at the window where the coloured glass glowed in spite of the windy sunless day. Harry was back. And she was going to be a secretary. She felt sick and cold.

She moved slowly to the stairs and sat on the polished wood, moving her sightless gaze to the row of felt slippers.

Then she lowered her head and wept.

9

The war came slowly to Gloucester. April thought it would entail hiding in the apple trees and shooting at Germans over the wall as they charged down Chichester Street in their funny policemen's hats. But as the months dragged by and not even one Zeppelin hove in sight over the cathedral spires, she felt let down. The seven years without Teddy had been the Slough of Despond, and like the Pilgrim, she thought anything, even disaster, would be a better state.

The Citizen printed Mr. Asquith's speech in full, and Will read it aloud to the whole family, sending over to thirty-three for the other Risings and assembling them solemnly in the kitchen as if they were already besieged.

' "If I am asked what we are fighting for . . ." ' Will had had to resort to glasses the previous year and he paused and looked over them at the gathering of women and children; Albert stood behind him reading silently over his shoulder. ' "... vindicate the principle that small nationalities —" '

'What does vindicate mean Daddy?' April interrupted.

Daisy corrected her scornfully, 'Vinegar silly. He said vinegar.'

Florence corrected in her quiet voice, 'No, it is vindicate dear. It means . . . er . . . what does it mean Will?'

Will hesitated and March said, 'It means justify. Make good. Let's listen, please!'

' ".... that small nationalities are not to be crushed in defiance of international good faith by the arbitrary will of a strong and overmastering great Power." '
Will breathed deeply and removed his glasses. Albert took the paper and continued to read silently. Will said, 'In other words, we're not going to let little Belgium be ground underfoot by those Germans and their Kaiser.'

Gran looked bewildered. 'Belgium? What's they to us? That's what I wanna know. Never 'ardly 'eard of Belgium.'

'It explains it here Gran.' Albert went to her chair and squatted by her while he told her about the Treaty of London signed right back in 1839. She tutted exasperation at the foolishness of it all and rested her liver-marked hand on her favourite grandchild's shoulder. March and May exchanged glances. May had completed her apprenticeship at Helen's Hair Salon in Saint Aldate Street, and March had been at Williams' for six years. Both wondered what difference the war would make to their lives.

Florence voiced all their questions. 'What will it mean? To us, Will? What will it mean to us?'

Will took her hand and rubbed it comfortingly, but it was Gran who answered the question.

'Nuthin' at all,' she said scornfully. 'Not nuthin' at all. The wars out in Africa didn't alter nuthin' for us, and neither will this one.'

And it seemed she was right. Germany walked over Belgium and trenches were dug on the Western Front and it seemed like stalemate. Nobody was terribly interested in the Russian advance on the Eastern front, so nobody was very surprised when, on April's thirteenth birthday, news came through that they had been driven far back into their own country again. The horrors of Gallipoli and Mesopotamia were all so far away. A hospital was opened in Great Western Road: a series of wooden huts in which were practised the first

185

ghastly attempts at skin grafting and piecing together broken faces. Food was short, but then it had never been plentiful. A munitions factory was opened in Brockworth which was a few miles past Bridget's house in Barnwood. A light railway ran to it from the station for transporting shells; Bridget told the Risings that the noise reminded her of California subway which she enjoyed. Mr. Edward arrived at the office in King's Street groaning because he had not been able to sleep.

Social life was more exciting: when a dance was in aid of Army welfare, Florence could hardly insist on a chaperone for her girls. It would be impugning the characters of those poor soldiers and they had surely suffered enough. So March, May and Sibbie soon were used to going out alone and being asked to dance by young men who had not been introduced. Albert refused to accompany them.

Otherwise Gloucester became a little more shabby and definitely less genteel. People with money were apt to take it to Cheltenham when it came to spending. The Promenade there was full of expensive, good quality shops, and customers were still treated with deference and not mere civility.

Ready-made clothes were Will's anathema. Denton's on the Cross supplied ready-made shirt-blouses and gym-slips for the girls at the high school. The Co-op could sell half a dozen navy-blue melton cloth winter coats in less time than it took him to measure one up. He undertook alterations for both shops, but alterations were well known to be slave labour. He paid Albert a wage; Florence, Sylv and his mother worked for their board and keep, he had no money to pay them. Of course once the war was over all the young men who had lived in uniform for so long would want suits. Meanwhile the Risings kept their head above water; March paid half the rent and May gave her mother five shillings a week towards the food. They were certainly not 'rising' any more.

Things were no better in the Barton and early in 1915 David surprised everyone by joining up. Mrs. Daker sold haberdashery, eked a precarious living, and blamed May for it.

Will had time on his hands and he was bored. He accepted that nothing would ever be the same without Teddy, but his spirit still craved the simple happiness which was its birthright. He rented some shooting on Robinswood Hill and he and Albert tried for a rabbit occasionally. He insisted on Florence taking a walk with him Sunday evenings after church, and he still loved the way she clung to his arm as they strolled through the park. It made him feel strong and protective. But then, when they got home, there was supper and May chattering about the wounded soldiers who had gathered at the back of the church behind the pillars where their poor faces could not be seen; and Florence would go to her room. And he to his.

He could not avoid Hettie Luker. She sat at her door in the summer evenings as she always had, calling across to Lottie or his own mother. When he took off his cap and stopped to speak to her, she had a way of watching his mouth and smiling that almost set him on fire. But though at first she had tried to persuade him to meet her in the stables at the Mews Lane entrance, he had always said 'Better not'. He could feel Sylv watching him and it was as if he had to spend the rest of his life proving to her that Dick had lied and there was nothing at all between himself and Hettie. Hettie appeared to hold no grudge. Her smile was always there for him. He could have gone mad with jealousy when Alf began boasting about his prowess again in the Lamb and Flag.

'Forty-five y'know Will. It's a good age to make a woman pregnant, you gotta admit. B'God, it en't for want of trying, I'll tell you that!'

Will could imagine and wished he could not.

He said, 'Seen the Citizen, Alf? Those poor devils are still on the beaches in Turkey. Thank God they sent the Colonials in there.'

'Ah. No-one in their right minds 'ud want to be out in that lot, eh? Some silly sod sent our Fred a white feather in the post yesty. He din't like it at all. I says to 'im I says, you stop at 'ome and keep the job going m'lad. Else we'll all be in the bloody wuk-'ouse!' Alf laughed and slapped his thigh. 'Our Fred in't too pleased about new babby. Not that much pleases 'im these days. 'E was all right when 'e could dash around in that blasted car of 'is, but since we went back to dray work, 'is face is like a yard o' pump water.'

'Things aren't the same,' Will said. 'Nothing's the same any more.'

Alf laughed again. He had something to laugh at after all. 'Old age, that's what got into you Will. Now drink up and get back to that pretty little woman of yours an' see what you can do!'

'Flo isn't the same either . . .' Will knew he'd drunk too much because tears gathered in his throat. 'She hasn't been the same since Teddy went.'

Alf recognised his mood and slipped easily into it. 'You're right there Will. 'E was a bright little whip-persnapper. Everyone did think the world o' that kid o' yours.' He clapped Will's shoulder. 'Give 'er another one, man! Blimey, if I can do, so can you. Same age as my old Het, in't she?'

Will did not bother to answer him. He walked home unsteadily, thinking of Hettie's infidelity and the loss of Teddy.

'Still got Albert,' he muttered as he bolted the garden door behind him. 'Still got our Albert. And little April.'

In January Mr. Asquith decided that Lord Kitchener's volunteers were not sufficient to continue with the war, and the word conscription was printed in the Citizen. Fred Luker did not wait for his papers to arrive.

When March came out of the office in King's Street at six o'clock one bitterly cold February night, he was waiting for her beneath a gas lamp. She tried to brush past him as she had brushed past him so often before, but he would have none of it.

He fell into step beside her, his rough clothes contrasting oddly with her immaculately tailored suit. She was still thin, and shapeless, but her carriage was like her mother's and she looked a lady.

'I want a word with you March. If you please,' he said curtly, no longer slurring his words, every consonant sharp.

March said, 'I'm tired. I've been at work since half-past eight this morning.'

'I haven't.'

She refused to ask why not. She had not seen Fred Luker alone since that acrimonious meeting when she was fourteen. When they had been in each other's company she had realised he was making a great effort to 'better' himself. The old type of cab driver had disappeared; the new ones were more like chauffeurs in decent uniforms. But when the Lukers had sold off the Austin because of petrol shortage he had seemed to revert to type again.

He said irritably, 'I've signed on. Joined up. I'm going to be a gunner. Artillery.'

She stopped in her tracks. Her feet were so cold she couldn't feel them, and the tip of her nose could be like Lottie's for all she knew, but she forgot all that in sheer surprise.

'Why?'

He shrugged, suddenly embarrassed. 'They'd have taken me soon anyway. Besides ... I can't stick Chichester Street any longer.'

It was galling that so often Fred Luker's feelings mirrored her own.

She said, 'You fool. You've built up that business and now it'll go. Look at Daker's.'

189

He smiled, pleased she was showing interest. 'I thought about that. Pa will keep it going. Somehow. Just enough for me to have something to start on when I get back. And I'll be getting to know a lot more about mechanics.' His eyes gleamed at her in the lamplight. 'Don't you see March? I'll come out with a damned sight more than when I go in.' He took a deep breath. 'I'm going to buy a charrybang when I get out. When this lot's over. You see.'

'If you come out.' The war might not have affected them yet, but the casualty lists in the paper were evidence that they affected others.

'Christamighty March! I'll come out! You know the Lukers — they come out of anything!'

She looked at him for an instant, then turned up her collar and breathed into it to warm her nose. They rounded the cattle market past the Saracen's Head. He cleared his throat.

'It's like this March. I want to know where I stand with you. Before I go.'

She quickened her pace and straightened her back to ramrod stiffness. He hurried to keep up with her.

'Look here March — you might as well talk to me because I'm not going to let you go till you do!' Determination made him breathe heavily. 'I'm going off to the Front dammit all! You could at least give me a civil answer!'

She crossed the road ahead of him, her boots making the wooden blocks of the road squelch slightly. He stamped after her.

'You still think you're the high and mighty Risings, don't you?' A train rattled over the bridge, sending gobs of steam to enshroud them; the stink of sulphur was in their nostrils. March used the concealment to rub her nose frantically on her sleeve. Just like Lottie Jenner, she thought furiously, blaming Fred for that too.

'You're not rising any more!' he yelled as they

190

emerged into Northgate Street and turned by the pillar box. 'More like sinking I'd say! Yes, a damned sight more like sinking!'

'How *dare* you speak to me like that, Fred Luker,' she whirled on him furiously. 'How dare you raise your voice —'

'It was the bloody train making such a rattle,' he said sulkily.

'*And* swear! Who do you think you *are*?'

'Never mind all that, March. You didn't bother about keeping me in my place when you wanted me to teach you to drive, did you?' She drew in a breath and he went on hastily, 'All right, all right. We were kids then. And you wanted a favour of me. And you were right sweet to me. And you knew I loved you. Don't shake your head like that March, you knew it, kid or no kid. And I haven't changed — in that way. I still love you.'

She said quickly but in a low voice, 'Well, I don't love you. I'm sorry Freddy. I've tried to show you these last few years without being . . . hurtful. I can't help my feelings.'

Suddenly he caught her arm and held her back; she tried to shake him off and could not.

He said grimly, 'You'll never love anyone except your Albert — I've known that for a long time March!' He held her harder still as she struggled furiously, her face screwed up against even hearing him. 'But I think, up to a point, you *can* help your feelings, March! Yes, I'd say you can help them very well indeed!'

She kicked at him with her boots, only just holding herself from screaming because there might be people in the darkness. He shoved her roughly against the Goodrichs' wall and pinned her there with the weight of his body. The closeness of him was overwhelming and she knew she was near hysteria.

He said, 'Dammit, you'll listen to me if it's the last thing you do!' He grabbed her arms as her hands went for his face. 'You'd help your feelings all right, my girl,

191

if I had a bit of cash, wouldn't you? That's why you never really broke with me — not proper you didn't. In case I struck it rich with the taxi. Wasn't that it March? Eh? Eh?'

He spoke right into her face whichever way she turned it. She gasped a sob. 'Get away — get away —'

'Why? Is there just a bit of feeling there you can't help, March? Marcie?' He pushed his mouth against hers before she could turn it again. He laughed breathlessly. 'There is — Christamighty, there is! You felt something then, all those years back, when you gave me your little-girl kisses!'

With a gigantic convulsion she pushed him off and began to stumble up the road. He ran with her, holding her arm to support her but not attempting to stop her again. They came to a gas lamp and she turned her face away in case he should see the tears and the running nose.

He said, 'March, just listen. I want you to marry me. One day I'll be rich, I promise you that. Then . . . when I'm rich . . . will you marry me?'

She tried to go faster but she had a stitch and her breath was like a dog's. She slowed enough to pant, 'I hate you! You shouldn't have said . . . what you did. It's only natural for a sister to love her brother! I hate you —'

He interrupted impatiently, 'I don't care about Albert. What goes on with you two — that's up to you. You can't marry him, that's for sure. And I'm the only person in the world who will understand about him. Christ, by the time I come home on leave he'll be gone too —'

He stopped as she halted and leaned over with a groan. She had spent sleepless nights already, praying fervently that Albert would never be called on to fight. She closed her eyes.

Fred released her arm at last and drew away. After a while she began to walk up the street and then he followed at a distance. She held her side, telling herself she had a stitch. She still hated him because just when she needed his support most he let her go on alone. Somehow she got indoors and left her coat and beret on the newel post, desperate to join Albert in the kitchen. And when she opened the door from the dark passage on to light and warmth, there he was laughing with Father over an awkward customer.

She looked at them all, seeing them anew. Mother was pouring tea for April and May, Aunt Sylv, still Mother's shadow, was buttering toast and cutting it into triangles, Daze was chasing a tea-leaf floating in her cup. March found her eyes were burning from the sudden change of temperature.

They often made her feel isolated and different, but tonight they made her feel lonely. If only it weren't so long until her week's summer holiday with Aunt Lizzie. If only Mr. Williams would give her two weeks' annual holiday instead of just one. If only Fred Luker hadn't said that about Albert. If only she had been content to stay in the workroom with Father so that it did not seem as though she had actually profited by Teddy's death. If only . . . if only. . . .

Florence said, 'Come by the fire March dear, you look perished. How good it is to have you home. Now we are all together.' Her look warmed March's very soul, and her words included Teddy; even Aunt Sylv's husband and dead baby. As March sipped the tea which Florence handed to her, she knew that in one way Fred had been wrong: the Risings would never sink. Florence would hold them up.

News of the surrender at Kut arrived two weeks before Albert left for France. 'It's up to you now son!' Will said heartily, clapping him on the shoulder. 'Can't get anywhere against the Turks, so you'll have to see what you can do with the Huns!'

Albert grinned dutifully. Florence said, 'At least

you're fighting Christians. Those barbarians out there make me shudder!'

Albert did not have much opinion of Christians after the King's School, but he hugged his mother reassuringly and said over her head, 'We might get in another shot at the rabbits before I go, eh Dad?'

'Good practice!'

They all combined to make Albert's departure seem no more than a holiday venture. Florence had the look of a frightened horse at times and was refusing food again. March also picked hopelessly at her meals.

Gloucester boasted two hills besides the Pitch: Robinswood on the south-west edge of the city, Churchdown on the north-east. Compared with the surrounding Cotswolds and the far Malverns, they were mere tumps, but they were full of coppices and dells, and after five minutes' clambering, Will and Albert felt themselves as deep in the country as they had felt on their Kempley trips. The weather had been wet since April's fourteenth birthday, but now a watery sun lit up every drop of water and made it a pearl. The rabbits would soon come out and begin to feed. The two men, both wearing breeches with stout socks pulled over them, squatted comfortably among some bushes, guns over their knees. The silence was companionable, broken at last by Will with a deep sigh of regret.

'You're the best tailor in the city Albert,' he said suddenly. 'You've got a knack for cutting. Dammit, that costume you made March eight years ago still looks as good now as new.'

Albert shrugged, too apprehensive at the immediate future to share his father's feelings of frustration. 'I was fairly good at arithmetic. It's just arithmetic.'

'And something more. Don't know what. Flair they call it.' He sighed again. 'Damned waste. That's all I can say.'

'Not just the war, Dad. Business wasn't too good anyway.'

'And that's the fault of the war too, son. Don't you forget it!' A third sigh elicited no response from Albert. Will said, 'I'm getting stiff. Where are the little blighters?'

Albert grinned, relieved. 'Let's move up. That dell's a bit shady, maybe they'll be out further up. In the sun.'

They stood up and began climbing. Will panted. 'One thing. You're going at the best time of year. Summer ahead. They say the mud and cold are worse than the German bullets.'

Albert laughed. 'Hope so Dad. We've had plenty of mud and cold in our lives and they haven't done us much harm, have they?'

They both laughed. Anyone could put up with mud and cold after all. Then Will said, 'Mind you. I don't blame Harry for keeping out of it. Wish tailors came under the reserved occupation thing, same as railway signalmen.'

'Same here,' Albert agreed, but without passion. He was going and that was that.

'Don't blame anyone for keeping out of it,' Will gasped, stumbling over a molehill. 'It's not our war. Damned French . . . all their doing. And the Russians of course. Nothing but trouble where the Russians are. Look at the Crimea.'

'What about Belgium though Dad?' Albert paused, seeing a movement ahead. He brought his rifle slowly up.

'Fat lot of good we've done the Belgians,' said Will, halting too and following the direction of Albert's barrel with his eyes. 'They're done for. Good and proper. Been better for them if we'd let the Kaiser take 'em over in the first place.'

Albert's gun fired and threw him back a pace. They both stared. Will said, 'You've got him son! You got him! There's some meat for the pot!' He lifted his head

195

and pointed his beard to the sky as he laughed triumphantly. 'My God. The Germans had better watch out when you get over there, hadn't they? Eh? E Albert?'

Albert shouldered his gun and put an arm on his father's arm as they trudged up to collect their kill. It couldn't be too bad out there after all. He could shoot a gun and he could put up with mud and cold. It wouldn't be too bad.

March suffered badly after Albert's departure, but still she suffered silently. She was too grieved for an outburst of temper, though this was what her reined spirit required. Her small spites towards Rags, Daze, Gladys Luker were not enough to give catharsis. She knew she was on the way to becoming an embittered old maid.

Two days after Albert had gone, Harry called, obviously at his behest. They made much of him, April spearing bread on the toasting fork and almost burning herself at the range in her eagerness to make his tea, Will coming in from the workroom to discuss the contents of the *Citizen* with him. March watched it cynically. She had had yet one more day of dull boredom at the office. Miss Pym had no intention of permitting her to become more than a dogsbody, and with Bridget's father awaiting his commission there was hardly any work for March to do.

Harry ate his toast and told them they mustn't worry about Albert because he could look after himself better than most. Then he pulled out his fat turnip watch and declared he'd have to run for the train.

'Would you walk round to the station with me, March?' he asked. 'It's a pleasant evening and I'd be glad of your company.'

March had no wish to accompany Harry Hughes anywhere, but Will, doubtless primed by Albert, joined his encouragement to Harry's. Sulkily she fetched her short coat from the hall and they went down the path in single file. It was bad enough with Harry fidgeting about

196

behind her between the laurels, but much worse when he skipped to the outside once on the pavement. March almost longed for Fred Luker's unthinking ill manners; in an odd way they bred ease between them.

She said crossly, 'I thought you were in a hurry. We'd better step it out hadn't we?'

'Train isn't until seven-twenty,' he replied, insisting on taking her unwilling arm.

'I thought you said you'd have to run for it,' she reminded him ungraciously. 'If I'd realised we had plenty of time I'd have waited for April. The walk would have done her good.'

'Actually, I thought it would be a good thing if we were on our own, March.' He snuggled her elbow into his jacket with horrible intimacy. 'We can talk about Albert and —'

'I don't wish to talk about Albert, thank you Harry!' March jerked herself free. 'And if you wouldn't mind I would prefer to walk separately. I am afraid I am not used to the smell of the grease you use on the signal levers.'

Harry flushed at the intentional insult. 'I — I washed and changed before I came, March. I apologise if —'

'It's not your fault of course.' She considered making a joke about Albert's army uniform and its particular smell, but Harry was not thick-skinned and would realise she was furious that he was here and Albert was not.

He stumbled, half in the gutter and half out, in an effort to preserve a little space between them. 'It — it's just that — I thought with Albert away, we might do something together, March. Summer's coming and there are some pretty walks around Churchdown. You could come out on the train and —'

'We try to spend as much time as possible with Mother. I'm sorry Harry.'

He said quickly, almost jealously, 'You find time to go to the hospital dances.'

It was too much for her and she replied coolly, 'Yes. Of

course you could come too. Only it's for men in uniform.'

He flushed darkly and was silent as they took the high pavement beneath the railway bridge; then as they turned into George Street, he mumbled, 'Albert would like to think we still see something of each other. That's all.'

She thought of Albert in his rough, ill-cut khaki with the flat cap making a triangle of his pale, ascetic face. He was taller than any of them now, with May's slenderness and April's curly red-gold hair. He had kissed her cheek before he left and told her that she was not only his cleverest sister — he was proud of her position as secretary to Bridget's father and she had never told him how menial it was in reality — but the most elegant too.

She said quietly, 'You know you are always welcome at home, Harry. Surely you saw that this afternoon.'

Mollified, he nodded vigorously. 'I feel as much at ease with your family as my own, March. More so.' He stared at the outline of the station buildings against the cold April sky, needing an excuse for his damp eyes. 'He said. . .Albert said. . . he would miss me most of all,' he told her gruffly.

March felt pain like a physical wound in her chest and bile rose in her throat. She mustn't lose her temper. Not here in the street with people passing and that man in the bathchair. . . .

She said tightly, 'I must go. Goodbye.'

She waited for no answer and almost ran back to Northgate Street. Harry stood and watched her with his jaw hanging, she saw him as she turned the corner. She did not wave. How she hated him; how she hated Albert. Everyone. The war was not just in France, it was here in her very soul. In her work which she had schemed for and wanted above everything . . . except the price she paid for it. And in her feeling for Harry, who had recovered after the disgrace of his expulsion and was consequently in a job that kept him out of the army.

A voice spoke behind her, making her jump. 'Penny for 'em March Rising! Or are they worth more than that?'

It was Sibbie Luker, still May's best friend and therefore over-familiar with all the family. She had come straight from the pickle factory in Worcester Street where she worked from seven in the morning until seven at night. The handkerchief which bound her hair away from the dangers of the machinery was in her hand and her abundant mouse-brown tresses were loose. She looked what she was — common.

March said shortly, 'I've been to see Harry Hughes on to the train.'

Sibbie darted speculative sideways glances at her, then suddenly said, 'Poor old Harry. I'll go and have a word with him too.' She suddenly changed her voice and mimicked the captain who drilled the young recruits in the barrack square at Bearland. 'Carry on March!' She giggled. 'Not that you'd know how I reckon!' Then she turned and ran back, calling Harry's name loudly. March hurried on, determined not to walk home with Sibbie Luker. Yes, they were the people she hated most. The Lukers.

Harry stopped as he heard his name shrieked down the length of George Street. Other people halted too but Sibbie Luker didn't care about that. He waited for her to come up, her brown hair — almost March's colour — flying about her face, and the smell of vinegar about her surely drowning any trace of signal grease that might still hang about him.

He said, 'What's up? Something wrong with March?'

She shook her head and hung on to his arm while she panted her breath back.

'Shan't see much of you now, shall I?' she gasped. 'Thought I'd say — good luck!'

He had to smile. After all she was half Rising, practically living there with May. And she was pretty and lively and warm.

He said, 'You're the only one to say that. Everyone gave Albert all their luck.'

'As bad for you as for him, I reckon.' She sucked in a huge breath and relaxed, smiling back at him. Her lips were bright red from the continual nibbling she always gave them. She jerked her head sideways. 'Come on, else you'll miss your train. I'll come on to the platform and give you a wave.'

'That'd be nice.'

He offered her his arm and she dimpled at him as she took it.

'Don't mind the smell then?' she asked with charming frankness.

He sniffed, closing his eyes in simulated delight. 'Heavenly,' he murmured. They both laughed.

He hung through the window of the train and admired the swell of her breasts and the blue of her eyes. She kept smiling and showing her teeth, then, as the guard blew his whistle and waved his green flag, she grabbed the door handle, pulled it open and jumped into the carriage.

'What are you doing?' he said, startled.

'Coming with you!' A porter chased the train and slammed the door disapprovingly. She bit on her lip, grinning like a mischievous child. 'Never bin on a train, and it's a nice evening and —'

He was appalled; still the conventional law-abiding Harry. 'You haven't got a ticket! And what about your people — they'll be expecting you home!'

She gave him a shove and he sat down hard. 'Don't be a kill-joy Harry Hughes! My folks expect me when they see me! And surely you can buy me a ticket the other end?' She sat by him and hugged his arm. 'I couldn't bear to let you go alone Harry. You looked so . . . alone!' She laughed at this. 'Enjoy things when you can Harry. Christamighty, we might be dead tomorrow!'

And with another impulsive move she reached up, dragged down his head and put her open mouth to his.

Shocked, he pulled back, but then, staring mesmerised at her open face — not so much frank now as downright brazen — he was caught by her mood. Albert was gone and March made any future calls to Chichester House an uncomfortable prospect. And Sibbie was here. He put his arm around her waist and squeezed until she shrieked for mercy. After that it was easy.

David was wounded.

Mrs. Daker had the news from the War Office and closed the shop immediately so that she could rock and keen in the back parlour while interested neighbours took it in turns to offer consolation. Tolly Hall, calling for thread for his mother who now took in sewing, brought the news to Chichester House, and an unwilling May went down that same evening to pat Mrs. Daker's shoulder and assure her it might very easily be worse.

She had a letter from David a week later and read extracts to the family as soon as she got home from work. With her golden curls tipped well over her forehead she was a walking advertisement for Helen's Hair Fashions, and her beautiful skin was strangely unlined by the expression of deep sympathy she so often wore. At least ten of the disfigured soldiers at the Great Western Hospital were madly in love with her and she was something of an expert in dealing with them.

'It's shrapnel. In the right thigh it seems. He's a little vague. . . .'

Florence said, 'He does not wish to pain you, dearest.'

April, never one for the proprieties, said in agony, 'It must hurt there.' She touched her own groin through the thick folds of her petticoats. 'Poor David. Will he be able to walk?'

'He's using crutches at the moment darling.' May smiled bracingly at April. 'It's good news really. He'll be invalided out of the army now.'

April's face changed expression. 'I hadn't thought of that. Oh May, you'll be able to get married now.'

For an instant May looked startled, then she said comfortably, 'He'll need time to recuperate, April dear. We'll have to see.'

Will lifted Rags off the chair by the empty range and put him gently on to the floor; Rags was an old man now. 'I'll be glad to see David Daker back. We helped each other out before, perhaps we can do it again. Business couldn't be much worse. Still, David can do most of his work sitting down. If necessary.' Will himself sat down and put his feet in the fender, although the June sunshine shone through the open kitchen door, bringing with it all the scents of the garden which Albert would have loved so much.

March said with suppressed violence, 'Trust David Daker to fall on his feet. Just a year out there and now he'll be safe home, probably with a pension, and everyone telling him how marvellous he is!'

Florence said reprovingly, 'March dear. Poor David is wounded.'

March replied inconsequentially, 'Yes. But Harry Hughes isn't!'

April's face was still radiant. She asked, 'How soon will he be home, May? We could have him here and nurse him, couldn't we Mother?'

Florence gave her gentle, sad smile but it was May who said quickly, 'Of course we couldn't April. Whatever would Mrs. Daker say? Anyway, he says here it will be two or three months before he's allowed out of hospital.'

Sibbie arrived then, hatless as usual, smiling even as she chewed her underlip.

'Good evening Mrs. Rising . . . and Mr. Rising.' Her smile widened as she looked at Will. It always did. It worried him no longer, but it seemed to imply a special intimacy between them. She stayed by the door, looking towards May and March now. 'I called to say I won't be able to manage the Saturday hospital dance.'

May's reaction was immediate. 'Oh, Sib. It won't be

so much fun without you. Why can't you come?'

'Some people — friends of the family — have invited me out to tea. At Churchdown.' Sibbie looked around, but the Risings were basically incurious and accepted this unlikely statement.

March said crossly, 'I would hardly call the hospital dances fun, May.' And April said, 'David can go to them when he gets back, can't he May? Will I be able to come too?'

Sibbie was staring at May. 'You've heard from David? Oh — oh May. Is he coming home?'

May stood up and handed the letter to Sibbie. 'I'll walk down the garden with you while you read it.' The two girls drifted out, Sibbie opening the stiff paper avidly.

March said, 'Strange, isn't it, how May is always otherwise engaged when it's time to wash up.'

April smiled beatifically. 'I'll do it by myself tonight March. I'm making up a new poem and I can say it out loud.' Will laughed fondly and April's smile turned fully on him. 'Well, I'll say it to Rags then Daddy!'

He looked over his spectacles. 'I love you, little April,' he said out of the blue.

April was now the tallest girl in Chichester Street and nobody there allowed her to forget it. She dimpled, thoroughly pleased. 'I'm nearly as tall as you,' she reminded him.

He shook his head. 'You'll always be little April to me.'

Albert's letters were peculiarly unsatisfying. He wasn't allowed to say much. When news came through of the attacks along the Somme, the family could make more sense of the letters they had received earlier. But the details Florence wanted to hear — what kind of food he had and how he slept — were missing. He commented on the lack of trees, flowers, birds. 'The shelling makes everything a desert,' he wrote. They simply could not imagine that. The *Citizen* quoted Ludendorff as saying the German troops were absolutely exhausted. Mr. Lloyd George took over from Mr. Asquith and there was a wave of optimism. The boys playing in the gutters of the Barton sang, 'Bugger orf Ludendorff'. But then little Rumania was defeated and nothing seemed changed.

A week before March's annual holiday in Bath, a telegram arrived from Uncle Edwin to say that Aunt Lizzie had collapsed and had been admitted to a sanatorium near Chippenham. Mr. Edward Williams — Bridget's father — had by this time obtained his commission and March asked old Mr. Williams if she could leave immediately to be with her aunt.

'If my son were not away, I have no doubt you would persuade him to grant you compassionate leave, Miss Rising.' The alderman had never entirely believed Edward's flimsy reasons for employing this young girl. 'I am a harder nut to crack.'

March swallowed and went back to her cast-iron three-bank typewriter, determined not to beg. She had never really cared for the way Bridget's father obviously indulged her either; it was a constant reminder that her position as his secretary had not been gained on merit alone. But now she wished with all her heart he was here. The alderman was right, he would have let her go.

They had news of Aunt Lizzie's death on the Friday evening before March was to travel to Bath. She would not believe it, even when Florence looked out the clothes they had worn to Teddy's funeral. Aunt Lizzie could not have left this life without a last intimate chat, a last smile, a last promise that next year she would be fit enough to ride in a motor car and that March should drive it.

The beauty of Bath, displayed as it had been that first time from the railway station, tore at her heart. Summer was heavy in the old Roman town; the tiny cafés had put tables out on the pavements in a continental way; punts were on the river. There was a terrible poignancy to such gaiety.

Uncle Edwin met them, looking old and frail in his black. He was bent as if literally a broken man. He escorted them into the sitting-room and stood watching them while Rose brought in tea.

'It seems only yesterday . . .' he gazed at April standing erect by her mother's chair. 'Yet you were in a cradle and your sisters just little girls.'

May took his arm and led him to his old chair by the window.

'We sat here, d'you remember Uncle Edwin? You and Albert played dominoes and I fell asleep.'

And March remembered how she had sat with Aunt Lizzie and been the special pampered child for the first time. And how jealous Albert had been. It was over. Over for always.

The coffin was open on the table in the dining-room, and after tea they all filed respectfully past it. It was yet another blow to March. She had expected a welling grief that in itself would be an assuagement. She imagined being escorted to her room prostrate, weeping; May staying with her and April being sent up with a light supper. But it did not happen. The waxen figure among the satin ruffles was a shell, just as Mother had always said. The life had gone — the soul — the person: Aunt Lizzie.

Tense to the point of shaking, she lay in bed that night deliberately remembering, in an effort to find the release of tears. A few sentimental drops coursed down her cheeks but that was all. Next door she could hear April weeping and being comforted by May. April, who had hardly known Aunt Lizzie! Angrily she turned in bed, then much later heard her mother talking quietly to May. They were sharing a room and her father was in the bed she herself had had when she had been ill all those years ago.

When at last the house creaked confidentially to itself, she got up and wrapped herself in a shawl and went downstairs as quietly as she could. She had no idea what she wanted to do, but her steps took her into the dining-room again. She felt no fear, not even awe as she stood just inside the door, looking at the outline of the coffin in the dim light of a bead of gas above the mantelpiece. If anything, her mood was one of reproach. She wanted Aunt Lizzie to be there so that she could say to her 'You promised so much, and now you've gone without fulfilling anything —' but before she could approach the table and look again, Uncle Edwin's voice spoke from a chair in the corner.

'I knew you'd come,' he said. 'I've been waiting.'

He stood up slowly and painfully and walked into the aura of light. He was still dressed and March guessed he would not change now until after the funeral tomorrow. His prominent eyes looked blank and staring.

'You're Lizzie. You're Lizzie all over again, my dear. I always said that, didn't I? I told you that when you were a little girl.'

She nodded but could find no words to reply.

He looked into the coffin. 'She couldn't have any more children. She lost them — every one, you know, my child. Every one. When you came that winter of 1902 it was as if you were her child. She saw it and so did I.' He held out an arm and March came slowly towards him and looked down at the mask of his wife. Nothing stirred inside her.

He whispered, 'While you are alive March, she cannot be dead. Remember that. Do not grieve. It is my comfort and it must be yours too.'

He put his flaccid arm on her shoulder. It was heavy.

'You can have anything that was hers, my dear. Anything. You know that, do you not?'

She took her eyes from the figure in the coffin and made herself look at him. His stare was still blank yet he seemed to be waiting for her comprehension, so she nodded again.

He went on in the same sibilant hoarse voice. 'I told you once you can turn to me at any time. For anything. I want you to turn to me, March. Do you understand?'

Again she nodded. He seemed to be giving the words a significance they did not have. She wondered whether she ought to ask for something special. Was there a brooch or necklace that had been a favourite of Aunt Lizzie's?

He repeated insistently, 'Will you? Will you promise to turn to me? Will you?'

She forced a voice from her throat. 'Of course Uncle. Of course.'

'On her soul, March. On my Lizzie's soul.'

He slid the heavy arm from her shoulder and found her hand and drew it over the coffin. She was frightened at last. But then quite suddenly, he placed her hand on the edge of the oak, went to the gas jet and turned it higher. He smiled almost normally.

'Thank you March. Tomorrow, we shall sustain each other. And when the time is right you will come to me. Won't you?'

She removed her hand and clutched her shawl tightly around her shoulders.

'I will Uncle. Of course.'

'I knew you would. I knew you'd come tonight. God bless you March.' He straightened his bent back with an effort. 'Now, off to bed with you. We don't want you catching another cold.'

He followed her into the hall and closed the dining-room door with a click. When she was halfway up the stairs, he said quietly into the darkness, 'Remember, everything that was hers will be yours one day, my dear. Everything.'

She did not wonder what he meant. Obviously Aunt Lizzie had spoken to him on the subject and he had written his will accordingly. She dropped the shawl on to the floor and got into bed, drawing the clothes tightly around her. He was an old man and did not look strong. Would the house and everything belong to her eventually? They could all live in Bath then. And Albert would be with them again.

She fell asleep quickly and with a smile on her face.

10

After the formality of receiving their Bibles from Miss
Pettinger, the leavers that year congregated as usual
behind the coke heap. Gladys was sure of a job with
Sibbie in the pickle factory, but many local girls were
now employed in a munitions factory at Brockworth
and Gladys yearned to join them.

'Go on April, let's 'ave a go,' she urged, pushing the
ubiquitous Daisy back to her own side of the playground. 'They picks you up in a lorry every morning
and brings you back at night. What d'you think?'

'I think my dad won't let me,' April said gloomily. She
knew Will was planning to apprentice her as a dress-
maker and the prospect did not attract her very much;
on the other hand it certainly did not repel her like the
idea of the munitions factory. Gunpowder choking your
lungs and your skin turning yellow. . . . But officially
she had to seem eager to make shells.

' 'E will if you goes on at 'im long enough,' Gladys
said with truth. April could usually get her own way
with her father.

Daisy once again scrambled up the sliding coke pile
and lifted her red face over the top.

'Get off!' snapped Gladys. 'When you're fourteen
you can come this side. Till then —'

'Miss Pettinger sent me!' gasped Daze furiously. 'So
now then Gladys Luker!' She wiped a filthy hand on her
pinafore. 'Miss Pettinger wants our April in her room.
Right away! An' if 'er says what a long time I bin with

the message, I'm a-goin' to tell 'er you pushed me down the pile — an' you're not allowed 'ere anyways!'

Gladys made a sound of disgust and raised enquiring brows at April, who shrugged with a *sang froid* she certainly did not feel and moved off briskly while trying to look unhurried.

Miss Pettinger had a visitor with her. At first April did not recognise the tall thin figure standing by the window, dressed in the black bombazine that had been almost a uniform of respectable ladies ten years before. Then she came forward and put a pair of pince-nez on her nose. It was Miss Midwinter.

April had not seen her old teacher since she left the little private school with Teddy seven years before, but immediately she was back in that special aura. Miss Midwinter was wearing her pince-nez, therefore the pupil should stand. April was already standing, so she bobbed a small curtsey. Her amazement was complete when Miss Midwinter actually held out a gloved hand and shook April's limp one.

'My dear child. I've been hearing all about you from Miss Pettinger. You have fulfilled your early promise.' Miss Midwinter actually smiled as she made this pronouncement. She picked up April's familiar red school report and tapped it on Miss Pettinger's desk. 'An excellent record my dear. I am proud to have started you along the Road to Knowledge.'

This was too much for practical Miss Pettinger. She shuffled some papers to show she had work to do.

'Miss Midwinter has come here with a proposal to put to you, April,' she said matter-of-factly. 'Perhaps you would both like to sit down.'

April waited until Miss Midwinter billowed down on one of the hard school chairs, then fetched another for herself. Miss Pettinger's hands fidgeted among her papers. They were red and knuckly and it crossed April's mind that they accomplished very varied work besides instructing. They inflicted punishment that was extremely painful even when just, they stoked the coke stove and mopped up various messes. And on occasions — few and far between — they soothed. There were many calls on them, so it was not altogether surprising when Miss Pettinger again took the field.

'Miss Midwinter has a place in her school for a pupil teacher, April. Your name occurred to her and —'

'I have *always* had you in mind, April,' Miss Midwinter amended austerely. 'Your conduct pleased me a great deal when you were with me. You are a member of an old and respected family —'

'And you are leaving school at fourteen,' Miss Pettinger took over blandly, 'which of course most of Miss Midwinter's pupils do not.' She smiled frostily. 'I daresay most of your girls continue their education at the girls' high school, Miss Midwinter?'

In the pause April said innocently, 'Bridget goes there. Bridget Williams — you remember, Miss Midwinter?'

Miss Midwinter regained her aplomb. 'And your dear sister works for Alderman Williams. As his personal secretary I understand.'

It was obvious Miss Midwinter had already spoken to the Williams. April lowered her eyes. Bridget by the sound of it. According to Bridget the Risings were still the next in line to the Royal Family.

Miss Midwinter swept on grandly, 'You will want to discuss it with your parents, my dear. And then perhaps you will all come to see me together.' She rose and gathered her bag and a lacy scarf while April skipped to the door and held it open. She swept out. 'On Tuesday,' she commanded finally.

Before then Miss Pettinger called at Chichester House and put the matter in very plain terms. 'Miss Midwinter will be getting a helper —' she refused to use the term pupil teacher '— at a very low cost.' She

210

looked straightly at Florence, then at Will as an afterthought. 'On the other hand, April will get excellent training and if she is still of a mind to teach in two or three years, I will give her the necessary experience to make her an uncertificated teacher.' She sighed. 'Who knows, by then there may be some way she can obtain a certificate.'

Will was exultant, this was a badly needed fillip for his pride.

'I knew I was right to send the two babies to that little school,' he said to Florence as soon as Miss Pettinger left. 'My goodness Flo, it'll be something to have a teacher for a daughter, eh? And our March private secretary to the mayor. May probably owning her own business before long. And Albert fighting for King and country.' His eyes grew moist. 'Something to be proud of, eh?'

Florence smiled at him, thinking how selfish she was to wish for the old days at number thirty-three, with the flaking ceilings and Aunt Lizzie's lace curtains. She nodded. Then looked at April questioningly.

April said, 'If I can be a teacher one day and make you proud of me —'

Florence said quickly, 'We shall always be proud of you, April. Whatever you choose to do.'

Will said, 'That's settled then. Perhaps things are looking up. At long last.'

David came home. And April was the first to see him.

Not the least of her reasons for inclining towards the work at Midland Road was that it would mean she would pass the Barton shop twice each day. Before David's arrival she called regularly on her father's behalf, and Mrs. Daker, who disliked her the least of all the Risings, was able to tell her the exact date and time that David would arrive. She got to the shop at four-thirty on that date, her hair, put up for the authority of her position, falling out from beneath her old sailor hat, one of May's dresses straining across her shoulders.

David was sitting huddled by a small fire in the back parlour and did not stand up. His face, turned momentarily towards her in greeting, was more guarded than ever, the eyes burning in the waxy paleness.

'Little April Rising, by all that's good and true!' He managed a grin. 'I thought it might be your sister when I heard the shop bell.'

April was as usual suddenly shy in his presence. 'May doesn't leave the salon until gone six. Seven some nights. She — she'll be so pleased — so happy . . . oh David, how are you?'

He said lightly, 'I think I might have a slight chill. Nothing to speak of. Sit down Primrose. Sit down.'

She was delighted by the name and obediently pulled up a chair.

'It's not cold David. I haven't even got a jacket. You must be ill.' She leaned forward, her concern deeper than May's ready sympathy. 'What about your leg?'

'I walk with a stick. Hoppity kick.' He grinned again. 'Teddy would have enjoyed that little rhyme. Yes?'

'Oh David. I can't bear it. You were so strong.'

He said roughly, 'I'm one of the lucky ones, Sweet Primrose, and don't you forget it. I'm home. I'm alive. I can walk fairly well. See. Hear. One day I'll feel warm again.' He forced himself back from the fire and looked at her properly. She breathed fast and tried to smile. He nodded as if satisfied. 'Yes. You're just as beautiful as ever, though you look as if you might be falling apart slightly this afternoon.' He took her hand quickly at her look of dismay and held it between his. The chill of him was instantly communicated. 'Is it because you're pleased to see me, little April? Could it be that?'

She was completely breathless. 'You know it is, David. Oh David. I've prayed and prayed that you would be safe.'

'And I am.' Again the light mocking tone. 'And now enough of me, Primrose. Tell me about you. May wrote that you were a skivvy teacher at that awful hole in Midland Road.'

She gasped a laugh. 'I suppose that is it exactly! Did May really say that?'

'Of course not. She made it sound good — as May always does. She says that you'll end up as headmistress.' He released her and stretched for the fire again. Impulsively she got up and lifted the smoking coal with the poker to produce a little blaze. He grinned wryly, 'Ah . . . April. I would have had to wait for ever for news from you.'

She said steadily, 'I wrote to you. Every week.'

He glanced sideways, surprised. 'I got two letters. Poems. No more.'

'I tore them up after I'd written them. Didn't you like the poems?'

For answer he fumbled for his wallet and produced two familiar pieces of paper. He watched her as she blushed deeply, then replaced them and pulled out a wad of pink notepaper.

'May's letters,' he said briefly.

The blush receded; she was well pleased to be included with May. Then he pulled out a single sheet. 'Sibbie Luker.' His smile was back. 'Was there ever such a lucky man? Letters from three beautiful girls.' He opened Sibbie's letter and glanced at it. 'Do you go with them to the dances at the hospital, little Primrose?'

'Not yet. Mother says I am too young to go without a chaperone. And Harry cannot take us because he is not in uniform.' She ducked her head. 'You could take us David.'

'But shall not. May is very popular I assume.'

'The soldiers often call. There is one called Marcel. They are terribly wounded, David. May would not — would not —'

'No. I understand.' He looked at Sibbie's letter intently. 'How will she feel about me walking with a stick — hoppity kick?'

213

Distress brought her to her knees by his chair. 'How can you ask that? She loves you, David!'

He looked into the eager young face, blue eyes full of pain. Then he leaned over and kissed the wide forehead.

'Of course. Of course little April. It's so simple, isn't it?' He looked and saw her close her eyes as her mouth worked uncontrollably; he sat up straight, tipping his head and sniffing exaggeratedly, 'Oh, you smell wonderful, young lady! D'you know that? Robin's starch and Puritan soap and a touch of lavender bag and the merest hint of camphor about the hat!'

He kept his head back with a fixed ecstatic expression while she laughed vexedly and stood up.

'I'll tell May you're here. But you must come round, David. Please come like you used to. Not tonight because I can see you're still so tired and cold, but tomorrow. Will you come tomorrow to tea and supper?'

He returned to the fire. 'Very well. I'll come tomorrow.'

'I'll call for you after school. Oh David — welcome — welcome home!'

She went through the shop in a happy whirlwind, even blowing a kiss to Mrs. Daker as that lady went through a tray of ribbons with a customer. As she ran up Barton Street she kept her face lifted to the autumn sun.

'Thank God,' she said inside her head. 'If you'll just send Albert and Fred back home, we — we'll —' she could think of no offering enormous enough to bargain with. 'We'll be so grateful,' she finished lamely. Then she was in Eastgate Street and there was Marshall's toy shop. After all, God had Teddy. He could not want more.

David waited until seven, when surely April would

have told May and she would be round to see him, then he stood up with difficulty and got into his jacket. Mrs. Daker was horrified.

'You're just going out when I am cooking supper?'

'It seems I have to, dear Mamma. I am engaged to be married if you recall.'

'So?'

He shrugged. 'If she will not come to see me, I must go to her,' he said briefly as he limped through the tiny kitchen.

It was hard going; further than he remembered. The sun slanted down Chichester Street: the Luker woman and Mrs. Turpin were still in their doorways and Lottie Jenner making for the Lamb and Flag with great determination. Either they had forgotten him or thought him of no account; none of them acknowledged his passing. It occurred to him that they were used to wounded men limping their ways towards the Rising house.

He went to the kitchen door, led there by sounds of chatter, and was welcomed vociferously again by April, with real pleasure by Will and Florence, but with some restraint by March and May and — he saw later when the excitement died down — by Sibbie Luker.

May was all apologies.

'April said you would come tomorrow evening, dear. We're going to a dance at the hospital — Mr. Luker is taking us in the trap. We really can't let them down. I'm so very sorry David. Oh dear. . . .' She looked at him with genuine distress, then brightened. 'But of course, you're in your uniform! How lucky — you can come with us!'

'And I'm wounded too. How fortunate.'

There was an uncomfortable pause, then March said, 'Do we have to go, May? This is the first time we've seen David for ages.'

'Darling, I know you don't enjoy going.' May kissed her sister's cheek. 'But they look forward so much to

215

seeing us. Think of Albert.'

David smiled at March. 'Yes. Do not feel you are putting me about, March. I promised my mother I would be home for supper.'

May looked relieved. 'Oh, that is all right then I suppose. And it's marvellous to see you David dear!'

He stayed long enough to watch them drive off. Sibbie could have been mistaken for a Rising now, so long had she associated with them and modelled herself on them. Her hair was still mouse-brown, but her pale blue eyes fringed with very dark lashes were striking, and her mouth, which she constantly pouted or nibbled, was full and more luscious than the sensitive Rising mouth. She smiled prettily at David and said she was sorry he couldn't come with them, and he smiled back and said if he'd known she was going he would have made different arrangements. Everyone laughed and Sibbie made a moue and bit her bottom lip.

David watched them down the road; like three white gardenias in a flower pot they looked. He made his farewells to Will and Florence. April walked with him down the garden to Mews Lane because he could not face Mrs. Luker and Mrs. Turpin again. They hardly spoke. She wished she had told him about the dance. He looked very cold and his face twisted as he leaned on his stick.

She said quickly, 'I'll call for you tomorrow after school. Half-past four.' And turned and ran indoors in case he thought she noticed his pain.

He stumbled into Mews Lane, and there, leaning against the wall of the stables, was Sibbie Luker. She smiled, showing white teeth.

'I said I felt sick. Pa dropped me off home and I came through the back. I thought you wouldn't want to walk down Chichester Street again.'

'Very perspicacious of you Sibbie.'

She said, 'D'you get my letter?'

'Yes.'

'I wasn't boasting. There's others now. Harry Hughes for one. I know exactly what I'm doing David.'

'I'll bet you do.'

She smiled again then turned and opened the stable door and led the way inside. David limped after her. In the corner lay April's red scooter and over one of the beams hung a rope from which Teddy had swung. Sibbie took David's free hand and drew him into the complete blackness of a stall where remnants of old straw still lay.

David was not gentle and he laughed when she cried out.

'Come down into the pit with me Sibbie Luker,' he murmured, crushing her hard on the brick floor beneath the straw. 'Come on. It's what you've always wanted, isn't it?'

And Sibbie remembered the nail in her back and told herself that David's anger was better than his disinterest.

The year drew to a close. There was the silent grief of Teddy's birthday and a quieter Christmas than usual without Albert or the prospect of a visit from Aunt Lizzie. Uncle Edwin, pressingly invited by Florence, declined to leave Bath but suggested that this summer it might be possible for March to visit him 'as promised'. Florence was puzzled by this but did not go into it. In many ways March had seemed more settled and contented since the funeral and Florence supposed that Edwin had 'promised' some of Lizzie's things — maybe even a small cash gift. Things like that mattered to March.

The engagement between May and David continued much as it had before the war. May had decided they had best wait until David could get the business on its feet again. There was small hope of that and in any case he appeared to have very little interest in the business.

217

Mrs. Daker still sold her buttons and thimbles, and when April called in with ointment, strawberries, books of poems, even buttercups gathered from the railway bank, David was nearly always sitting before the fire drinking scalding tea.

He was unfailingly pleased to see her however, and encouraged her to talk. It was to him she spoke of the books she read, the poems she wrote, the children she taught. She confided in him almost completely. Not quite. He was still May's.

May herself was in a dither. When Marcel Beauvais from Ostend proposed to her beneath the frost-encrusted apple tree, she thought it was the most romantic thing in the world. But then, she could remind him gently that she was already engaged to be married. She would be twenty-one in the spring, and the only thing she was sure of was that she did not want to be married to any one man. Yet she wanted to be married. It was crazy. She told Sibbie how she felt and Sibbie had difficulty in checking her laughter.

'My dear darling May . . .' she hung on to May's arm, gasping. 'I know *exactly* what you mean!'

It was one comfort.

Then at the end of January, Albert came home on leave.

He did not have David Daker's facility for putting on a face. It was obvious to his family that his experiences in the trenches had been more — much more — than uncomfortable. His ability to find happiness in a flower or a simple joke had gone for ever. When Will rallied him heartily, 'You showed 'em then lad, eh? You showed the Hun!' Albert crouched over his knees and studied the oilcloth as if his life depended on it. He showed a little pleasure however when Harry called and even asked him to stay the night.

'Now hang on old man,' Harry held up his hand. 'I start late turn tomorrow afternoon. We can't all swan around like you, you know.'

March watched angrily as Albert grinned without resentment.

'Well, you don't have to get back tonight at any rate. We could walk down to the river. Have a pint at the Saracen's Head.'

Harry raised his brows at this suggestion and said, 'Nice barmaid there, eh old man?'

March said sharply, 'You can't possibly go out tonight Albert. It's going to snow!'

'What difference does that make?' Albert smiled. 'Remember how we used to have snow fights, Harry? Remember Evensong that time when we hid snowballs in our cassocks and shoved 'em down —'

Harry looked uncomfortable; the days at the King's School had been expunged from his list of memories. Unlike Albert. All he could do was remember. Every sentence began 'Do you remember —' as if they had been the happiest days of his life.

Harry stayed and they walked as far as Sandhurst in the pitch darkness, talking foolishly like overgrown schoolboys. The next morning Harry produced a bottle of rum and they lay on their beds still drinking and talking. Harry, unused to liquor, was soon giggling.

'And what are the mam'selles like, Albert? Eh? What are the bits of French skirt like? Compared with here?'

The rum had an unwelcome effect on Albert, driving him back to places he had no wish for. He shook his head fiercely.

'Don't know what you mean, old man. When you're off duty there are prostitutes. Don't know about them.'

'Oh come on Albert! You must know! If I can manage it in Churchdown surely you can manage something in la belle France!'

Albert leaned on one elbow. 'How do you mean?'

Harry, bursting with importance and the longing to boast, said smugly, 'I've got a girl.' He pumped out a laugh. 'I've had a girl. I've got a girl. And I can have her again any time I want.'

There was a long silence while Albert assimilated this. Then he frowned. 'I thought you and March were friends. Can't have anything like that going on when you and March —'

Harry flumped back on to the bed. 'Oh she wouldn't have anything to do with me, old man. I tried. Don't think I didn't try. But March never thought much of me you know. I meant to tell you before — right at the beginning . . . anyway I'm all right now. Quite all right. Thanks very much.'

There was another long silence, then Albert said painfully, 'Who is it? Anyone I might know?'

Harry was convulsed again. 'I should think so. I should think you might know her any time you so wish!' He rolled over and looked across the intervening space at his friend. 'It's Sibbie Luker, old man! Marvellous she is — an absolute corker! If you like I'll put in a word.' He leered drunkenly. 'I'm not possessive Albert. Not where you're concerned, old man. Always been pals, always will be.'

Albert shifted on to his back and stared at the ceiling with his blue eyes.

'No thanks, old man. Thanks all the same.'

'Any time. Any time, old man.'

'Thanks. . . . Time you were going, old man.'

Harry sat up, hiccoughing loudly. 'You're right. As ever. Walk to the station with me, old man?'

Albert said dreamily, 'Not now, old man. I'm tired. G'night.'

Harry chuckled again as he staggered to the wash-stand and splashed his face and combed his hair. By the time he left the room, Albert was asleep. And they talked about licentious soldiery!

Alderman Williams was at a Council meeting and Miss Pym had a cold. At three o'clock March pushed her remaining work into a drawer and left the office. The snow still held off but the low yellow-grey sky kept people off the streets and she was home in ten minutes flat. The house appeared to be empty. Florence had left a stew in the slow oven on the left of the range and was doubtless sitting with Aunty Sylv. Will might be anywhere looking for work. And she had doubtless passed Albert as he went for another aimless walk. She sobbed with frustration, then paused as a sound came from above.

Albert sat on the edge of his bed cleaning his revolver. There was no sign of Harry but the stench of rum was everywhere. March thinned her lips disapprovingly.

'Honestly. . .Albert. I don't know why you're so keen on that wretched Harry Hughes. If Mother could smell this room, what d'you think she'd say?'

He looked at her blankly, then tipped some oil on to his rag and began on the barrel of the gun. He did not use his whole hand as March did when she cleaned the top stair rods, twisting the slim brass through the Brasso as quickly as possible; he used one finger swathed in the cloth and very slowly and gently rubbed it along the length of the barrel.

She said, 'Are you all right?'

He nodded.

'I left work early. Thought I might see you walking back from the station with Harry.'

'No. I didn't go. I was tired.'

'Have you slept?' she asked in a kinder tone.

'Yes. I think so. I was lying down.'

'Would you like some fresh air? We could walk down to Fearis' and buy some muffins for tea.'

'All right.' He rubbed on however. 'March. Do I smell?'

'What of? No, of course you don't.'

'It smells out there all the time. I thought I could still smell it.'

'You've had about fifty baths anyway. It's that rotten drink I suppose Harry bought.'

She sat on the other bed and watched him. He stopped

221

rubbing and held the gun up, examining it carefully.

'I haven't shot anyone yet, March. Honestly,' he said.

'Well, point it the other way. I don't want to be your first victim.'

'It's not loaded. I've got cartridges though.' He looked thoughtful. 'I could kill myself if I wanted to. Some of the chaps shoot themselves in the foot. So that they're sent home.'

She got up and went to the closet.

'Come on. Here's your tunic and cap. Put the gun on the wash-stand, you can finish it later. Take the brolly. It might snow.'

She got him dressed and down the stairs. He leaned heavily on his father's big black umbrella as they negotiated the path between the laurels. When they were in the street she took his arm, thankful the weather kept Hettie Luker and Aunt Sylv indoors.

He did not speak and his weight grew heavy on her arm. They turned into Northgate Street and trailed behind a small party of men from the hospital walking into town. There were two wheel-chairs pushed by nurses, three or four men on crutches with the white of bandages showing beneath their caps. March held Albert back. She could imagine what their faces would be like.

The road dropped away beneath them and the high pavement with its rickety iron railings was close to the metal girders of the railway bridge above. March made a small cooee to get an echo and provoke a response from Albert, but he looked straight ahead, apparently not even hearing her. There came the unmistakable snort of an approaching train. The bridge trembled and the usual reverberations were everywhere; smoke and steam descended to cut off the light. They were in a murky tunnel of noise.

Suddenly Albert screamed. She could not hear him but his gaping mouth and distended nostrils and eyes told her what was happening. Clutching the umbrella he turned frantically, ran along the railings until he came to a gap and jumped the four or five feet down into the road. Horrified, March followed him from above, calling fruitlessly into the bellow of sound, hanging over the railings with outstretched hand.

Albert ignored her, not seeing her; he flung himself full length along the tram lines and brought the umbrella to his shoulders. Sighting along it towards the group of soldiers, he began to make explosive noises between his teeth. At first these were inaudible, then as the train receded into the distance, they could be heard plainly. 'Putch! Putch! Putch-ch-ch!'

He scrabbled to his feet and ran crouching until he was beneath the soldiers and wheelchairs. He pointed the umbrella. 'Got you!' he screamed. 'Got the bloody lot of you — filthy, bloody swine — buggers —'

March reached him. She lifted her skirt and scrambled anyhow over the railings, landing by his side with a spine-jarring thump. She encircled him with her arms and held him to her with all the fierce strength of her thin frame. He struggled for an instant, then as suddenly as it had begun so it ended. He turned into her neck and began to weep.

One of the nurses joined her and helped the two of them back on to the pavement.

'It's shell shock. You know, do you?' she asked in a low voice. 'He should see a doctor.'

'I'll see to it. I'll see to it. Thank you — thank you very much. I'm so sorry if it has upset anyone —'

'Please. We understand. May we help you home?'

March moved her head so that she could see past Albert's cap.

'No. I can manage. We can manage. Come Albert. Come my dear.'

She led him down Mews Lane. Someone had hooked the umbrella over her arm and it was a frightful struggle

223

to straighten her hat and go on down the rough passage, with Albert's stumbling feet threatening to trip her every inch of the way.

'Come on. Come on dearest,' she whispered, thrusting at the garden door with her foot and easing him down the path. She prayed her parents would still be out and the back door open. Her prayers were answered. She sat Albert by the range and made hot tea and held it to his shaking lips. Then she filled bottles and urged him upstairs.

Once in bed he seemed to recover a little.

'I'm all right now March. All right now. If only I could sleep. I can't sleep you know. Not properly.'

'You'll sleep my darling boy. Close your eyes.'

'Don't leave me March.'

'I won't leave you.'

'As soon as I sleep, you'll go. I know you will.'

She threw her coat on to the other bed and unhooked her skirt. In her petticoat she climbed in beside him and took his head on her shoulder as she'd done when they were children.

'I'm not going to leave you, Albert. Go to sleep.'

He smiled and lifted his mouth for her kiss.

'March. I love you. I'd forgotten.'

'I know my darling. I know. Go to sleep.'

And she held him to her and stroked his ginger hair and smiled through her tears. He was hers. She would get him out of the Army if it meant shooting him in the foot. And he would be hers always.

But she reckoned without Albert. The next day she did not go back to the office, too scornful of her job even to send an excuse. She told Albert that he was not going back to France, that she would engineer it somehow. He shook his head quite gently.

'March, I shall go back. It's all right now. I'm clear and up straight again. I know now why I'm doing it. Remember what I said all those years ago March? You said you'd die for me and I said—'

'I remember. We were children.'

'It's all right March, I know that. But I've got to have things clear — clear and simple. And that's all it is, isn't it? That I'd die for you.'

'I want you here Albert. Alive and here.'

He was silent, looking down at the oilcloth again in a way that frightened her. Then he said, 'Please March. Let me go.'

She whispered, 'I — I don't understand, Albert.'

He shook his head helplessly. 'I don't understand either. But perhaps if I stay now, I won't be the sort of person you can love.' He waited while she protested, then went on, 'You think it could not be so. At this moment that is what you honestly think. But later...' he looked up suddenly. 'March. You despise Harry, don't you?'

She swallowed, not wanting to answer in case she forfeited his precious exclusive love.

He smiled. 'If I stay my dear, I might become like Harry one day.'

She drew away and looked into his face. For an instant she saw him as others must see him, the everyday anonymity of him, the pale ginger hair, mild blue eyes, thin high cheek bones. If he stayed he would always look like that. Perhaps.

She kissed him quietly. 'All I ask is ... come back Albert. Please.'

He held her again. But he did not reply.

It was strange how the family took this burgeoning love so calmly. Of course March knew it had always been there and the others must have seen it too. Now they closed ranks to give March and Albert the precious time they needed. March did not go back to the office and neither Will nor Flo pressed her to do so. Harry was dealt with in the front parlour by May or April, and after two calls he stayed away. The threatened snow arrived and closed them off from the rest of the world. They cleared a path to the winter cabbage patch with much laughter and returned to make cocoa for Florence and Will and talk of other times.

March was transported into a world of delight that she had never guessed could exist for her. She knew that in the midst of his terror she was somehow making Albert happy, and this increased her own happiness to a point where she could only just support it. All this love just created more. Florence spoke freely of Teddy. They sang around the piano in the bandy room and remembered Aunt Lizzie calling them all 'beautiful'. Gran came over and held the hand of her favourite.

Quite suddenly it was over. Early one morning they congregated in the kitchen for the last time. Albert kissed them all, even his father.

Will said, 'After.... It'll be better, son. We'll start again. A brass plate — "Rising and Son". What d'you think of that?'

'We'll make our own designs Dad,' Albert agreed. They hit each other on the shoulder.

Florence smiled. 'You're a mutual admiration society,' she said.

They were always pleased when Florence teased them. Albert said, 'We're a mutual admiration society Mother!'

March was the only one to accompany him to the station. She held his arm high because he had to shoulder his kitbag, and they went down Mews Lane to avoid seeing people.

'We're like an old married couple,' Albert said, smiling at her without embarrassment.

'Yes,' said March, thinking only that she mustn't cry. It was one of the qualities Albert appreciated in her; she did not weep tears of sadness, only of temper. She must make it easy for him to leave.

No-one they knew was on the platform, and amid the many parting couples they were completely anonymous. The train arrived from Cheltenham and Albert found a compartment and stowed his bag in the netted rack above his seat, then let down the window and hung through it. March tugged off her gloves and put her fingers in his.

They did not speak until the train began to move, then he said above the hissing steam, 'Thank you March. Thank you.'

She opened her eyes wide, willing the tears to subside. An iron-tyred trolley passed by, shaking the platform. She was running alongside the moving carriage; Albert's fingers had loosened but hers still gripped.

He leaned out at a dangerous angle and their mouths touched jerkily.

'Let me go March!' he shouted. 'Now!'

She forced her hand open and stood still. He went from her in a cloud of steam, snatching off his cap and waving it as if he were going the short distance to Newent or somewhere similar.

Carefully she counted the dark blue and white Mazawatee tea advertisements on the sooted brick walls of the station. There were thirty-seven.

April smiled at Mrs. Daker as she went through the shop, and received a blown kiss in return above the head of a customer. In the back parlour, David was reading the *Citizen*: casualties for the month of January.

'You look better today,' April said, ignoring his reading matter. 'And your mother looks very happy too. She blew me a kiss!'

'She calls you a little bit of spring in winter,' David said mockingly.

April was used to these moods by now. She said briskly, 'And you call me Miss Primrose. Very nice.' She sat down opposite him and produced a drawing from her bag. 'I wanted you to see this protrait of my employer.' It was a ghastly caricature drawn by one of

227

the younger children, recognisable only because of the enormous pince-nez.

David smiled obediently. 'How many more like this?'

'Seven. I had seven of the naughty ones this afternoon. So I asked them for pictures of people they disliked. Four of them did Miss Midwinter. Three the Kaiser.'

His smile widened a little. 'You'll get the sack of course. You know that.'

She opened her bag wider so that he could see the other pictures. 'I've absconded with the evidence,' she assured him. 'My word against theirs.' At last his smile became a grin and she relaxed. 'You really are better, David.'

'I've got some new medicine.' He reached for it from the mantelpiece. A brandy bottle. She tightened her mouth, but before she could speak, he said, 'How is May?'

'Well. A little depressed since Albert left. You will be with us on Sunday as usual again, so you will see for yourself.'

He let that go, merely taking a mouthful of brandy direct from the bottle.

'And March?' he asked afterwards.

April frowned. 'Like a tightly coiled spring.' She stood up as if she could not bear to watch him with the bottle. 'March cannot . . . cannot . . . receive our help. She shuts herself off from what we could give her. Mother — you know Mother, David — she pours love out to her and it could be a soothing balm. But March won't — cannot take it.'

He looked at her straight back and carefully put the bottle on the floor out of sight. 'You are very perceptive, April.'

She thought he was still mocking her and she said angrily, 'If that is what I am — then I cannot help it! And it hurts, David!'

'It's the difference between you and May.' He spoke

almost to himself and then laughed abruptly. 'Don't ever be a nurse Miss Primrose — you're much too subjective.'

There was a short silence while she considered asking him what he meant, then did not. She came and sat down again, registered that the bottle had disappeared, and said, 'David. You still won't talk about the war. I know that. But how is it . . . how will it be . . . for Albert?'

His eyes were without expression. 'Ask Fred Luker when he comes home on leave.'

She smiled slightly. 'I can't do that. Fred is good with cars and you and Albert are good with cloth.' She stood up again and got ready to go. 'You see, Mr. Luker came in for a word with Albert and he said —' she lengthened her face and used Alf Luker's voice exactly, 'Fred do make 'is bloody gun talk! Bloody talk!' She tried to grin down at him. 'And of course that makes sense. Because a gun is a machine like a motor car. But cloth. . .' she stopped on a question.

David shook his head. 'There's more to it than that, little April. Much more. Albert. . .Albert will be all right.'

She said passionately, 'I don't believe you! And I'm not little any more! I'm almost as tall as you, David Daker!'

And she was gone, pushing clumsily through Mrs. Daker's little kitchen into the back alley and slamming the door behind her.

March knew that old Charles Williams was angry with her for taking leave of absence during that last week in January, yet she refused to tell him that her brother had been home on leave. Even so, when written notice that her employment would cease in mid-February was placed on her desk by a triumphant Miss Pym, the shock of disgrace made her physically ill. She emerged from the tiny lavatory on the half-landing, still white and shaking, and asked to see Mr. Williams. Miss Pym informed her that the alderman was at the Guildhall, but would grant her an interview the next day. March threw down the letter.

'You can be my messenger then. I won't be here. That was all I wished to tell him.'

Miss Pym drew in her chin. 'You realise you will forfeit one week's salary by such a foolish action?'

'A week's salary? Is that all?'

March walked down the stairs with a sense of release. She had wanted the post urgently enough to blackmail a small girl ten years ago, and because of that it had always been dust and ashes in her mouth. She was well rid of it.

But although her family uttered no word of reproach, she knew their feelings. To be 'given notice' was not to be given references, and it was unlikely March would obtain another position of equivalent importance. She told herself she was happy back in the workroom sewing the occasional button-hole and tidying up after her father, but then Sibbie arrived one evening in March, half-excited, half-subdued, and announced that 'every cloud had a silver lining'. After some fidgeting and embarrassment she explained that dear little Bridget Williams had put in a good word for her and she had a job in King's Street at guess where — Williams and Son!

Politeness could not hide the general astonishment; only March kept an expressionless face. Sibbie explained that she was sick to death of the pickle factory and Gladys said munitions were no better, so she'd been trying to get an office job for some time. And she was so sorry that March's bad luck had turned to good for her, but she simply could not let such a chance slip through her fingers.

It was May who said, 'Of course you couldn't, Sib. March would have recommended you herself if she'd any idea that you wanted a job like that.'

Later, even Florence expressed surprise at the appointment.

March said bitterly, 'You know how she got the job, don't you?'

May said defensively, 'She's a hard worker March —'

'She certainly is!' March made for the door. 'But she can't type or do shorthand or add up a column of figures!'

April looked at May. 'What did March mean?'

'Nothing darling. Gossip. Sibbie is sometimes a little over-friendly with the soldiers. . .you know.'

Florence nodded. 'Single girls cannot be too careful, May. I've always said this.'

Surprisingly, Will spoke up. 'Sibbie Luker — all the Lukers — are good generous people. Very generous.'

The very next week news of the Passchendaele assault began to come through. The dreaded name Ypres was mentioned again, and after the gas attacks two years before everyone knew that no good could come of it. The casualty lists lengthened and were published weekly instead of monthly.

Albert's named appeared in April, two days after the War Office telegram arrived. Albert Edward Rising. It described him as a beloved son but it did not say that he left a sister as good as a widow. It made no mention of his simple straightforward love for Rags the cat, the daffodils at Newent, an organ note soaring into the fan-vaulted ceiling of Gloucester cathedral. To most people he was as anonymous in death as in life.

Yet as a postscript, perhaps as an offering, Harry Hughes enlisted that same day, was sent out to France and was never heard of again.

11

March could shed no tears. It was as if the discipline
she had laid on herself at Albert's leave-taking stayed
like a curse to desiccate and wither. Grief took her as it
had taken Florence and Sylvia; she could do nothing.
For hours she sat in the workroom staring at the needle
in her hand. Obediently she would lay the kitchen
table and take her place with the others, but unless
prompted she forgot to eat. Nobody was over-anxious
on her behalf; they were all paralysed by Albert's
senseless death, and though they knew March's grief
was more intense, they felt the least they could do was
to allow her to suffer it quietly and in privacy.

Helplessly, drearily they went about the business of
celebrating April's and May's birthdays. For April,
Florence boiled eggs and sat the cosies on them as she
had always done on special occasions, but no-one
made any comment. When it was May's turn she gave
her a pair of stockings almost surreptitiously, as if it
were an act to be ashamed of. May held her mother's
thin face to hers for longer than usual.

'We shall be happy again,' Florence murmured
steadily. 'Don't be cast down, my dearest.'

May whispered, 'So long as we have you. . . .'

Grief came differently for the other Risings. Gran,
bent and nearly double now, recalled the old days lugubriously.

'Plenty o' men about then there were,' she said,
remembering the kitchen table at Kempley surrounded

by Jack and Wallie, Will and Albert. 'Now look at us. All women save Will. 'E got the 'ole kit and caboodle of us on 'is shoulders I reckon. All my other boys scattered to the winds. My ole man dead and buried. And now two gran'sons. . .ah-eh. . .ah-eh. . .' she lifted her head piteously to Florence. 'I allus said we'd be proud of 'im. I allus said it. And Christamighty we can be proud of 'im right enough. Can't we? 'Tis all we got. Our bloody pride.'

'Be quiet our Mother,' Will said sharply.

But Flo took the almost bald head in her hands for a moment.

'They've gone to a better place Gran. We know that.'

'Ah. . .ah, my beauty.'

Will, looking at them, felt the terrible weight of them all for the first time in his life. His mother, Sylv and little Daisy. Florence, May, March and April. And only April and May working.

March knew that what she was experiencing was a form of madness. She was in a wasteland amid such desolation and isolation that the existence of her own dwindling body seemed an offence. A displacement of air that was unnecessary. The obvious solution occurred to her at intervals during the endless days and nights. But even desperation took an effort. Aunt Sylv probably had an ancient supply of laudanum and she could beg a little over a period of time until she had sufficient. There was the railway line; but that meant leaving the house which she never did now. There was the gas stove, but someone else was always within range of its lethal hiss. She knew that one day fairly soon, she would make the effort. She could not even look forward to it because looking forward needed energy.

On June 22nd Fred Luker came home on ten days' leave. There had been other leaves which he had spent in France; no-one in Chichester Street had seen him since he joined up eighteen months previously. There was a grand get-together at the Lamb and Flag — the singing could be heard from the front bedroom at Chichester House — and the next day he presented himself, neatly uniformed, to offer Florence his condolences. He saw no sign of March and sent her his regards.

He then spent three days in the Forest of Dean talking to the small mine-owners there with whom he and his father had dealt before the war. He was more self-assured now and saw that the old business of hawking coal around on the dray wasted precious man-hours. He suggested that in the future peace, the surface coal-mines might join in a co-operative to supply large concerns like the schools, the Gas and Coke companies, the engineering firms sprouting along the Bristol Road.

Cautiously the Forest miners told him they would need something in writing from such large concerns. Fred spent another three days in Gloucester sounding things out from that side. Nobody could see the end of the war, and no-one was interested in discussing peace until it came. And then they would want something binding in writing from the miners. It looked like a deadlock, but Fred knew it wasn't. He spoke the same language as the miners and could talk them round the next time; and if not, they were a gullible lot. Pragmatism and dishonesty were often the same thing.

The day before his leave was up he called again at Chichester House. This time March was in the kitchen with her parents. He was shocked at the sight of her; not just her thinness but her bowed shoulders and blank face. On her part March felt a definite sense of shock penetrating the depth of her madness when she glanced up briefly and took in the familiar yet foreign figure before her. Fred seemed taller than when he bent over his precious Austin. His shoulders were very wide and his neck thick and strong. He reminded her of the caricatures of John Bull that abounded in the press: pugnacious, thickset, completely determined.

He took a chair opposite Will and watched them almost clinically. They were like figures in a dream.

He said deliberately, 'I wondered if you had any news of Harry Hughes?'

March became still. Fred's voice was the same, rough to the point of harshness, yet with a note of authority that was new. His attack was the same too. Perhaps even more direct. Brutal.

Will shook his head. 'He's been gone about six weeks. It was a sudden decision. When he heard. . .when he heard. . . .'

Fred said, 'When he heard about Albert's death. Yes.' He glanced at March. 'You knew he was friendly with Sibbie? He told her he wanted to be wherever Albert was. He told her that Albert was the best friend he'd ever had or would ever have.' He cleared his throat. 'I wanted to tell you that. It might help.'

Florence also glanced at March, then murmured, 'We see so little of Sibbie now and had no idea she saw anything of poor Harry. Probably then, she is worried by the lack of news?'

March stared at the floor. Sibbie and Harry. Sibbie and old Charles Williams. She didn't care about it any more. It didn't matter.

Fred nodded. 'Yes. She was so worried she went out to Longford and called on his father. But he had heard nothing either.'

Florence poured the obligatory tea and answered questions about April and May. No-one mentioned March's name; Fred did not speak directly to her and her parents broke through her silence only with a smile. But when it was time for him to leave, Fred tucked his cap under his left arm and held his right hand towards her.

'I'll go the back way Mrs. Rising. Thank you for the tea. March, will you walk through the garden with me?'

March looked up without full comprehension and he repeated slowly, 'Come on March. You won't need a jacket, the sun is so warm.'

She shook her head dumbly. He picked up her limp hand.

'Yes. I want to talk to you.' He looked at Florence. 'You can spare March for half an hour, Mrs. Rising?'

Florence smiled encouragement. It would do March good to get outside. 'Of course Fred. March dear, a little air will be good for you.' She took March's elbow and urged her up. March walked like an automaton by Fred's side. 'Give our regards to Mrs. Luker —' Florence opened the door and the heartless sunshine poured in.

Will said, 'Yes. Our regards to your mother, Fred.'

Fred did not reply.

The garden was burgeoning; the currants and gooseberries behind the nets sent a heady smell across the rough grass. Albert's fruit bushes. They would be called Albert's fruit bushes always. March staggered a litle, leaning more heavily on Fred. The rough khaki beneath her fingers was terrifyingly familiar. She felt a mounting pressure in her throat.

'You're quiet Marcie.' Fred's voice was gentle as he used her special name. 'Won't you say anything to me?'

Fred had been to the same places as Albert had been. Fred knew what it was like; knew that some men shot themselves in the feet in order to be sent home. March turned her head so that he could not see her face. She had done that before. When her nose had been running.

He said quietly, 'Please speak to me Marcie. Tell me that I should be dead. That it should be Albert here with you. Say anything you like.'

Of course. Fred knew about her feelings for Albert. Fred knew about her bitter anger. Fred knew . . . everything.

They came to the miniature apple orchard where the tiny apples were already dropping into the grass beneath. Fred stopped beneath the biggest tree.

236

'Albert would be pleased with this crop I reckon. He loved the garden didn't he?'

March tucked her chin on to her chest and bore heavily on the rough khaki arm. She wondered whether she might fall down.

Fred went on. 'Not as much as he loved you though Marcie, eh? Our Sib told me about his last leave.'

She choked and cringed lower.

He said, suddenly brusque, 'Stand up straight March! 'Tisn't like you to cower and grovel, it isn't in your nature. You had what you wanted from life. You had someone's complete . . . *self*! If Albert had lived you'd have lost him again — oh yes you would. To Harry. Or someone like Harry.' He opened the gate into the lane, pulled her through and shut it with a bang. 'You know that, March. And even if you'd kept him it would have been like having a tame dog about the place! That's not for you.'

She turned, her hand raised to strike him and he caught it in his.

'Be angry in a minute March, but listen first! You've got him — don't you see? You've got him now, for always! No-one can take him away from you! Can't you understand that's why *I'm* so bloody angry?'

She stared at him, eyes wide, then shudderingly, she let the spring in her relax. He watched her carefully. Her shallow breathing became deeper and quicker by the second.

He said, 'Come on. In here if you're going to cry.'

He pushed at the old stable door with his shoulder and drew her into the musty gloom. She looked wildly around her. There was April's old scooter and a rope hanging from a beam. Her breathing was fast, too fast and convulsive. Fred. Fred was here. In khaki. Understanding everything.

She gasped a scream as she collapsed, and he caught her and held her tightly as if he expected grief to disintegrate her slight body. Indeed the sobs that racked her might easily have done physical damage without his supporting hand on her rib cage, his shoulder for her jerking head. For five long minutes the gale blew itself past crisis point, leaving her as weak as a kitten. Now his hold was different; he cradled her, rubbing his thumb along her spine, wiping his cheek to hers to clear the tears. It seemed natural that after a period of this soothing, he should begin to kiss her. First her eyes and then her ear lobe, back to her eyes and down her long thin nose and then her trembling, shaking mouth.

She did not protest. The uncontrollable passion of her grief spent, something else flickered into life; a physical feeling that was not unlike the beginnings of temper. She let it take its course. Soon there would be a time when she had to make a decision: to stop or go on. For now it did not matter. The warm mouth came back to hers, and this time she was conscious of it. Her own lips moved beneath it, tremulously but with a definite response. At once, the soothing hands slid up her back and held her head to steady it, and the kissing went on. She permitted it deliberately; the moment for decision was still not upon her, and meanwhile the warm hands and mouth did not intrude into her grief but were a kind of homage to it.

Fred waited for the sudden tension in her spine. It did not come. He leaned away from her at last and looked into her face. It looked back at him, the mouth open on a sob, the eyes swollen and half-closed.

He said, 'I'll make it all right for you Marcie. Just trust me.'

She made a sound of protest as he laid her in the straw, but that was because it was cold and she wanted his warmth back with her. She welcomed him when he lowered himself on to her, not even realising that the moment of decision had come and gone. There was no room in the world for anything except him; he was no longer Fred Luker who had given her driving lessons. He was a nameless someone who knew everything and did

238

not condemn. His complete acceptance of herself was the balm she needed, and once she accepted that, his expertise awakened every suppressed instinct within her. She gave herself to that first experience of sex as she had given herself to her tempers as a child; with an abandon that was exhausting, exhilarating and brought complete peace.

She lay still again while Fred cradled her.

'My darling. My beautiful darling.' He was near tears because she made no effort to rearrange her clothes. He ran his hand along the slim length of her leg. 'I've always loved you Marcie. Always. But I never knew how much.'

She looked up at him. 'Tell me. How much? How much do you love me?'

'Oh Christamighty Marcie. More than anything. Anyone.'

'More than Sibbie?'

He laughed hoarsely. 'More than any o' that lot. You're part of me now Marcie. I can't tell you how much I love you. You're my life.'

She sat up slowly and began to button her blouse. As his hand still stroked her she trembled with remembered joy.

'I'm glad you don't love me better than life. You must live. You must live. If I am your life then you must live. Do you hear me?'

He said steadily, 'I hear you Marcie. I'll come back. I promise you. And if you'll trust me, I'll make everything all right for you again. That's a promise too.'

She stood up eventually and let him pick the straw from her hair and clothes. Then she left him quickly, frightened that this sense of peace would go if she stayed too long and realised what she had done.

She slept the whole night through and her dreams of Albert were no longer nightmares that stayed with her when she woke. Now, he seemed faceless, almost formless. He was with her as a warmth and comfort. It was as if she was absorbing the essence of him. Wasn't that what Fred had said? That she had him for ever now?

She did not go to the station to see Fred off. It was a Saturday and Hettie, Alf, Sibbie and Gladys made a retinue which grew as it progressed. Lottie came 'for the fun of it' and Daze tagged after Gladys to hear about the goings-on at the munitions factory. There were plenty of noisy tears and good luck wishes, but no-one seriously thought Fred was in any real danger. The Lukers could survive anything, even old Ludendorff and the Kaiser. Sibbie swung her mother's arm on the way home and Hettie remembered how happy she had been with Will Rising. And how he had ditched her the minute his sister got wind of the affair.

Sibbie grinned sideways, pumping her mother's arm painfully.

'Ah . . . I was just thinking something, our Mam. Us Lukers. We're a fine lot aren't we? Not quite good enough to be loved, but good enough for plenty else, eh?'

Hettie sniffed back her tears and looked reproving. 'Now our Sib. You can't 'ave it all ways my girl and you've chose —'

'Oh ah. I can Ma. I can have it as many ways as I choose — you wait and see.' She laughed. 'Just you remember, we're better than a lot of folks round here. D'you know that? Better than most.'

Suddenly Hettie was infected with her daughter's resilience and laughed through her streaming eyes.

'Not just better girlie. We're the best!'

They swung into Chichester Street still laughing. Indefatigable.

Will was drunk and he knew it. He was often drunk these nights, and everyone understood and did their best for him. But tonight nobody's best was good enough. He wanted Hettie. Or Florence. He wanted Albert or Teddy. Or old Mr. Daker. Even Harry Hughes would have done.

Lottie was not in the Lamb and Flag, and Alf Luker was helping with a moonlight flit. Will drew in great lungfuls of the September evening air and reeled against Goodrich's wall, then followed the bricks down to thirty-three.

'Ma?' He hammered on the door, then squatted on the boot-scraper. 'Ma, come and let me in! Give me some bread and cheese and onion so's the girls — ladies — can't smell my breath! Come on Ma, come on —' the door opened and he fell in. His mother supported him with difficulty.

'No, Will. No food tonight. There en't none 'ere.'

'Cruel. Cruel, Mother. Where's our Sylv? Oh, with Flo as per usual, I'll be bound.'

'Yes. She's keeping Flo comp'ny. Like she do most nights when you're at the public.' Gran looked down the hall. 'Now come on our Will, stand up. That's it. Off you go and 'ave a bit o'walk. Walk it off afore you goes in. Nice night like this — do you good. Come on now —'

'I wanted a bit o' company Ma. Talk. About Teddy and Albert and poor ole Pa.'

'Not tonight Will. Dessay that young Daker 'ud be glad of a chat though. Why dun't you go and keep 'im company. Our May en't too keen, is she?'

'What d'you mean? They're engaged aren't they?'

'Engaged! Look over those glasses son. Our May dun't want to marry the lad.'

He had bundled himself down the steps by this time and stood on the path, surveying her hazily.

'Bin understood for years Ma. Years. Fixed up when she was fourteen or something.'

'More's the pity.'

'Like me and Florrie they are. Same as us.'

'Is that what you want for May then our Will? Same as what you got with Florrie?' Old Mrs. Rising's eyes, faded and rheumy, fixed him for an instant then flickered away. 'You get on down the Barton for an hour, our Will. Talk to that young Daker.'

241

There seemed nothing else to do. Stinking of whisky, he avoided the Cross and went down past the Army hospital which now sprawled over land owned by the railway company, and approached Barton Street along the embankment. Soldiers and girls were everywhere, looking at the full moon and at each other. A portable gramophone blared, 'Pack up your troubles in your old kitbag and smile...smile...smile....' Will wept maudlin tears and thought how he would take poor wounded David Daker over to the Waggoner and buy him a whisky and talk about his old man who had stood on his head. And maybe about Albert. Oh, and May. Cheer the lad up.

He went down the side way and tapped on the kitchen door. Nothing happened so he went in. The place was deserted. Kitchen and parlour were neat and tidy for the night. Will stood in the middle of the shop looking around indecisively, wondering whether he should write a note. The next instant his spine jarred with shock as a sneering laugh came from behind the workroom door. He was still facing towards it, eyes wide, when it was followed by a scream; a female scream. Then another laugh, triumphant yet cynical. He lifted the counter flap and shoved at the door in sudden panic; when it gave he hung on to the knob and went with it, almost falling into the small, dark room. And then he had to continue to hang on grimly, bent nearly double to absorb the physical shock of what he saw.

There was David Daker, white-faced, eyes like chips of coal, shirt sleeves rolled to the elbow, crouched above the cutting table as if bringing his peculiar concentration to bear on one of his paper patterns. But the pattern was Sibbie Luker. Her milky body lay spread-eagled before him in complete abandon, the red marks of his fingers still blotching the perfect skin. Her arms were upflung in surrender and her head hung from the edge of the table so that Will saw her face in reverse, contorted and horrific.

She recognised him before he recognised her. She screamed again, her scream enunciating the words, 'Oh no!' Then she jack-knifed her naked body and began to cry piteously. For a long second they stayed like that: Will staring incredulously; David leaning with assumed nonchalance against the edge of the table, Sibbie huddled upon it, naked and weeping.

Then Will said, 'Get your clothes on Sibbie. You're coming with me.' He went into the room and presented the girl with his back. 'And as for you —' he addressed David scornfully. 'Your liaison with my family is at an end. If ever you try to speak to any of us again — and that includes Miss Luker — I will report you to the police immediately.'

David said insolently, 'For what? Making the most of the local whore?'

Will felt quite sober. He breathed deeply twice.

'For perverted practices, more like. You dirty swine — you —'

David said coldly. 'Be quiet man. You don't know what you're talking about. You don't know anything, do you? How old are you — forty-five, fifty? All that time — all those years — and you haven't learned a thing!'

Will hardly heard him. 'To think — to think I wanted you to marry May!'

'Not really.' David's smile was chilling. 'You thought you did. You thought you did the Dakers a good turn — helping us out when my father died — permitting me to fall in love with your daughter. But you never really forgot we were Jews did you?'

Sibbie said, 'I'm ready Mr. Rising.'

Will turned. She was so like Hettie, a hurt and damaged Hettie. He tried to sound gallant as he crooked his arm.

'Come on then. We don't want to stay longer than we have to.'

She took his arm timidly and he escorted her through the shop, parlour and kitchen. He knew it was the last

243

time he would see the place where he had first started tailoring. David made no attempt to follow. They walked the length of the Barton and Eastgate Street without speaking, but in the quiet of the Catholic churchyard she began to weep again and collapsed on to a flat tombstone, pulling him to a stop. He had to remind himself that she was a woman of twenty-four; she looked such a child sitting there knuckling her eyes.

He said sternly, 'Now, now Sibbie. All over and done with. Try to forget it. Turn over a new leaf. Let this be a lesson to you.'

She said in a small voice, 'You — you know about me, Mr. Rising?'

'Know about you?'

'What he said. David Daker. You already knew what I — that I —'

He said briskly, 'I know you've been a silly girl Sibbie. Letting attention go to your head and —'

She burst out weeping again. 'You'll never respect me now! I can't bear it! That you of all people — the one person in the world I look up to — care about —' She threw herself from side to side and Will stood awkwardly by her and held her steady against his right leg.

He said sensibly, 'Of course I respect you Sibbie — I'm probably the one person who can understand you, my child. For one thing I've always been a second father to you — isn't that so?'

'May and me have shared everything. Always. And when you were good to Ma I used to pretend you were my father.'

He sucked in a quick breath. 'Yes. Well. Then you know I can understand you — your warmth. And sympathy. Because . . . because of —'

'Because I'm like Mam?'

He swallowed his next breath and tried to continue smoothly. 'You hardly deserved to come up against someone like Daker. He's returned from the war with a crazy streak in him. Maybe it will caution you Sibbie — as it has certainly cautioned me.'

'Is it really the end of him and May?' Sibbie asked without distress. 'I think it's best. He's a funny one Mr. Rising. Real funny.'

He tried not to think what she meant and knew he would think of it often. The white flesh, so familiar yet so young and taut; the red finger-marks . . . everywhere.

He said quickly, 'We must both forget him, Sibbie. He won't trouble us any more, he's got some shame.' Thank God May had escaped that. He felt sick at the thought of May on the cutting table. Yet he had seen Sibbie Luker there and had not felt sick exactly.

She said pathetically, 'I loved him 'cos of May, see. I know it sounds wrong, but that's why I let him do it. Because of May.'

Will remembered she had met the young swine under his roof in the first place. 'I understand, Sibbie. I told you, I understand. Now come along like a good girl and let's get you home.'

It was almost dark. She stood up and took his arm again and leaned on him as they went down Mews Lane.

She whispered, 'There's only been him and the alderman. You do believe that?'

'The alderman?' Will was shocked again, not unpleasurably. 'D'you mean old Charles Williams? He must be seventy if he's a day!'

Sibbie said simply, 'I like older men. They're kinder.' She swallowed. 'I thought you knew about him.'

'No. I. . .March insinuated. I wouldn't listen.'

Again she wept. 'Oh God. What must you *think* —'

They were outside her gate. He held her up.

'Why? Why did you do it, Sibbie?'

'I don't know. They gave me presents. I don't love them. Only one man I've ever loved. And I've lost him now.'

She was crying so much, so wholeheartedly, he had to

245

put his head down to hear her. Suddenly she seized his cap and held it hard as she kissed him.

'There!' she choked. 'I know I've lost you so I might as well take what I can anyhow!' She clung to him like a leech. 'Oh Will — I've always loved you — I wouldn't lie to you — ever since I was a little girl.'

Hettie had used that phrase, he recalled. 'I wouldn't lie to you. . . .' He put his arms around her waist and let her kiss him again.

He knew he was drunk. Very drunk indeed. The night sky reeled around him. He tasted her tongue and felt her sharp teeth and melting body. Then, tantalisingly, she pulled away from him and was gone, and the slap of the wooden door against its jamb made him sway. He stood there, waiting for the world to settle. Then a voice spoke from the complete blackness ahead of him.

'Still at it then Will?'

Will literally left the ground, turning a half-circle in the air to face the speaker.

'Who the hell is it?'

Some of the blackness gathered itself together and materialised beneath the moon. It was Dick. Sylv's ne'er-do-well husband who had disappeared ten years ago and had been presumed gone for ever by everyone except Sylv herself.

He said prosaically, 'Me. Bad penny.' He stood before Will drooping slightly from the shoulder, shabby, ill-kempt and . . . in khaki. 'I were just leaving. Said me goodbyes and were off.'

Will waited for his thumping heart to settle and his thoughts to turn over again properly. This — this — soldier — had been in talking to Flo and Sylv.

Will said roughly, 'Didn't even think to say hello to me — is that it? Christamighty, is that a uniform or what?'

Dick shrugged. 'Petty offenders were given the chance to join up. I joined up. Now I'm on the run.'

Will's fuddled mind searched back. 'You were over with our mam, weren't you? An hour or so back? She

246

wanted to get rid of me so she could fetch Sylv without me knowing.'

'I bring trouble,' Dick reminded him. 'I'm a deserter, Will.'

Will refused to be shocked; he returned to his gripe. 'Christamighty. Sometimes I think none of you want me in this bloody family at all.' The whisky made him believe what he said; he was head of the Risings and should have been consulted about Dick.

Dick said, 'They calls it 'arbouring. The military police know about Sylv 'cos I put 'er name down as me nex' o' kin. Once they've searched thirty-three they'll be over —'

'You're my sister's husband,' Will stated, full of righteous indignation. 'If I can't help. . . . Sylv was good to Flo when Teddy died. Did you hear about Teddy? And Albert? We got to stick together Dick.'

Dick shuffled. 'Thought you'd call me a coward.'

'We've heard enough. Nobody says much but we've heard. Albert. Fred Luker. David Daker.' He remembered this evening and stopped.

Dick misunderstood his benevolence. 'You dun't 'ave to worry about me saying nuthin' Will. I wun't say a word about that little girl —'

Will exploded. 'D'you think I'm offering you a bed because I think you'd tell tales? God, Dick, I haven't done a thing! Drunk too much but nothing else! Not since you left! Ten bloody years innit? Can you say the same?'

Dick shuffled again. 'Dun't want no bed Will. Mebbe the stables.'

Will was galvanised into decision-making. 'Right. The stables it shall be. Though you're welcome to the best bed in the house if you want it. No-one can say I've turned my back on my own.' The thought of giving Dick sanctuary uplifted him. He remembered another time when he had given Dick's wife similar sanctuary; his ennui finally disappeared. He sprinted through the garden, leaving Dick skulking in the back lane, and burst in on a gloomy gathering in the kitchen. Sylvia and Florrie were sitting stoically as usual while his mother waved her apron like a banner, prophesying doom for them all. April patted her uncomfortably, March stood by Florence's chair with an expression of withdrawn disgust, and May, practical as usual, brewed tea.

Will said, 'Quick. Jump to it. We want a mattress and bedding down in the stable for Sylv and her husband. Stop that crying Mother and take some tea down to Dick. Sylvia —' but Sylvia, her stolid courage melting with gratitude, was weeping at last.

Will enjoyed the furore which he created. He stood in the middle of the kitchen, legs slightly apart, and gave out his orders like a general. The women, thankful to have something to do, scurried at his bidding. He was making things happen tonight in a way he hadn't done for years. Sibbie. Now Dick. April picked up a pillow and ran ahead of him, echoing his feelings with the uncanny knack she had when she said, 'It's quite an adventure really isn't it?'

No-one mentioned the fact that they were breaking the law. It was the autumn of 1917 and everyone was revolted by the war.

The next morning was Sunday and they all slept late, including Sylv and Dick in their makeshift bed in the stables. The constables found them there, took the bedding as evidence of collusion, and led Dick back to the familiarity of prison. Will, descending hastily in his nightshirt, was apprised of the situation by a policeman in a ready-made Co-op suit. 'It won't come to much Mr. Rising,' he said reassuringly. 'You'll get a chalking-off in court of course. That sort of thing. You'll live it down.'

'My business won't,' Will retorted bitterly.

He could blame nothing on Sylv, or even Dick. It

had been his own doing. It had been the drink. Sometimes he wondered whether the whole episode with Sibbie had been the drink too.

He told them about David's banishment that afternoon. April took a Sunday School class occasionally and she sat with her gloved hands clasping her prayer book very tightly as her father informed them that David Daker was not fit to consort with respectable people any more. May took the news submissively, as if she might already suspect as much. March was completely indifferent, Florence surprised and horrified.

April said clearly, 'Why? What's he done?'

'That I am not at liberty to tell you,' Will said ponderously. 'But I must make it quite clear it is not some small peccadillo. It puts him beyond the pale.'

April said conversationally to her mother, 'Perhaps he harboured a deserter. That would make him a traitor to King and country, wouldn't it?'

'April —' Florence warned.

Will flushed darkly. 'I wish I could think that young Daker cared enough for any other human being to give them succour. But he sees people as — as — carrion —'

April burst out, 'How can you say that Father? How *can* you? David was injured caring for people! He gave his leg just as Albert gave his *life*!'

Will was deeply angry with his younger daughter as he had never been before. 'Don't mention Albert's name in the same breath as his!' he thundered. 'And kindly take my word for this whole sordid business child!'

'I am *not* a child! Everyone thinks I am, but I am not!'

Florence said, 'April. Dearest.'

April looked at May. 'You won't listen to this will you May? You know yourself that David is the sweetest kindest man in the whole world!'

May put her arm around the shaking shoulders.

'You have always idolised him dearest. Like another brother. But I know what Papa means. I sometimes had the feeling . . .' she searched for words, looking into

249

April's tortured blue eyes. 'I sometimes felt that as far as David was concerned, I was an — an object. A valuable, precious object, but nevertheless . . . now listen darling, please! He treated me that way. He used to take me off the shelf, polish me and put me back —'

'I hate you all!' April said hysterically. 'You've always been awful to David — you've none of you understood him! He'd die for any of you — willingly. And he'd die before he'd admit it! You can't see anything — you're so blind and stupid and —'

'Be silent!' It was Florence's voice, level as ever, yet it halted April in mid-flow. Everyone was staring at her incredulously, even March, who years ago had been only too wont to burst out in just as uncontrolled a manner.

Florence pitched her voice lower still. 'Whatever you think April — however you feel — you have to take your father's word about this business. You know he is never unfair or unjust and that he is not a bigoted man. Now go away for half an hour — into the garden if you like. Think about what has been said. And then come back and tell us your thoughts, sensibly and without rancour.'

It was the longest speech Florence had made since Albert's death. April kept her lips together and breathed quickly through her nose, but she took the advice. And she thought about the prayer they had just said in Sunday School 'for the brave men who, with their courage and true valour, defend us from the evil foe. . . .' April pivoted on her low strap shoes and stared at the lush greenery around her. Who exactly were the foe? Where were they? At the beginning of the war she had been a child and everything had been neat. She should have known better. She should have known when Teddy had been taken away, that nothing — ever — was neat.

On Monday night Will went to the Lamb and Flag as usual and immediately knew that something was different. Lottie held his arm even after he had bought her a gin, and told him repeatedly he was an honest man if no-one else in the world could say the same. Alf guffawed at all his jokes and said that any time he wanted to drop in for a chinwag, there was always someone there, even if it was only Het or Sib. Mr. Goodrich, fetching a jug of stout for his old mother, pumped his hand as if they hadn't met for years.

Only after Lottie stumbled from the snug for an unexpected lying-in, did Will see that she had been sitting on that night's copy of the *Cheltenham Echo*. He glanced at it idly while Alf went for more beer. There was the usual news, American soldiers landing in France, French soldiers throwing down their rifles, Russian soldiers fighting each other, the poor bloody British managing as best they could with the new tanks supposed to be supporting them; and someone called General Allenby doing something in Palestine. Will wondered what Palestine had to do with the war.

His gaze went idly on through the lesser headlines and suddenly he sat up and glanced over the partition to where Alf was telling a pair of soldiers about Fred and his talking machine gun. For the moment no-one realised that Will Rising was alone in the snug reading a newspaper. He glanced down again. 'Gloucester tailor turns traitor,' it said. The words had to be consciously focused. He could barely discern the text and he adjusted his spectacles frantically rather than lift the paper under the light. 'On the night of September tenth, a deserter from the ranks of the Somerset Light Infantry was apprehended on the premises of. . . .'

Will wet his lips and sat on the paper himself. He was sweating. If it hadn't been for the headlines he might have imagined the article was strictly factual — the word 'harbour' did not appear. But that stark and catchy line slanted the whole report. Made it 'newsworthy'. The sweat dried cold and he felt sick. It was so easy to remember those few words, 'Gloucester tailor turns traitor.' Nobody who knew him would take them seriously, but his present business depended on people who did not know him that well. All his old customers bought ready-made clothes; he needed the nouveau riche with 'county' aspirations. And they would remember that he had been labelled traitor.

Alf's voice said above him, 'I'm just off Will. . . . You all right me old mate? You look a bit green.'

Will made a face at his glass. Had Alf brought in the *Echo*? Or had it been Lottie? Or even Sid Goodrich who never gossiped yet had obviously known about it.

Will stumbled into the street by the light of an enormous circular harvest moon. He wanted to go somewhere and cry because the whole world was against him: even his little April.

A hand gripped his arm and held him from falling into the gutter.

'Come on my handsome. Just here. Lean on the wall and take some good deep breaths.'

It was Sibbie Luker's hand and Sibbie Luker's voice and smell and — and essence. He obeyed her, sobbing openly. She continued to hold him.

She whispered, 'Sat'y I cried on you. Now you cry on me Will. Go on, cry it all out.' He tried to tell her about the paper and she put a finger on his lips. 'I know. Pa told me. One bloody thing after another.' She did not remove the finger, it moved back and forth across his lips. 'It makes what I got to say worse. But I have to say it Will. Otherwise you might write me off for good an' all. And I wouldn't want that.'

'I'd never write you off Sib. I told you, you're like another daughter to me —' he stopped speaking because her finger was now inside his mouth.

She laughed. 'I don't think so Will. You're not like a father to me anyway. Not now.'

His weeping stopped but he was still breathless. She was pressed against him and her hand came away from his mouth and explored his face slowly. It was a sensual experience new to Will. His liaison with Hettie had been boisterous and innocent by comparison. He was almost frightened. But certainly not miserable any longer.

She went on softly. 'Listen Will. Yesterday old Charles Williams offered to buy me one of them little bungalows down by the canal. My own place, Will. The deeds 'ud be in my name.'

It took a minute to sink in and then Will removed some of his weight from her and took a sharp breath.

She flattened her palm on his cheek and held on to him.

'I knew you'd be shocked. In a minute you'll walk away from me — you're bound to. I'm a kept woman now and you've been trained to keep away from kept women. But later on Will, just think. My own place. I can sell it for a couple of hundred probably. Or keep it. As soon as the old man's dead, I'm free.'

He jerked his head away from her hand and tried to take a step. He staggered and fetched up against the rough bricks of Goodrich's wall. She laughed again.

'Yes, I know. It'll take some getting used to. Probably even poor old Ma will disown me. But I don't care Will. You'll get used to the idea — all of you — and you'll come to me because I'll be the only one among the lot of you with a bit of money and my own place.' He took another shambling step and another. There were two yards between them. Her whisper reached him even when he'd trebled that distance.

'Don't forget last Saturday night, will you my love? How you saw me bruised and naked and at the mercy of all men — yes, even you. Because one day you'll wonder just who is master and who is slave. I promise you that Will Rising. I promise you that!'

That night he dreamed vividly. Sibbie was indeed naked and covered in red marks. He was rubbing salve into them. Very gently.

12

A letter arrived from Uncle Edwin asking Florence to 'spare' March for a visit. He knew that April would be back at school and May as busy as ever, but from her last letter he gathered that March was still at home, and if this was so, perhaps Florence and she would like to come and have a week or two in Bath. Florence's name was apparently an afterthought.

March said, 'Not yet Mamma. I feel so unwell all the time.'

Florence was anxious. 'I thought you seemed so much better since Fred Luker came home on leave.'

March flashed, 'What do you mean?'

'Nothing in particular March. I was grateful to Fred for talking to you and helping you to accept Albert's loss.'

'I'll never get over Albert's death,' March said fiercely.

'I did not say you would get over it dear.'

'My being unwell has nothing to do with Fred!' March swallowed a mouthful of bile determinedly. 'I'm run down, that's all.'

'Quite. That is why this invitation has come at a fortuitous time. Now listen to me dear. You were Lizzie's favourite niece and I am sure Edwin has in mind that one day you will inherit some of her things.'

March stood up. 'I must go Mother,' she gasped.

Alarmed, Florence half-rose also but March waved her down and made for the back privy. Ten minutes later she returned, insisting it was the margarine.

'Horrid stuff. I'll never get used to it,' she shuddered.

Flo was still anxious. 'Some arrowroot,' she said. 'You must take arrowroot and lie down.'

So the subject of visiting Uncle Edwin was shelved.

Florence's anxiety was not only for March. The other two girls were looking 'pale and peaky' as she informed them often. April, starting her second year at Midland Road, had no more illusions as to her real position in the school. In case she had been nurturing secret ambitions, Miss Midwinter informed her that when she and her sister retired, the school would be sold as a going concern. 'In fact child, when the right buyer comes along, we shall not hesitate. Our retirement depends upon it as you will realise.' She did not assure April that the new owners would be persuaded to keep her on as 'pupil teacher'.

April longed to call in at the Barton and talk it over with David, but had eventually succumbed to Florence's pleas and promised not to try to see him. Nevertheless she still hoped she might encounter him accidentally. She was always re-buttoning her shoe outside Daker's, or standing to watch a train thunder over the level crossing.

May was frankly lonely. Her engagement to David had served as protection only for a long time now, yet without it she felt bound to turn down other male friendship. For one thing she discovered that she could not even imagine the kind of man she wanted to marry. She had loved so many: Teddy, Albert, David and all her many suitors among the wounded soldiers. But none of them exclusively.

She was not a stupid girl and this discovery horrified her. She asked April whether she was shallow and her sister's passionate reassurance to the contrary did not entirely convince her. Her chief morale-booster —

255

Sibbie — was no longer around. Disgraced for ever by her own action. May had wept when the news was brought to Chichester House by Lottie Jenner. March said scornfully, 'You're well rid of Sibbie Luker. She was nothing but a sycophant.' May had looked up the word. Had Sibbie really sucked up to her for her own gains? But what exactly had she gained? Except a spurious friendship with Bridget Williams which she must have used in some way to ingratiate herself with old Mr. Williams. May said later with defiance, 'Sycophant or no sycophant, I miss her most terribly.'

Florence arranged a holiday for the three girls with Aunt Sylv and Daisy.

'There's poor Sylvia with her husband in prison. March still grieving for Albert. And though April and May have taken everything in their stride I can see they are both below par.' She looked at Will. 'You too my dear. Would it be possible for you to have a few days away?'

'Of course not,' Will said irritably. 'And I don't see how Sylvia can do it either. Nor March. Neither of them have done much work for me over the last two months so neither of them have been paid!' Florence's surprise did not escape him, though he did not look at her. 'And as for April and May, they are our breadwinners. Do you think they can throw up their jobs just for a week's change?'

Florence said quietly, 'No, I don't think that, Will. But I think if I spoke to Miss Midwinter, she might let April —'

'The girl has just had four weeks' holiday Flo!' Will let his ennui erupt into impatience.

'I could try.' Florence refused to be ruffled, which annoyed Will more than ever. 'And if not, then May and March could go. May has had no annual holiday from the salon this year.'

'Good God woman! I just told you that March has no money for any holiday! Nor Sylv —'

Florence's voice dropped a tone. 'I have a little put by, Will. The fare to Weymouth is eight and fourpence and they could get rooms for ten shillings. Sylvia is a careful housekeeper. I think she could feed them for another pound. That is under five pounds all told. For the five of them.'

Will stared. 'And you have saved five pounds?'

'Yes.'

He tried to laugh. 'I'll have to cut down on your housekeeping.'

She flushed slightly. Will's donations were minimal. She said, 'Mrs. Hall gave me a little work my dear. Now I no longer help you, the afternoons are long and I was glad —'

'Kitty Hall? Gave you work?'

Florence's flush deepened. 'Blankets to darn. Very easy.'

There was a pause, then Will said, 'Prison blankets. My God. My wife darning prison blankets.'

Florence pleaded, 'It did not last long Will. And I've had in mind for some time . . . since we lost dear Albert . . . that the girls would need a holiday.'

Will went to his chair, lifted out Rags and dropped him to the floor. It was typical of Flo that she wanted a holiday for everyone save herself. At one time that would have made him weep with love.

He settled himself heavily. 'Please yourself my dear. You earned the money and managed to save it. Spend it how you wish.'

He tried to feel benevolent. There were men — Alf Luker only just down the road — who would have 'borrowed' that money for whisky. After all it was his by right. Everything of Florrie's was his by right. But he had always been a fair and just man. Always.

Miss Midwinter was a match for Florence. Smilingly she treated the suggestion of a further week off from school as merely ludicrous.

'The maternal instinct Mrs. Rising . . . I am always dealing with it as you might imagine. But of course April is a woman now and must take on a woman's responsibilities.' She led the way through the tiny yard that was the playground. 'We are quite pleased with her, you will be glad to hear. Quite pleased.' She glanced through a window where April could be heard chanting 'Mrs. D. Mrs. I. Mrs. F.F.I. Mrs. C. Mrs. U. Mrs. L.T.Y.' 'Yes. Quite pleased.'

April kissed her mother warmly that night and laughed with genuine amusement.

'Thank you for trying, Mamma. Miss Midwinter admits that your maternal feelings are natural and a credit to you, but might be a little confining for me!' Even March raised a smile. April went on mischievously. 'If you could hear what she thinks of the maternal feelings of some of her parents you would be thankful that she knows you are a Rhys-Davies!' Florence was bewildered. 'Oh Mamma,' April reminded her with mock severity. 'Have you not realised that a Rhys-Davies is simply incapable of having anything but fine feelings?'

Florence tutted ruefully but was thankful that May's salon had agreed to her week off when she wanted it.

'And dear Sylvia has agreed to go on the understanding that she looks after you — you are not to do a thing, she says!'

In fact they all embarked on the Weymouth week for Florence's sake more than their own; only Daze was as excited as they all should have been at the prospect of a holiday by the sea. Miss Pettinger had secured her a position as mother's help to Mrs. Woodward at the chemist's, but the baby was not due until November and Daze was bored.

Weymouth was as they had imagined from Florence's description. She had gone there with Grandma Rhys-Davies as a small girl and had been enchanted by the watering-place strung along the deep bay with its bathing machines and clock and its pierrot show. The pierrots had given way to a concert party known as the Happy Hey Days. Aunt Sylv promised that if their money allowed they would go to the show. Daze jumped up and down with excitement. May, smiling at her, went straight to the tiny box office and booked seats for that very night.

'My treat,' she told them, pressing Daisy's hand warningly in case March should feel affronted. But March stood apart as usual, drooping a little in the warm September sun and looking definitely 'pale and peaky'.

Sylvia nodded acceptance. She had thought May should have paid for her own railway ticket at least. Flo had always been soft with her.

'We'll 'ave a 'igh tea then,' she said. 'Kippers and some o' the cherry cake Gran put in my case.' Daze was permitted to jump unrestrained. 'But this wun't 'appen every night my girl! Tomorrow when it gets dark, we can 'ave a game o' cards.'

They strolled along the prom, Daze and Aunt Sylv trailing some way behind March and May. May was fascinated by the fashions. She squeezed March's arm, aghast as a girl not much younger than they were themselves passed by wearing a dress without sleeves.

'That simply is not decent,' May murmured. 'I wonder whether Mother would let us make something similar for next summer? So short and simple.'

March murmured without interest, 'Grecian.'

'Greasy?'

'Modelled on Greek costumes,' March explained impatiently. 'All right if you've got nice arms.'

May giggled. 'Imagine Lottie Jenner. Or Aunt Sylv.'

March said, 'May. I think I must go back to our rooms. The sun is so hot.'

May was immediately all concern, fetched the key from Aunt Sylv and escorted her sister back to their furnished rooms above a banana warehouse. March lay on one of the beds, her forehead damp and her hands slightly shaking.

'Darling, you're ill. Oh March, you poor darling. What can I do?'

'Go away,' whispered March ungratefully. 'Oh. And fetch me a pail.'

May arrived with an enamel slop-pail which March used as soon as she was alone. She lay back exhausted and thanked God that the others were going out tonight. She could take her mother's ardent advice and rest.

Even without March — perhaps because of that — the evening was an unqualified success. The Happy Hey Days were a bunch of bright young things with little talent but a lot of enthusiasm, carried almost entirely by someone called Monty Gould. May, constantly referring to the programme, saw that the comedian who walked jauntily onto the platform wearing one of the new trilby hats, twirling a cane and saying, 'I was walking down the street the other day when . . .' was called Monty Gould. The young man who leaned against the piano and sang to the pianist to 'Come into the garden Maud,' was also called Monty Gould. The male half of the Dancing Duo was the same.

Monty Gould had the audience on his side from the very beginning. He made them laugh, he made them cry, he had them jigging and breathless with his tap dancing. When he came to the edge of the stage and asked them to join in a song for 'our boys in France' they cleared their throats and smiled mistily.

Even so the beginning of the chorus was ragged, and May's clear soprano rang true above his pleasing tenor.

'Keep the Home Fires burning . . . while our hearts are yearning. . . .'

He turned immediately in her direction, not pausing but letting a smile lighten his dark, handsome face as he sang more strongly to offer her encouragement. A few determined singers accompanied them but after a faltering hesitation May responded to Monty Gould's encouragement and soared away as she so often did in the bandy room. 'Till the boys come home.'

When the song was over there was a moment's hush, then clapping broke out almost frantically, and amid its roar Monty Gould ran to the side of the stage, took the steps in one bound and found his way to May. He took her hand and urged her to her feet. The wavering spotlight played on them and the applause continued for the beautiful blonde girl who looked like an angel. May dimpled exquisitely, just as she had in the Corn Exchange after singing 'I'm a dainty dancing fairy' and then the young man turned towards her and lowered his head to her hand in a way that the Belgian soldiers had never dared do because of their poor faces.

May looked down at the smooth dark head, so unlike David's wiry mop, felt the dry hand on hers, so unlike David's nervously clammy fingers, then looked into the brown eyes as they lifted to hers. She felt a small thrill begin in her throat and tremble down her spine. His eyes were clear brown like Florence's and March's . . . and Teddy's. Yes, Teddy's, because they were filled with laughter. She stared into them with parted lips, and helplessly her own smile widened and the next instant they were laughing joyously. As if they shared a joke; or the war had ended; or they had come into a joint fortune.

The audience might have thought the whole thing was rigged, except that Aunt Sylv stood up and detached the young man in no uncertain manner, sending him back to the stage and sitting the young lady down with two unmistakable gestures. Laughter broke out everywhere. Undeterred, Monty Gould parodied the walk of the browbeaten clown of the moving pictures, Charlie Chaplin. He spoke a word to the pianist, turned and, completely transformed, sang to May, 'We have come to the end of a perfect day, to the end of a journey home. . . .' May, breathless, told herself it meant nothing, but did not believe herself.

Aunt Sylv was furious.

'If your mamma could have seen that little exhibition,' she muttered as they left the theatre, meeting familiar smiles from complete strangers, 'I just don't know what she would have said!'

May squeezed her aunt's ample arm. 'Dear Aunt Sylv. She wouldn't have objected too much, I think. Not when she saw . . . him.'

They emerged into the September night. The moon hung over the shallow water of Weymouth Bay, providing a pathway straight to France and the unbelievable horrors over there.

'And why might that be?' Aunt Sylv asked with unaccustomed sarcasm.

May sighed at the moonlight.

'Because he was like Teddy. And everything Teddy did, Mamma understood.' She squeezed again with affection. 'And darling Aunt Sylv, I know you understand too. Of all people, you understand.'

Aunt Sylv stopped looking around for Daze and joined her niece in staring at the moon. 'A-a-ah,' she sighed.

Daze appeared, dragging Mr. Gould behind her. May and Aunt Sylv hung on to each other.

'He was looking for you, our May!' Daze said, grinning from ear to ear, her sailor hat falling off her head, her hair ribbon sliding away. 'I saw him and told him I was your cousin and he asked me to — to —'

Mr. Gould was not so dynamic outside the brightly lit confines of the small theatre. Now there was something else about him; something small boy and appealing.

'I wanted to thank you.' He did not let go Daze's hand and the pair of them looked more than ever like something from a silent film. 'The show tonight — there's never been one like it. And it was your doing.'

May swallowed. 'Not at all Mr. . . . .Gould. I shouldn't have pushed myself forward like that.'

'You were natural. That was what they liked. In all that tawdriness, you were natural.' He smiled nervously at Aunt Sylv. 'You have the advantage of me, ladies. My name being in the programme.'

Aunt Sylv was silently cautious as always, but Daze shouted, 'This is me mam. That's May Rising. Me cousin.'

May expanded quickly, 'Mrs. Turpin . . . we're pleased to meet you, Mr. Gould.' She pulled Daisy to her. 'We have to go now dear.' Mr. Gould looked vulnerable without Daisy's sticky hand in his. May swallowed her natural sympathy. 'Thank you Mr. Gould. Good night.'

He recovered himself. 'But not goodbye surely? Mrs. Turpin — are you here for the week?'

Aunt Sylv made a noise like a cross sow. Daisy, hugging May's hand now, said, 'The 'ole week. Innit lovely?'

'Yes. Yes.' He spoke simply. 'We change our repertoire on Wednesday. May I offer you some seats? It would give me great encouragement to know I have well-wishers in the audience.'

Daisy said,'What about March?' She ignored May's shushing sounds. 'March is May's sister and is proper poorly tonight. But by Wednesday she might be better.'

'Four seats,' Mr. Gould promised beseechingly.

Surprisingly it was Aunt Sylv who said brusquely, 'I don't see why not. Give March a bit of a treat wouldn't it?' She began to draw the two girls away.

May said more graciously, 'Thank you Mr. Gould.' And then when his beautiful Teddy-smile dawned, she added, 'I shall look forward to it.'

March was not enchanted by the news of her unexpected treat on Wednesday; drained yet still queasy, she could think of no prospect that could possibly enchant her. While May and Daisy cleared away their

263

supper and laid the breakfast for the next morning, Aunty Sylv visited her niece in the tiny bedroom which she was sharing with May.

' 'Tisn't very roomy our March,' Sylvia said, tidying around as she knew Florence would have done had she been here. 'But 'twill do for a week I reckon, eh?'

March said weakly, 'There are a lot of rustling noises underneath. I hope snakes don't come in with the bananas.'

Aunt Sylv crouched down, adjusted the chamber-pot to where the sagging bed springs gave it more clearance, and listened.

'Shouldn't 'ardly think so. Monkey mebbe. I'll ask the men tomorrow.' She sat back on her heels. 'Lovely smell they makes mind, don't they?'

March tried to close her nose against the sickly-sweet banana smell. She remembered Albert telling her his trick for not smelling Gran's boiling sheep's heads, and weak tears rose to her eyes.

Aunt Sylv said abruptly, 'Who's the father, our March? Come on, you can tell me. I bin through all this remember. Just tell me an' I'll make sure 'e gives you a ring and makes it all legal and proper.'

March was completely shocked. So shocked she forgot her weakness and sat bolt upright on the hard flock mattress to stare at Aunt Sylv as if she'd announced the end of the world. Which, as far as March was concerned, she had.

Aunt Sylv levered herself up on to the other bed with difficulty and held her big shoulders close to her chest.

'Come on my girl. I know babby-symptoms when I sees them. Lucky for you I'm the only one 'oo does.'

March's face changed slowly and subtly from blank amazement to realisation and then to horror. She made no attempt to cover up.

'Oh no . . . oh no . . .' she whispered.

Aunt Sylv said matter-of-factly, 'Funny 'ow things work out. Now, if Sibbie Luker was still friendly with your May, she would a known a month ago and it would a been all round Chichester Street and 'alfway to Bristol by now.'

March breathed, 'I can't believe it — I can't!'

'You know 'ow babbies come our March? Flo 'as *told* you 'asn't she?'

'No. May. May knows, Sibbie told her years ago. Oh God. I thought it had to be dozens of times.'

Aunt Sylv was genuinely surprised. 'Why? Christa-mighty, I thought you girls was supposed to be so quick and bright an' all. Think about it a bit our March. Once is enough.'

March never doubted her aunt's diagnosis. Now it was given she saw that there was no other answer.

'Din't you miss?' the incredulous voice went on. 'Din't you put two and two together when you missed?'

March suddenly collapsed over her crooked knees. 'I never keep account of — of that. And when I realised how late ... I thought it was because I was ill.' She began to weep noisily. 'Since Albert died I haven't always ... it hasn't always ...'

Aunt Sylv stood up and patted the thin back quickly.

'Now, now, girlie. Cry quiet if you must. We don't want May or Daze in asking questions. There, there.'

Aunt Sylv was no expert with comfort, but March was rarely receptive to it either. She suffered the thumps and choked back her sobs somehow. For a few minutes more she hugged her knees, her forehead pressed close to them. Her aunt stayed awkwardly above her, waiting.

Then March drew a breath and spoke quickly. 'He made me. I wasn't well — it was all so terrible after Albert was killed. It didn't seem to matter. Nothing seemed to matter.'

Aunt Sylv was on familiar ground again. She nodded. 'It's a bit o' comfort. An' you thinks to yourself, it can't do no-one no 'arm.'

It hadn't been quite like that but March moved her

head in agreement. The turbulent copulation with Fred in the stable had been a comfort, yes. But it had been a triumph too. And an erotic delight which — especially now — she dared not admit.

There was another pause. From the other side of the door they heard May and Daze go into a duet. 'We have come to the end of a purr — fect day. . . .' March said desperately, 'What am I going to do?'

Aunt Sylv repeated, 'Tell me 'oo it was. I'll go and see them —'

'I can't! I can't!'

The rough voice humoured the panic-stricken one.

'Was it Harry Hughes? He's the only one I can think of and if it was 'im we're sunk 'cos I reckon 'e's dead and gone with Albert. If it were one o' they soldiers from the 'ospital then —'

'Oh my God! Of course it wasn't Harry!' March raised a ravaged face for an instant then buried it again. 'It was Fred Luker.'

Aunt Sylv could not hide her surprise.

'Fred Luker? You? Oh I know he always trailed after you when you were a kid. But I didn't think you gave two straws for 'im!'

'I don't — I don't — I told you —'

'Yes. Yes, you told me.' Aunt Sylv registered that the singing next door had stopped. 'That's almost as bad as Harry Hughes, but not quite. End o' June 'e were 'ome weren't 'e? 'Tis just past two months. Lottie Jenner might be able to do something. There might be time.'

'What d'you mean?'

'Get rid of it. Lottie's done a few in 'er time.'

March sat up and shook her head. 'Not Lottie Jenner. No. Not that.' How could she explain that they had always looked down on Lottie.

Aunt Sylv said, 'Well, you can write to Fred. He'd get leave and be 'ome in three or four weeks I daresay.'

March found herself in a curious state of mind. It was the only thing to do. Write to Fred and tell him he had to marry her. It was degrading and everything she hated. Yet . . . she did not entirely hate the idea. If she had a choice it would be different of course. But she had no choice. Fred had no choice. They must be married as soon as possible. Just for an instant she let herself remember Fred's hand moving along the inside of her thigh. She shivered.

'I'll write,' she said in a low voice. 'I'll write tomorrow.'

Aunt Sylv stared down at the red-brown head. 'Are you sure child? Can you really marry one of the Lukers and make a go of it?'

March lifted her shoulders, shrugging off the large hand.

'I've got no choice, have I?' she asked.

Aunt Sylv had had no choice either. The father of her three children had already been married to someone else. She sighed deeply.

'No. Not really March. You ain't got no choice.'

As it happened March did not have to wait until Wednesday to meet Mr. Gould. The next afternoon, as they lay in canvas chairs on the fine golden sand, he stopped before them and tipped his straw boater charmingly.

'This is a lucky meeting!' he said, his eyes on May. 'I thought as the afternoon was so bright, I would take the air.'

Aunt Sylv gave a dry, cynical cough. March, who was composing a rough draft of her letter in pencil, looked up unwelcomingly. Daze, who might have oiled the situation as she had the previous evening, was nowhere in sight. May did her best. Mr. Gould touched March's unresponsive hand and looked baffled.

May smiled. 'Have you time to fetch a chair and sit with us, Mr. Gould? We should be glad of your company.'

'It would be the greatest pleasure, Miss Rising.'

He almost sprinted along the beach to the stack of chairs. May said happily, 'What a charming coincidence. We were rather dull by ourselves, weren't we?'

Aunt Sylv lengthened her mouth in a kind of smile. March said, 'I was not dull, May. I was writing home.'

'Darling March. But do take the trouble to talk to Mr. Gould. I want you to tell me if he reminds you of . . . someone.'

March put away her notepad and pencil ungraciously, but hardly needed to open her mouth. Aunt Sylv limited herself as always to monosyllables. Mr. Gould and May were quite capable of sustaining a conversation throughout the long golden September afternoon; and did so. Many facts emerged. He was twenty-eight to her twenty-two. He had a 'weak chest' so was unable to serve his country, but as the Happy Hey Days had performed in all the barrack halls in England he liked to think that in his small way —

'You probably do more for the spirit of our cause than many a serving soldier!' May said enthusiastically.

'Thank you Miss Rising. Thank you.' His colour deepened gratefully. 'We played Bournemouth last week and at the end of our last performance I was handed a white feather.'

'Oh my goodness,' May said, hands to face.

'It was a frightful experience. And on stage too.'

'I wish I'd been there,' May declared passionately. 'I would have stood up and announced to the whole auditorium that in spite of being medically unfit to serve in the field, you were doing more than your bit to keep our fighting spirit high!' Her cheeks flushed, like his, and her blue eyes flashed. She looked magnificent.

He sighed. 'Ah Miss Rising. . . . Actually Miss Maud Davenport, who does several numbers with me, did go to the front of the stage and say something of the sort.'

May paused, ravaged suddenly with an unaccustomed emotion which she hardly recognised as jealousy. 'I am so glad,' she said at last.

He saw at once that he had erred. So he then told her that the 'company' was his only family. Both his parents had died when he was small, and he had been brought up by grandparents in North London who had sent him to a small private school where 'drama' had been prominent on the curriculum.

'My younger sister went to a private school also,' May breathed, delighted to find another link between them. 'She teaches there now. Our brother went with her.' She lowered her voice. 'He died when he was six.'

'How frightful! Yet . . . you *knew* him. And you have sisters too. I have no-one.'

Daze returned and pestered to be taken to the Punch and Judy show. Mr. Gould and May strolled along the sand with her and stood on the outskirts of the crowd, smiling at Judy's squawks but hardly hearing them. May told him about Albert and how terribly March missed him, and that was why she was out of sorts. She told him about Florence saving up so that they could have this week away. She even mentioned the decline in Will's business. He said, 'I envy you your family, Miss May.'

She noticed the change in address and dimpled. 'I would like to share them. They would be most happy to welcome you if you are ever in Gloucester, Mr. Gould. The house is always full of callers.'

'It would indeed be a pleasure.' He smiled absently at the vociferous applause all around them for Punch's antics, then added abruptly, 'And is there a special caller, Miss May? I cannot believe you are not engaged to some lucky man.'

May, too, smiled over the heads of the crowd towards the striped box with its tiny stage.

'Well . . . I am not. And there is no special caller.' She turned to him and her polite smile disappeared. 'There was someone. Yes. As a matter of fact he was a childhood sweetheart. We were expected — everyone expected . . . I had a ring. But the connection was meaningless and when my father forebade it earlier this summer, I will confess I was relieved.' She added in a low voice, 'I have told no-one else how I feel. They realise that I am not heartbroken. But I have told no-one that I am . . . relieved.'

He looked at her with a gaze that was now steadfast.

'I am honoured that you have told me,' he said. The crowd began to break up and he changed again from serious to mischievous. 'Let's run from your cousin! Wave to her — yes, she's seen! Now come on!'

At once the moment was transformed into fun. Daisy ran screaming after them and Mr. Gould pulled May behind the bathing-machines, then expertly beneath the promenade where the paddle boats were stacked. They emerged the other side, doubled back gasping with laughter, and slowed to a respectable walk as they came within sight of March and Aunt Sylv.

March made another effort. 'Did Daisy enjoy the show? Where is she?'

Mr. Gould spoke up to cover May's threatened giggles. 'She enjoyed it a great deal from the sound of her applause. She was with us a moment ago.' He glanced around innocently as Daisy came panting up, hurling accusations. 'Ah, there you are child!' he boomed in music-hall tones. 'Rescued at last from the Perils of Punch!'

March and Aunt Sylv exchanged glances as the other three were finally convulsed by their own laughter.

By Wednesday afternoon March's letter was in the post and she felt a great deal better. Strangely, when she thought of her future it was with a small thrill of something like excitement. Perhaps it was because she suddenly had a future. Or perhaps May's twitterings were infectious. Even March could see that May had never felt like this before. Aunt Sylv said straight out, 'The girl's head over heels in love.' And May herself did not deny it. She could think of nothing and no-one but Monty

Gould. She wanted to touch that sleek dark hair and look into those light brown eyes again . . . drown in them. . . it was the most romantic thing that had ever happened to her. Yet she had known of its possibility. That was why she had waited . . . yes, she saw quite clearly that it was all ordained.

They returned from the beach after another accidental meeting with Mr. Gould, to find the afternoon post waiting for them on the dark stairs that led up to their rooms. Florence's handwriting was recognised immediately. The envelope was addressed to Aunt Sylv, and while the kettle boiled for tea she slit it open and passed it to March to read aloud to them all.

March did not get very far. Reading on while May commented, 'Darling Mamma, the notepaper even smells of her!' she stopped suddenly and drew in a shuddering breath. May said, 'What is it March dear?' But March could not reply. May took the paper from her numb fingers and read it for herself. Tragically she looked up at Aunt Sylv. 'It's Fred Luker. He's listed as missing believed killed. Poor Mrs. Luker is taken ill and Sibbie is back home looking after them all.'

Daisy said perfunctorily, 'Poor old Fred. Still, he might be all right I suppose.' She glanced at her mother. 'Will we be allowed to speak to Sibbie our Mam? If she's there all the time it will be difficult not to.'

Aunt Sylv said tersely, 'We'll see. Now go and make the tea our Daze — two spoonfuls 'll be enough mind. And May, take this sixpence and pop down to that shop that sells off buns at closing time.'

May was surprised. 'We've got bread and butter.' She saw Aunt Sylv's expression and nodded. 'I won't be long.' She went through the kitchen. 'Don't go in for a bit, Daze dear. This sort of thing makes March remember Albert all over again. She's very upset.'

She was so upset that there was no question of her going to the show. The news seemed to bring on one of her queasy turns again. Aunt Sylv put her to bed with

271

the tea when it was made and said she would trust May and Daisy to behave themselves for the evening and she would be outside the theatre at nine o'clock sharp to meet them. May was so thankful that March's sudden relapse did not bar her from seeing Mr. Gould that she spared very little thought to Fred Luker's predicament or the effect it had had on her sister. The slightest thing upset poor March these days and at one time she and Fred had been quite friendly.

May and Daisy sat in the front row holding hands, prepared to enjoy every second of the evening. Which they did. Monty Gould concluded the show with a song generally sung by a saucy soubrette in music hall who would cast her eye to her partner or even up to the boxes. Monty Gould sang it seriously to everyone there, even the harassed usher. 'I love you dearly, dearly and I hope that you love me. . . .' Only then did May discover that she and Daisy were still hanging on to each other for dear life. She looked round and grinned sheepishly, wishing that it were April sitting there sharing these precious moments. Then she saw tears in Daisy's eyes. She smiled, and the fourteen-year-old smiled back then sawed at her nose with the back of her hand. 'In't 'e lovely our May?' she whispered. 'In't 'e the loveliest man you've ever seen?' And May hugged the thin shoulders suddenly.

Aunt Sylv did not waste time with idle regrets or even grief.

'Pretty kettle of fish this is,' she remarked, going into the small bedroom as May and Daze had left. 'But to be honest my girl, I couldn't see much hope of happiness for you with Fred Luker.'

March, lying frozen in the bed, staring at the ceiling, said cruelly, 'You should know about that. You never had much out of your marriage, did you?'

Aunt Sylv looked at her sharply, surprised by this show of spirit. 'Don't you be too sure of that March

Rising, neither. Dick an' me, we were 'appy enough when we was allowed to be. We was two of a kind. You and Fred Luker — chalk and cheese.'

March turned her head and stared at the window instead. 'Doesn't matter now. We won't get the chance to find out.'

Aunt Sylv folded her arms. 'It'll 'ave to be Lottie Jenner, that's all. She won't talk. I'll see 'er an' —'

'Not yet.'

Aunt Sylv said warningly, 'Once you're much over three months you can't do nothing March. And Flo mustn't know — it 'ud kill 'er —'

'All right, all right. I'm talking about a day or two. Not a month, not even a week. Just two days after this week.'

Aunt Sylv was unaccountably nervous. 'What you thinking about girl? You can't do nothing yourself mind. An' if you start jumping about . . . it gen'lly strengthens you whatever they do say.'

March said, 'It doesn't look as if I've got the energy to do much jumping about, does it?'

'Then what? I don't want nothing 'appening March. Flo trusted me with you two girls.'

March turned her head into the pillow and her voice was muffled.

'There's someone who might help me. My uncle in Bath. On the way home I'll call on him. It'll be all right Aunt Sylv. Letty and Rose are in the house, even Mother couldn't object to me spending a night there. After all, I was Aunt Lizzie's favourite niece.' She sobbed, suddenly remembering Aunt Lizzie. And Albert. And Fred Luker.

Aunt Sylv said doubtfully, 'I don't know what that old man can do, I'm sure.'

March said fiercely, 'He's got money. And money can buy anything!'

Aunt Sylv did not argue with that.

*　　*　　*

273

The following afternoon Monty Gould proposed marriage to May and was accepted instantly. They discussed arrangements in a sort of trance. They were both over twenty-one, but he would come to Gloucester and ask her father's permission formally. Everything was going to be absolutely straightforward. Everything was going to be absolutely wonderful.

Aunt Sylv said crossly she wished she had never come to Weymouth in the first place and what Flo was going to say she couldn't guess. Daisy hugged her and told her that she was as pleased as Punch about the whole thing really. She smiled unwillingly.

When May was asleep that night March punched her pillow and stared dry-eyed at her own abdomen. 'I hate you Fred Luker,' she whispered with absolute conviction. 'You promised . . . you promised. . . .' And then she almost physically shut him out of her thoughts and lay down, hands over the place where 'it' must be. She did not have time to think about Fred now. Somehow she had to persuade a great deal of money out of Uncle Edwin. Enough for her to go away on a long holiday by herself. The difficulties were enormous. And not only in Bath either. Mother would protest in amazement at the idea of her daughter traipsing around the country on her own.

March tightened her mouth. She was twenty-four. She was a woman.

A sudden wave of nausea made her hold her breath and when it had passed she was cold and shivering. Oh God . . . she was a woman.

13

Will and Florence found it difficult to understand just what had happened at Weymouth. Sylvia, suddenly cowardly, had gone straight in to number thirty-three, and May, in a state of euphoria, seemed hardly to notice she had arrived home without her sister.

'Mamma — April — Father — it has been the most wonderful week of my life. I have to tell you — I know you will say it is too sudden — but that is the way it was, so I must tell the truth.'

Florence said, 'Darling girl. It is wonderful to see you. Leave the suitcase there, April, and let us have tea. Is March having hers with Granny?'

May settled herself at the table with an expression of bliss.

'Boiled eggs! And no-one's birthday! Oh Mamma, it's as if you knew there was something special to celebrate! Sit by me April — how beautiful you are darling, your hair is so much curlier than mine and when it's loose like that . . . March is in Bath, Mamma.'

'In Bath? On her own?'

'She was anxious about Uncle Edwin and said she had been selfish to have a week at the seaside when she should have been comforting him. But that's not what I want to tell you. I have the most wonderful news —' she decapitated her egg as if she expected a rabbit to leap from it, then smiled as if it had. 'I have met the man I am going to marry. In Weymouth. He is beautiful — he reminded me of Teddy when first we met. But there is also something of Papa about him. His name is Montague Gould. Monty for short. Isn't that sweet Mamma? Monty. It sounds so right don't you think? May and Monty. Oh my dears, I am so happy!' And as if to prove it beyond doubt two tears collected and rolled on to her cheeks.

April was the first to respond. She gave a sort of squeak and flung her arms around May, sweeping both their eggs out of the cups and setting them rolling across the tablecloth oozing yolk. Florence sat very still, staring down at a leaf floating in her tea. Will finished stirring his and replaced the spoon with a clatter, leaning back in his chair and saying, 'Well! Whatever next? Goes away for a few days by the sea and comes back going to get married! To a perfect stranger!'

May was not put out. Laughing in spite of her tears, looking through April's spread hair, she said, 'Perfect is the right word Daddy. Perfect for me.' She turned her blue eyes on her mother. 'Oh Mamma, I do love him so. He's made everything so — so right for me!'

Florence looked up and smiled slightly. 'Wasn't anything right before?' she asked gently. 'You have been our ray of sunshine, May. I did not know things were not . . . right.'

'How could they be, Mamma? All that has happened —' she reached out beyond April's shoulder and caught her mother's hand stretched towards her. 'But now . . . there's a meaning to all that. I know now why I was put on the earth. It's so difficult to explain.'

April said passionately, 'I know what you mean May.'

'I think we do too. Don't we Will?' Florence turned her gentle face down the table. Will shrugged almost irritably, but May knew she had all the support that was necessary. She began on a description of Monty's charms.

Will said gruffly, 'Why isn't the fellow in uniform? Not one of these conchies is he?'

'Of course not Daddy! He has a weak chest and was

not fit enough for the army. But my goodness, he does more for the country than many a soldier, yes, I can say that in all truth Mamma! If you could see him perform —'

'Perform? What is he? Some circus fellow?'

'Daddy, please don't be horrid. Monty is — is —' she knew that he was a music hall artiste, but could guess the reaction that would provoke. 'He is an actor,' she said with dignity.

Only April was delighted with this information. Florence looked worried, Will did not like it. He was suddenly insanely jealous. His sons had been taken from him and now he was to lose his daughter.

'I cannot allow a daughter of mine to run off with an actor fellow,' he said pompously.

May, still holding her mother's hand, responded to the gentle pressure and simply laughed. 'Daddy. Just let me tell you about him. The way he held the audience in the palm of his hand, yet is so alone. No family. I want him to belong to ours. I want you all to feel —' she swallowed and gripped her mother's fingers tightly. 'I want you to feel that Monty is another son.' She sobbed. 'Oh my dears, there is room here for a son, surely? Papa darling, he is completely different from David. So willing to love and be loved! To be with Monty is like being in the sunshine.' She turned to Florence impulsively, hardly realising that April had withdrawn herself. 'Mamma, d'you remember how it was with Teddy? That feeling of happiness — of something exciting about to happen — of everything being amusing and — and fun?' She saw that Florence remembered only too well. 'That is how it is with Monty!'

Florence tried to maintain her smile. 'I think you are in love, my darling girl.'

There was little more to be said. Will asked unanswerable questions about the young man's income and Florence wondered worriedly how May would manage to make a home in theatrical digs, but they could see that May was determined. The questions were shelved until Monty's arrival next weekend; speculation — the enjoyable kind — was embarked on.

April, ready to dislike the young man because he was different from David, was forced to kiss her sister's peach-like cheek. She said sturdily, 'I hope he knows how lucky he is!'

May held her sister to her. 'We are both so lucky,' she said quietly. 'We thought how easy it would have been to miss each other. If the company had not got that week's booking at Weymouth. If Mother had not persuaded March and me to take a week's holiday. It is terrifying to think by what a narrow margin we found each other.'

Will remembered thinking how lucky it was that smallpox had driven Flo out to Kempley. But now the memory was a tinny echo and meant little. In some ways it put him against the match. He looked from one to another of his family; it was at moments like that he felt most alone.

'And as for March . . .' he growled. 'I've got an order for a suit so I hope she won't hang about in Bath too long.'

March continued to rehearse what she would say to Uncle Edwin as she walked past the abbey and began the long climb up the terraces of Bath. Aunt Sylv had given her sufficient money for a cab and checked that she could use her railway ticket the next day, but March did not know what might happen at this interview; she kept the florin where it was, inside her glove, in case she needed to buy food or a bed for the night. She swallowed on a dry mouth: Uncle Edwin had always said she was like Aunt Lizzie; would he now believe that she was also consumptive — a fact to be kept from her family — and needed six months' rest? She swallowed again. At least she wasn't going to be sick. When the saliva ran, that was the time to find the water closet.

She pulled the doorbell with a hand that trembled slightly. She had left a Gladstone bag at the station with a few of her things rifled from the big case she shared with May, and she suddenly felt ridiculous standing there in a linen coat and skirt she had made herself, as if she had called for a casual hour instead of on a desperate mission. But when Letty opened the door and immediately exclaimed her delight, her nervousness disappeared and she was able to lie calmly.

'Letty, is my uncle at home? I took a cab in between trains hoping to have an hour or so with him.'

'Oh Miss March — Miss March! He'll be that glad to see you! Oh this is a lovely surprise I'll be bound! Come in, come in. We haven't seen anything so pleasing since — since —' she lowered her eyes. 'Since you know when.'

March patted her shoulder. She had been the only one of the Rising children to treat Letty and Rose as servants and not equals, and strangely enough they loved her for it.

'Never mind, Letty. I'm here now. Where is my uncle?'

'In the dining-room, Miss. He spends a lot of time there these days.' Letty dropped her voice sepulchrally. 'Where 'er coffin was.'

March nodded as if it was the most natural thing in the world, though her heart sank when she remembered how oddly Uncle Edwin had behaved in that room before the funeral. Letty did not announce her, seeming almost reluctant to approach the door, and March paused before knocking and looked back.

'Letty, is there a fire in the sitting-room? No? Then ask Rose to light one, will you? And we'll have tea in there like the old days.'

Letty paused, one foot on the basement steps. She and Rose both suffered from rheumatism and were not used to coal-carrying any more. But March had a look of the mistress about her, and it was nice to feel there was a hand on the helm again just for an afternoon. Letty smiled and creaked downward.

Uncle Edwin was sitting with his back to the door, staring across the gleaming expanse of the dining-table to the window beyond. The room, which had seemed so bright when Aunt Lizzie presided over meals, was in reality all heavy mahogany and stifling velvet. March could smell the dust. She said timidly, 'Uncle... it is me. March. Come to see you as I promised.'

He turned slowly like a mechanical figure on a stand. His face had sunk cadaverously, his hair was sparse and iron grey, and his eyes, colourless and dull, stared at her expressionlessly for a long moment without surprise. Then he held out a hand.

'I've been waiting for you. Sit down.'

She took his hand, looking around for a chair. They were tucked neatly beneath the table, but when she moved to go to one, he kept her by him, looking up at her. She stood next to him uncomfortably.

He whispered, 'It's time. We've waited a full year. That is enough surely?'

'I should have come sooner Uncle. But you heard we lost....' Her voice trailed away.

He said, 'Your mother wrote to me. You know grief now, my dear.'

She nodded. He drew her closer and put the back of her hand to his cheek. She could feel the roughness of stubble.

He said, 'We will comfort each other, March.'

'If only that could be so, Uncle.'

'Of course it can be so, dearest. Do you not remember our words of last year? That is why you have come. It will take time. It will not be easy. There is a difference in our ages and I am no longer strong. But it has always been there, March ... between us ... the understanding.'

Her lips were as dry as parchment. 'Yes Uncle,' she whispered, hardly knowing what he meant, yet remembering the presents and the kisses and the sense of power.

He droned on. 'Before Lizzie left me, I knew that you were meant to take her place. And then she commanded it.'

'Commanded —?'

'On her last day. She said you were to have everything that was hers. Everything. I did not understand her at first. I thought — her clothes, jewellery. She came to me empty-handed, March, the Rhys-Davies never had a penny.'

'So I understand Uncle.'

'But then I knew. When we stood here together, March, I knew. And I saw that you knew too.' He rubbed her hand harder and she tried not to flinch away. 'Lizzie intended you to inherit *me*, March. That was her last wish.' As he spoke he seemed to be gaining energy from somewhere. His beard rasped on her hand agonisingly and his voice was stronger. March was paralysed with horror. Tears of pain started to her eyes and she swallowed and swallowed again, desperately.

He said, 'I sit here often March, thinking back. And I see that when you arrived that first time, as a child, she recognised something in you that was a facsimile. She began training you then, my dear, to take her place. Talking to you. Telling you about her background. About me —'

'She never spoke of your affairs, Uncle.'

'She was never disloyal, I know that. But she spoke of the way to . . .' he chuckled softly, '. . .to *manage* me. Did she not? Gentle persuasion — did she not tell you to use gentle persuasion?'

The highlighted memory, once so precious and secret between her and Aunt Lizzie, now made her gasp with horror.

'I see she did.' He removed her hand at last and looked down at it. 'My dear, I have made you bleed!' They both stared down at the prominent metacarpals, the middle one traced by a line of bloody graze. Then Uncle Edwin put his mouth to it and sucked. The pain leapt up her arm and she gave a little cry. 'My dear, I am sorry . . . sorry . . .' he kissed frantically with puckered lips and then touched her hand with extended tongue. 'Is that better?'

She longed to pull away and run from the house, back to the security of Florence.

She whispered, 'Much better Uncle. Much better.'

He saw her tears and tried to stand up to take her in his arms. Somehow she moved naturally towards the door and said shakily, 'I've asked Letty to light a fire in the front room. Shall we go in and have tea now?'

She did not wait for his reply but went into the front room. It was warm there, in any case, after the sun of the day. She spread her hands to the blaze of the newly-lit fire and when Uncle Edwin came in she was drawing up one of the many small tables to accommodate the tray which Letty had just brought in. She smiled up at him. 'This is nice,' she said. 'See, Letty has fetched us some muffins. Like old times.'

She must be careful. Very careful. Until she knew exactly what he intended she must give away nothing.

In the event Monty Gould arrived at Chichester House before March, clutching roses for Florence and some precious tobacco for Will and a book of Keats' poems for April. It was a very good beginning.

May's tales of her family had been based on a lifetime's memories and had ill-prepared Monty for the stark reality of the small, plump man wearing glasses, surrounded by three thin women. April had a cold and was less vivid than usual, and Florence, far from being the dark elegant creature May had described, was an old lady. Chichester House itself was too large and draughty and though October was still a week away, Monty was glad to congregate with the others around the kitchen range. Everything was shabby and depressing. Only May shone like a candle through it all. The sooner he married her and got her away from this, the better.

As for the Risings, they saw an extremely good-looking, well-dressed young man. Inclined to flamboyance at first, he soon discarded that manner like a change of costume, and became simple and straightforward. In his wide-eyed frankness, Florence did indeed see Teddy. In his comradeliness, Will glimpsed Albert. When he nodded over the newspaper April sensed her father.

Will said bluffly, 'Have to take you along to my shoot my boy. Robinswood Hill. Nice bit of country and we might get a rabbit for the pot.' He had not gone to Robinswood since his trips with Albert.

'I say. Thanks a lot sir. I'd enjoy that.'

They brought home a rabbit each and Will was in good spirits.

'We've settled it all May. Your young man seems set on a Christmas wedding, so the sooner you see about the banns the better.'

Florence was secretly horrified, May overjoyed.

'Oh Daddy — I knew you'd love him. I knew it!' She hugged her father's arm, sensing that his enthusiasm would diminish if she hugged Monty.

Florence said quietly, 'So soon? I had not thought to lose you so soon.'

It was Monty, with his unerring instinct for saying the right thing, who picked up her hand. 'Please do not talk of losing May, Mrs. Rising. This will always be her home and she will often be in it.'

Will nodded. 'Young Monty has persuaded me that there is a lot to be said for racketing around the country, Flo. They can often racket this way!'

May smiled encouragingly at her mother. 'Listen. I'm going to go up and light the candles on the piano and we'll have a sing-song in the bandy room. I want you to hear Monty sing.'

April said, 'The candles are nearly gone. Shall I light the gas?'

May shook her head. 'No. Just the candles. I'll bring some more.'

When they gathered ten minutes later, April understood May's insistence on doing without gas. The candles flickered on her golden hair as she accompanied Monty, and they made his brown eyes luminous. He sang alone at first, his light tenor sounding like Albert's in the closeness of the room. Then they sang in duet; all the old favourites. 'We have come to the end of a perfect day.' 'Keep the Home Fires burning.' 'Come into the garden Maud.' April watched her mother and wanted to weep.

Monty left on Monday morning from the Midland station. He was playing in Blackpool that evening; it was a long engagement and he promised to find digs for two. They had already advanced the date of their wedding to November.

May leaned up to the carriage window and kissed him chastely and he murmured, 'Thank you for everything darling. They're just as you said — a wonderful family — a beautiful home —'

May smiled. 'They adored you darling. And when you shot that rabbit —'

'I was a gamekeeper in a play once.' He grinned at her horrified expression. 'Nothing else to it darling.'

May wept a little as she walked on afterwards to Helen's. It made her look pale and interesting and Helen, as well as some of the more privileged clientele, thought it was terribly romantic. She hoped it would snow on her wedding day. She began composing a letter to Monty telling him this and describing the snowflakes as 'confetti from heaven'. Perhaps he might write a song of that name.

At five-thirty on Tuesday a telegram arrived from

March. It said 'Married today. New Inn 7 pm. Love March and Edwin.'

Florence read it twice before taking it through to Will in the workroom. He was reading the paper but bundled it hastily behind the sewing machine as she entered. The enormity of March's message did not get through.

'What does she mean?' He looked accusingly over his spectacles as if Florence was keeping something from him. 'Married? Is she married? Who has she married?'

Florence felt a sensation creeping up her spine and knew it to be a species of fear.

'Look at the signature.'

He looked and his frown deepened. 'We knew she was with Edwin of course. But has he had the audacity to agree to her marrying someone? I've never liked his manner where March is concerned, but if he thinks he can step into my shoes —'

'He wouldn't . . . he wouldn't . . .'

'I'm not so sure. And what does this mean? New Inn. Do they mean our New Inn? If she has got married, then she's ashamed of him. Won't bring him here. New Inn indeed?'

Florence said without hope, 'It might be Edwin who has remarried.' She looked through the window. 'Here is April. Perhaps she can help.'

But April could not and neither could May when she arrived. The telegram was taken over to number thirty-three and read to Aunt Sylv and Gran Rising. The former said sharply, 'What does Flo make of it?'

April shook her head. 'Nothing. We don't know what to make of it.'

Aunt Sylv looked as if she might say something signifi-cant, but all that she actually managed was, 'Looks as if March might put in an appearance about seven o'clock. You'll know then I s'ppose.'

'Yes,' April said. There seemed little doubt that March had married someone in fact. And May was marrying her actor. April felt a twinge of something like fear.

* * *

By seven, they were all assembled in the kitchen. The minutes ticked by and no-one came. May dismissed it as a joke. Florence said, 'If nothing happens, you must go to Bath tomorrow Will, and bring her back. I don't like her staying there now that Aunt Lizzie has gone.'

And then just before eight, the door bell jangled in the hall. April flew to the door and in the dim light saw that March stood there alone.

'Oh thank goodness!' She drew her sister inside gratefully. 'We wondered what to expect. We're all here waiting for you — come on.'

March did not hang back. She saved her exclamations until she reached the kitchen door by which time they sounded theatrical.

'Why are you here? Didn't you get my wire? The New Inn at seven o'clock — I wrote it quite clearly and the clerk read it back to me. We've been waiting for you. Edwin has ordered the most sumptuous dinner —' She ran out of breath and took another quickly before anyone could speak. 'At half-past seven he let me take the car and come to fetch you! Yes my very own car — what d'you think of that? It's a Wolseley. Grey with a darling tonneau. April you'll love it! You must come and stay with us and I'll teach you to drive.'

It was Gran who stopped the flow. Her voice came out in a squawk which rivalled her own cockerel back at Kempley.

'You've married your uncle? Is that what you're saying girl? You've married that old man?'

March, her tirade silenced, swallowed two or three times and ran her tongue around her lips. Then she drew herself up.

'Edwin and I have always been close. Yes, close. He

286

is shy and retiring otherwise he would have come and asked properly Papa. He — he needs a companion —' she shook her head at Flo's exclamation of horror. 'I am fond of him. Truly. And the best way seemed to be —'

Will said wildly, 'It's against the law! A niece cannot marry her uncle!'

'There is no blood relationship Papa. We have been married in the Baptist church today. Quite legally —'

'In Bath?'

'We did not think you would wish it to be here.' March slipped off a glove and displayed her ring. Her hand was yellowy white and a scar ran down its length. 'Please don't be angry. Come back with me and eat a meal. Please. I cannot bear it if you turn against me — I cannot bear it!'

There was another silence. They stared at her ring. Then May said, 'Oh March. Oh darling. What have you done?'

March looked at her desperately. 'The only thing I could do! The only possible thing! I have nothing — I *am* nothing! Uncle Edwin has always loved me!' She took a step towards her mother and saw the distaste in the brown eyes. Her hand clenched, the bones standing out skeletally. She said in a choking voice, 'Very well. If you will not celebrate with me — or wish me well — I'll have to manage on my own.'

Aunt Sylv said, 'March — wait a bit — sit down and talk to your ma and pa. Tell them —'

'No!' said March harshly. 'No Aunt Sylv! If they can't accept my marriage, I don't wish to talk to them again!'

Gran spoke in her hard old voice. 'Leave 'er be Sylv. She's made 'er bed. Now let 'er lie on it.'

March laughed wildly. 'It's — a very comfortable bed thank you Grandmother! More comfortable than any bed I shall find with you!'

And she turned and left Chichester House.

*   *   *

October came in wet and windy, the Indian summer giving up almost overnight to winter. It became obvious that the much-vaunted capture of little Passchendaele had cost too much; April heard a rumour from Gladys Luker — who had it from Sibbie, who had it from old Charles Williams — that the German casualty list was far lower than the British. If killing men was what the war was about, then Passchendaele, Messine, Ypres, counted for little. April felt a sinking frustration and guessed that David had felt the same all along. If only she could talk to him . . . he would understand that the events in her family — the high romance of May's sudden match and the sordid pragmatism of March's — were like shadows of the war. David understood things like that.

April missed March more than she had thought possible. When Albert had come home and given himself so whole-heartedly to his family again through March, her sister's happiness had been a revelation to April. She had been permitted to love March as she had very occasionally loved her when they were children. They had talked of very ordinary things: school affairs and the possibility of buying a second-hand car after the war. When the news of Albert's death had driven March into the waste lands, April had always hoped that she might be the one March would turn to. She was home each evening long before May, and tried to do the things May did so well. She cut her sister's bread for her, stirred her tea, fetched a cushion. That guardianship was not only taken from her suddenly, it was proved to have been useless; March had evidently not even noticed April's special care and love.

April felt she might be taking over March's role of frustrated emptiness; looking ahead to May's departure, it seemed almost inevitable. It was impossible to take May's place, with her ranks of followers. April was still too young in Florence's opinion for the dances at the hospital, and in any case May's ready sympathy was not hers. She could have given her life to one of May's pathetic young men, but a kiss and a loving glance were quite beyond her.

She threw herself into the work at Midland Road and felt guilty because she enjoyed it. Gladys put her feelings in a nutshell when she asked one Sunday afternoon as they walked home from the church: 'Don't you feel left out o' things April?'

She did. She felt that the great events of the world were passing over her head.

Gladys went on scornfully, 'There were a whole lot of us weren't there? Daze, you, me, Bridget Williams — stuck-up donkey — and Tolly Hall. An' your Teddy of course. An' I'm the only one out o the lot of you that's doing any bloody thing about the war effort!'

It was true. Bridget was at the high school and Tolly had actually won a bursary to the Crypt School. Daisy was now ensconced at the chemist's and was allowed to serve in the shop when they were busy. She talked high and mightily about getting shop work later on when the baby was old enough to be left.

Gladys turned the knife in the wound. 'I bet ole Teddy would 'a lied about his age and been in the trenches by now!'

April said feebly, 'Don't be silly Glad. Teddy wouldn't be fifteen till Christmas Eve.' But she wouldn't have put anything past Teddy.

As if to reinforce her feelings of inadequacy, Kitty Hall arrived that very evening with a pile of blankets for Florence to darn. Tearfully she confided that Tolly wished to join a group of volunteer schoolboys forming an ambulance corps. The boys had already raised enough money to buy an ambulance and were talking to the Red Cross about the scheme. Kitty's husband, Barty, was inclined to think the whole thing would make a man out of little Tolly and refused to interfere. Kitty had all Florence's sympathy but the only comfort she could offer — and perhaps the best — was a murmured, 'They won't consider it my dear. Boys of fifteen — it would be ridiculous.'

April wasn't so sure. She met Bridget a few days later and found her enthusiastic about Tolly's scheme. Bridget had gradually transferred much of her hero-worship from the image of murdered Teddy to Tolly Hall, who had shared so much of Teddy's short life, and she tried hard to inject quiet Tolly with a little of Teddy's adventurous spirit.

So it was that when April saw the advertisement in the Citizen she was ripe for some sort of rebellion. It said, 'Give your hair to the war effort!' And underneath in smaller print it offered to send one whole pound to the Red Cross for every length of hair donated. The address given was in Alvin Street, a narrow ancient thorough-fare of slums running between Worcester Street and the cathedral. April sauntered that way when she came out of school. The number given was enamelled on a peeling doorway next to a second-hand furniture shop. She intended merely to enquire for further details, but as soon as she opened the door on to a bare, noisome hallway, she was lost. A squat Italian woman appeared from beneath the stairs which rose out of the hall; her eyes ran over April's respectable figure and took in the mass of hair beneath the knitted beret. She said, 'Y-e-es?'

April said nervously, 'There was a piece in the paper. About — er — giving one's — er — hair for the Red Cross.'

The woman's face cracked into a congratulatory beam and she seized April's hands and made a sort of obeisance over them as she overwhelmed her with praise. April could not get a word in. She was led down some basement steps and into what had been a coal cellar. Two or three chairs stood around a tall mirror. A man was having a shave, wrapped in a sheet. April backed away.

'I did not realise — a gentleman's barber shop —'

'We wish to show our patriotism my child — just as you!' She dusted a chair and ushered April into it. 'But how to do it? All we have is our skill with the scissors. Then we must use this skill, yes? Just as you have just your hair perhaps? Now the cover-up —' April was swathed in the sheet whipped from the other customer. 'The hat over here . . . the hair pins. A-a-ah. Papa! Look at this beautiful hair. Two pieces would you say? Three?' She pushed her face before April's. 'How does that seem to you child? Three pounds for the Red Cross. And you will hardly notice it. The hair is so thick and curly it will twirl around your face so and so —' She did things with a greasy comb and April, staring appalled into the long mirror, saw that her hair did indeed twist and twirl becomingly over her ears and forehead. Rather Byronesque.

She swallowed. 'Three pounds.' It was a great deal of money.

'So. We will begin.'

The barber left his customer and came over. Wordlessly he clubbed April's hair close to the neck and handed three large tresses to his wife who immediately went to a table, bound the cut ends and dripped wax on to them from a candle. It took no longer than five minutes. April would have put her hands to her face in horror had they been free. As it was, she clenched them fiercely beneath the enveloping sheet and tried not to cry. The man, still without a word, went back to his customer, and the woman, holding the three swatches of hair up in delight, came back to April. She saw her distress and cooed congratulations while she laid the tresses carefully out of April's sight and picked up scissors.

'Now, my angel of mercy . . . we make you very pretty.'

With small flips of comb and scissors, she began. The hair was taken up the nape of the neck at the back and into a feathery fringe in front. April, swallowing and feeling sick, watched a transformation in the mirror. It took longer than that first frightful severance. Fifteen — twenty minutes. The woman was carried away by her own artistry.

'Now my child. You shampoo tonight. And as the hair dries, you comb it this way. Up. Always up. You understand?' April nodded dumbly and allowed herself to be uncovered and led back up the stairs. She stood in the street outside the chipped door feeling vulnerable . . . cold . . . bald! She couldn't go home, she couldn't face them. May would be appalled and sympathetic. Florence would be horrified. And Will . . . April and her father had not been very close since the David débâcle, but he would still be hurt about her hair.

She scurried from Worcester Street into the Northgate like a criminal. Then suddenly turned past the cattle market and began to run in earnest; towards the Barton. She did not ask herself why; she just ran. It had been a grey, rain-filled day and was almost dusk; a light shone from Daker's window, illuminating the boxes of cottons and silks. She held her side and breathed deeply. Then opened the door and went in.

The bell pinged and the thick smell of cloth enfolded her reassuringly, just as it did in Will's workroom. David was behind the counter, measuring ribbon on the brass rule set into the wood. His customer blocked April from his view. She turned her back and fingered a roll of silk, praying Mrs. Daker would not come to serve her.

Luck held. The customer said, 'That was barely the two yards, you know.' And David murmured something and obviously added another inch because there came a satisfied grunt and the customer continued, 'I measured carefully but there are the turnings and so on.'

'Quite.'

April had not heard David's voice for nearly three months and the monosyllable started her heart beating violently. She had an impulse to lean her head down on to the silk and restrained herself with an effort.

He had to pass her to open the door for the customer, but his back was towards her back and he gave no indication of recognition. Behind the counter again there was a short silence. She waited for him to ask whether he could help her and rehearsed how she would turn and whip off her beret in one movement and say brightly, 'What do you think?'

Then he spoke very quietly. 'What are you doing here April?'

She felt her strength disappear through the soles of her feet and the tips of her fingers. Her carefully rehearsed greeting went to the winds. She only half-turned. 'How did you know?' she asked weakly.

He shrugged impatiently. 'How could I not know. Idiot.'

He looked the same. Gaunt. Still haunted.

He said unemotionally, 'Christ. Why are you here? Surely your father told you never to speak to me again?'

She whispered, 'David. I'm so sorry. So sorry.'

'Did he tell you why?'

She shook her head and he laughed shortly. 'Of course not. So why are you here?'

She said painfully, 'I was glad. Glad. When Daddy refused to let May continue with the engagement. I was glad. I'm sorry David.'

'You'd better go.' He did not move. His hands on the polished wood were clenched. 'Go on.'

She went slowly towards him. 'I've always loved you. Ever since — ever since March's birthday party. I wouldn't have hurt you for anything David, but — but — if you are hurt, I could help you.'

He stared for a long moment, his eyes wide and burning black. Then he held out one clenched fist as if he could stop her advance.

'You don't know what you're talking about, little girl. Christ, you're as bad as your father aren't you? Tarred with the same stupid, ignorant brush! Love. Sympathy. Consolation. You and your family make me sick. Sick!'

He did indeed look as if he might throw up then and there.

She stopped, breathing quickly. 'David, don't send me away. I can help you. You know I can help you, whatever it is that is gnawing —'

He gave a sort of growl of sheer rage and slammed his fist on to the counter. 'Be quiet! Every word you say makes it worse — can't you see that? Christ, I thought you were the one who had a little — a little —'

'Perception. You said I was perceptive.'

'Don't remind me of my own words for God's sake. You could dredge up enough absurdities to get me committed — just as your father would like to get me committed.'

She was horrified. 'Daddy? No — no, he wouldn't even —'

'Just go away, April Rising. Go away and keep away like Daddy told you! Go and tell the casualties at the hospital how brave they are — how wonderful. They might believe you although you don't know what you're talking about. You're fifteen April! For God's sake, you're fifteen — and you come in here —'

She was weeping, not covering her face which contorted pitifully as the tears rolled down it. He groaned.

She whispered, 'I can't help being fifteen. Not knowing . . . anything. I *do* know I love you! And I do know that you don't love me! That is enough . . . that is enough.' Suddenly she remembered something and reached up to pull off her beret. 'I tried to help. I tried to do something . . . *something*. They're going to pay three pounds to the Red Cross for my hair.'

There was a thick silence in the shop. Somewhere to the rear Mrs. Daker rattled a saucepan against the gas stove. David stared.

Then he said, 'Where did you go?'

'A barber's shop. In Alvin Street.'

'You know they won't give a penny to the Red Cross?'

'I did think about that. But I'm sure they will. She —

294

she was an Italian and they're very patriotic. And anyway . . . that was what I intended.'

'So that makes it good? Your intentions were good so that makes the whole thing dinky-doo? Does it?' His voice was savage and she began to cry again.

'David, I know it sounds silly. But you *must* understand. I'm — I'm *trying* —'

'Did it occur to you that *if* they give three pounds to the Red Cross they are doubtless getting ten more out of the deal? Do you honestly still believe that people do something for nothing?' He dropped his forehead suddenly on to his raised fists. 'I thought you were intelligent. That's what I meant by perceptive, I expect. Intelligent. And you're stupid. You're stupider than May and I wouldn't have believed anyone in the world could be stupider than May!'

She sobbed, standing helpless and vulnerable with her hands by her side, one of them clutching the beret. He did not dare look up and see her; the short curly hair around the face that was heart-shaped instead of oval, the drowned violet eyes . . . he willed her to go. To leave him in peace.

But not April. She said at last, 'What should I have done then? Kept my hair?'

He breathed twice then said, 'Gone to the Red Cross yourself. Offered the — the stuff — direct. If they're not actually selling it they probably know the best market. Oh God, I don't know. Go home April.'

She blurted, 'Tolly Hall is younger than me and he's going to join a medical unit and —'

'Go *home* April!'

'I'm nearly sixteen, David. And people can get married at sixteen.'

'If you don't get out I'll just leave you here.' He began to turn towards the door into the little back parlour.

She said desperately, 'All right I'll go. But . . . but I'll do something David. I'll make you proud of me — I'll do something!'

She dashed the back of her hand across her face and blundered out of the shop. She stood a moment, collecting herself. Luckily the street was almost empty and she rammed on her beret and gloves and hunched her shoulders protectively around her naked ear lobes. But from the depths of her misery rose a new determination. She *was* going to do something positive about her life and David would be proud of her. Purposefully she made for the Black Dog Inn where the bus dropped Gladys every evening.

It was another week before April could present her family with a *fait accompli*. They had been appalled and admiring about her hair and it had been May's consoling kisses that had hurt most of all. She could not tell them then of her intentions in case they eroded them with their understanding caution. As May had shampooed with her own special Cuticura soap, first assuring her how pretty her new curls looked, then exclaiming when they were wet, 'Oh my dearest girl, there's nothing here — absolutely nothing *here*!' April had decided to keep it all to herself until she had actually arranged it. And that was what she did.

Eight days later she addressed them as they gathered at the supper table.

'I've left Miss Midwinter darlings. Today actually. And on Monday I start on the bench next to Gladys. At the munitions factory. Filling shells.' She laughed artificially. 'I had to do something about . . . it.'

Nobody argued. May had bought some satin slippers that very day from a girl who worked at Slade's Shoes in the Promenade at Cheltenham and found it hard to think of anything else. Florence extended a hand, smiling a small, inverted, dismayed smile, and April knelt before her and let her denuded head be patted lovingly.

Will said heavily, 'March lost her position. May's giving hers up. Now you. All three girls.'

May protested vigorously. 'Papa, how can you say

that? Poor March was most unfairly treated — that was made obvious when Sibbie Luker was taken on by that awful old man! And as for me —'

Will shook his head. 'I know. I know. Excuses — reasons — for every one of you! But see it from my point of view for once. My business has run itself into the ground. I'd give anything for the chances you girls have had. And don't blame Sibbie for seizing the opportunity March made available to her.'

Florence was moved to protest. 'Will my dear! May was criticising Sibbie for more than that, as you well know! There now —' she dropped a kiss on April's head. 'Let there be no more talk . . . defeatist talk don't they call it? We must be . . . forward looking. May is going to be married to a dear boy who will look after her and make her life interesting. And April is going to help to win the war. What more could we ask, Will?'

Will was in no mood to be optimistic. He said, 'I could wish for my sons. And for my other daughter who has sold herself more blatantly than Sibbie Luker could ever do —'

'Will! Please!' Florence was ashen-faced, the hand on April's curls suddenly clenched.

Will was not prostrate with apology as he would have been at one time. He thumped himself heavily on to his chair and looked at the table without joy. 'Blackcurrant jam again,' he grumbled. 'I thought we might have dripping toast today. Something seasonal.'

May tried to bring the atmosphere back to normal. 'Blackcurrants are very good for you Papa,' she said briskly, taking over the teapot while Florence controlled herself and April scrambled into her place. 'And we shall need to have plenty of it for April this winter. The girls at the factory turn quite yellow, some of them. It's something to do with breathing the T.N.T.'

April began to eat silently. Her news had not had the effect she had feared. But the sudden eruption of resentment from her father had been like a bursting boil. She glanced at him from beneath her new fringe. She knew he thought of her as his special child; she knew he thought that she had let him down. Was there no way that you could please one person without displeasing another?

Muddled and angry, April munched obediently through her blackcurrant jam sandwich. She didn't care if she turned bright yellow. She would be proud to do so. May simply did not understand .

14

March told Edwin of her pregnancy in the middle of November. His delighted astonishment knew no bounds.

She was sitting in Aunt Lizzie's chair next to the fire in the sitting-room; it was her favourite place in the whole house. He held out his hands to draw her to her feet and when she declined to move, he knelt on the hearth-rug and put his head in her lap in an attitude of worship that was balm to her soul. She rested her own head on the antimacassar and laid reluctant fingers on his hair; encouraged, he slid his hands into the small of her back and pressed his cheek to her stomach. She allowed him to stay there while she counted twenty fairly slowly, then said gently through his murmurings, 'Edwin dear. Do you think it is quite safe to put pressure on baby?' And he immediately staggered to his feet, fetched her a footstool, drew a chair to her side and patted her shoulder. She saw that his face was wet with tears.

He said, 'Are you certain about this dear heart? Tell me everything. When did you know?'

'Oh Edwin . . . it would be indelicate to speak of it.' She turned her head towards the fire. His breath stank.

'But dearest,' he was remembering, calculating. 'If you haven't seen Doctor Maine, you cannot know. After all, I have been only once to your bed.'

She took a sharp breath to show him she did not approve of such frankness. She did not let herself remember that one night.

'Edwin. Dearest.'

'You must let the doctor examine you, March. You cannot know for certain.'

She sat forward and held her hands to the blaze. 'I knew that night, Edwin. That is why I have ... abstained ... ever since. I was thinking of your son, Edwin. There must be no risk.'

'March. Child. How could you have known such a thing.'

'I knew, I tell you!' She rounded on him angrily. 'A woman does know these things. And I have been proved right!'

He fell to his knees again and gathered her to him. 'I'm sorry my love. Sorry.' She let him kiss her, keeping still and unresisting as she had when a child. The kiss went on and on. Not until she tasted his foul tongue did she realise where it was leading and pushed him away.

'No Edwin!' she said sharply.

He was thoroughly roused. 'Why not sweetheart? Why not? It is perfectly safe — put your trust in me, March. I know about these things —'

'Is that why your first wife lost four children?' She spoke clearly and cuttingly, knowing she had to put an end to his advances once and for all. He stared up at her. 'Yes, did it occur to you that it might have been your fault? Four miscarriages?' She was all righteous indignation, believing in herself with complete self-delusion. 'My God. I've done my duty, haven't I? I'm bearing you a son Edwin! Isn't that enough for you?'

He was reduced to tears again, holding her hand and begging for forgiveness. Letty came in with the tea things and caught him still at it. She glanced at March, noting the high flush and the hand still protectively across the abdomen.

March said, 'Thank you Letty. Take the coal bucket with you please.' And as soon as the door closed, 'Would you pour the tea Edwin,' she asked. 'I am so tired today. I don't know why.'

'My darling ...' Edwin fussed around her and she

300

watched him with a half-smile.

'I hope you're not going to treat me like an invalid, Edwin,' she said. 'I'm perfectly healthy you know.'

And she was. When the sickness had gone she had recovered very quickly from the separation with her family which she thought at first would kill her. And she had a new defiance too which helped her enormously when Letty gave her those queer looks, or the neighbours cut her, or her life in Bath with an old man became so boring she wanted to scream. She would show them all.

When the baby was born her family would come round: Florence would be unable to resist the call of grandmotherhood. March might drive down to Gloucester in the Wolseley and take them all out for a spin. Yes, she'd show the Risings all right. And she'd show Fred Luker too, dead or alive. She'd show him that she could do better without him. He might be able to transport her to a plane where everything was wonderful, but she'd show him that even after that experience, she could manage — she could manage. . . .

Montague Gould married May Rising in the distinguished Saint Catherine's church at the top of Wotton Pitch. It was a proper wedding. Will borrowed twenty pounds from Sid Goodrich and hired the Cadena for the breakfast. Monty backed a lucky horse and used his winnings to buy real champagne, some of which he drank from May's slipper. The Citizen printed a long list of guests which still did not hide the absence of the bride's older sister. It provided a bit more gossip to add to the story of traitorous goings-on at Chichester House. May did not care. She was so happy she could hardly believe it. As she hugged April in the privacy of her bedroom before the ceremony, she tried for a moment to pretend that she missed March.

'March and Sibbie,' she sighed, adjusting her veil. 'I never thought I would get married without them being

there, April.' Then she smiled at their mirrored faces.
They both knew that March's unhappiness would
have cast a shadow on the proceedings. May hugged
April. 'You're here, that's the important thing. And
after all —' she re-adjusted the veil. 'Sibbie shared
everything a little too freely. Perhaps it is better she
doesn't share Monty!'

They both laughed at such a ridiculous idea and
went downstairs to join Florence and Will. The mood
was one of hectic excitement. Will was enjoying
himself; Monty had won him over completely.
Florence could have wished for a quieter, more
serious occasion, but she too trusted Monty by now.
April, in her long straight muslin dress, came into her
own for the first time. Her short curls, threaded with
a blue ribbon, completed the picture of a Regency
lady. She was confident in her own beauty and knew
the contented self-assurance that May had always
known. Monty's friends — members of the 'Company'
— flocked around her admiringly. She remembered
the scene in Daker's shop just three weeks previously, and knew that the trembling, vulnerable girl of
that day had gone. Her love for David was rejected
but she could still be proud of it. She tipped her head
in a way Teddy had had — 'leadin with his chin' Will
had called it — and smiled as she caught May's
flowers. In spite of everything, she was a Rising and
could rely on that if nothing else.

For May it was a whirl of excitement that matched
the froth on her father's beer, the bubbles of the
champagne. When she and Monty waved their goodbyes through the train window, she knew she had
memories she would treasure for ever. But the future
held more.

Monty kissed her and she snuggled into his arms
without any of the reservations she'd felt with David.
Monty never invaded her. His kiss was companionable as well as sensual. She sighed ecstatically and

302

together they watched the telegraph poles whizz past the window of their compartment hypnotically enchanted.

It was only momentarily annoying when the compartment door slid open and two soldiers clumped in to join them. They glanced coldly at Monty and he thumped his chest and coughed. May intuitively took her cue. 'Is it bad again dearest?' She took the snowy handkerchief from his breast pocket and made a to-do about shaking it out. 'Lean your head back and hold this to your mouth.'

The soldiers exchanged glances. One of them leaned forward. 'It's this fog, lady. Shouldn't be out in it.'

May's smile was gentle and resigned. 'I'm afraid we have no choice — er — Corporal. My husband is on urgent war work.'

Monty held her hand and squeezed it.

When they were at last in the privacy of their bedroom in Blackpool he thanked her and she tried to explain.

'You are brother to me as well as husband. You are everything. I want to be everything to you my darling.'

'You are, May. Oh you are.'

She remembered all the things Sibbie had told her about men and made even the unhooking of her stays into a ritual. Incredulous and delighted, Monty carried her to bed.

'You are my darling. Oh you are,' he murmured. They were a perfect match.

March's letter shocked May as much as it did Will and Florence. She showed it to Monty after the evening performance.

'I didn't think she really loved Uncle Edwin. Not in that way.' She looked at Monty, distressed. 'I assumed it was an . . . an arrangement. For companionship. Or something of the kind.'

Monty shrugged. 'The arrangement was extended, presumably.'

May was appalled. 'You make it sound so mercenary. Like Sibyl. No Monty, it's not like that. March told me once that Uncle Edwin had promised to leave her everything when he died. She had no need to sleep with him for money!'

Monty, bored with the subject of March and her unlikely marriage, kissed his wife and made love to her in his usual satisfactory manner. Much later, however, she returned to the subject as she held him in her arms. 'Monty. . . .'

'Yes, my darling.'

'It would be nice to have a baby wouldn't it? Like March.'

He shook his head against her shoulder. 'Not a bit sweetie. You get fat and haggard and then you go through a lot of pain . . . I couldn't bear that.'

'It would be me bearing it Monty. And I wouldn't mind a bit if it meant having a baby at the end of it.'

'With a maid to do the napkins like March will have?' He kissed her. 'I want you with me dearest. Always. Just you and me.'

She laughed adoringly and kissed the top of his head. 'You're to be husband, brother, father and . . . baby. Is that it?'

'Yes please May.' He glinted his brown eyes up at her before fastening his mouth on her nipple. Still laughing, she rocked him against her. He would change his mind. Of course.

Will's reaction to March's news was red-faced and blunt.

'It's disgusting! She led us to believe she was going to be a companion to the man! They've been married less than three months —' he rounded on Florence. 'Christamighty woman! You do realise this will make us grandparents and cousins in one fell swoop, do you?'

Florence's emotions were far more complicated. She said hesitantly, 'At least it *is* a marriage. I thought

March might intend taking all and giving nothing.' She shook her head. 'I should go to her. I think her pride will not let her come home after what happened that night.'

'You won't get a welcome from Edwin if you go,' Will warned. 'He was always a queer devil. I remember him lurking about when I took the children there first. Hardly spoke a word.'

Florence frowned, finding it too difficult to comprehend. 'Lizzie could never keep a child you know.'

'I do know. And how he must be boasting now. An old man of over sixty.'

Florence made no reply and somehow her silence angered Will more than a reproof would have done. Or perhaps it was Edwin, fifteen years older than himself, enjoying married bliss while he — while he lived like a monk. And in more ways than one. They did not need to make any vows of poverty.

Determined to do something, to break through Florence's reserve somehow, he snapped suddenly, 'I can't run this place any more, Flo. We'll go back to thirty-three. Live with Mother.'

He hoped she would protest or at any rate appear dismayed. But she looked up at him and gave one of her rare smiles.

'Oh Will. How wise of you dearest. We should have done it before. But now, with May and March gone, it's ridiculous to stay here. And Sylvia will be delighted.'

Will went to the door, unable to stay in the room with her any more. Teddy . . . Albert . . . two of the girls . . . and now the house. And she didn't care.

He reverted to the subject of March savagely. 'She's nothing more than a whore!' His voice rose. 'Your daughter is nothing more than a whore!'

That would hurt her. He slammed the door between them and knew that would hurt.

April found no great satisfaction in working at the munitions factory at Brockworth. At first there was a sense of comradeship with the other girls which was sufficient to convince her she had done the right thing. Gladys, thrilled to have a special friend to work with, drew her into the clannish atmosphere of the shell shop on the first day. She was never introduced formally, but names attached themselves to faces beneath the head-scarves: Mavis ... Clara ... Ginnie. They were what Gladys called 'good sorts' and would forge your name for you in the book if you were late and give you a 'lend' of some of their special cream which bleached the yellow out of the skin. Then there was Connie who was a bit of a toff, and went for a walk well away from the shed during the dinner break so that she could smoke her little cigars. And Stella who smiled secretively as she confided what her ma got up to while her pa was away in France. Stella had bored a hole in the ceiling so she could get a bird's eye view of her ma's bed. It seemed very like the Lukers! There was a lot of jumping and laughing.

But this comradeship was not quite enough. April could not treat the whole thing as a bit of fun as Gladys did. She was not, after all, very proud of her bright orange fringe which proclaimed her as a war worker for all and sundry to see. When they missed the bus because Gladys overslept, the orange hair enabled them to get a lift on the light railway which ran direct from the station along the London Road and out to Brockworth. The engine-driver hauled them both into his cab, pinched their bottoms and called them names. April did not find it as amusing as Gladys obviously did.

The work itself was physically hard. Some of the girls could fill sixty shells in a day and sing as they did so. April, frightened to open her mouth in case she breathed down the poisonous T.N.T., could manage thirty shells if she worked non-stop. The stiff oilskins which they wore did not help movement. She was exhausted.

Connie watched her pick over her dinner one day just before Christmas. It was carrots floating in stewed lamb and called Lancashire Hotpot.

'Come on outside for a turn with me youngster,' she said brusquely, climbing over the bench and clumping off without waiting for April's yea or nay. April looked at Gladys, startled, then followed willy nilly. Connie trudged across the gravelled yard where the bus would collect them that evening, and on to the rough grass beyond. Then she felt inside her overall and produced her gold cigar case.

'Come on. Have one. Do you good.' She lit a short cheroot and passed it to April who puffed experimentally. 'You're wishing you'd never come, aren't you?'

April puffed and breathed in and choked. Connie thumped her back peremptorily.

'Sorry.' April's eyes poured tears. She tried to grin. 'How is this supposed to do me good?'

'Nerves.'

They trudged and April puffed and coughed occasionally. It was better out here under a grey sky full of snow than in the shed where they ate dinner. In one week's time it was Christmas and they would have two days off work. In six days it was Teddy's birthday. He would have been fifteen.

Connie said, 'Finished? Time to go in. Tell yourself that the more bloody shells you fill the sooner the war will end.'

April was shocked at the aristocratic way Connie said 'bloody'. She tried to match her *sang froid*. 'Vital war work. Yes.'

Connie shook her head. 'No. That sounds as though you approved of the war.' She ground her cigar under the heel of her rubber boot. 'That's what's getting you down, d'you see? Making these things which will kill more men.'

'Is it?' April hadn't thought that far; she was always too tired to think.

'I expect so. You taught little kids before, didn't you?' Connie grinned, her teeth very white in her yellow face. 'That was war work. You could teach them not to fight wars. Good stuff. Now you've swapped to something else. Not good stuff. So just tell yourself that the next shell you fill might be the one to end the war. You'll be all right then.'

April dropped the rest of her cigar and stepped on it in imitation of Connie. She felt better. Whether it was the cigar or the philosophy, she did not know.

The move back to thirty-three went smoothly, and if Will had thought it a punishment for his two remaining womenfolk he had to revise that thought quickly. They and the three 'other Risings' found it a relief. A concentration of their forces as it were. As Gran said, 'There we was, a-rattlin' about over 'ere, and you a-rattlin' about over there. And 'ere we all are as snug as bugs in rugs. No more rattlin'!'

Florence held out against taking her old room, but when they followed Alf Luker over with the big bedstead, she discovered Gran had emptied it of all traces of her things and directed Alf there in spite of protests. April slept with her mother and Will went into the attic room immediately above them.

Florence said softly that first night, 'Well my dear child, here we are again. Where we started together, you and I. Except that you were in a drawer then.' April loved her mother talking like this and encouraged her to go on. Florence put her head back and looked at the ceiling. 'See the cracks? What do you think they look like?'

April studied them seriously. 'A map of Norway?'

It was wonderful to hear her mother's delighted laughter.

The old terraced house had gone downhill badly in the ten years since they left it. Neither Gran nor Aunt Sylv had much interest in housekeeping for its own sake, but now that Florence and April were installed they all found it worthwhile. With a will the four women set to work. Kitty Hall brought them some paint pots with prison paint still left in them. They thinned it assiduously and began on the hall. Will, giving up all pretence at working in his old front room, walked the streets rather than witness their concerted energy. He had half-hoped that his mother and sister might drag Flo down to their level, but he remembered now how Sylvia had raised herself when she'd stayed with Flo before. And it was happening again. By the time May visited them at Christmas the old house looked sprucer than it had in their day, and May was ecstatic in her appreciation.

'I wish Monty could see this!' she exclaimed. 'You've done wonders. We were so anxious when we heard you were coming back here.'

Will said defensively, 'Why didn't he come down for Christmas May? Thought he might be slumming it? Was that it?'

'There's a rehearsal for the Boxing Day performance.' May kissed her father placatingly on the top of his head. 'Actually I didn't ask him to come. I wanted you all to myself. Just for once.'

Nobody commented on this, though there might have been a connection in Aunt Sylv's next remark. 'Ah. Another new year next week. Nineteen eighteen — sounds kind of queer don't it? Mebbe it will be the last year of the war. Then they'll let my Dick out o' prison.'

Will stared down at his hands and noticed for the first time a liver mark across his knuckles. And he wasn't fifty yet. He'd never stand living in this place with Dick, that was certain.

May said, 'It's strange about love, isn't it? I didn't understand before and now I do. Dear Aunt Sylv.'

She made it sound as if she and Sylvia were in a special club. Yet all the women there knew what she meant. And so did Will.

The move back across the street brought one small ray of comfort to the only man of the family. Hettie Luker still called most evenings to drink her stout in the kitchen with Gran and Sylv. The old lure of warmth and comfort and laughter was gone for him, but occasionally she would mention Sibbie's name, forbidden though it was. He listened avidly and said nothing. In the face of his silence, Hettie eventually became defiant.

'She's got a nice little place down there,' she addressed Gran, but Will knew she was talking to him. 'It's made of wood and it's got a verandah overlooking the canal. You can watch the barges go up to the match works. There's sailing boats now too. One of her friends took her out in a skiff last summer. Lady's life.'

Gran said sourly, 'So I 'ear. Price is a bit 'igh for most of us I reckon.'

Hettie snapped, 'It's no more than what we've paid most of our married lives. You 'ad seven young uns. So did I. An' we ain't got no nice little 'ouses by the water.'

Sylvia said pacifically, 'She was always a generous girl was Sibbie. She used to share her sangwidges with our May and gev her a lovely bottle of bath salts one birthday. I'll always remember that.'

Hettie looked mollified but continued to attack. 'An' there's May going from pillar to post in those theatrical lodgings, not a stick nor stone to call her own —'

Sylvia said firmly, 'May's 'appy. And she knows she's making her husband happy.'

Hettie was silenced. Will stood up and went to the door; there was no more to be heard that night. He said suddenly, 'Daresay Sibbie makes a lot of people happy.'

They all stared after him. And Hettie smiled.

March woke to a prickling sensation in her groin. It was half-past three by Aunt Lizzie's little carriage clock. She switched off her torch and lay down again, knowing quite well what it was and not wanting to admit it even to herself. Doctor Maine had never examined her properly, and had used the information she had given him to forecast that the date of the baby's birth would be June the twelfth. It was now March the twenty-third. Babies born after only six months carrying never lived, so March could not permit her baby to be born just yet. The prickling sensation swept from her left thigh across her swollen pelvis to her right groin. She savaged her lip and turned over. Edwin would never believe her. He'd know . . . he'd turn her out.

But there was nothing at all she could do about it. Fred Luker had impregnated her on June the twenty-third, and exactly nine months later she was going to give birth. The pains grew steadily stronger. She bore them until first light and then rang for Letty, but before the thump of Letty's bedsocked feet sounded in the attic above, she heard Edwin move next door. With a gasp she arched her back and hit the wall behind the bed with her fist. He arrived immediately, hunched with anxiety, his old-fashioned nightcap pulled down to his ears.

'What is it my love? A bad night?'

He came close to the bed and saw March's twisted body and waxen face. 'My God. Something's gone wrong!' His panic was contagious. 'It's Lizzie all over again — oh God, oh God! What have I done to be punished like this?'

Letty bundled through the door and took in the situation at a glance. 'I'll go for the doctor,' she volunteered, pulling curling papers out of her hair as she spoke. 'Get Rose up, will you sir? She'll make tea for madam. And yourself.'

March was alone again. She had never imagined pain like this; she would not be able to stand it for long. It was supposed to go away occasionally, she was certain of that. This was incessant. Every few minutes it flared to a crescendo, but it never went away. It was half-past six now and this had started at half-past three. Three hours.

The doctor came and shook his head at her. 'Much too soon,' he grumbled as he examined her. 'Hardly dilated. Nothing much. I'll send a nurse. Relax for a while. You might not be in labour yet. It's too soon.'

Tea arrived, but March had no spare time to drink. Letty tried to hold her head and put the rim of the cup to her lips, but before the hot liquid reached her she screamed and twisted, spilling the tea over the sheet in her effort to get away from the pain. She was vaguely conscious of the arrival of the nurse, but time had no meaning any more. There was only one meaning. She was being punished for her wrong-doing. It was amazingly clear to her now, that everything that had happened in the past year had been a punishment. Losing Albert had been a punishment for betraying Harry . . . just as losing Teddy had been a punishment for blackmailing Bridget. And losing Fred had been a punishment for that ecstasy in the stable. And this — this was a punishment for deceiving her uncle, and, in a way, her dear Aunt Lizzie.

She fought it until she was too exhausted to fight any more, then she jerked and whimpered and called for her mother. Florence became a symbol of purity and goodness that might beat the evil in herself.

'Mother!' she cried, opening her eyes and seeing only the nurse's washed-out grey ones above her. 'Mamma . . . I want my mamma!'

'Not long now dearie,' said the nurse reassuringly. 'You're doing nicely. Very nicely.' She went to the windows and pulled the curtains across the late afternoon dusk. A small coherent part of March's mind did a sum: it must be fourteen hours since this began. She whispered, 'I can't go on. Why don't I die?'

The nurse actually laughed. 'My goodness, we're not going to die dearie! What a thing to say!' She bustled back to the bed and did something unspeakable between March's crooked knees. 'Time to start work, I think. Yes, I think we can get down to it now.'

March's son was born at six o'clock the next morning and weighed just under seven pounds. Edwin, on his knees in the dining-room, did not question anything. Lizzie had heard his prayers and had permitted him to keep this child. The nurse made no comment and Doctor Maine assumed that Edwin must have known all along. When he came to the bedroom and knelt again to weep on the back of March's hand, she knew breathlessly that she had got away with it. Pain had been sufficient punishment and in the circumstances, although the memory was still too near, it had been worth it. They both looked down into the cot where the tiny boy child slept, his groping hands pinioned within the bindings. His scraggly hair was inclined to be ginger and March had noticed that his eyes were pale blue.

She said, 'I'd like to call him Albert Frederick.'

Edwin would have agreed to anything and he had always known of her devotion to her older brother.

He whispered reverently, 'Little Albert.'

Suddenly March understood how her mother had felt about Teddy. It came to her like an epiphany, startling and clear. She reached down and put the flat of her hand gently on the baby's head. There was an instant connection; he became part of her as he had not been when he was actually inside her body. She leaned down and stared at him. He was ginger like Albert . . . he could be Albert again.

She said, 'Leave me now Edwin, I must feed him.'

'I'll stay dearest. Don't worry about me.'

She lifted the baby and held him to her shoulder as she said calmly, 'No. Leave me Edwin dear. I would prefer it.'

She waited until he stumbled to his feet and retreated. Then she began to undo the bindings around her breast.

It was perhaps because of her intense joy in little Albert, that March began to feel homesick. She and Edwin were now officially Baptists so there was no christening which might have tempted Will and

Florence to bury the hatchet. March's note on the reverse side of the formal card announcing the birth did not elicit more than a stilted letter from Florence saying that they were thankful for March's safe delivery. It was obviously written against Will's wishes. Unexpectedly it was followed by a letter from April sending her love and hugs for her darling nephew.

March begged Edwin to permit her to invite April to stay.

'I realise you cannot countenance my mother and father yet,' she said in a conciliatory voice, although she had refused to discuss their attitude with Edwin at all since the awful night when she had returned to the New Inn alone. 'But April is so sweet. And she would love to see Albert.'

Edwin said pompously, 'I doubt very much whether she would be allowed to accept any invitation I might offer, March. But in any case sweetheart, I do not wish her to be leaning over my son, infecting him with the explosive material which must cling to her.'

'Edwin! She is the cleanest, most fussy —'

'I think not, March. My son is too precious to risk anything.'

That was another thing. Edwin never referred to Albert as their son, always his. It forced March to remember that in fact he did not belong to Edwin at all — a fact which her initial self-deception now made almost impossible to believe, even secretly. More and more she inclined to the more acceptable idea that the baby was a reincarnation of the dead Albert. It made her more homesick. It made Edwin more repulsive.

The summer dragged on. Startlingly, in spite of the Allies making no noticeable headway, it became apparent that the Germans could not maintain their enormous front. Rumour had it that Ludendorff was making some attempt at peace negotiations. In Gloucester, April began to see an end to her work and it was like a promise of light in darkness. In London at the Variety in Deptford, May saw peace as a personal salvation also. In the relaxed atmosphere of a country not at war, Monty's lack of uniform would not be held against him and he would get engagements that were suited to his talents. She might rent a little house in Gloucester near her mother and become pregnant. To be home again and with a baby would be heaven.

And in Bath, March knew that the peace would provide her with an excuse to go home. Not even Edwin would begrudge her that.

15

Saint Catherine's was for weddings, ancient Saint John's for thanksgivings. On that afternoon of November the eleventh, it was crowded with the irreligious hordes from the streets around the North-gate for a special service of praise. Many had not even read the notice outside, but had crept in to kneel in the dark interior to weep for one reason or another. Hettie Luker was there with four of her children, praying superstitiously with crossed fingers for Fred and her other boys. It would be like Fate that would, to keep her hoping for the last fourteen months then pole-axe them all right at the end. The soldiers from the Great Western Hospital were packed into the front; they had been notified of the service and had turned out in what uniform their torsoes could support. The smell of disinfectant combated the woodworm and dry rot odour of the church itself. They sat dumbly, their twisted faces turned to the altar candles perhaps envying the ones who had 'given their all'. Their nurses provided splashes of red and white colour that remained in April's memory for many Armistice days to come. White flesh and red blood.

April and Florence sat near the back, alone at first, then joined by Aunt Sylv and Daze. As the service progressed, not understood by most of the congregation, yet soothing in its very ancientness, April put her head on her hands and wept difficult, repressed tears that made an agony of her throat and hurt her head behind her eyes and felt as if they were wrung from her innards through her mother's old wooden mangle. She wept for them all, May and March as much as Teddy and Albert. But mostly she wept for Florence, who did not lower her head but knelt upright and stared at the starry candles until her pupils were mere pinpoints in her beautiful ravaged face. To April she represented all the losses of the war, and more. She seemed suffering itself.

Afterwards, subdued and silent, they trailed back home. Gladys left her mother and walked with April and Daze; Florence and Sylvia linked arms. From London Road a solitary figure hurried ahead of the Saint Catherine congregation: it was Bridget. 'I had to be with you,' she said apologetically to Florence. 'Mother says I can stay if you don't mind.' Florence laid her gloved hand briefly on the smart velvet bonnet. 'We're glad to have you,' she said.

Gran and Will were in the kitchen of number thirty-three, a pot of tea and piles of toast waiting. Will was half-ashamed of opting out of church, half-defiant. Church was not for him, yet he needed something, some outlet for relief or regret or whatever it was that welled in him. It was he who suggested that they visit the Cross as darkness fell.

'There'll be singing. And they're burning dummies.'

'Pagan rites,' murmured Bridget, her eyes kindling in spite of herself. She was half-sorry the war was over before she could accompany Tolly Hall to France in his brand new ambulance, wearing a nurse's outfit not unlike the one she'd had as a child.

Florence said, 'I think I would prefer to be quiet, Will dear. Take the girls why don't you?'

April was surprised to find she wanted to go. She said, 'Will you be all right Mother?'

'Leave 'er be,' Gran said, shooing them all into the passage. She closed the door on the hubbub of finding coats, hats and gloves. 'We got our mem'ries to sort

317

out. Eh Flo? An' that's about all we got I reckon. Mem'ries.'

Florence gave her gentle smile. 'It's all anyone has, Gran,' she said.

The Cross was jammed with people and Will had to burrow a passage through them for the girls to see anything. Keeping close to the wall of the Bank, they wormed along until they were almost beneath the effigies that were supposed to represent Hindenburg and the Kaiser. From Westgate Street people were still pulling logs and whole trees to heap on the pyre. The fire brigade stood ready to water the walls of Dentons, and the roar of voices singing 'Pack up your troubles' rose to a squeak now and then as railway detonators went off, factory hooters wailed and through it all the church bells clanged incessantly.

The noise literally scattered the wits; tears accompanied crazy laughter, strangers embraced. April found herself clasped to the bosom of an enormous woman smelling of rancid fat. She hugged her in return and was passed back to a man in overalls who was yodelling. The others had disappeared, engulfed in the maelstrom of bodies; it was the forfeit to be paid, the loss of individual identity to the whole. At first April paid it gladly, lifting her voice with the others, weeping and laughing and embracing indiscriminately as the pile of wood was fired and the flames licked around the dangling effigies.

The mass hysteria was so complete as to be physical; she felt that without everyone else around her holding her together, she would literally disintegrate and run into the gutters of the Cross like rainwater. Soldiers, lightermen from the canal stinking of beer, gypsies from the Westgate waste land, housewives and boys and girls older and younger than she was herself, swung her round, shouted at her, grinned and sobbed. The firemen played a spray of water around the fire so that rainbows flickered across the old stonework of the buildings and raucous screams arose here and there as people were wetted. April caught a glimpse of Gladys riding high on someone's shoulders, then Daisy swung past. Of Will or Bridget there was no more sign.

It was licensed madness . . . chaos.

Suddenly April was in a pocket of emptiness; still, panting, deserted. She felt her own heart beating with a heavy metronome menace as she looked into the cloudy, moonless sky. There was a pressure in the air, as if the city huddled around the firelit scene, containing it as it had contained other madnesses. The leaping flames and crazy faces linked Centurion, Conqueror and Cavalier. And now the Kaiser. In a sudden panic she pushed through towards Eastgate Street. Hands pulled at her clothes like briars, but now she fought them off as if she were trapped in a nightmare. Long ago she had lost her hat and her short curls stood on end. She clutched at them with both hands and opened her mouth to scream. And a voice said, 'It's all right April. I've got you.'

It was David Daker.

She held him with her hands and flung her strong young body against his, determined he should not leave her. They reeled backwards and he gasped as his leg took their combined weights.

'April . . . it's all right! What the hell — Christ what the hell are you doing here? Does your mother know where you are?'

'Yes. Yes of course. Oh David . . . I was frightened. And there you were. Like you always were. Oh I love you!' She tipped back her head and bellowed into the uproar. 'I love you! I love you!'

'For Christ's sake!' He backed again and came to a wall where he leaned. In the lurid light his face was chalky. 'You're mad. Let me go —'

'No!' She tightened her hold convulsively. 'You must let me hold you — I don't care if I'm hurting you. You must suffer for me —' she was hysterical. And nearly as tall as he was. She pulled at his neck and kissed him. He became very still, the typical Daker stillness.

'Why were you frightened?' he shouted at last. 'Did someone . . . did something happen?'

She shook her head violently. 'It was the night. No moon. Like witchcraft.'

He nodded, understanding. 'It might have been a night like this when they burned Bishop Hooper,' he said.

'Oh David . . .' she looked at him through tears. 'I do love you. Why don't you love me?'

'Because I mustn't.' He edged back behind a buttress of Saint Nicholas' church and she, clinging to him, went as well. 'You — you're at the Brockworth factory,' he panted. 'Tolly Hall told me.'

'Yes. A year I've been there. David —'

He went on roughly. 'Straight after you came to the shop that time. After you'd given your hair. You little idiot. Sometimes I could kill you —'

Hope was resurrected. 'I don't care about that, David. What did you mean, you mustn't love me?'

'It's my good deed. My one good deed.'

She did not understand him and the cacophony was too great for discussion. She said, 'I wish we could stay here for ever like this.' Her tears were beginning again, the mangle turning. There was a concerted shriek as the ships' sirens down on the canal blasted off in unison. David suddenly bawled 'Blast it! Blast and damn it! I mustn't love you — I mustn't!'

Rockets shot into the air and in their light she saw his dark face descending on hers. He kissed her. Not as she had kissed him with puckered lips and a little smacking noise, but slowly, with penetration as if he would enter her body then and there. She was startled at first, her eyes opening wide, trying to see into his. Then as the kiss went on and his hands moved gently and persuasively to her waist, she relaxed against him tremblingly.

320

And then it was over. He removed her limp arms from his neck and pushed her gently back against the buttress. And left. He did not ask how she would get home, he did not say goodbye. There was a long moment when she felt his pain as an agony in her chest, then he was gone.

She stood where she was, bumped by people, wetted by the firemen's water, her face burning and her body a pulsating cluster of nerve-ends. She did not know what she wanted, only that whatever it was was all-consuming. After a while she began to walk towards her home, and as her passion cooled enough to permit her to think of David without trembling, she knew that she had won him. Somehow. He might try to persuade her otherwise. Because of May. Because of his dark moods. It didn't matter what he said. He knew and she knew.

She reached number thirty-three in a dream of tremulous delight, almost frightened by the strength of her own happiness. And there, where he had crawled, was the body of Rags who was the same age as April herself. She leaned over him, her hands pressed to her mouth to keep back the vomit. He must have ventured too far from his quiet backwater; his rear end was squashed and exuded unmentionable bloody entrails. She ran for her mother and they wrapped the poor body in an old sheet and laid it in the wash-house.

Then they wept together, holding each other as they rarely did. It seemed a final farewell to the war. To death itself. A last sacrifice to the gods. They had a right . . . they had earned the right now . . . to happiness.

Will watched the three dummies burning amidst the rainbow spray of water and felt none of the catharsis of everyone around him. Christamighty, what had it all been for? The ashes floated down and were knocked to the road and stamped on like so many of his hopes. For the umpteenth time he paraded the list of his losses through his mind: old Daker, Teddy, Albert, Harry, his own father. As an aftermath there was the sourness that now existed in the remnants of his family life. May and March gone, little April turned against him. And Flo . . . Flo. Tailor turned traitor. Tailor turned traitor. What was he supposed to *do* . . . how was he supposed to *live*? All he wanted was a little happiness. He was starved, shrivelled for want of it.

He turned to go home, and there, waiting for him, as naturally as if it were a daily occurrence, was Sibbie Luker.

She grinned widely, not trying to speak through the din, not advancing, jostled on all sides, separated from him by linked arms yet unmistakably waiting for him to look round and see her. He felt his face stretch wide and a frisson run through him from top to toe, before someone shoved him on the shoulder and sent him sideways between two shrieking women holding their skirts to their thighs and attempting the can-can. He thought he had lost her in the crowd and then she was lifted high and her face was turned to his again, still smiling, but asking for nothing.

He watched her for a long moment before the hands that held her slid beneath her armpits. She was more beautiful than he remembered, with Hettie's wildness minus her unkemptness. Her mass of hair was loose around her shoulders just as it used to be when she came straight from the pickle factory; but her skin was whiter than April's, her lips as juicy red as always, her eyes violet in the flaring firelight. She was as vivid as the flames and rainbows, and like the flames and rainbows she belonged to everyone.

He caught up with her far down Southgate Street, nearly at the infirmary gates. She had her back to the wall of a house, her arms spread-eagled, the one hand clasping a window ledge as if she was frightened of being swept away. People still milled around, but thinly, and he knew her attitude was a challenge to him. He could pass her by, or he could take her as she was. There could be no apologies, no alteration to her way of life.

He stood before her, panting yet not exhausted. Slowly he put his hands on the wall, either side of her head, and lowered his body to hers. It was like coming home.

She whispered against his ear, 'Are you sure? You must be sure.'

He couldn't find words to reply but he did not move, and after a while she put her mouth to his and he kissed her with a deliberation that was a commitment in itself. She let him finish then tipped her head and began to caress him with her parted lips. Not with Hettie — certainly not with Flo — had he known such an innocently erotic embrace. He slid his hands over her thick flannel coat, letting her take all his weight so that she groaned softly.

'Christamighty Sib! You've got no drawers!' he discovered. They were the first words he had spoken to her and she tried to laugh against the pressure of him. And suddenly he was infected with laughter too. The happiness that he had craved came to him — realised because this girl that he lusted for was as careless and carefree and amoral as her mother before her. He saw the evil phrase 'kept woman' in a new light. Sibbie had been kept . . . for him. To compensate for Hettie, who had compensated for Flo.

He put his arms around her waist and held her to him in a huge bear hug, his beard pointing to the moonless sky as he laughed. And at last she took her arms from the wall and clasped him too, and her laugh became triumphant. She knew she could have summoned him to her almost any time during the past year, but this had been worth waiting for. He had come to her. She laughed with him until they were both fighting for breath. Then she gasped, 'Now Will Rising. D'you want to come and have some supper with me in my little house by the canal? Or d'you want to go straight back home to your family?'

He did not have to answer. They swung down Southgate Street together and over the level crossing into Bristol Road. And David Daker, roaming the streets like a caged animal, saw them and watched them until they were out of sight, with his black eyes narrowed.

And then he too went home, thinking of April. For the first time he permitted himself the luxury of thinking of April exclusively. Surely Will Rising and Sibbie Luker being together meant that he was entitled to think of April without sullying her sweet eagerness. He told himself sternly that two wrongs could not make a right; the fact that April's father had succumbed to Sibyl Luker's importunings did not whitewash what he himself had done. Yet somehow it made his . . . what had Will called it? — perversion . . . possibly forgivable.

And he knew that April would forgive him. That had been the trouble from the beginning. April would always understand and forgive. She needed protection from herself.

But now. Was it different now?

She had responded to his kiss. He sweated when he remembered it. At first she had been frightened; then she had trusted him; then she had responded. She was as unlike May as it was possible for a sister to be. She was completely unconscious of self, where May was conscious of little else. May had married an actor; perhaps together they would enact out the rest of their lives. It seemed suitable. But April . . . April was different.

He walked past the Pump rooms and followed the railway line to Barton Street. His head ached and his heart thumped and he did know what he could do. Then, after all his soul-searching, he remembered how she had come to see him last year, against her father's wishes. To show him her hair. Unbidden, a small smile appeared on his frozen face. It came to him with complete certainty that the matter was out of his hands now. April must know that he wanted her, and that would be enough. Of course he could go away . . . run away. But he knew he would not do that. His roots were in Gloucester just as hers were. Besides . . . he was much too curious to leave now.

As he unlocked the shop door and let himself in, he began to chuckle. He was ten years older than she was, but she had lived with older people for so long that it did not matter. It would be interesting to see what she would do next. Interesting. Exciting.

His mother, upstairs, sat bolt upright in bed and listened. She had not thought the Armistice would make any difference to David at all, yet here he was laughing his head off as if he'd won the war all by himself!

May and Monty spent Armistice night in Piccadilly Circus with thousands of others, and by the time they dragged themselves back to their digs in Kilburn, Monty was as drunk as a lord and May not much better. He would have slept immediately, but she, remembering her dream of peace, kissed him incessantly until he was sufficiently awake to want her.

'We mustn't . . . we mustn't . . .' he grumbled as she moved seductively against him. 'I'm not prepared Mamie . . . don't do that.'

But she went on doing it. 'It'll be all right baby. There. Mamma's baby. There then.'

He giggled helplessly into her neck. 'Have your wicked way woman! I am powerless against you,' he declaimed in a slurred voice.

'Quite powerless.'

She smiled ecstatically into the darkness of the small cramped room. A baby conceived on Armistice night. If it was a girl she would call her Hope. If a boy . . . if a boy . . . Victor. It was all happening just as she had planned.

March, unwilling to wean Albert, was tied to the house that night, and Edwin, dutiful as ever, stayed with her. They watched through the sitting-room window as fireworks lit the sky and Letty and Rose came up the area steps and waved to them before scurrying into the darkness. March held Albert to the glass though he was half-asleep.

'I can tell him later that he saw the Armistice celebrations,' she replied to Edwin's protestations. 'It won't hurt him. He can have his ten o'clock feed a little early to make up for being disturbed.'

'You should wean the child, March,' Edwin said austerely, refusing to move from his chair when she began to unbutton her blouse, though he knew she liked to be on her own during feed-time. 'He is eight months old now and quite strong enough to manage a cup.'

March did not protest too vehemently. She still hoped that Edwin might let her go home for a few days soon. 'I enjoy feeding him, Edwin dear. It is my duty.' She closed her eyes as the first pain shot through her breast. Then it was all right. Even when, towards the end of the feed, Albert closed his new teeth on her nipple she only laughed.

Edwin said, 'You have other duties March. To me. Those you neglect.' He got up and pulled the curtains across the windows though she was behind a screen. He turned up the gas. Her breast ballooned through the opening of her blouse. He sat down by her.

She said in a low voice, 'Edwin. You know how I feel. We have been blessed with Albert. I think — I think that is enough.'

'Well, I do not.' He stretched in his chair, desire making him more than usually pompous. 'You are a young woman, March, and it would seem I am still potent. I could have more sons. I want more sons.'

She held Albert very close. He had never been as direct as this before. She dropped her voice to a whisper. 'We will see dearest.' When she went into her own room, Edwin was standing by her bed, disgustingly naked.

'No Edwin,' she said faintly. 'I cannot. I am still feeding —'

'Tomorrow you will finish. Rose shall take over with watered cow's milk. Come March. Come my darling. Let Edwin take care of you again.'

She had to hold herself against fighting him. Her tears seemed to inflame him and her unwillingness was put down to modesty. It seemed to take a very long time before it was over and he lay panting beside her. She leapt out of bed and donned her nightgown with trembling hands. When she slid in again very gently, he was asleep, still naked and stinking. She lay on the very edge of the bed, her sobs dry now and terrified. At midnight Rose and Letty returned and went breathily upstairs and she heard Rose crooning gently to the baby. Then the long hours of night went on. There was nothing she could do. Illness would mean he would be with her all the time . . . she couldn't bear that. She looked into the future and it was like a long dark tunnel.

Men came home sporadically all through November and December and still there was no news of Fred. Nor Uncle Dick. Nor Gran Rising's sons. Neither Sylvia nor Gran pined however. They were realists to the core and both knew that though they loved their menfolk they were often better off without them. It was different for Hettie. Fred could pull the business together. Fred would sort out his father and his brothers . . . make sure Gladys didn't follow in her sister's footsteps . . . take the strap to Henry when he stole, Hettie needed Fred badly.

He arrived in time for Christmas, eighteen months since he had been home last. He held court at the Lamb and Flag and though he recounted the barest outlines of his life in a labour camp in Silesia, it was all around the street the next day that he had lived behind German lines as a Polish peasant, outwitting the Hun right, left and centre. He presented himself at number thirty-three and was accosted by April, all agog.

He smiled grimly. 'Well. I reckon I did outwit them in a way April. I stayed alive. Not many did that.'

She said, 'We're so proud of you Fred. You and David. You won the war for us.'

He shrugged. 'Dunno about that. Listen kid. March — tell me about March.'

April, sentient in her love for David, hardly knew where to begin. They were in the passage of number thirty-three; no longer was there the delightful privacy of all the rooms in Chichester House. She glanced towards the kitchen.

'She was lonely after Albert died. Then you. We all thought you were dead. So . . . so —'

'So she ups and marries her uncle.'

'Fred, try to understand. They're happy.'

'Have you seen them April? Ma tells me none of you have seen March since she was married.'

'It's difficult to explain Fred. Father was so hurt you see. But we know she is all right. She writes to me quite often. About Albert Frederick. He sounds perfectly beautiful.'

'Albert Frederick?' Fred frowned, looking more like John Bull than ever.

April said, 'The baby. Named for Albert. And for you I suppose Fred. I hadn't thought of that before.'

Fred said slowly, 'My God. She had a baby. That was something Ma didn't mention.'

April felt suddenly uncomfortable. 'Perhaps she didn't know. We don't talk about it a great deal actually.' She bit her lip. 'Actually Fred we haven't seen him. I wanted to visit but apparently Edwin did not think it a good idea because I was working at the munitions and —'

'Albert Frederick.' Fred looked past April into the dim recesses of the passage. 'Albert Frederick. Yes.

That . . . that's nice for March.'

April felt on surer ground. 'Very nice,' she agreed enthusiastically. 'March is going to have him photographed for his first birthday.'

'When is that?'

'March the twenty-fourth. I'll bring a copy over for you to see, Fred, shall I?'

He grinned, his teeth as white as his mother's in the dim passage. 'I can't wait till March kid. I'm getting a new car tomorrow. I'll pop down and see them all. Sort something out.' He reached behind him and pulled open the front door. 'Perhaps she'd like to come back with me. Spend Christmas with her family. Like old times, eh?'

He went into the street and April hung on to the door, looking at him doubtfully.

'I don't think she'll do that Fred. She would hate to come back to this house again.'

His grin was indefatigable.

'We'll see. Wouldn't hurt to get one of the attics ready though.'

April went back inside, still puzzled. But then she too grinned, leaning against the newly painted wall, closing her eyes, turning her face to the ceiling in sheer gratitude. Fred home. And David . . . David in love with her. Her father came down the stairs.

'Hello my little April.' He took his hat from the stand and struggled into his overcoat. 'Are you saying your prayers again?'

'Yes Daddy. Yes, I am.' She felt guilty as she belatedly helped him with his coat. She could always get her own way with Will; everyone believed that. But she would need prayers to help her with this. She said, 'Daddy, even if I do things that might hurt you, I still love you. You know that, don't you?'

He turned and planted a kiss on her nose. She was the same height as himself and more like him than any of his children.

He said, 'I hope so, kitten. And . . . and if I do things . . .

sometimes . . . that don't seem right to you . . . well, the same applies.'

She laughed. How could he ever do anything that wasn't quite right? She held the door for him. 'Where are you going just at tea time?'

'See a man about a dog.'

It was one of Monty's silly comic phrases. Will had adopted many of them lately. 'I was walking down the street the other day. . . .' 'That's no lady, that's my wife.' Flo would tighten her mouth and look reproving, but she knew it showed his fondness for May's husband. For them all. Since the move to number thirty-three, Will was like his old self.

16

Fred drove his new car with care, hardly noticing the bare countryside of winter, certainly not taking any pleasure from it. The car, a bull-nosed Morris, had belonged to one of the archdeacons in the cathedral close and had been laid up for two years because of the petrol shortage. Fred had worked on it for two days before he went to the fuel dump at Churchdown and bartered for black-market petrol. He had no wish at all to be stranded on his way to Bath. He knew exactly what he had to do and had planned the day with the precision of a battle offensive. The element of surprise was everything. He dared not give March time to think, to plan, to scheme towards a compromise. The two days he had spent on the car had been risky; April might have written to her sister to tell her of his return. But Fred had always felt a relationship between machines and the Risings. He had made his first real contact with March through the Delage. If his present car broke down now, so would his hope of gaining March.

He felt his way through the gears, getting to know the machine through his senses just as he knew the woman. At Almondsbury he stopped to let the engine cool. He took two of the cans from the back seat and topped up the petrol tank. Then he went into the George Hotel and booked a room for that night. He sat on the running board of the Morris and let his thoughts take a different direction while he smoked a cigarette and consciously rested. He thought of the miners down in the Forest of Dean and how he would organise them.

There had been coal fields in Silesia and a man who came to the labour camp to negotiate with the Germans about their fuel. One of the Germans had worked in London before the war and described the man as a 'fly one'. Fred had put in a question now and then and built up a fairly accurate picture of the man. He was what Fritz called an 'entrepreneur'. He sold his fuel at very much more than he paid the miners. Yet they could not manage without him. Fred studied the end of his cigarette. Warmth and food. They were basic human necessities which had to be supplied whatever was happening in the world. And war made them desperate necessities. He narrowed his eyes against the thin spiral of smoke. Warmth and food had to be transported. And these entrepreneur-blokes were go-betweens.

It was all so logical that it pleased mechanically-minded Fred with its sheer balance; he saw it as the sources of need and supply being perhaps a few degrees apart, and himself a pendulum swinging between them. At the same time this logical sequence of events conveyed no calm and tranquillity to him; there was an urgency to the business that brought him to his feet. If he could see his opportunity, so could others. This business with March must be settled quickly for more than one reason; he must get down to the Forest. In both cases — March and the miners — there was no time for diplomacy. Frontal attacks were called for.

He found the address without difficulty and drew up behind a grey Wolseley. Letty answered his ring immediately. Behind her, Edwin was settling a magnificent fur coat on to March's shoulders and was himself dressed to go out. There was a short, uncertain pause, they all stared for a startled instant, then March put a hand to her mouth just as Letty said, 'Was there something sir?'

332

Fred said nothing; when he spoke it must be only to attack. March said faintly, 'Fred. Freddy. My God. Is it really you?'

Edwin frowned. 'Do you know this man, March?'

Fred noted the word man. Not gentleman. March swallowed visibly.

'Edwin. . . of course. It's Fred Luker. You remember our neighbours in Chichester Street — the Lukers?' She looked again at Fred. 'I cannot believe this. You were presumed dead.' Her voice took on a note of accusation.

Edwin said pompously, 'Mr. Luker. Yes, the name is familiar. Well, as you see. young man, we are just about to take a drive. However, we can postpone it for a —'

March said suddenly, 'Fred, why have you come? Are they all right at home? Mamma —'

Fred stepped inside, took the edge of the door from a surprised Letty, and shut it behind him.

'Your family are very well March. Very well indeed. Happy.' He saw a door on his left and went swiftly to it. 'Shall we go in here?'

Edwin tucked his chin into his collar disapprovingly. March dithered for a moment then hastily followed Fred into the sitting-room. The fire, banked for their return, smoked blackly behind the guard. Fred glanced around him, taking in the carpet, curtains, upholstery; the sheer comfort of the place brought a grim smile to his face. March hadn't changed. He watched her closely. She went behind a chair near to the fire, her chair perhaps, a spoon-backed velvet thing. She held on to it for dear life and met his gaze with something like fear in her own.

'Why *have* you come Fred? What has happened?'

She expected an emergency; anything else would have been heralded by a letter. Well, this was an emergency.

He waited until Edwin closed the door then said flatly, 'Plenty has been happening by what I hear. But. . .for now, I've come to take you home. Where you belong.'

March's eyes widened and she looked frozen where she was. Edwin gulped in a huge breath. 'Look here my man — you are talking to my wife. If you have something to say, we will listen. But make no mistake, she belongs here. This is her home.'

Fred said in the same unemotional voice, 'No. She has stayed here with her baby to spare others. Her home is with the father of her child.' Nobody spoke. Shock stretched Edwin's old face almost free of wrinkles. Fred gestured at March. 'Go and pack. Get the baby. Come back here.'

March made a small whimpering sound but did not move. Edwin stood in front of the door as if barring it, his breathing very audible, blood now pumping up his neck. He spoke at last, explosively, saliva slurring his words. 'Get out you. . . . That's all I'll say to you, neighbour or no neighbour! Missing in action or not! Just get out before I call the police!'

Fred looked coolly at him. 'Listen. It's not your fault. I could lie and tell you her mother is ill and she's needed at home. But this has got to be final. There's no time for lies. The baby is mine. Mine and March's. I was home on leave in June 1917. Work it out for yourself.'

March whimpered again and slumped over the back of the chair. Edwin, dribbling chin thrust forward, stared for a long time at the hard, pugnacious face before him, then turned slowly towards her.

'Is this true? My God . . . is this true March?'

The question was answered by her silence, her bowed head, the hunched shoulders beneath the fur coat.

Fred repeated quietly, 'Fetch the boy, March. Pack your things.'

There was a pause; the two men continued to look at March. At last she lifted her head slowly, met Edwin's intense gaze and flinched visibly.

'This is my home!' She spoke tremulously to him. 'Aunty Lizzie wanted me to have everything. Edwin you know what she said — she —'

'You. . . .' Edwin spoke on an indrawn breath of disgust. 'You . . . *bitch!*' He breathed out and spittle frothed his colourless lips. 'There was never any love — there was never *anything!*'

'It was mine!' she protested, her voice rising with self-justification as she realised she had said the wrong thing, taken the wrong attitude. March could not backtrack, it was not in her nature. 'You told me yourself it was mine! And, my God, I've paid for it! Deny that if you can!'

'So . . . a whore as well as a bitch!'

He looked as if he would fall over where he stood. Fred said quickly for the third time, 'March, do as I say. Go and pack.'

Edwin rounded on him with a snarl like a cornered animal. 'She shall not take anything! Take *her* with you for God's sake! And your bastard child! But she came here with nothing and that is how she will leave!'

That took the spirit out of March. She clung frantically to the chair as if she would never be parted from it.

Fred's voice was hard as he used words he had used before. 'Stand up straight March! You are mine and what I have is yours. We have a son too. Fetch him and let us go.'

Edwin swung round again and watched as she straightened slowly and began to make for the door like an invalid. Perhaps he hoped she would plead with him, but as her hand went out for the door knob, acknowledging defeat he said pettishly, 'Don't think you can take that coat my girl! Paid for with my money is that coat!'

She stood still and let the coat slide from her shoulders to the floor, then she left the room. The two men faced each other across the fireplace.

Fred nodded his head at the chair. 'Sit down. It's hit you hard. D'you want a drink? Whisky?'

Edwin said, 'If I were a younger man I would kill you. I

should kill you. My wife . . . my son. You don't know what you're doing. That is your only excuse.'

Fred gave a wintry smile. 'I know exactly what I'm doing. I've always known I wanted March Rising and I've got her. Now sit down and let me ring for that woman to bring a drink.'

'No! Letty — Rose . . . they mustn't know.'

Fred shrugged. 'Suits me. She's coming back to Gloucester for a visit then — that should satisfy them.' He glanced at the floor. 'In that case you'd better let her take the coat, hadn't you? If she walks out in the stuff she came in, they're going to wonder.'

Edwin sat down abruptly. 'She can have the coat. Nothing else.' He looked up. 'I can't believe this. She's above you. You're common.'

Fred snorted half a laugh. 'Yes. You're right. But I know March like I know my car. And I can manage her. Just like I manage my car.'

Edwin made a sound of disgust and put his head in his hands.

After a while March came through the door again, carrying Albert over one shoulder and wearing the linen suit, very tight across the chest now. Fred looked hard at the baby, noted the blue eyes and gingery hair and smiled again. Then he leaned down, picked up the fur coat and draped it over March's shoulders. 'It's very kind of you to spare your wife for a visit to her family,' he said, directing his voice at the open door.

He guided her into the hall, picked up the Gladstone bag she indicated at the bottom of the stairs and opened the front door. She waited at the top of the steps as if not trusting herself to descend them safely; he put a hand under her arm and they went down together to the waiting Morris. She did not glance at the Wolseley in front. She handed Albert to Fred and slid into the front seat of the small car as if it were a limousine. Fred held his son, smelled the baby smell of him, looked over his copper-gold head at the slim ankle on the running board, and smiled again.

He couldn't stop smiling, even when March began to cry as they drove through Bath.

'What have you done Fred Luker! My God, I've got nothing! No blankets for Albert. No clothes. Nothing!'

If she expected Fred to tell her that she had him, she was disappointed. He guffawed loudly above the sound of the engine.

'You've got the coat girl! Reckon that'll fetch two or three hundred! Just what we need to start the business!'

She felt as if he'd turned a cold-water hose on her.

'Business?'

'Our business girl. We're going to make money, remember?'

'So it was the coat you wanted, not me?' The old familiar temper stirred in her like a resurrection. 'You're hateful Fred Rising! You come back to life — turn up — claim Albert and me as if we're left luggage! And all you can think of is how much money you'll make from Edwin's fur coat!'

'No. Oh no. That's not all I can think of, March. I've booked a room at the George in Almondsbury. I'm thinking a lot about that. I hope you slept well last night because you're not going to do much sleeping at the George.'

'How dare you speak to me like that!'

'As if you were a whore?' He looked at her sideways. 'I knew that a long time ago March. I've bought kisses from you. I've bought your favours, often. But I didn't buy you that day in your stable, did I March?'

She sobbed, 'You're hateful Fred Rising! Hateful!'

'Because I know all about you?' He stopped smiling and said seriously, 'You're a fool March. The only person in the world who really knows you and still loves you — what more could you want?'

Her sobs died away. 'Do you really love me Fred?'

'Yes,' he said flatly.

'How much?' she asked as she had asked before.

'Enough to make a fortune for you. To buy you clothes and a car and make you the most important woman in Gloucester. I was going to do it on my own, but he cropped up.' He jerked his head at Albert. 'So we do it together now March. The first thing we did together was get that coat. I'll show you the next thing when we get to the George.'

She sat haughtily silent for two minutes. Then she pulled down Albert's bonnet and ran her mouth sensuously over his head.

'You showed me that before,' she said with a curious mixture of repressiveness and provocation.

'That was just a beginning, March.'

That night Albert cried lustily for Letty's attentions and for the first time in his short life was ignored.

'Let him get on with it,' Fred advised. 'His racket covers ours.' He put his warm hand on the inside of her thigh and felt her instant response. Albert screamed in the corner and the bed creaked ominously. March surrendered to Fred with the same fierce abandon with which she had surrendered to her tempers. Her physical loathing for Edwin, her cerebral devotion for Albert, her maternal obsession for baby Albert all went into the long sexual intensity of that night. Fred might know, he might love her in spite of everything, but that did not mean he could understand or forgive. There was a fierce aggression in his love-making that matched her own. It seemed right that it should be orchestrated by the furious yells of their son. It seemed right that when at last the baby fell into an exhausted sleep, they should also feel quieter, more tender.

He said, 'Marcie. Tell me you love me. You've never said it.'

'You know I do. How could I . . . you know I do.'

'Say it.' He held her against his neck and stroked her long brown hair. She closed her eyes and tears filled her lids.

'I love you Freddie. Don't leave me again. You won't will you?'

'Marcie. . .Marcie. I'll never be far away. That, I promise.'

'But. . . . What shall we do Freddie? If we live together — the disgrace! I don't think I could bear it. And Albert —'

'We can't live together girl. I'm not going to make you that kind of important woman. Not like our Sib.' He felt her flinch and held her more tightly, 'We're going to play Edwin's game for a bit. It won't hurt us. You're going to have a long stay with your ma. Tell her what you like. Tell her he's got something catching and you've taken Albert away for his safety — she'll understand that. And he won't start no divorce, you could see that. So we'll have two or three years' grace.'

'Two or three years? Fred, you just told me you'd never leave me —'

'I said I wouldn't be far away. And I won't be. I'll be over the road. I'll be coming over each day to see if you'll give me a hand with my new business. Typing, suchlike. Your ma will be pleased to think you've got an interest. She'll be pleased when I take you and the baby out for a drive on a Sunday afternoon.'

She was silent, secure in his arms, feeling a faint relief that perhaps she hadn't burnt quite all her boats. She turned her head and tasted his neck. There were bristles even on his throat.

'Have you got a typewriter then Freddie?'

His laugh vibrated in her mouth. 'Not yet. It's one of the things the coat will buy. You can choose it.'

'Oh Fred. It's such a lovely coat too.'

'Good job. It's got to buy you a complete wardrobe. You can't turn up at your ma's without a change of clothes. And for the babby too.'

'Don't call him babby please Fred.'

'Albert Frederick then.' He put his hand under her chin. 'Thank you for that Marcie. When April told me

339

that, I knew I had to come for you.'

'Oh Freddie. Shall we go to sleep now?'

'In a minute, Marcie. In a minute.'

The next morning while she fed Albert, he told her the bare outline of his thirteen months in Silesia, but more of his plans to sell coal. At first she was horrified.

'Coal? You're going back to coal-hauling? I thought you wanted to get a char-a-banc. Or another taxi?'

'The boys can do that side. I've got bigger fish to fry. And you can help me, March. Edward Williams is back from the war. I want you to call on him.'

She was aghast. 'I was dismissed from the office!'

'Not by him. He's got cause to dislike the change made by his father.' He grinned sideways at March. 'You know the alderman has paid for Sibbie's bungalow down by the canal?'

'I don't want to talk about that please, Freddie.'

'All right by me. But you've got influence there Marcie. I want you to use it.' He came behind her and ran his fingers down the length of her spine. She said nothing and he reached around and removed her nipple from Albert's mouth.

'Fred — really —'

They tussled and Albert roared.

'Fred —!'

'Say you'll go and see Edward Williams.'

'All right!' Order was restored. 'That was despicable Fred! No, don't laugh, I mean it. It was blackmail.'

'I shall be using it often Marcie. On everyone. It's how business is done. And it seemed to work on you.'

'I don't know whether you're serious or not.' But Marcie smiled too. Because it suddenly struck her that if Fred was going to take on all that desperate manipulation that life seemed to call for, the guilt would at last be taken away from her shoulders. She sighed. 'I hope it's all going to work out as you say Freddie.'

He put his arms around them both. 'Of course it is Marcie! Of course it is!' She had never seen him like this before: jubilant. Another thought occurred to her; the war had taken, but it had given too. Fred had gone away sullen, discontented; an underdog. He had come back confident and assured and very much master of his fate.

She said, surprised, 'Freddie, I really do love you. You . . . you've given me back something. Myself.'

His smile died and he drew back, encircling her still, but leaving her free to lift Albert and turn him into her other breast.

He said quietly, 'You couldn't have said anything nicer to me Marcie. If I don't do anything else in life, that would be enough. To give you back yourself.'

She glanced up from the sucking baby, slightly alarmed. 'But you will do something else in life, won't you Freddie? You meant what you said about the business?'

He laughed again, falling against the bed and rolling about helplessly. She was reminded that in spite of his self-assurance he was still a Luker: lots of noise, lots of laughter, thumping bed-springs.

He said, 'Oh Marcie. . . my Marcie. You'll never change. We'll make such a pair. Such a pair my girl. No-one will beat us!'

It was surprising how well the family took her unannounced arrival. She had known her mother and April would succumb immediately to Albert's charms, but she had wondered about Will. However, after the straight look he could barely restrain his pleasure in his first grandchild. There were a few sarcasms: 'How did you persuade Edwin to let you loose?' and 'I thought you would arrive in your own car and try to impress us.' But they were said with a smile, and he held Albert as he had always held his own babies, with casual expertise. On Christmas Day he did not have to see a man about a dog, and he surveyed them all with obvious pleasure. 'We're beginning to look something like a family again. Eh April? Eh little April?'

May did not come home for Christmas, but in mid-January a letter arrived from her addressed exclusively to Florence. Florence read it with a little smile. May too was expecting a child. She hugged the news to herself for the rest of the day. How pleased darling Will would be, especially if it was another boy. Will was made for family life, for children and their endless routines and demands.

It was a Monday morning and as she carried the smalls across the yard to the wash-house it started to snow, the gritty flakes showing up against the dark grey of the gasometer. Both Granny and Sylvia were out 'doing the rough' at their various houses and she had the place to herself, just as it had been in the old days.

She dippered some hot water from the copper into the sink and began to squeeze Will's combinations, combs very gently. What enormous satisfaction there was in the small things of life, and how everything turned full circle if you could only wait patiently for long enough. March had called her son Albert. Would May call hers Teddy? Flo smiled gently at the thought. How incredible it was, this life. How incredible and how indestructible.

April tidied up her classroom at the Midland Road School with meticulous care. Miss Alicia was suffering from a 'touch of the bronchials' and she had taken over her room and her work. She knew that immediately she left, Miss Midwinter would make a tour of inspection and if so much as a piece of cotton obtruded itself from the tiny work baskets, there would be a stern reprimand. 'A neat classroom is the sign of a good teacher' was one of her many maxims. But April could not summon a hint of impatience for the whole frustrating experience that was Midland Road School; she was too happy to mind what happened in her day-to-day existence.

In any case her teaching days would soon be over. There would be no pupillage at Chichester Street Elementary now; certainly no training college when she was eighteen. She must marry David when she was seventeen and work with him in the shop. In her crazy exultation on Armistice Day it had not occurred to her that David Daker could actually need her. But during her secret and tentative visits to the shop since, she had realised that she could make David laugh even when his leg was hurting him most; and when he was laughing she could encourage him to handle cloth again and begin to sketch designs.

At the beginning of December he had spent a whole afternoon in his cutting room and two weeks later had produced a loose velvet jacket for her with what he called 'raglan sleeves' and a stand-up collar that framed her short curls to perfection. While he had worked, she had minded the shop and was heartily congratulated by Mrs. Daker herself on taking the princely sum of thirty-five shillings in three hours. It amounted to a clear profit of five shillings. In a nine-hour day there were three lots of five shillings. Fifteen shillings a day, six days a week. It was a fortune!

In the New Year when it was too cold for snow, old Doctor Green died of the Gloucester disease, bronchial pneumonia. Kitty Hall, one-time maid and wet nurse for the doctor, came to April tearfully and asked whether young Mr. Daker could make her a loose jacket and matching skirt in black velvet to cover her very ample proportions. For the funeral. No expense to be spared for her dear Doctor Green.

For decency's sake, April held the tape measure while David measured her, then made tea and held Kitty's hand as she offered stumbling solace.

'You're born to this job April,' sighed Kitty at last, standing up to leave. 'You can put Daker's back on the map, like it was in the old days when your father did his apprenticeship here.' She patted her nose and looked at April over her workmanlike handkerchief. 'But your ma's going to get to hear of it dearie. I won't breathe a word. But someone will.'

343

April swallowed her own forebodings on this score. 'I think Mamma would understand,' she said. But neither of them really meant Florence.

Kitty sighed again. 'Wish my Tolly was home. Not only for my own sake dearie, but for yours. I've always said to him that now Teddy has gone, he must keep an eye on you. You and him got on well when you were kiddies didn't you? But what with him going to the Crypt and that Bridget Williams going to high school — well, they seem to be thrown together. She's even talking of joining him in France you know!' Kitty's mouth thinned disapprovingly. 'I told her he'll be home before she's halfway across the Channel! He calls it mopping-up operations, I call it dogsbodying. Those Frenchies are using him and the other boys to skivvy for them in their military hospitals!'

April ushered her to the door and let her smile linger as she closed it, like the Cheshire Cat's. David, hiding behind the cutting-room door, said, 'You're indispensable, April Rising! What should I have done with her if you hadn't been here? Does she ever stop talking?'

'A coat and skirt!' said April gleefully. 'That's seven guineas at least David! Seven guineas!' She sobered suddenly. 'Doctor Green's always been good to us. Isn't it strange — and wonderful — that even now . . .' she faltered to a stop and David put the palm of his hand against her cheek, which was all he dared to do with his mother in the kitchen and customers liable to come in at any moment.

So April tidied up her classroom carefully but with great speed, because David was waiting for her and she could stay there only an hour in case Florence grew suspicious. She slid into her old indestructible melton coat because the green velvet jacket was another of her many secrets, pulled her knitted beret down to meet the collar, and went out through the tradesmen's door into the snow and early darkness.

The subway reminded her of Teddy and Bridget and

March and she was glad again that March was home with baby Albert and appeared to be so content. April was realising her old dream of replacing May as March's nearest sister, and it was with joy — and surprise — that she saw her ministrations being accepted with warm appreciation.

Only this morning March had taken her early morning teacup from April's eager hands with tears in her eyes. 'Darling . . . if you knew. It's so good to be home!' She drank her tea and looked at the smears on the side of the cup with a smile. 'Dear April. You didn't wash this cup in soda water did you? Didn't Mother ever tell you that china washed that way would never hold tea smears?' She laughed at April's downcast face and put the cup down to hug her. 'I'd rather have tea made by you than any other kind, whatever the cup!'

April skirted the park to the Spa Pump rooms so that she could see the beginning of the new memorial to the fallen soldiers of the war. Albert's name would be there of course. And poor Harry Hughes'. But not David's and not Fred's. Her bargaining with God had done some good.

Someone else was staring at the enormous marble slabs piled in readiness. It was Connie. Connie, who smoked cheroots and made the last shell to be fired in the war. April watched her as she stood there, obviously 'County' in her tweeds and brogues, a small felt hat pulled firmly over her hair, hiding it as effectively as the head-scarf had done in the factory. Then she reached into her sleeve and produced a handkerchief and dabbed quickly at her face. She was crying. Carefully, swallowing her own tears, April retreated and turned down Arthur Street. Who would have thought it? Connie had lost someone in the war. How amazing that Stella had not found that out; Stella who had cut a hole in the ceiling so that she could watch her mother being unfaithful to her father.

Luckily there was no-one in the shop, because nothing

could have stopped her going straight to the counter and saying to David, 'I love you. I love you so much David.'

David looked at her, still not believing after two months that it was happening and he was permitting it to happen: the constant secret visits, the interest in the business, the sudden outbursts — as now — of her strangely adult, passionate love.

He said in his objective way, 'Why don't I remind you you're only sixteen and don't know the meaning of the word love?'

'Because you've given up all that protesting. Because you knew all along that I fell in love with you at March's fourteenth birthday party. Why wouldn't you allow yourself to see it, David?'

He shrugged. 'Perhaps I did. Perhaps I encouraged it. To feed my ego. I wouldn't face up to the fact that the one sister found me faintly repulsive, but I suppose I knew that too. So —'

'You are not to talk like that David!' April's colour flamed, not for her own pride, but for his.

She broke the rule that he had made by his example, and came close to him, putting her arms around his waist and holding him forcibly to her.

'David, listen. I think you and May were in love with an idea. May's idea was wrong from the very beginning, but yours . . . yours was killed in the war.' She regarded him straightly from twelve inches away. 'That's why you turned to Sibbie.' He jerked physically and would have torn away from her but she had been prepared and held grimly to him. 'Don't — don't hurt yourself my darling. Did you think I didn't guess? Did you think I didn't know how it was? To lose an idea — to go from the highest to the lowest? Ah David . . . David . . . that was when my love changed, from adoration to understanding.'

He was still now, very still within her arms. She loosened her hold and he stayed where he was, his eyes burning into hers. She whispered, 'On my way here I

346

saw Connie. She worked at the munitions factory. She was hard . . . tough as nails. But now — ten minutes ago — she was by the new war memorial, and she was crying. Perhaps I should be there crying too . . . we lost Teddy and Albert after all. But — but — I'm happy David. It's selfish, maybe it's wrong. But I can't help myself. I'm happy.'

She cupped his head in her hands and he did not resist her. Very slowly she brought their mouths together. She kissed him as he had kissed her two months ago on Armistice Day. Deliberately she built passion between them, making her body soft against his hardness, exploring his mouth with her tongue. His hands came to her shoulder blades tentatively at first, then harder until it was as if he tried to mould her body to his own. And then, when she thought she must cry out with wanting him, a peculiar sound came from upstairs. A hoarse, croaking sound that made them pause, then draw apart and look at each other, she wildly, he with a hint of his ironic smile.

He said softly, 'It's all right. It's my mother. Singing.'

April listened, identified it, nodded and then smiled into David's eyes, so brilliantly that he blinked.

'Isn't that beautiful? I've never heard her sing before. She is always weighted with unhappiness. Oh David . . . isn't that beautiful?'

He did not take his eyes off her. 'Yes,' he said.

'Everything is.' Her face contracted with sudden conscience. 'Except for Connie. Except for . . . so many.'

'There is always beauty my darling.' He massaged her shoulder blades in a friendly way as he let her go. 'Oh April. I do love you so.'

She was radiant again. 'That's the first time you've really told me that David. That's the first time you've treated me like a woman and not a child.'

He smiled. 'You're seventeen in eleven weeks, April.'

'Yes. Seventeen. We could get married then if Pa would give his consent.'

David drew her to him again and kissed her. 'He will.'

'You know he will not. You are treating me like a child again.'

'No. This is one promise I can make to you my Primrose Sweet. If you still wish to marry me when you are seventeen, I will see your father and he will agree to it.'

'I — I almost believe you David! I feel you could do anything!'

'When I am with you I too feel I could do anything.' He laughed. 'But that one thing, I certainly can do.' Another kiss and then he said solemnly, 'April. Will you marry me? Please?'

Her reaction was that of a schoolgirl. And as her weight bowled him against the counter so that he winced with the pain in his leg, he recalled the day of his father's death when he had thought there would be no more happiness for him. He had not known then that as his father had departed this world, so April Rising had entered it, bringing with her an ample supply of the daisies of happiness. And he had dared to be embittered.

'Primrose. Sweet Primrose,' he murmured.

THE END

THE DAFFODILS
OF NEWENT

Chapter One

It was June the twenty-first, the longest day of 1919, and April Rising's wedding day. She woke at five o'clock and lay still in the bed she was sharing with her visiting sister May, watching the morning light around the edge of the blind in their attic bedroom, her body burning with fever one moment, shivering with panic the next. Eight months before on Armistice night, when she had still been sixteen, David Daker admitted his love for her in a kiss which had at last accepted that she was no longer a little girl. Now, only just seventeen, she had penetrated his post-war withdrawn soul, and together they had overcome the considerable family opposition to their marriage. She had no idea how it had been done, but here she was seven hours away from a proper white wedding with her two sisters as attendants.

She sat up very carefully so as not to disturb May who was, after all, seven months pregnant. Naturally May, innately indolent, merely puffed a little sigh and slid a hand over her abdomen. She was as beautiful as ever, her blonde baby-fine hair curled in wisps over her shoulders like the illustrations of Rapunzel in the book of fairy tales belonging to Mother. April smiled affectionately, hoping that she would have children, and as gracefully as May seemed to be having this one.

April's other sister, March, asleep next door with her baby son, had looked so thin and haggard when she had come home at Christmas.

April pushed her feet into the felt slippers Mother had made so long ago, and crept quietly out of the bedroom and down the stairs to her father's workroom where the dresses hung limply from their padded hangers. Her own, cream satin cut on the cross in panels that swathed themselves to her, was March's creation, inspired by sketches and descriptive letters from May. The two attendants' gowns were entirely May's idea, and had been copied down to the tiny roll hems from some Grecian dresses she had seen in Weymouth during the war. They were sleeveless and straight up and down like silken sacks. Will Rising, the girl's father, had refused to make them: 'I'm a tailor, not a French blouse maker,' he had protested. So May had come down three weeks ago and she and March had cut and stitched and talked as they never had before. May, engrossed in her own pregnancy, was flatteringly deferential to March, who had already 'gone through it'.

April let her fingers brush lightly against the fine materials and linger on her mother's grey chiffon, then she moved to the window. Through the frosted glass, inlaid with her father's name and trade, the sun was already warm. She put her fingers to the W. of 'W. Rising' and traced it carefully. She had not been close to her father since he had condemned David Daker two years ago, but before then she had been his favourite daughter. She thought that now he had forgiven David everything would be all right again.

She touched her fingers to her lips and smiled. Of course it would be all right.

She slid the catch of the sash window and lifted the bottom half with infinite care. There was a slight rattle from the weighted pulleys but no squeaks; Mother always soaped the cords. April put out her head and turned it to the left to stare up the street – Chichester Street – to the portly window of the Lamb and Flag leering across the road to Mr Goodrich's dairy. Behind that lay the playground of Chichester Street Elementary School where April Rising and Gladys Luker had sat on the coke pile and exchanged secrets. Beyond that still lay the silent streets of Gloucester: North, East, South and West converging at the Cross, supine in the early sunshine, waiting for whoever would tread them that day, be it Roman, Cromwellian, or the three Rising girls on their way to a wedding. April smiled at the thought, always conscious of her place in the long queue of Gloucestrians.

She straightened her neck painfully and looked at the house opposite, hoping one of the Luker family might be up and about and would pull aside their tattered curtains and wave to her on her wedding morning. But even energetic Fred was using the wedding as an excuse to lie in, and Gladys, exhausted after a week at the pickle factory, would not wake for another four hours at least. As for young Henry, he wasn't interested in weddings. And Sibbie was no longer welcome in her old home. Sibbie Luker was now the scarlet woman of Gloucester and owned her own house and did not care tuppence that her father barred his door to her.

So April turned her head to the right and stared towards the top of the road where Chichester House lay behind its high brick wall. Chichester House . . . where she had spent ten of her seventeen years . . . She smiled and pulled back from the window. She knew now what she wanted to do with her sudden gift of time and solitude. She wanted to walk in the garden of Chichester House again and remember her two dead brothers, Albert and Teddy.

She slid into the hall and reached into the darkness under the stairs for her old Melton coat. Upstairs someone used a chamber-pot and she froze, thinking it was Will and he would come down to investigate her own furtive movements. There was a creak of bed springs and silence. Huddling her coat over her cambric nightdress she turned the hefty key in the front door and eased it open. Morning smells of lilac and baking bread and vinegar from the pickle factory rushed into the house. She inhaled them blissfully and set off across the road for her old home.

It had not been Will Rising using the chamber-pot. He was awake before his youngest daughter, but not in the same house. Fretfully at four in the morning he turned in bed, hunching a shoulder towards his companion, and snapped, 'I'm not discussing it any more, woman! It's too late now. She's getting married tomorrow . . . Christamighty, this *morning* . . . d'you realize it's four-a-bloody clock? I'll have to go Sib, they'll be about early this morning and April's sure to bring me a cup of tea in bed as it's the last time—'

Sibyl Luker looked at the back of the ginger head

8

with unusual exasperation. 'That's what I'm trying to tell you, Will, but you won't listen. It needn't *be* the last time. It *mustn't* be the last time! You know what David Daker is like as well as I do – ' she caught her breath, unable to resist the provocative remark even during such a serious conversation, ' – well, perhaps not quite as well as I do—'

Will growled in his throat warningly, 'Sibbie!'

'Well . . .' Sibbie changed tactics and snuggled up to the unresponsive back. 'Will, darling Will. You always listen to your Sibbie. Why are you turning a deaf ear now? April is only seventeen, my darling. Seven*teen*!'

'I know how old my daughter is, thank you, Sibbie.'

'And you know what David is,' she said, swiftly abandoning her cajoling in sudden pique at his closing ranks on her. She – Sibbie Luker – who had always shared everything the Risings had. She moved away from him, hoisted herself up in the bed and folded her arms over her naked breasts. 'You yourself called him a pervert, Will. Do I have to remind you of that!'

Tiredness and anxiety made him snap back. 'Yet you let him do . . . whatever he did! Is it – is it perhaps that you can't stand the thought of any of your lovers going to someone else?'

Tears started in her eyes. 'Will. How could you say that? I've never taken – I've always shared. I could have made you leave your Saint Florence and come to me—'

'Don't be too sure of that, my girl!'

'But I didn't try! I didn't want that! I wanted you to

9

be happy, Will – that's all I've ever wanted! For you to be happy!'

She was crying in earnest and he turned and gathered her to him. Tears and laughter were always near the surface for Will Rising, they were as natural to him as bubbles to a spring. When they were suppressed, that was when he turned sour. Now he wept and let himself be comforted and then he laughed as she wriggled under him like a kitten and kissed his face with her tongue.

'Sibbie . . .' he crooned. 'Little Sibbie Luker. Kept woman. Kept for Will Rising. All these years . . . kept woman. For Will Rising.'

She waited until after, when he was spent and exhausted. Then she whispered against his mouth, 'Why, Will? Tell me why you've allowed this marriage? And don't give me any cock and bull about it being for old man Daker's sake. You wouldn't let David marry May. And April is your favourite.'

Will groaned, seeing the clock standing at five to five and knowing he must get up and leave for home. There seemed nothing for it but to tell the truth.

'David knows about us. He saw us that night. Armistice night. He told me that if I didn't agree to him marrying April, he'd tell her about you and me.'

She was very still, gazing into his face two inches away, knowing that with his near sight he couldn't focus hers.

'That's blackmail,' she said softly, with a kind of admiration.

'I don't know what it's called. But that's what he said.' He raised his head and drew it back so that he could see her. His beard trembled slightly and his resemblance to the Old King was striking. 'What could I do, Sib?' he pleaded. 'What could I *do*?'

'Nothing. But I wish you'd told me sooner. I could have done something.'

'What?'

'Warned her. Told her about David and me.'

'She knows, Sib. She guessed. It didn't make any difference. You don't understand April. When she loves, she loves. Not even death . . . she's still so close to Teddy.'

Sibbie said stonily, 'I should have told her exactly what he used to do to me. Not even you know that, Will Rising.'

'Oh God . . . Sib . . .'

'God's not going to help you over this. I could have done.'

He massaged her abdomen helplessly. And she lay still and thought about David Daker who wanted one of the Risings so much he was willing to blackmail for her.

Will said, 'Sib, I have to go. Really. Now.'

'Then go.' She gathered the neat square head to her shoulder. 'And Will . . . dear Will . . . I hope it goes well today. I wish I could be with you, I'm half Rising myself. But I'll think of you all the time, darling.' She put him from her and slid out of bed, standing proud and naked for an instant in the pale five o'clock light. 'I think I'll go out too. I shan't sleep any more. I'll walk along the canal bank and think of last night. And tonight.'

'Oh Sib . . .' He grinned as he dragged on his short

summer pants. After all it wasn't the end of the world. Naturally David would treat April quite differently from the way he'd treat Sibbie Luker, and there was a good chance the marriage would work out. If it did not, she could come home again as March had come home. Home to her father who would look after her without recriminations; even with understanding.

And meanwhile he had Sibbie. And because of having Sibbie he somehow had Florence again. His own quiet, gentle nun. His to protect and cherish as nuns should be. No more anger because of her purity, no more . . . degradation. With Sibbie love wasn't carnal and wicked. It was fun.

He strode along the canal bank into Bristol Road. Musing philosophically along these lines, he worried no more about April.

The blackcurrants were as big as the gooseberries and had a bluish tinge to them like black opals. The gooseberries themselves were all ruby red and sweet. April picked them and savoured them slowly as she wandered past the fruit enclosure to the group of gnarled apple trees, standing in the long grass like petrified dancers. How Albert had loved this garden. The long hours of solitude he had spent in it, thinking maybe of Harry Hughes, maybe of his beloved March. He had only to lift his neat golden head to see the cathedral spires where he had sung as a choirboy, and to sniff the air blowing up Westgate Street from Newent and Kempley and the countryside of his roots. April bent and picked up two tiny hard green apples fallen from the trees. She felt she knew Albert far better in death than she had done in life; he was easier to love as the ten years between them grew less. But of course he belonged to March. Just as Teddy had belonged to her.

She hurried down the path to the gate which led into Mews Lane. Teddy too had loved the garden, but as a rampager not a nurturer. Teddy would have gathered the hard little windfalls as ammunition for his catapult. They would have played David and Goliath. She would have stood on the wall and been Goliath and he would have made her fall off and crash into the pile of grass cuttings beneath – several times. Dear Teddy, instigator of so many games and so much trouble and so very much love; forever a child of six years old. Peter Pan. She hung on to the gate and looked all around the garden. In the eighteen months since the Risings had left Chichester House there had been three itinerant tenants, none of whom had done anything outside. The place was empty again and had a derelict air which fitted well with the war-deprived street and the gently decaying area around it. To April it looked like a shrine.

She turned to go into the stable and froze where she was. Walking down the cobbled lane, picking her way daintily on low-heeled satin shoes, was Sibbie Luker.

For two pins, April the courageous, April who had her beautiful red-gold hair cut off for the war effort and worked in the poisonous powders of the munitions factory, would have run. She was wearing her felt slippers, her old school coat over her nightie; her short curls were not yet washed and brushed and she was in a private world of her own. But Sibbie had seen and recognized her and was smiling without embarrassment as if the last two years hadn't happened. Everyone knew about Sibbie Luker: she had stolen May's childhood sweetheart from her, she had taken March's treasured job as secretary to Alderman Williams, she had bargained with her . . . yes, with her *body* . . . until he bought her the small wooden bungalow alongside the canal. And everyone also knew what went on there night after night. Even Harry Hughes, poor dead Harry who had been Albert's best friend, even he had been one of her . . . men. April felt her cheeks flame at the thought. But she couldn't run.

Sibbie said, 'Well, look who's here! Isn't that lucky – I was just going to sneak in and see Ma while Pa's still sleeping and can't throw me out – ' she laughed merrily at that, ' – and I was hoping Ma would give you a message. And here you are!'

April found she was the one who had to make excuses.

'I couldn't sleep—'

'Shouldn't think so!'

' – And I wanted to see the – the garden – just once more.'

'Oh April! You haven't changed, have you? I remember you standing in that kitchen over there – ' she jerked her head towards the back door, ' – and talking out loud. And when I asked who you were talking to, you told me. God.'

April recalled the Sibbie of then, her golden head a shade darker than May's, lighter than March's. She had always been in the house, part of the family, whispering to May, 'We always shares everything May, dun't we May? Dun't we?'

April swallowed sudden tears and said unthinkingly, 'May still misses you, Sibbie.'

Sibbie smiled, pleased. 'Course she does. She'll never have another friend like me. And I won't have one like her. Underneath we're still the same.'

There was a pause, uncomfortable for April, considering for Sibbie. Then the older girl said, 'You see, April, May knew. Long before I showed her, she knew there was something wrong with David Daker.'

April opened the gate and moved swiftly up the garden path again. 'I don't want to hear,' she said. 'Goodbye Sibbie.'

But Sibbie, unencumbered by slippers and long nightie, got ahead of her without difficulty.

'You must hear, April. I've always thought the world of you. And I know something about David that you don't.'

April tried to pass her left, then right. Sibbie grabbed her coat and stopped her. April clapped her hands over her ears.

'I know!' she said, her eyes wide and very dark blue staring furiously at Sibbie. 'I know you and he had – had an *affaire*—' She pronounced the word in the French way and Sibbie burst out laughing.

'Is that what it was?' She sobered and shook April gently. 'Oh April . . . don't make anything of *that*! That doesn't matter. If he was all right that would be a good guarantee for you.' She tried to put her free arm around the Melton shoulders, but April backed away. 'Listen April. Do you want children? Babies?' She shook her again, impatiently. 'Oh for God's sake don't look like that! You're as bad as your mother! Do you want kids or don't you?' April did not answer. She had backed right up to the gate now and was stuck there. She was taller than Sibbie and stronger too, but she could not bring herself to wrench away physically from the confining hand.

Sibbie sighed. 'Well, it doesn't matter. I'm just telling you, my girl, that if you marry him you won't have any. Do you understand that?'

'Go away Sibbie!' April gasped. 'Please go away and leave me in peace!'

Sibbie stepped back and dusted her gloved hands fastidiously.

'Righty-ho duckie. If that's what you desire. ' She put on a mincing, affected voice to hide her hurt. 'Don't say I didn't warn you though, will you? It's that shrapnel in his poor little groin, don't you know. Oh he'll give you a marvellous time – don't worry about that. But there won't be any results.' She tinkled a laugh, stopped dusting her hands and smoothed her fitted powder-blue coat instead. 'Maybe that will suit you. I don't know.' She looked critically at April. 'If I were you dearie, I'd get May to Marcel your hair and put a dab of rouge on your face. You Risings never knew how to make the best of yourselves.' She sighed dramatically and stepped around April and into Mews Lane. 'Toodle pip!' she concluded. And was gone.

May's actor husband, Monty, arrived at midday. No-one had found time to meet him from the Paddington train, so he burst in on them unannounced and in his

16

rôle as one-of-the-family immediately slotted into place.

'Mamma—' He embraced Florence with a sort of passionate reverence. 'Will!' He shook Will's hand in both of his. 'My beautiful sisters!' He couldn't get near them for curling tongs and safety pins. May extended her neck to present her face and he kissed it without embarrassment. 'Darling May. I can see you're in the thick of it. I want to hear everything. May I change behind this screen-thing while you talk?'

In the event he did most of the talking. Will loved it; another man, a son practically, in the house again. He sent Daisy to the Jug and Bottle for beer and did not avoid Florrie's disapproving look.

'Special occasion, my love. Special occasion.'

She looked beautiful in the chiffon May had made for her; like a blue-grey cloud. He cupped her thin face in his needle-pocked hands and kissed her and she laughed forgivingly and fetched glasses.

'Want some help, son?' He passed a glass around the screen and caught a glimpse of Monty's sinewy legs. Some sort of dancer wasn't he? A bit of everything: actor, singer, dancer. And his legs weren't that much better than Will's own short, hairy pair.

'Thanks Dad.' Monty took the glass, grinned, flapped his shirt tail at Will. He knew his father-in-law loved the familiarity. Florence was so . . . formal. They all worshipped her of course, but sometimes Monty wondered just what went on in that marriage. Five children and she still looked like a nun.

Will said, 'How long can you stay, Monty? Time for a spot of shooting on Robinswood? D'you remember the last time I took you up there? First time too wasn't it? You bagged a handy rabbit.' Will had a rabbit shoot on one of Gloucester's two small hills. He never used it now, but he liked to talk about it.

'No R in the month, Dad. Besides I have to get back for tonight's performance. We closed last night at ten-thirty, open again at seven tonight.'

May removed the last pin that had held April's swirling skirt in place and put it on the kitchen table with the others from her mouth. She stretched luxuriously and put her hands beneath her abdomen. The Grecian dress revealed her size for the first time.

'Well . . . we're ready now . . . and in good time.' She went behind the screen. 'D'you want any help now darling?' In the spurious privacy she wound her arms around Monty's neck and kissed him with relish. He snapped his braces over his shoulders and put his arms round her enormous waist. They began to giggle.

March spat out her pins and looked irritated. 'Will you stop it, you two!' She pulled at her own straight tunic, dissatisfied. 'I wonder if these sleeveless dresses were such a good idea, May. I've never noticed before how arms go in before they go out.'

May emerged, deliciously flushed. 'They're all the thing in London, March. And arms are made that way. April don't *touch* your hair, it's perfect! No, not even to put on the veil, I'll do that. I'm the hairdresser of the family.'

Monty folded the screen against the door and they stood around April in an admiring circle. The screen crashed inwards as Gran opened the door. There was pandemonium, then Gran, Aunty Sylv, Daisy and

Hettie Luker crowded in. Hettie liked the way the panels of the dress were on the 'bee-ass'. She said, 'They sort of outline the – the – chest.' She glanced nervously at Florence.

May said matter-of-factly, 'Yes, April's got a nicer bust than March or me. Although mine is all right at the moment.' She laughed unaffectedly and Florence wondered wryly how darling May could say such things with such perfect innocence.

'Well.' March was not enjoying it. She never liked crowds and she was worried about letting Hettie take over Albert-Frederick. 'I suppose we'd better go.' She kissed April's cheek awkwardly. 'Dear April. I hope you'll be happy. If anyone can be, it will be you.'

Her words were significant to everyone there, and April reddened slightly as she returned the kiss. She decided on frankness and looked at her father as she spoke.

'Listen . . . everyone. Just believe me. I know David better than anyone. Better than he knows himself. Please trust me.'

The short speech lifted some of Will's hurt. Of course she was wrong; she had no idea what sort of man David Daker really was. He himself would never have guessed that the dark, suave chap with the constant half-smile was anything more than a reserved young man – a bit like Albert – who would come out of himself in time. The war hadn't helped of course, but he'd been one of the lucky ones really, invalided out before the casualty list could get him. He should have come back to his father's small drapery in the Barton and started the tailoring side up again – with

Will's benevolent help – and everything would have been as it was before. Maybe he would have married May, maybe not. Probably not. But before any decision could be made, Will had discovered David's true nature. He had discovered him and Sibbie in that tiny cutting-room of his behind the shop; with Sibbie spread out on the cutting table like a paper pattern.

Will felt his mouth go dry at the recollection and he glanced at the clock on the mantelpiece. Another ten or eleven hours and he'd be with Sibbie again. Meanwhile he'd put on a good face today, knowing that he was right and that April would soon be home again, weeping and hurt and needing him as she had when she'd fallen as a child. And her public statement – so like April – absolved him of present responsibility somehow.

They walked round to ancient Saint John's. May and Monty had been married at the fashionable Saint Catherine's at the top of Wotton Pitch, but April was a Sunday School teacher at Saint John's and loved the sooty, grimy old workaday church. The Lukers came out in force to wish her well and to admire their own two representatives at the wedding, Fred in his civilian suit and Gladys in a gaudy copy of the new sleeveless creations. Gran Goodrich popped out of the shop, dragging her son behind her, and the patrons crowded out of the Lamb and Flag to raise a cheer for Will Rising who'd had it rough in the past. April held her father's arm so hard it hurt, and Will, thinking nerves were overtaking her, patted her hand with his free one and said, 'There, there, little April. You're not far from

20

home, you know. And the door will always be open.'
And April smiled wryly, relieved that her father did
not after all need comfort from her.

And then her sisters were fussing over her again in
the porch and the dark cave of Saint John's nave was
before her, the sooty windows casting purple and
orange lights over the scant congregation. She remembered the Armistice Day service with a clutch of her
heart; then someone next to the splash of vicar-white
by the altar turned and looked at her. David Daker's
face, giving nothing away to the world, opened for her
with a kind of terror. He couldn't believe it either. He
couldn't believe that happiness could still exist after so
much death and stench and degradation. She had to
convince him that it could and did.

She and Will paused, waiting for the first organ
notes; everyone looked round and smiled at her beauty
and her dress and her short orange-gold curls and
her ridiculous, unfeminine height which dwarfed her
strong, square father. And while their eyes were still
on her, she stretched out the hand holding the tiny
nosegay of primroses, and curved the slender arm
towards David as if inviting him to her. There was a
small gasp throughout the church; Florence put her
ready handkerchief to her mouth to hide its tremor,
and Gran clutched at Aunty Sylv feeling, suddenly,
that she was an old woman. And then, while April
followed that curving arm with her whole body, the
organ notes reverberated, and David turned fully
towards her, acknowledging her gesture, and held out
both his hands and waited like that while she paced
slowly towards him. Then he gathered her to him.

Daisy said afterwards it was the most romantic thing she'd ever seen; even more romantic than the meeting between May and Monty.

The Breakfast was at the Cadena; Will had found the money from somewhere to 'do' for May and April. It was a fairly quiet affair, just the family and a few very old friends: Gladys and Fred Luker, Bridget Williams and Tollie Hall. David's best man was someone no-one had seen before, a man met at the hospital where David had been 'patched up' as he put it. His undisguisedly foreign name was Emmanuel Stein. He and Mrs Daker sat together, looking very Jewish in this Aryan gathering. Even Florence's darkness could not compare with their olive-skinned difference. April sat by the strange lamenting woman who was now her mother-in-law and smiled at her tentatively.

'You don't mind too much, Mrs Daker?'

'Mind? Why should I mind?' asked Mrs Daker lugubriously. 'He has to marry some time and if it must be a Rising then you—'

She might have been going to say that April was the best of a bad bunch, but David, hovering protectively, swooped in. 'April, take Manny onto the verandah. Show him the view. I'll say goodbye to Mother, then we must leave.' They were spending a week in Scarborough.

Manny Stein stood up immediately. 'Gloucester is a very interesting and ancient city,' he pronounced dutifully. 'And I shall be obliged indeed if Miss . . . Mrs Daker will describe it to me.'

*   *   *

March said, 'Don't be ridiculous Fred. Of course I can't come away for a week to the Forest. What would happen to Albert-Frederick?'

'Your mother would be delighted to look after him. Anyway May won't go back to London for a bit.' Fred Luker folded a slice of ham in four, speared it on his fork and put it in his mouth. He spoke through it. 'You've got the perfect excuse, Marcie. You've been doing all these letters for me and I am going down to see the coal-miners themselves, so you could come with me to take notes. Nobody would think anything of it.'

March said tightly, 'Kindly do not speak with your mouth full.'

'And kindly don't call me ridiculous. And kindly come with me next week to the Forest of Dean.'

March breathed quickly. 'Why should I?'

He turned and looked at her, chewing slowly and rhythmically. On her other side Aunty Vi Rising cut her ham into postage-stamp squares and spread each one with mustard. 'Because you're the mother of my son,' Fred said quietly, but not quietly enough for March. 'And because in the eyes of God we are man and wife, and because we haven't been together since I rescued you from Edwin Tomms last January. And because I thought you would want to.'

March held her knife and fork so hard it shook slightly. She studied her plate.

'Rescued me? Is that how you saw it? Smashed my life to pieces – that's how it seemed to me.'

Aunty Vi said, 'What's smashed, dear? I din't 'ear nothin'. What was it?'

Fred smiled. 'You want a row, don't you, March? I wouldn't mind one either. Come down to the Forest with me and—'

March put down her cutlery with a clatter and turned her back on Aunty Vi. 'I don't want to. That's the other thing. I don't *want* to.'

'We all 'as to do a lot of things we dun't want to,' Aunty Vi mourned. 'D'you think I want to stay on at that dead 'ole with the boys? But 'oo else would 'ave 'em? They couldn't come yer. They'd be in trouble afore you could turn round. Poachin's bad enough, but yer, 'twould be out-and-out thievin'.'

Fred kept smiling. 'I don't believe you, Marcie. Remember that night at the George after we'd left Edwin? D'you remember that? You wanted to be with me then, didn't you?'

March did not flinch but the anger seemed to go out of her. She kept her tea-brown eyes on Fred's blue ones and spoke softly and reasonably. 'Maybe I did. But now . . . I've had enough of men, Fred. You don't know what it was like with Edwin. Pestering. It was disgusting. Now things are good. I want to be with Mother and Dad. Quietly.'

His smile died. 'You've had six months with them, Marcie.'

'I want it to go on. Six years. Sixteen.'

Aunty Vi's eyes watered with too much mustard. 'I'll be dead in sixteen years,' she said painfully.

March dabbed at her mouth with her napkin; her arms, naked in the fashionable tunic, were still thin but beautifully shaped. She said with a new assurance, 'This is how I want my life now, Fred.'

He smiled again and leaned towards her, taking her napkin from her hand and pressing the knuckles between his thumb and forefinger.

'If you don't come with me, Marcie, you'll be sorry,' he said pleasantly.

March stayed very still. Vi began to cough.

'Let me get you some water, Miss Rising,' Fred said and stood up. March looked at her hand and saw the dark bruise already spreading.

Monty said, 'May – sweetheart – I'll have to leave. Really.'

'I can't bear it,' May said with every appearance of bearing it very well. 'I simply can't bear it. You haven't felt Victor kick once. Put your hand on him – he must know that his daddy is here.'

He touched the front of her tunic dress lightly and she immediately covered his hand with her own and pushed it over the curve. Gran saw it and tut-tutted audibly.

'You are brazen, May Gould,' Monty laughed, putting his mouth to her exquisite neck. 'You tricked me into having this baby and now you want to show everyone—'

'Baby, darling, honey,' she crooned at him. 'How could a *woman* trick a *man* into having a baby. Silly billy.' She kissed his ear lightly and whispered, 'And hasn't it been wonderful since?'

He lifted his head, pretending to be outraged. 'You really *are* brazen May! I don't know what you mean!' He couldn't hold the pose and spluttered with laughter as he looked into the clarity of her eyes. They fed each other scraps of meat on the end of a fork. Gran muttered to Aunty Sylv, 'If that's how they go on in London . . .' and Aunty Sylv muttered back, 'They're happy, those two. That's what matters.'

Monty said, 'I wish you wouldn't keep calling him Victor. Suppose it's a girl?'

'It has to be a boy. For Mother.'

'It's *our* baby, May!'

'Of course. Why do you think he's called Victor?' May looked at him and the laughter was between them again. 'It was victory night that night in more ways than one!'

Monty said, 'I really have to go, May!'

'You don't mind me staying on a few days? They'll miss April more than they realize.'

'I mind like hell. But I'll put up with it somehow.' He kissed her again. 'No, you're not to come with me to the station. Fred Luker said he'd take me round in his car, and I don't want any sad station farewells.'

May, who had no intention of leaving the Cadena until after April did, smiled beatifically. 'Monty, you're wonderful. I love you. I love you, baby-darling. Sweetheart. Mother's baby.'

Gran said, aghast, 'Look at them now! It's indecent.'

'They're all right,' replied Aunty Sylv.

April said, 'The Cloisters have a very beautiful fan vaulted ceiling . . . Did you know David before the hospital, Mr Stein?'

'No, Miss . . . Mrs Daker. And only two weeks in

the hospital. We were the only two Jewish patients, you see.'

'I see.' David had never made friends easily; perhaps his army friends had been killed. That he should be forced to choose this stranger to stand by him at his wedding was evidence of his . . . alone-ness. She swallowed on the pain of it. He would never be alone again.

'To the right you can see where Bishop Hooper was burned,' she said huskily.

'Hooper?'

'Reformation. One of our – Anglican – martyrs.' April straightened and took a deep breath. It was hot beneath the glass of the verandah and the potted palms smelled of mushrooms. 'He was burned at the stake. He burned and burned but would not die.' She turned away. 'He did eventually, of course.'

'David tells me you are a teacher, Mrs Daker.'

'A pupil teacher. That is all.'

'You should go to college and become trained.'

'Married women teachers are not allowed in Gloucester,' she said shortly.

'Ah. I see. So you help David with the small shop, yes?'

Why did he make it sound second-rate? 'Yes. Oh most certainly. Yes.' She smiled, trying to show him that nothing could be more wonderful than helping David with the small shop. He blinked, dazzled. David Daker had told him of the Rising girls, their two dead brothers, their ill-assorted parents. He had been disappointed: the father was stocky, bulldog, a typical British type; the mother, far from being beautiful, was thin and bent though she still had a certain elegance. The brothers – how could he know? But the girls themselves were merely fair and pretty and under-nourished. Until now. Suddenly he saw this one, as . . . quite extraordinary.

David said, 'Christ. When will this be over?'

'Soon, my darling. I'll get out of this ridiculous dress and we'll catch Fred as soon as he gets back from taking Monty to the station.'

'And everyone will come with us and throw rice. And that dress is not ridiculous. It is virginal and very pro-vocative. It is moulded rather than sewn. I shall get the pattern from May and make all your dresses from it.'

'We can catch an earlier train and change at Cheltenham. Let's do that, David.'

'I love you, Primrose Sweet. I love you. I love you. I love you.'

'David, stop it. You don't have to . . . it's *happening*. Just believe that and everything will be wonderful.'

'What's the matter? Something has happened. What is it?'

She almost told him about Sibbie. Maybe she would. Later. When they were at Scarborough. Tonight.

'Nothing. Everything is perfect. I love you. Oh, David, I do love you so much. Ever since that first time. When I was five—' She recalled him waiting for her on the landing outside the bathroom door at Chichester House. Full of menace and glorious attraction. Devil Daker she had called him. She shook.

He whispered, 'I feel like Mr Rochester marrying Jane Eyre when he's got a mad wife locked in an upstairs room.'

She knew exactly what he meant but she still whispered back, 'You haven't got a wife – anywhere. Have you?'

'No. But there's something mad somewhere.'

She looked into his dark, secret face and her heart accelerated.

'That's what makes it . . . like it is,' she said in a low voice. He encircled her wrist with thumb and forefinger and felt her pulse race. He squeezed, his eyes on her face. She smiled at him. He, too, blinked.

Fred did not wait at the Great Western Railway station and Monty walked the length of the Up platform, counting the Mazawattee tea signs just as his sister-in-law had before him, and hating the hiatus between one life and another. May's deliberate provocation had made him tingle, and he cursed himself for not demanding her immediate return to their shabby London digs. He ran through his two numbers for tonight's show: 'I love you dearly, dearly and I hope that you love me,' May's favourite; and 'Come into the garden Maud,' which he would sing with Maud Davenport. May pretended to be jealous of Maud, but knew there was no need to be. Darling May. Beautiful, wonderful May, who could enter into any rôle he chose to play. He paced past a bench full of waiting passengers and automatically straightened his back, pushed his bowler to the back of his head, lightened his step. There was an altercation at the ticket barrier and a young woman in a blue single-button coat, with a cloche right over her ears and a fringe into her eyes, hurried through. She reminded him of May; almost as fair, almost as blue-eyed, certainly slimmer around the middle. She came up to him breathlessly.

'Is it Monty?' She parted full lips and her tongue and teeth glistened visibly. 'I met my brother – you left your brolly in his taxi!' She produced an umbrella with a flourish. It wasn't his. He considered an umbrella made him look like a businessman instead of an actor. He said, 'You must be . . .'

'Sibbie Luker. May's erstwhile friend.' Sibbie laughed. 'Don't be frightened. I won't eat you.'

If it had been anyone else, Monty might have donned his man-of-the-world rôle. But Sibbie Luker was different. She had hurt May.

He said coldly, 'It's not mine. The umbrella.' He raised his bowler courteously. 'I'm sorry you have had an unnecessary walk. Good day.'

Sibbie stared at him, her mouth even wider.

'My God. You're cutting me. Aren't you? May's husband – cutting her best friend!'

'Good day, Miss Luker.'

'May would hate you for it.'

He turned and walked up the platform past the bench. She was one step behind him, talking still. Heads turned.

'It's no good. You can't get away from me. I didn't have a walk here. I had a run. And I do not run after men, they run after me.'

He was furious. 'Not this one, Miss Luker. I am May's husband.'

'Ah!' She stopped suddenly and her exclamation made him stop too. The people on the bench tried to look away. 'Ah,' Sibbie repeated. 'So. That is how you see yourself, is it? Of course you have no background of your own, have you? So May is not your wife first and foremost, you are her husband. Loyal. True. Good son-in-law to William and Florence Rising, brother-in-law to April and March.' She put a long gloved finger to her full bottom lip. 'What does that make our relationship, I wonder?' She held up a hand, palm facing him. 'Of course we have a relationship. I am half Rising, I have always shared everything with May—'

'So I heard,' he interjected against his better judgement.

'Ah, so you know about David.' She laughed, bending over, her hand now on her beautifully flat abdomen. 'But you don't know about the . . . other connection.' She straightened and sobered and considered him, narrow-eyed. 'I could tell you, I suppose. You wouldn't let on in case it hurt May. Maybe I will tell you one day, then you'd see that there is some relationship between us. But not now. Here's your train anyway.'

It came puffing in, filling the station with sooty smoke and heat. People got up and porters cantered nonchalantly alongside the running board. He went to an empty carriage and swung himself in. She was behind him.

'Look here—' he began angrily. Another passenger pushed in behind and Sibbie cannoned into Monty and held them both upright.

'Darling Monty. I really must go,' she said as if he were detaining her. 'Have a good journey. Are you sure about the umbrella?'

He hadn't felt such a complete ass since he'd been sent those damned white feathers in 1917. He shoved her to the door where she clung, laughing into his face. The man behind said jovially, 'Better close the door, lady! Give him a kiss quick!'

Sibbie obeyed, planting her open mouth over Monty's and flicking her tongue across his cringing lips before she turned and leapt gracefully to the platform.

'Goodbye darling. Hope you can sleep without me!'

She skipped up the platform and through the barrier, waving the umbrella like a sword. Monty sat down, hot and dishevelled and thoroughly out of countenance.

Once in London Road again, Sibbie's smile disappeared.

'One day it'll be different, my lad,' she murmured, making for the Cross where she would be able to see them leave the Cadena. 'One day I'll be head of that family. You'll see.'

It had been a long journey and they arrived at the tiny boarding house near the harbour very late, so there was no supper, not even a cup of cocoa. David undressed in the large draughty bathroom and put on his new pyjamas and the dressing gown he'd had in hospital and padded back down the landing. April peered over the top of the sheet, looking about twelve years old.

'Darling, don't look like that. It's late and we're tired. Go to sleep.' He wondered how he'd summoned the evil courage to marry her. He pulled back the covers to climb in beside her. She was naked.

'April!'

'Don't make me ashamed,' she whispered. 'I knew you'd say it was late. I knew—'

'Oh April. My darling girl. You don't have to. We've got all our lives—'

'I want to, David. I want *you*. Everyone saying I'm so young and thinking I just want you to look after me. It's so *funny*. Honestly, David, what I said back at the Cadena was true. I've wanted you – *wanted* you – since I was five years old.'

'It's a physical impossibility.' He began to stroke her body with his left hand, holding her with his right. He put his fingers lightly on her chin and followed an invisible line beneath it, down her neck, between her breasts, over her abdomen and back again.

'David. Please—' she said urgently.

'Plenty of time, Primrose. Plenty of time.'

She shivered and shook as if she had an ague. At last he slid his fingers between her legs and kissed her as she groaned in ecstasy. Much later he whispered, 'Is that enough, my darling?'

'I'm tired, David. I'm tired.'

'Then that's enough. Go to sleep, Primrose.'

'David, it was lovely. But why—'

'I told you. There's time. You were happy, darling?'

'Yes. Yes of course.'

It was true. But she also felt a faint shame. And something else. Was it fear? She turned over and pressed herself against his pyjamas and felt him wince as his leg hurt. She wouldn't tell him about Sibbie. Not now. Perhaps not ever. He held her and kissed her and told her he worshipped her. The shame went away. She slept.

Chapter Two

Fred Luker thought long and hard about March Tomms' repudiation of him at the wedding. In one way it suited him well; he was an ambitious man determined to make a great deal of money in the shortest possible time, and a divorce scandal would not help his business interests. If March had begged him to end the farcical muddle of her marriage to her great-uncle, he would have done so because he loved her. But he could love her just as easily while she was in the ambivalent position she was in now. Only he, Edwin Tomms her husband, and March herself, knew that her marriage was at an end. Edwin was a minor public figure in his home town of Bath and, ironically, wished to avoid a scandal as much as Fred did. Ostensibly March was paying a protracted visit to her old home to help her mother who was not strong; it was lucky in a way that Florence had not been strong since her last pregnancy sixteen years ago. Nobody thought it odd that although she had April, Gran Rising and Aunty Sylv to help run the small house in Chichester Street, she should also need her eldest daughter plus her first grandchild, Albert-Frederick.

Yes, the arrangement suited Fred Luker very well. He had March and her son under his eye without having to provide a home for them. It was March's attitude recently which was fast getting under his skin.

Fred had been obsessed with March Rising since he was sixteen years old. She had picked him up, dropped him, used him shamelessly; he had smarted and trembled and waited for her . . . until 1917. He had come home on leave after her brother Albert's death in the Somme, and found March changed for ever. The spiky independence he had loved had been beaten out of her by grief; she was withdrawn, half mad, contemplating suicide. She had turned to him then, thankful to be able to surrender her tortured spirit to someone who knew her as well as he did, who accepted her failings and loved her for them. And when he had returned from the dead last Christmas and driven down to Bath to take her – by force if necessary – from her marriage of convenience, she had turned to him again, giving herself to him with a joyful abandon that meant – that must have meant – she loved him.

And since then . . . what had happened? He had talked to her about his business prospects, not only in an effort to take her out of herself, but because he needed her interest and encouragement; she had been patently bored. He had asked her to contact her old employer, Mr Edward Williams, with a view to a loan. It wouldn't have been difficult, Bridget Williams was April's best friend. But she hadn't done it. He had wanted her to buy a typewriter so that she could use her skills in writing letters for him; she had shelved the whole idea. And now, when he had swallowed his pride yet again and asked her to spend a few days with him in Dean Forest, she had turned him down flat. He was back to square one: trailing round after March's favours like the love-sick oaf he had been before the war. And he too had changed since the war; since he had returned from the Silesian prison camp alive, *and* in his right mind. Yes, he was quite a different kettle of fish from the Fred Luker of pre-1914 who had tended his father's dray horse and tinkered with cars in his spare time and smelled accordingly.

So on the Monday morning following April's wedding, he drove once more to Bath, taking the same route he'd taken before when he'd gone to fetch March from her husband-uncle. His mood too was not dissimilar. There was a small, calculating smile on his normally rather set face, and his pale blue Luker eyes were narrowed in thought as well as against the strong June sunshine. He was almost certain he had found a way to kill two birds with one stone. He needed ready cash; and he needed to teach March a lesson. Maybe, with luck, the two went together.

He changed into second gear to take the long hill down into the heart of Bristol and his smile widened as the small, bull-nosed Morris edged its way around the drays and vans delivering in Whiteladies Road. Not so long ago he had driven his father's dray, sitting up behind the carthorse, catching the flies she flicked off with her tail. A servant: that's what he had been, no more than a servant. When he had bought the Army transport truck at the surplus sale in Aldershot, converted it into a charry and used it for outings and excursions, he was still a servant. His father insisted it was independence, no-one breathing down your neck, open air, your own master. But the fact remained, someone hired you, someone paid you. That made you a servant.

Now an entrepreneur . . . that was something different. Fred negotiated the cobbled dock roads and took the road for Bath and Wells. Entrepreneur. He had learned a smattering of the lingo when he was a prisoner and that's what Fritz had called himself as he negotiated sales between the Silesian coal-miners and the iron foundries, milking them both, courted by both during wartime shortages, touching his cap to no-one. And that was what Fred was going to do. He had promises from the pickle factory where Gladys his sister had put in a word for him; Bartie Hall, a warder at Gloucester Prison, said that if the price was right the prison governor would be pleased to buy from an old soldier. And he had been to the Forest of Dean and talked to the Freeminers down there three times already. They were a slow lot, but if he could flash some money under their noses, they'd agree to supply him.

The countryside levelled out alongside the dreaming Avon, so different from the turbulent Gloucester Severn. A signpost told him he was approaching the tiny village of Keynsham; he slowed, noting the huge chocolate factory on his left. Then he rolled down into the lovely basin of Bath itself.

Edwin Tomms was already a successful ironmonger when he married Elizabeth Rhys-Davies in 1868. He gave her a beautiful house in Bath, every comfort, her own carriage and two maids . . . besides four miscarriages. In the absence of any children of their own, Elizabeth – Aunt Lizzie – had taken a great interest in her orphaned niece's family. Florence had married far beneath herself, as had her poor dead mother, but William Rising had ambition and he was good-looking and a real family man. Lizzie liked him, loved and admired gentle Florence, adored the children. When Teddy was born and Florrie nearly died, she took them in for two months, and after that the links between the two families were strong.

But March was her favourite. March was darker than the other girls, more like the Rhys-Davieses than the Risings. March had aspirations and she loved to hear about her great-grandfather who had somehow been gypped out of his inheritance by something called an entail. And Uncle Edwin could see the Rhys-Davies in her too. He could see Lizzie as a young girl, as she had been when he first married her. He had coveted March when she was just a child and had bought her affection with presents. And after her darling Aunt Lizzie had died he had married her and been with her through the terrible premature birth of Albert-Frederick.

Then Fred Luker appeared last January and told him that Albert-Frederick was not a premature baby at all and was therefore not his child. Edwin thought he would go out of his mind. He determined to alter his will so that neither March nor her bastard son would get a penny. He waited to die.

But death did not come and neither did madness. He found he was saner than he'd been since Lizzie's death. Then he had lived in a half-world, convinced that March would come as Lizzie's successor. When she arrived on his doorstep that September afternoon, he had not been surprised. Lizzie had wanted March to have everything. Surely everything was Edwin. In fact March's arrival confirmed his madness and enabled him to live in it while she stayed with him.

Since her sudden departure he was able to understand why she had come to him and why she had stayed. Some of his egomania was dissipated forcibly. He saw that when Lizzie had begged him to give 'everything' to March, she had not included her husband. He saw that March had not been conceived and born simply for him. She was not Lizzie made young again. She was half Rising, and from somewhere deep in the Rising side of the family she had inherited a calculating nature. She had ingratiated herself with dear Lizzie just to get her worldly goods, and when Lizzie had died she had cut herself off from her uncle for over a year, and then suddenly descended on him when there was no-one else to save her from total disgrace.

His need for vengeance gave him energy. He had retired from the management of his three shops in Bath, but now he returned to them and interfered whenever possible. He became a pillar of the Baptist church where he and March had been married. He was on the governing board for three of the village schools in the area. And he waited.

Perhaps because he was so certain an opportunity for revenge would come, he did not turn Fred away when Letty announced him. Letty, a stout fifty now, had dropped a few sly comments about Mrs Tomms' prolonged absence from Bath, and sounded disappointed at a possible return.

'That Mr Luker's at the door, master. The one what took the missis back to Glawster with him.'

Shock held Edwin rigid for a moment, then he forced himself to say jovially, 'Ah, news of your mistress at last, Letty! Good. Show him in and then bring the port.' Edwin did not drink but he regularly produced port for his visitors. It was how he had got on the school boards.

Letty was disappointed at this reaction. From the look of the master's face when Miss March – Mrs Tomms in company – went off with that common chap last winter, Letty had hoped for a speedy scandal. As she said to Rose down in their basement kitchen, 'I can 'ear it brewing. Everythin' fine and dandy on top, and poison underneath!' Rose had said comfortably, 'Whoever got Baby Albert, got Miss March. An' I s'pose you en't suggesting that Master en't the legal guardian of that dear little lad?' That had silenced Letty. She dared not voice her suspicions, but she had them all the same. Albert-Frederick hadn't looked like a seven-month babby to *her*. But Rose worshipped the child to the extent that his whole background must be snowy white. So Letty showed in *Mister* Luker with a sarcastic little bob and muttered to herself as she went for the port that fine feathers never made fair lady, nor gentleman.

Edwin dropped his geniality with the closing of the door and did not stand up. He was sitting in the spoon back chair that had been Lizzie's favourite, then March's. It looked out over a railinged park where the summer leaves were jumping and jerking under a shower.

'Well? What do you want this time? You're not getting any of her things. And the child can die of cold for all I care!'

Fred grinned. He would rather a frontal attack any day. Nevertheless, in view of Letty's imminent return, he prevaricated.

'Nice view you've got from here. March was describing it to her mother the other day.'

Edwin looked at the straight square-shouldered figure outlined against the window. He was surprised it didn't collapse under the barrage of sheer hatred he was directing at it. But then, this upstart had survived other more tangible barrages quite recently. That was the trouble with the war. Servants thought they could be gentlemen.

Letty came into the room without knocking and Fred went on blandly, 'March is always talking of you. She is very homesick. But as you know her mother is not strong—'

'Will that be all sir?' Letty asked hopefully, putting the tray on a small table and clicking the single glass ostentatiously.

'Unless Mr Luker can stay for high tea?' Edwin asked, heavily sarcastic.

Fred resisted the temptation to accept. 'I'm booked in at a place in Almondsbury. Where March and I stayed last time we left here,' he said, watching Edwin for a reaction. Gnarled fingers curled slightly on the knife-edged thigh, that was all.

'Off you go then Letty. Remember I have the School Management Committee Meeting tonight, so I shall want my light grey top coat carefully brushed.'

'Yessir.' If Letty had been five stone lighter her departure might have been described as a flounce. She closed the door behind her with a click.

Fred leaned forward. 'So. You are still keeping up appearances. I'm glad of that.'

'Are you?' Edwin wetted his lips. 'What was all that nonsense about March being homesick?'

'Nonsense?' Fred feigned astonishment as he took a seat on the other side of the grate without waiting longer for an invitation. 'Nonsense? Did you really think poor March left here without a qualm? Naturally she has to be with her mother at a time like this. But just as naturally she misses her home very much.'

'Pity I'm in it, then she could come back. Is that what she thinks?' Edwin laughed unpleasantly. 'Well, she needn't think that. I've made a cast-iron will to keep her and the brat out of Bath, let alone this house!'

Fred lowered his head and did not speak for some time. Then he said quietly, 'I can understand, yes I think I can understand. But surely while you are alive that does not hold good? Surely you would allow her to come back here and see you?'

Edwin frowned, looking for the trap. 'I wouldn't give her house room here. She's a whore!'

'So you said before. I hoped that after a few weeks to reconsider you would see the dilemma March was in—'

'A few weeks? The girl has been gone for six months! And if I reconsidered for six years it would make no difference.'

'I raped her of course. You realize that I expect. She is very like her mother. Fastidious.'

There was a pause. Edwin's breathing became fast and audible.

'I had the devil's own job . . . certainly. You raped her, you say? How you have the gall to sit there and—'

Fred's head came up. 'Naturally I assumed you guessed that. After living with her for eighteen months.' He shrugged helplessly. 'I can feel sorry for the girl in a way. There she was pregnant and me presumed dead . . . besides, she wouldn't want *me* . . . beneath her. She turned to the person she loved best. You.'

There was a longer pause. At last Edwin said on an indrawn breath, 'Are you trying to tell me she wants to come back?'

'No.'

'Then what the deuce is this about?'

Fred smiled. 'Were you going to pour some of that port, sir?'

Edwin stared. Fred was not the sort to call anyone sir out of uniform. 'Not until I know what this visit is for,' he said bluntly.

Fred shrugged again. 'I wanted to see if you were keeping up appearances. Obviously you are, and with great success. School Management Committee, eh?'

'Naturally a man in my position – respected—'

'Quite. How long can you go on like this without . . . a visit at least from March?'

'Indefinitely I should think.'

'I shouldn't. Gossip. It might have started already.'

'I won't have that woman in my house!'

'Besides, if I were you, I would insist on my conjugal rights now and then.'

The pause this time was so long it seemed it would never end. Fred dropped his head again and studied his hands. They were short and blunt, a mechanic's hands. But a mechanic had to have sensitive hands as well as strong ones. Fred could almost feel his way around Edwin's mind.

The old man whispered at last, 'What you are saying is . . .'

Fred took a breath, sat up, stared ahead with his blue eyes as frank and open as they knew how to be.

'I am saying that you won't keep up this pretence of being respectably married if you don't have March here. And if you have her here you might as well sleep with her.'

The whisper was hoarse. 'She wouldn't let me. It was difficult enough before. But now—'

'I can get her down here. How you – arrange things – afterwards, is up to you.' Fred watched the old man lick his lips. 'She won't like it of course. But a great many wives don't like it. There's not much they can do about it.'

'My God. I could punish her for what she's done. I could make her—'

Fred closed his mind quickly to the thought of March and the old man and said, 'She wouldn't stay for long. You understand that. I could only persuade her into it for a short time. But that should be enough to establish that you are still respectably married. Very much married.'

'Quite. Quite. A great many people in Bath were

surprised when I took such a young wife. And when she produced the child—'

'Quite,' echoed Fred dryly, watching the old fool delude himself all over again. How easy it was. How pathetically easy.

'When could you – er – persuade her to come down?'

'Next week if you like. Or the one after. Any time.'

'Next week would suit me fine. I'll have to cancel my attendance at the Sunday School midsummer picnic. I wouldn't want to leave her alone. For a minute.'

'No. That would be unwise. I would bring her down and fetch her of course.'

'They will realize then that you are simply a messenger.'

'Quite,' Fred said again. 'A taxi driver. That's what I am.'

Edwin rubbed his hands nervously on his trouser legs, stared suspiciously at the young man, and turned to the port.

'Yes. March told me you drove a cab. Yes. Perhaps a small glass of—? Before you go back to Gloucester?'

'By all means. Won't you join me?'

'I don't.' Edwin poured and passed and watched Fred toss it back like medicine. 'I expect you . . . you must have regretted what you did . . . wanted to make recompense in some way . . .'

Fred put the glass in the grate. 'Regretted raping March, d'you mean?' He remembered for a sweet second her passionate acceptance of him in the stables of Chichester House that summer. Two years ago. He

46

had battered down her grief, not her body. 'No, Edwin. I never regretted that. I couldn't regret something like that.'

The old man flushed up. 'I thought . . . I understood you to mean that you felt this whole thing was your fault. If March had not been pregnant surely none of it would have happened?'

'Oh, that. True. It wouldn't, would it? Which would have been a pity.'

'A pity? So much misery? Not only for me – you said March was unhappy.'

Fred shrugged. 'A little unhappiness never hurt anyone. And if none of it had happened, well, I couldn't have arranged this little reconciliation, could I?'

Edwin was not unintelligent all the time. He stared again, then his flush deepened to puce and having reached asphyxiation level, receded until he was yellow-white.

'What do you want?' he asked finally in a dead voice.

'Some of March's inheritance. Five hundred pounds.'

'She *is* a whore. So, she's willing to sell herself for five hundred pounds, is she? I could get a girl in Bristol for five shillings. Tell her that.'

'Don't be a fool. She knows nothing of this. Not even that I'm here. Don't you think what I'm offering you is worth five hundred pounds? That sum is nothing to you.'

'As I just said – you dirty, common criminal – I can get a woman just as beautiful and more amenable than March Rising for—'

47

'But you don't get only March for that money, Edwin. You get your name. And more. You get a reputation as rather an old dog. Young woman like March coming home for a week because she can't live without you. Good God, what's five hundred pounds in those circumstances? Think, Edwin. Think!'

Edwin thought, long and hard. It seemed to cause him a great deal of pain. While he thought, Fred revealed his supreme confidence in the final decision by going to the port bottle and pouring himself another glass and tossing it down after the first one.

Eventually Edwin controlled his breathing and said in a low voice, 'You are despicable. If she knew what you are doing she would hate you.'

'I'm willing to risk that,' Fred said. He went to the window. 'Looks like the rain has stopped. I'll have to get off. I've got people to visit tonight. Business. A cheque will do.'

'I shall tell her.'

'Tell her what you like.'

Edwin went heavily to a drawer in a side table equipped with silver-topped ink bottles. He withdrew a pen. 'How do I know she'll come? Your powers of persuasion might not be as great as you seem to think.'

'If she doesn't come, you've lost five hundred pounds,' Fred said carelessly. He came and stood over the table and his face lost its easy-going expression. 'Write it,' he said brutally. 'You've got no choice.'

Fred Luker left Royal Parade at three-fifteen and drove immediately to the branch of the West of England Bank in Milsom Street. He cashed Edwin's cheque, came out and went on over Pulteney Bridge, then turned and drove along the other side of the river, glancing now and then to his right where the view of the abbey was breathtaking. When he rejoined the Bristol Road he began to laugh. He thought about what he had done. The old man was right, it was despicable. March would be angry and outraged, she might even hate him for a time. But not for long. He threw back his head and laughed aloud and then decided it was his lucky day, so he swung the Morris in through the gates of the chocolate factory and asked a scurrying worker to direct him to the manager's office. He got in there without much difficulty and found what he called an 'officer type' sitting behind the desk.

'My name is Luker, sir,' he said, standing straight, almost at attention. 'I'm trying to start a coal business. Got relations with a small surface coal-mine down in Dean Forest. I'm selling what I can in small lots, but I reckon I could supply a place like this at a competitive price.'

The officer type surveyed him without pleasure.

'Your own business, eh? You chaps come out of the army with ideas above your station. We've got our own railway siding, man. Our fuel is delivered by a reputable Bristol firm.'

Fred let his shoulders droop. 'Thought I'd give it a try, sir. My job was gone see, when I got out. Parents . . . wife . . . you know how it is.'

The officer type frowned. 'Well. No harm in trying I suppose. How did you propose getting the stuff here? Long way from the Forest of Dean.'

'The mine is near Whitecroft, sir. We haul the coal

by dray to the coal siding there and train it into Gloucester and Stroud.'

'Sounds expensive. Three loadings. Stand at ease, man.'

Fred spread his feet obediently. 'We want the business, sir, so we keep our price down. We've got a couple of factories in Gloucester who are using us in a month or two. Trial period of six months. If the bills are less and the service good . . . who knows. I've got a possible market in Stroud – on my way there now.'

'And you came to Bath specially to see me?'

'Well . . . yes, sir. I heard you'd got your own siding, see, and I thought that would probably keep the cost down further. Like I said sir, I gave it a try. Sorry to have wasted your time.' He brought his hands from behind his back.

'How did you get here – er – Luker, was it? Train?'

'No sir. I drove. Car's outside.'

'Car eh? Thought you were penniless.'

'Had it before the war, sir. Morris. I'll have to get rid of it once I've scouted around for business.' He permitted himself a smile. 'I used to run a cab service in Gloucester. And the haulage. No call for it now – others got in while I was away. But I've still got the car and a dray and a cart-horse.'

'Hm. Enterprising sort of chap aren't you? What kind of prices are you offering?'

'Depends on the size of the order. The bigger it comes the lower the price. We do steam coal at a pound a ton for a train load. More than that – well, I'd work out a special price.'

The officer type stared at him, lifted his top lip and

very delicately gnawed his lower lip. 'Hmmm . . .' he said through his nose. 'Hmm . . . I'd have to talk to our accountant. Storeman. Those sort of chaps. Where can I get in touch with you – er – Luker?'

Fred put his cap under his arm and felt in his inside pocket for the card printed 'F. Luker, 17, Chichester Street, Gloucester'. His fingers touched the ten pound notes there and he smiled slightly.

'Right. My name is Porterman. Captain Porterman, though I don't use the rank now of course.' He stood up and came around the desk. 'I'd like to think I could give one of our chaps a chance. I'm not making any promises you understand, but I'll be in touch. How's that? Does it make the journey worthwhile?' He guffawed, quite certain it did. Fred let his smile widen into a grin.

'Gosh. Thanks sir. Thanks Captain. It's great to talk to someone like you. Gentleman.'

He got outside somehow before he laughed again. And he kept the laughter within limits until he was negotiating Bristol's narrow streets. Then all the way up Whiteladies Road and Blackboy Hill could be heard Fred Luker's raucous mirth.

May went to Helene's Hair Salon in Saint Aldate Street to gossip to her old friends and to use the telephone there to ring Monty in the Kilburn Music Hall. Madame Helene assured her that if she came back to Gloucester she could have her old job back, baby or no baby, and May dimpled and said she might well take her seriously. Amid the protestations May let her secret wish take voice. 'I – we – might well move back home,' she confided to Madame. 'Obviously now that we are having a baby we must have a home. I can't follow my husband around any more. And Gloucester is fairly central.'

Madame waved her hands as she believed Parisiennes did. 'My dear Miss May! Then I shall hold you to this! In six months – a year – when there is a vacancy here, I shall remind you of your promise.'

'Madame, no promise!' May laughed, blushing, knowing that it was all empty talk, but very pleasing to her ear. 'If . . . if . . . if . . . oh you know I should be glad to help you out.'

Later in the privacy of the tiny office with accounts and appointment books littering the shelf, she used the greasy wall telephone. 'May I speak to . . . is that you Monty? You beast, putting on that ghastly voice! You – what did you say ? Will I come to where with you? Bed? Oh *Monty*! You are incorrigible!' She spluttered into the mouthpiece, then caught sight of herself in a small mirror above the gas lamp. Immediately she peered forward and began to rewind her front curls on a finger.

'Darling, I'm so glad, full houses both nights? Well of course it was for you, Maud is no oil-painting you know, they'd hardly want an encore from her. What did you sing?'

She leaned back and tucked in her chin, studying her reflection for any sign of her neck falling in. At last Monty finished talking and she smiled into the mirror and said, 'Listen darling. I'm going to see some new houses this afternoon at Longford. Houses. *Houses*, darling. They're building some marvellous new ones at Longford. They're in twos so they're called semi-detached.' She made her smile into a grimace and looked at her teeth. She quite liked her teeth.

'Well Monty, we must live somewhere when the baby is born. Yes, I know we live somewhere now dear, but we can't bring up a baby in a bed-sitting room or theatrical digs. It didn't take you long to pop down here for April's wedding. I *know* it's further from Blackpool darling, but you're not at Blackpool very long.' She put her lips together and sighed audibly into the mouthpiece. 'What? Of course we'll have to talk it over, Monty. That's what we're doing now. Oh I *know* you don't buy a house like you buy a pound of potatoes! But you can get loans for houses. You remember Bridget Williams? Well, her father is an auctioneer and they are acting as agents for these new houses and they will arrange a . . . what did you say Monty? Well, we've got *some* savings haven't we dear? Surely. But we can't have spent all . . . nothing at all? I don't believe you. Darling I'll have to go, Madame is knocking on the door. Yes of course I do dear. Do you? Oh good. Oh Monty. Oh . . . goodbye.'

March found to her surprise that she was quite glad to see Fred Luker when he called the following Thursday evening.

Since April's wedding life at number thirty-three Chichester Street had seemed anti-climactic, to say the least. Will was always out somewhere 'seeing a man about a dog', Florence looked even more pale and thin than usual, and May was suddenly out of sorts. But it was Aunt Sylv who thoroughly got on March's nerves.

Sylvia was the one who had diagnosed her pregnancy while they were on holiday in Weymouth two years previously, and though they had never spoken of it since March slipped away to see her Uncle Edwin, Sylvia's wise, lizard eyes spoke much louder than words. Sylvia knew the truth about her marriage to Edwin; it therefore followed that Sylvia knew Fred had taken her from Bath practically by force, and she and Albert-Frederick were back in Gloucester for good.

It hadn't been so bad until now; April's sudden declaration on her seventeenth birthday that she was going to marry David Daker, had taken the family's attention well away from March and her baby son. But now April was gone. March devoted herself assiduously to Albert-Frederick, deliberately seeing in him her dear, dead brother, Albert, but she remembered vividly and constantly her battle of wills with Fred at the wedding. She hoped she had hurt him. But then if she had hurt him enough perhaps their peculiar relationship was at an end? Not that it would make much difference to her as things were; she was neither fish, fowl, nor good red herring. And it wasn't going to take much longer for everyone in the street to know that.

So, when March came downstairs that Thursday evening and found Fred chatting amiably to Florence and Gran in the kitchen, she could not help feeling a small leap of pleasure somewhere in her chest cavity. Fred's love for her was the only positive thing in her life, apart from her small son. He knew she was nervous, edgy, bad-tempered; he had told her he loved her with all her faults. He couldn't retract all that, not now.

He stood up as she came into the kitchen, watching her to see whether she was noting this refinement. He was shorter than Albert had been; his neck was thick and his shoulders were heavy and slightly bowed from the years of delivering coal. But his fair, slightly gingery hair and blue eyes were not unlike Albert's. She smiled at him. She was glad she had changed her blouse and re-pinned her own long chestnut-brown hair.

He said heartily, 'The very person I hoped to see. I was just saying to your mother that I need a little business advice, March.'

She couldn't resist parrying this blatant invitation.

'I know nothing of business—'

But he swept on smoothly. 'I wanted to ask you what Edward Williams would have done if he'd been faced with the sort of problem I've got at the moment. After all you were his secretary for ten years—'

'Nine,' March corrected. 'And he never discussed his business problems with me. I typed his correspondence. Inventories. That sort of thing.' She wondered why she was talking like this. She would like to walk up London Road with Fred now and listen to the late cuckoos on the Pitch. Florence rescued her.

'I don't know anything about business either, dear. But I do know that you need some air. And Fred has just asked me whether he can walk you down to the river for an hour to discuss this new contract he has got. Why don't you go? It would do you good.'

March sighed as if with martyred resignation. She

went upstairs to fetch her short jacket and to bite some colour into her pale lips; her face needed no help, two spots of colour emphasized her high thin cheekbones. She half-smiled at her reflection: she was excited.

With unerring instinct Fred led her across the road to Chichester House.

'We can't go in there—' March hung back, suddenly afraid. 'It's nothing to do with us any more, Fred.'

'Nobody's there now. Can't afford the rent or the upkeep of such a big place.' Fred grinned easily as he pushed open the door in the wall. 'Your April often walks here, didn't you know?'

The garden was the same: blackcurrants, gooseberries, loganberries, raspberries in the enclosure; giant rhubarb leaves, beds of mint, the rosemary and lavender bushes. They sat on the front steps and she began to feel the tension going out of her.

'Have you been to the Forest yet?' She tipped her face towards the evening sunshine and closed her eyes. The warmth soothed through her lids and into her head. She knew he hadn't gone yet; when he asked her again, she would go with him.

'No. I went to Bath instead.'

Her eyes flew open and she turned to look at him. 'To *Bath*?'

'Ever heard of the chocolate factory at Keynsham? One of these model places, like Bourneville.'

He began to tell her about Captain Porterman, making it sound much more definite than it had been. 'You see what this means, March? I've got to organize that rabble down in the Forest. Organize them properly. I need two train loads of coal every week.'

'So you're going down there soon – next week? I think I could come with you then actually.'

'Not this time, my love. It might be rough. Next time, certainly.' He sensed her incipient umbrage. 'I shall be going down often. I'd rather you and I were together when I'm not up to my eyes in work.' He lifted her hand to his lips. 'Besides I want you to do something for me next week. Something very important, March. Will you do it?'

'How can I do anything? I'm stuck in the house day after day with Albert-Frederick—'

'I need some money, March. Will you get it for me?'

'Don't be absurd Fred. You know I haven't got any money.'

'Your husband is a rich man, March.'

She took a breath and held it, looking at him. Then she let it go. 'You went to see Edwin,' she said with a kind of horror. 'You tried to get money out of Edwin.'

'I went to see Edwin with a proposition, March. As – as an intermediary if you like.' March liked long words. He held on to her hand and massaged the knuckles with his thumb; her bones were too near the surface of her skin. He felt a tenderness for her that almost undermined his intention. But March herself had set the pattern for their relationship: it had always been a duel. Only with her brother had March achieved an entirely loving relationship. And Fred did not wish to be March's brother-figure.

She was angry; bewildered too. 'What right had you to see Edwin without consulting me first, Fred? What have you done?'

He pressed her hand a little harder. 'I've every right to act on your behalf, March. As I told you last Saturday, in the eyes of God—'

'But without telling me? In the eyes of the *law* I am still married to Edwin Tomms!'

'Quite. You are in an impossible situation, Marcie. I felt I had to do something about it.'

The small flutter happened again inside her chest. There was only one thing Fred could have seen Edwin about and that was divorce. Divorce was a disgrace, it terrified her. But if Fred had actually managed it so that she was the innocent party . . . after all, the whole world could see that she had done her duty by her elderly husband . . . Fred was devious and clever, he might have arranged something. And then, one day, a long time in the future to give her time to recover from the past ten years, Fred would marry her. She did not even ask herself whether she loved him; it was enough now that he loved her.

She said again, all anger gone, 'What have you done, Fred?'

'Found his weak spot, Marcie. That's what I've done. His reputation in Bath – it's more important to him than hating you and Albert-Frederick. More important than hating me even!' He laughed and lifted her hand again to his face. It smelled of powder from the baby. His son, named for Albert Rising and Fred Luker; he still had to remind himself of that. He put his cheek to her palm.

'He wants to go on being respected – and admired as being a bit of an old dog for getting himself a young wife and a fine strapping son.' The hand was withdrawn and he said quickly, 'He's failing, March – he won't last long. If you'll do this he'll alter his will again in your favour. He knows as well as you do that it was your aunt's wish you should inherit everything—'

'What have you *done,* Fred?' The anger was back in her voice, and fear too. She couldn't face Edwin again; not after the frightful denouement last Christmas when Fred had arrived and told him the brutal fact of Albert-Frederick's parentage.

'Listen, Marcie. A week. That's all he wants. Just so that people will be convinced you haven't left him. Take a few drives with him – be seen around the town with him—'

'*No!* How *could* you *do* this, Fred? It was you who took me away from him – rescued me—'

'And it was you who told me only last Saturday that I hadn't rescued you at all. I'd smashed up your comfortable existence—'

'Oh God! I hate you, Fred Luker – I hate you—' She stood up, poised for flight. But he would not release her hand. He stood up too and pulled her to him. She was shaking violently but did not immediately pull away; she needed him, she needed his strength of will.

He said in a low voice, 'I thought you'd do this for me, Marcie. We planned so much – that night we spent at the George, d'you remember—' How could she forget that wonderful night when she had escaped from Edwin and given over to Fred the responsibility for herself, her son and her happiness. 'I told you I would keep that promise I made to you in the war,

Marcie. I want to keep it. But I can't do it without you, my darling. I want to be rich – successful – only for you, Marcie. We'll live in that house in Barnwood just as I said – we'll have a car bigger than the Williams' – we'll have tennis parties—'

'Fred – I can't – I can't—' But there was pleading now mixed with the anger and outrage. 'I can't face him!'

'Not a full week then, Marcie. Just a few days.'

'He won't change his will. And if he does he'll probably live for years!'

'Darling girl, he's seventy-six. And not much bigger than your mother!'

She stood there within his arms, still trembling, searching for a loophole. She found it. 'But you need money now – you asked me to get money for you now.'

'He'll let us have some on account, Marcie. ' He felt her tighten and released her hand at last to stroke her hair. 'That's why I am so certain he will change his will, my dearest. We talked reasonably, he wanted to know how you were – and the boy.'

She wanted to raise her fists and pummel his chest; she wanted to tell him she did not believe him. But then she would have nothing. And he was asking her to help him; he was kissing her and the scent of the lavender was overpowering.

She whimpered, 'I don't know what to do, Fred. I don't know.'

'Then let me tell you what to do, Marcie. Let me drive you down to Bath for a few days – not quite the week – let Rose take Albert-Frederick off your hands for a while. You're tired. It will do you good to get away from Gloucester. Let poor old Edwin show you off to his friends. Let me bring you home—'

'I can't bear to say anything about money. You'll have to do all that, Fred.'

'Of course, Marcie. I wouldn't dream—'

'It's your responsibility. Your doing. If you think it's all right for me to go there again. And Albert-Frederick – don't forget *he's* your responsibility too, Fred.'

'I know. Oh Marcie, if only I hadn't been taken prisoner that summer. I'd've had compassionate leave and we'd have been married and probably been able to afford a little cottage somewhere—'

March leaned against his chest so that he had to continue his kissing on top of her head. She wasn't absolutely certain that a tiny cottage with Fred was exactly what she had wanted back in 1917, or now. Perhaps there had been some kind of rhyme or reason to the awfulness of that summer after all? And if there had, then Fred's idea wasn't quite so appalling.

She lifted her face and kissed him briefly.

'I'll have to go home now Fred. I don't want Mother running up and down stairs to Albert-Frederick.'

Strangely, she slept better that night than she usually did. If only it weren't for Edwin, she would quite look forward to returning to Bath. It was a city she loved, and a life-style she would have loved anywhere. Fred was right, Rose would take the baby right off her hands; and there would be meat or fish every day and twice a day if she wanted it. And it would just show Aunty Sylv.

Chapter Three

It was true May was out of sorts. She had been home to Florence several times since the beginning of her pregnancy and though she missed Monty when she was in Gloucester, she missed Gloucester even more when she was away from it. The two small rooms in Chestnut Grove just off the Kilburn High Street were pleasant enough. The garden backed on to the railway, but then the railway was only a stone's throw from Chichester Street. Kilburn High Street was quite as busy and interesting as Northgate Street; but Kilburn was not the sort of place in which May wanted to begin building a proper family life. She couldn't see herself hanging nappies in the garden there and pushing a pram down to the shops. She wanted to be among her own where she would be the centre of a small, admiring group of neighbours and friends; where she and March could meet in the park and thread the small streets on the other side of the railway into the Barton where April was, and go on down to the cathedral teashop or back to see Florence and Gran.

The *Citizen* were doing a feature on the new houses at Longford. Barely a mile down Worcester Street and there they were: a little village of them with black and white gables like Tudor cottages, and diamond-

paned windows and quite some way from the treach-
erous flood area of Twigworth. But because there was
that faint – very faint – risk, they were reasonably
priced. Two hundred and fifty pounds; a deposit of
£24 secured one of them immediately. May had let
her imagination run riot until the phone call from
Madame Helene's. She had wandered around the
Northgate Furniture Mart and chosen a delightful
round table for the dining-room; furnished the
sitting-room with big squashy chairs upholstered in
plush, and chosen a double bed for the front bedroom.
She could see it. Cream wallpaper, a rose-coloured
satin bedspread . . . and then Monty had been so
unreasonable.

Naturally she had expected reluctance. He did not
want her living a hundred miles from where he was.
Naturally she had expected his caution about buying
a property; the only people she knew who owned their
own houses were the Williamses and Sibbie Luker –
and Sibbie hardly counted. But that Monty didn't have
£24 in the world was incredible. They spent hardly
any of his money did they? And then, when he'd said
that Gloucester was the last place on earth he'd want
to live, it seemed practically an insult. How did he
think she would feel if they settled in London and
he went off to – to Timbuctoo? The concert party –
the Happy Hey Days – were never long in one place.

She talked to Florence about it. Florence was
sympathetic but adamant.

'Darling child, you know there is nothing I should
like better than to have you near. But that is mere self-
ishness. Your place is with your husband. You don't

need me to tell you that.' She smiled and her face was lit by love. May's heart contracted at its sallow thinness and she nearly said, 'I shall have Monty, God willing, most of my life, but you . . . how long shall I have you?' But she knew that no argument would sway Florence in this. Florence's list of priorities was immutable, husband and children always came first.

However, Monty would listen to Will and Will was more easily persuadable. But to May's surprise, when she tackled her father, he pursed his lips disapprovingly.

'Stay on? Here?'

'For a while, Pa. Until we could save enough to get this house I'm telling you about.'

Will thought about it. True, he would enjoy having Monty at weekends and when he was 'resting'. But if May was in Gloucester all the time there was more risk of her meeting Sibbie.

He said consideringly, 'Look here May, you know how your mother and me 'ud feel having you near. But you wanted this actor chappie and you can't desert him now—'

'Daddy! I wouldn't desert him for the *world*! I *adore* Monty – you know that. I've *explained* it to you.'

'Yes child. All right. But I don't quite see it like that. A woman marries a man's work in a way.' Will put his finger in his watch pocket and leaned back on his heels. 'Your mother . . . what should I have done without her?'

'I can't button-hole for Monty!' May cried, exasperated.

'But you can be with him when he has to go to these out-of-the-way places. It's all you *can* do for him. Imagine how he must feel – talk about lonely—'

'Oh Pa. I'm sorry. Don't make me cry, please. I can't *bear* to think of darling Monty like that. He *was* lonely till he met me. No parents. No family.'

So when she telephoned Monty next time at the Kilburn Empire, she was quite determined to fall in with whatever he wished. Nevertheless it was quite a shock to hear that he had left the Happy Hey Days.

'Left them?' He had been with the small concert party off and on since before the war. As he so often told her, they were his family.

'Darling, listen. So much has happened.' The line seemed to be under water and May blocked her free ear with the flat of her palm. 'You've heard of the Mincing Light Opera Company? No? May, they are *the* people to be with! Absolutely. Tophole orchestra, first-class singers . . . Came to the show last week and heard me sing . . . round to the green room afterwards . . . supper. My darling girl – a real opera supper. Can you believe it, May? '

'Darling, of course I can. I've always said you have the best light baritone I've ever—'

'Only snag was, I had to be ready by this Sunday. Opening at Scarborough on Monday.'

'Scarborough? That's where April—'

'So can you be back tomorrow sweetie? We'll have to pack up here and Maud wants to give a little party on stage after Saturday night.'

'Of course Monty darling. Of course . . . how sweet

of Maud. They'll miss you terribly!' May was smugly pleased about that. Maud Davenport's duets with Monty had always irked her. She added doubtfully, 'Darling, are you sure it will be all right for me to travel all the way to Scarborough? The birth is only six weeks away.'

Monty misunderstood her reluctance and rushed in with reassurance. 'Darling, you know it hardly shows! And they'll love it – it's supposed to be lucky to have a baby born on tour, you know.'

'But Monty, it's so far!'

'We don't have to change, sweetie. They shunt our coach off at Crewe and York and the next train picks us up and—'

'What about digs?'

'They send a man ahead. All arranged. Oh May, isn't it marvellous? It's an important little company you know. Mostly G and S. It's *Yeomen* and *Gondoliers* next week but they use the alternative titles *The Merryman and His Maid* and *The King of Barantaria*. Don't you think there's something rather top-drawer about that?'

'Oh yes darling. Rather.' May removed her hand from her ear and nibbled at the finger of her glove. It was much too early for a premature birth but supposing she got a giddy turn this evening? She couldn't possibly go to London tomorrow and then right on up to Scarborough the day after.

'So I'll see you tomorrow darling? Meet you. Paddington. The midday train?'

'Lovely, Monty. I'll be there. Unless anything really awful happens.'

It never occurred to Monty that anything could. His fair, delicate, ethereal May, once so prone to chesty colds, was as strong as a horse and had been since her visit to Bath in 1902.

May walked slowly down Saint Aldate Street, feeling herself being torn in two. Love and pride for Monty vied with her lazy unwillingness to join him and push her way through life again. Here, Pa saw to some things, Mother to the rest. Gran and Aunt Sylv were in the background, March and April available. It wasn't fair of Monty to expect her to leave such security just at the moment and struggle with luggage and porters and dirty trains. A voice broke through her thoughts.

'Well. Are you going to cut me dead then, May? You've been very careful not to go anywhere I might be, but I didn't imagine that if we met face to face you'd pretend I didn't exist!'

May's head jerked, puppet-like. Sibbie was standing before her, obviously about to turn into the tiny teashop on the corner. She wore a beautiful, semi-fitted coat with a single button fastening and long lapels; her hat was like a helmet and emphasized her vivid face with its rouged cheeks and bright red mouth and mascara'd eyes. May had seen such hats in London, but Sibbie must be the only woman in Gloucester wearing one.

She said, 'Sibbie! I – I didn't see you!'

'Didn't recognize me – is that what you mean?' Sibbie seemed very aggressive. Certainly it was the first time she and May had met since her self-exile to her bungalow by the canal, but April had run into her several times and insisted that Sibbie invariably smiled and waved.

May stammered awkwardly, 'You look very well, Sibbie.'

Sibbie eyed May scornfully. May pregnant was even more exquisite than May virginal, but she was not smart.

She said, 'You probably think I look like a tart.' She held up an elegantly gloved hand. 'Don't worry. I'm not offended. I like the way I look, and so do . . . others.' She smiled and brushed an invisible speck from her coat. 'Your husband for instance.'

May gasped. 'Monty? You've met Monty?'

'You couldn't be bothered to see him off two weeks ago. Someone had to!' Sibbie's smile widened. She reached for the door handle of the teashop. Inside, Will saw her, half stood up, spotted May and sat down again.

May repeated stupidly, 'You saw Monty off? But you don't know him!'

'I introduced myself. Your best friend. Told him we shared everything.' Sibbie laughed. 'So of course he let me kiss him goodbye.'

She opened the door and disappeared inside. May stared after her, glimpsed her father and would have run to him if Sibbie hadn't been there. She felt tears and panic threaten her. First David, now Monty. She clenched her hands and walked quickly down to Chichester Street and along to number thirty-three, hardly hearing Snotty Lottie's greeting or seeing the youngest Luker batting a ball against the wall of the Lamb and Flag.

Florence looked up from a blanket she was darning. 'Well May? How was Monty?'

May took a deep breath, looked at her mother's pricked fingers as they worked at the prison blanket Kitty Hall had brought round, and let her breath go again.

'He's got the most marvellous chance Mamma! With the Mincing Light Opera Company – serious singing at last. But I have to pack and go back to London tomorrow. We leave for Scarborough on Sunday . . . there's so much to do . . .'

Fred took the long way round to Parkend in the Forest of Dean because he wanted to call at Lydney railway station and enquire about coal trains going across the bridge over the Severn.

As early as 1917 Fred had investigated the possibilities of obtaining coal cheaply from the Forest Freeminers. During the wartime shortages it had been one way to keep his father's coal-delivery business going and Fred, on leave from his machine-gun nest in France, had enjoyed hammering the best bargain he could from the small, family-owned businesses in the ancient Royal Forest. Apart from the big Cannop Colliery in the centre of the seam, all the mines were tiny surface ones, needing no drainage pumps, no gas detectors. A pick, a shovel, a horse and cart – or even a wheelbarrow – were all that a man needed to dig his own coal. The trees had been there millions of years before the Crown annexed them as a hunting ground and to supply naval timbers. They had been packing their dead branches into humus, the humus into peat, the peat into sparkling black coal which was discovered as a side-line when the first miners dug for iron.

When Fred had seen for himself how casually inefficient that side-line was, he had spoken to the Freeminers of a co-operative; and had got nowhere. The Freeminers cherished their ancient rights, believing that only in them could they retain precious independence. Fred had cursed them for stupidity, but he had not forgotten them. During the long boredom of his incarceration in Silesia he had taken stock of his past life and future prospects, and the dream of being one of the new breed of 'middle men' had been born. He had dealt with coal in small amounts, he had worn a leather back protector and humped it all over Gloucester. There was money in coal, it was the heart of England. And the Freeminers of the Forest were waiting.

He did not let himself think about March. He had last seen her mounting the steps of the house in Bath, clutching Albert-Frederick over her shoulder and saying in a voice that Letty could not miss, 'Come for me tomorrow if Mother gets worse, mind, Fred.' He didn't want to remember that.

Now and then he had flashing glimpses of the Severn on his left and the presence of such a wide band of water between himself and March seemed to help him to separate her from himself in his thoughts.

The station master at Lydney was helpful and Fred turned north and drove up through Bream and Whitecroft to the tiny pub where he had taken half a dozen of the few remaining Freeminers several times before. The place was called the Gavellers Arms and boasted two rooms, both floors smothered in dirty sawdust and stinking of stale beer. Only one of the miners was present, a man called Danby, who had been spokesman for the others before. He rose from a seat in the window; he was dressed in leather breeches and collarless shirt. He held his cap in his hands and used it as a reason for not taking Fred's outstretched hand.

'Dun't bring no good news, Mister. 'Tuthers were for not putting in a face at all. But I said as we'd promised Luker to meet 'im 'ere and 'im bein' a prisoner of the 'Uns an' all, 'twere on'y decent to—'

Fred interrupted this rambling apology with upraised hand.

'Tell me about it when you've downed a pint, Danby.' He turned away immediately so that Danby could not see his taut face. He was ready to explode with sheer frustrated rage. The stupid ignorant fools had backed down. He'd got them to the point of being interested and assumed that he could carry the day and because he hadn't pressed home his advantage immediately with cash . . . well, he'd show Danby the five hundred. And then they'd bloody well pay for their own lethargy. He'd bleed them all white. He'd suck their blood until—

'Here we are, Mister Danby. Hereford hops. Nothing quite like 'em, eh?' He let Danby see his wallet as he paid for the beer. He asked for whisky himself. He sat down. 'Cold feet eh? Tell 'em it's all set up. The pickle factory in Gloucester. And—' He grinned tightly. 'And the bloody chocolate factory at Bristol. Keynsham. Ever heard of it? They bloody eat coal! Your chaps will have to dig twenty-four hours a day to keep them supplied! Paid in advance too, so I can let you all have some money.'

Danby picked up his tankard and drank deep. Froth coated his upper lip and he blew through his nostrils like a horse and cleared it.

''Sno good, mister. See, you dun't understan' the Forest. We'm in'pennant down yer. We got 'nuff to feed ourselves and our fam'lies. We dun't need no more, see. We . . . we'm in'pennant.'

Fred made a further effort to control his anger; he was not as tall as Danby but his shoulders were as powerful and they hunched forward as if holding himself in. His pale blue eyes stared hard at the face opposite him, despising it, hating it.

'That was one of the reasons I chose the Forest Freeminers. I could have gone to Coalpit Heath – any of the small mines around Bristol—'

'They 'ouldn't 'a lissened to ee, mister.'

Fred forced his shoulders back; this man was not quite so stupid as he had at first thought.

'You led me to believe you were interested.'

Danby made a movement that might have been a shrug and drank again. 'Us let 'ee go on. Aye. No 'arm in lissening.' He put down his tankard and looked keenly across the table. 'Lissen yer, mister. You get one to do it, the rest'll follow. That's all the incouragement I kin give you.'

'Well? Why not you then?'

'I got no sons to 'elp. I might dig ten 'undred a day. No more. Where'll that get ee?'

'No bloody where.'

'See?'

'Is there someone then? Someone who would lead the rest of the stupid sheep?'

Danby's expression hardened and he stood up. 'No, no-one.'

'Then why the hell did you just say—'

'Tellin' ee. Tha's all.'

The man shambled out without another word, either goodbye or thanks. Fred could hardly credit he had gone for good and waited, fuming, for a further ten minutes before investigating. Danby had gone. Like some animal he had left his watering-hole. The whole damned scheme was gone . . . down the drain. Fred drank his whisky and another. The landlord looked at him knowingly.

'Thought you 'ad 'em in the bag mi'boy, eh? Eh? Come down from Glawster throwing your weight about.' He laughed. 'Wait till you knows 'em like I knows 'em. You'll 'ave to squat yourself a bit o' land and dig the black stuff up with your own shovel. That's the only way you'll do it.'

Fred bought a third whisky and downed it. 'Squat?' he asked.

'Build. Draw smoke between sunset and sunrise and it's yourn.'

The old man laughed again. 'Make sure it's on a seam though, mi'boy. Make sure o' that. An' I don't reckon you'd know coal unless 'twere burning in your grate. Eh? Eh mi'boy?'

Fred licked around his mouth, tasting again the sharpness of the drink. He said slowly, 'No. No, that I wouldn't, Dad. That I wouldn't.'

He went outside and cleared some kids off the car. He got in and began to drive north towards Mitchel Dean, Longhope and Newent, towards where Will Rising had lived. And where Will's sister, the bovine Vi, still lived. Fred had never enjoyed feeling a fool, even in the days when he had known he was one. He was certain now that he was no fool, simply because he had emerged from the war unscathed. And he intended to show those ignorant Freeminers of Dean just that.

Edwin came into the sitting-room dressed in a pearl grey dust coat and carrying a cap. March was in Aunt Lizzie's spoon-back chair holding Albert-Frederick on her lap while she pointed out the waving trees in the park opposite the window. She looked up, coldly enquiring.

'I think we'd better take a drive.' Edwin did not look in her direction but went straight to the window, effectively blocking her view. 'The purpose of this visit is to show your world and mine that we are still married. It was our custom to drive out most afternoons.'

'I did not imagine you would have time,' she murmured. 'So many committees and functions—'

'Get your coat. And make ready your – your bastard son – and come!' Edwin's voice shook with rage. 'And if you think you can shelter behind him and Rose for the whole week, you had better think again, madam!'

March, who had shared Rose's bed next to the cot for the three nights she had been at Bath, stood up with dignity.

'I explained to you. Albert is used to sleeping with me—'

'Then his cot must be moved into our room! There is nothing else for it! What do you think Rose and Letty must say down in the basement?'

'I think they will assume that you are too old for—'

Edwin whirled round. 'Get your coat March! Quickly!'

March left the room.

The cottage on the Newent–Kempley Road was like a pigsty. Fred was used to near slum living; Hettie Luker cooked and washed after a fashion, she rarely cleaned. But this dirt was different. This was farmyard dirty. He was reminded of one of his rare conversations with Albert Rising in the coke yard at Chichester Elementary. Albert had been trying to describe the carefree enjoyment of life in the tied cottage at Kempley. 'Gran says they're as happy as pigs in shit,' he had laughed, flushing slightly, but knowing that Fred Luker of all people might understand. Fred had understood, but he still hadn't been prepared for the cottage which Vi Rising shared with her brother Wallie before he disappeared, and now with the four boys she and Sylvia had collected twenty years before. There was actually a pig asleep on the broken armchair in the kitchen and the smell was sharp and noisome.

Luckily the boys were all out working in the large

market garden that kept them in this state of filthy plenty. He knew they must live well, they were all as large as oxen.

'Just thought I'd drop in,' he bawled, shaking his head when Vi made movements to oust the pig from the chair. 'I wanted to have a chat with you. About old Forest customs.'

'Dun't 'ave to shout then Mister. I en't deaf. An' I dun't know nuthin' about Forest folk neither. We'm Newent.'

The way she spoke the Great Wall of China might have crossed the few miles between Newent and the Forest boundaries. And she must have very sharp ears indeed if she could hear a normal voice through the grunting of the pig and the cackling of the hens. He smiled propitiation.

'Call me Fred, Aunty Vi. I remember you when you came to Gloucester with Aunty Sylv after your father's funeral.'

'I never did. Never bin there till April's wedding. Never ast me. Wouldna gone anyway. Nasty noisy place.'

He swallowed and decided to come to the point. 'I thought you might know something about squatter's rights in the Forest. Talking to a chap in the Gavellers—'

'The Gavellers? Dun't want to go there Mister. Man was killed there back in 84. 'E was from Kempley and 'e smiled at one of the Forest girls. They shot 'im in the Gavellers. Sawdust is still stained they do say.'

Remembering the Gavellers Arms Fred would not have been surprised at anything.

'So you do know something about the Forest then?'

Vi scratched the pig's head gloomily. 'Only bad things. They buried 'im. Nuthin' were ever said.'

Fred frowned. 'Made an impression on you, Aunty Vi.'

'Ah. It did that. Pa used to tell us never to look at a Forest boy.' She scratched her head and added casually, 'It were Pa's brother what got shot y'see. An' nine months later Pa went down to St Briavels and brought Austen 'ome with 'im.'

Fred stared at her. Austen was another of Gran Rising's progeny and when the old home near Newent had been broken up after Grampy Rising's death, Austen and Jack had disappeared to the Rhondda coal mines.

He said slowly, 'Sounds to me as if Austen is your cousin, not your brother, Aunty Vi.'

She shrugged. 'Cousin, brother. 'Tes all the same when we wuz brought up under the same roof. Washed under the same pump. Ett off the same table. Slep' in the same—'

'So Austen was born in the Forest of Dean?'

Aunty Vi was suddenly cagey. 'I dunno about that. I never said 'e were my cousin neither. What for you so int'rested in Austen all of a sudden Mister? 'E wudn't one o' they conchies y'know. 'E were in a reserved occ'pation – the coal mines wuz jest the same as the army an' 'im and Jack 'ad bin miners since nineteen nought six!'

'Couldn't have done without miners, Aunty Vi, and that's a fact.' Fred forced himself to go over to the pig and pat its bristly back. It made a noise between a snort and a squeal and Vi smiled lovingly.

'No. I'm interested in this squatting business. Seems like if you can build yourself a house overnight you can claim the surrounding land. Something like that.'

'Thinking of living down in Dean then, are you? Dun't do it Mister, they'm a rough lot and no mistake.'

'But is it true? Does it happen these days?'

'Draw smoke twixt sunset and sunrise,' she incanted. 'Aye. I can 'member it 'appening. But for Forest folk. Not strangers.'

'And if your hearth – your fire – happened to be near a coal seam, could you mine that coal under the old Freemining laws?'

'If you're Forest. Yes. You got to be borned in St Briavels. That's what the mining law do say.'

He stared at her until she said uncomfortably, 'You can take some greens back with you. And some bacon. And there's a 'are what bin 'anging—'

He thanked her hastily and made his farewells. He could smell the cottage interior on his clothes; but he didn't care.

Edwin drove towards Bradford-on-Avon and stopped the car on one of the wooded banks. The river ran through green fields with a serenity and sparkle that reminded March vividly of Aunt Lizzie. She wondered how on earth that wonderful woman had been happy with this awful creature. Four miscarriages . . .

Edwin said, 'Is the child asleep?'

March glanced into the back seat and nodded.

'Good. Come here.' He made an ungainly grab at her, knocking her hat askew and hurting her breast. She gave a tiny, startled scream and held him off somehow. He grappled, panting furiously. He got his clawing fingers in the neck of her blouse and pulled hard; buttons flew everywhere and her camisole was revealed. He tugged at that.

'Edwin!' Her voice wobbled furiously. 'What do you think you are *doing*! Let me go this minute – d'you hear—'

'Whore!' he gasped. 'Harlot! You've been sold to me for five hundred sovereigns and you're not worth—'

'Sold?' Her voice wobbled up a register incredulously. 'What do you mean – sold?'

'Marital relations! That's what he said! And you promised to obey me – only two years ago – love, honour and obey! And I am *commanding* you now – commanding you!' He reared up behind the steering-wheel and flung the frail weight of his body on to her. The remembered smell of him almost made her vomit. She flung back her head and screamed at the top of her voice. Albert-Frederick woke immediately and joined his howls to hers. Like a scene in a farce, a courting couple hidden among the long grass on the river's edge also knelt up hesitatingly and stared at the rocking Wolseley.

March sobbed, 'Those people – my God – they can see everything!' Edwin glanced behind him and saw that they could indeed see everything. He whipped March's coat over her breasts. She immediately reached over her seat and took Albert on to her lap.

Edwin sat there, breathing fast, not looking at the courting couple. After a while they disappeared and Edwin got out and wound the handle. They jogged on to the sandy road.

Albert-Frederick stopped crying but refused to take his face out of March's neck. She said tensely, 'Edwin, I came here for the sake of your reputation only. If Frederick Luker said otherwise, he is a liar and a cheat.'

'You knew that already. You concocted this scheme together. I'm the donkey and you're the carrot . . . I accepted that. But I paid your – your *lover* – five hundred pounds to eat the carrot.'

She cried out at his coarseness and Fred's treachery. She imagined them talking together, working it all out. A carrot, to be bought and paid for and eaten. Not that the truth was much better. She might have guessed that in order to persuade Edwin to change his will in her favour, she would have to sleep with him. She hadn't used her intelligence; once again March Rising had been stupid. She huddled over Albert-Frederick's sunbonnet and was achingly silent.

It seemed to encourage Edwin, and he pulled off the road again. The car was silent; there was birdsong and Albert-Frederick's uncontrollable hiccoughing. He turned to her.

She said in a low voice, 'Edwin. Not again. I swear to you that if you lay a finger on me, I will let the Reverend Gough at the chapel know that we are living separately and that Albert is not your child. I swear that to you.'

'You have as much to lose as I have!'

'No. I shall go home. You will stay here.'

'I mean the money. I'll not pay any more to your fancy man. Not a penny more.'

'I should hate you if you did. Fred Luker can come and fetch me home but I shall not speak to him and I shall have nothing more to do with him. I swear that to you too.'

'Don't pretend you didn't know he had that money out of me. I won't believe you, March. After all, what was our marriage in the first place but a sale!'

To her own surprise, March began to cry on to Albert-Frederick's bonnet. 'Edwin, I made a mistake. I grant you that. Not just one mistake . . . I've done nothing but make mistakes. Ever since I was a child. All I can say is, I'm sorry. I'll stay for the rest of this week and save your face for you. If you want me to I'll come again on those terms. But there must be nothing else to it. I must be your great-niece again – never your wife.'

'He implied that when he needed money you would sleep with me—'

'He is nothing to do with me, Edwin. I don't care what he said. If I come to Bath again it will be of my own free will and because you have asked me. Nothing to do with Fred Luker. Now. Let us go home. Please.'

There was a long pause. Albert-Frederick buried his head in her shoulder and struck out behind him with a tiny fist. Edwin watched her slow tears and thought of the things he could say that would hurt her even more. But now he was tired and it did not seem worth it.

'Will you really come again? Sometimes?'

'I don't know – I can't promise—' She thought of Fred whom she had lost. Or never had. 'I expect so.'

'I will be an uncle to you, March. Just an uncle.'

He waited for her reply and when it did not come he got out again and cranked the Wolseley, and they chugged back slowly, just in time for tea.

March told herself she should be used to loneliness now, and anyway how could she be lonely when she had Albert-Frederick. But the tears would not stop and she pretended to Letty that she had a summer cold.

Fred had no difficulty in persuading Will to accompany him to the Lamb and Flag.

'Haven't got to see a man about a dog tonight have you Will?' he asked jocularly. Will shook his head and got into his new summer alpaca jacket. He did not much care for the way Fred Luker had started to call him Will instead of Mr Rising, and to turn his own little jokes against him. On the other hand Fred had shown him some of the money he now had, and Will knew he could be generous down at the Public.

The two men trudged down Chichester Street in the summer twilight and Fred explained briefly.

'If I can get hold of your brothers, I might be able to make our fortunes, old man,' he said, keeping up the jocular tone. 'Apparently the old custom still holds good in the Forest. And your Vi tells me that Austen is a St Briavels man. Couldn't be better.'

Will swung himself into the Lamb and Flag and went to the public bar.

'Two glasses full to the brim.' He nodded to Sid

Goodrich and Snotty Lottie. 'Don't be daft, Fred. Those old laws are gone and done for now. Some landlord 'ud soon come along and pitch you off his property—'

'It's Crown land, Will. All of it owned by George the bloomin' Fifth. Everyone's there with 'is permission. One more or less isn't going to make that much difference.'

'The miners themselves wouldn't stand for it. They're a funny lot Fred.'

'Don't I know it. Bugger me . . .' He took a breath and began to tell Will about that first visit to the Forest during his leave in 1917, then about the entrepreneur in the prison camp in Silesia.

Will said, 'Ah . . Silesia might be one thing. Dean is another.'

'Get one of them working and the others will follow. If Vi can remember her father talking about Austen's begetting, so will others. Don't you see Will, I've got a handle there. I'm not breaking any of their bloody laws – if Austen'll come in with me I'm using a Forest man to do my squat for me. And if there's any trouble we shall start digging around the Gavellers Arms – see if we can find any old skeletons.' Fred pushed money over the bar. 'Will, listen. I've got to get started quickly. If I don't I'm going to lose the contacts I've made. You've got to help me.'

'Me? What can I do Fred? I'm no miner—'

'Come with me to South Wales. Find your two brothers. Talk them into coming back and working for me. With me. A partnership if you like.'

'They wouldn't know the meaning of the word.

They're . . .' Will searched for words to describe his brothers.

'Like Vi?' suggested Fred. 'Then they'll work for me. Just find them for me, Will. I'll do the rest.'

Will laughed into his glass and drank. 'I'm not coming with you on any wild goose chase, Fred. When you came out of the army and bought that transport car you had the right idea. You can get another one – Henry's practically old enough to drive – and between you—'

'Will. You'd better come with me. Tomorrow.'

'What? Hey – who the devil d'you think you're—'

'Tomorrow, Will. Otherwise Florence might get to know about the man and his dog. Sorry . . . bitch.'

There was an electric silence.

Fred pushed a sovereign over the bar.

'Keep 'em going with that,' he instructed. 'I'm off, lads. I might have some work for you soon.' He touched Will on the shoulder and grinned when the alpaca jacket seemed to shrink away. 'Till tomorrow Will. Be ready early. Sevenish.'

He went outside. He had drunk too much and had too little food. He stuck his fingers down his throat and vomited into the gutter. Then he walked back down to number seventeen to see what Hettie had been cooking.

May had to admit that the members of the Mincing Light Opera Company were very friendly and definitely a cut above the Happy Hey Days lot. They gave her the seat next to the lavatory door because she needed to pass water rather frequently these days. Every time she went in and lifted the seat and saw the rails flashing by, down the long tube, she felt rather peculiar and had to pull out the small basin and hang her head over it for a few minutes. It worried Monty and she refused to tell him it was because of last night's party. She refused to talk to him very much at all. He had not noticed that, which was aggravating but not surprising, with one of the company an ex-Minstrel who still had his ukelele and insisted on playing 'Yankee Doodle went to London, riding on a pony . . .' because it was American Independence Day whatever that was.

Monty didn't know either, and when the day was explained, he said, 'I'm surprised it's a time for rejoicing. I should have thought the poor things regretted it more each year. To think they could have been part of our glorious Empire and they turned it down!' The ex-Minstrel laughed uproariously at this and so did one of the ladies, but the others nodded and of course May knew exactly what Monty meant; darling Monty, whose ideas and feelings ran exactly parallel with her own. She smiled at him fondly and then remembered she was furious and hurt and straightened her face. 'Dearest girl, have you got a pain?' he asked anxiously. She gave him a straight look from her very blue eyes and turned to look out of the window.

They were two hours at Crewe awaiting an engine to pick them up and take them on to York. The Company contralto, who had the biggest chest May had ever seen, got out a small meths stove and made tea and people came to their carriage and sipped it delicately from bakelite picnic cups as if they were in a drawing-room using bone china. The ex-Minstrel took a small mouthful of the remaining leaves, tipped his head back and made a horrible, gargling, choking noise. 'Helps to keep the tone gravelly,' he explained to Monty and May. There were other groups of coaches stationed in the same siding, and after the tea, Monty lifted May down carefully on to the ballast and they took a short stroll up and down while Monty read off the various Companies emblazoned on each coach.

'Reserved for North Company. *East Lynne*.' Monty sighed and squeezed her arm. 'This is Theatre my darling girl. Concert parties are all very well, but this is top-drawer.' He stopped suddenly and gazed at a compartment window framed in damask curtains where a gentleman and lady sat eating chicken drumsticks from napkins. 'Is that . . . is that Beerbohm *Tree*?' he breathed. May took great delight in saying shortly, 'Beerbohm Tree died during the war. Even I know that!'

'I thought he looked rather wooden,' riposted Monty immediately.

'Very amusing,' May acknowledged and had great difficulty in not laughing.

Fred waited until they had negotiated the narrow streets out of Bath before asking March any questions. She looked tired, her hair, normally glossy brown with lights everywhere in it, was simply brown. And she was so thin. She was wearing the jacket that her blasted brother had made her long before the war and she barely filled it out. He thought fiercely, 'Dammit all. I will make a pile somehow. The old man will die and I'll marry her and make her the greatest lady in Gloucester. Dammit, I will do it.' And he said aloud, 'This is the place. One of those model factories it is. I'll have to buy the first load on the open market but after that . . .' She said not a word and he asked abruptly, 'Well? Was it . . . unpleasant?'

She didn't give him a glance but held Albert-Frederick so that he could stand on her lap and look over her shoulder at the passing countryside.

He said impatiently, 'I can see you're in a temper. Shout at me if you want to. It was the only way I could get the old man to take you back and pay the money. Dammit all, you only had to open your legs! It's happened before, nothing to look deathly about!'

Still she was silent, and his words, perforce shouted above the engine note, seemed to hang hideously in the air between them. Albert-Frederick bounced joyfully, leaned forward and gave his mother one of his special, wet kisses. Fred saw from the corner of his eye a slow tear gather on her lashes. He swallowed. She never cried. March shouted and screamed and hit out in all directions. She did not cry.

He said, 'Go on. Tell me I'm a swine. Swear at me.' He waited and she said nothing. Albert subsided onto his well-padded bottom and she cuddled him down against her shoulder to go to sleep. On the top of his sunbonnet was a circular damp patch. Her tears? He drove on, giving her time, hoping that the sights and sounds of Bristol would take her out of herself.

As they approached Thornbury he said, 'Next stop Almondsbury. I'm going to buy you a lemonade and a sandwich. You need building up.' He felt a sudden tense quality in her stillness and added hastily, 'It's all right, I haven't booked us in at the George. I thought you should arrive back the same day I collected you.' She relaxed imperceptibly and he frowned. Twice – just twice – he had made love to March Rising, but each time she had wanted it.

He parked outside the George and fetched refreshments on a tray. Albert-Frederick slept soundly. Fred sat on the running board and drew at his beer, and his mood hardened as her silence continued.

'Look, you'd better know what's been happening in your absence. You need not make any comment, in fact I'd prefer you not to. Bit of a mess at the moment, but it's going to work out. I'm going to make it work out. Then perhaps you'll understand why I did . . . what I did.' He looked up. She was staring through the windscreen, an uneaten ham sandwich in her hand. He went on carefully, 'They backed out. The Freeminers. They thought I was an idiot with a big mouth and they listened to me as . . . as an entertainment. Like they'd have listened to Monty Gould. When it came down to it, they weren't there, so the money stayed in my pocket.'

He thought he heard a sound from her and glanced up again. She was as before. He drank again and continued. 'I heard about the old Forest custom – you probably know it. You build a fire grate and get smoke rising from it during the night and you can lay claim to a certain section of land. It was done a lot two or three hundred years ago. No reason why it can't be done again. But I need local men to help me. So . . . your father and me, we went down to the Rhondda yesterday and found your uncles. Jack and Austen. They're over at number thirty-three right now, and tomorrow I'm taking 'em down to Whitecroft and Parkend – that's where most of the open-cast mines are.'

There was a definite sound from above him this time, and looking up again he saw on the immobile face what might have been an expression of scorn.

'I know I can't dig out enough to make it worthwhile. I know all that, March. But once I can show the other pig-headed fools what I'm prepared to do . . . your father says it will mean a summons. He can't understand that the scale of business I'm prepared to do will make a summons worthwhile.' He counted on his fingers. 'There are at least a dozen Freeminers still pulling coal out of those seams. The mines drain down into the middle of the basin where the big Cannop Colliery pumps out the water. So the surface mines require no pumps. There's no problem with gas – no overheads at all. Each of those dozen Freeminers has a family who will help. They say they're not interested in money, but the sort of money I can make for them . . .' He put his glass on the running board and slapped his knee. 'Well, that's it March. I'm going to be working my guts out for the next year or two. After that . . .' He pushed himself upright and looked down at the top of her hat. 'Will you be all right over there with your mother for a year or two?' he asked roughly. 'There won't be much you can do to help me. Bit of typing perhaps. I'm going to get Sib to talk to Old Man William, so you need not worry about that.'

She spoke quietly, 'I'll be all right. It's what I want. More than anything in the world. To be with Mother.' She seemed to relax into her bucket seat at last.

He was embarrassed with her; just as he had been embarrassed as a young lad when she had been so far above him, so much in possession of that great mystery, herself.

He said, 'Be a bit crowded for a few nights. Your uncles . . . But I'll have 'em out by next week.'

She inclined her head and kissed the top of Albert-Frederick's sunbonnet. He got in beside her and drove carefully back through all the lovely Severn villages. He was this side of the river again now; not separated from March at all. Yet separated completely.

He remembered how she had been after Albert's death; withdrawn and hurt so badly he had imagined he had seen her body gently bleeding. That time he had forced her to put all her agony into sexual fervour, and – curiously – come to terms with both pain and passion. Now, glancing almost nervously at her, he wondered whether he might have done better to cook up some story for Florence Rising and book a night at the George.

But it was too late now. She would come round. Eventually.

Chapter Four

April had expected that sharing a home with her mother-in-law would prove very difficult at first. The shop and cutting-room facing the Barton were very small, the parlour and kitchen behind them smaller still. Mrs Daker, well known for her strange, cantankerous ways and her dislike of the Risings in general, had ruled the roost at 'Daker's' since her husband had died on the same day as April's own birth. On the other hand, during the frequent visits April had made to the shop as a schoolgirl, and because of her staunch friendship with David, ostracized by the rest of the Risings, the old lady had nurtured a soft spot for the harum-scarum girl with the cropped hair and hand-me-down clothes. April had an open, frank manner that ignored any awkwardness and permitted her to say such things as 'Lovely day, Mrs Daker,' when it was raining outside, and even 'I like to hear you sing, Mrs Daker – it sounds like hope.' So that, although the two women were wary still at sharing such close accommodation, there was careful circumspection on each side and a respect that might one day – with luck – develop into a kind of love.

What April had not expected was to find any awkwardness in the small front bedroom above the shop. There she had imagined a closeness with David that would be like the merging of their souls. She had imagined intimate looks that spoke a thousand words. She had imagined small and tender jokes, such as they shared long before marriage. April had looked forward to the day when she could give herself to David and he could give himself to her.

But she found that there had been more intimacy between them when they had not shared a bedroom. Nightly she gave herself to David, offering herself with a curiously innocent abandon which she shared with May; and because David did not give himself, there was always a small secret part of her that carried shame. He induced a physical ecstasy in her that she could not have imagined before, but because he did not share it with her she was reminded obscenely of Sibbie's words . . . 'he'll give you a good time'. Their love-making was something reserved entirely for the bedroom, it did not carry over during the day to be remembered in small smiles or even pretended archness. They had to work hard to resurrect their easy, tender friendship during breakfast; after supper they discarded that with their clothes.

They were . . . busy. During their honeymoon they walked the cliffs to Flamborough Head where the wind from Scandinavia made speech impossible. They went into the long fish sheds on the old quay and saw the lines of girls in their kerchiefs and big oilskin aprons gutting the herring so quickly it was difficult to follow their hands. David refused to swim because of his wound, but he sat on the beach and watched while April swam alone, lying on the water with her eyes closed against the sun while the ice of the North

Sea seeped through to her bones. When David towelled her dry, she said suddenly, 'Oh David, I love you so!' But there was bewilderment in her voice, and when he said, 'Do you my darling?' she was convinced it was her fault that he held back from her.

That night, as May got ready to attend the farewell party on the stage at Kilburn and March returned home from Bath, and Will and Sibbie cavorted in the wooden bungalow on the canal bank, and the uncles sat with Gran and Sylv and Florence and talked of the old days when Albert and Teddy had been alive . . . on the last night of their honeymoon, April wept and at last tried to talk to David.

'It's wonderful darling. Like heaven. But you're not there with me.' He kissed her and held her close.

'Don't say that, Primrose. You are my only hope of heaven.' His voice was deliberately light; his daytime voice. She tried to look into his face and could not.

'What on earth d'you mean darling?'

'If I present myself alone at those pearly gates, they'll surely turn me away. But if I'm with you—'

She was suddenly impatient. 'Oh David, be serious. Please. I know . . . I know what should be done. Tell me why . . . why . . . you won't do it!'

There was a silence. She pushed at his chest, wanting desperately to see his face in the frail light from the gas jet, but he held her to him fiercely. She whispered at last, 'It doesn't matter. I'm sorry—'

'No! It does matter – let me tell you. You must never think I don't love you with my whole self, April – that phrase, consumed with love. I know what it means.

93

It's like a fire, my love for you, and sometimes I think it will destroy me!'

She gave a small cry and encircled him with her arms, kissing his throat, holding him as if she expected his body to be ripped from her physically. 'I won't let it happen – I won't let it!'

'It's all right my love, my little love . . .' He found himself comforting her, stroking her hair. '. . . You are also my salvation, April . . .' He forced a laugh. '. . . As I said, my passport to heaven.'

She fumbled desperately with the problem of her husband. 'David, I do understand. When you came home first and nothing had changed . . . I mean, you had changed, your whole world had become hell and there we were – blind – not seeing what was happening. You could hear screaming and smell burning, and we just laughed and—'

He was amazed at her perception; he had known she felt for him, agonized for him, but that she *knew* and could find words to name something that, to him, had been nameless, was amazing.

He murmured, 'So you gave your beautiful hair to the Red Cross and went to work in the munitions factory.'

She clung harder. 'It was puny. I know it was stupid – you told me off, d'you remember? But I was trying to tell you that I wanted to be with you – I was trying to reach you—'

'In hell, Primrose?'

'Yes. In hell.'

'No-one can be with you in hell, my darling. That's what hell is. Isolation. If someone joins you, it is no

94

longer hell.' He kissed the top of her head. 'You did something much better than joining me, April. You forced me to think of someone else. Something else. That's why you are my salvation. Can you understand that?'

'I think so.' She rubbed his spine, feeling each vertebra with tenderness. 'That's why you married me. You saw it was selfish to keep me waiting any longer.'

'Oh Primrose. Sometimes you're as wise as a seventy-year-old crone! Then you say something like that and I am reminded that you are seventeen.'

'And you are twenty-eight, David! *Not* eighty!'

'I can be both. Like you.' At last he took her shoulders and held her away from him. 'Listen. It seemed right – it *was* right – at first, to keep away from you. Then there was Armistice night and I . . . you . . .'

'You realized that over half of me was grown-up, David.'

'Yes. All right. So then you pestered me unmercifully – yes you did – don't deny it—'

'I don't deny it.'

'And I was weak enough – wicked enough – to give in. But I made conditions for myself. You were seventeen. I could not bear to see you big with child.'

She whimpered a laugh. 'Big with child. Like the Bible.'

'Just like the Bible. A pact. A biblical pact.'

April was silent. She too had bargained with God. For David's life. For Fred Luker's life. For happiness.

He said at last, 'Now do you understand, April?'

'Yes,' she whispered. 'But I don't think you're right.

To make a baby together would be . . . would *be* heaven.'

'And then? To bring a child up in this rotten world? Wouldn't that be hell?'

She looked into his dark eyes and saw the bleakness returning, but still she tried. 'Does that mean . . . do you never want to have children, David?'

He answered her with a question that was a cry for help. 'Am I not enough for you, April?'

And she responded instantly. 'Always. Always and always, my dearest.'

She would have slept then, friendly in his arms. But when he caressed her, she felt she had to prove something. She moved against him, opening her mouth to his, responding to his touch like a finely tuned instrument. And the next morning their dual selves were waiting for them again, their dual intimacies which somehow could not be fused.

But if she had to prove something to him in the bedroom, it was as if he had to prove something to her in the shop. His uncaring attitude to the business disappeared on their return to Gloucester. True to his word, he made April a replica of her wedding frock in peacock-blue silk. He made her a blouse in shantung with enormous sleeves, like bat wings, called magyar sleeves because the Hungarian gypsies who went around with their hands permanently on their hips, wore them. He bought a wax model and draped it with one of the new up-and-down frocks and stood it in the window which had for so long displayed only gent's suiting.

People began to flock to Daker's. Sometimes they

stood in the Barton and gazed at the dummy and hid smiles behind their gloves. Sometimes they came inside for a reel of cotton to see April's latest creation. Soon they were ordering blouses and dresses for themselves. Will, forcing himself to go through the door he had vowed never to open again, said jokingly, 'You're going to put me out of business, April!'

She said quickly, 'It's nothing to do with me, Daddy. It's David. He's working so hard.'

Will nodded and said acutely and with regret, 'It's a new world, April. In my day I had my name on the window and that was all. Now, it's different. You put your goods in the window these days. David is showing off his work on a beautiful girl and everyone wants to look like you, my darling.'

She made a face. 'So I'm the goods in the window, am I?'

He laughed with her, but noted something in her eyes that made him think to himself: she'll soon be back home . . . she's not happy.

Florence spooned bread and milk into her grandson's rosy mouth and tried not to watch March over-anxiously as she sat at the table, her hands listlessly in her lap. Albert-Frederick tried to take the spoon in his own fat fingers and blew milky bubbles as it escaped him yet again. March did not laugh with her mother; she hardly seemed to notice her baby.

'March dear, I think this child could do with a walk this afternoon. He's getting bored with being in the house every day.' Florence wiped at the milky face and gave over the empty spoon. Albert-Frederick banged on the tray of his chair. Florence went on loudly, 'It's overcrowded here with Jack and Austen. Let's go to the park. We could walk along Spa Road, through the sunken garden and sit under Raikes' monument.'

March focused her, then took the spoon and stood up. 'Yes. All right, if you like.' Albert-Frederick yelled his frustration and she slapped at his grasping hand.

Florence could contain her anxiety no longer. 'Are you worried about poor Edwin, my dear?'

'No, of course not.' March widened her eyes like a frightened horse; very much as Florence had noticed April widening hers lately.

She said decidedly, 'Then you must be missing your sisters.'

March nodded gratefully. 'Especially dear April,' she agreed.

They put Albert-Frederick in the pushchair and lifted it down the steps, pausing ritualistically for him to point out the boot-scraper and Grampa's name on the window. And as they did so the telegraph boy's red bicycle turned into Chichester Street and bowled towards them. March put her hand to her breast; she would never forget the War Office telegram about Albert as long as she lived. The boy scraped the toe of his boot along the gutter and pulled up in a flurry of dust. Albert-Frederick sneezed.

Florence tore at the envelope and spread the paper. 'Can't see . . . glasses,' she said faintly. March took the flimsy sheet. 'It's all right. No reply.' She out-stared the boy who was standing there brazenly waiting for a tip, then turned to her mother. 'It's from Monty. It says "Victor has started his journey stop all's well stop more news later stop Monty."' She folded the paper and gave it to Florence. 'What a waste of money. However, May told me he was being paid twenty pounds a week! Twenty pounds – imagine it!'

Florence said, 'May, in labour. Oh March – oh darling – poor little May!' She turned. 'I really think we should go back inside and wait for the next wire.'

March looked determined. 'Oh no Mamma. You're not going to sit and worry for the rest of the day. There's nothing at all we can do about it. We'll walk to the park, then we'll come back down the Barton and tell April. By the time we reach the house, there might be some more news.'

Florence's black cotton gloves fluttered about her throat uncertainly. Then she nodded. The two women moved off down the street, stopping to let people speak to Albert-Frederick: Granny Goodrich, Hetty Luker, Daisy coming home for her half-day from Woodward's the chemist. It was like a royal progression.

They were in Manchester. There were fifteen theatres in the city, fifteen companies needing theatrical diggings. Mr Brockwell who went in advance and 'fixed them up', had allocated Monty and May to a house where there were already five children, on the grounds that the landlady must know how to deliver them. Mrs Turner put three saucepans full of water on the gas stove, and sent her five out to play. They ran up and down the back alley behind the house, shouting and screaming; she ran up and down the stairs flapping her apron and asking Monty where the doctor could have got to.

May was wonderful at first. She woke in the early hours to a strange, tearing sensation in her groin that was not too painful at all. When she got out to sit on the chamber-pot, she found her nightdress stained and she woke Monty excitedly. He went down and made tea and they sat up talking about the advantages and disadvantages of boarding-schools until Mr Turner went to the iron foundry at six o'clock. May could still feel objective about the lump in her abdomen, and after Sibbie's disclosure or boast or whatever it had been, she had come to wonder whether she might have let Monty feel neglected. He had told her once that he was the only baby she must have, and it was true she had practically seduced him when he was drunk on Armistice night. So she seriously considered letting Victor go to one of the new kindergartens when he was three. Or four. Or perhaps six. But that was before he was actually born.

At midday the tearing sensations had a clawing quality to them and extended around her back and down her legs. They made her feel terribly tired, yet ensured that she could not sleep. She told Monty he had better go for the doctor and send a telegram to Chichester Street. 'Make it amusing,' she instructed. 'Mother mustn't worry.'

But by the time Monty returned, May was writhing at regular intervals, and as she writhed, beads of sweat appeared on her upper lip and tears of fright came into the corners of her eyes. It was then that Mrs Turner began running up and down the stairs and the screaming of the children suddenly seemed unbearable.

In between pains May gripped Monty's hands desperately.

'Darling boy, I don't want you to see me like this, but I can't manage without you . . . Could anything be wrong d'you think? Surely a little pressure from inside couldn't be like this? He's been kicking and moving about for ages now and there's been no *pain* . . . oh – oh Monty it's coming again . . . oh dear God . . . oh Mamma . . . Mamma!'

Monty tried to cradle her and was amazed at her strength as she pushed him from her to reach up and grab the brass bed rail and pull her contorted body up as if she could draw it away from the pain.

The doctor arrived, young and raw, and insisted on Mrs Turner's presence while he examined his patient. Mrs Turner, veteran of five births, had not actually seen one. She held her throat with one hand, her stomach with the other and very obviously fought against heaving.

'By no means dilated,' the doctor said nervously. 'Try to relax a little Mrs . . . er . . . Gould. You are working against your contractions.'

He lacked the simple language and the authority of a midwife and May ignored him and thrashed about helplessly.

Mrs Turner gasped, 'Hot water . . . downstairs . . .'

Monty hovered at the top of the landing. 'Isn't there anything you can *do*? She can't go on like this. My God, if I'd thought – we'll never have any more. Just get us through this and we'll never—'

The doctor said, 'Ether tends to slow things down, of course.' He bit his lip as May choked a scream behind the door. 'She could do with some nursing care.'

'Anything. We've got cash. When – who – where—'

'I'll send someone.' The doctor couldn't wait to get away. He edged past Monty and went down the stairs in a rush. Monty hesitated, listening to him speaking to Mrs Turner, then went into the bedroom.

Fred turned out of Northgate Street and bounced down Mews Lane to the stables where his younger brother, Henry, was currying the big dray horse which was all that was left of old Alf Luker's livery business. It was six weeks since his abortive meeting with Danby in the Gavellers Arms, and he was ready to make his bid to 'squat'. Austen had come with him on his furtive search for a site with a likely 'coal dig' as he put it, and when he had found it, Fred had gone to great lengths to conceal their tracks. Since then he had quietly supplied the spot with enough food and equipment to keep them going for a week if necessary, and tonight was the night. Somehow they had to comply with that ridiculous law and build a fireplace, a skeleton dwelling around it, and a chimney.

He parked the small charabanc within reach of the outside tap.

'Good wash Henry, soon as you can.' He climbed out stiffly and stretched himself, then plucked a sovereign from his jacket pocket and spun it in the air towards his brother. 'Oddfellows' dinner at Cheltenham Town Hall. Made a collection for me after. It's yours.'

Henry, prepared to be resentful and sullen, caught

it and grinned delightedly. 'Right business to be in, Fred,' he said cockily. 'Dunno why you waste so much time down in the Forest.'

'I'm not wasting my time, boy, don't worry about that.' Fred slid out of his jacket and folded it over one arm; his shirt was stained with sweat; it was a hot day. 'Going to be gone for a few days this time. I want you to take over the charrie. Right?'

Henry glowed. He was still sixteen and had only driven the charabanc while Fred sat critically next to him.

Fred went on, 'Our Glad has got the booking list and she'll tell you exactly when to leave and what to do. You listen to every word she says, our Henry. D'you hear me?'

'Ah. An' I won't be familiar. An' I'll change me shirt and wear your jacket and touch me cap and say wanna wipe y'r feet on me ass kind sir – and—' He dodged Fred's hand and went to the tap. 'An' why is our Glad doing all this booking bizz then, our Fred? What happened to the true romance story with you-know-'oo?'

This time Fred went after him and got him by the top of his right ear. Henry yelped and danced.

'You will never talk about Mrs Tomms disrespectfully my lad unless you want to feel the full force of my—'

'I didn't say nothing 'bout March Rising, our Fred—'

'Then you will say nothing in future either!' Fred sent him spinning back to the tap, dusted his hands and continued. 'Gladys doesn't enjoy the pickle factory any more than our Sib did. If we can get her interested in the business we might keep her off the streets.'

Henry rubbed his ear ruefully. 'You en't got a very high opinion of your fam'ly, 'as you, our brud?'

Fred picked his jacket up from where he'd dumped it on the bonnet of the charabanc. 'I haven't got much of an opinion of anyone, Henry. Anyone at all,' he said. And went to change into his working clothes.

By the time he had picked up the two uncles, Jack and Austen Rising, it was four o'clock. He packed them into the Morris together with overalls and beer bottles, and drove to the Cross, then turned down Westgate Street and headed for Newnham-on-Severn. Florence and March, returning along Eastgate Street from a call on April in the Barton, saw them and smiled at each other, thankful that the house would be theirs at tea-time. They had both searched unobtrusively for Albert's name on the new War Memorial at the park, and finding it, had felt the usual terrible pang.

Monty said wildly, 'My God, it's four-thirty! He promised he'd send a nurse – you can't go on like this my darling!'

May became rigid yet again, fighting a pain, then suddenly sat bolt upright clutching at herself. Terror held her face still.

'Monty – Monty! Something has happened – oh my darling, I've lost it – I've lost it!'

He pushed back the clothes. May's nightdress was saturated. He ran to the door and shouted for Mrs

Turner and she stumbled up the stairs, yellow-faced and apprehensive.

''Tis the waters missis. They'm broke, that's all. Should be a mite easier now. More room like.'

Monty was inordinately grateful to her, especially as it seemed she was right about the pain. May lay exhaustedly on the pillows and sipped tea and could be held to his shoulder.

'It's still there . . . Monty, it will come back. I know.'

'Not so badly, sweetheart. The nurse should be here and she will help you. Try not to—'

'Monty, I can't bear it.' May lifted her ravaged face and looked at him. 'I simply can't bear it. I've tried to be s-s-sensible – not to say anything – but you shouldn't have *kissed* her! If you love me how can you look at another woman?'

'Sweetheart, are you delirious? What do you mean?'

'S-s-sibbie said – she said you'd kissed her. After April's wedding. On the station platform.'

He was aghast. 'I *knew* something was between us! She is a wicked evil woman, May! And you believed her – oh my darling girl, do you think I could ever *see* another woman when I have known you?' He was so distressed he began to weep. 'Oh May – beautiful May. You cannot think so poorly of me that you really think—'

May pulled his head to her breast as she had done so often and he wept there like a child. Then a pain came upon her suddenly and she closed her eyes and bit her lip till it bled so as not to disturb him. The midwife came upon them in that pose: wife in the midst of a contraction, husband weeping all over her. She clapped her hands like an angry schoolteacher and thrust Monty from the room. Then she was out of her coat, into her white apron and starched headgear, hot water was sent for and poured into ewer then into basin – May always wondered why – hands were washed, scolding instructions begun. May thought of Snotty Lottie who had delivered all Florence's children with the well-known twisting emergence for which she was locally famous, and prayed that this woman had the same expertise.

Fred turned the Morris carefully off the Blakeney road into a track which skirted the Forest School at Parkend. He ordered the Risings out into the ankle-deep bracken and loaded them with the beer and clothing. Then he led them straight into the Forest along an unmarked way which, it seemed, he knew very well. They stumbled after him for over half an hour, rolling on unseen logs, slipping on leaves that were damp even in the height of summer. Jack and Austen kept up a steady stream of curses.

''Ow much bluggy further then Fred-lad?' bawled Jack at last, as he went down on one knee over a hidden stone. 'Sodd'n' 'ell, din't expec' this sort o' caper. Ee said ee wanted our expert 'elp. Not a bluggy forced march!'

'Nearly there,' Fred said briefly over his shoulder. 'And keep your voice down for Christ's sake. This is supposed to be secret.'

'No need for language,' Jack said mildly, picking himself up and shouldering his sack of beer bottles.

'Christamighty, we could've stayed in the Rhondda and 'eard clean talk at least.'

'Shut up, our Jack,' Austen advised. 'We cum this far . . . I've seen it, remember. 'Tis good coal.'

They emerged into a glade filled with sun and dissected by a tiny crystal-clear stream. In front of them the packed leaves rose sharply into a solid wall of oaks. Near the stream was a large tarpaulin-covered heap.

'Good.' Fred went around the dell like a sniffing dog. 'No-one's disturbed a thing. I left one or two traps around.' He got back to the tarpaulin, removed some stones which weighted it and flung it back. A pile of stores was revealed, tinned food, shovels and picks, candles and tobacco, camp beds, blankets. He grinned at them above the glorious jumble. 'Think I did my bit all right then? It's taken me a dozen trips to supply this, *and* I never took the same route twice. Did *you* remember it, Austen?'

'Bluggered if I did Fred-lad,' Austen grinned, stepped over the stream and dug his hand into the leafy loam. 'Come and look at this, our Jack. Ever seen anything like it?' Among the handful of loam, coal dust sparkled wickedly.

'Christamighty,' breathed Jack. ''Tis there. 'Tis just *there*!'

Fred grinned again. 'No tunnels, no gas, no floods. You just dig the stuff out. And it's ours if we can get up some sort of shack before tomorrow morning and light a fire.'

'No-one can see us, Fred. 'Oo's to know whether we does it or no?'

''Tis the Forest law,' Fred announced righteously.

'And we're not going to start by breaking any laws!'

He watched sardonically as they cavorted about like schoolboys, grabbing shovels and starting to dig willynilly, jumping the stream in their cumbersome boots, slipping on the bank, falling in the water. Then he walked into the sun and started to mark out a rough foundation with the heel of his boot.

It was Sylvia who broke the silence as they sat around the empty grate that evening long after Albert-Frederick had gone to bed.

'It would be tonight of all nights the men are missing,' she grumbled. ''Twould 'ave taken our minds off our May if they'd been cluttering up the place like usual.'

Will said good-humouredly, 'Don't I count as one of the men then? Or perhaps I'm not cluttering the place up quite sufficiently.' He sprawled out in his chair and Sylvia laughed obediently. Florence glanced at March and spoke almost apologetically, 'We do tend to take a long time in labour, Sylvia dear. I don't think we need worry unduly.'

But Sylvia had lost her baby girl in this very house, and she still considered May to be delicate.

'I just 'ope 'er man will remember to send another wire,' she fretted. 'These actor fellows are a flighty lot when all's said and done.'

'Monty's all right,' declared Will stoutly, thinking of his other two sons-in-law. 'He'll just be coming off stage now.' He had acquired one or two professional terms and liked to air them occasionally.

Sylvia looked across the room disbelievingly. ''E

wouldn't go on and do his songs tonight, surely? Not with his wife in labour?'

March spoke for the first time. 'Why not? May won't want him hanging around, I assure you.'

Sylvia thought of her husband, Dick Turpin, waiting outside her bedroom door, suffering the agony with her. They thought they had fine feelings, these in-laws of hers, but when it came down to it they could be a cold lot.

Will looked at his watch; Sibbie would be waiting, but he couldn't leave them like this. 'Where's our April? I thought you said you'd called in to tell her this afternoon? I did think she'd be down with us.'

Nobody answered him.

David said, 'Darling, I expect you want to walk along to Chichester Street for news. I'll get my stick.'

'No. I don't want to do that, David.' April had a strange set and stubborn look to her normally mobile face. 'I want to go to bed.'

David glanced at his mother, glasses on the end of her nose, reading that night's *Citizen*. A small smile lifted her inverted mouth.

'Very well dear. You go on up. I'll be with you in a moment.'

He made a show of locking up and putting out the breakfast cups and saucers. He was trembling with desire. The shop door pinged against its lock as he had one foot on the bottom stair. Cursing under his breath he stumbled through the dark room and unbolted it. A dark figure, vaguely familiar, stood there.

'Manny Stein – by all that's holy! What brings you here?'

David backed in and Manny followed. His stilted courtesy, his black hat which he constantly raised and lowered, his bag . . . all proclaimed him foreign.

'I was nearby . . . had to look you up . . . your charming wife . . .'

Mrs Daker became very Jewish and pressed him into her own chair. David called April. She came downstairs, her blue eyes black with pupil, the summer dressing-gown wrapped around her thinness revealing almost as much as it hid.

'Mr Stein – all right then – Manny—' She held out a hand and he took it in both of his. It was very hot and damp. David, watching, saw his reaction; the awareness in his dark face. April sat down quickly.

Manny Stein said, 'I have a job in your line. In London it is called the rag trade. Here it has more dignity—' He gestured towards the shop where the window announced bespoke tailoring.

'Welcome, welcome to the business, whatever it is called,' David said in a dry voice. 'We shall have to share ideas. April is a great one for innovation. Perhaps you should talk to her.'

'Don't be absurd, David.' April tinkled a laugh. 'Manny deals with ready-made clothing I dare say.'

'Yes. Certainly. But my wholesaler also supplies embroidery materials. Tapestry stands. I see you have a haberdashery line . . .'

'You're selling? At this hour?' David's brows went up. Manny Stein flushed.

'No. I had business in Cheltenham. And I thought—'

'Mr Stein must stay with us this night!' Mrs Daker brought in tea. 'He can have my bed with pleasure. I hardly close my eyes now.'

'I wouldn't dream of it, Mrs Daker. I have in any case reserved a room at the Bell Inn, but my train leaves at eight o'clock tomorrow.'

They looked at him anew. The Bell Inn. David said, 'You sound prosperous, old chap. Is it a sign of the times?'

'Indeed yes.' Manny nodded briskly. 'Always after a war there is a boom in fashion – luxury trades in general. And the new modes for ladies are very easy to copy.' He smiled at April. 'As your sisters knew when they made their wedding gowns.'

David waited for April's comments and when they did not come he said, 'Is there any possibility of you staying till a later train tomorrow, old man? I'd be interested to see anything you have.'

Manny suppressed a smile. 'But certainly David. For a friend, anything.'

April stood up. 'If we're seeing you tomorrow, Manny, will you excuse me now? I'm very tired.' Her cheekbones beneath the huge dark eyes looked unusually prominent. He scrambled to his feet and bowed ridiculously from the shoulders. She smiled tightly and avoided David's eyes as she went to the stairs. There was a short silence, then the voices droned on beneath her.

Angry and shaking she lay between the sheets, hours from sleep. At midnight she heard chairs scraping and David came up the stairs. He crept into their room, closed the door softly and began to undress by the light from the bead of gas in the popping mantle.

'I'm not asleep. Turn up the gas, David,' she commanded levelly.

He did as he was bid and looked down at her with the half-smile that always twisted at her heart with its strange mixture of love and sadness.

'Still awake, baby? Did we disturb you with our talk?'

'I have not been to sleep yet. And I am not a baby.'

He paused in the act of pulling off his tie and his smile became cajoling. 'I knew something was wrong. You were stiff with irritability.'

'I told you, I wanted to come to bed.'

'I know. We were going to bed if you recall. And Manny arrived. He was my best man at our wedding, Primrose.'

'He is a salesman. He came for business.'

'It crossed my mind. But . . . there is friendship too.'

She burst out furiously, 'He convinced you with that tale of the Bell! I could tell – you and your mother – you believed him!'

'Hush darling. He is still downstairs.'

'I don't care if he is here! In this room with us! He was laughing at you!'

'What does it matter, April? Surely you are interested to see some of his lines? It could be good for *our* business – which seems to absorb you fairly thoroughly!'

'Sometimes. Yes. Certainly. Now – tonight – I was interested in something else!'

His smile appeared again and he began on his shirt

buttons. 'Darling girl. Did you think for one moment that I put Manny Stein before you—'

She bunched herself into a corner of the bed, clasping the clothes around her. 'Don't come near me, David! I mean it – keep away—'

He stood there, braces dangling. 'I thought it was what you wanted. April, what on earth is the matter with you tonight?'

'Don't you know? There was a time when you would have known – instinctively you would have known what was the *matter* with me! That man . . . looking at me . . . making me feel . . . I don't want to be looked at, David! I don't want to be the goods in your shop window! My sister is having – has probably had – a baby! Tonight!' She was panting with anger and her voice was loud. 'I want a baby! I want a *baby*! D'you hear me?'

He continued to remove his trousers. 'I imagine most of the Barton heard you, Primrose.' He reached for his nightshirt. 'Manny is probably enjoying it very much. I don't see how he could help looking at you when you came down in that ridiculous dressing-gown—'

'I hoped he might take the hint. That we were going to bed – together. Like husbands and wives do!'

He picked up his trousers and put the legs seam to seam with great care. 'I thought you understood how I felt about you, April. And about children. We talked at Scarborough—'

'I'm too young and the world is too wicked! That was it, wasn't it? But I'm not too young. And it's up to us to make a world fit for our children. And if my sisters can—'

He looked up, suddenly angry. 'Do you have to copy May in everything?'

He had missed the point again. She almost stammered with rage as she searched for words to wound. Then she said, 'You didn't object when I picked you up after she'd dropped you!'

He finished smoothing his trousers over the bed rail. She sat up straight and held out her arms. 'I didn't mean that, David. I'm sorry.'

He turned and looked at her. As before, she was naked, her body thin but perfectly formed. He said through his teeth, 'Are you tormenting me deliberately April? Are you?' He grabbed at her and pulled her against him so that they were eye to eye. She said something in a gasping voice which he did not hear and he put his mouth on hers and forced her down again. She cried out against him and twisted to free a trapped leg. He pulled up his nightshirt and rammed into her furiously.

So for a few seconds of frantic activity. Then he collapsed and lay with his face in the pillow. And she stared at the gas globe until her vision starred.

Then, slowly, she closed her knees together and straightened her legs into the bed; next she turned on to one elbow and put her hand on David's springy hair where it grew into the nape of his neck. She leaned down and kissed the top vertebra in his spine. Stroked and kissed. Whispered into his ear, 'David. I love you. I love you, my darling. And you love me. That is all that matters. Without that I would want to die.'

He let her murmur for a long time, then, not looking up, he put an arm across her and lifted his head onto her breast. She held him, stroking, kissing, murmuring; far into the night.

All the way home from the theatre Monty prayed it would be over. It couldn't have happened during the performance because one of the little Turners had promised to run round with the news; but it might have happened in the last half an hour while he took off his make-up and wended his way through the streets of back-to-back houses, forcing his steps to slow each time they involuntarily quickened.

The light was on in the front bedroom.

Of course the light would be on; May would be waiting for him, wanting to show him the baby and kiss him and tell him never again. And then, like a blow across his face, came the scream.

He took three more paces to the next gas lamp, and hung on. The scream appeared to have been unheard by anyone else; the street remained deserted and uncaring; even the dust and smell of compacted humanity had been blown away by that single note that held the depths of exhaustion in its basic pleas. Monty muttered, 'Please God . . . please . . .'

Nothing else happened. It could have been the birth scream. He listened for the cry of a child. Nothing. He remembered the ex-Minstrel who was called Frank O'Rourke saying jokingly, 'Don't let it get the better of you, old man. It's always worse for the father!' Certainly Monty would infinitely prefer to be bearing this pain rather than listening to May bearing it.

He pushed his hat to the back of his head and laid

his forehead against the cast-iron lamp post. 'Please God . . . please God,' he muttered again. Then he straightened, marched another six paces to the front door on the street, found it, unlocked and let himself in to the cabbage smelling hall. Mrs Turner appeared at the other end of it, silhouetted in a square of light from the kitchen.

'Is it you, Mr Gould? I hoped the doctor . . .'

'You've called him again?' Monty hurried down the passage, divesting himself of hat and coat as he went.

'Twice sir. She's real bad. Weak, see. Seems she's very narrow – I noticed it myself when you arrived. Too much in front and not enough at the sides I said to my Bert.'

'Who is with her now?'

'Midwife. Reckon the doctor will want her in 'ospital.'

'Oh my God. My God.'

The front door opened again and the young doctor came in with a rush and went straight upstairs. Monty returned to the newel post and hung on to it.

It was very dark in Dean Forest that night. Fred worked stripped to the waist and gleamed whitely with sweat; the others eyed him askance and left their braces over their vests. They could have been mistaken for the wild boar that had once roamed these parts, grunting and digging and snorting and smelling. As one of them barrowed stone from a convenient ruined wall nearby, another shovelled and slapped at a big board of mortar and a third spread and sludged and bedded carefully. Occasionally they would stop one by one and reach for the bottles stacked in the stream. They spoke no word.

At three-thirty, Monty sat on the stairs and put his head on his knees. The doctor was still with May but all sounds had now ceased and Monty was certain she was dead. He tried to pray and could not. He tried to recall her face and it wavered behind his lids, a blur of angel-blonde hair, creamy skin and blue blue eyes; the intrinsic May was not there. Desperately he tried to instil his image with a persona; if he could not then she really was dead. He could keep her alive by force of will, but he must *see* her.

Mrs Turner said, 'Cuppa tea sir. Come on now, drink up.' He was angry with her for interrupting his concentration and gestured the cup to the step by his right leg. 'Gawd, what a night,' she went on in a half-moan, half-whisper. 'You en't going to forget this night for some time to come, are you sir?'

He did not reply and after a hesitant moment she backed down the stairs and disappeared again into the kitchen. As if at a signal the bedroom door opened and the doctor, shirt-sleeved, sweating and not quite so young as before, appeared on the landing and signalled him to come up. He kicked over his cup, ignored it and scrambled up the stairs.

'The position is – ' the doctor looked completely done up '– forced to anaesthetize to alleviate the weariness . . .' How could he use such long words at a time like this? 'Now we need her to be alert in order to . . .' She wasn't dead. May was alive.

'No time for fainting spells, man!' The doctor was

extremely unsympathetic, he jerked Monty upright. 'You have a part to play!'

His words could not have been better chosen. Monty listened hard to the producer of this particular drama and knew it was the part of his life. He took a deep breath and went into the bedroom.

He was prepared for blood, for smells, for disarray; there was none of that. Each time May disturbed the covering sheet, the nurse straightened it. Later she untucked the bottom and rolled it up for the doctor to examine his patient. There was no sign of blood and the smell was of strong antiseptic. But if Monty was disappointed, May's thin face, 'pale and peaky' as Florence always insisted, her damp-dark hair, her half-closed drugged eyes were drama enough.

'Monty . . .' Her voice was a thread of distress.

'It's all right my darling.' He crouched by the bed and took her hands in his. His eyes filled with tears.

'I don't want you to see . . . Please.'

'The doctor—' they didn't even know his name – 'he wants me to be with you for a few minutes, my sweetheart. That's all.' He kissed her knuckles. 'May. You have to start bearing down, darling. Next time you must bear down as hard as you can.'

'I know. She said that.' May let her eyes roll towards the nurse at the end of the bed. 'I can't. I can't do it, Monty. I'm too tired.'

'Of course you can do it, my beautiful. You've had a nice sleep.'

'They think I slept. But I didn't.'

Monty smiled at her. 'You'll be all right now I'm here. We'll do it together, May.' He made his voice confident. 'I'm going to hold your hands and they will hold your feet and we'll work really hard.'

The nurse said in a low voice, 'I think it's now.'

She rolled back the sheet expertly and exposed May's distended abdomen. Monty glanced over his shoulder and nearly shrieked in horror. The smooth white belly he knew and loved, suddenly had a life of its own. Grotesquely it contracted and convulsed and at the same time May gave a soft moan and closed her eyes as if trying to leave her body to manage alone. The doctor and nurse took a leg each and crooked it expertly and the doctor said, 'Now. Now if you please Mrs Gould. *Now!*' They pressed hard on the slim, race-horse legs and Monty averted his eyes, his part forgotten, his hands already slackening their hold on May's limp fingers. The doctor snapped, 'Come on Mr Gould. A little encouragement—' and the nurse cut across him with a single loud command, 'Push!'

Monty's voice rose to a trembling crescendo, his 'part' forgotten in sheer terror. 'May? May, wake up darling. Please wake up. May . . . please . . .' The transparent eyelids trembled and he shook her hands with frantic fussiness, like a pestering child. 'May! It's Monty. Open your eyes. You have to—'

The eyes opened and looked at him, first with puzzlement, then with the automatic reassurance they always brought to him. The doctor's voice stated his requirements once again with careful precision; the nurse repeated ringingly, 'Push!' and Monty stared at her, frightened, his clear brown eyes like Teddy's eyes when he was in trouble. Darling Teddy and darling Monty. Always wanting help . . . She gripped his hands in her long fingers, braced her heels on she knew not what and began to work.

The trees seemed to wake up slowly that morning of August the twelfth. It was going to be hot again and the leaves of the oak that had supplied so many navies sheltered one beneath another, very still, conserving their strength for the parched day ahead.

The small dell, which had been so beautiful in the evening sun the night before, appeared completely desecrated in the first of that morning's light. The banks of the stream had been broken down by trampling boots and the thick pad of leaves covering the right-hand bank had been churned into an open wound of fern roots, brambles, broken stone, dollops of cement, discarded timbers, empty bottles, even clothing. The strange construction overlooking this waste in no way resembled a hovel, let alone a cottage; it might have been a giant clothes-horse set about a miniature blacksmith's forge. And the men still moving around in a trance of weariness were feeding the forge with pathetic offerings of bracken and twigs.

Fred straightened his back.

'Right. The matches.'

Jack lumbered over to the trampled tarpaulin and grovelled through some loose candles, balls of twine and an assortment of cutlery.

'Austen!' he growled out of the side of his mouth. 'You 'ad 'em. Where b'ist?' Austen shook his head, incapable of speech. 'You were lighting the bluggy lantern—' Jack scrabbled futilely again and Fred galvanized himself into action, leapt through the open timber frame and snatched at the box of lucifers protruding from the tobacco tin.

'Christamighty,' he grumbled, setting light to the kindling. 'Lose the lot if I relied on anyone else wouldn't I? Sun will be coming through them trees any minute now—' As he spoke, one single piercing ray came through the tangle of waist-high fern behind the tin chimney, shone across the stream and spotlighted the point where Austen had shovelled out the coal-grit. Everyone looked towards it and seemed to stop breathing. Then there was a crackle, a spurt of flame, and a steady line of smoke, unwavering in the still air, rose steadily upwards. They watched it, tipping their heads until it surmounted the trees around them, a banner for anyone to see.

They looked at each other. They didn't have the energy to cheer.

And in Manchester, at number eleven Jubilee Walk, May gave the final push that expelled Victor Gould from the safety of her womb. And Monty did the classic thing, and fainted. May did not worry. Relaxed and instantly recovered, she lay back and watched with a little smile as the doctor saw to Monty and the nurse to Victor, and her eyes were oftener on Victor than on Monty. When they gave her the small wrinkled bundle, she was glad that Monty could not see her. It was a moment that excluded him completely. She looked at her son and knew how Florence had felt at Teddy's birth; how March had felt at Albert-Frederick's. *This* was what life was about. This was the ultimate fulfilment. There was no need for more. She was indulgent when Monty came to her, pale and apologetic and completely adoring.

'Darling boy. It must have been simply dreadful for you. I won't let it happen again, I promise.'

The nurse looked at her sharply. Monty, who had been about to beg her never to have another child, was taken aback and murmured, 'You might change your mind, dearest.'

She kissed him maternally. 'Don't worry baby. I won't. Two babies are quite enough for me.'

The nurse said, 'Mr Gould has been a tower of strength, Mrs Gould. An absolute tower of strength.'

May smiled, unable to explain that it was Monty's final weakness that had called forth her own strength. 'Yes. Yes, he would be,' she said.

Monty kissed her and let them usher him outside while they 'made her beautiful'. As if you could improve on perfection. He frowned, remembering how his 'part' had slipped away from him in those final minutes, then just as suddenly felt glad. It had been one of the rare times of his life when he had not been acting, when he had been utterly sincere.

Nobody connected with the Risings had attended the Victory Parade of the previous month in London, yet four weeks later they did indeed celebrate their personal victories in a variety of ways. Victor William, child of the Armistice, was born. Fred squatted on his coal seam and named it Marsh Cottage after March. And David triumphed over his own dark soul and let April see his final weakness.

Chapter Five

By 1923, when April was twenty-one and had been married for four years, an enormous change had somehow occurred in the Western world which was, sometimes pathetically, mirrored in the microcosm of narrow provincial life in Gloucester. Suzanne Lenglen was not only winning every singles match at Wimbledon, but she had brought the new fashion for freedom in women's clothes to its peak. April, who had joined the Hucclecote Tennis Club with her old friend Bridget Williams, wore a bandeau on and off court, and in the short skirts her husband made for her, worn with pale lavender stockings and long, cuban-heeled shoes, she had become one of the leaders of the social set in the city. She smoked her cigarettes in a long jade holder and blew perfect concentric smoke rings for her young nephews. David too was well-known, not only as a designer of women's clothes. He lectured at local church halls and institutes for the Worker's Educational Association. His subjects were diverse but not unconnected: Fabric and Design was closely linked to the Political History of the Industrial Revolution, and his art students left their course with a thorough knowledge of conditions in eighteenth-century weaving sheds.

Meanwhile their marriage had settled into a

pattern which both thought completely secure and immutable. April accepted that – for whatever reason – David did not want children, and she continued to demonstrate nightly that he was all in all to her. And David, still 'fighting his demons' as she put it, encouraged her to lead the city's social set from a long way in front. They were both conscious that there were limits to their undoubted happiness. David especially knew that beyond those limits was a precipice and a bottomless pit. So they worked at establishing their secure pattern and keeping within its boundaries, and a small incident that summer showed them how important those boundaries were.

March and May continued their patterns along very similar lines. May and Monty had acquired a house at last in a London suburb; and officially March still shared a beautiful home in Bath with her husband. But both girls preferred to spend most of their time at the shabby old terraced house in Chichester Street, where Florence, thinner still, conducted life with a gentle baton and provided just the right mixture of love, tenderness and asceticism that the varied Risings needed.

March, the pain of Fred's treachery scabbed over with bitterness, worked hard towards some sort of reconciliation with her uncle-husband in the hope of a solid reward after his death. She had visited him five times since that fateful week in 1919; the third time he had spoken of asking Mr Hazelbank to call. Mr Hazelbank was the Tomms' solicitor. He mentioned the proposed call each time March left him now, as if to ensure her return; but Mr Hazelbank had not come.

May was, as usual, enjoying life thoroughly. Victor

was handsome and lively and very intelligent; Monty was as devoted as ever; the new house was fun and they led a hectic life there, so that it was good to return to Gloucester now and then for a rest and to give Victor a taste of ordinary routine. May had the best of both worlds. Just as her father had.

May and March never discussed current affairs; their father and April did, though separately and at great variance. April, at home with David and her mother-in-law one evening that early summer, held forth with only surface objectivity.

'No. Actually I don't particularly mind I haven't got a vote. Most girls of my age aren't capable of making an intelligent choice. March will have a vote next year and she'll vote for Mr Baldwin's party because he looks like Papa!'

David, busy with his sketch-pad near the kitchen window, grinned appreciatively at this remark, but said gently, 'I didn't ask whether you minded, Primrose. I asked whether you considered it a fair arrangement. Men at twenty-one and women at thirty?'

April made a face. 'Of course it's un*fair*,' she agreed. 'But then, everything is, isn't it?'

David glanced up, pencil poised, wondering if April meant anything personal by that unusual cynicism. Mrs Daker sighed as if she was in front of the Wailing Wall, put down the evening edition of the *Citizen* and removed her glasses.

'President Wilson has lost,' she announced. 'America does not join the League.' She lifted her shoulders to her ears. 'It is in any case doomed.'

'But Mother, it is the hope of Europe!' April took up new cudgels, glancing at David for support in this at least. He treated the present as if it were already history and therefore merely interesting. But David narrowed his eyes, measured her – or something – with his thumb on his pencil and continued to draw.

Mrs Daker shook her head. 'Mr Wilson had no place for a Jewish nation in his plans,' she said.

'That might have come later, Mother. If only we can have a long enough peace, anything can be worked out. Negotiated.' She watched David irritably as he went on drawing. 'Well. What do you think?' she asked at last.

He flashed her an amused smile but did not stop work. 'I think the Dough boys and girls know what they're doing,' David said. 'They're a practical people, dealing in actualities and not hopes.'

'But the League is a practical idea!' April protested.

David shrugged. 'The concept of a re-formed Europe is asking for trouble. This new Czechoslovakia for instance – how many races – three, four? Rumanians, Slovaks, Germans. And as for the Polish Corridor – a red rag to a bull.'

'If you mean Germany is the bull, you must see you're wrong. They're a beaten nation.'

'They weren't beaten, Primrose. We made a peace treaty with them and it's not the same thing.' He grinned. 'Come and look at this and tell me what you think.' He showed her his sketch, putting the tip of the pencil on the knob that was the head of his figure. 'This is what the cloche hat does for design – incorporates the whole body, head and all, into one long line.'

'Ugly,' pronounced Mrs Daker. 'The female frame is not meant to look like a snake's. It is composed of different . . . features. The hat sets off the head. Then come the shoulders and the bosom.'

'But Mother, this is fashion!' April turned her enthusiasm into a channel where they could all agree. 'You have a genius for a son – David, if you make the hat even deeper – bring that tiny brim right down over the ears—'

David whooped with delight as he sketched in two short strokes at the top of his drawing. 'Mother, you have a genius for a daughter-in-law!' he declared.

'Of course there must be no sign of hair,' April mentioned.

'The shingle is the thing by which we catch the market . . .' David petered out helplessly and April finished for him.

'By which we catch the market with a zing!'

They clutched each other, laughing, and Mrs Daker said with a smirk, 'I have two lunatics for a son and his wife. That is what I have!'

Will, on the other hand, was perfectly satisfied with the state of things. Contrary to David's prediction, he thought America ought to keep out of their affairs from now on, even to the extent of forgetting the national debt.

'The least they could do,' he grumbled over his stout in the Lamb and Flag. 'Coming into the war when it was practically over—'

Lottie looked into her empty glass, then over the wall of the snug to where Will, Alf Luker and Sid Goodrich were putting the world to rights.

'Time to toast young April then, is it, Will?' She put her glass onto the counter. 'I did bring her into the world, so let me join you. I wouldn't mind a drop of gin if it's a special occasion.'

Will, quite used to her gambits, was undisturbed. 'First I've heard about it then Lottie.' But he signalled to the landlord all the same. His geniality had not abated since Armistice Day; Sibbie brought him business as well as pleasure, and life at number thirty-three was pleasant with just himself and the women. And young Albert-Frederick of course. What a nib, into everything.

Lottie feigned astonishment. 'Nothing in the oven yet?' she asked with her usual coarseness. 'How long she bin married then, Will?'

'Four years.' April was the one small speck in the clear blue sky of his content. She had not come home yet. March was still there most of the time; when Edwin was ill she always went to nurse him but it was never for long. April, on the other hand, called for an hour at a time and was always anxious to get back to David Daker. He passed Lottie her gin and looked into her knowing eyes. 'Maybe they won't have any family,' he said defiantly. 'It's not unknown these days.'

'Ah,' she agreed. 'Young April's spreading her wings and that's a fact. Them dresses she wears! And she smokes like a chimney!'

'They all do. She's a modern girl, Lottie.'

Lottie wiped away her dewdrop with the back of her hand and stuck her nose in her glass. When she surfaced she said lugubriously, 'It's not the life your

April wants, take my word for it. Made for mother-hood that girl was. Made.'

Will felt a pang at his heart. The thought of April with David Daker was still horrific to him; he had been almost relieved when Sibbie told him what the shrapnel wound had done to him. But the alternative of April being deprived of a child and trying to forget her need in what he called 'flapping' was even worse. He growled unguardedly, 'I always said that young Daker wasn't right for her – always said that.'

Lottie's eyes brightened, this was much more like it. She decided to roll up her sleeves metaphorically and chance her arm.

'Don't want to take too much notice of Sibbie Luker, Will,' she advised. 'David Daker wasn't the first one she'd sampled, and he won't be the last neither. I reckon most of the good citizens of Gloucester 'ave 'ad a conducted tour around that young lady, so 'tidn't no good holding it against David Daker.'

She watched with enjoyment as a dark flush spread up Will Rising's neck and into his face. She liked Will well enough and had felt sorry for him in the past married to the Rhys-Davies purity, but it wouldn't hurt him now and then to be reminded that he was in no position to be smug about the way he'd arranged things.

He muttered, 'Sibbie Luker is like her mother. Honest and straightforward as the day—'

'Casts their light over everyone d'you mean, Will?' asked Lottie innocently. 'Ah, I reckon you're right there.' She had gone far enough and subsided onto her seat again to talk to the dull but worthy Granny Goodrich from the dairy.

After a pause Will turned heartily to Granny's widower son, Sid, and told him what a good chap Baldwin was.

'It's his pipe,' he stated didactically. 'Shows him to be a regular Englishman. Not to be hurried or rushed into anything. Steady. That's Stanley Baldwin. Steady.'

'Ah. We need someone like that at the helm.' Sid nodded over his own pipe. 'D'you know, I had someone come in the shop the other day and ask me if I wanted to join the International Labour Party. What d'you think of that, Mr Rising?'

'Damned cheek,' Will exploded. 'Artisans like us –' he included Sid in the term – generously, as he was only a shopkeeper – 'our own men – that's us. Even before Lloyd George did away with the workhouse!'

'I reckon we did ought to band together though,' Alf Luker said into his tankard. 'D'you know what? All those young 'uns what fought for King and country, lot of 'em en't got no jobs and if they en't got anyone to fight for 'em they don't allus draw any money.' He supped deep. 'I reckon we ought to band together.'

'Unions you mean,' Will said scornfully. 'Get over to Russia if you want that sort of thing, Alf. Christamighty, your Fred en't doing so badly on his own.'

Alf's rheumy eyes went from his beer to the stained counter top and up along the roll of honour on the wall behind the bar.

'Our Fred's different,' he said at last. 'Dunno where 'e gets it from – not me nor 'Ettie. 'Im and Sib, they's the same. Determined. 'Ard as nails. They'se a union all to themselves an' tha's a fac'.'

They were back to Sibbie again. Sometimes Will thought everything began and ended with Sibbie Luker.

But he wished Lottie hadn't said what she'd said. Sibbie might have been a naughty girl before she took him, but since then – five years almost – she'd not looked at another man. Surely.

May was on one of her frequent visits to Gloucester. She brought presents for everyone, although it was less than a month since she'd scattered her largesse before. There was a steam engine for Albert-Frederick who was displaying an inordinate interest in all things mechanical. There was perfume for March and April, a box of dates for Gran and Aunt Sylv, ridiculous lace hankies for Florence, an enamelled daisy brooch for Daze, tobacco for Will. May was dressed, not entirely in fashion, in trailing silk, Victor was handsome and stalwart in velvet. May was no penny-pincher, Monty was still getting good parts in the kind of operettas that were all the go now, and she spent whatever he gave her.

But the news she brought with her now was of the house.

'My dears, it's absolutely delightful. Practically inside Bushey Park – not far from Hampton Court, April, which you'll just adore. We have to be near London, you see. All the big shows are there.' She snatched four-year-old Victor from the floor where

Albert was accusing him of 'interfering' with the new steam engine. 'Baby, you wouldn't like it anyway.' She kissed the protesting child. 'Well then, Mummy will buy you one all for yourself.'

'You spoil him, May,' March disapproved. 'He's not really interested anyway, it's just because it's Albert's.'

May said, 'And as Albert won't share his toys, I'll have to buy Victor one of his own.'

April put her cigarette in an ashtray and knelt on the floor. 'Darling, let's show Victor how it works, shall we?' she cajoled her older nephew.

March too knelt down. 'You will share the toys that Aunt May brings you,' she told her son tightly. 'Give the engine to Victor.'

May instantly regretted her small dig. 'Oh don't be silly March. You're right. Victor isn't really interested.'

'I am! I am!' Victor shouted.

'He'll break it,' Albert looked up at March defiantly, then saw her expression and repeated without hope, 'Mummy, he'll *break* it!'

He hung on to the steam engine and March gripped it and forced it from his fingers and passed it to Victor. Albert did not cry. He watched with all his eyes as Victor turned the small brass model over and over. May slid him to the floor.

'Listen. Girls. I've had the most marvellous idea. How about if I ask Mamma to look after Victor – you do the same, March – and we three go up to London together? Just for a weekend. Monty is up at Harrogate until next week and we could have a wonderful time, just the three of us. You'll love the house and I can take you into town and show you the sights . . . oh do say yes!'

April sparkled immediately. 'It would be rather marvellous,' she agreed. She had her hand casually on Albert's left shoulder blade and she pressed it as she turned to him. 'You'd love having Grandma all to yourself, wouldn't you Albie?'

'Don't call him that please April.' March levered herself back into her chair. 'And I'm not sure that Mother is up to looking after two children.'

'Aunt Sylv will do most of it,' May said. 'And Mother would *adore* to think of her three chickens painting London town red!'

April squatted by Albert, picked up her cigarette and blew a thoughtful ring. 'What do you say, March?'

'We'll see what Mother thinks.'

It was as good as an enthusiastic agreement coming from March. April released Albert and hugged May's knees and May tickled Victor's velvet stomach until he doubled up with giggles, dropped the steam engine on to the floor where the flywheel snapped off.

'What a good job Uncle Fred can mend that sort of thing.' April smiled at Albert and handed him her cigarette holder. 'Here darling. See if you can make a smoke ring like Aunty April.'

He looked at March and shook his head dumbly, his mouth drawn in to bottle a sob. May was telling everyone that darling Victor hadn't meant it and March was ignoring the steam engine and frowning angry disapproval at April.

April jumped up and put the engine on the mantel-piece. 'For Fred,' she remarked, then went to the gramophone.

'Let's hear that song again, May, shall we? Albie – come and dance with me—' She wound furiously and placed the needle. The strains of Kern's 'Look for the Silver Lining' filled the old bandy room. She took Albert in her arms and sang the words to him significantly. He encircled her neck with his thin arms and smiled at her adoringly.

Later Florence joined them with a tray of tea things and May sat at the piano and played the latest craze, 'Kitten on the Keys'.

And at the Midland Hotel in Manchester, the leader of the resident dance band, a young man called Henry Hall, played the same number as his solo, and received no less applause. Music, Modes, and Money were the new vogue. And the Risings were dabbling in all three.

Fred heard of the proposed London weekend from his sister, Sibbie, and was not a bit pleased.

'A few years ago neither Will nor Florence would have permitted them to go up there alone! I'm surprised at that sop May calls a husband. As for Daker—'

Sibbie lay back in her chaise-longue and laughed raucously.

'Hark at who's talking! My God our Fred, I've heard about you! No woman is safe when you're around and you've got the cheek—'

'You know how I feel about March.' He looked at her coldly. He had never confided in her because he didn't trust her an inch, but she had been living at home all through the years when March Rising had occupied his every waking thought. 'The other women . . . they're nothing.'

'Then they should be.' She stopped laughing and went to the mantelpiece to pick up her cigarettes. 'You think I waste my time with Will Rising, but I don't spend my life with him. I've got other . . . contacts. Contacts who are very generous. You could make certain that your – er – ladies – are just as useful to you.'

'It's different for a man.'

'Rubbish. Some of these rich bitches are on permanent heat for someone like you. Instead of blackmailing me into getting concessions for you from my poor old alderman, you should be looking around for bored wives with rich husbands.'

He shrugged. 'Maybe.' He took the gold automatic lighter she offered him and lit her cigarette with ill grace. 'Meanwhile, can't you have a word with Will? Make him see what folly it is to let those girls loose in London on their own?'

'I want Will to be happy.' She blew smoke through her nostrils. 'Funny. Nobody believes that. Even Ma thinks I do it for some kind of revenge.'

Fred watched her curiously as she rearranged herself on the sofa. Her movements were automatically sensual now; she couldn't help herself.

'Do you love him then? Are you trying to tell me you love a man old enough to be your father?'

She gestured widely with her cigarette, tipped her head back and studied the ceiling. 'What the hell is love, Fred? Do *you* know? I certainly don't. I wanted to belong to the Rising family. I tried to do that by sharing what was May's. Her sandwiches at school, her soap, her love affair. When that went wrong I had to think up something else. And there was Will. He was unhappy, Fred. Now he's happy.' She lifted her head and looked at him. 'Is that love?'

He shrugged again. 'I wouldn't know. I meant the other thing. Bed.'

'Oh. Is that all? I enjoy it well enough. And he – he adores it!' She laughed her harsh laugh again. 'I enjoy it with anyone, Fred. But he . . . that's why if you ever tell him about the others, I'll kill you.'

He pulled down his mouth in mock terror. 'You do the small things I ask of you, Sib, and he'll never know. It's up to you.'

She laughed again, drew on her cigarette and stood up.

'I adore being blackmailed,' she said and came to stand very close to Fred before blowing out her smoke.

He stood his ground. 'Talk to Will then,' he said.

'I might do.' She put her hands on his shoulders and kissed him slowly. 'Yes, I might do.' She let her hands slide across his back until her glowing cigarette touched his ear lobe. He sprang back, cursing. And she went to the window and stood looking out at the sluggish waters of the canal. 'Yes. All right.'

But Will's adjurations came too late to baulk the plans of his three daughters. David, always encouraging April to enjoy herself, was all for the weekend, and March and May, devoted mothers though they were, began to look forward intensely to two whole days without their offspring. They went up by train on Friday afternoon, arriving at the suburban terminus of Hampton Court in the red glow of a perfect May sunset. A taxi took them through Bushey Park to the row of villas – amazingly like the ones at Longford – on the other side. May conducted them through the rooms with housewifely pride and for the first time since her return to Gloucester, March felt a pang of envy for her sister. She had imagined that the joy of caring for a lovely home had been stamped out of her by the unhappiness she had known at Bath. For four years now she had been in retreat in the shabby old-fashioned terraced house in Gloucester which did not even belong to her father. Now in May's small house she saw all her heart's desire. She could imagine herself and Albert in something similar, entertaining friends, working in the garden. Almost timidly she asked May whether she could cook supper in the laboratory-like kitchen. May agreed happily. April laid the table in the dining-room where French windows led on to a lawn; May collapsed in an armchair in the 'lounge' and shouted instructions to her sisters.

The next day she spent an hour on the telephone, 'rallying the forces' as she put it. As a result, a taxi arrived just before lunch and disgorged a young man who introduced himself as 'Eugene'.

'You're May – I've heard all about you. I was with Monty before the war in a juggling act. Has he told you? I'm in the chorus line now my dear – the very best I could do I'm afraid. But I'm not wanted this evening so—'

'It's most awfully kind of you.' May had actually

spoken to Frank O'Rourke, the ex-Minstrel of Mincing Light Opera days. She felt confused and a little bothered by the arrival of this stranger. After all she was responsible for her sisters. And might darling easy-going Monty object? She said, 'I thought Frank might squire the three of us around the sights . . . you know.'

'I do indeed.' Eugene eyed March and April appreciatively. 'Frank mentioned that you were a corker, Mrs Gould, and I shouldn't have thought it possible that there were any more at home like you. I'd have been quite wrong of course.'

April had met young men like this at the tennis club. But there she was always with David – or they knew about David. They knew she belonged to someone else and therefore their banter was permissible. Bereft of David, she felt unsafe and very vulnerable.

Eugene said he would take them 'out on the town' and bundled them all into the waiting taxi. They went through countless suburbs and into Hill Street while Eugene put May at her ease by countless familiar reminiscences.

At Hill Street he found he did not have enough money for the taxi, which did not surprise May in the least. She dug into her handbag and turned to follow her sisters into a very dark house lit by shaded lamps and impregnated with incense fumes. People were everywhere and it was necessary to slide around the walls in order to reach the small tables loaded with food. Armed with a finger of toast topped with pâté and olives, April found herself propelled forward into a central clearing. Sitting on a chair remarkably like a throne was an Indian princess. A lady-in-waiting crouched at her feet. They both wore gold embroidered saris and were hung with jewels.

Someone enquired April's name and murmured an introduction. A man said, 'I am the Maharanee's aide-de-camp. She would deem it an honour if you drink with her.' Champagne was poured into a glass and topped with what April knew to be *crème de menthe*. Someone said, 'You must meet Captain Mahbou.' And her hand was taken between dark fingers, pale at the ends. Suddenly there was an opening in the crowd at the end of which was a grand piano. The Maharanee clapped her hands with childish delight as a young man in evening clothes and white gloves appeared and bowed very low. The ADC gave some orders and more joss sticks were lit and twirled their smoke gaily into the heavy air. The young man sat at the piano and removed his gloves. May appeared behind Captain Mahbou and whispered, 'That's David Plunkett Green,' and the next minute the huge reception room was filled with the minor wail of 'Harlem Blues'. There was dancing. A girl in a silver dress did a shimmy alone before the throne. Eugene said, 'Time to go. How about tea on the river somewhere?'

They went outside and there was another taxi. Eugene got in, so did Captain Mahbou and someone called Rupert. April found herself sitting on Captain Mahbou's large, whitish, greyish palm. She shifted hastily and said, 'I am married you know.' He smiled like a hungry wolf and said, 'I am married several times. It is of no account.' March said firmly, 'We are all married. And it is of great account to us!' Rupert seemed to find this an unusual statement. He called March 'Goddess' and spoke to her of someone called Rose Marie who was on in Leicester Square. Her silence went down very well with him and by the time they reached Maidenhead he was on his knees before her, elbows in her lap. May and Eugene continued to chatter theatre shop, exchanging gossip like Gran and Hettie Luker in the wash-house on a Monday. And April thought determinedly of David, and how she would make all this into a very funny story for his entertainment when she got home. And how she would never leave him again.

They left the taxi at the Dumb Bell hotel and went in for tea. There was dancing to a three-piece band and Captain Mahbou took April around the floor in a sort of crouching run, holding her so close she could scarcely breathe. They left the Dumb Bell and took Eugene to the theatre and they stayed until the first interval. There were no seats; they stood at the back of a box and Rupert held March's hand to his face and murmured 'Goddess' occasionally. Captain Mahbou put a protective hand on April's bottom again and smiled widely at her every time she looked at him. His white teeth in the darkness of the box quite dazzled her; she was not used to White Lady cocktails, nor champagne and *crème de menthe*.

May, a little disconsolate without Eugene, wanted to go home when they left, but the men protested vehemently.

'It's only nine o'clock!' Rupert was appalled. 'Let's go to Wembley Fun Fair!'

They stopped en route to drink more cocktails and

as the ground then seemed unsteady beneath their feet, it was a natural choice to take a boat at the River Caves which was luckily the first sideshow they came to. They sprawled about on the hard duckboards and floated through dark caverns past scenes from various nightmares: Orpheus and the Underworld, the Bottomless Pit, besides various gibbeted bodies and writhing chained prisoners on an island. Here, Rupert decided they must land and release the captives. He leapt ashore and held the curved prow of the skiff while the girls scrambled out, followed ponderously by the Captain. They spent half an hour chopping at the papier mâché chains with the Captain's sword, and, sweating and triumphant, returned to the water to find the skiff had floated away. Furious shouts came from the entrance.

Captain Mahbou said, 'It will be bad for the Maharanee if I am found.' April whispered, 'Take off your shoes everyone. Quickly, follow me!' She waded into the knee-deep water and as the lights went on and the hunters stamped through the river maze, she led her small band around the back of the island and past the single amazed attendant at the gate. 'Quick – run!' she ordered, setting a good example. They all ran in different directions and April found herself on a road she had never seen before. She leaned against some railings and put her shoes on and a taxi cruised to a halt near her.

'Selway Gardens. Next to Bushey Park,' she ordered.

The driver looked at her bedraggled state. 'Got enough money, miss?'

'Of course,' April replied haughtily. 'I am a personal friend of the Maharanee of – of—'

'Ah.' The taxi driver nodded. 'I thought I knew that smell.'

May had reached home before she did and was making cocoa in the immaculate kitchen. They waited anxiously for March and when at last she arrived, they stared at each other incredulously.

'Did it really happen?' asked March. 'I can't believe it.'

May apologized. 'I didn't know, girls. I mean usually when Monty rings up friends, we have a meal or go to the zoo with Victor. Are you all right?'

'Of course,' said both girls in unison.

April recounted her conversation with the taxi driver and they sniffed each other and began to giggle.

But the next morning they felt awful. Eugene telephoned and brought a subdued Rupert for afternoon tea. They walked slowly through the park and caught a bus to Hampton Court. It was a day of fitful sunshine and the ancient house held occasional hollows of sheer menace within its golden walls. April felt again the sense of being a mere dot in the enormous wheel of time; from the utter meaninglessness of yesterday, she viewed the equal meaninglessness of her present life with David. She wasn't really helping him. Four years they had been married; the business was prospering well, they were inseparable, yet he was still lonely.

'Darling, what is it?' May asked anxiously. 'Do you feel sick?'

April looked at her two sisters and said, 'It seems

so pointless sometimes. I wish I could die . . . now.'

May was horrified. Rupert said, 'It's a hangover, old fruit. I wish I could die with you.'

Eugene shuddered. 'It's this place. Let's stroll over to the Wick and have some more tea. And ices.'

But March took her arm and held it close against her side. 'I know exactly what you mean,' she said in a low voice. 'But there's no way out. You have to keep on and on.'

April felt tears flood her eyes and she held tightly to March as they walked back to the gatehouse.

'We should have tackled the maze. That would have cheered us up,' said Rupert.

'April could have rescued us again.' May tried to rally her sister. 'She was marvellous last night, Eugene. Really marvellous.'

They sat around a small iron table and Rupert lifted his tea cup solemnly. 'I'd rather have a hangover with you than with anyone else I know,' he said.

It raised a wan smile all round.

But the weekend in London had a lasting effect on the three Rising girls. They had sampled the delights of the jazz age and found they left a sour taste as well as a rocking insecurity.

March continued to receive letters from Rupert for some time, and his ridiculous adoration reminded her yet again of Fred Luker's treachery and the arid years that had elapsed since then. She thought of Edwin, bed-ridden but still alive at eighty, promising her that if she kept visiting him he would make a new will in her favour. She thought of Albert-Frederick growing less like his uncle and more like his father every day.

And she wished that Rupert could be older and more serious and be wealthy as well.

April told David of her 'conquest' and wished she hadn't when he looked at her searchingly as he laughed.

And May, inexplicably and quite simply, wanted to go home.

Indirectly it had its effect on Fred Luker also. Over the past four years he had tried again and again to win March back to their passionate and sparring relationship. At first his failure to do so had hurt him, then when she continued to visit Edwin in Bath, he was angry and frustrated: if she had resented his arrangement so much, why did she continue it? But all the time he had known that between Gloucester and Bath she was safe; safe for him when he had 'made his pile'.

Then two things happened at once. Captain Marcus Porterman informed him almost casually that he had arranged to take future coal consignments from the Welsh collieries. Someone he had been in the army with had bought a controlling interest in a mine and officers must stick together. And on the same day, Fred heard about March's trip to London.

There was nothing he could do about that other than approach Sibbie, and that proved useless. He was tired of feeling guilty where March was concerned, so he chose to see her trip – alone and unchaperoned by Albert-Frederick – as disloyalty. Simmering with rage he went to see Porterman to suggest a compromise: a half-and-half arrangement perhaps. The weekly coal train to Keynsham made Fred's business very profitable indeed; without it he would just make ends meet, maybe not even that. He had more enemies among his band of miners than friends. The Freeminers of the Forest of Dean did not take kindly to his arrival, nor to his bland assurances that he had observed all their laws. When he introduced Austen Rising to them at the Gavellers Arms, he noticed one or two of the older men exchange glances. He smiled as he told the younger men that Austen was 'St Briavels born'. Then he turned to the others. 'Isn't that so, gentlemen? We don't want to hang out any dirty washing, but I think you will bear me out?'

He had had no more difficulties and within a month he was fulfilling the contract he had made with Porterman and with the pickle factory besides half a dozen local hauliers. But they did not like him for his veiled blackmail and they would enjoy seeing him go down, even if it meant losing the good living he had given them.

Captain Porterman said, 'Look here Luker, I made my position plain in the letter. I didn't expect to see you two days later. I'm sorry about it, but Fawcett Jones was my commanding officer and he approached me personally.'

'You gave the contract to me, Porterman, and now you're backing out. That's all I know.'

The good Captain coloured angrily. 'No need to cut up rough, Luker. Nothing was signed.'

'A word of a gentleman. I thought it was binding.'

'No place for gentlemen in business, old man.' Porterman tried to sound genial. 'Wife's having a party at the weekend for Fawcett-Jones. Perhaps you'd like to pop in and put him wise as to tonnage and price?' He saw Fred's expression and swept on, 'These place cards – she asked me to drop them in to the house this morning and I rather overlooked them. You pass it on your way back to Bristol. Think you could drop them in for me? Just give them to the maid, no need to see Leonie.'

Fred was about to tell him what to do with his place cards, then checked himself. Leonie. Probably a fancy name for a stuck-up dowager with a moustache as luxuriant as her husband's. On the other hand, it was worth a try – he had nothing to lose.

'No trouble at all, old man,' he said with a familiarity that was insulting. 'A pleasure, in fact.'

Leonie Porterman was nearly forty, childless and bored. She had married above herself socially, but Marcus Porterman was her inferior in everything else. When her maid told her that Mr Luker wished to see her on a personal matter, she was immediately interested.

'I've heard about you, Mr Luker. My husband admires your business acumen very much.'

'And I've heard about you.' Porterman had never mentioned her before today. She was a short, thickset woman, very dark; but no moustache. 'I didn't imagine you could be so . . .' He let his voice die, swallowed visibly, took her hand and bent his head to it with deliberate clumsiness.

She didn't pull away. They stood holding hands in front of the low fire. There were twin windows either side of the chimney breast; outside, willow trees and lawns, inside, flock paper and armchairs like big boxes.

She tinkled a laugh. 'I've read about people like you. Isn't it called animal magnetism?'

He roughened his voice. 'I don't know. I've never felt like this before. God . . . you're beautiful. I'm sorry – I don't know anything about women.'

She smiled delightedly. 'You must let me teach you. I know quite a lot about them.'

He thought of all the women he had known: he thought of March, remote and aristocratic. He risked saying, 'I don't want to know about other women. Just you.'

She drew a little breath but did not turn away. 'You'd better sit down, Mr Luker. I'll ring for tea. Or would you like something stronger?'

'Whisky. Neat please.'

'My God, you're very direct. Could I have my hand back please?'

'Oh . . . must you?'

'Not really.'

They walked together to the side table containing decanters and glasses. She poured some whisky into a glass, drank from it and gave it to him. He managed to toss it back without taking his pale blue eyes off her.

She said in a low voice, 'Stop looking at me like that, Mr Luker.'

He whispered, 'Why?'

'Because I like it rather too much.'

He couldn't believe it would be this easy. He had imagined getting a foot in; inviting her to meet him at a roadhouse somewhere. He had been here exactly ten minutes.

He didn't have to pretend any more; desire flamed

in him quite suddenly as it often did. He put his finger in the whisky glass, wiped it across her lips and put his mouth to hers. When he lifted his head her eyes were closed and she would have fallen if he hadn't held her.

'God . . . this is marvellous.' She looked at him. 'I've dreamed of this sort of thing. Dreamed. Have you read any Lawrence?'

'No.'

'Good. I want it to be natural. You're so natural, Luker. Earthy.'

But it was she who slid her hand inside his baggy trousers and found the opening in his pants.

'My God,' she whispered.

'Yes,' he whispered back.

They lay on the rug in front of the summer fire and he was rough with her because he knew instinctively that was what she wanted.

Afterwards they lay quietly side by side and he trailed his fingers languidly across her breasts.

'I wish . . . I wish . . .'

'What do you wish, my gorgeous Luker?'

'I wish this could go on for ever.'

'I don't see why it can't. With pauses for meals and things of course.'

He lifted his head. 'Didn't you know? I've finished here. The Captain has given me the old heave-ho.'

She propped herself on one elbow and stared down at him. She was no fool, this woman. Fred held his breath.

She smiled. 'I think he'll retract that, Luker. He'll be pleased I've found myself a friend. I get bored, you know, and that worries him. So . . . while we're such good friends, I think you'll find that Captain Porterman will buy all his coal from you.'

He held her gaze for a long second, letting her read whatever she wanted in his face. Then he reached up and took her head in his hands and kissed her, rolling over on to her as he did so.

'What, again?' she asked.

'We've only just started, Mrs Porterman. And we've got a long way to go.'

He drove home slowly and unsmiling. He had saved his business and he had somehow scored over March, but it gave him no pleasure. And then he found the forgotten place cards in the map pocket on the door. At last he began to laugh.

Chapter Six

In the spring of the following year, when Mr MacDonald had struck a Lab–Lib pact and formed the first Labour government, April and David moved to a new shop in fashionable Eastgate Street, almost opposite the market. Manny Stein called himself a partner now, and brought them large orders from London, besides plenty of ready-made stock. It was the most exclusive shop in Gloucester and second only to Jaeger and County Clothes in Cheltenham. In an upstairs workshop with a skylight overlooking the work going on in the new Kings Square, David designed and cut his couturier outfits. In the big sitting-room with its armchairs, ashtrays, gas fire and a view of the busy street outside, they entertained their many friends and acquaintances. Would-be politicians and intellectuals gathered to discuss the work of Albert Mansbridge, the Webbs, Dr Marie Stopes, besides who was what in Gloucester, the clothes they wore, the things they said.

It was after one of these evenings that Tollie Hall joined the International Labour Party. And Bridget Williams suddenly spoke of women's rights and meant nothing political at all, as most of the young men present soon discovered. And it was during one of these evenings, when May was home for Easter and March had left Albert-Frederick with Florence, that an amateur photographer snapped the three girls laughing together against a background of cut flowers from the shop. The picture appeared in the *Citizen* the next night under the heading 'Daffodil time again. But these Gloucester daffodils are with us all the year round.' They were all old married women now, but collectively they were still known, with much admiration, as 'the Rising girls'.

Albert-Frederick sat on the coke pile in the playground of Chichester Street Elementary, and dreamed of his aunt. He had adored April for as long as he could remember and had been passionately in love with her since last year when she had danced with him and sung 'Look for the Silver Lining' and had understood so exactly how he felt. Whenever he had a spare moment, he deliberately thought of April and her short golden curls and her smoke rings. He thought of them running away together and living in a very sunny place with fruit to eat and a real stream and a model railway. He knew that was what she wanted. He knew that she was unhappy.

A voice said, 'Oy! What you doin' up there? You're not allowed up there!'

It was one of the huge boys who would be leaving in the summer. Albert-Frederick slithered off the coke pile quickly and stood before him, looking at the ground.

'Well? What were you *doin*'?'

'Thinking. I was thinking.'

'Filthy little sod. I can guess what you was thinkin' too. Get up in that corner.'

He shoved Albert around the coke pile and behind the boys' lavatory. Albert began to whimper in terror.

'Come on. Take off y'r jersey!' Hands seized his new grey jersey knitted by Gran Rising, and tugged. 'Down with your breeches!' The hands snapped his braces to his knees. He felt his pants pushed down. He began to scream and squirm unsuccessfully; his trousers were trapping him around his knees. The next minute, horny fingers were shoved brutally up his back passage; he screamed in earnest like a stuck pig.

'What the hell—' A new voice cut through his terror. His captor was removed from him very suddenly and there was a scrabbling crash of body on coke. The voice said tensely, 'Get out! Go on, get out you little swine! If ever I catch you interfering with – with anyone – again, I'll make you wish you hadn't been born! Understand?'

The big boy was whimpering now. 'You broke me arm! You rotten . . . let me *go*! Yes – yes, I understand – course I understand . . . but they got to know 'oo's boss! You dun the same, Mr Luker – I 'eard about you! 'E's a soppy little bugger – 'e's got to learn—'

Fred Luker said tensely, 'Just get out. Clear off.'

There was a moment's silence and Albert knew they were alone together. He continued to cry.

Fred said sternly, 'Stop that. Pull up your breeches. Make yourself presentable. And come with me.'

He marched Albert into Miss Pettinger's office without pausing to knock. The headmistress, in the midst of collating the school bills for that term – including the pile of coke in the yard – did not look up.

'Outside,' she said calmly. 'And knock. Then wait for me to tell you to come in.'

Fred took a moment to admire this leathery woman whom the years merely made stronger. His hands and backside recalled her ministrations of twenty years ago; he would have liked Albert to stay with her. But it was not to be. What had been good enough for Fred Luker was not necessarily good for his son.

He said, 'Sorry. No time, Miss Pettinger.'

She looked up at that and managed a wintry smile. 'Oh, it's Fred Luker, isn't it? Have you come to offer me some cheap coal?'

There wasn't much she didn't know, this one. Fred wondered what else she might guess after this interview.

'No miss. I've come to say that I'm taking young Albert Tomms home to his mother. And if she takes any notice of what I say to her, he won't be coming back.'

Miss Pettinger looked at the hiccupping boy, then at the grim-faced man. She put down her pen and laced her fingers.

'Now we will stop that crying and be quite quiet.' She waited again and Albert's breathing became normal. 'Good boy. Sit down while I talk to Mr Luker.'

Albert looked around for a chair. Uncle Fred was standing right in front of the only one besides Miss Pettinger's. It was unthinkable to disobey, so he sat on the floor. Miss Pettinger did not look at him.

'Are you complaining about my school? Or about my pupil?' she asked gently.

'I am complaining about another pupil, miss. No names, no pack drill. No tales. He was interfering with this boy.'

'You witnessed the interference?'

'Yes.'

'Then you must tell me the name of the perpetrator. And I will deal with the matter. Your duty is done, Fred. I thank you.'

'Sorry miss. I'm taking Albert home.'

'Don't you think that amounts to interference too?'

Fred felt himself flushing. 'I'm a friend of the family, miss. I'm very fond of the boy.'

'I don't doubt that. He is a likeable boy. But you have no right—'

'Sorry miss. I'm taking him home. You can't stop me.'

'Probably not. I don't intend to try. But I think you will find that Mrs Tomms would prefer to see me on this matter.'

Fred nodded curtly, took Albert's flaccid hand and pulled him to his feet. He walked the length of Chichester Street knowing that in this as in so many other things, Miss Pettinger was right. March would tell him to mind his own business and she would take Albert straight back to whatever he had to face next time behind the coke pile.

But Fred knew nothing of the first Albert's ordeal at the hands of the bishop many years ago. Fred knew very little indeed of the bargain that March had struck with her Uncle Edwin when she had been only four-teen, to free her beloved brother from the excesses of being the bishop's page. All Fred knew was that March had barely spoken to him for the past four years and would certainly oppose him on principle.

He found the household in its usual state of calm and quiet routine. Sylvia Rising and the old lady were out at their scrubbing jobs, Florence sat in the dining-room button-holing industriously for Will who was in the workroom making a suit for one of the younger Council members. March was 'doing upstairs'.

Florence, who answered his knock, led the way down to the kitchen. She did not ask unnecessary questions; it was obvious that Albert was upset about something but unhurt physically. Automatically she boiled milk for cocoa and put a hand on his shoulder in silent sympathy.

'A bit of an upset in the school yard, Mrs Rising.'

Fred had long ago joined the conspiracy to shield Florence from worry. 'But while I'm here I'd like a word with March.'

'She's polishing in the bandy room, Fred. Do go up. Albert and I will have some cocoa together and be happy and chatty.' She picked up a postcard from behind the tea caddy and put it on the table in front of the boy. 'Look darling. A card from Victor. It's Charlie Chaplin, isn't it?'

Albert forgot his troubles on the instant. 'Victor 'ud rather go to the pictures than play with his toys,' he commented, peering at the clown in his bowler hat. 'Bet he couldn't read what it says.' He spelled out laboriously. 'Comic Cuts.'

Fred, hearing this as he closed the kitchen door, felt a surge of unusual pride. Dammit, Albert was only six years old and he could read. His son.

March looked up from the piano with a fine mixture of expressions on her face. Guilt because she was looking through sheet music rather than polishing, wariness because it was a man's step and men were not frequent visitors in this house, then baleful aggression.

'What do you want?'

Fred held out a pacific hand. 'Listen, March. I've brought the boy home from school—' He hung on to her physically as she made for the door in a surge of panic. 'He's all right. Drinking cocoa with your mother. Quite all right.'

'Then why—? What business—?' She backed to the piano again as she snapped questions.

'It's not the right place for him, March. That's why. And it is my business as you very well know.'

'I haven't noticed you making it your business over the past six years.'

He shrugged. 'I thought I made it very much my business when I brought you home from Bath.'

For the first time she spoke of that second visit to Bath. 'You forfeited any rights you had – to me or to Albert – when you sent me back there.' She seemed to regret her words and made a dismissive gesture. 'That's all over anyway. Why have you brought Albert home?'

'It's not over. Not for me. I still love you, March.'

She looked at him and put a hand to her throat. Then she whispered, 'Why have you brought Albert home?'

Fred said deliberately, 'He was being buggered by a thirteen-year-old.' He thought how Leonie would have enjoyed his words. March did not. The effect on her was frightening. The colour drained from her face, her mouth opened as the skin tightened around it, her eyes pulled sideways, oriental fashion.

He went to her and put his arms around her and she did not pull away. 'You don't know what I'm on about darling, do you? One of the jack-me-lads had the boy's trousers down and his fingers up his backside. Nothing to worry about, it's happened to all of us, but I couldn't stand there and see—'

'Nothing to worry about?' Her eyes were glazed. 'You don't understand. Oh Fred . . . he's downstairs?'

'Yes. And he's all right. It's something boys do—'

'I know! Oh God, I know!'

She was shaking like a leaf and he held her very close, her remembered smell bringing his old feelings for her back with a rush. He had schemed for the moment when she would turn to him again, now it was here he was unprepared. He murmured, 'It's all right now, March . . . all right,' not even thinking of Albert-Frederick any more.

She said wildly, 'It's not all right! He can't go back there – I won't let him – but what else, where else – oh God, it can't happen again – it can't!'

'What can't happen again, Marcie?'

'Edwin. I can't ask him again—' It was Edwin who had saved her brother Albert from similar ignominy, and though Fred did not know that, he realized with her words that he had the key to March's gratitude and therefore . . . love. What a fool he had been not to see it before.

He said strongly, 'Of course you can't ask Edwin, Marcie. There's no need. I can look after my own son. He shall go to Marley – it's got a good reputation.'

'Marley?' Her trembling abated. 'Albert at Marley? They have a uniform. And they learn French.' She became very still. 'It's an expensive school. Very expensive.'

'The money's nothing. Only the best is good enough for Albert-Frederick.'

'Oh . . . Fred. He would love it there. He's never liked Chichester Street – he's like my brother Albert, you see. A bit lonely.'

'If he doesn't like Marley, he can try somewhere else.'

She moved away from him to stare into his face. 'You've done that well? I mean, I wouldn't want you to risk your business or anything.'

'Why not? Parents do risk their businesses for their children.'

'Oh Fred. You've hardly . . . looked at him.'

'I thought that was what you wanted, Marcie. But I have looked at him. And wanted to help.' He held out his hands and she put hers into them. 'I'll give you the cash. Then you can pay the fees yourself.'

She gazed at him. Her transparent brown eyes held an expression he hadn't seen for some time: hope.

She said, 'Thank you for – for bringing him home, Fred.' She dropped her gaze. 'I'd better go down to him now.'

'All right. But tonight, when he's in bed, will you come for a drive? Not far—'

'I'm playing tennis with April. At Hucclecote.'

'Then I'll take you there. And bring you home.'

They both remembered that the first time Fred had taken her anywhere it had been to Bridget Williams' house at Hucclecote. They shared so much. She smiled and nodded.

May was restless. Over Christmas and New Year Monty had been in pantomime at the Fortune, and their lives had been as nearly regular as they had been since their marriage. It did not suit either of them and when the season finished Monty made no attempt to get another part. They went to parties, taking Victor with them, and afterwards lay in bed till midday. Their money dwindled rapidly. Monty discovered the delights of the racecourse. He was lucky at first and they lived the high life. At not quite five years old, Victor could order a lunch running into four courses and a wine to go with each course. He could interpret the semaphore of the tic-tac men and knew how to place a bet. He was quick, intelligent and lively, and the bond between him and his mother was so deep as to make outward show rarely necessary. They could exchange a small smiling glance that excluded the whole world, including Monty. He was aware of it and was jealous, and did not know it.

They had a row.

It was Sunday and they woke at eleven and made indolent love until they heard Victor going downstairs to feed his goldfish. Immediately May prepared to get out of bed. Monty detained her.

'Not yet Mamma . . . Monty wants Mamma . . .' It was their usual way of talking but May wriggled free and reached for her satin negligée.

'Don't be silly darling. Victor is about.'

'Monty wants—' He giggled, still drunk from the night before, made a grab across the bed and pulled her down again. She was suddenly angry.

'Monty! You're hurting – don't be so ridiculous! I want to cook a proper lunch today and take Victor for a walk in the park – *Monty*—'

She tore free and retied her negligée. Monty sank back in the pillows pretending to cry. It had always worked before.

'Stay there then baby.' May made an effort. 'I'll bring you a nice cup of tea in bed. How's that?'

She left without waiting for a reply. It was with conscious pleasure that she joined Victor in their modern lounge and watched the goldfish surface for their ant eggs. The child looked up briefly and smiled.

'When we go to Grandma's next, may I take Pipsqueak and Wilfrid?' He followed the swimming fish around the bulbous tank with interested eyes. 'I want to show Albert that toys are silly.'

'Darling. You don't really think toys are silly, do you?'

'Not silly. But not important. Albert thinks they are important. He's never been to the races. Nothing.'

May reflected that perhaps Albert was a good influence on her precocious son. She nodded. 'Of course you may take Wilfrid and Pipsqueak to

Gloucester, if you can think of a way of carrying them.'

'Easy-peezy,' Victor said airily. 'They can go in your flour jar.'

'What about my flour?' But May was laughing as usual. Teddy had rhymed words just as inconsequentially as Victor did.

He smiled cockily. 'Throw it away,' he advised.

They were both laughing when Monty came into the room. He stood swaying for a moment, holding the door jamb, naked and unnoticed. The laughter abated somewhat and he announced pathetically, 'Monty *needs* Mamma!' He came behind his wife, undid her negligée with a wild flip of his hand and cupped her breast, trying unsuccessfully to get his mouth to it. She staggered back, caught her heel in her satin hem and sprawled onto the sofa. Monty fell on top of her. She screamed and he laughed and began to kiss her. They struggled and fell to the floor. It was like a scene from one of the silent films that were all the rage, except that the hero should then have charged in and removed the would-be rapist with a well-aimed fist. Instead Victor leapt onto his father's bare back, dug his nicely manicured nails into the base of the slim neck, pushed his sharp knees into the kidneys and braced himself with eyes shut and teeth bared. Monty sobered very suddenly and got off May. He then reached around and tore at his son and held him up at eye-level.

'What the *hell* d'you think you're doing?' he yelled furiously.

'I hate you!' shouted Victor. 'You were hurting

Mummy – you took off her clothes! I hate you!' He began to scream.

Monty shook him like a puppy and the child gathered breath and spat vigorously. Monty then dropped him and aimed a swipe at his head which missed. Meanwhile May had gathered herself and her trailing negligée together and joined in the general shouting match. As the full impact of Monty's aggression was realized she launched herself at him, a she-cat in defence of her young. Monty recoiled, fended her off by the simple expedient of pushing her back on the sofa, turned and left the room with what dignity he could muster.

May and Victor calmed down gradually and an air of embarrassment seemed to settle between them. Outside the bay window, the people next door were returning from church; a middle-aged couple with grown-up children. They eyed May's rather smeary windows curiously and talked in high, unnatural voices as they walked up their own garden path and let themselves into their house. The sun poured into the cheerful little room, glinting off the fish bowl, the fireplace with its chrome companion-set, the oval bevelled mirror. It was just as always; yet it was as it had never been before. May thought she could not bear it.

'Mamma . . .' Victor whimpered. 'I'm frightened.'

May wanted to say, 'So am I darling,' but of course did not. Instead she smiled warmly. 'How ridiculous! Whatever is there to be frightened of?' She stood up and held out her hand. 'Come on. Breakfast and lots of tea. Then we'll go upstairs and pack.'

'Where are we going?' wavered Victor.

She pretended astonishment. 'I thought you wanted to show Pipsqueak and Wilfrid to Albert? We're going to stay with Grandma of course.'

Victor was instantly comforted. 'Oh . . . yi pee-pipee!' He held her hand and they went into the kitchen. 'Ackcherly Mummy, Albert is my favourite cousin,' he said.

'Actually, he's your only cousin,' May said, laughing.

Monty, listening from the bathroom, felt a terrible aching gulf where his stomach should be. It was partly because he was going to be sick, and partly because he knew he had lost a little piece of May.

Somehow they managed to organize a picnic by the river. It was August Bank Holiday and Fred's mystery tour for the Gloucester Indian Club Swingers had been cancelled, so he took them to Rodley. 'Rodley on the Mud' Will Rising called it, and Gran grumbled incessantly. 'Why we 'ad to come 'ere when we've got the park right under our noses I'll never know.' But they were there because the uncles, Jack and Austen, could join them from the opposite bank; and the children could swim and scream; and Fred could see March in a swimming-costume.

Aunty Sylv and Florence, Hettie Luker and her Gladys, Kitty Hall and Tollie, unpacked the food under half a dozen strategically placed umbrellas. Inside the coach the girls changed into their bathing-dresses and hats and put on rubber shoes to wade and slide through the mud to the turgid water. April turned

163

to survey the back of her bathing-dress and remarked, 'Good job Captain Mahbou can't see this,' and March giggled and said, 'It's barely decent,' and was glad that Fred would see her in her modest affair. May laughed gaily, she was very gay this holiday, and said she just wished Eugene could see them all as he would go absolutely tollymollary. Bridget Williams, fresh from her training college, with a job at a school in Tuffley, wore a brief, pleated tennis skirt and over-shirt. 'I know it's not a bathing-dress,' she said coolly. 'I want to look human, thank you very much.'

They emerged from the charabanc amid applause. Will leaned his head on Florence's knee and tipped his bowler to shield his eyes. Sibbie possessed what she called a one-piece which she wore to swim from the canal bank. He wished she could have been here today. David kissed the end of April's nose and told her she was a credit to the firm; April replied quickly, 'Good job you can't get in the water darling – you wouldn't be safe with me!' Fred murmured to March, 'You're beautiful . . . beautiful . . .' She said, 'I can't swim very well . . .' and he replied, 'I'll keep you afloat.'

Tollie flicked his quick eyes over the three Rising girls and then let them rest for a little longer on Bridget. He wondered when she would decide to marry him. Not for a while . . . she enjoyed having him on a string with a dozen others, and her excuse was that in Gloucestershire married women were not permitted to teach. He couldn't imagine his life without his mother or Bridget to tell him what to do, to wear, to eat, to say. But nobody could tell him what to think. Jack and Austen rubbed their hands as they dived into the charabanc to change into their ancient costumes. They made the most of the Forest girls, but their own family had 'class' and could be cuddled and kissed quite freely up to a point which limited avuncular behaviour. And Gladys Luker wasn't exactly family anyway.

The men all followed Jack and Austen and the girls began to scream their way through the oozing slime. Here the Severn flooded every winter and the water meadows yielded their rich alluvium annually over thousands of years. However hot the summer, only a thin crust dried on top and this broke like a biscuit under the rubber bathing-shoes. The Rodley mud was supposed to be very good for the skin and was heated and used on the faces of many wealthy ladies who would pay money for it. In its natural state, now and then disturbed by the frantic escape of a browsing eel, it was rather too plentiful to be inviting. Sinking to calf depth at each step the girls assured each other in piercing shrieks that it was medicinal, but their groping feet still cringed at their unsteady hold, and when Gladys wailed, 'What if we disappears? Like the man at the Picturedrome in *The Sinking Sands of Assam*?' May gave a shriek and led the retreat.

They were too late. Coming towards them at full pelt were the males of the party, Victor and Albert-Frederick in hot pursuit. Fred led the way. They followed him in flat dives from the low bank, crouching and launching themselves off like seals on to the already churned mud. Fred aimed himself at March, caught her around the knees and brought her down on top of him to continue into the river. Austen and Jack carried Gladys off; Albert and Victor claimed May and April. The river churned and swirled as if with a shoal of elvers. Albert and April dived and surfaced again and again; Victor splashed with his mother in the shallows; Gladys screamed and clutched at her bathing-suit and Austen's raucous laughter could be heard practically down river to Bristol.

Fred said, 'March, I love you. I want you. I can't go on like this. Come away with me, please darling.'

They did the new side-stroke so that they could face each other in the water; the current took them quickly away from the rest.

'Oh Fred—' March's open mouth shipped water and she coughed and spluttered. He took her head on his chest and drew her into the bank. They held on to a willow branch and laughed. It was as if their long four-year estrangement had never been; any awkwardness had been lost in the old awareness.

She said gaspingly, 'Fred, it would get about – these things always do. It was bad enough when you brought me back from Bath that time, but that's forgotten now—'

He interrupted. 'Listen, Marcie. You've never seen Marsh Cottage – I named it for you, you know. We've moved out of there – Jack and Austen are with a chap named Danby now. I sometimes sleep there – use it as an office. Come down with me next week—'

'Fred, I'm going to Bath next week.'

'To that old man?'

'You know why I go. I've explained. He's promised to change his will again. And he's over eighty now.'

'And has he done it yet?'

'No. But—'

'Exactly. He'll be dead one of these days and he still won't have changed it. Can't you see he's got you on a string? We don't need him any more, March.'

Her face became serious beneath the close-fitting cap.

'I thought . . . I thought you might want to marry me because of that money, Fred.'

He released the branch and took her round the waist. She too let go her hold and they sank beneath the water. When they surfaced he was kissing her. She spluttered again and reached for a handhold on the bank. They lugged themselves up on to the grass.

Fred kissed her again through her spluttering and her protests.

'Listen woman,' he panted. 'It's you I want. You—'

'All right – all *right* Fred!' But she was laughing again, glowing like the carefree girl she'd never been. 'All right, I'll come with you. Yes – yes – I promise! Yes, I do love you – I do!' She softened suddenly, 'Oh Fred . . . I do . . .'

He kissed her slowly, then began to tell her how they would arrange their trip to Marsh Cottage. She nodded.

'Darling, I think we'd better go back. Edwin doesn't matter but I wouldn't want Mother or Dad to think there was anything between us.'

Fred smiled, thinking of Will Rising and Sibbie. But he said, 'All right, Marcie. We'll go back and swim with the others.'

In the event March did not want to get in the water

again, so they walked along the bank to where April and May were towelling the boys. Fred felt a triumph that effervesced into schoolboy tomfoolery; he suddenly leaned down, whipped April's rubber bathing-shoe from her foot and ran with it back to the river. Once there he hurled it to the middle of the stream. It became the object of a game they put on for the entertainment of the others. April ploughed through the mud again, laughing and calling him names; he brought her down with a flying tackle and rolled her in the ooze until she looked like one of the popular nigger minstrels. He spat mud and went for her again in the shallows, then they both set off for the shoe, which was bobbing blearily in mid-stream.

April was an expert swimmer. She had for a time belonged to the Ladies Swimming Club at Barton Baths – when she had needed an excuse for looking into the shop window at Daker's – and had learned the new Australian crawl. Fred, less expert, scrambled through the water without finesse but at a good rate. His strong grip wrenched the shoe from her scrabbling fingers and he held it aloft with a gasping cry of triumph while she squeaked and pushed herself out of the water like a leaping salmon. 'Race you for it!' he panted and set out for the opposite bank.

The stage was taken by Bridget and Tollie who swam around each other warily. When Gladys left the river, shouting abuse at Austen and clutching her bathing-dress to her, Bridget suddenly dived. The next moment Austen disappeared with a shout of surprise. When he surfaced, blowing like a whale, Bridget was already up and announcing to the world that he had left her no modesty whatso*ever*! She too clutched her sodden shirt and it was plain to see someone had ripped it from her shoulder. Eyes sparkling, she screamed at Tollie to defend her honour. Austen began to shamble out of the water circumspectly. Bridget said, 'Oh never mind darling.' She encircled Tollie's neck and presented her legs on top of the water. 'I'm too tired. Carry me out.' Tollie crooked his arms and complied.

On the other bank in another mud bath, April surrendered too.

'Keep the shoe . . . drown me if you must . . . I'm exhausted!' Her laughing gasps ended in a long-drawn-out moan as she threw herself supine on to the warm slime, arms stretched above her head, eyes closing against the burning sun.

'Poor little April Rising,' Fred mocked, squatting by her, lifting one limp foot, beginning to shove on the mud-filled shoe. 'Poor helpless little April Rising—'

'April Daker,' she corrected lazily. 'I'm a married woman now remember, Fred.'

'Poor little April Rising. Pretending to be a married woman—'

Her eyes opened, her smile died. 'What do you mean by that?'

He knelt over her, a supporting arm either side of her head. His own pale blue eyes grinned into her darker ones. 'I mean you're still the schoolgirl. That's what I mean. You might be taller than most of us, with a missis to your name and fancy frocks on your back and your own bank account and your silver cigarette case—'

She relaxed, grinning back. 'Oh shut up, Fred Luker. Businessman of Gloucester. Sharp as they come – hard as nails—'

He lifted a casual hand and plopped a dollop of mud onto her face. She refused to flinch. 'Delicious,' she said, licking it daintily from her upper lip. 'Chocolate flavoured if I'm not mistaken.'

He collapsed on top of her, laughing again 'Oh you're beautiful! Lovely! The best of the Rising collection. Come on. Move. Albert's halfway across the river and March will blame me if he gets swept too far downstream.'

She was up immediately, searching the water anxiously.

'Stay there darling!' she called to the dog-paddling boy. 'Aunty April's coming for you!'

She plunged into the river, Fred forgotten. He watched her admiringly, still smiling. He wanted March more than any other woman in the world, but he knew his teasing words just now had been right. Somehow the goodness of Florence, the passion of Will, the discrimination and sentiment of March, Albert and May, the daring of young Teddy – somehow they had been perfectly combined in April. She was the best of the Risings.

He glanced at the opposite bank and saw David Daker's eyes on her. Then he looked further and saw March watching Albert. April reached him and they began to cavort together. March subsided and let the gaze move to Fred as he stood there, caked in mud, like some primeval being. She didn't smile.

He gave a roar like a lion and dived into the water.

She was jealous. She was actually jealous. Almost as jealous as David Daker.

Albert had been immediately happy at Marley Close school, but he was even happier when his cousin joined him 'for a week or two'. Like April and Teddy before them, the two boys discovered that their family connections earned them special attention from the untrained teacher who owned the old house on the Twigworth Road and strove to keep it intact by running one of the new-fangled kindergartens. Arnold Baxter was the second son of a second son; his brother had died at Ypres, his father in a TB sanatorium. His uncle was a solicitor in Gloucester, pompous and not very successful, and there were many sons who would inherit his money.

Arnold, shell-shocked and unqualified for anything, huddled in the big four-square Georgian house at Twigworth for nearly a year. Then, like a gift from heaven, a French nurse who had met him at the field hospital in Armentières visited England and looked him up. She had read of the work of Froebel and judged very shrewdly that English opinion was swinging towards German intellectualism in a kind of reaction from the four years of forced antagonism. She also realized the potential of the big house and grounds near a city which provided scantily for its infant population. In any case she was fond of Arnold and very sorry for him, and there were no prospects for her in France. She was nearly forty and he was twenty-two, but he was grateful to her for marrying him. They were happy, and the children in their

kindergarten were happy. By 1924 it had a preparatory department with a growing reputation, enhanced
if anything by astronomical fees.

'To play is to learn,' trilled Mrs Baxter in her
accented English as she led a trail of six-year-olds to
clean the lawn of daisies. 'To learn is to play,' echoed
her young husband, not entirely inaccurately, as
he tinkered with the boiler in the basement, shadowed
by Albert Tomms whose grandmother was a Rhys-
Davies.

Victor dismembered his daisy during rest-time that
afternoon.

'The whole *thing* is called the calyx,' he told his
cousin knowledgeably. 'Each separate piece is called a
sepal.'

'You mean petal,' corrected Albert, lying on his
back and dreaming of driving an engine.

'No I don't. These are petals.' He sprinkled white
scraps over Albert's face. 'You ought to listen to Mrs
Baxter, Albert. She tells you about real things.'

'Engines are real things. Arnold was in one of the
tanks in the war. They're real things.'

Victor didn't give up. 'Have you ever seen your
Mummy without any clothes on?' he demanded. The
thought of Aunty March without clothes was so funny
he began to laugh.

'No. And neither have you.' Albert turned his head
to grin back. Sometimes Victor was so silly he had to
laugh.

'Yes I have. And my Daddy. His thing was as long
as this.' Victor spread his arms wide. He saw the
success of this confidence and went on boastfully,

'And my Mummy's chests were as huge as balloons.'

Albert's laughter was checked. When he had swum with Aunty April in the river he had noticed that her chests floated on the water like balloons. He said unguardedly, 'I'd like to see Aunty April without any clothes on.'

Victor said, 'Easy-peezy. I'll ask her if you can.'

He was rewarded by a faceful of torn-up grass and a red-faced Albert saying, 'I didn't mean it! Stupid little idiot!'

Sibbie Luker had never liked March. It was unfair of her because if March had not vacated her job as typist to old Alderman Williams, Sibbie would not have got it and then would never have owned her own bungalow and been her own mistress. Perhaps a natural antipathy had been exacerbated by guilt; whatever it was, Sibbie made no secret to her brother that she did not like March Rising and was not happy that he was friendly with her again.

'What difference does it make to you?' Fred asked, surprised to see her in the tiny office he now had in Kings Square. 'And how do you know we're friendly again?'

Sibbie jerked her head to the window; Gladys had tactfully 'gone for her grub' when Sibbie arrived. 'Gladys told me what you were getting up to at the picnic.' She paused while he gave a few opinions on family gossip, then added, 'It wouldn't be seemly if anything permanent came of it, Fred.'

'Seemly? What the hell do you know about seemliness?'

She said with dignity, 'I know about it even if I don't appear to be seemly.' She sat down on Gladys' typing stool and faced him squarely. 'Look here Fred, I mean it. You can't marry March and that's that.'

'Out of it, Sib. Go on. Out. I'm not discussing my affairs with anyone, let alone you.'

She sighed patiently. 'Fred, I don't like discussing my affairs either. But as it's you . . . when Florence Rising dies I'm going to marry Will.'

'You . . . what?' He stared, then leaned back in his chair and laughed uproariously. 'Pull the other one, Sib. Go on, here it is—' He stuck his leg out accommodatingly and she kicked it.

'Shut up Fred. I mean it. She's older than him and the next bad winter will take her. I shall marry Will and all those girls will be my stepdaughters. That amuses me a lot. But it won't amuse me one bit to have you as a stepson.'

'Why not?' He went on laughing, holding out his arms and mewling 'Mamma' at her in the most infuriating manner.

She stood up and pulled her hat down over her ears. She could have killed him.

'You don't understand, do you . . . you oaf. I've always wanted this – to be head of the Risings. You'll spoil that if you've married into them first—'

'I thought you only wanted to make Will happy.'

'So I do. But I want this as well. Oh it's no good talking to you, Fred. This is for all of us – Ma went to bed with Will long before I did and then he dropped her and it nearly broke her heart. This is for her as well – and for me – and for you and Glad and all the poor

174

bloody Lukers who have been down there somewhere—' She stabbed a gloved finger at the torn
oilcloth.

He said slowly, 'You're mad.'

'If you want to call me mad, all right. But can't you
see that you mustn't marry March?'

'No. I can't see that at all, Sib. And if you think Will
Rising would marry you – put you in Florence's place
– you really are mad.'

'He loves me!'

'He might do. But he worships Florence.'

'When she's gone he'll worship me. You'll see.
Everyone will see.' She turned and went to the door.
'One more chance, Fred. Promise me you won't marry
March Rising. Take her to bed if you like. But don't
marry her.'

'Clear off, little sister,' Fred said briefly.

She left. And made straight for Chichester Street.

It was not so hot as it had been on the day of the
picnic and Albert and Victor were playing with
Teddy's old iron hoop up and down the pavement.
Sibbie marched straight past them and knocked on the
open door of number thirty-three.

Victor, suave man of the world, but still intensely
curious, said, 'May we help you? The lady of the house
is resting.'

Sibbie could easily have thoroughly disliked him
but he was May's child. She leaned down. 'I'd like a
word with Mrs Tomms. Could you ask her to step
over the road for five minutes? Tell her it is very
important.'

She did not wait for an answer but ran across to the

garden door of Chichester House and let herself through. Very quickly March's head appeared, her eyes startled and full of enquiry. She flushed angrily when she saw who it was.

'You!' March was not one to bandy words, she turned immediately and would have gone except that Sibbie said quietly, 'It's about Fred. And you'd better listen.'

March hung on to the door against her instinct. And in that time Sibbie did her work.

'Before you get any friendlier with my brother you'd better hear about him. He's had plenty of girls in his time – you probably knew that. But now, there's a special one. And you won't be able to break it up. He'll tell you it's a business arrangement, but he enjoys his business as you know. Her name is Leonie Porterman and she lives at Keynsham.'

Again March looked at May's old friend, a fleeting glance that told Sibbie she had heard the name Porterman before. Sibbie did not overplay her hand. She stood there staring back at March, convincing her with silence. March seemed to droop, then again she turned to go. Something made Sibbie start forward. 'It wouldn't have done, you know, March. Not you and Fred. You're not matched – not matched at all.' Then the heavy door clunked shut.

March told herself she should be grateful she was saved from making a complete fool of herself all over again. She did not write to Fred or get in touch with him, but the day before they were to have gone down to Marsh Cottage, she left for Edwin and Bath. As the train drew out she and Albert waved through the window at May, April and Victor getting smaller and smaller on the platform.

'We'll be going back to Grandma and Grampa soon, won't we, Mother?' Albert asked anxiously.

'Of course, son. Of course,' March said and smiled at him. Rose had written that Mr Tomms did not come downstairs any more, so it could not possibly be long before he died. But she would not leave him now until he did, whether he changed his will or not. At last she would keep her wedding vows: for richer or poorer, till death do us part.

A wire came from Monty in his usual extravagant vein.

'Please forgive me and come home stop I love you and always will stop cannot live without you stop broken-hearted Monty.'

May put it with the others, but knew she couldn't hold out much longer. Nobody understood her any more like Monty. She was thirty, a married woman with a growing son, the young soldiers who had flocked after her in Chichester House were gone. There were no Eugenes or Ruperts in Gloucester. She needed Monty's adulation.

She decided to leave Victor with her mother for a few days and have a second honeymoon in the semi-detached house at Bushey. She half-closed her eyes and pictured the bright, neat lounge, the bathroom, the modern kitchen. It would be heaven to be home. She and Monty could lie in bed all day and maybe she would become pregnant again. She thought of her words at Jubilee Road after Victor's birth, and smiled.

Of course there must be more children. Pregnancy suited her.

She sent a wire saying, 'Meet me Paddington two fifteen' and caught the ten forty-five from the Great Western Railways station. It was October the tenth. She wore a new coat, thin blue wool with a single button fastening and lapels down to her abdomen, and a blue straw cloche chosen by April, cream gloves and low-heeled court shoes. Cloche hats did not suit her, she still had her long hair which was too thick to be contained neatly; her feet and ankles were so narrow they needed more support than the cut-away court shoes and before she had walked the length of the platform she had raised a blister on her right heel. Crossly she settled herself into a corner seat. No-one had come to see her off and she suddenly felt very hard done by.

However, May loved travelling and by the time the snorting engine pulled past Old Oak Common, she was smiling again. It would be lovely to see Monty. She wondered whether he would be wearing his new plus-fours. He looked marvellous in them, he had such well-shaped legs. He would hold out his arm and they would walk down to the lawn at Paddington and people would turn and stare at them and wonder who they were. She simply must not limp, it would spoil everything.

He was wearing plus-fours and a terribly sporting sort of cap. She put her arms around his neck and kissed him for a long time, standing on one leg with her blistered heel waving in the cool air. When she drew away she was horrified, and thrilled, to find his eyes swimming with tears.

'Monty . . . baby . . . Mamma's back.'

'Oh my darling. Oh my wonderful girl. What have I done? I love you – insanely – you must believe that.'

'I believe it, darling.' She kissed him again. 'Oh I've missed you so much. I didn't realize how much till I saw you standing there looking so beautiful—' She kissed him again. People were looking and smiling. 'Baby, have you got a part yet? You didn't mention in your wires—'

'No. No, I haven't. I'm getting too old for the younger parts and they say I'm not mature enough for—'

'Baby, don't *worry*! Panto rehearsals will start soon.'

'They've started, May.'

'Oh . . .' She kissed him. 'Mamma's poor baby then. We'll find something, don't worry. Let's go home and go to bed. We can have supper there. Like we used to before Victor. D'you remember?'

'Oh May. Oh God, May—' The tears were running down his face. She glanced nervously at the audience and reached in her sleeve for a handkerchief. A pang of uneasiness clutched her diaphragm.

'Darling,' her voice became urgent. 'Please. Let's get home. Never mind the underground. A cab—'

'May, it's no good. It's no good.' He seized the handkerchief and coughed into it. 'You'll have to go back, darling. There's nowhere . . . nowhere at all . . .'

She said sternly, 'Monty, tell me what has happened.'

'I thought . . . money. It would please you if I

won a lot of money. Epsom . . . I went to Epsom. And greyhound racing. And car—'

'We've lost money before, Monty. We'll win it next time.'

'It wasn't money exactly.' He looked at her and gripped her hands. 'May, don't hate me. Please don't hate me.'

'I could never hate you, Monty.'

'I lost the house. Our house at Bushey Park, May. It's gone. Lock, stock and barrel. I'm staying with Maud Davenport and her mother. There's no room . . . nowhere. You'll have to go back to your mother, darling – thank God you didn't bring the boy. May – I'm so sorry – don't look like that—'

'It couldn't . . . not the house.'

'I had to, May. I'll explain—'

'I don't want to listen. What about Victor's toys? Our things – my clothes – that lamp we bought—'

'Darling, it had to go as it stood. A debt of honour is not like . . . it's not a legal debt—'

'Well then—'

'It's collected by people who don't care how they get it. They knock you about, May—'

'And you just let it *go*? In case they knocked you about?'

'May, try to understand.'

She understood only one thing. She turned and walked back to the ticket barrier. 'When is the next train to Gloucester?' she asked in a high voice. The audience dispersed. The show was over.

* * *

It was at this time that the newspapers published a letter by a certain Comrade Zinoviev containing instructions to British Bolsheviks in their work of subversion in Britain. The following General Election returned Mr Baldwin's 'plus-four boys' with unprecedented relief. Tollie Hall said to David Daker, 'It was too soon anyway. In another five years it will be a different story.' He dreamed of a revolution and a new Britain; it made the office at Williams Auctioneers just bearable.

Chapter Seven

In November that year, Monty Gould came to live with his wife and son in Gloucester. He was in debt, depressed, and resentful of his 'luck'. Luck was a word much in use that year; most people were down on theirs. May made him promise to give up gambling on the grounds that it would upset her mother. She went back to work with Madame Helen and passed on all her tips to Monty. As he never had any money, she had to assume he was breaking his promise. She went to see Mrs Baxter who agreed to take Victor on special terms as he was almost a Rhys-Davies. She told Monty she would never forgive him; but privately she thought that next summer when she had saved up £24 which would secure one of the Longford houses, she might try very hard to 'take him back'. A little punishment wouldn't hurt him now.

April flipped the curtain of the changing booth and presented herself to David and Manny. Her dress was like a fringed lampshade hanging from beneath her armpits. Her curly hair had been slicked down into the nape of her neck; the sides brought forward on her cheeks in two rigid curls.

'What do you think?'

It was David's latest creation, the hair-style as well as the dress.

Manny Stein moistened his lips. 'Good. Very good.'

'David?' April was not interested in Manny's opinion. She stood close to David and deliberately batted her lashes.

He grinned. 'It'll do.'

She pouted. 'It's supposed to drive you mad, darling.'

'Wicked woman. Go and change this minute.'

She flipped back through the curtain and behind her heard Manny Stein say, 'It drives *me* mad.'

David ignored that. 'The thing is, can you sell it?'

Manny said, 'I could sell a gross if April would come and model it.'

She waited, unconsciously holding her breath. Then David said smoothly, 'Sorry old man, that's not on. I couldn't spare April.'

Manny Stein said resignedly, 'Well. I think I can still sell a gross!'

April's joyous laugh rang out over the curtain. 'Darling David. You're such a spoil-sport. Manny might have got quite a price if I'd gone with the frock!'

Neither man returned her laugh to her and she looked at the pier glass in the booth and made a face at herself. She was nearly twenty-three and she and David had been married for a long time. She shouldn't be always trying to look for reassurances of his continued love.

Sibbie opened the door to Fred and sighed as she recognized him in the early twilight.

'Look Fred, if you've come to have another go at me about March clearing off to Bath, just leave it, will you? I've had a trying day and I'm not in the mood.'

'Oh?' He shouldered past her into the neat sitting-room. Will's pipe lay in the hearth. He picked it up. 'Careless. Not like you, Sib. Or are you trying to get the feeling that he's already your husband?'

She snatched the pipe from him and put it on the mantelpiece. 'I'm serious Fred. I don't want you needling me any more. I had nothing to do with March's leaving Gloucester and I don't know anything more about it. At a guess I would say March had news that her uncle was dying and dashed off to get her hands on some cash. You know what she's like as well as I do.'

He did. And it was possible. He would never completely understand how March's mind worked. Maybe his foolery with April had upset her that day and she was trying to punish him. He had decided to let her stew for a bit; but it was nearly Christmas. Surely she'd be home for Christmas.

He said, 'Nothing to do with March, little sister. A lot to do with you. I want you to have another go at Edward Williams.'

She sighed again, this time with exaggerated patience.

'I've told you, Fred. I can't. Not while his father is alive.'

'Why not?'

'Charles Williams is my benefactor after all,' she said with Victorian primness. Fred laughed scornfully.

'No well, seriously Fred, Edward Williams knows about me and his father. He's not likely to—'

'In other words, you're good with old men. The younger ones see through you.'

Her face tightened. 'You really are a swine. The point is that Edward is a good man – yes, there is such an animal, Fred. And though he's got that awful wife, he's still faithful to her. And if he changes his mind he doesn't want to follow in his father's footsteps.'

Fred grinned. 'I can think of another way of putting that, Sib. Anyway your other old man – Will Rising – didn't seem to mind going from mother to daughter.' He leaned easily away as Sibbie aimed a swipe at him. 'Pull yourself together, girl,' he advised. 'Charles is practically senile now. Edward will be an alderman one day like his father. I want him in my pocket. I've got other interests now and I need someone in the Council Chamber behind me. He'll be at the Mayor's Masked Ball at Christmas, and I know the alderman always takes you, so go to it.'

Sibbie sat down suddenly in front of her bright fire. She said, 'I'll make a bargain with you, Fred. You want Edward Williams. I want Monty Gould.'

He did not take her seriously at first. 'Wrapped for Christmas?'

'How you like. Bring him round here one night and I'll have another go with Puritan Edward.'

He went to the fire and kicked at a coal. Ash fell into the hearth and she leaned down immediately to sweep it up.

He said slowly, 'What about May?'

'We've always shared everything, May and me.'

'You bitch,' he said.

'Aren't I just?' She smiled at him, cheerful again. 'We'll see how I manage with younger men, Fred. Shall we?'

The new flat above Daker's Gowns was vast compared with the huddled living quarters in the Barton. When the shop was closed April was often very conscious of the emptiness below them; she was glad that the entrance via the fire escape into the alley behind Eastgate Street did not take them through the ghostly, carpeted showroom with its papier mâché models gleaming in the reflected street lamps. Next to the flat was David's big cutting-room and on the other side was a gap in the roofs and then the living quarters of the Bishop family who owned the Bon Marché. In the freedom that such private isolation gave them, April sometimes did outrageous things. She hardly knew why she did them. At the back of her mind she had a vague idea that she must 'hold' David by such ploys. Now she undressed very slowly while he lay in bed, his knees crooked to support a book. She was wearing the very latest French knickers and stood fiddling with the button, waiting for him to look up. He did not. She recalled the enormous awareness that had existed between them when she had been just a child.

'Did I put out the gas?' she asked rhetorically and flitted into the big living-room which May called a lounge. The gas was out. She walked between the big square chairs and the ashtrays on stalks and into the tiny hall, then through to the cutting-room. The uncurtained skylights were full of stars. She went to one of them and looked through and down. She could see the new Post Office and the plane trees which lined the cattle market. It was bitterly cold. She shivered and put her hands over her bare breasts. How long must she stay here before David came to investigate?

He said behind her, 'What are you doing out here like this? You'll freeze.'

She turned, her face lighting. 'David. Darling. Come and look at the city just before Christmas. I think it might snow.'

'Come to bed. Ridiculous child.'

'Don't you like my new knickers?'

'I adore them. I adore you. Now come to bed.'

'Hold me David. I'm cold.'

He came to her and put his arms lightly around her waist. 'You're not in the least cold.' He kissed her nose. 'D'you know something, Primrose? You're growing up into the most frightful flirt.'

She pouted. 'Only with you. And that's allowed.'

'No. With others. Poor Manny—'

'Poor Manny indeed. When I think how he wriggled his way into the business—'

'And Fred. We all know Fred belongs to March but the way you annexed him at that picnic in the summer! I thought May would scratch out your eyes!'

'Oh *David*! Fred's practically my brother!'

'And this man you met last year in London? Captain wotsit?'

She was reduced to giggles, leaning her forehead on his chin. 'I wish you could have seen that.' She looked up, pretending shock. 'Maybe you're right though, darling. D'you know what Victor told me?'

'What's that, Primrose?' He was as indulgent as an elderly uncle.

'He told me that Albert wants to see me without any clothes on!'

'You didn't—'

'David, of course I didn't! He's six years old!'

'I wouldn't put it past you, April.' David smiled, black eyes gleaming with amusement. 'What did you tell the little so-and-so?'

She looked prim. 'I told him I take my clothes off in front of Uncle David *only*.'

He held her to him quite suddenly, looking into her eyes without laughter or indulgence.

'Darling . . . darling Primrose . . .'

Immediately her hands went to his head in reassurance. 'It's all right, David. All right.'

'I want – I want—'

She stared at him, one hand stroking his dark hair down into the nape of his neck. 'What do you want, David?' she whispered. 'You've got me . . . you know that.'

'I want to make you pregnant.'

The words, simple enough in themselves, were shocking between them. The wish had been spoken by April five years before and never mentioned again. Their sex life had been erotic and sterile. It seemed to her she had to work constantly to eradicate her spoken wish from their lives, and she had done it by changing herself. By becoming the decade's innocent and outrageous symbol – a flapper. To hear now that her wish was also David's was cataclysmic. It was a sudden wrenching-away of the superficiality of those five years. She forgot her nakedness and the provocation of her French knickers. She went on holding his head, stroking it, and gradually on her face a smile dawned. She let it grow until it seemed to engulf the two of them in the sheer radiance of her happiness.

'Then . . . then you will,' she whispered. 'Oh my dear David.'

His voice shook uncontrollably. 'You know it's not . . . the shrapnel . . .'

'That you want to – it is enough.'

She meant it then. But afterwards as he lay face down beside her, his hands clenched on the pillow, she knew it was not enough for him. She pretended not to know that he had failed and kissed his ear, murmuring, 'Good night darling, it was perfect.' Then she lay very still on her back. She had read in a medical book by Dr Marie Stopes who was all the rage, that even an invisible speck of semen could fertilize a baby. When she was certain David was asleep, she pushed her pillow beneath her buttocks in an effort to encourage that speck into her womb.

Edwin had a relapse just before Christmas, so there was no question of March going home even if she had wished to. Rose made up a truckle bed for her in his room and put Albert into the other double bedroom on the first floor. They shared the nursing between them, and Letty took and fetched Albert from the small school in town which did not associate play and learning in any way at all. A week before Christmas when Rose crept downstairs to start on the grates, March crawled even more exhaustedly in by the side of her son to get two hours sleep before dawn. He curled against her, warming her with his body.

'I don't like it here, Mamma,' he whispered.

Somehow she controlled herself. 'You'll enjoy it after a while, darling,' she whispered. 'Bath is a beautiful place.'

'But you're busy with – with Papa – all the time. And Letty is very boring.'

She said sleepily, 'Your Uncle Albert called her Petty Letty.'

Albert giggled. 'I'll tell Victor that when I get home.'

Home. It sounded like heaven to March. And of course heaven was barred to her. If only Edwin would send for Mr Hazelbank. If only . . . so many things.

She whispered, 'We'll stay for Christmas, darling. Try to make your uncle – I mean your father – happy for Christmas.'

Albert saw nothing odd in this. A mixture of the Baxters' freedom of thought and his old-fashioned Sunday School, he said self-righteously, 'Yes. We have to make sacrifices at Christmas for Jesus Christ's sake.'

'Amen,' said March, and fell asleep.

Florence went down with the Spanish flu and had to take to her bed and resume her daily meal of raw chopped liver. Gran creaked up with a pan of coals from the range each morning for her fire; May put a clean cloth over the card table near the armchair and brought in a dainty breakfast tray. Florence surveyed the tiny glass of snowdrops flanking her poached egg, and smiled. 'Oh May. Where on earth did you get them?'

'We grow them in pots along the window sill. At the salon.' May poured tea and set the teapot in the hearth. 'Now darling, I'll be home at five. Promise me you'll eat your liver at midday. Aunty Sylv says that yesterday you dithered with it.'

'I promise,' Florence croaked through her raw throat. 'Now darling girl, wrap up warmly. These bitter winds will go to your chest.'

May smiled gaily as she went out, but that night her face was gloomy as she collapsed onto the bed in the attic which she shared with Monty.

'We're so *busy*! I know you think hairdressing is a pleasant pastime for me, but it's frightfully hard work. I'm on my feet all day, then when I get home half the time Jack and Austen are sprawled out in front of the fire.'

'Only at weekends darling. Come on, let me undress you and put you to bed. Like I used to.'

'If that's all the help you can suggest, never mind!' May said, exasperated. 'You could undress Victor if you must undress someone!'

'I do enough for him, May,' protested Monty. 'It's the most awful drag out to that wretched school. I don't know why you don't let him go to Chichester Street. And I've had to go out shooting with your father most of the day.'

'Oh my God.' Will hardly ever visited his rabbit shoot on Robinswood Hill. 'Oh my God, you *have* had a hard day!'

Monty was not used to sarcasm from beautiful May. 'Darling, please be kind to poor Monty,' he said, kneeling down to slip off her shoes.

She moved her feet away. 'I've told you. I'm tired.'

'We could have another baby,' he suggested.

'What? When we haven't got a home for ourselves? You must be mad!'

Monty flushed. 'I think I'll go down to the Lamb and Flag then. It's only half-past nine.'

'You do that. Let me get a decent sleep for once.'

'I might not come back,' he threatened childishly.

She went to the dressing-table and unpinned her hair. 'I think I could spare you for one night. Quite easily.'

Monty left the room and banged the door and Florence heard him go past her room like a whirlwind. She had become very fond of her son-in-law since his terrible misfortune last autumn. It seemed to make him so much like her own Will during the war when he had been so down on his 'luck'. She hoped that in the quiet routine of Gloucester life he could find his old happiness again. Just as Will had.

Fred was in the Lamb and Flag. He tried to think about Edward Williams and how he could use him in the future. He needed to expand. His activities as an entrepreneur had proved very rewarding: Fred had a gift for manipulating people and then organizing them, and then making sure they were grateful to him. There seemed no reason why he could not extend his particular talent. The only trouble was, thoughts of March constantly got in the way. He kept remembering her at Rodley, clinging to him, laughing and making him laugh. Hell's teeth, surely she hadn't cleared off to Bath in a fit of pique because he had rough-housed with April?

When Monty Gould came in, eyes, glittering and face flushed, Fred recognized his mood only too well.

He bought him three drinks in quick succession. Monty had drunk a great deal in London and had been almost permanently and happily intoxicated. Tonight, drinking whisky 'medicinally' as he put it himself, he became more morose by the minute.

'Something must change m'luck pretty soon, Fred. One horse – one decent bet – that's all I need.'

Fred swilled his beer in his glass, staring down into it as if all the answers were there. 'A man makes his own luck. You have to take life in two hands and twist it the way you want it to go.'

These were words Monty wanted to hear but his voice was still plaintive. 'How can I do that down here, old man? That's what I want to know. Don't expect me to start digging coal or gravel or whatever it is you're digging now, do you? I'm an actor, Fred. I want to act.'

'Exactly. That's what I'm saying. Act a part to get a part. Who could help you?'

'Maud could help. Maud Davenport. The Happy Hey Days are booked for a summer season at Blackpool. Maud could get me my old place. But May . . . May won't let me go and ask Maud. Never liked Maud.'

'There you are. You've got to act two parts. One for May. One for Maud.'

Monty giggled. 'One for May. One for Maud. All for Monty!' He sobered. 'I'm not going home tonight, Fred. Show her. Can I come over . . . stay with you?'

Fred grinned. Sometimes Fate played right into his hands so neatly it was unbelievable.

'Sorry, old man. But I know where you can go. Relative of mine.'

He led Monty out of the pub and down Northgate Street. Like a lamb to the slaughter.

Sibbie opened the door of the bungalow wearing her new eau-de-Nil satin nightdress; Monty recoiled and so did she.

'You din't say, Fred – you din't say it was your sister. I can't – May's tole me about you!'

Sibbie recovered immediately. It was lucky she had no-one else with her that night – very lucky. She pretended terror. 'What on earth has happened? Fred, what are you doing here with May's husband? Is something wrong with May? Oh my God – that's it, isn't it? May's ill and she needs me with her—' She backed into the warm, well-lit living-room as she spoke. Monty, nudged by Fred, followed.

'Nothing is the matter with May, Miss Luker,' he said with what he hoped was dignity. 'Your brother offered me a bed for the night and I suppose this is his idea of a joke.'

She rounded on Fred. 'How could you, Fred? Do you think I have no feelings? Do you think Monty has no feelings? I have already tried to befriend him once and was rebuffed—' She hurled herself on to the chaise-longue and burst into tears.

Fred said stiffly, 'I had no idea you two had met

before. Monty needed somewhere to sleep and you have a sofa. I couldn't take him home with me – you know what it's like over there. Sorry I've put my foot in it.' He jerked his head at the door. 'Come on. We'll go. You'll have to make it up with May.'

'We can't leave her like . . . like this . . . old man . . .' Monty felt unsteady on his feet. It was very warm in the room and very cold outside. It was a long way to walk back to May's anger and all the problems of thirty-three Chichester Street. He cleared his throat. 'Miss Luker, it would seem I owe you an apology.'

Fred said, 'Well, I'm off. You're over twenty-one. Please yourself.' He opened the door, slid through it and closed it quickly behind him. Monty looked helplessly down at the shaking satin shoulders.

'Please Miss Luker . . . please . . .' he stammered, out of his depth. He was too drunk to choose a rôle and much too drunk to realize that Sibbie had already chosen one for them both.

She flung herself upright and dashed away her tears. 'I'm sorry,' she said bravely. 'I really am. I suppose Fred thinks it's a joke but – ' she looked up at him through drowned eyes ' – you see Monty, I really was part of the Rising family and this sort of thing really hurts.'

'I'm sorry,' he repeated miserably. 'Everything seems to have gone wrong lately . . . everything.'

She got up slowly and went to a chiffonier glittering with cut glass. 'I heard about the house. Last autumn. If only things had been different . . . I could have helped.'

'You?' He stared at the back that was so like May's. Even their movements were identical.

She shrugged. 'I have some money. I don't want it. You could have had it.' She carried a drink to him. 'Here. Drink this and sit down for five minutes. You look all in.'

'I am. Completely.' He collapsed and allowed her to crouch before him with the drink. 'I don't know which way to turn.' He could see down the front of the nightdress. He seized the drink and tossed it back. She was still there. 'It's generous of you to suggest . . . it was an enormous debt.'

She shrugged again and the nightdress did a shimmy on its own. 'You can hold them at bay with small payments.' She grinned. 'I know about things like that.' She stood up just before he fell forward on to her. She refilled his glass and put it in the grate. 'That's a nightcap. Drink it then go to sleep on the sofa.' She went to the door of her room. 'And remember, if you need help in the future and you can bear to ask me—' She disappeared in the midst of his protestations. He looked at the door, heard her moving about inside and tried to curb his imagination. He drank the whisky, helped himself to more, paced about the room, held the mantelpiece and leaned over groaning. He wanted to be sick. Was there a bathroom? Where was the kitchen? He blundered into her room. She held his head over the chamber-pot and wiped his face afterwards.

'I smell terrible,' he groaned, hating himself.

'Poor baby,' Sibbie crooned. 'Come into bed and let me get you warm.' She drew off his trousers and jacket and wound herself around him, holding his head against her breast like May always used to, but never

196

did now. He slept blissfully and when he woke at eight o'clock the next morning they were both naked. He did what she wanted him to do, groaning aloud with the pain in his head, forgetting it only momentarily as they shared a brief orgasm.

But Sibbie was blindingly happy. She had felt triumph when she had first slept with Will Rising on Armistice night, but nothing compared with this. As Monty Gould grunted guiltily on top of her, she smiled blindly at the ceiling. 'We're together again, May,' she whispered ecstatically. 'Together again at last.'

Chapter Eight

April, Bridget, Tollie, David and Manny Stein went to one of the Cadena's famous tea dances. David did not dance but he wanted to enjoy watching the impact of April's lampshade dress. He was not disappointed. William Bishop, who was rumoured to be about to expand his Bon Marché into most of the new Kings Square, approached him with an enquiry. David led him through the tables to walk around the balustrades and look down on the Saturday shoppers in the restaurant below.

Tollie held April gingerly as they fox-trotted unadventurously.

'What you don't seem to understand, April,' he said, 'is that if only there are enough Labour members – prospective members that is – they are bound to be voted in. Now that the working-class man has a vote he will obviously return a working-class representative.'

'There's no guarantee of that,' April said without much interest. 'They've only got to look at what happened before. Mr MacDonald couldn't make it work even with the help of the Liberals so—'

'It wasn't the time,' Tollie said eagerly. 'But now . . . things are getting worse. Baldwin is hopeless. Did you read all that drivel about the Coal Commission last year? You see, if it goes on like this there'll be an uprising in less than twelve months.'

April opened her eyes wide. 'D'you mean a revolution? Like in Russia?'

'The same.'

'Oh Tollie. This is *England*.'

'Exactly. A land fit for heroes.' He laughed. She looked at him uncertainly and laughed too.

Bridget held him very tightly indeed. 'I saw you laughing together Tollie, don't try to deny it. April is my best friend. My very best friend, but if you think you can play fast and loose – even with my best friend – *especially* with my best friend—'

Tollie said wearily, 'Do you ever think of anything but sex, Bridget? Anything at all?'

'Yes. I think of your advancement. Daddy says he needs someone for the antiques. And I told him—'

'I wish you wouldn't, Bridget. I'm not interested in antiques. I'm not interested in the auctioneering business at all.'

'What are you interested in, Tollie? Apparently it's not sex. So just what is it?'

'Politics. I'm going to go in for politics. Socialist politics.'

If he thought he might put her off, he was wrong. She was silent, staring at him while they circled the floor again. Then she said, 'Darling. Of course. It's absolutely you. And I can help you. I know so many people. You'll be one of the intellectuals like that man with the funny name.'

'Chiozza Money,' he supplied glumly.

'Do you know him, Tollie?'

'Not personally.'

'You will. You'll know them all.' She threw back her head triumphantly. 'And what is more my dear, they will know you.'

Tollie felt his heart like lead inside his chest.

Manny Stein drank his tea and put down his cup to take April's fingers in his. She tried to free herself and could not.

'April, listen to me. David will return in a moment, I haven't long. Leave him. Come away with me. You know I love you and I can give you anything you want.'

She drew in her breath and horror widened her eyes as Tollie's threat of revolution had not. She might have 'flirted' with Manny as David had said, but that she had pushed him to this point appalled her.

'Manny. You don't know what you are saying. Truly. Please let us forget it – you did not speak.'

He did not release her hands. 'I knew of course you would try to put me off. You are besotted with David. It is a childhood passion which is meaningless now, April. You are a woman, not a child. You do not love him – perhaps you do not love me either. Yet. But I can love enough for both of us—'

'Manny, please don't say any more. You make me hate myself.'

That surprised him. His dark, covetous eyes sharpened. 'You? Hate yourself? That is ridiculous, April—'

'I have teased you, Manny. I know it, and you must realize it now before you say any more. I did not mean to hurt you, to make you believe there was anything more than affection on both our sides.'

'My darling. I have loved you since I saw you first. There was never mere affection on my side. And if there is that much on yours—'

She tugged furiously at her hands. 'I am going to leave you now. Where is David? I want to go home.'

Manny restrained her with difficulty. Over Bridget's shoulder Tollie raised his eyebrows. Manny said quietly but with great force, 'Listen to me, April, and think over what I say. This is a shock to you. Yes. But I have known about you and David from the very beginning. I heard your argument that night, not long after you were married, when I called at the Barton shop. Do you remember?'

'I remember. Oh God—'

'David cannot give you a child. I can.' She tugged again, half standing, scraping her chair. 'I will release you now, April. But I want you to think over my words. You are the toast of Gloucester. I can make you the toast of London and a mother also.'

She jerked and was free. David came to meet her as she ran between the tables. He took her arm and felt her tremble.

'Bridget will bring your coat, darling,' he said smoothly. 'Let us go on and make some tea, shall we?' The shop was across the road; even so it was odd to walk through crowded Northgate Street on a Saturday afternoon in January in a dress like a lampshade. David made nothing of it. They went straight through the showrooms where the assistants hurriedly stood up from gilt-backed chairs and pretended to be sorting through the ready-mades. David did not let go April's elbow till they were at the top of the stairs, then he turned her to face him. His expression was tense.

'What happened, Primrose? Did Manny make a pass?'

She tried to laugh and to control her shaking. 'Yes. I suppose that's what it was. Forget it, David.'

'What did he say?'

'Nothing. Absolutely nothing. Really.' She put her face on his shoulder, unwilling to meet his eyes. She thought of Manny Stein at the bottom of the narrow stairs in the Barton, listening. She shook.

'My God. I *told* you. Before Christmas I told you that you were leading him on—'

'How?' Her voice was a sob. 'That's not fair, David. I don't like the man – never did. But he was your best man – your friend in hospital—'

'What did he *say*?'

'I can't even remember. Nothing much. I'm being silly.' She turned her face into his neck, willing him to put his arms around her.

'I'll chuck him out. There's nothing binding in the partnership, it's a sort of gentleman's agreement.'

'David, I won't hear of it. If I did encourage him – without meaning to – it's so unfair!' She forced herself to straighten and look at him directly; he made no attempt to hold her. 'I've choked him off now. There'll be nothing else. You can't send him away because I've got the heeby-jeebies. I'm sorry darling.' She turned and went into the sitting-room. 'You see, he won't come over with the others.'

But he did. He crouched by the gas fire with a toasting-fork looking more like Mephistopheles than usual. And when April glanced at him he smiled as if they shared a secret.

She went into the bathroom and splashed her face with water. If only . . . if only . . . she and David could have a baby.

It was March's thirty-second birthday. Dr Maine came in the morning and pronounced Edwin fit enough to partake in 'suitable celebrations'. March smiled and clenched her hands behind her back to stop them from clenching around Edwin's scrawny throat. It had occurred to her several times that it might be possible to hasten his end, although poison had been in her mind rather than physical violence. Not only had he kept her running up and down stairs all day and all night, but Mr Hazelbank had still not been summoned.

She said smoothly, 'Rest now my dear. When Albert comes home from school there is a special cake.'

The two men chortled like silly children. It was as if Edwin knew that his good health and careful nursing depended on Mr Hazelbank being always in the offing, as it were. Every day Albert pleaded, 'Mother, when are we going home?' And March replied impatiently now, 'For goodness' sake Albert! When we can – just as soon as we can! How many times must I tell you!'

She saw the doctor out and went down to the kitchen for Edwin's hot chocolate. It infuriated her to see Letty sitting doing nothing. 'You can come up with me and fetch the night's linen, Letty,' she said.

'Laundry. Rose's job,' Letty said insolently.

'Not today. Rose has been up all night—'

'She's younger than me!'

'So am I. And I pay you to do what I say!'

'*You* don't pay me, Miss March!'

March fumed. So soon this woman would have the last laugh. But not yet. 'No. But I can soon stop you being paid, Letty. So come on!'

They went upstairs in mutual dislike. Edwin, on the other hand, seemed livelier than usual. He sipped his chocolate and put it on the tray. 'Ah Letty. When you fetch Master Albert from school, do not take him for a walk. There is a special cake for tea – ' he looked archly at his wife ' – we'll have a little party. You and Rose must come up—' He stopped speaking and closed his eyes. They stared at him, puzzled; he whined and whimpered but was rarely abrupt. His head settled into the piled pillows, a pulse throbbed in his neck and was still.

March rushed at him furiously and felt for his heart; there was none. She shook him. 'Edwin! Edwin – wake up this instant! Do you hear me?' She went on shaking him until Letty removed her hands.

'It's no good, Miss March. He's gone. Lovely way to go too, with the both of us by him and him so happy.' Tears spouted from her eyes. 'Don't take on so,' she said to herself as well as March.

March crouched by the bed sobbing noisily. If Letty hadn't known her as a child in one of her tantrums, she'd have thought the girl really was frantic with grief. March looked up.

'I can't bear it! I can't *bear* it, Letty! Get Dr Maine

– quick, quick, there might be a chance! The silly fool said he was better – get him!'

'Don't be silly, Miss. Come on now.' Letty got March up on her feet, feeling a twinge of sympathy in spite of herself. 'We'll go and have a cup of tea and send Rose for the doctor and someone to lay out. Come on now. It's been expected long enough.'

March suddenly felt very tired. Whatever she did turned out to be wrong. She might have guessed this would, too. She allowed herself to be led out of the room.

Fred sat one side of his desk and looked at Leonie Porterman sitting on the other side. Her hair was shingled so short it was like a man's; her make-up was heavy. It was March's birthday and she had not even come home for that; he thought he hated Leonie Porterman, yet he knew that he would sleep with her tonight.

He said, 'I will not have you coming to the office to see me, Leonie. I've told you before. I've got friends in Gloucester – good friends – but if you continue to flaunt our relationship to the skies, they will have to drop me.'

'Oh stop being such a Filthy Luker!' She smiled at her oft-repeated pun. 'Everyone knows about us anyway. D'you know, when Marcus and I had our last row he told me that we're known as "Three in a Bed Unlimited"! That's rather good, don't you think?'

'I don't suppose Marcus thought so.'

'He says he'll buy you out. Killing, isn't it? He'll pay you money not to see me again. If you could push the offer high enough, Luker, we might elope on it!'

'Oh shut up Lee, do. And clear off, there's a good girl. I'm going down to the Forest in a minute.'

'I'll come with you. I like that place down there. It's earthy. Reminds me of the gamekeeper's cottage in *Lady Chatterley*. Did you read that book, Luker?'

'Yes, I did.'

'What did you think of it?'

'Filth.'

'Exactly. Your sort of book!' She laughed uproariously as she lifted her skirt to adjust a suspender. She added, 'Shall we go in my car or yours?'

'Go? Where?'

'Marsh Cottage. You just said—'

'Leonie, I am going alone. I am selling the cottage to one of the miners and I can't have you tagging along.'

She pulled down her skirt and surveyed him through narrowed eyes. 'You'll be coming to Keynsham tonight I hope, Luker. It's Wednesday.'

Was there a hint of menace in her voice? He said levelly, 'I'm busy tonight, Lee.'

'Very. Same here. As usual.'

She wasn't going to let him off; and it was March's birthday. He couldn't bear the thought of Leonie Porterman on March's birthday. He stood up and reached for his jacket on the back of the chair.

'Right. I'm off then.'

'Don't be late tonight then, Luker. I wouldn't want Marcus to get his coal from *anyone* else now.'

He watched her sturdy figure go past the window. Yes, she had been threatening him. He went to the small mirror that Gladys used and struggled with his collar stud, nearly choking himself with his suppressed anger. The sooner Sibbie delivered Edward Williams to him, the better.

While Fred talked to Leonie Porterman, April went for a bath. She rarely bathed during the day, but David had promised to take the afternoon off, hire a car and drive her to Bath to wish March a happy birthday. Like Fred, April had assumed March would be home, first for Christmas, then for her birthday. When her weekly letters to Florence contained no such news, April planned this surprise visit.

She sang as she wallowed in scented water. Gracie Fields' record of 'Sally' was still very popular and the only way to imitate those clear soprano tones was to use the steamy acoustics of the bathroom. She was into the second verse, wavering slightly as she descended the scale for '. . . don't ever wander . . . away from the alley and me . . .' when the door knob rattled, the door opened, and Manny Stein stood there.

April was shocked. She relied on the isolation of the flat to wander around half-dressed and leave the bathroom door unlocked. She had avoided Manny since that day in January and when she could not, her manner had been heavily repressive. Before then she might have laughed as she grabbed her face-cloth to hide her upper parts; now she did not. What was worse, he did not move.

'Get out!' she snapped. 'How dare you—'

He said, 'I knocked first. I didn't realize you were taking a bath.'

'Now you do. So go.'

'David said you were upstairs. He did not seem to object.'

'*Go!*'

'I simply want to know whether you have thought about what I said eight weeks ago in the Cadena.'

'It was absurd. Ridiculous. Get out!'

'April, you cannot dismiss my – my declaration—' He smiled slightly at the word. 'You cannot dismiss *me* like that. My love for you is absolutely consuming. I look at you lying there and I hardly know what to do.'

'I'll scream.'

'And no-one will hear.' He took a step inside and closed the door behind him. 'Let me talk to you. Explain. Please take away that face-cloth.'

She felt her outrage turn to fear. There was something crazy in his face, in his quiet request.

She forced reasonableness into her own voice. 'Listen. Manny. I can't talk like this – I simply cannot. I shall panic and there will be the most frightful scene and we shall never be able to meet again. Go into the living-room and sit down. I will be with you in three minutes.'

'April, I dream of you. Every night. And all day long. I am obsessed.'

'Two minutes. I promise you, Manny—'

The door opened again and David stood there. He saw his wife sitting in the bath, precariously modest, talking smilingly with a man.

He said tensely, 'Stein. It's you. Get out of this flat. This building. And don't come back.'

'I must talk to April. Surely you understand that? Surely you—'

He got no further. David caught his arm and swung him through the door, hooked his gammy leg around the immaculate ankles and felled him in the tiny hall. April screamed with fright, leapt up, grabbed a towel and crowded behind David. Manny picked himself up with difficulty. He had hit his head as he went down.

He said, 'I thought you were lame. Or is it an excuse you use when it comes to impregnating your wife properly?'

David hit him open-handed across the mouth. He began to bleed. He dabbed it with his handkerchief and laughed.

'For someone who professes to abhor physical violence, you are doing well this afternoon, my friend.' He stared at David. 'My friend,' he repeated. He looked beyond the open door and smiled slightly. 'Adieu, fair April. I shall be waiting. If ever you need me.' He left.

April sat on the edge of the bath, not knowing whether to laugh or cry or be sick. She let concern for David overtake all three emotions.

'Darling. Are you all right? Your leg—'

David surveyed her without any expression on his face. 'My leg is very good for ejecting suitors. As that one pointed out. What is more important – are you all right?'

'Of course. But I don't quite know what might have happened if you hadn't arrived when you did.'

'I think I know. He would have – what was his word? – impregnated you.'

'David!' She stared up at him, dismayed. The towel had fallen and she retrieved it fumblingly, embarrassed to be naked in front of him. 'It wouldn't have come to that!'

'Wouldn't it? Surely it's what you want? Oh, you might have put up a bit of a fight, of course, but—'

'*David!* Don't talk like this – please.'

'Why not? You're a passionate female, April – face up to it. Erotic too. D'you know, some of the things you've done – and let me do – have shocked me. Does that surprise you? A soldier with two years' experience in French brothels, shocked by a schoolgirl in his home town.'

She was weeping. He said savagely, 'Get into the bedroom. Go on. Now.'

'But David . . . we're going to Bath to see March . . .'

He pulled her up and shoved her ahead of him into the bedroom. She lay on the bed on her side, watching him in horror as he pulled off his clothes. There was no tenderness. After less than three minutes she felt something eject into her. She had never felt that before. He got off her and stood at the side of the bed, his anger still burning in him almost visibly.

'There! Are you satisfied? Have I *impregnated* you now?'

She held her crutch fiercely, her eyes like stars. 'David – there was something! I felt something!' She lifted her buttocks slightly. 'I *knew* Sibbie Luker was wrong all the time! I knew—'

His hands ripped hers away. 'What do you mean – Sibbie Luker?'

'Nothing—' She flinched from the anger in his eyes;

it had been hot, now it was frozen. 'Nothing, David!'

He pulled her upright and shook her hard. 'Tell me! Tell me what you meant. You've been discussing me with Sibbie Luker. Just as you discussed me with Manny Stein!'

'No! No, David. Darling – really—'

He pulled her on to the floor and she fell to her knees.

'Tell me now! Otherwise you can get out of here and go with him!'

She sobbed. 'I hate him, David. I always have. But he's Jewish and I thought if I showed my dislike it would hurt you and your mother! After the Cadena – in January – I thought you understood!'

'You know me better than that, Primrose. That's the trouble with you, you've always known me – seen through me. And you talked me over with Sibbie – comparing notes, was that it?'

'No! Never!' She hung from his hands like a drooping flower. 'David, please let me lie down to let the semen—'

'You fool! Don't you realize that's happened before? Twice before, to be exact. Just twice in six years! Christ! Surely you told Sibbie *that*? Surely you used one of your wonderful long words – impotent – that's the word, April. That's what they call it in those books you read – impotent!'

He flung her hands from him and she collapsed against the leg of the bed. There was a long, sobbing silence. He went to the window and looked out.

She said, 'Sibbie found me in the garden of Chichester House. The morning we were married. She said there would be no children. That is all. I didn't listen.'

He took a long, trembling breath. 'You should have. Anyway, you know by now. Six years this June we've been doing our stuff, April. You and me. Some stuff, eh? We could give lessons.'

'Please David . . .'

He turned and went to the door briskly. 'Look. I don't want to see you again today. Maybe not for a week or two. Is that clear? If you want to stay away for good, that's OK with me. I shall understand. Obviously. If you want to find Manny . . . well, that won't be difficult. He's waiting over the road. I can't say *that* will be all right by me, but I suppose it's what I deserve.' He went out, shutting the door carefully behind him. She heard the door in the hall close similarly, then his muffled footsteps on the stairs. Slowly she stood up and began to dress. It was difficult because she couldn't stop crying.

Dr Maine was kind.

'Please don't distress yourself any more, Mrs Tomms. Your husband was a very lucky man. I understand entirely why you spent so much time with your parents.' He smiled knowingly. 'Sick mother, certainly. Also a very demanding husband, yes? Mr Tomms was very fond of boasting, you know . . . yes, boasting. But when you were needed you returned to look after him. And of course he took advantage of that too.' He patted her shoulder. 'I hope I may continue to be of service to you.'

March stared stonily ahead. 'I shall have to go home

after the funeral, Doctor. I cannot afford to live here.'

'My dear, you will be a wealthy woman. A very wealthy woman.'

The front door bell rang and she stood up. 'I believe that will be the undertaker. You will excuse me.'

'Don't forget I am always ready to attend you, my dear Mrs Tomms.'

'I won't forget.'

March wondered how long he would remember. Once the will was read everyone would be only too anxious to forget 'dear Mrs Tomms'. She ushered him out. Rose was keening in the basement and Letty had gone to meet Albert from school and take him for an afternoon tea at Kunzels. She dealt with the undertakers. She thought bleakly that if Edwin weren't already dead, she really would kill him now. With her bare hands.

Fred thought of Leonie and March and his strangely empty life and wondered what had gone wrong. When had the intricate and marvellous business of making money turned sour? Had it been when his manipulation of people had rebounded, like twisted elastic, and he had found that one trick – just as one good turn – deserved another?

He gritted his teeth with annoyance as he drove over the Cross, swerving to avoid some stupid girl wandering along in a dream. Then he saw it was April. He pulled up the car outside Dentons and jumped out.

'April?' She turned and he saw fear in her face. 'April, what the devil is the matter? Where are you going? It's not that warm – where's your coat?' He had a moment of panic. Something had happened to March. Life would never be the same.

But she relaxed and smiled. 'Sorry. I thought it was . . . someone else. Sorry. I didn't mean to . . . sorry.'

April rarely apologized. And there were smudges on her face; no rouge or mascara, just smudges.

He repeated, 'Where are you going? D'you want a lift?' A bicycle came close and he took her arm and held her flat to the Morris. She was shaking like a leaf.

'You're cold. Get in. There's a rug on the back seat. I'll take you home.' Which was ridiculous. The shop was just around the corner.

But she got in and when he reached back for the rug, she huddled herself in it as if she was ill. He realized that must be it; she was ill. A dray pulled by two horses lumbered past them, full of beer kegs. He drew out behind it but could not pass.

'I'll go down College Green and into Northgate that way,' he said.

She shook even more. 'No. No, I don't want to go home. I – I don't know where to go.'

He glanced sideways. 'Are you ill, April? Have you got a chill?'

'No. I'm cold. But it's warm in here. The sun comes through the windows and . . .' Her voice trailed away. She was crying.

He said, 'I'm going to the Forest. Come with me.' He saw her nod and freed one hand from the wheel to clutch hers. 'Don't cry, little April. I can't do anything about it while I'm driving.'

She went on crying. 'That's what's good. I didn't want to be alone. But I don't want . . . I don't want . . .'

She hiccupped mightily and tried to laugh. 'Oh God. Daddy used to call me little April. Even when I was taller than he was. Oh I wish I was little again. Oh Fred, I don't want to be grown-up.'

'Well, I don't want to be a kid again, thanks very much.' He pulled out and overtook the dray at last. The gypsy encampment down on Westgate fields smoked sootily ahead of them. 'I got plenty of beatings when I was a kid. I remember Miss Pettinger beating me for swearing. And Pa leathered me regular for one thing and another. Don't wish that on me again, April.'

She hiccupped another obedient giggle. 'All right Fred.' She found a handkerchief and wiped at her face. 'Thanks for picking me up. Am I going to be a nuisance? Are you going to do some of your coal business?'

'No. I'm going to hand the key of Marsh Cottage to one of the Freeminers. You haven't seen the cottage we built have you, April? Me and your uncles.' He grinned at her. 'The architect's nightmare, we should have called it. Tell you what, I'll take the Newent road. That will take you back to your childhood.'

'Oh, Fred. You are good to us all. D'you remember when you collected Teddy and me from the infirmary when we had our tonsils out? You and Sibbie and Gladys were like our family.' She inverted her mouth apologetically. 'How is Sibbie, Fred?'

'Flourishing. She talks about the past too. She—' He grinned again, ruefully. 'She still thinks of herself as part of your family.'

At Lassington he stopped the car and they got out

and looked at the famous oak tree, already propped in ten places. As they walked back to the car, Fred suddenly dived into the hedgerow and came up with a daffodil bud. 'The first of the Newent daffs,' he said, presenting it to her. 'We got here before the gypsies.' She held it against her face and he knew she was near tears again. 'Come on. Across country to Bulley and then to Mitcheldean.'

He drove slowly, pointing out landmarks as if to a child. 'Westbury over there – Rodley the other side of the river. We'll have another picnic there this summer, shall we? Down that road is Flaxley Abbey and Speech House. The Forest is like a little country in itself.'

'They mined iron long before coal,' April mentioned, trying to make an effort. 'And the oaks went to the Navy for years. David's got a book about it.' Her voice faded again. She sniffed the daffodil pushed through the button-hole of her blouse and her eyes filled up.

Fred said matter-of-factly, 'You and David have quarrelled. Quarrels are soon mended, April.'

'Yes. Yes, I know. But . . . the cause of this one will always be there.' She straightened her back and took a deep breath. 'Never mind. We'll manage.'

Fred felt a definite urge to murder David Daker. He said shortly, 'If the cause you are talking about is my sister, forget it. It doesn't matter.'

She glanced at him and then gasped a little laugh. 'It's a good job I know about Sibbie, Fred, otherwise you could have just put your foot in it.'

He laughed too. 'Sorry. Didn't think of it like that. You'd have to know about Sibbie, I suppose.'

'Yes.' She didn't want to talk about Sibbie. Her unguarded remark to David about Sibbie had revealed much more important secrets: the secrets of David's mind. She said suddenly, 'Did I flirt with you at the picnic last summer, Fred?'

He was going to say yes. Then he saw her white knuckles on her knees. 'No. We were like a couple of kids. Does David think you flirted with me?'

'Not just you. Others. You see . . . Manny Stein made an absolute fool of himself this afternoon. David found him. Us.'

Fred frowned and turned into the track leading to Marsh Cottage. He switched off the engine and leaned back, letting the silence wash into the car like a balm.

He said at last, 'So. David was rattled by what he saw, and because he was rattled, he accused you of flirting with everyone, and you had a row.'

'More or less. I suppose that's it. Yes.'

The simple definition had its effect; he watched her lean back too, wind down her window, comb her fingers through her hair.

She tried to laugh wryly. 'David said I was erotic. Me!'

He shrugged, determined to take it all very casually. 'Like your father, I suppose.'

She turned at that, startled. 'Like *Daddy*?'

He could have bitten his tongue. 'Your father had five children after all, April. And he always seems to me . . . affectionate. In some ways he was more of a mother to you kids than your mother!'

She laughed more genuinely, knowing what he meant. 'We were lucky he was always *there*. It made us very close. Like David.' She swallowed. 'Perhaps it is possible to be too close.'

He got out and helped her from the car as March had taught him to do so many years ago. She kept the rug around her shoulders and declined his helping hand over the rough parts. She jumped lightly from log to log in the marshy places. When they came to the dell she exclaimed with delight, slipped out of her shoes and paddled down the stream.

There was no sign of Danby. They went into the house and he let her look round while he lit a fire. She was entranced with everything.

'It's like playing at house! Those beds along the walls – and the table and chairs. Oh Fred you were so clever – you deserve to make a fortune!'

Nobody had given him such unstinted praise. He found himself telling her about the treks to the dell to supply what had to be one gigantic endeavour. He told her about that first trickle of smoke which had climbed along the first sunbeam and was his public claim to the land. He couldn't explain about Austen's irregular birth and the way he had used it to lever the other miners into working for him, so she saw him as entirely romantic, entirely idealistic. For the first time he did not enjoy deceiving another person: even when he had tricked March into the Bath visit he had felt a certain pleasure because he had scored off her. So he took one of the palliasses from the bunks and threw it down by the fire. 'Come on, sit here while I make tea. You paddled in your stockings – ridiculous girl. Take them off and dry them.'

She did so and he watched her from the corner of

his eye, marvelling at her unselfconsciousness. Was this what David called flirting? She had the natural, clumsy grace of a colt, all legs and arms and a certain lack of co-ordination. He brewed the tea, opened a can of milk and stirred it in. She had had army tea with David. She sipped, stretched her long, bare legs, sipped again, and without warning, put her cup down and began to sob as if her heart would break.

Fred said, 'Now come on, old girl. Out with it. What's been happening exactly?'

She put her head in her hands and rocked to and fro like Mrs Daker did. It seemed to help. She blurted suddenly through her fingers, 'It would be all right if we could have a baby. Oh Fred, if only we could have a baby! I'd give anything – do anything – to give David a baby!'

It was all clear. He remembered something Sibbie had said once.

He said uncomfortably, 'You're still young, April. You'll start a family soon.'

'No.' She rocked again. 'No. After this awful business with Manny he . . . we . . .' She shook her head and started again. 'I thought we might then. But he said it didn't mean anything. He said because of the shrapnel he can't . . . he said he's impotent. Oh God, Fred, if I had a baby I think he'd be all right. I think the demons would go away for ever. I think he might be whole again!'

He let her get on with it for five minutes. She rocked a bit more, and was still again, weeping quietly.

At last he said, 'Let's get this absolutely straight, April. This afternoon David made love to you.'

She was silent for so long he thought he had got it wrong. Then she said, 'Made love. I suppose you might call it that.'

'Well, did he or didn't he?'

She looked at him and smiled slightly and sadly at his directness. 'We had intercourse. There was no love in it.'

'Has it happened before?'

She answered again as if he were a doctor searching for a diagnosis. 'Twice.' She made a face. 'Just twice.'

'But this time . . . you might be pregnant. That would prove him wrong, wouldn't it?'

'Of course. That's what I've been at some pains to explain to you.'

He said severely, 'Don't take that tone with me, girl. I was the one who held you when you were sick after your tonsils, remember.'

She puffed a helpless laugh. 'Oh Fred. Be serious.'

'I was never more so. If you find out in a couple of months that you are pregnant, he will know it was because of this afternoon. Am I right or not?'

'You are right. But if it didn't happen before—'

'Then obviously, you make assurance doubly sure.' He looked at her and she looked back at him quite blankly. She did not know what he was talking about.

He said carefully, 'A donor. You need a donor. This new artificial insemination thing – you've heard of it? The semen is taken from a donor.'

'My God, Fred. What the hell are you suggesting?'

He grinned easily. 'Hang on to your hat, girl. I'm suggesting something that might make you run out of here very quickly. I am suggesting that I could be your donor.'

She was silent, staring at him, assimilating what he had said. She was not shocked, but she was adamant.

'No. I'm not going to run, Fred. I'm honoured – if I follow you correctly then I really am honoured. But you see . . . I couldn't.'

'Then that's all right. Let me pour you some more tea.'

He did so and she drank it. The middle of the fire fell in and he crawled towards it and threw on two logs. It crackled comfortingly.

She said, 'You must think me ridiculous. One minute I say I would do anything to help David to get over . . . this. And the next . . . I could agree here and now, Fred. But when we actually . . . when you . . . I should fight you off. Instinctively. Can you understand?'

'Of course. I'm not hurt, little April. I shall go on loving you as a brother, and I hope you will go on loving me as a sister.' He sat very still, frightened to disturb her. 'But, if ever you change your mind . . . well, it wouldn't be disloyal – not with me as the donor, would it? I'm a brother but not a brother. Can *you* understand?'

'Yes. Yes, I can. And you're absolutely right. Absolutely.'

He sat on, wetting his lips carefully, watching the shining length of her shin bone as it splayed into the arch of her foot.

She said, 'Would it work the first time? I mean . . . we couldn't do it more than once.'

He nearly told her that it worked first time with March, but did not. He shrugged his shoulders just enough so that she could feel it.

She took a deep breath. 'Your . . . your Freeminer is a long time coming for the key.'

'Yes. He won't come now. I'll have to drive by his place and drop it in.'

'Oh. Then we ought to go.'

'We'll have to wait till this fire goes down.'

They were silent again, looking into the heart of it. April said very quietly, 'I'm frightened, Fred. I'm sorry but I'm really frightened. There's so much to think of and no time.'

'What is there to think of? It's a solution. Which you can either take or not take. That's all.'

'David . . . oh, David would be so *happy*.'

'Perhaps that is the answer. David's happiness.'

'But it would be a trick. A secret from him.'

'A secret, yes. A trick? I'm not sure. You see, April, if it really did happen this afternoon, how will you ever know whether it's a trick or not? Whether it's David's—'

'Then I ought to wait and see.'

He was silent and it was she who eventually said, 'But – if he's right and there's no baby, I might never have another opportunity.'

He moved away from her, propped himself on his hands and spoke consideringly. 'What you need to realize, April, is that the baby, one way or another, is yours. If it has been made by David, then that is fine. Wonderful. If by a donor, then that is all he is. A donor. Do you see what I am saying? A donor is not the same as a father. The baby is yours in any case. You choose the father. And your choice will always be David because half of you is David anyway.'

He heard her quickly indrawn breath and knew he had said the right thing and wondered where the words had come from. He leaned forward, shook some leaves and dirt out of his turn-ups, got up and went to the window above the yellow sink. It was getting dusk, but dusk came early in this tree-filled land. He did not want to look at his watch; it must be past five o'clock. Danby wouldn't come now. But how long before David began an official search?

He turned and looked down at April. She was clutching her crooked knees now, still staring at the dying fire. She glanced up, met his eyes and gave a small, sickly grin. He saw she was incapable of making that final decision. He walked briskly to the door, bolted it, found an old newspaper and pushed it over the window.

She said, 'Fred, listen. Must it be now?'

'Yes. You know it must be now. Or never.'

'Fred, I can't take off my clothes. I couldn't bear that.'

He wanted so much to laugh. To hold her and kiss her all over and make her enjoy it. He was almost certain he could.

He said, 'It might be difficult, little April.'

She half-smiled to oblige him. 'You know what I mean. Only my knickers. You mustn't . . . look.'

'All right.'

She wriggled about and did something, then lay down on the palliasse. Her face was set. He slid out of his jacket and waistcoat, slipped his braces off his shoulders, stepped out of his trousers. She averted her eyes. He knelt between her legs.

'I – I'll try not to push you away, Fred,' she gasped. 'But if . . . you will understand, won't you?'

He couldn't help grinning down at her then. 'Darling, it's not that serious. Really.'

Tears formed in her eyes. 'Probably not for you, Fred. For me it's more than just serious. It – it's damnation.'

The words did not have impact for him then. He was very gentle, very careful, propping himself on his elbows and watching her for any sign of revulsion. He kept up a steady, insidious rhythm, and saw her being absorbed into it, fists unclenching and holding his shoulders, lips relaxing and parting as her breathing quickened. He knew it could only happen once for her and he timed the whole operation with an objectivity which did nothing to lessen his enjoyment.

But then, when it was indeed happening, she flung her arms above her head suddenly; her body arched to his; she tipped her head far back and her eyes opened and stared at the wall behind her with a terrible intensity.

'David!'

The cry was hoarse and cracked; it was a plea, but there was no hope in it. Fred found himself glancing up at the wall, half expecting to see David there, turning from them in disgust. The wall was of course empty; but he knew it had not been empty for April. She had chosen damnation.

He thought she would be inconsolable afterwards;

he expected tears and despair and remorse and an endless need for justification of her decision. But there were no tears and hardly any words. She lay quite still, her knees crooked and firmly together as if holding herself in while he dressed. Her eyes were open and followed his movements curiously but without any resentment; she looked friendly still.

He knelt by her head. 'I dug some latrines up in the bank, April. I'm going there now. There's a bucket under the sink if you want it.'

She smiled and shook her head and lay very still.

'Are you all right, my dear?'

'Yes. Yes of course. I must stay here for a few minutes more, Fred. You go on. I'm perfectly all right.'

'April. Please don't feel guilty. You *know* you weren't unfaithful. I know about infidelity. You weren't unfaithful to David.'

She smiled again, kindly, as if to reassure him. 'Like going to the doctor's, Fred?'

'Well . . .'

She laughed. 'Go on Fred. I'm all right.'

He went. When he returned she was ready to leave, the rug around her shoulders, the fire damped out, the room already cold and empty and dark. She had put her stockings and shoes back on and combed her hair. Without her usual make-up she looked as she had looked on her wedding day; a schoolgirl in adult clothing.

He held the door and they looked around them, knowing they would never come here again. She went ahead of him along the track. She did not jump from log to log this time, she went very carefully indeed. He tucked her into the car and drove on to Parkend and Danby's cottage. He pushed the key through the door; he couldn't see the burly Freeminer now and haggle with him. Anyway he didn't want anything for the cottage now; it was above price.

As the words came into his mind, he knew that there was the answer for him. What had happened was above price. April's act this afternoon had been for love; nothing more, nothing less. He looked at her as she sat waiting for him in the car and felt a pang of pure envy. He would never know love as she knew it, as David Daker must know it.

He slid in beside her and she gave him that smile again. She said, 'So. It's gone, Fred. Marsh Cottage – your cottage. I'll never forget it. Thank you for taking me there.'

He shrugged. 'It could have been anywhere. The place doesn't matter.'

'Oh, it does. It couldn't have been anywhere, Fred. Any more than it could have been anyone. Only you, dear Fred. Only you. And only the place which you built yourself with your own hands.' She leaned across and kissed his cheek. 'I'll never forget . . . never.'

He drove away towards Lydney. There were tears on his face because he felt he had shared that love.

Fred dropped her in Westgate Street so that she could walk through to the cathedral. He kept asking her if she would be all right and in the end she promised that at eight o'clock that night she would light the lamp in the bedroom which looked into the Northgate.

'Will you go out especially to see it then, Fred?' she asked.

'Of course. David might . . . you don't know what might happen. If it's not lit I shall come straight up. Is that clear?'

'Quite clear.' She put her hand through the car window and he shook it formally. Then she walked down College Green and into the Cathedral Close. She kept her thighs as close together as she could. The west door was standing open and she slipped into the candle-lit nave and stood very still, surveying its magnificence with new eyes. So often she had come here: when Albert was singing a solo; when she had been confirmed; when she had wanted to pray especially hard for David. And now, when she was pregnant.

She walked with her funny gait up the central aisle, staring at the massed organ pipes above her, feeling the old tombs beneath her feet. She felt in perfect communion with the universe. There was no need for the complication of words which would entail pleas and supplications and explanations. She existed in space and there was a place for her; she wasn't lost or overlooked; she had an essential importance.

She reached the roped-off chancel and knelt where she had knelt for her confirmation. And that was where David found her half an hour later, as he made the rounds of her special places for the tenth time that day.

He knelt by her and put his arms around her and his head on her shoulder.

'Will you forgive me?' he asked.

She wasn't surprised to see him. Such a perfect moment had to be shared with him. She turned her body towards him and told him what she had learned that day. 'There's no need,' she whispered. 'I am never going to ask your forgiveness for what I have done, David. You must not ask me for mine. We must put our faith – entirely – in our love. There is no other way.'

David, the intellectual, the wisely objective, held his young wife and could not speak. When his voice returned he said very humbly, 'Can you tell me what you mean, darling?' He looked at the high altar. 'I think I understand. But is it the same understanding as yours?'

She smiled at him, an ordinary everyday smile that had nothing ethereal about it.

'Oh David, how could you? You know I'm hopeless at explaining things.' She sighed. 'I think I mean that we – you and me – are imperfect. Very imperfect. We can't rely on one another. That sounds awful David, but we must accept it, mustn't we? It is . . . possible . . . for us to betray one another—'

'No!' he whispered. 'I promise you that—'

She put her hand over his mouth; her voice became stern. 'You must not make any promises. And I won't either. That doesn't – mustn't – matter. Promises. What we do and why do it. What does matter is our love. So long as we've got that . . . so long as we can hold that above water . . . there need be no misunderstandings, no need for forgiveness. There. Have I explained it properly?'

'Yes, April.' He helped her to her feet. Then asked

with a dry mouth, 'Did I . . . back there this morning
. . . did I drown our love?'

'No.' She began to walk back down the nave,
leaning heavily on his arm. 'Did I?'

'No.'

They emerged into the darkness. For the first time
April could remember, there was no physical awareness between them; they clung to each other and
hardly felt movement and limbs. Perhaps because of
that, they were closer than they had been since their
wedding day.

Chapter Nine

The next day April went to Bath to be with March.

David drove her down and they parted with a sense of fitness that had some relief in it. The intensity of that communion in the cathedral was impossible to maintain, and the new relationship which they must now find was just out of their reach. A pause was necessary. They had not been parted since April and March had gone to London to stay with May. April needed to assimilate what had happened and to come to terms with it. Once in Bath with March she put aside her own concerns; she placed the whole problem squarely in the lap of God. If she was pregnant, then only He knew . . . anything. And if she wasn't pregnant, He had decreed it and she must accept that too. David left her fearfully. He knew that she had had some sort of revelation during their day of separation and he assumed it to have been entirely spiritual. He wondered – when she came back to earth – whether she would still want to be married to him.

April did not go with March to the funeral. Letty and Rose, who had lived with Edwin so long, went to the ceremony at the chapel and supported March to the graveside. April stayed behind to look after Albert. He was just seven years old and had given up hoping that they would ever return to Gloucester and Marley School and Victor, but with April's arrival he realized that the old man he'd had to call Papa had really gone for ever and they would be going back to Grandma and Grampa soon. He simply could not understand his mother's irritable gloom; he knew she had been as bored as he had with Edwin Tomms.

He helped April put parsley around the plates of bloater paste sandwiches and risked a few questions.

'Aunty April, why is it called funeral meats? It's fish paste sandwiches and cake.'

'Ye olde custom,' April informed him with exaggerated lugubriousness so that he knew it was all right to laugh. 'And probably all your poor Mamma could afford with the money tied up right, left and centre.'

Albert ate a sandwich reflectively. 'Mummy says we'll be like church mice. D'you think we will be?'

'I don't know, Albie. It won't matter anyway. You'll come back and live with Grandma and Grandpa. You won't mind that, will you?'

'I'll *love* it!' Albert raced around the big dining-room table blowing crumbs from his mouth indiscriminately. 'I'll be so hap-hap-happy!' He jumped knees first onto a chair. 'And Victor loves mice! He'll put us in a cage and keep us safe!' He laughed hysterically and for the first time in a week.

April picked him up and hugged him.

'I can smell bloater on you. Here, chew some parsley.'

They both chewed parsley and giggled. Albert kept his arms around his aunt's neck and snuffled into it.

She smelled delicious; even her hands which were definitely bloatery.

'I wish we could go away and live on an island,' he said. 'Just you and me.'

She sobered, thinking about it. She said, 'D'you know, Albie, so do I.' She kissed him. 'The awful thing is, I couldn't live without Uncle David. And you couldn't live without Mummy. But I know exactly what you mean.'

He let her put him down and give him another sprig of parsley. For a moment he felt a pang of sadness; but it was a happy sadness because he shared it with his aunt.

March stared at Mr Hazelbank as if he had gone mad. 'Are you sure that is Edwin's last will?' she asked.

'Certainly, Mrs Tomms. Unless you have found something in the house, that is the last will and testament of your late husband. Everything is yours unconditionally. It is only to be expected surely?'

April leaned forward. 'Are you all right, March? You are so pale my dear.'

March said faintly, 'But the date . . . it's only just after Aunt Lizzie's death.'

'Darling, you know it was Aunt Lizzie's wish. That you should have everything. And there has been no need for Uncle . . . for Edwin to change that, has there?'

Dr Maine, who had been assiduously attentive during the proceedings, picked up March's clenched hand and encircled her wrist with his fingers.

'Shocked condition . . .' he mumbled, fumbling in his waistcoat pocket for his watch.

March wrenched her hand away. 'I'm perfectly all right thank you, Doctor!' she snapped. 'It's just that . . .' She looked at Mr Hazelbank. 'I rather thought Letty and Rose . . . they've been with him – us – for so long.'

Mr Hazelbank smiled. 'I dare say your husband knew they could rely on your generosity, dear lady.'

March heard the unction in his voice; this was the first time any of Edwin's contemporaries had called her 'dear lady'. It confirmed, more than anything else, that she was rich. Perhaps rich was too precise a word – comfortably off. She looked around the dining-room at the table where Aunt Lizzie had lain in her coffin and Uncle Edwin had claimed his niece.

She put a hand on April's arm. April was the ugly duckling who had turned into a swan. Was March going to be the church mouse that turned into a well-fed, purring cat? Had it all been worthwhile after all? The shame, the indignities, the sheer boredom and drudgery at the end – if she could emerge from them independent of everyone – *everyone* including Fred Luker – wouldn't it be worthwhile?

She said cautiously, 'There *might* be another will – something more recent – around the house—'

Mr Hazelbank's smile became indulgent. 'I rather doubt it, dear lady. Your late husband consulted me in all his affairs, I do assure you. But if you should find . . . send for me immediately and I will act for you. As I shall be delighted to act for you in all things.'

March inclined her head and stared down at her

lap. First Dr Maine, then Mr Hazelbank; professional men, touting for her patronage. She wouldn't be in the least surprised if Fred Luker proposed to her the minute he heard about this news. She must start spring-cleaning the house, and do it alone. If there was a later will, and surely there must be, then she must be the one to find it.

April was all sisterly concern.

'Darling, you really do look done up. Now just sit there – wasn't it Aunt Lizzie's favourite chair? Put your feet up and let me look after you for a bit. You've obviously been run off your feet . . .' She fussed and grumbled and asked about Albert's school and told March about Florence's illness and May's job, anything to divert her mind. Still March continued to stare blankly before her and April concluded contritely, 'I never thought you would be so frightfully cut up when Uncle Edwin – sorry darling – *Edwin* – died. How stupid I was. As if love has limits. *I* should know that! Oh March, you must have hated leaving him so much to look after Mother.'

March stood up and went to the window. 'Not really. There were difficulties.'

April, with all her new knowledge, understood. She said, 'Come and sit down, darling. Let me look after you for once. Please.'

'I can't. I must be doing something. Don't worry about me, little sister. It's my way.' She turned resolutely. 'I'm going to start on his room. No – I want to do it alone.'

'But March, not now darling! It's getting dark and you've had such a trying day.'

'Don't worry, April. I'll be an hour. No more. Go downstairs and look after the old girls, will you? I can't seem to bear the sight of them any more. And – and April.'

'Yes darling?'

'In an hour can you call me? And can we sit here and have bread and milk together?'

'Oh March . . . of course.'

They both remembered the days when Florence had sent them ailing to bed with bread and milk.

That spring and summer Sibbie Luker reached a new height of well-being that made her almost beautiful. She did not make the mistake of approaching Monty again; she guessed that guilt would sour any future meeting she might engineer. But she had possessed him, however half-heartedly, and the confidence she gained from the brief encounter swept her on to conquer Bridget's father, Edward Williams, with ease.

In May, 'young Mr Edward', as he was still called at the auctioneering firm in King Street, took his seat in the City Council Chamber. Fred immediately thumbed through Leonie's many acquaintances in his mental notebook, chose one with a large gravel quarry in the Cotswolds and contacted him with a proposition. He was a reserved man, another war survivor who was a defeatist, and had inherited the gravel pit when it was thriving, since when he had sat back and watched it decline. His name was Walter Lanyon, he had been in the same regiment as Marcus Porterman and he seemed to come to Leonie's parties to get a good square meal. He disapproved strongly of

Fred's blatant association with Leonie, but when he heard his terms he realized he might afford a smallholding with the profits and he could then live as he wanted to; as a recluse.

So in June Fred Luker secured a contract to supply materials for the new council estate being built to the south of Gloucester, known locally as the White City. The deal was made on a friendly basis; Edward Williams had a high opinion of the Risings and had always encouraged Bridget's friendship with April. And he was aware that the Lukers were almost an off-shoot of the Risings, deplorable though his wife considered that connection. When Edward succumbed to Sibbie's charms he offset guilt and self-disgust with the undeniable fact that Sibbie did not 'do it' only for money. Like his father before him, Edward discovered that Sibbie brought real affection with her. After thirty years of sterile marriage – apart from Bridget's conception – Edward Williams thought he might be falling in love again. So he listened to Fred's application sympathetically and swayed his fellow councillors with him. Had he not done so, Fred would not have hesitated to threaten him. But it did not come to that.

Meanwhile Sibbie bloomed like a flower. If the Rising girls were likened to daffodils, she could be likened to something hardier and brighter, a buttercup, maybe even a dandelion. She took no money from Edward because old Charles Williams paid her a regular income and other men who flocked around the small bungalow were more than generous. She had achieved the sort of power she had always wanted; she was making two men very happy – Will Rising and Edward Williams; and she was helping her brother Fred. Life that summer of 1925 was very sweet for Sibbie Luker.

Indirectly her seduction of Monty helped him too.

Terrified that he would meet her again, ashamed of facing Fred, unable to look May and Victor in the eyes, he left for London after a few weeks. There was a room for him at Maud Davenport's, as there always had been, and he let her comfort him. He told May that he was looking for work and it was not long before Maud secured a niche for him with Happy Hey Days again. This time he did not have a solo act; he was Maud's accompanist in one spot, and during the finale he was permitted to sing a duet with her. They had a summer season at Bournemouth, but he thought it was best if May kept her job at Madame Helene's. Just until he got himself settled.

April stayed with March until all the Bath business was settled up. This took longer than it might have done because March refused to sell the house until she had personally dusted every corner of it. Eventually they returned to Gloucester in June, a huge pantechnicon of furniture going ahead of them to be stored in Stayte's furniture repository in Arthur Street until such time as March could buy her own house in Gloucester. Letty and Rose were pensioned off and in an excess of gratitude for the many 'keepsakes' from the house, came to see them off at the station.

March hung out of the window, trying to shield Albert's eyes from possible smuts.

'You'll write to me, Albert?' Rose's eyes swam

with tears. 'You won't forget old Rose, will you?'

'Not likely. Nor Petty Letty,' Albert said with unaccustomed cheek, simply because he wanted to report that particular *mot juste* to Victor. Letty decided to smile.

April said, 'We'll come and see you anyway. Take care of yourselves—'

'Rose, we're leaving.' March tried to disentangle Rose's arms from Albert's neck. 'Your skirt in the running board—' Rose dropped back and was enveloped in steam. March collapsed onto her seat. 'Well that's that. We shan't see them again. Albert, come in and pull up the window please.'

April slid out of her hip-length cardigan, rolled it up and put it on the sagging rack. 'They're not that old, darling. And Bath's not that far away.'

'I shan't go there again, April. That chapter is closed. Albert, come in this minute.'

'Then another one is beginning,' April said rallyingly. 'Cheer up darling. Everything is going to be marvellous for you now.' She smiled. 'I'm beginning a new chapter too. You're not alone in that.'

March tugged at the back of Albert's pullover. She was practically certain Edwin had not left another will, and she felt quite different now about the last eight years. Edwin, after all, had honoured Aunt Lizzie's wishes whatever he might have implied; and he had been motivated by fear, probably, just as she had. Fear of being old alone, dying alone. She was glad now that she had stayed with him, almost regretful at the ending of that chapter.

'Yes. A new chapter. It frightens me in a way.

Albert, will you come *in*! The wind is blowing my hair all which-ways.' She opened her eyes at April. 'And you too? Of course you've been ages away from home and I know what that means to you. You and David are so close. Closer than Monty and May. Closer than Ma and Pa even.'

'I suppose that's what I meant. Yes.' She was certain about the baby now, but David must be the first to know. She stood up and hauled Albert in by force. 'Albie, do as your mother says!'

He looked round at her in surprise, but then sat down in the circle of her arm. Everything in Albert Tomms' world was absolutely and completely all right.

David had written to her almost every day. His letters made no reference at all to their terrible day in March; that physical cleft followed by the spiritual reunion transcended mere words perhaps, but she was conscious that he was frightened to mention it. His letters told her of daily events in the workroom and the shop; Manny had obviously gone for ever with all his contacts – though again this wasn't mentioned. David had been to London himself but he was no salesman; amid the witty observations and asides she gathered that he was retrenching. The Eastgate Street shop would provide them with a comfortable living; the original tailoring premises in the Barton, now a haberdashery, provided Mrs Daker with an interest and an income. But some of their plans would have to be abandoned; a chain of exclusive gown shops in the south-west, as Manny had foreseen, would remain a dream. And the house in the country, where they could entertain their less fortunate friends, must be shelved. 'Obviously Gloucester, which spawned us, is not going to let us go,' he wrote wryly.

April read his letters in the privacy of her room overlooking Bath's beautiful gardens, and sometimes she laughed aloud. His comments on Bridget and Tollie Hall's strange courtship, his vignettes of Florence and Kitty Hall sitting in the small back yard at Chichester Street drinking tea sedately, Aunty Sylv and Gran trudging home from their scrubbing jobs, May and Victor at Marley School's sports day . . . they were touching and funny. He ended one letter: 'Sometimes I ask myself why the confines of this narrow-minded city are not only acceptable but welcome, like a comfortable jacket that unexpectedly looks well too. Then I know why. Because every small incident, every sight, every harsh vowel sound, is illumined and made beautiful by you.'

It was the nearest he came to declaring his love. He did not visit her during the three months she was absent. He very carefully exerted no pressure on her at all, giving her breathing space, a chance to reassess their marriage; even to end it.

She wrote back just as obliquely. She saw the spring and summer literally unfold in Bath and she described it leaf by leaf, pigeon by pigeon, as each tiny symptom of her pregnancy revealed itself. And the nearest *she* came to declaring her love and announcing the baby was: 'The narrow confines of home are what we both need now, David. Our lives are going to be quite different and we shall have to have dependable old life-lines to guide us.' She did not realize how abstruse she was being; she thought he must read between the lines and know.

He met them at the station in a cab driven by Fred's brother, Henry. The luggage was strapped on to the boot-flap and Albert permitted to sit next to the driver. March sat between David and April.

'How is Victor? Has school finished for the summer? How is Grandma? I've got ten engine numbers and a number one Meccano set.'

David said heartily, 'Everyone is very well. What about you three?'

'We're OK. Will Uncle Fred help me with my meccano, Henry?'

March said, 'Do not use that abominable Americanism please, Albert. And Uncle Fred is much too busy to help you with anything.'

Henry said easily, 'You're right there. Up to his eyes he is, fixing deals for the council now, would you believe it.'

'The city council?' asked March in spite of herself.

'The big time, that's what it is,' Henry said cockily. 'Everythin' 'e touches turns to gold. Gladys says it's only 'cos o' the Portermans. Lose them and 'e loses the lot *she* says.'

March sat up very straight. 'I see.'

They drove past Clarence Street and around the long sweep of the cattle market. The plane trees were immobile in the summer sunshine and the smell of dung and vinegar drifted reassuringly into the cab. As they dipped into the low road beneath the London

Road railway bridge, Albert hung out and shouted his name and had to be dragged in and reprimanded again.

He turned a sunny face to his mother. 'I just wanted to tell Gloucester I was back,' he said. 'Did you hear the echo? That's the reply, you see.'

April and David exchanged a smile across March.

They left her and Albert and most of the luggage at Chichester Street and went straight home. April had intended staying with her mother for an hour but suddenly she had to tell David as soon as possible. She had to take that anxiety out of his dark eyes.

The flat was meticulously tidy and clean.

'Your mother's been,' she said, walking round, touching familiar objects, looking out of the window and exclaiming at the new buildings in Kings Square, then the sweet familiarity of Eastgate market.

'No. I've kept it like this in case you came back unexpectedly.' He smiled at her again. 'I'm getting finicky, I keep dusting and polishing every blasted thing.'

He wouldn't let her into the kitchen; he had a meal in the oven.

'You're nervous,' she said. 'Stop it, David. I had to stay with March – she's been working herself silly – but I'd have come back after the funeral if I could.'

'You said our lives would be different. Of course I've been nervous – *am* nervous. I don't know what the hell you've got in mind, Primrose.'

'Didn't you guess?'

'You want to go to London and sell our lines? I

remember you said something about it once – a year ago now I expect—'

'Idiot. How can I go to London when I shall be so busy here? How can I be any kind of shop window for selling your designs when my shape will be all wrong?' She looked at him and swallowed fiercely; he trusted her so, that was what hurt. It would never occur to him that she could betray him. She whispered, 'David, we're going to have a baby. Next December. I thought you must guess.'

He stared at her for so long that she thought she must be wrong, he must have known about Fred all the time. And then he held out his arms, still silent, and his black, guarded eyes filled with tears. She had never seen him weep. She stood within his embrace and kissed his ear and his neck, and then led him to a chair and sat on the arm with his head on her breast.

At last he spoke in a muffled voice. 'I'm sorry darling. It's just that . . . I wanted so much to give you a child and I thought I never could.'

She whispered, 'And I wanted to give *you* a child, David. That is why I did it.'

He hardly heard her words, and if he had would not have questioned them. It was not the moment for questions. They held on to each other for a long time and when at last they parted, smiling almost sheepishly, they still constantly touched each other as if for reassurance. Everything was sweet and poignant, every action significant. They ate David's meal and washed up. They sat together talking far into the night. David's happiness shone from him unreservedly and April was sure that his dark places were lightened for ever.

But when they went to bed at last and he began to caress her, she drew away.

'Forgive me darling, do you mind? We've waited for so long for this baby, don't let's risk . . . anything. You do understand, David? You're not hurt?'

'Primrose, how could you hurt me? How could you *ever* hurt me?' He took her hand and held it between them. When he slept April stared into the darkness and prayed earnestly.

'Please God, make it his. Please God . . . please . . .'

Fred heard of March's return to Gloucester with mixed feelings. It was almost a year since the picnic at Rodley when they had been so close, almost a year since she had deserted him. He had been forced to see it as desertion because there was no other explanation. No letter, nothing. Sibbie's interpretation was the only one: March had heard that Edwin was failing and had decided to play the part of the devoted wife in the hope of getting some cash out of him. In a way he understood her. After all, for almost as long as she could remember, the Bath inheritance had been her birthright. Her Aunt Lizzie had made no secret of that. But that she had gone on the day before their trip to Marsh Cottage and without a word . . . that made it the sort of rebuff she knew he would understand. More than a rebuff, a deliberate insult.

His pride made him stay away, stay silent, immerse himself in work, degrade himself with Leonie Porterman. And then April had turned to him.

April was a new dimension in Fred's life. He had always taken her for granted: the kid sister who had a crush on David Daker. He had been 'fond' of April. At the Rodley picnic he had admired her. At Marsh Cottage he had loved her, yet had known humbly that his love fell far short of hers for Daker. If her love was a model, then his for March came nowhere near it. But then . . . nobody else's did . . . nobody else's could, dammitall.

Maybe that didn't matter. Maybe he and March were as much in love, in a different way. A sparring way. Often an angry way. What they lacked in tenderness, perhaps they made up for in a kind of total awareness. Fred shook his head angrily, unused to introspection, simply knowing that his feelings were confused and it was April's fault. He had to see March and he had to see April and he did not know which he ought to see first. It would make a difference, somehow he was certain of that. He wanted – almost desperately – to know whether April was pregnant or not. If she was, in a peculiar way his pride would be restored . . . or rather, wouldn't matter any more. He would feel he had helped to make April happy again; he had redressed some of his wrongs . . . Monty . . . March . . . even Marcus Porterman. He could go to March and tell her he understood her damaged soul as no-one else would ever understand it; he could tell her he loved her and wanted her and they had been meant for each other always. He could almost borrow some of April's tenderness and woo March yet again; but differently this time. Without anger; without challenge.

He would see April first.

But he needed to see her alone to find out whether she was pregnant, and she never seemed to be alone. He went into the shop twice, pretending he was choosing a birthday present for his mother, but she was never there. Neither was David. Presumably they were closeted together idyllically upstairs. Did that mean she was pregnant or she wasn't? She had been in Bath for three months and as far as he knew David hadn't visited her there; they had a lot of leeway to make up. The fact that they were inseparable now could mean anything. Anything at all. And time was passing; twice he had seen March walking down Chichester Street with Albert and his heart had contracted at the sight of her. But she hadn't seen him; or worse, she had seen him and pretended not to. It was like that other time all over again; the time when he had tricked her into going to Bath and she had not spoken to him or looked at him all the way home, and Albert's sunbonnet had grown wet with her tears.

Then, over a week after March's return, he left the car outside the King's Street office and walked round to see his mother at midday. It was Saturday and Victor and Albert were scuffling together in Mews Lane, just outside the Chichester House stables where Albert had been conceived. Fred hovered by the rear entrance to number seventeen and watched his son.

Albert was tall for seven and superficially very much like his dead uncle. Only Fred knew that the fair gingery hair and blue eyes came from the Lukers and not the Risings; it was a secret he would have to keep all his life and for the first time it irked him. He would

246

be proud to claim this boy as his flesh and blood; proud to go to the Marley School sports day, as May had done to see Victor, and make deprecatory jokes about Albert's undoubted prowess. 'Takes after me for running – I had to scarper out of trouble often enough!' Victor might be witty and clever beyond his years, but Albert could have laid him in the dust any time he wanted during their mock fight. He just didn't want to. Fred conveniently forgot the difference in the boys' ages and wondered fleetingly where Albert had got his gentle streak from. Maybe there was something of the Rising in him after all. April Rising.

Victor was spluttering helplessly with laughter, making no attempt to return the volley of light slaps from his cousin, sheltering behind upraised elbows and reeling dramatically every time Albert's fingers touched him. Albert too was grinning from ear to ear as he practised the fancy footwork of the great Jack Dempsey as seen at the Picturedrome with April and David that week.

'Mouse eh?' he panted. 'Do I feel like a mouse then, Victor Gould or Mould or whatever your name is? Does this feel like a mouse? Or this? Or this?'

Victor yelped and crouched and cried out, 'Mercy – mercy, great mouse – yowps! – I mean *church* mouse! Quite different, old man – I mean old mouse – cripes alive, mercy on us!' He reached the ground and knelt there as if in obeisance, checking his laughter to say, 'Church mice is nice!' then exploding again uncontrollably.

Albert folded his arms and surveyed his victim severely. 'That's better. I might be poor as a church mouse but I'm still older than you, bigger than you and sensibler than you!'

Victor looked up. 'Did you say smellier than me, oh great mouse?' He gathered himself up and ran, laughing and yelling again, with Albert in fist-shaking pursuit, through the gate of Chichester House and into the derelict, overgrown garden.

And Fred went in to see his mother with a considering frown on his face. He was frowning as much at himself as at this new aspect of the March problem. Had he really forgotten the business of the money? Or had he assumed that March had got something, if not everything, of her inheritance? He frowned again because he could not answer his own questions. Then he wondered if that was answer enough; if the money – or lack of it – simply did not matter.

This thought was surprisingly comforting, as if some of April's feeling was already rubbing off on him. So-called Christians were eternally assuring each other and everyone else that money did not matter. He'd never believed them before.

He couldn't wait to get over to March and tell her this. He was glad she was as poor as a church mouse because now she would know he loved her entirely for herself. He imagined himself telling her this and her melting into his arms. If he could catch her alone, in her room, he could undress her then and there – he was expert at that because it was one of Leonie's rituals – and they could wedge a chair under the door handle and lie together on her bed and the years would evaporate with all their bitterness and wasted time. And it occurred to him also that he could get news of

April over at number thirty-three. Two birds with one stone.

Henry had told him about Albert's precious meccano; on the way back to the office he bought a more advanced set and spent the afternoon making and un-making the suggested models to ensure it was all intact. He called at number thirty-three that evening at seven-thirty when he was fairly sure Albert would be in bed.

He was a little too early. May and March were in the kitchen with their sons, feeding them a supper of bread and milk.

He greeted the boys. Then May. Then March. 'And how is your mother?' he asked formally.

May replied because March had turned the tap on at the sink.

'The same. She says she is well but I doubt she weighs six stone.'

Florence had never looked heavier than six stone to Fred. He said, 'And how are you, March? And Albert?'

March made no reply. He ached to tell her that he understood how she felt; the last ten months wasted on that old man. Albert said, 'We're OK.' And March said in a withdrawn voice, 'I have asked you before not to use that silly word, Albert!' And Fred thought of the last time he had been with her on the river bank, cradling her in his arms, wet, bedraggled in that ridiculous swimming-dress. He felt suddenly powerful; at last he was in the position he had always promised himself; and so incidentally was March. He had money and influence and March had none. Neither of them were tied legally; he could rescue her properly this time; give her all the things she so badly wanted.

May collapsed into a chair and put her elbows on the table. 'I can tell you it's marvellous to have them back. What with going to the salon every day, fetching Victor from school, worrying about Monty and Mother . . . it's just too much for me.'

Fred ignored that and addressed March's back. 'It's been a sad time for you. You must have been thankful to have April. How is she?'

March made no reply and Victor giggled into the quietness. 'Aunty Ape. Aunty Ape played a jape!' Albert clattered down his spoon, leaned across the table and aimed a swipe at his cousin. May intervened with horror.

'Albert! We do not hit each other in this house, *if* you please!' She put an arm round Victor. 'Did he hurt you, darling? '

March came to life.

'Of course Albert didn't hurt Victor. Now come on, boys. Into the dining-room to say good night to Grandma and Great Grandma and Aunty Sylvia.' She glanced at May. 'I'll take them up, May.' She did not look at Fred.

May kissed Victor and sat back, indolently toying with the spoon in his empty dish. 'Well Fred. And how is the big business tycoon?'

Fred noted the antagonism and knew it was linked with Sibbie. May and Sibbie had been like sisters, which must now make their estrangement worse. He hoped it was that; he hoped that fool Monty hadn't felt bound to confess.

He stared at her. 'Flourishing thanks, May. And how is Monty?'

She pushed at the spoon moodily but she did not flush so it was all right, she didn't know about Monty and Sib, thank God. He went to the door. 'I'd better go. You didn't answer just now, is April all right?'

'Fine. Radiant actually.'

He looked over his shoulder. 'What does that mean exactly?'

The defences went up; May did not trust Fred. 'Nothing in particular. She's glad we're all together again I expect.' She got up and went to the sink, dismissing him, and he closed the door behind him and stood in the passage for a moment, considering. If April were pregnant he was so much part of the Rising family that he could take March by storm; force her if necessary. But surely May would have told him just then? May was usually so frank and open that she seemed almost simple.

He took the stairs quietly, two at a time. Albert and Victor were sharing one of the attic rooms and he looked in just as Victor had lifted his nightshirt at Albert and March had caught him a resounding slap across his buttocks.

'I'll teach you to stop those dirty tricks!' she said furiously as the child subsided onto his bed with a yelp of surprise.

'Now now—' Fred entered and scooped Victor under the clothes, grinning privately at him to show it was all good fun.

March said, 'What are you doing up here? The boys have already said good night—'

Fred interrupted smoothly. 'I missed Albert's birthday.' He produced the flat box from inside his jacket. 'Here you are, old son. Instruction book with it. It's slightly up on the one you've already got—'

Albert was delirious. 'How did you know I'd got one? Oh Uncle Fred – it's corking marvellous – honestly! Look at the *tools* – oh cripes—'

'Don't swear please Albert!'

'My birthday in seven weeks, Uncle Fred,' Victor mentioned helpfully.

'You've thoroughly unsettled them, I hope you know!'

He looked at March and wondered whether her hectic flush and general tension were good signs or bad ones.

'Let them look at it, March.' He took her elbow and got her out on the landing. 'Might as well go in here – your room, is it? I want to talk to you anyway. When we've . . . finished . . . we can slip in and tuck them up. How's that?'

She pulled away. She was visibly trembling now. He felt her anger and wished it were not there. He was used to it; sometimes it was good, a sign of passion in her. But for now, tonight, he longed for a quiet acceptance of their love; their eventual good fortune which had been so long – so very long – in coming.

She made no move so he pushed at the opposite door and went inside. The room was like a cell, white honeycomb bedspread over an iron bedstead, a single worn rug on the highly polished oilcloth, thick lace curtains and a black blind half unfurled against the low-level sunshine. A virgin's room. An old maid's room.

March spoke from behind him. 'Just what do you think you're doing, Fred? This is my *room*!'

'Yes. Yes, I see.' He walked slowly to the window and looked down on Chichester Street. He said, 'March, I'm sorry.'

He heard her draw in a breath and hold it. 'Sorry? How do you mean?' She sounded tentative, almost hopeful.

He gestured around the room 'This,' he said vaguely. He turned and grimaced to hide the fact that for two pins he could have burst into tears like a soppy kid. 'It's been awful hasn't it, Marcie? Over seven years of it. Tied to that mean old swine in Bath. Putting up with Christ knows what in the hope of softening him up. And all for nothing.'

She frowned, puzzled rather than annoyed.

'Hardly for nothing, Fred. Surely that's why you're here?'

They stared at each other uncomprehendingly. Fred made one of his flat-handed gestures as if trying to wipe a slate clean. 'I'm here to ask you to marry me, Marcie.'

Colour came into her pale face. Her eyes burned at him. He saw her swallow before she said very carefully, 'Why didn't you come sooner, Fred? We've been home well over a week. You knew that. You saw me in town the other day with Albert.'

'Of course I knew. I wanted to give you time to unpack!' He couldn't meet her feverish eyes. 'Dammit all Marcie, I'm asking you to *marry* me! We've had to wait all this time, what does a week matter?'

'It might matter a great deal. A great deal.' He thought for a moment she was going to cry and he hoped she would. He could comfort her then, he could call on the new tenderness inside him. But she clenched her hands into fists at her side and went on, 'It would matter if during that week you had heard that my circumstances had changed.'

He saw his opening and blundered in. 'That's what I wanted to talk to you about, Marcie. When I heard the boys larking about this afternoon—'

'Larking?'

'In Mews Lane. Victor was teasing Albert about, well, about your changed circumstances – and it came to me quite suddenly that you and I have been wrong all along. Money doesn't matter. It really doesn't, Marcie—'

'Not a bit. Not when you've got enough.'

'Well . . . yes, all right then. And we have.'

'So you didn't come to ask for my hand when I returned from Bath because you thought Edwin had left me penniless.' March spoke very clearly and next door the boys fell silent. 'When you discovered that was not the case you couldn't wait to come over here and tell me that money doesn't matter. How touching.'

Fred said quietly, 'Drop your voice, Albert is listening.' He brushed past her and shut the door then faced her again angrily. 'Listen Marcie. I don't know what you got from Edwin and I don't care any more. He's dead, that's what counts. We can get married – legally. We've been married in the sight of God for—'

'Please don't keep bringing God into this, Fred. You don't know what you're talking about. Be honest and admit it's Edwin's money you're interested in, not me.'

'That's not true, Marcie. You might not believe me but I honestly thought you were penniless.'

'And you were sorry for me?'

There was no pleasing the woman. He did what he should have done in the beginning: took her by her upper arms and held her very hard while he kissed her. It was like kissing his mother's clothes-post. Yet he knew she wanted to respond; he could feel her holding back deliberately.

'What is it, Marcie? What's the matter?'

She closed her eyes in a gesture of surrender, then opened them quickly. 'I don't trust you, Fred. I can't trust you. Ever again.'

He shook her slightly. 'Trust me? Trust me to do what, Marcie? You know me and I know you. So we both know what we can trust and what we can't. That is enough. It has to be enough.'

He kissed her again and felt her tremble against him. Desire flamed in him and he forgot resolutions of tenderness, mutual forgiveness, and began frantically on the row of buttons that ran from the neck to waist seams at the back of her sloppy blouse. Just for a second he thought he had won; she gasped and fell against him and his hand slid expertly beneath her bust-bodice and reached under her arm. And then she tightened in a kind of instinctive reaction against his expertise. Her head jerked back and she stared wide-eyed into his face six inches from her own. Whether she saw ardour or just plain lust, he never knew, but she thrust against him hard and held him literally at arms' length, looking for something she obviously couldn't find.

At last, when he reached for her again, she shook her head.

'No Fred. I suppose that is what trust boils down to. Knowledge of someone. And I don't know you. Not any more.'

'Christamighty, March. You know enough. You know that we should be together. You knew that at Rodley. Then you pulled back – just like you're pulling back now.' He put his hand under her outstretched arms and cupped her breast. 'Come to me, March. Now. Like you did before in Chichester House stables. And at the George—'

She slapped his hand furiously. 'My name isn't Leonie Porterman, Fred! I don't come running every time you beckon!' She turned her back and went to the window. Her open blouse sagged between her prominent shoulder blades; she was much too thin. She made an obvious effort to control herself and said in a quiet voice, 'Leonie Porterman is the reason I don't trust you, Fred. Don't know you. That's why I'm not sure whether you asked me to marry you because you thought I was poor. Or very well off.'

He was shocked into a temporary silence. The passion which had sparked between them, died. After a while he said softly, 'When did you hear about Leonie?'

She sighed deeply. 'After Rodley. Why do you think I stayed in Bath? There was nothing for me here.'

'And there was something in Bath?'

'Edwin needed me. He was dying. You might not believe me but I'm glad I stayed with him to the end.'

'Especially as it appears you got what you wanted all along. His money.'

He could not seem to goad her. She lifted her shoulders and let them fall. 'He never changed his will as he told us he would. After Aunt Lizzie died he left me everything, just as she wanted. He never changed that.' She glanced at him quickly. 'That's why I'm glad I stayed. He did what she wanted. He saw that if he punished me for what I had done, he would also punish her. When I realized that, I also realized that he – *he* – could be trusted.'

There was another silence. He said, 'Who told you about Leonie Porterman?'

'Sibbie.'

He heard his breath whistle in his mouth and cleared his throat.

'What I've done . . . it's always been for you, Marcie.'

'What you've done, and what you've made me do too?' she asked bitterly. She rounded on him. 'Fred. I thought I needed you. Ever since Albert died I believed that. You told me it was true and I believed you. Now . . . now I don't need you—'

'You still want me. I could tell – just now—'

'That – that's disgusting! I don't want any of that ever again!'

He said steadily, 'I won't see Leonie. I won't touch a penny of your money. I'll never interfere between you and Albert-Frederick—'

'You certainly won't!' Her eyes were very wide and

clear. 'You can break two of those promises and I could bear it. But I cannot risk you breaking that one, Fred. Albert-Frederick is all I have. You must not come between us!'

'I have a right to see to his upbringing, March.'

She heard the threat in his voice and it was the final straw. He tried to retract. 'I didn't mean—' But she was already pushing past him to get to the door. He grabbed at her arm, but the time for physical persuasion had gone. She paused on the landing and reached behind her in a frantic effort to re-button her blouse; he made a move to help her and she left it, running down the stairs uncaringly just to get away from him.

He stood in the doorway for a moment feeling, for the first time, completely defeated by March's stubborn nature. Then he turned and went back to the window and tried to recapture his former sense of her courage and pathos. But the tenderness had gone and as he searched for it, consciously trying to force it back into being, he realized that next door the boys were quarrelling again. Someone fell on the floor with a bump, then Victor's voice said shrilly and without its accustomed humour: 'He only gave it to you because he wants to be your mother's new sweetheart!' There was another bump and Albert's reply, muffled, but still audible, came through the wall. 'She only wants me. She told me so. Uncle Fred always gives me presents at Christmas and birthdays. So sucks to you.'

The last of what Fred privately called his 'softness' went from him. Grimly, he was glad that when it came to serious matters Albert-Frederick did not allow Victor to get the upper hand. Even more grimly he planned his next move: he would pay a visit to Sibbie and give her the thrashing of her life.

And then he would console himself with Leonie Porterman.

Chapter Ten

A few days later, another proposal of marriage was made and turned down, though not so irrevocably as Fred's.

After the Zinoviev letters, Tollie's political interests had taken a severe bend to the left. He received certain instructions from the British Communist Party, all of which advised him to conform, to melt into his background, to support the present regime, and to wait for the Day. Tollie obeyed without difficulty, but when the next instruction came he had the strangest feeling of being hoist with his own petard. It was obvious the Party had been doing some investigating; this was disturbing but it was also a compliment because it meant they were taking him seriously. They had found out about Bridget; her father; her grandfather; her ambitions. They thought she was the perfect cover for their latest recruit and it turned out that by 'cover' they meant 'wife'. He must marry as soon as possible and produce a large family.

He had long resigned himself to the fact that one day he would marry Bridget, but that day never seemed to draw closer because for one thing Tollie was afraid Bridget might swallow him whole once she was married to him, and for another Bridget herself was having far too good a time to tie herself down to one man. The other problem was that she had oft stated that she had no intention whatever of producing 'brats'.

However, Tollie took the project seriously. He used the office telephone to ring Bridget and suggest a picnic after work. An hour later she was in King's Street, a large wicker basket of food on the dickey seat of her three-wheeled Morgan.

'Where shall we go?' she asked gaily. Her school, small, private and very exclusive, closed early for the summer, and three months stretched deliciously ahead of her. 'You demanded the picnic so you must choose!'

Tollie had never demanded anything in his life, but lately he had found it expedient to share Bridget's fantasy.

'Just drive up to the Cotswolds and let's see where we get to!' He climbed in beside her and kissed her cheek. 'You smell nice.'

'You smell of the office. I'm going to tell Daddy to give you some decent jobs. I don't see why you can't get out and about a bit now. You must know all the background.'

A few months ago he would have deprecated. Now he said, 'I'd like to specialize in the books actually, Bridie. Any chance d'you think?'

She flashed him a sideways glance, surprised and pleased. 'Of course. If that's what you want, that's what you'll get.' She sighed dramatically. 'You always do get what you want, Tollie Hall, don't you?'

Tollie thought wryly of the first time Bridget had seduced him. He had been fourteen to her sixteen.

Obediently he leaned across and began to nibble her ear lobe. She screamed and swerved the car around a vegetable cart, then took it very fast over a level crossing. They bumped madly. He knew better than to protest. He just laughed into her ear.

'You're incorrigible darling,' she panted, enjoying herself very much. 'Just wait till we find a quiet place, will you?'

He knew it was hopeless to talk about the book department of Williams' or even Bridget's school. He directed her carefully up Robinswood Road, through Painswick and past Bull's Cross towards Miserden. At a certain point they turned off into the ferny woods. She would have thrown herself on him immediately but he kissed her, held her off and suggested a walk.

'Darling . . .' She pouted at him. 'Couldn't we walk later?'

'No. Now. Come on. I know what I'm doing.'

She was surprised again, but not entirely averse to his new masterful manner. They wandered through the fern until they came to the lip of an enormous quarry. It was empty with a strange, cathedral beauty of its own. Tollie had come here with April and David Daker after a political meeting at Cheltenham and he had earmarked it for future solitude. It was the ideal spot for a proposal.

They sat down and surveyed it.

'It's a bit awesome, isn't it?' Bridget shivered. 'Hold me, Tollie, I'm frightened.'

Bridget had been frightened only twice in her life; once when March blackmailed her when she was eight years old, and a few weeks later when Teddy Rising had died and it had been her fault. But she knew full well when a really feminine girl should be frightened, which was almost the same thing.

Tollie held her tenderly.

'Marry me, Bridie, and I'll look after you,' he said.

She was unmoved. 'Well of course you will, darling. It will be marvellous.'

He drew away. 'Then you will?' He fumbled with one hand for the ring.

'Will what, Tollie?'

'Marry me. I just asked you to marry me, Bridie.'

'Oh darling, you are so funny. We've always known we would get married one day.'

'Not one day, Bridie. A definite day. Next month – isn't July a specially good month for weddings?'

'No. June, my sweet idiot. June brides. Surely you've heard of June brides? What's that you've got there darling – a ring! Tollie, you've bought a ring – you're serious!'

He slid it on her finger. 'When?'

She spread her hand admiringly; it was a single small diamond.

'A solitaire,' she said dramatically. 'It's beautiful, Tollie. How sweet of you darling. Not that I can wear it publicly of course. I'll put it on a chain around my neck.'

'What d'you mean? I want everyone to know we're engaged.'

'Don't be silly darling. You know married teachers are taboo.'

He did know and it had always been his safeguard.

He said stubbornly, 'Then you must leave teaching. If we're going to get married next month, Bridie, you can't keep it a secret.'

'Next month? Who said anything about next month?'

'You did. July, you said.'

'Don't be absurd darling, of course I didn't. We can't get married for ages yet. We haven't got any money – anywhere to live—'

'Bridie, we can't go on like this.'

'Why not? It's marvellous, Tollie.' She snuggled up to him, still holding her hand above their heads so that the sunlight caught the diamond chip.

'No Bridie!' He wrested her away. 'No more of that till we're married.'

'Don't be ridiculous darling. Why ever not? It's 1925!'

'It's still wrong.'

'No such word. Don't be cruel to your Bridie. Feel how my heart is hammering away—' She slid his hand beneath her blouse. He pulled it back as if he'd been stung.

'No, Bridie.'

But she was adamant and he had never stood against her. She fumbled in her bag, handed him a packet so that he could 'take precautions'. Tollie turned his back on her and did his own fumbling, and then had a brilliant idea.

'Ready, darling?'

He turned to find her naked among the fern. Shielding himself with one hand he crouched by her.

'Ready, Bridie,' he whispered.

After all, he had his orders. Everything was fair in love and war, and this was both.

Fred got no satisfaction at all from his punishment of his sister. He dared not risk bruising her too much in case repercussions from Edward Williams rebounded on him; anyway, her brazen frankness on being found out matched his own.

'I had to stop you somehow darling,' she said, nursing her arm where Fred had twisted it savagely behind her back. 'You'd have done the same if I'd got in your way.'

'How the hell you can see March and me as a stumbling-block to any of your plans—'

'Well, in the end it wasn't even that.' She slid the bodice of her dress off her shoulders and supported her arm above her head. 'It just wouldn't *do*, Fred. You and March. Oil and water. She's a prude and you're not. You *need* Leonie Porterman.'

He hit out at her head in frustrated rage. She swung with the punch and her shingled bob hung over her bare uplifted arm in an attitude of complete surrender.

He ground out, 'You know nothing about me – nothing!'

She looked at him through her hair and smiled. 'You're a man, aren't you?' She extended her arm. 'Kiss it better, Freddie. Kiss it better for Sib.'

He slapped the arm away. 'Save that rubbish for your old men.'

Her pale blue eyes were challenging. 'I wish you weren't my brother, Fred. I wish you were one of my men. It would be so . . . relaxing.'

'Relaxing?'

She laughed. 'You're such a wicked man, Fred. You'd make me feel innocent again. Dammit it, compared with you, I am innocent!'

He looked at her. Her petticoat was satin and strained across her breast provocatively; her mouth was open on her laugh and he could see the separate pearls of her teeth and the redness of her tongue. He understood her sexual attraction.

'You . . . you bitch!' And then he had to laugh with her, because, after all, they were two of a kind.

So he could not sublimate his anger and disappointment at March in thrashing Sibbie; there was still pleasure to be found with Leonie but she never failed to remind him of the hold she had over him. The gentleness that had seemed to be softening his life, had gone. He hardly knew what he wanted any more.

He heard of April's pregnancy from Will one night in the Lamb and Flag, and immediately his spirits lifted. He bought a whisky for Will and watched the ginger beard flip to the ceiling as he tossed it back. The old man plonked his glass on the bar and grinned like an excited schoolboy.

'I was delighted about Albert. And Victor of course. Florrie and I . . . we were both delighted. But this . . . little April . . . after all this time!' He leaned confidingly towards Fred. 'Kept a very soft spot for little April, I did. Jealous as a snake when she married Daker – well, you know I didn't care for him o'course. You know most things about us Risings, don't you Fred lad?' The grin developed into a laugh. Then Will sobered. 'I was glad at first . . . no babies . . . shrapnel in the groin y'know. Then. Well. She's like Florrie, a natural mother. Loves her nephews. It didn't seem right that she should be married to someone who couldn't . . . I mean . . . you know what I mean, Fred.'

'I know,' Fred agreed, grinning himself because he was the only one who did know. He and April. 'I'd like to see her. Congratulate her. And Daker, of course.'

'Why not?' Will spread his hands expansively. 'We'll go round now my boy. Take a bottle and wet the baby's head, eh? That the idea?'

'No.' Fred knew suddenly what he wanted to do. He wanted to see April alone. He wanted to reassure her. Be the big brother. He wanted to tell her that if she ever needed him, he would be there. 'No, we won't intrude, Will. I shall run into April some time. It's late.'

'Quite right. Consid'rate. Long evenings made me forget . . . prob'ly already in bed. Like we should be. Eh Fred? Eh?'

'That's right Will, that's right.'

But it wasn't that easy. April was surrounded by family and friends and rarely seen without David. Fred finally had to make his own opportunity.

One hot Sunday in July, Tollie called for April and David and drove them out to Barnwood to watch the tennis. Fred followed them at a discreet distance, paid his entry fee and lurked in the club house, peering out of the windows now and then to check on her presence. It was like an oven in the wooden, tin-roofed building. He sweated, tore off his tie, removed his hat and wiped his forehead and wondered what the hell he thought he was playing at.

At four o'clock tea was served and the ladies began to move discreetly to the wooden lavatories set well away from the courts. When April emerged, holding her hat and lifting her hair to catch a faint breeze, Fred was waiting for her.

'Fred! I didn't know you were here! Come and have some tea.'

She seemed genuinely pleased to see him, yet at the same time very anxious to get back to the others. He shook his head, smiling to put her at her ease.

'No tea thanks, April. I hoped we could talk for a few minutes. Alone.'

She swung her hat by the brim, fanning herself exaggeratedly. For the first time it struck him that he might not be welcome; that her practically sequestered state since her return from Bath might have been engineered to keep him at bay.

He said quickly, 'I want to talk, April. Just that.'

'Of course.' She glanced at David. He was sitting in a steamer chair, his bad leg supported, his head on one side as he listened to Tollie's political jargon. 'But won't they – everyone – think it rather odd if we stand here jawing on our own?'

'Walk down to the church with me then. The cars are parked there. You can tell David you needed some shade.' She still hesitated and he said, 'You owe me that much, April.' And then immediately wished he hadn't.

'Of course,' she said again. She fell into step by his side, still swinging her hat, and as her arm brushed the thin material of her summer frock the slight swelling of her abdomen showed for an instant. Fred had a crazy impulse to put his hand there, gently and tenderly to feel the outline of his child.

He said abruptly, 'I understand I can congratulate you.'

She looked at him and gave him a brief smile, then studied her white, low-heeled slippers again. 'You can congratulate both of us please, Fred. David and me.'

He drew a long breath and stood back while she took a narrow turn in the ancient footpath. Aspen leaves hung limply above them and the smell of warm foliage was heady. They came to a stile and she put her elbows on it and surveyed the old grey church beyond. She seemed hardly conscious of his presence, let alone his part in this baby.

He said deliberately, 'What about me? Aren't I to be congratulated too?'

She became very still. He looked at the back of her neck where the short hair curled into the nape and wanted to touch there too. He had hardly put his hands on this girl; he had been decent all the way through. Now he wished he hadn't.

She said quietly, 'Fred, we made a bargain. This is David's baby.'

'That remains to be seen, surely?' He heard the sharp edge on his voice and wondered what he was doing. He had come here to talk peacefully with April about the baby, to show his pleasure, to cement their trust and friendship. He was ruining everything.

She pushed herself off the stile and stood very straight.

'Is your car parked over there? We'd better say

goodbye now, David will wonder what has become of me.'

He flushed at such an obvious dismissal.

'I'm sorry, April. But what do you expect when you hide from me like you've been doing? I can't publicly announce anything, but I thought privately – between ourselves – we could acknowledge the fact that—'

'This is David's baby!' She lost her cool-cucumber dignity and turned to him, as flushed as he was. 'Can't you see that any sort of private conversation between us is out of the question! That had to be part of the bargain – I thought you realized that.'

'What happened to the brotherly feeling? You were my sister if you remember and I—'

'What we did couldn't have – have happened otherwise, Fred.' The flush made her beautiful. Luscious. Practically edible. Her eyes were violet, dark with huge pupils. 'But when we decided to do that, Fred, we stopped being brother and sister. Surely you see that?'

'What did we become? Lovers?'

There were tears in the eyes; tears of anger. She paused, then spoke cuttingly. 'You've done plenty of deals, Fred. Has love ever entered into them?' She saw the pain in his face and made a dismissing gesture with her hat. 'Oh Fred . . . listen. If you'd given me money for some reason, you wouldn't *mention* it again. Don't you see? A gift is just that. A gift. There is always gratitude, but it must be unspoken.

'I told you how I felt . . . then. That day. I can't speak of it again, ever.'

'Is that why you've been avoiding me?'

'Have I?' The tears came to nothing; she couldn't even be angry with him for long. She frowned, thinking about it. 'I don't think consciously I've avoided you. But obviously I haven't sought you out—'

'You never sought me out, April. I didn't seek you out either. But we met. Often. That day in Westgate Street when I nearly ran over you in the Morris . . . if that happened again . . . if you have another row with David and I see you, will you get in the car with me and let me drive you to the country?'

Momentarily the frown deepened, telling him his hypothesis was in bad taste. 'Of course not. That would be practically . . . a conspiracy.'

'Was it a conspiracy before?'

She blurted, exasperated, 'It . . . *happened*, Fred! Nothing was planned! But I . . . we have to forget it now. Can't you understand that?'

He said levelly, 'All I understand is that you're going to go on avoiding me. I had a sister – a friend. I'm not going to have her any more.' He thought, first March, now April.

She said nothing but she turned her face away from his slightly, unable to meet his eyes. He had a view of her profile, so much less austere than March's or Florence's, less fine than May's. A hand seemed to have gently brushed the nose and upper lip towards the wide forehead. She was imperfect in a perfect way.

He said, 'So this is goodbye then, April?'

She made a small negating gesture. 'Not quite so dramatic as that, Fred. Just—'

'I've got nothing to lose,' he went on as if she hadn't

spoken. 'I'll say goodbye the way I want to say it.'

He took her firmly by the shoulders and turned her to him and kissed her. In a way it was like kissing March. A clothes-post. In another way it was quite different. There was nothing in April that responded to him. Nothing at all. He let her go.

'Goodbye then,' he said, as if his kiss had been merely brotherly. He leapt the stile in a way that David never could and grinned at her over his shoulder. 'One thing, whether you want to or not, you can't very well forget me, can you?' He let his gaze slide to her abdomen, then he didn't look at her again. Damn all the Risings . . . at least the Rising women. He could do without them.

Tollie Hall and Bridget Williams were married in September of that year. Both families had been resigned to the match for some years and Edward Williams had always accepted Tollie, as he had the Lukers, as an extension of the Rising family. But Alice Williams thinned her mouth to an invisible line for the ceremony and made no effort to smile at anxious little Kitty, let alone the upright Bartholomew Hall, warder at Gloucester Prison.

April went back to the sumptuous house in Barnwood to help Bridget change into her going-away outfit, and felt that she too was saying goodbye to a way of life. It was doubtful whether she would ever enter this bedroom again where she and Bridget had talked and laughed and wept. Bridget had consoled herself after Teddy's death with his best friend, Tollie, but April had never realized Bridget felt enough for

Tollie to actually marry him. Yet here they were, married.

April sighed. 'It's a funny old life.'

'My God. You sound like your Aunty Sylv. What's funny about it? You try to make it fun, yes. But it always catches up on you in the end.'

April made a face at her friend. 'Wedding day talk?'

'I don't know, I've never been married before. Your wedding day was different, April. I've never seen anyone so happy. You were transported somehow.'

'Surely you're happy, Bridie?' April was suddenly anxious.

'I suppose so. I'm being sick all the time at the moment, so it's rather difficult to decide.'

'You're . . . Bridie, you don't mean—?'

'Of course I mean. You don't think I'd be getting married yet if I weren't pregnant, do you? I'm having a marvellous thing with Maurice Foster at the tennis club at the moment. He dances like an angel. I suppose in a month or two I won't be able to get around the floor. Oh well, never mind, you and I can get together and swap symptoms!'

April forced herself to kiss her friend and smile congratulations and only as they went downstairs did she say, 'What about Tollie?'

Bridget snapped, 'What about Tollie? He tricked me – I swear he arranged the whole thing so that I'd have to give up teaching and marry him.'

April hung back and watched as Bridget received admiration from the guests for her red dress with the dropped waistline and matching silk coat. Bridget knew, as well as April did, that Tollie Hall would never trick anyone. Besides, somehow April had always had the impression that Tollie was rather a reluctant suitor.

In November of that early winter, a new department was set up at Williams'. It dealt with rare second-hand books. It was run by the young Bartholomew Hall, who was something of a scholar and had a quiet yet confident bearing that was well suited to the impoverished gentry he mostly dealt with. The firm bought him a small car and he went to all the sales in the county. People liked and respected him. He had married Mr Edward's daughter and got her in the family way immediately, which was another feather in his cap. She had always been a bossy, wild sort of a girl; he would be good for her.

It was in November too, that March moved into her house. A house of her own, just as she had always wanted, just as Fred had promised her. And she had done it without Fred.

March had listened hard to the idle gossip that abounded between Gran, Aunt Sylv and Hettie once Flo had retired to her room. Hettie saw no reason to be ashamed of the way Fred used his liaison with Leonie Porterman to further his own ends. She hinted at Sibbie's comfortable position with a kind of defiance, but it was different for a man. She giggled unashamedly that Fred had to eat the icing before he could get to the cake. March heard and understood. Fred could have given up his scandalous association with Captain Porterman's wife and returned to number thirty-three with another proposal. He chose instead to continue the affair quite flagrantly. It was his way of showing March that not only did he not want her money, he did not want her either.

March hardly dared to admit to herself how hurt she was. She looked back over her life and saw that when she had given in to pain, she had usually leaned on Fred. And each time that had happened, he had let her down. When she had fought back and taken her fate in her own hands, she had found some kind of solution. She decided to fight back now.

The house was only twenty minutes' walk from Chichester Street. The three girls went to see it one grey afternoon with Florence on April's arm, each imagining she was helping the other. April wore an olive green hip-length jacket, very full, with a matching beret; she managed to look like a Parisian artist. March was severe in a tailored costume. May wore a tweed coat with a big fur collar. Florence knew how gaunt she looked and had pulled a veil over her cloche hat and under her chin.

They walked slowly up London Road to the top of the Pitch, down the other side to Barnwood Road, and there, just off to the right, was a quiet cul-de-sac of spacious houses with their own large gardens, called Bedford Close. March had seen the discreet For Sale sign back in the early autumn and had fretted and fumed for six weeks while the Bath house was sold and the estate settled up. Florence assured her that there were plenty of houses to be had that were just as nice, but March wanted that one. It was on the way to the Williams' place at Hucclecote and it had its own tennis court, yet it was close to Florence and Will. No other house would do. The Rising women walked around its big empty rooms on November the fifth, with a kind of awe.

'Albie could have one of the upstairs attics for his train set,' April discovered with delight, panting as she reached the second floor.

'This room is big enough for a grand piano,' May exclaimed, breathing deeply on the stale air in the sitting room, and admiring its french windows looking on to the garden, and its beautifully moulded cornice.

March said, 'I must get Jack down for a few days to sort out the tennis court. We can have tennis parties next summer, girls. Won't it be wonderful?'

May marvelled, 'The kitchen is so light. Of course the gasometer takes all our sunshine, but this one is particularly bright.'

'It reminds me of Chichester House,' Florence nodded.

It was the final seal of approval.

Even so, it was to Bridget's old-fashioned flat in Wellington Square that the young marrieds of Gloucester flocked that winter. Bridget armed her guests with paint pots and brushes and dared them to do their worst on her high walls and ceilings. Afterwards they would play charades until the small hours, even hide-and-seek in the railinged gardens in the square. A new and daring card game called strip poker was introduced, and the residents in Brunswick Road were shocked to see Maurice Foster running past their windows just before Christmas, dressed in just his shirt and combinations. Then, quite suddenly, Bridget lost her figure and her interest in parties.

April's baby was late. It was due on 23 December and she was still on her feet through Christmas and its aftermath.

'He wants to be a 1926 baby,' she said in reply to the many exclamations of 'Are you still about – you must be so fed *up*!'

Sure enough on the last day of December, at midday, her waters broke without warning. She was determined that her baby would be born without fuss, and kept going for an hour afterwards without calling down for David, but then she was forced to lie on the bed because her legs would no longer support her. There were plenty of old wives' tales about dry births, and she tried to dismiss them from her mind as her contractions became more grindingly painful. David called young Dr Green whose father had brought Teddy into the world, and he said she was 'nowhere near' and to call him the next morning. So Florence, frail as a cobweb, came to sit by the bedside and tell David not to worry.

As the hooters in the docks blared out for the New Year, April sweated and panted and twisted on the bed in the flat above the new Kings Square.

'Darling, hang on. Is it very awful?' David asked, looking in agony towards Florence.

'Yes,' gasped April. 'And I'm enjoying every minute of it. D'you hear? I'm having a baby! I'm having your baby, David! It's the most wonderful thing in the world!'

Florence took her hands and remembered her own

lonely births where the pain had not worried her so much as the indignity. And David gathered April to him and whispered, 'D'you think I care about that any more? It's you, April . . . you're the one. Just be all right!'

Grey dawn did not break until past seven on the first of January, and showed that there had been a fall of snow in the night. April asked her mother to go to the skylights in David's cutting-room and fetch her some. Florence brought it in a saucer and together they examined the transparent crystals just as they had when April was a small girl. Then another contraction dragged April into her own special no man's land and she clutched at her mother's hand so that the snow slipped onto the pillow. Both women ignored it but when the pain had passed, April rolled her forehead in its icy coldness and seemed to gain some relief.

David was busy with callers. Will came every hour, his expression accusing each time he glanced at David. Tollie was at Tewkesbury, but Bridget risked driving her Morgan over the icy roads to bring grapes and a bottle of gin. March left Albert with Aunty Sylv and came to sit anxiously by the bed, remembering only too well how it had been for her eight years ago. When she returned to Chichester Street, it was the turn of Gran and Sylv to trudge round under their black umbrellas. May arrived after Helene's had closed at six, expecting to greet her new nephew or niece, and was horrified to find April still 'nowhere near'.

'This is longer than I was!' she said to her father in the living-room as he tried to get a light from the gas

278

fire for his pipe. 'Shouldn't the doctor be here by now, Daddy?'

'He's looked at her twice. Something's not dilated, whatever that means.' The pipe would not draw and he looked pathetically at his middle daughter. 'May, she's going to be all right isn't she? We were so close and this blasted husband of hers—'

'Dad, of *course* she's going to be all right! As for David – that's all water under the bridge!' May paced irritably, tired as usual these days. 'I suppose the doctor knows what he's doing?'

'His father saw your mother through Teddy. And that was the worst thing I've ever known.' Will stared gloomily at the gas radiants. He jerked his head at the bedroom. 'She's like your mother. Won't cry out.'

'Oh God. What can we *do*?'

Will sat up. 'Snotty Lottie. That's what we can do. She'll know if there's anything wrong.' He hustled to his feet, his pipe rolling unheeded to the floor. 'I'll go for her. She'll be in the Lamb and Flag. Bridget Williams brought some gin. Get it open for Lottie, our May. Have a sip yourself, you look done in.'

May screwed up her face and did as she was bid. She felt so much better that she had another glass with Lottie, then with her father. Unable to stand, she sprawled in one of the box-like chairs; she hadn't felt like this since she and Monty had lived it up in their lovely little house in Bushey Park. She looked at the empty glass on the wide arm of the chair and saw again Victor's fish bowl and the oval mirror and the thick, thick carpet. Tears came into her eyes.

David stood in front of her.

'She's going to be all right, May. Don't cry, please don't cry. Lottie says she's going to be all right.'

She couldn't stop crying. She wanted Monty; she wanted another baby and all the fuss and attention that went with it.

David said, 'Don't go out without something to keep out the cold. Have some of this gin . . .' She had some more and staggered down the fire escape more adroitly than she would have done sober. She realized that it was very late, everywhere was closed, even the public houses. She skidded grandly around the Cross and started down Northgate Street. There was a cat in the road and she called 'Rags?' and then remembered that Rags had died on Armistice night and wept more tears. The snow built up on her fur collar and melted against the warmth of her neck. She was so tired; always tired these days. The opening of Saint John's Lane loomed on her left and she wondered how she would ever reach the railway bridge and the turning into Chichester Street.

A voice called, 'May! Is that you, May?'

She turned, thankful for any diversion. A snowy figure hurried towards her from the Cross, at first looking so much like April that May gasped, then materializing, galoshed and hooded, as Sibbie Luker.

'May, what's happening? Your father has been with April most of the day and when I tried to enquire, March opened the door and told me to mind my own business!'

May drew herself up to her full height. 'And so you should, Sibbie Luker! April is our sister. Nothing to do with you.'

Sibbie drew back and her muffled figure seemed to harden, black against the snow. She barked a laugh. 'You know better than that, May! Rising business is my business!'

But May, belligerent with gin, was not embarrassed or cowed. 'David is married to April please remember, Sibbie. He wouldn't look at you now, believe me!'

'Perhaps I'm not talking about David Daker! Perhaps I dropped David Daker when you did, May! Yes, I think I did. I wanted a bigger share of your family. And I got it! What concerns Will Rising, concerns me, and don't you ever forget that again!'

May stood erect and magnificent for a few seconds longer while Sibbie's words seeped into her fuddled brain. Then she sagged, her beautiful neck sank between her shoulder blades, and the snowy collar met the snowy hat. In between, as out of a helmet, May's small face glared, pinched and disbelieving.

Sibbie glared back briefly, still rigid with the anger that May's unexpected attack had sparked; then common sense prevailed and she realized she had made a tactical error. Will would be deeply hurt and angered by what she had done. It might spoil . . . everything.

She drew nearer to May. 'Oh May, surely you don't begrudge me an interest in your family? You never used to. We shared everything, don't you remember? Your banana sandwiches and your darling mamma's umbrella and – and – I've always looked on your father as – as a kind of uncle—'

May took a step away and nearly slid over in the snow with her own uncertainty. Had she misunderstood? That day Will had been in the teashop . . . had he been meeting Sibbie?

Sibbie laughed sympathetically. 'Darling May. D'you know, I do believe you're the slightest bit tiddly. That's why you seem so strange, isn't it? You've been drinking April's health, has she had the baby? What is it? Is she all right?' Sibbie purposely raised her voice to the one she had used as an excited schoolgirl; her consonants disappearing as her accent slipped into broad Gloucester.

May was partially reassured. 'Oh Sib . . . of course I'm not tiddly! And April – poor little April – forty-eight hours—'

'Well, you were a long time weren't you, May? Gladys told me it was terrible for you. And among strangers too. At least April's got her family with her.'

'That's true.' Incredibly May began to feel as she had felt in the old days, with Sibbie like an echo by her side. 'But of course, I had Monty . . .' She caught herself up in case Sibbie should mention that disgraceful – and hurtful – incident when she had forced a kiss on poor Monty. Sibbie must not share Monty in any way whatever. Monty was entirely May's.

'Of course you did,' Sibbie said in her oddly persuasive burr. 'I've never known a man so devoted as your Monty.' She smiled, and in the lamplight her teeth looked very white and pointed.

May said, 'I must go. Victor will be wondering . . .'

'Yes. I'll walk round with you, dearest May. Call in on Mother.'

'There's no need . . .' But Sibbie had taken her arm

and was helping her along the high pavement beneath the railway bridge where the drips from the ballast above were forming long icicles already. It was surprising how easy it was to cover the distance with Sibbie's hand beneath her elbow. When they reached number thirty-three she hesitated, and Sibbie seized the moment to embrace her fondly as in the old days.

'Darling May.' Her hands, suddenly ungloved, slipped warmly under the icy fur collar and around May's damp neck. 'It's been so long, and I've missed you so much.'

May felt tears gather in her eyes again. 'Oh Sib . . . so long . . . we're getting old . . .'

'That doesn't matter. We shall get old together.' Frozen cheek touched frozen cheek and May put her arms around her old friend and held her close. In spite of Monty so far away, in spite of poor April in the throes of childbirth, in spite of *everything*, she felt comforted.

Young Dr Green said, 'I'm afraid it will be a forceps job. Lottie – you can boil them up for me if you will. Kindly wash your hands first.'

Lottie used her sleeve, her nose dripping freely as it always did in times of stress.

'No need for them things, doctor sir. The 'ead be crowned ben't it? Let me 'ave a go. C'mon now. No need to worry. If I can't do no good, you can tinker around as much as you like.'

The doctor remembered tales his father had told, and stood over the ancient crow-like woman while she washed her gnarled hands. There were so many cracks and crevices in the palms it was absurd to hope they could ever approach sterility, but at least a token show for the sake of his reputation . . .

Lottie left the soap on her hands and sat confidently on the end of the bed. 'Next time, little April. Next time. Just do your best and old Lottie 'ull do the rest.'

The voice came through faintly to April's consciousness and the rhyme reminded her of Teddy. It was as if he were here in the room with her, just as he had been so often when they were ill together. She tried to tell Florence and no words would come. It was infinitely reassuring when her mother leaned close and said quietly, 'I know, my darling. He's been with us all the time.'

She did not feel Lottie's expert hands, nor hear the grunts of satisfaction coming from the old woman as the bent fingers touched tiny temples, but she obeyed the command as best she could when the time came, and with the last atom of her strength she bore down. Lottie did not waste her time or the baby's strength by useless tugging. Young Dr Green watched, fascinated, as the fingers slid further and hooked beneath a minuscule armpit. And then he witnessed Lottie's famous twisting action come into its own. The baby corkscrewed and slithered on to its waiting rubber sheet; April groaned her trembling relief; Lottie wiped her nose and pushed the shoulder blades in one action; air pumped into new lungs and the baby cried.

Florence whispered, 'She's perfect, my darling. A perfect little girl. You've got a daughter, April.'

It was as if Teddy was laughing somewhere and April laughed with him.

'Davina,' she whispered to Teddy and her mother. 'David's daughter. Davina.'

Florence said, 'Of course, darling. Davina. Little Davie.'

And Teddy, who of course must know everything, went on laughing.

The next day, suffering badly from a hangover and the emotional business of welcoming a girl into the male ranks of the younger generation, May decided that her life could not continue as it had for the past year. Monty came to Gloucester once a month with chocolates for Florence and tobacco for Will and flowers for May herself. They were wonderful weekends, he spent enough money to keep them all for a week, and Victor was invariably sick on the Monday after a visit from his father. But May had been brought up in a household where man and wife lived and worked together. Even now, when her father was so often out on business, he was still there to deal with the daily round in a way that most men were not.

He got in the coal each morning and chopped Flo's liver for her lunch with just the right amount of onion to make it bearable. When she had been recovering from last year's influenza, he had carried her downstairs every day and back to bed every night. May was not to know that his tenderness towards his wife was in direct proportion to his physical feeling for Sibbie. Nevertheless a hint of threat stayed in her mind after her meeting with Sibbie on the first night of the New Year, and strengthened her determination to change her own way of life. She wrote to Monty who was in pantomime at Bognor and told him to find a flat suitable for the three of them. Victor was openly rebellious.

'I don't want to leave Gramp and Gramma!' he screamed at his mother. And he certainly did not want to leave Albert, so recently returned to him from Bath. But May was inclining to the view that Albert was a bad influence on her young son. March had complained several times that Victor was 'rude'; May knew of course that Albie, eighteen months older than Victor, was the real culprit. The boys saw far too much of each other, both back at Marley where discipline was lax, sleeping together until March moved out of Chichester Street then half the time insisting on exchange visits. They were babies, but they would grow up.

The reunion was doomed from the start. Monty was used now to having a companion who fed him his cues. In the old days May had fulfilled that role and others besides. He would have died for May and enjoyed watching himself do it. But then Victor had been born, and Monty had gradually realized that his son was superseding him in May's order of priority. When Sibbie had held him closely, he had felt again the warmth that appreciation always gave him. He had repaid her – albeit guiltily – the way she obviously wanted, and though he had not been able to face her again, the warmth lingered. He needed more of it.

Maud Davenport supplied it.

She did not require a companion in bed; she required what she had had from him before May appeared on the scene. He ranked alongside her at rehearsals; if there was any altercation Monty was automatically on Maud's side; he chaperoned her everywhere. In return he was treated like a favourite son. His tie was tied for him, he had a cup of tea in bed every morning, baths were run and towels were heated.

She was inconsolable when he landed a tiny part in the panto at Bognor. He felt the same. But the dame of the panto was an elderly clown called Desmond Oakfield. Monty had diggings with him and two other unattached men. But Desmond favoured Monty.

'My guess is, my dear – ' he used a lorgnette to emphasize his words ' – you have sung in opera. Am I right? Just don't tell me I'm wrong.'

Monty smiled charmingly and admitted it.

'I knew it. When you sang that chorus with me, I could hear it. There's training there. Don't tell me I'm wrong.'

Monty had never had formal training; he made deprecating sounds. Desmond tapped him lightly with his lorgnette.

'Mock modest. You need someone to blow your trumpet for you, dear boy. May I volunteer?'

'Too kind, Mr Oakfield,' Monty murmured.

'Desmond. The name is Desmond.'

May interrupted this partnership brutally. She arrived at the theatrical lodging after curtain-up. She was tired, Victor was tired, they were both homesick. She was used to theatre landladies and when she rang the bell she arranged herself suitably, her bag on one side, her good-looking son on the other. When Mrs Townsend opened the door she saw a frail, rather

Edwardian beauty, golden hair escaping in tendrils from her hat; she recognized her instantly as a Wronged Wife.

May held out her hands. 'Mrs Townsend! I would know you anywhere from my husband's letters! I want to thank you for looking after him for me while I was detained – at my parents' home.'

Mrs Townsend was overcome at being part of this drama. Obviously this beautiful lady knew nothing of Desmond. She did not suspect she was a wronged wife. Mrs Townsend ushered her into the front room which doubled as sitting and dining-room for 'the theatricals'. A fire was burning and a kettle was on the trivet for them to make their own cocoa, the usual late supper was laid on a cardboard-stiff cloth. Mrs Townsend gestured widely and said she would get Townsend to take the cases up. Then she whisked herself away to sort out the sleeping arrangements. Both Desmond and Mr Gould had double-bedded rooms and had been tactful enough to rumple the bedding each morning. She flung back the sheets and investigated thoroughly, then breathed a sigh of relief. Maybe she had been wrong.

Wrong or right, May was having none of it. The next day was Sunday and she had Monty and Victor out of the diggings ten minutes after breakfast. There had been no joyful meeting the night before; May and Victor had already retired when Monty and his fellow actors returned, and they announced their arrival only by a note propped against the cheese dish. They were firmly asleep in the middle of the feather bed and Monty had had great difficulty in squeezing himself alongside Victor. The temptation to tiptoe along the landing to Desmond's room was almost overwhelming. The atmosphere at breakfast was completely artificial. May would have liked to fire a great many questions, but she had discovered before that it was very difficult to carry on any acrimony in the company of actors.

Desmond made a great fuss of Victor, keeping him on his knee while May fitted his coat over his shoulders and calling him 'my pretty' and 'baby bird' in a way May found revolting but which Victor exploited to the full. He showed May half a sovereign as they walked along the promenade looking for house-agents that might be open on Sundays. 'He'll give me another one if we go back to tea, Mummy,' he said. 'I don't want you to have anything to do with that man!' May snapped, cold and hungry after her sketchy breakfast. 'He's not a nice man at all!' And Monty, not knowing whether to be pleased or sorry at the sudden arrival of his family, said uncomfortably, 'He's not bad, May. Heart of gold.'

She did the best she could, but she hated every moment of her first month in Bognor and wondered why on earth she'd come. Monty tried to 'keep in' as he put it, with Desmond Oakfield, which meant that they did in fact see plenty of him and his lorgnette and his half-sovereigns. The only decent school for Victor would not take him until his seventh birthday, which was not until July. May could have enjoyed herself with Victor on his own; she could have striven for a renewal of her old relationship with Monty on his own, but as a threesome they no longer jelled.

After a particularly wet day in February, the sheer ennui of their situation came to a head. In front of Victor the bickering crescendoed into something more.

'What exactly do you want from me, May?' Monty said with more weariness than anger. 'I've begged your forgiveness over and over again for losing the Bushey Park house. But you're determined to punish me for the rest of my life—'

May was aghast. 'That's not true, Monty! Surely you haven't felt that all this time? Oh my dear . . . ' She turned swiftly to Victor. 'Darling, please go to bed now. Daddy and I have to talk.'

Monty, with a parental attitude far ahead of his time, put out a restraining hand. 'Let him stay. We're together in this problem. He might as well know what is happening and why.'

'He doesn't understand, Monty!'

Victor said, 'I do. Mummy and me want to live in Gloucester and Daddy doesn't.'

His parents were temporarily silenced. They had not realized themselves how simple the problem was.

Victor said, 'We could live with Grandma and you could come at weekends. Like before.'

Monty glanced at May. 'We ought to be together more than that, Victor. That's why your mother brought you down here last month.'

May said, 'Well . . . we are a *family*. That's how families live. Together.'

'We don't have to be a replica of your family, May.'

'I know . . . I know.' May wandered to the window and looked out helplessly. The lamp lighter was doing his round; it was nearly time for Monty to go to the theatre.

She said, 'I think I'm fed up with you being an actor, Monty. It's too uncertain. When you've got a job, the money is marvellous but we spend it as we get it, then when there's no job we have to rely on Mother and Dad—'

'I know.' Monty came behind her and touched the nape of her neck. 'I hate that too. But what's to be done?'

'You could give it up surely? Fred would get you a job in Gloucester and we could rent a little house—'

Monty laughed. 'Oh May. Can you imagine it? Digging coal with Jack and Austen? Or even helping Gladys with the books nine till six and a half-day on Saturday—'

Victor said with innocent acumen, 'Daddy couldn't act that part!'

Monty picked him up and sat him on his shoulders; it was a rare union between them. May, looking at them laughing together, felt suddenly isolated. And from that feeling was born an absolute determination to woo Monty away from the theatre and into a permanent home in Gloucester. She went to them and circled them with her arms. It wouldn't be so bad. She would work on it slowly, going home with Victor for long periods, joining Monty when she thought it . . . necessary. Something had gone out of their marriage, but she could put it back. She was certain of that.

Tollie was pleased, and not really surprised, at the way the birth of his first child paralleled the political situation. The first day Bridget felt movement inside her, the government withdrew their subsidies to the coal industry. Tollie watched, fascinated, as his wife swelled in time with the escalating problem. As the mine-owners one by one declared that reduced demand required lower wages for the workers, so Bridget grew rapidly like an inflating balloon. Maurice Foster stopped calling and at the same time Mr MacDonald warned that if the miners came out on strike so would the railways and the engineers. As Mr Baldwin assured the country that no-one would starve, Bridget went into labour. And when the news came through on their cumbersome crystal wireless set that the fields in Durham and Wales were no longer working, and that – as the Lord Mayor gloomily put it to Councillor Edwards – 'the balloon has gone up', so Bridget's balloon also went up and she produced a baby daughter.

She was on her feet, or rather on her *chaise longue* in time for Tollie to join the ranks of the 'plus-four boys' who were to break the national strike with which he so ardently and so secretly sympathized. In a week it was all over and would have been without Tollie driving the tram from Longford to Worcester Street, but he took on himself some of the blame for its failure. He remembered the successful 'putsch' in Berlin six years before, and cursed the jolly phlegm of the English.

Four weeks later when only the miners hung grimly on to their principles, Bridget asked querulously, 'Darling, what are we going to call it?' She measured her waist with her hands and wondered how soon her milk would dry up and her breasts return to their normal size. 'What about Marianne? Or Jacquetta?'

Tollie walked over to the new perambulator being rocked proudly by his mother, and looked into it. He had remained curiously detached from this child of his; she had been a means to the end of obeying his instructions from the Party and that was all. He had been pleased when her carrying had meant there were no more calls from Maurice Foster and no more all-night parties in the flat, but he had had little interest in Bridget's symptoms. Now, reflected in Kitty's face, he saw the protective love and tenderness which had umbrellaed him all his life and had been extended to Teddy Rising and Teddy's mother and all the Risings. He remembered the enormous influence this love brought with it, and he looked at the tiny, bonneted occupant of the baby carriage with sudden interest. Could such a love influence this child as it had influenced him? Was this where his teaching could begin?

He said, 'Let's call her something real, Bridie. None of your fancy modern names mean much.'

'Oh God.' Bridget looked bored to death. 'Is it to be Martha or Mary?'

'No. No, let's call her Olga.'

The harsh unusualness of the name pleased Bridget. She considered it, her lower lip thrust provocatively forward. There was no way she could match the charm of Davina. But Olga had a distinction of its own.

'Olga Hall,' she murmured experimentally. 'Olga Hall.'

Kitty clinched it. 'It's such an ugly name. I've never heard it before.'

'I like it,' said Bridget. 'Olga she shall be.'

April came home from her first visit to the tiny Olga Hall. She was amused at the baby's amazing likeness to Tollie.

'The same quiet brown-ness – d'you know what I mean David?'

David grinned. 'Exactly.'

'There's nothing of Bridie about her at all. Tollie has always been so self-effacing.'

'Don't let him fool you, April. Underneath that quiet, subdued exterior is a banked fire.'

'Oh David. I grew up with Tollie Hall, remember.'

'Nevertheless . . . How did Bridie seem? As unbearable as ever?'

April smiled. 'You never liked her, did you?'

'Not very much. She tried to be so damned over-bearing, but if it hadn't been for the Risings she'd have been invisible.'

'Oh David,' April repeated, laughing helplessly. She stood up and smoothed her thin voile dress. She was as slim as ever, her hip bones showed through the thin material.

'I must go and feed Davie. Then I'm going to bed. This hot weather makes me so tired.'

David frowned his concern. 'Don't you think you should put Davie on a bottle now, Primrose? It's a bit much for you surely?'

She dropped an apologetic kiss on to the top of his head. His hair was getting sparse and unexpectedly she felt tears of tenderness clog her throat.

'I just love doing it darling. But I expect you're right. I'll talk to Dr Green.'

She trailed into the bedroom, stepping out of her shoes and unbuttoning her dress as she went. She loved the summer, she always had. It must be the breast-feeding that was making her feel like a piece of chewed string.

She leaned over Davina's crib. The child was beginning to stir, her innate rhythm telling her it was time for her ten o'clock feed. She had been a model baby, placid and content, with none of David's restlessness. April stared at her, seeing again the baby's complete dissimilarity from David. Many babies had fair hair and blue eyes, but it was now obvious that this baby was not going to change. And David was not like Tollie Hall, he was a strong, dominant character who surely should have stamped some of his characteristics on his child.

Davina stretched delightfully and opened her eyes at her mother. She clenched her fists and gurgled recognition. It was such a recent accomplishment that April momentarily forgot her sadness and laughed as she picked her up and settled them both on the bed.

'Mamma's been to see Olga Hall,' she said as the baby sucked busily. 'She'll probably be your best friend later on. You'll be a bit older than her but that won't matter. Her mummy was two years older than me and it didn't make any difference.' She felt the tears collecting again and cleared her throat angrily. 'And her daddy is the same age as your Uncle Teddy. But you'll never know Uncle Teddy.' Suddenly she bowed over the tiny blonde head and sobs racked her body.

David came in like a whirlwind.

'What is it? What is it, my darling girl?'

But she couldn't tell him. She couldn't tell herself. She had to pretend it was the heat. Or the breast-feeding. Or remembering Teddy. That was what it must be, after all. That was what it had to be.

David took the baby and changed her nappy expertly. As usual she burped obediently and curled on to her side preparatory to sleeping the night almost through. David came back to April and put out a hand to stop her buttoning her dress. He knelt on the bedroom floor between her knees and put his head between her breasts.

She stroked his hair lightly. 'David. Darling. I'm all right now you know. It was just . . . the heat.'

He slid his hands around her waist and massaged the base of her spine. 'We'll buy a bottle tomorrow, darling. Don't worry about it. Relax.'

She took a breath and held it while his thumbs moved into her groin. 'David . . . please. Not while I'm still . . . David, no.'

'Yes, Primrose.' He moved his mouth over her breast and into her neck. 'We've been apart too long. Much too long. No more feeding, no more worrying.' Expertly he straightened his wrists, pulling her dress and knickers over her buttocks. She was filled with panic and fell back on the bed, digging her elbows into the counterpane and dragging herself away from him.

'David . . . David, I'm frightened!'

'I know.' He spoke calmly but he followed her on to the bed and began caressing her naked body insistently. 'I know, my darling. It's strange, isn't it? I was the one who used to be frightened. And your love – your physical need for me – forced me to hide that fear. To pretend. To simulate. Oh April . . .' He moved his hand behind her shoulder blade and held her to him while he kissed her. The combination of tenderness and adoration was too much for her. Tears poured down her face.

Still he would not release her.

'Listen, darling.' He ignored her weeping and put his mouth to her ear. 'Listen. I'm not frightened any more. Because of Davie. Surely you can understand that? I can admit to you now that if I try to make love to you, I might – I probably shall – fail. It doesn't worry me any more, April. I want to go on trying. Surely you won't let your fear come between us, April?'

'You don't understand – you don't – ' She tried to stop her blubbering in case it disturbed Davina.

He said, 'Is it because the last time – when Davie was conceived – I took you in anger? Is that it, April?'

'No. Oh no David.' She clung to him suddenly, burying her wet face in his neck and kissing him frantically. 'Never think that. I knew – even then – I knew it was love. Darling, I can't explain.'

'You think that because I succeeded last time and made a baby inside you, it will hurt me all over again if next time I fail.'

'I suppose so,' she agreed miserably. She did not let herself remember Davina's actual conception, but contrarily, the absolute sterility of the experience was with her still. In her agony of conscience in Marsh

Cottage, she had hardly been conscious that Davie had been made without love; now the sheer irony of it seemed to freeze her soul.

He lifted her chin from beneath his and kissed her gently. 'It won't,' he whispered. Then he kissed her again. And then again. Gradually she responded, unfolding for him in a kind of half-remembered dream. And this time he did not fail.

Much later he murmured, 'Darling. It's so soon. Perhaps I was selfish. If you're pregnant again, your health . . .'

She rolled over and kissed him. 'Don't worry, David. You're quite right. It's much too soon. I couldn't possibly get pregnant when I'm still breast-feeding. It doesn't happen.'

He chuckled sleepily. 'You've been reading your books again, Primrose.'

She almost contradicted him, then let her head nod on his shoulder. He roused himself when she was silent and leaned on an elbow to look at her.

'There will be other times, darling. I'm not saying it will be all right always, but there will be other times.' He grinned at the silent crib. 'Davina is living proof of that.'

She met his eyes and forced herself to hold his gaze.

'D'you remember when she was being born, David? You said all that mattered to you was . . . me.'

'You know I meant it, darling. Do you doubt it now?'

'No. No. But it's how I feel. You are everything to me, David. Even now – even now that Davie is actually here – you are *everything*. I don't want

298

more children. I don't want another baby, David.'

He stared down at her, his black eyes searching her face for a clue to the enigma he thought he had always known. There was no clue save for a desperate intensity to be believed.

He smoothed her hair and cupped her face protectively.

'Don't think ahead, April. Just let us be thankful we have each other. And Davie.'

She held his hand where it was and turned her face to kiss the palm. They held each other and eventually slept.

April was not in the least surprised to find a few weeks later that she was not pregnant. It seemed to her that love and the conception of children had very little to do with each other.

Chapter Eleven

Davina Daker was four years old. It had snowed during the night and snow nearly drove her mad with the sort of suppressed pleasure that in other people erupted as excitement. Davina's excitement made her grin from ear to ear incessantly, so that her cheeks looked ready to burst. Her father called her his 'little apple' and she did indeed have the rounded goodness of that fruit.

Her grandparents were giving her a party, and at her own request they were walking the long way round to Chichester Street. Everything looked so much nicer with its covering of snow. The dustbins in the alley behind the Hippodrome were fat white mushrooms, and the trees in the cattle market were lacy against the black of the auctioneer's shed. David lifted her onto the wall to walk along its length and make footprints in the fresh snow there, and April ran ahead over Northgate Street and threw snowballs at them, missing each time to make them laugh. Davina knew she was the happiest person in the world because it was simply impossible for anyone to contain any more happiness than was inside her. She couldn't even call out when they were beneath the railway bridge; she stood stock still and listened while her parents did it for her and the echo bounced back from the icicled roof. 'Dav . . . eeena! Dav . . . eeena!' There were a few other people about and they looked and smiled at her.

They went straight into Will's workroom as arranged. Will lifted Davina onto the cutting-table and Florence began to unbutton her leather gaiters with the button-hook. 'Your fairy dress is ready,' she said conspiratorially. 'Shall Mummy and Daddy have a cup of tea while we dress you?'

'Yes,' said Davina, shining-eyed.

Florence slid her feet into her black dancing shoes with the elastic that criss-crossed up her legs over her white socks. Then she began to fix a crêpe paper tutu around the tiny waist. In the corner the wings waited, fashioned on thin wire.

Will was in his element, once again head of a big family, surrounded by eager children. He insisted on fixing Davie's crown and bowing low to her. He glanced at Flo to exchange proud smiles. Flo was like a girl again, as arrow-thin and aristocratic as when he had first set eyes on her at Kempley churchyard back in the eighties. He did not see that her dark hair was iron-grey and her back bent; happiness had given Will rose-coloured spectacles.

He said, 'How's that then, Davie?'

Davina nodded her head experimentally and the crown did not fall off. 'It's luvverly,' she breathed.

'And so are you,' Florence said. Will nodded. This child had none of the Daker darkness in her, body or soul; she was all Rising, just as April had been at her age.

'We're lucky,' he said, reaching for Florence's hand. She smiled. 'Haven't I always told you that?'

301

David sat at the kitchen table and drew the early edition of the *Citizen* towards him. He had not really known the Risings until their move to Chichester House, and this kitchen had no memories for him. He held the paper up and watched April over the top of it. She moved around preparing the tea with a mature grace that he was now accustomed to, but which struck him anew in these different surroundings. He tried to date the change in her from girl to woman.

'Four years,' he murmured. 'Four years ago.'

She lit the gas and turned to smile at him, the match still in her hand. 'It seems incredible, doesn't it? I can hardly remember a time when we didn't have her. What did we use to *do* all day, David?'

'You'll burn your fingers.' She blew out the match and threw it on the range. He grinned. 'I'm glad you're not entirely sensible!'

She looked at him in astonishment 'Sensible? You've never called me that, darling. I don't think I like it. It sounds very dull.'

'You're never dull, Primrose. But you have changed. You are different. I can't put my finger on it.'

She reached cups and saucers from the dresser, turning down her mouth humorously. 'You're trying to tell me I'm getting old.' She shook her head. 'One minute I'm a child-bride, the next an ancient wife.'

He rustled the *Citizen* dismissively. 'Stop fishing for compliments, Primrose. Whatever age you are, I am going to be eleven years older. Always.'

'Poor old man.' She poured tea and placed his cup squarely on the page in front of him. He sighed.

'That *is* childish.'

'You weren't reading. You were watching me.'

'Admiringly.'

'No. Like you watch some of your students. Objectively. Clinically. It makes them squirm.'

'It didn't make you squirm.'

'No.' She met his eyes above her teacup and saw there everything she had ever wanted to see in David's face. No more secrets. No more demons. Davie had done that.

She said breathlessly, unable to sustain the moment, 'If I've changed, what about you? University tutorials in Cheltenham, Gloucester and Bristol – now *that's* what I call sensible!'

He recognized her mood. It happened often; it had been happening – as he said – for four years. He laughed and reached reassuringly for her hand. 'You call it sensible, I call it education, Tollie calls it politics and my mother calls it getting above my station.'

She laughed too, then suddenly lifted his knuckles to her lips. 'Oh David . . . I knew it always. You're a very clever man.'

'Not clever. No. Otherwise we would be wealthy and I would understand you.'

She chose to ignore the last half of his remark and held his hand to her cheek consideringly.

'You know a lot. You read everything in the newspapers and you listen to the wireless, then you sort of stand back and fit everything together like a jigsaw puzzle. And when it doesn't fit you know it is wrong. Somehow.'

'It's called forming an opinion. Everyone does it. You do it.'

'No. Not in the same way. I feel things are wrong or right. And often I don't feel . . . correctly.'

He watched her again and she thought she might squirm at any minute. Then he said abruptly, 'And what do you feel about us, Primrose? You and me?'

'I feel we are the luckiest people in the world. We are indivisible.'

There was a long pause. Then he released his hand and put it flat on the newspaper in front of him. She frowned.

'David, what is it? Don't *you* feel we are indivisible?'

'Of course.' He smiled. 'I'd like to lock the door and make love to you in front of that range.'

'Oh David. It's Davie's birthday party.'

'Four years ago you couldn't have spoken those words . . . we are indivisible. You would have come round this table and kissed me. That's what I meant when I said you had changed.'

She laughed, stood up and went round the table. She made the kiss long and lingering but then she straightened with a businesslike sigh.

'I'd better go upstairs darling. Really. We'll be together tonight.'

'Yes.' He touched her fingertips with his mouth. 'Yes. We're together every night, Primrose.'

He watched her go through the kitchen door, then return to blow him a kiss. 'Don't stay too long reading. Davie will expect you.'

He nodded and turned back to the paper to skim the headlines about the young Prince of Wales, who seemed set to follow his illustrious grandfather's example as far as ladies were concerned. David sighed and reached for his recently acquired spectacles in order to scan the small print. He was confronted by a list of wills and bequests which reminded him obscurely of something April had said a long time ago. Davina had been given to them by God. He frowned . . . a trite belief doubtless shared by every mother. But April was wont to make bargains with God on a strangely personal basis. He remembered her before the high altar in the cathedral that ghastly evening in 1925; he remembered her calm certainty and assurance. Had she in fact fretted and prayed herself into a conviction that if she were pregnant, it was a special, never-to-be-repeated dispensation?

David gnawed his lip and shoved his glasses higher up his nose. It was hard to pinpoint the change in his beautiful wife. There was a barrier – a flimsy veil of a barrier – between them. She had been an impulsive girl; now she was a mature woman. Just as loving, just as responsive. But . . . He drew in a breath and straightened his shoulders. The impulsive young girl had so often seduced her older husband. He remembered her skipping around the flat in french knickers and nothing else, deliberately provoking him. She no longer did that. Of course there was Davie to consider. But she no longer seduced him; he seduced her.

His eye was taken by the last will and testament of Alderman Charles Williams. He saw that Sibbie shared a large slice of his inheritance with Edward Williams. Sibbie was wealthy in her own right. He smiled grimly and wondered what she would do with her money. He hoped she wouldn't succeed in buying

Will Rising at last. It would hurt April unbearably.

Upstairs, April stood inside the door of the bandy room for a few minutes, surveying her family and friends with smiling affection. She was unconscious of any barrier, however flimsy, between herself and David; the instinctive survival element in her subconscious had successfully shifted any barrier there might have been away from the small, secure Daker trio, and firmly entrenched it around Fred Luker. It had been the only solution to an impossible situation for April. She no longer had a brother; David, Davina and April were one unit, Fred was an outsider. Every time she looked at Davie and saw the Luker element in her, so she turned her back more firmly on Fred. She had no idea˙ that this attitude had altered her feeling for David, unless it had deepened and strengthened her love still more. She was unable to look at her problems objectively and fit the pieces together 'like a jigsaw puzzle'. She felt her way intuitively.

Fred could not be completely ignored or forgotten; apart from his physical presence in her life and the local gossip about him which was rife, he had . . . perhaps . . . saved her marriage. So although he was thrust as far away as possible, he was a constant reminder of . . . betrayal. The woman who had lain with Fred Luker could not be quite the same with the man she loved, the man she had betrayed. She could respond to his ardour as she had always done, but she could not initiate it.

But as she stood there watching the inmates of the bandy room, she knew nothing of this. She fiddled in her handbag, got out her cigarettes and holder and began to smoke as usual. Davie was still downstairs being dressed by her adoring grandparents; the rest of April's world was here, secure, at least for the moment.

There was May, on one of her frequent visits home, sitting between the brass candlesticks of the piano, letting her hands stray over the yellow keys in an improvisation of her own. May had been involved in long-drawn out negotiations with Bridget and Tollie over the past few months in an effort to get Monty a job at Williams'. Looking at her now, April could see her sister's yearning to be home for good; to give up following Monty around the country and settling Victor into new schools. May was beginning to look . . . not old . . . matronly . . . her hair a more silvery blond. She must be thirty-six this year. April felt a small qualm at the passing of time. David was almost forty.

March, on the other hand, was thinner, with none of May's soft outlines. Her hair was still chestnut dark and very glossy, her movements quick and precise. Her eyes went constantly to Albert-Frederick, kneeling on the sofa with Victor, looking out of the snowy window towards the cathedral spires. Her glances were not overtly affectionate, she seemed to be checking up on him. It was as if she could overhear their murmured conversation, though had she done so she would not have been merely watching.

April kissed her two sisters and grinned at the boys. Victor was saying quietly, 'She used to be my mummy's best friend and now she's a kept woman . . .' Albie coloured as he met April's eyes, and Victor stopped his words with a hand over his mouth. April put an arm around each shoulder and said softly, 'If it's one of your naughty jokes you'd better keep it to yourselves.'

She went on to greet Bridget, pregnant for the third time, overweight and a little blowsy. Olga and Natasha sat on the floor at her feet, fighting over their dolls. Bridget was full of complaints as usual, looking strangely complacent at the same time.

'It's heartburn time, my dear. Did you suffer that way?'

'I think so. I can't remember really.'

'No. It's a long time for you darling, isn't it? Tollie says pregnancy suits me but of course he doesn't have to put up with it, does he? I hate him sometimes.'

'Bridie. You know you love being pregnant and you love dear Tollie.'

'Dear Tollie indeed. Bossy Tollie perhaps.'

'Bossy? Tollie?'

'You don't know him, April. He's very masterful.' Bridget's eyes sparkled and April chuckled and shook her head at her friend.

'You don't change, Bridie,' she said almost scoldingly.

She smiled across at Aunt Sylv, pouring lemonade into an assortment of glasses on the card table. Gran, nearing eighty, had chosen to take to her bed for the afternoon. The children would visit her in turn later, and she would receive them as Queen Victoria had received her grandchildren, with a kind of gracious disapproval.

The door opened and Will appeared, signalling to May. She began to play a triumphal march and in came Davina, angelic in white crêpe paper and tinsel. Davina's grin looked nearly painful, her fringe stuck out from her silver crown and she shouldered her wand like a soldier's rifle. Everyone clapped. Bridget snatched up Natasha and said, 'Look baby, look at the fairy queen.' And Olga said enviously, 'It's only Davie Daker.' Victor, enthralled and uninhibited, yelled, 'Three cheers for the Risings!' And May, proud of her handsome son who always said the right thing at the right time, laughed delightedly and called out, 'Take the fairy queen for the first dance then, Victor dear – the polka!'

April took Davina's wand from her and watched smilingly as Victor led her out with much aplomb. Then Albert was before her, bowing low. 'Aunty April, will you dance with me?'

Will and Flo passed them, dancing with exquisite ease. Will had tried to do the one-step with Sibbie to the music of her gramophone but nobody suited him like Flo. She was as light as a feather, quite literally. He glanced down at her, frowning slightly. It didn't mean anything of course, she'd always been light and after Sibbie who had plenty of flesh on her, she was bound to seem frail. But Flo . . . Flo who had been to death's door once in their lives together and had returned to him . . . if anything happened to Flo, he couldn't live on. He was quite certain of that. He could not bear to lose Flo. Nor Sibbie. He could not bear it.

Albert studied April's mouth, just level with his eyes. He wondered if he was going to swoon.

'I've been eating parsley,' he said abruptly to her throat.

She laughed. 'So. You didn't forget my words of wisdom! Now why would you be eating parsley? Is it bloater paste again?'

He was so pleased she remembered, he almost swooned again.

'I've started smoking. Properly. I've got a holder like yours and I can blow rings like you do.'

'Wicked child. If your mother finds out—'

'I do it in the attic. When I'm fixing my train set. Nobody comes up there, it's strictly private.'

Aunty April laughed again, flinging back her head like Grandpa did, exposing the white column of her throat where it plunged down into the neckline of her woollen dress. Albie felt the sweat cold under his arms.

The door opened and Uncle David appeared. Surprisingly, behind him came Fred Luker. Albert opened his eyes wide and looked for Victor to test his reaction. It was a long time since Fred Luker had been Uncle Fred to the boys; Victor referred to his wealth as 'ill-gotten gains' and told Albie lurid stories about his private life. Only Grandpa still called him Fred and went with him to the Lamb and Flag and laughed indulgently when Albert's mother pulled her disapproving face.

Aunty April's hand tightened suddenly and Albert forgot the intriguing arrival of Fred.

He blurted, 'I love you, Aunty April!'

'Do you darling? How marvellous. I say, can we sit down a minute?'

They sat down almost behind the piano. It was as if she wanted to be alone with him and Albie felt his heart flutter with a kind of panic. She was so beautiful; her legs so long, the swellings beneath her woollen jumper-thing so perfectly proportioned. He still dreamed of seeing her without clothes.

He said passionately, 'I'd do anything for you, Aunty April. Anything in the world.'

She looked at him properly and her dark blue eyes smiled warmly. She picked up his hand and sandwiched it between her own.

'Dear Albie. Thank you.' She considered, her head on one side. 'All right then. Will you look after Davie for me, darling?'

Coldness touched him. 'Are you going away, Aunty April?'

'No. I don't think so. But sometimes mothers can't help their own children. You wouldn't understand that—'

'Oh I do. I do.' There were links between him and March forged of steel, but she was rarely able to help him.

'Then will you keep an eye on her, Albie? If anyone seems to frighten her or—'

'I'll kill them, Aunty April,' he promised.

She laughed. 'Well, you need not go as far as that.' Unbelievably she leaned towards him and he knew she was going to kiss him. The reddened lips were a perfect Cupid's bow, and he anticipated how they would feel against his, very soft and slightly sticky. He couldn't bear it. He really would swoon.

'I have to go to the closet,' he said and stood up quickly, nearly hitting her chin with his shoulder.

David had to leave early to see to the shop. He was surprised when April, helping him with his coat and muffler in the narrow hallway, decided she would come with him.

'Primrose, you can't. Davie will feel deserted.' He held her by her shoulders. 'What has happened? Has Albie made a lewd suggestion?'

'Oh David. You are *ridic*ulous! I just want to be with you.' She scooped his hands away and pressed herself against his cold overcoat, then stood back, laughing. 'I'm being silly. Of course I can't leave Davie. I'll see you in an hour or two anyway.'

'True.' He poked his head and pecked at her and she clung again, but without passion. With a kind of desperation; as if they were shipwrecked and about to be torn apart. She stood at the door and waved to him, shivering in the cold. He gestured her to go inside, then tramped around the corner into London Road. The barrier – whatever it was – had suddenly become thicker, and she was trying to force herself through it. But what the devil could it be?

Sibbie Luker was taking advantage of a whole day without Will, to entertain Edward Williams. She put a pan of chestnuts beneath the fire and cooked a leg of pork with turnips.

'Barton Feast?' He was referring to the traditional meal served at the annual hiring fair.

'I have to celebrate my feasts when I can.' She had never tried to hide anything from Edward; he had known of her from his father and her long association with Will Rising had been part of her attraction. Edward Williams admired all things to do with the Rising family. She fished out the pan of chestnuts and swept the hearth again. The bungalow was kept impeccably.

'Isn't it strange, Edward – ' she removed the chestnuts one by one, blowing on her fingers ' – so many men say they love me, yet at Christmas and Easter, Bank holidays and Barton Feast, I am always on my own.'

He reached for her. 'Ah Sibbie. That won't always be.' He held her on his lap, protectively. He had endured a frigid wife for thirty years now, and his adored only child, Bridget, had grown away from him. This child-woman was just that: mistress and daughter to him. The meal was ready and waiting on the table but she did not push him away; she had never pushed him away.

He whispered, 'I've asked Alice for a divorce, Sibbie. I want to marry you.'

She drew away and stared at him. Sibbie was never shocked, but at that moment she was close to it.

'She wouldn't agree to it,' she breathed.

'Not yet, no. But I shall wear her down eventually.'

'But . . . she will cite me as co-respondent.'

'Yes. Would you mind very much? I shouldn't care a button.'

'But darling. You're a councillor. You'd have to resign – you don't know what it's like to be – to be—'

313

'Ostracized? No, I don't. I'm looking forward to it. It will set us apart. Isolate us. Together.'

Sibbie said nothing. She let him kiss her repeatedly until his passion was thoroughly aroused. She let him undress her and lie her on the hearth rug and she watched the glowing fire out of the corner of her eye and groaned occasionally and wondered whether she was pleased or not. What about Will? And what would Fred say if he knew he was in danger of losing his best 'contact'?

But . . . it was the first marriage proposal she had received and she couldn't help feeling a small thrill.

He said, 'Our dinner will be getting cold, my darling.'

'I love cold pork.'

'So do I. And cold turnips.'

'And as for cold roast chestnuts . . .' They laughed together and made love again. Edward Williams was only five years younger than Will Rising, but he had fought in the war with Sibbie's generation and she never thought of him as old.

Fred could almost smell himself smouldering with resentment. He managed to corner March alone in the kitchen and as he shut the door on the two of them, he had a glimpse of April Daker kissing her husband in the hall as if her very life depended on it. Fred decided he had had more than enough of being treated like the plague by the Rising girls. Two of the children here today had been fathered by him so he had a perfect right to come to the birthday party of one of them. He had been sorely tempted to stand in the middle of the bandy room and announce the fact to all and sundry. But Davina was so sweet and shy, and Albert-Frederick so tall and serious, and the peculiar tenderness generated all those years ago by April Daker in Marsh Cottage had nourished itself on the two children until it was the only thing that mattered to him. Making money . . . Leonie Porterman and the other women . . . they were appetites which he gorged in sporadic bursts and then forgot. Albie and Davie and his right to be near them, caring for them, that was what mattered.

March was making tea for the women. She had an enormous tray loaded with cups, saucers, spoons and was bending down to check that the gas was lighted beneath the kettle. She actually jerked upright and put her hand on her breast like Hedy Lamarr. She wasn't unlike Hedy Lamarr. Well, he could put on the drama too if necessary. He leaned his back against the door and surveyed her.

She visibly swallowed, then said tensely, 'What do you want? Why did you come here today?'

Fred wished he could tell her the real truth; he told half of it. 'Your father asked me. I accepted because I wanted to see my son with the rest of his family. When I bump into him accidentally in town he's awkward with me—'

'What do you expect? Everyone knows now – I'm surprised my father asked you – anyway, what do you mean you wanted to see . . . I don't understand.'

'You're supposed to be intelligent, March. I wanted to check up on Albert-Frederick. My son. Make sure he is happy.'

'He is not—' She whispered the denial hopelessly and did not finish it. He felt a pang of pity for her.

'March. Listen. Four years ago I asked you to marry me. Whatever you thought at the time you must know now that it wasn't because of your money.' He waited. She shrugged, still with that hopeless look about her. He went on carefully, 'You've got exactly what you always wanted, March – what I promised I would get for you. Do you remember? The house in Barnwood, the money. You hire a car when you want it. You help your mother out. You buy presents for your family. Everything. You've done it on your own and I know you well enough to be sure that gave you a great kick. Didn't it?' Still she said nothing. Almost automatically she turned off the gas and poured the contents of the kettle into the teapot. He let her finish. Then he said in a low voice, 'Is it enough, March? Are you satisfied?'

She caught hold of the handles of the tray but did not lift it. She said, 'I . . . manage. Very well.'

He remembered the sterile old maid's bedroom that had been hers in this house. For all her money and fine house was her new bedroom very much different?

He whispered, 'Such a waste. All that fire and passion wasted. Drying up. Shrivelling.'

Her head came up furiously. 'How dare you speak to me like that, Fred Luker! What right have you got to come here and insult me – try to wound and humiliate and—'

'Because I'm the only man you've really given yourself to, March. I'm not the only man you've loved. I know that. I know that I must always come second to your blasted brother . . . a corpse. But I'm the only man you've wanted. The only man—'

'Be quiet!' She really was outraged. She came around the table and gestured angrily for him to move from the door. 'Let me out! This minute. All you can think about is – is – lust and – and carnal passion and—'

He caught her flailing arm and held it hard. 'Will you marry me, March?'

She was still. Like a wary half-tamed animal.

'Marry you?' Her clear tea-brown eyes flicked over his face and then down to his hand on the sleeve of her dress. 'Why?'

Her wariness was infectious. He tightened his hold; he must say nothing about Albert-Frederick. If she thought he wanted to have any kind of say in the boy's upbringing, she'd be threatened, just as she'd been before.

He said, 'The usual reasons. Love.' But love was only one reason. The main one was that he and March were meant to be married. She was going against their destiny. His voice was flat, unemotional. She did not believe him.

'You mean you want another bedfellow? Isn't that Porterman woman enough for you?'

'March. Leave her out of it. We're talking about you and me—'

'How can *I* leave her out of it? You won't. You're still seeing her—'

'No.'

She was childishly triumphant. 'You are. Victor saw you both go into the Bell Hotel last week. He went

317

in and asked for your room number. Told the man you were his uncle and she was his aunt. Gave the name Luker. The man told him there were no Lukers registered in the hotel and the lady and gentleman he had just seen were Mr and Mrs Smith!'

Fred felt himself go cold. He twisted her arm fiercely. 'Now you're lying. He'd never have told you that cock and bull—'

'I heard him telling Albie. He's a dirty little monkey. But he doesn't make up things like that.'

'He told Albert?' Fred felt his heart contract painfully. He brought March close to him and stared into her eyes. 'You let him tell Albert? You denied it, I hope.'

'Of course I didn't deny it. I knew – it was true. Everyone knows—'

'But *Albert* . . . Godamighty, March . . . my son—'

She pushed against his chest and suddenly there were tears in her eyes. 'I knew that was why you asked me again to marry you. Your son. That's what's gnawing at you now, Fred, isn't it? Love . . . you don't love me. You probably want to take me to bed again. But you don't love me. Otherwise you'd have given up Leonie Porterman four years ago when I first told you I knew about her. Better still, you would never have got entangled with her in the first place—'

He shook her angrily. 'Did you put Victor up to following me?'

'Of course not. He does things like that. He's an underhand child. Devious.'

'Albert wasn't with him? You're sure of that?'

'I told you. He was whispering to Albie—'

'Why didn't you shut him up?'

'Why should I? Maybe – in this case – it was better for Albie to know the truth.'

'You bitch, March.' He altered his grip, took hold of both her wrists and clamped them behind her back. They were chest to chest. He could smell lavender and Pears soap and see the lines of discontent around her mouth. He said, 'Listen. You're to talk to Albert. About me. You're to put this – this piece of gossip – right. Do you understand me?'

She was breathing quickly, almost panting. 'I understand what you are saying. Yes. But the – the *gossip* – is true. Isn't it?'

He missed the near-pleading in her voice and heard only the disgust. His resentment flared into a defiance that he *knew* was absolutely justified.

'What d'you expect? A monk?' He used a term that Leonie had coined. 'A Lukerian. Is that it?' He laughed. 'You know – of all people – you know I'm not like that, March. Besides, Leonie Porterman is business. She has her husband in her pocket, and I need her husband. It's as simple as that.'

'That might have been true in the first place, but not now. You've no need . . . now. You're your own man now. You – you *like* her!' The tears had gone but her eyes were very bright.

He did not release her hands, but used his arms so that he was supporting her rather than imprisoning her. He whispered, 'You went to Edwin Tomms from necessity at first, March. But later . . . you told me . . . it was different.'

She said nothing and there was a long pause while

they gauged each other's breathing and being. Then his head came down to hers and she did not move away. The next moment the door opened hard against Fred's back; he jolted March two steps backwards and into the table. The teapot, balanced precariously on the edge of the tray, fell to the floor and smashed. March freed her hands, twisted, saw it, gave a sound between a moan and a scream and swung back to hit Fred hard on his left ear.

Aunt Sylv came in.

She surveyed them calmly, her lizard eyes un-condemning.

'You two up to your shenanigans again, are you?' she asked. 'I'll clear that mess up and leave you to it.'

Fred gave her a look of dislike, turned and left the kitchen. March said furiously, 'You always have to *interfere*!' and began to hurl broken china into a bucket. She remembered dissipating her temper in this very kitchen over thirty years ago by banging her head against the table leg. But her brother Albert, who had been the cause of it then, had understood and had not left her to erupt alone.

By the time she went into the hall, Fred had left. She went into her father's workroom and watched him through the letters in the frosted glass. He ploughed through the snow; over to number seventeen. He was not wearing a hat or a coat. She put her forehead against the cold glass and let the tears come.

It was bedtime; the party was over. May stood behind her mother's chair and brushed the long greyish hair over one hand, gathering it and returning it to the brush with a slow soothing rhythm. Florence closed her eyes. Will was seeing a man about a dog, Victor was in bed, Sylvia was reading the *Citizen* aloud to Gran. It was a time of complete peace.

May said, 'I suppose Fred would have given Monty a job. But that sordid business with Captain Porterman and his wife . . . Monty hates anything like that.'

'Of course darling. Monty is so open and honest.'

'But if Tollie really will need an assistant soon, that will be ideal. Bridget says he never has a spare minute. Although – ' May giggled naughtily ' – he must have some time with her by the look of things.'

'Really . . . May,' Florence protested weakly.

'Yes. Sorry Mamma. Anyway I don't think Monty could possibly have any objection to being Tollie's assistant. Do you?'

'Will it mean a financial loss to him, dear?'

'Not really. The salary is wretched of course, but Monty doesn't have many engagements now. We shall save a lot of money by living in Gloucester.'

Florence was watching herself in the mirror as her favourite daughter expounded more plans. There she was, looking dishevelled with her hair down, and there was darling May, frowning slightly, brushing and combing and brushing and talking and not realizing that her mother had gone away from the small vignette and was watching it from elsewhere. And as Florence watched, so she saw the tiny hiccup that jarred the mirror-image, then the froth of redness at the lips. She saw May drop the brush and scream and reach for something – a pillow-case – then the picture tipped back as if the mirror was falling over, and it was gone.

May sobbed, 'Mother – Mamma – my little Mamma please, please come back.' Florence had collapsed like a broken doll and May lifted her bodily and put her on the bed. Blood flowed from her mouth and gurgling sounds came from the nose. She wasn't dead.

Sobbing, May ran to the landing. 'Aunt *Sylv*!'

Sylv appeared from the wing room and broke into a lumbering trot. Halfway along the landing another door opened and Victor appeared. 'Mummy?' he said on a panic upward inflection.

'Get back to bed!' she screamed. 'Go on, I'll come in a minute!' She pushed Sylvia ahead of her into the front bedroom and watched as the big hands turned Florence on to her side. The blood flowed faster still.

Sylv panted, 'It's got to come away, she'll choke on it else. Christamighty 'ow 'ave she got so much!' She mopped desperately. 'Water – wring this out in the basin. Oh Christ . . . Jesus Christ . . . come and 'elp us now.'

May was crying loudly and despairingly. Gran appeared in the doorway. 'Go and fetch Lottie,' she rapped out, moving to the bed and supporting the limp body with her ancient one. 'Go on. Then see to your boy. He's near histry-errics.'

May ran as she was, home-made felt slippers and all, straight into the Lamb and Flag and bundled Lottie out.

'Nuthin' I kin do about lung flux,' grumbled the old woman, her shawl flapping around her in the bitter January wind. 'Jest got to let it come away—'

'Come and see, Lottie – just come and see,' sobbed May.

But it was over when they got back upstairs, and Florence was coming out of her faint and looking at them in some surprise.

'Am I going to die?' she asked weakly when she saw Victor shivering by the door. 'I'm not frightened, but I would like Will to be here.'

Someone had made tea but she couldn't drink it. Sylv said doubtfully, 'I'll go and look for 'im, Flo, but I en't sure . . .'

Victor tugged at May's hand and whispered in her ear. She glanced at him sharply and took him on to the landing. He told her Will's exact whereabouts. She felt the last dregs of reality slipping away from her.

'How do you know?' she breathed.

'Albie and me. We followed Gramps one night. Sorry Mummy.'

It was the first time she had hit Victor. He crumpled where he stood, holding the side of his head but not whimpering, somehow understanding why she had to do it.

'Sorry Mummy,' he repeated.

'Get back to bed. Go on. Now. I'll come and see you later.'

'Are you going . . . there?'

'Never mind.'

'But are you? I know the way.'

'So do I. Go to bed.'

It was a long walk down the Bristol road to the swing bridge and the small lane alongside the canal, and it was made longer by the wet snow underfoot.

May was tempted to call for April, but April was Will's favourite child; she couldn't do that to him – or to her. Besides, Sibbie was her friend, which somehow made it her responsibility. She ploughed on, tears warming her frozen face. She should have known years ago.

No lights were on in the wooden bungalow. She hammered at the door, then kicked it. Even when the gas was lit in the room beyond she kept kicking and hammering and crying. When the door swung back and light framed Sibbie, she could hardly speak.

'Tell him . . . tell him . . . oh tell him his wife's dying and needs him! Tell him that – go on!'

She turned and ran back the way she had come, unheeding of Sibbie's shouts. But she was exhausted after her long tramp and Sibbie was fresh. She caught May up long before the bridge.

'Wait. Oh wait May, please. You don't understand – I tried to tell you that night! I tried, my love – my only love – but you were drunk and you didn't – couldn't – understand. It's you, May. It's always been you. Please believe – believe—'

May tried to brush her aside, but she stood her ground. She was barefoot, her nightdress scarcely decent. Already she was shivering uncontrollably. Will came blundering up.

'Godamighty our May, what's up? Is it your mother?' His concern was such that he forgot his own position. He had pulled galoshes on to his feet, his hair was on end.

'She coughed blood. Pints of it. Lottie says she'll be all right, but she wants you. Oh God . . . Pa . . .'

He was recalled to the present. 'I'll explain all this

later, May. Come on now, rally round, girl. We've got to get home quick.'

He scooped May away from Sibbie and sloshed them both down the lane. Sibbie stayed where she was, keening like Mrs Daker.

'May . . . May . . . don't leave me. It's you, May. You . . .'

'She's deranged,' Will said briefly. 'I've been trying to help her. Deranged.'

'Oh Pa . . .' May did not know what to think or say or feel. Poor Pa, poor Sibbie, poor May. Or was it wicked father, even more wicked Sibbie, and stupid, silly May? And what about Sibbie's arms around her neck, Sibbie's bare feet blue in the snow, her body all too obvious in the satin nightie pressed to May's coat?

Will said, 'Forget all that. Tell me about Flo. Is she really going to be all right? I can't live without her, May. You know that. None of us can live without her.'

May nodded. That was true at any rate. That was real.

But again Florence rallied. White and shaken, she took to her bed once more and lay looking at the map of Norway on her ceiling and eating her raw liver. Dr Green had a quiet word with March and suggested perhaps she could take her mother to Spain or Italy. Terrified, yet fascinated, March began to make tentative plans. April would look after Albie for her. It could be arranged.

But March had planned – years ago – to take another dear invalid abroad to recuperate, and her plans had come to nothing. And March had been born under an unlucky star.

Chapter Twelve

As soon as Florence took to sitting in her chair, May flew back to Monty. It was the sort of half-and-half life she had been leading for the past four years while she paved the way towards Monty changing his life-style, but before the discovery of Will's perfidy she would have used Florence's illness as an excuse to make a protracted stay in Gloucester. Now she couldn't wait to get away from everything she held dear. Even in far-off Harrogate, surrounded by people she did not like very much, she could not throw off the horror of that night. She would sit by herself gazing out of the window in their rented rooms and shuddering convulsively.

Amazingly, Monty was not in the least surprised.

'Your father had to have an . . . outlet,' he said uncomfortably. Something made him explain this to May; she needed to know that men had to have that something. 'I know Florence is a wonderful woman, May, but you must realize they haven't slept together for years.'

'It's horrible. Horrible.'

Monty flushed. 'I'm sorry you think so.'

'I don't mean *that*. I mean Sibbie.'

'But you knew about Sibbie already, May. We've

talked about it before. Everyone in Gloucester knows about Sibbie.'

'Yes, yes of course. But with my *father*. She's my best friend—'

'She was your best friend, darling. Twenty years ago.'

'But underneath . . . oh, you don't understand.'

She didn't understand herself. Could it be that she was jealous of her own father? Victor, precocious child that he was, had to air his views with the same brand of innocence as his mother used to have.

'When I saw her through the window with Gramps, she looked like Marlene Dietrich. And that's enough to give anyone the shudders!'

May drew in her lips, hating the thought of Victor spying and seeing – what? But Monty fed his precocity as usual by roaring with laughter and swinging mock punches at his son's shoulders. The next minute they were all over the furniture and the landlady's aspidistra was on the floor. May was glad about their male rapport in one way. In another, it excluded her. She shuddered again. She needed someone. She needed . . . Sibbie.

April and March sat in the beautiful sitting-room at Bedford Close, admiring the first daffodils in the garden and discussing the proposed trip to Nice, which was as far south as they thought Florence could stand. Albert, true to his promise to 'keep an eye' on Davina, had taken her upstairs to his private domain to watch his train and locomotives making their complicated circuit. May was sitting by an open window of very second-class theatrical diggings in Harrogate, watching Monty and Victor play cricket in a small back yard. She would smile and clap and then return to the letter in her lap which was from Bridget Hall, née Williams.

For most of the letter Bridget described her latest pregnancy symptoms; her third baby was due any day now; but in the final paragraph she said that if Monty would like to write a formal letter of application to her father, a place might be found for him in the firm. 'Tollie badly needs some help with the rare books and Monty has a certain air about him. Get him to quote a bit of Shakespeare in the letter, Daddy loves Shakespeare. And he loves the Risings too and Monty is a Rising really, isn't he.' May smiled at that but decided not to show it to Monty, he wouldn't like it at all.

Outside another run was clocked up and she clapped obediently. She wondered how she could 'get' Monty to write a letter to Edward Williams, the idea of him being an assistant to Tollie had been all hers. And in any case did she particularly want to go back to Gloucester now? Knowing what she knew, it would be difficult, if not impossible. Suddenly she crumpled Bridget's letter and threw it in the empty coal bucket, leaned out of the window and called, 'Shall I score? You're doing so well . . .'

At number thirty-three Chichester Street, Kitty Hall was telling Florence that Bridget had in fact gone into the nursing home in the early hours of the morning.

Florence smiled rather anxiously and Aunt Sylv got her ponderous weight out of the chair and went to put the kettle on. It was one of Will's business days and the women prepared to relax and discuss the younger generation.

Edward Williams heard of the arrival of his third granddaughter at midday. He was not permitted to visit her at the exclusive nursing home in Brunswick Square, his wife could not bear to discuss any aspect of Bridget's unexpected fecundity, and Tollie was at home supervising Olga and Natasha. So Edward took his news down to Bristol Road to share with Sibbie.

'Edward! It's not your day. Is something wrong with Bridie? '

'Nothing. Another girl. I had to come and tell you.' He slammed the door of his car. 'I won't stay long darling. I had to tell someone. Can't I even have a cup of tea?'

'Oh Edward, of course. Come in. Is everything all right? Mother and baby?'

'Fine. She produces 'em like rabbits.' He was proud of that, Alice had been horrified by the whole business. 'Three in just under four years. Not bad, eh?'

Sibbie laughed as she fetched cups and saucers. She liked Edward Williams very much. She remembered how distasteful the seduction of his father had been; this was surely her just reward.

She said, 'Florence Rising had three in three years. Then there was only eight months between April and Teddy.'

'Impossible, darling.'

'Teddy was three months premature. She nearly died.'

'She was always delicate. Bridie is as strong as a horse.'

'It's Tollie who is the surprising one.' Sibbie poured tea, thoroughly enjoying herself.

Edward felt the same; he laughed. 'I reckon it's his way of getting out of the tea dances and the tennis parties and Bridie's silly flirts. Not that they meant anything.' He turned his mouth down. 'Poor baby, she did enjoy a little fling. Not much of that for her these days.'

'She loves it,' Sibbie said sagely. 'She's got a lot of me in her. She likes people to know that she's wanted. And a string of babies is one way of letting them know.'

They were both laughing uproariously at this remark when Will arrived. He had recognized the car as he came over the swing bridge and his alarm had had time to build into anger. He swung open the door with a deafening crash and made his entry like one of Monty's avenging stage heroes.

Sibbie did her best at first, though her heart wasn't in it.

'I think you know Councillor Williams?' She shot warning glances at Will, demanding his co-operation. 'He is just leaving—'

'How long has he been here, that's what I want to know!' Will said truculently. 'Like father like son, eh? I suppose you think you can buy your way into Miss Luker's good books just like he did before you! Is that it? Is that why you come sneaking around here behind my back making a damned nuisance of yourself!'

Edward, aware of the position, mumbled something and picked up his hat.

'Oh no you don't, my fine buck!' Will got between him and the door and adopted a crouching stance. 'You don't leave here just like that. Scot free. Oh no.'

Sibbie abandoned her good intentions. Ever since last January when May had caught them together, her feelings for Will had changed. She was bored with him at last.

'For goodness' sake Will, stop being so ridiculous! Edward and I have been having a cup of tea. Can't you see that!'

'Oh. So it's Edward, is it?' Will crouched lower than ever but now it looked as though he was cowering. 'Edward. Edward and Sibbie. And what else I wonder!'

'You should know, Will,' Sibbie said laconically.

He looked as though she had struck him physically. 'Sibbie!' he protested, his face twisted.

'Look here old man, I think I'll go, and let you discuss this with Sibbie.' Edward tried to touch one of the raised arms reassuringly. It came up automatically and hit him. Will gazed down at the result of his involuntary movement with surprise and horror.

Sibbie's self-control snapped.

'What the *hell* d'you think you're playing at, Will Rising?' She knelt by Edward and dabbed at his bloody nose. 'How dare you come in here – you're the usurper after all! This is my house and I have the deeds to prove it. And this gentleman is *my* caller – I suppose I have a right to have callers?'

'No!' shouted Will. 'Not the sort of caller he is!' He leaned against the back of a chair. His face was mottled. 'You know very well you belong to me, Sibbie! Ever since I rescued you from David Daker you have belonged to me!'

She was furious. 'I belong to no-one, Will,' she said, her voice shaking with sincerity. 'Only myself. You did not rescue me from David. I chose to come with you. I picked you. Don't you understand that after all these years? I have picked other men too when I have felt like it!'

Will sagged, his short legs buckling. His eyes became bulbous.

'And you picked . . . *him*?'

She held Edward close. 'He is different,' she said proudly. 'He is quite different from the rest of you. He has asked me to marry him.'

Will tried to laugh, but bile rose into his mouth. 'How can he marry you? He's got a wife already.'

Edward stood up. 'I'm getting a divorce. I love Sibbie. It's true we'll be married one day.'

Will looked from one to the other. The blood beat in his head. He had thought he would lose Florence and she had been saved for him. Now he knew that it had been an exchange: Florence for Sibbie. He was going to lose Sibbie.

She said calmly, 'It's true, Will. I love Edward. We are going to be married.'

The bile filled Will's mouth and made it impossible for him to reply. Something was pressing behind his eyes, trying to force them out of his head; his collar choked him. He tore at it with one hand, hearing his own breathing as a loud snore in the quiet room. Then he collapsed.

Aunt Sylv opened the door because Florence was arranging the first of the gypsies' daffodils in the dining-room. They called every April, their baskets bursting with the yellow trumpets, their greasy hair gleaming in the pale sunshine as they whined, 'First o' the Newent daffs, lady. Buy some for luck.' Sylv would have turned them away with short shrift, but Florence always liked to fill the house with daffodils.

So it was that when Edward Williams brought Will's body home, the house was filled with the scent of his favourite flower. He had likened April to a daffodil, he had gathered them around his home at Kempley, he was laid in the dining-room among them.

Edward Williams tried to explain and condole at the same time.

Florence, her Rhys-Davies heritage strong in her thin face, stopped him.

'Sibbie, did you say? Little Sibbie Luker?' She seemed to forget that Sibbie was the town's scarlet woman. She looked into Edward's embarrassed face and nodded. 'Hettie always made him happy too. Sibbie's mother. Perhaps it's a gift they have.'

'Mrs Rising, let me fetch your daughter – please—'

'Not yet. Let his mother be with him. And Lottie – fetch Lottie for me, would you? They will lay him out together. Then the girls can see him. And then he and I will be alone together.'

There seemed to be no sign of shock; it was almost as if she was thankful for what had happened. Gran exhibited the emotions Edward had expected, screams and wails and angry accusations against the absent Sibbie. Florence polished the dining-room table and laid blankets on it; then she banked the daffodils along window-ledge and mantelpiece.

Lottie arrived post haste, her eyes snapping; but then, as she looked at the stolid face of her old drinking partner, the wickedness went out of her. She put her knotty forefinger on Will's beard. 'Poor Will Rising. Poor daft Will Rising,' she said.

Florence paused at the door. 'He was rich, Lottie. Rich in love, rich in kindness, rich in joy. Nothing will be the same without him.'

She went to sit in her husband's workroom until the sheer busy-ness of the event should subside. April and March came to her there, tight with anxiety, and she calmed them. There was tea to be made with tea from the caddy emblazoned with the old King's likeness . . . or was it Will's likeness? They had always been so similar. There was bread and butter to be cut, the butter patted and stamped with Mr Goodrich's acorn stamp. There was a telegram to be sent to poor darling May. And there were the undertakers to call.

David and Mrs Daker arrived, then Alf Luker with messages from Hetty and Glad and Fred and Henry; then Kitty Hall. Beds were made up for the visitors the next day: Aunty Vi would come of course to pay her respects to her brother, and May and Victor should arrive by evening. Florence gave instructions in a low voice that did not tremble. When the girls said they would stay with her that night, she shook her head at first, then gave a small smile.

'Let it be April then. His daffodil girl.'

So April stayed.

She tried to persuade her mother to come to bed and Florence nodded. 'Perhaps later. You go on darling and make me a warm place. I must be with your father on my own for a little while. Don't worry about me. Not when I'm with him.'

About midnight April crept down the stairs and stood outside the dining-room door. She heard Florence's quiet voice talking . . . talking. After a while April went on down the passage to the kitchen where Aunt Sylv kept vigil, the kettle simmering hopefully on a bead of gas.

'She bin talking to him like that ever since she went in there at eleven,' Aunt Sylv said heavily. 'Talking and talking. As if she'd got to catch up on all the things she never said before.'

'Oh Aunty Sylv, what will happen to her?'

Sylvia came and put her muscular arm across April's shoulders as she sat at the table.

'"Tis better she be left than him. Much better. He couldn't 'a done nothing without her.'

'Why? It seems he had someone else anyway!' April couldn't keep the bitterness out of her voice. Sibbie Luker of all people, the reason why David had been ostracized so long ago.

Aunt Sylv massaged her niece's top vertebrae. 'That was 'ow he were, April love. He wanted the moon, but his feet stayed in the cow shit.'

April wept.

'Ah, don't cry, littl'un. He was happy – only in the war when he lost his boys was he ever unhappy. He

335

hardly knew what it was to be miserable. But he couldna done without his Florence. He'd have sunk right into the cow shit . . . hated himself. 'Twouldn't 'ave done, April.'

And in the dining-room Florence whispered, 'Wonderful memories, Will. Don't think I will ever forget them, my darling. We'll share them again very soon . . . so soon. D'you remember when I came to Kempley to get away from the smallpox in Gloucester? You called me a princess, Will. And you made me laugh. My life had been so drab until then, darling. You brought me light and colour and joy. How did you do it, Will, without any money . . . none of the things others consider important? It was in you like a light, wasn't it, dearest? You gave it to Teddy and I thought my heart would break when he went, then I knew I still had it in you. April's got it too, hasn't she? Thank you for sharing it with me, Will. Thank you.'

And in the little house on the canal bank, Sibbie wept into Edward Williams' shoulder.

'I never meant that to happen, Edward. He was always so good – to me and we laughed together . . . I never meant to . . .'

Fred Luker sat with his sister Sibbie in the darkest corner of Saint John's. In front of them in the coloured light coming through the sooty windows, people rustled and whispered discreetly. Will Rising had been a well-known figure in Gloucester, and his funeral turn-out was very respectable indeed. The *Citizen* reporter lingered at the door and people spelled their names carefully for him.

336

Fred glanced at Sibbie in the gloom. She looked like a drowned rat without make-up and in unbecoming black. He hadn't realized she thought so much of the old boy, and if she really was hoping to marry Edward Williams it was just as well he was out of the way, surely. But Sibbie was mourning her childhood which had gone for ever with Will Rising.

Fred wondered whether Will's death would affect him more personally. Would March give up her big house which meant so much to her and return to live with her mother? Or would that honour fall on May? It wouldn't make much difference either way, he could not keep a personal eye on his son wherever she was. Unless he married her.

And if Will's sudden absence did precipitate a marriage between Sibbie and Edward Williams, what then? Certainly his contracts would disappear. Anything supported by Edward would suffer with his disgrace, that was certain. Could he stand alone yet? He had the gravel pits on a bank overdraft, granted because of Edward Williams' contracts and Marcus Porterman's backing. He needed capital. He remembered Leonie's old and oft repeated joke about Marcus being willing to pay him to keep away from her. How serious was that? And how much could he be pushed to? Without Leonie, he would obviously be without Porterman himself. And Porterman gave the firm a shred of respectability as well as reliability. So he would have to replace Porterman.

He left that thread of a thought hanging in the gloom and thought about his private life. He had a private life . . . a little too private. He had a son and a daughter and no wife and no home. And the Risings had no male head any more. With her father gone and Leonie quite definitely out of the picture, could he batter down March's stubborn pride at last? That thread connected with the previous one and became the perfect solution. March had respectability and money; as far as business went it was the perfect union. She was the mother of his son. And he wanted her . . . he loved her . . . He gnawed his under-lip and glanced at Sibbie again, feeling suddenly that the long, long period of waiting was coming to an end.

Sibbie snuffled up at him, then caught his arm as there was a rustling entrance at the door. The *Citizen* reporter slid into a pew.

'I am the Resurrection and the Life, saith the Lord. Whosoever believeth in me shall not perish . . .'

The white blob of the cleric and the shining rosewood of the coffin appeared, then the mourners. Florence, Sylvia one side of her, Violet the other. Gran would be at home cutting sandwiches with Fred's own mother. March came next, the eldest surviving child, supported by her tall son – by their tall son. Then came Monty, taking all May's considerable weight. Then April, walking erect and slightly away from David so as not to put pressure on his gammy leg. Her chin was tilted as Will's had so often been, she looked very tall and thin in a straight black coat and skirt with her black cloche hiding every strand of hair. But on her lapel and at her waist and in her hand, were daffodils. The violent splash of colour in the grim old church was shocking. People turned their heads to look, and as they did, so she smiled. It occurred to Fred suddenly that if he married March, April would be his sister-in-law. She couldn't very well avoid him then.

The whole family sidled into pews and the pall-bearers placed the coffin. Will's favourite hymn was sung: 'Now the day is ended.' Clear and true, May's soprano led the singing. Beneath it was April's steady voice, and underneath that again could be heard March's. He was proud of them. Dammit, he was proud of all of them. He wanted to belong to their clan.

Beside him Sibbie began to sob. Fred lowered his head and felt tears rush to his eyes.

The hearse was drawn by horses as Will would have wished. Their black plumes nodded ahead of the more mundane cars, and people stood still on the pavement with bowed heads. To the Cross they went, and then down the length of Eastgate and over the level crossing to the Barton. So they came to the cemetery, edged with tall poplars like soldiers. Will was laid to rest quite near his youngest son, Teddy, but this time it did not rain as it had done at Teddy's funeral, and the spring sunshine sparkled everywhere as if Will was laughing. When the earth hit the coffin and the cry went up 'Dust to dust', Sibbie lifted her tear-stained face and met May's eyes across the chasm of the grave. Tentatively, tremblingly, May smiled. She could come back home now; the obstacle to her return to Gloucester had gone.

So March was baulked of the trip with her mother. Not only that, but Florence had chosen April to stay with her that first awful night. March clenched her hands and thought of her father with Sibbie Luker. It was just one more thing to keep the Lukers away from the Risings. Her mother might forgive; March never could.

She watched the earth cast on her father's coffin and the future stretched ahead of her, lonely and sterile. May would come home permanently probably, and live in Chichester Street; and Monty would get a job somewhere and he and Victor and May would be spoiled and pampered by Florence and Gran and Aunty Sylv. Like the prodigal daughter. No-one would realize that she, March, had lost her father twice over and her lover . . . countless times. She shivered and looked sideways at her son who was so like her dead, beloved brother. She still had him, she still had darling Albie. He had set his face in a model of David Daker's, eyes narrowed, jaw line grim; but at such close quarters she could see his mouth was shaking. She leaned towards him and took his hand; he was the one good thing to come out of her life. She could not regret him. She thought back to the terror and loneliness of her pregnancy and what it had meant: the marriage to Edwin, the ensuing degradation when Fred had come home and told Edwin the sordid truth. No . . . she could not regret any of it when she looked at Albert.

He turned his head and met her eyes, and the next minute his head was on her shoulder and he was shaking with silent sobs for the grandfather who had so ably taken the place of a father for him. March held him to her, and at last wept her own difficult tears.

Chapter Thirteen

The interview with Captain Marcus Porterman was cold and businesslike on Fred's side, stammering and outraged on his.

'I've told her I'd pay you a sum to keep away certainly! But – but – dammit all man, a chap says things in the heat of the moment—'

'How much are you willing to pay me, old man?' Fred remembered the condescension of this man at their first meeting; he spared him nothing. 'It'll have to be pretty good because although I can guarantee my absence, I shall have a helluva job to fend her off.'

'You insulting swine! Lee might have enjoyed slumming it for a while but I can assure you once she knows you've said these things she'll have finished with you for good and all! I shan't need to pay you a penny!'

'All right. Try it, Marcus old chap. If you think I have to make any running with your wife, you must be more of a fool than I thought.'

The wrangling went on for the best part of the morning after Will Rising's funeral. At the end of it Fred was richer by ten thousand guineas.

'I want a signed paper,' he said abruptly when he took the cheque. 'Stating that on this day I swore to have nothing more to do with Leonie Porterman—'

'*You* want a signed paper! My God, Luker, you've

got some gall. If you think I'm signing anything—'

'I shall sign it,' Fred said calmly. 'I want your signature as a witness. It's to your advantage after all. It will hold good in a court of law.'

He produced a document already prepared in his own handwriting and Marcus Porterman read it through, breathing heavily.

'Dammit. This says that neither of you must see each other. I thought you were going to take the responsibility for . . . fending her off, as you so elegantly put it.'

'This is it. This is a receipt for the ten thousand and an insurance policy for you. Don't you see?'

Porterman shook his head with a bewildered kind of cunning. 'Wouldn't look too good for you if this became public, certainly.' He scribbled his name under Fred's. Fred took it, folded it with the cheque and put them both into an inside pocket.

'Nor Leonie of course.' He smiled. 'And as you are Leonie's legal guardian, Marcus old man, you are responsible now for keeping her off my back. I suggest a world cruise.'

Porterman stared and began to splutter. 'I could have done that anyway without paying you ten thousand.'

Fred shrugged. 'Maybe. I wouldn't count on it. The shock of knowing that we've made this bargain behind her back might get Leonie on board a boat. But do it quickly, Marcus, for God's sake. Because once she's had time to think it all out, she won't like it one bit. She'll want to stay around to ruin the two of us, and she's brighter than you think.'

There was more spluttering, some vague threats, but eventually Captain Porterman left. Fred followed him soon after and kept an appointment with his bank manager. He explained the cheque briefly.

'Captain Porterman has to leave the firm rather quickly. His wife's health. This is a kind of compensation for loss of his support . . .'

Fred recalled March's expression as she stood at the graveside only yesterday. He knew her thoughts as if they were his own and he cursed Sibbie frequently, though without anger. There would always be something to come between him and March; they had started off on the wrong foot when they were just children. Leonie . . . Sibbie . . Albert-Frederick . . . it amounted to stubborn pride. He wondered how long to wait before he made his frontal attack on her. Because that was what it would have to be; the only way now to win March.

If Florence realized that Will's death had finally revealed his long betrayal to the world of Gloucester, she did not show it. She made his workroom into a small front parlour; the smoked glass panel with his name engraved into it came out of the window and was made into an elegant firescreen. It was replaced by clear glass which she refused to shroud with lace curtains or an aspidistra. That summer she sat in the open window most afternoons with her sewing or knitting, and the neighbours would come over and pass the time of day and ask how she was getting on.

'I miss my husband,' she always said frankly. 'But he's not far away.' And when they left her they said quietly, 'Won't be long before she joins him . . . she was older than him, wasn't she?'

May and Victor did not go back to Harrogate after the funeral, and Monty joined them when he had collected their things. Florence insisted they should have the dining-room for their own, and she moved out of the big front bedroom at last and took Will's smaller room. It seemed the ideal arrangement. Monty left the house at ten to nine each morning and returned at six each evening. May had got what she wanted. She wasn't quite her old self of course; she had lost her father after all, but she was still a devoted daughter to her mother. She saw that Florence ate her mandatory raw liver; she concocted a shopping list with her; she made sure that the three grandchildren visited regularly. There was no way she could ever resume her friendship with Sibbie now, but she could pretend she didn't care about that. She and April and March and Florence presented a united front to the world. Sibbie was never mentioned; she might never have existed. The few titters died away and the integrity of the Rising family was stronger than it had ever been; stronger than when Will himself had led it.

Fred entered the house in Bedford Close very quietly. March was giving one of her rare tennis parties and the garden milled with white frocks and flannels. It was breathlessly hot and had been for a week; a thunderstorm was overdue to clear the air. The front door stood open and he could see right through the large sitting-room to the open french doors. April was there, pushing her hair up at the back to cool her neck, her legs bare and bronzed after this scorching summer. March, head bound about with a ribbon like a Greek goddess, was moving around, pushing some kind of trolley; he could hear the clink of ice; her latest acquisition was a refrigerator. May, frankly fat without a corset, lay in the hammock laughing at Victor and Albie on court. Tollie was there, and Monty, and there were other children he didn't recognize.

He edged along the hall until he came to the staircase. He planned to wait in March's room until this beanfeast was over and she came to bed. Surprise tactics, a showdown. He took the stairs very carefully and slowly, two at a time, loosening his tie as he went. It was hotter still up here. He made for the front of the house and was then baulked. It was obviously March's room, overlooking Bedford Close itself, but it was in use as a cloakroom, the bed piled high with scarves and bags of all descriptions. It was also doubling as a nursery. In a cradle near the window lay Bridget Hall's latest, Beatrice, after Beatrice Webb.

Fred cursed and went to another door. Thank God it was empty and was evidently Albie's room. There was that bloody steam engine he'd mended once, and bits of what looked like a motor cycle on the bed. March would certainly create about that unless Albie got rid of it before she saw it.

From below came April's voice, suddenly raised. He went to the door and listened.

'Bridie, are you sure you're all right?'

Then Bridget Hall: 'Of course I'm not all right April! I'm going to be sick, how can I be all right if I'm going to be sick?'

There were two sets of footfalls on the stair carpet and the bathroom door crashed open. There were awful glugging sounds. April's voice said soothingly, 'There, there darling . . . poor old Bridie . . . it's too soon, much too soon.' Bridget's voice gasped, 'Tell that to Tollie, not me!'

Fred turned back into the room in disgust. Surely she wasn't pregnant again? They were like a pair of rabbits, she and her Tollie.

He waited, sitting on Albie's bed, hands dangling between his knees. An hour passed leadenly. He got up and went into the bathroom himself, then wandered into a room at the back of the house from where he could see the tennis court. They were beginning to pack up. He watched them through the muslin curtains, sharply critical. May could take some tips from Sibbie on how to keep her figure; Monty was just a suit of clothes, and Tollie Hall was . . . what was Tollie Hall? A meek good small boy, always careful of his mother; but what now?

He realized they would be fetching their clothes from March's room and retired again to Albie's bed, wondering what the hell he would say if the boy came in. People seemed to be marching interminably up and down the landing. Then April's voice sang out, 'I'll just collect Davie,' and Albie's door opened and she came in.

'It's all right – all right—' He stood up and held out his hand. 'Don't say anything. Please April.'

Her colour drained away, confirming for him that she was frightened of him. He felt the old resentment against the Risings return; what would she say –

or even do – if he succeeded in marrying her sister?

She said through stiff lips, 'Where is Davie? Albie and Davie, where are they?'

He looked at her incredulously. 'You don't think I've harmed either of them, do you? Hell's teeth April, what goes on in that mind of yours?'

'I . . . nothing. Where *are* they? They were coming up here—'

'For Christ's sake April! I don't know where they are. I've been here for . . . I've been here for some time. Haven't seen them.'

'Then why are you here?'

'I want to see March. Surprise her.'

'Oh.' Her shoulders dropped in relief. She pushed her hair back off her forehead; it was dark with sweat. 'I'll tell her.'

'I said I want to surprise her, April. Look, shut the door a second, will you? Someone's going to come barging in and the whole idea is to catch her off-guard.'

She turned and pushed the door to automatically, then faced him again, still suspicious. 'Why?'

He took a breath. 'I'm going to ask her to marry me.'

She was surprised out of her defensive attitude at last. 'She won't do it, Fred. Four years ago perhaps, after Edwin's death . . .'

'I asked her then. There was something in the way. I've cleared that up now.'

A faint flush showed in her neck. 'She won't do it, Fred. You don't understand March.'

'I understand only too well. Sibbie.' He shook his

head. 'Listen April. March and I have had an . . . understanding . . . for years now. There's always something that holds us back. Now March is on her own and she's not happy – yes, I know that too. I've got to convince her that she should forget Sibbie's existence and marry me. I can do it.'

A smile appeared in April's wary eyes. 'I think you might, Fred. I think . . . it would be wonderful if you could. Wonderful for March.'

He said deliberately, 'What about you, April? How would you feel? It would be much more difficult to treat me like a leper if I were your brother-in-law.'

The flush deepened. 'Fred . . . I know. I'm sorry. That time we talked, when I was still pregnant, at Hucclecote church – d'you remember?'

'Of course I remember. The big brush-off.'

Her eyes darkened. 'There was no other way, Fred. I couldn't . . . divide my loyalties. And over the years I knew you were trying to see Davie. When she was with Mother or Dad, you always seemed to bump into them. Then last winter, at her birthday party . . . and today . . .'

'I shall see more of her if I am married to your sister.'

'But then you will *be* my brother, don't you see? And if you are married to March you won't ever be tempted to . . . ' She trailed off, meeting the real pain in his face.

He said slowly, 'You haven't trusted me then, April?'

'Fred . . . please try to understand. If it had been just my life – but it was David's. And Davie's. And there

348

was talk about your – your business methods. Fred, I'm sorry.'

He drew in a breath and let it go. Then he spoke in measured tones. 'April. Whether March agrees to marry me or not, Davina belongs to you and David. Understand that, once and for all. I shall always love her . . . be interested in her . . . help her if I'm asked. I can't help that. But she does not belong to me.'

There was a long silence. April's flush died away and her darkened eyes cleared to sky-blue. At last she said, 'You make me feel pretty humble, Fred. I won't apologize any more. But . . . oh Fred, I wish you luck. I really do wish you luck.' She came close and her lips touched his cheek. And then she left.

Eventually so did everyone else. He moved at last, opened the door and went down the landing to March's room. All the clothes had gone. He looked through the window: March and Albie were waving at the gate. He wrinkled his nose at the stink of face powder and stripped off his jacket and shirt before collapsing on the bed.

David said, 'Well, my beautiful women. Did you have a nice afternoon? Who won?'

'Mummy won. And Albie's new siding goes unnerneaf the floor and comes up by the window and there's a buffer stop right *there*!' Davina's voice crescendoed with amazement and delight at such ingenuity; David laughed, picked her up and kissed her.

'In other words you watched ten minutes of tennis, then you and Albie played trains for the rest of the afternoon. You're as bad as he is for mechanical contraptions. I don't know where you get it from!'

April looked at him quickly, then remembered her special news and relaxed. 'I know where she gets her antisocial streak from, David Daker!' She encircled them both with her arms. 'Although you're not any more, are you? Oh darlings, what a marvellous pair you are! David and Davina. My family.'

Davina gurgled and ruffled her mother's hair and David tried to look at her properly and could not.

'What's happened? Something nice, I can tell.'

'Tell you later.' April kicked off her shoes and going towards the kitchen sang out over her shoulder, 'Put Davie in the bath would you darling? Then I'll have one and we'll have supper and go to bed.'

'It's six o'clock!' David sat his daughter astride his shoulders and followed April. 'Aren't you well?'

'Never better. I want you to come to bed too.'

He stood in the kitchen doorway, absently unbuckling Davie's sandals which were right beneath his nose. 'Tollie's coming round. There was a library auctioned – Harkworth Hall I think – and he found a first edition of Mary Wolstenholme.'

'How interesting,' April said without any interest at all. She rolled lettuce in a cloth and began to snip the tails from a bunch of radishes. 'I suppose we can spare him half an hour.'

'Generous of you,' David murmured, making it sound like a request for further information. April said nothing, and as Davie was now patting his head and calling 'Gee-up!' he went on into the bathroom.

In the event April postponed her bath and urged

Tollie to stay to supper. She felt a luxuriant freedom from the pressure of time; they had plenty, she and David. She went about getting the meal, clearing it, watching the two men enthusing about some book with the same half comprehending enjoyment she had felt before Davie's birth, when the big living-room of the flat had always been full of people. She knew that somehow this afternoon she had been released from a bondage but she did not – dared not – investigate this knowledge too deeply in case it proved false. Rightly or wrongly she had been bound to Fred; now she was not. It was absurd because if Fred's suit with March was successful she would be doubly bound to him, through Davie's blood and through March's marriage contract. Yet it wasn't so. By revealing his lifelong feeling for March it was as if he had turned his back on April and Davie, indeed his solemn words had confirmed that.

April washed up at the shallow yellow sink, promising herself as usual that she would clean the mottled brass tap tomorrow, then she grinned exuberantly and fetched the Brasso from the cleaning cupboard. From the living-room Tollie's serious voice was interrupted by one of David's explosive laughs that held none of the old cynicism. April sawed away with the Brasso rag and let her grin widen. David was getting younger, not older; he was just about her own age now.

That night she danced for him as she had done long before Davie's birth. With the age-old allure of Salome, she let her tennis skirt drop to the floor and twirled around the bed as she divested herself of her blouse and brassière. David could hardly believe it.

'What has happened? Something has happened.'

He watched her from the bed, half-amused, half-anxious at such a sudden reversion.

She paused, pointed one long elegant leg and looked down its length. 'I often used to dance for you. Don't you remember?'

'Of course I remember. But you're a mother now. And I'm a father.'

He wanted to lean forward and pull her to him and cover her with kisses, but it wasn't possible that her reserve had vanished through a single day. He forced himself to lie there and smile at her.

She smiled brilliantly back at him. 'Yes, that's true.' She held on to the bed rail with one hand, raised the other high above her head and pretended to lift on to ballet points. 'I polished the tap tonight,' she said breathlessly. 'I haven't done it for years. It looks like solid gold.'

'Is that your news?'

She gurgled. 'No. My news is that Fred is going to ask March to marry him.' She left the foot of the bed and leaned over him. 'He's been in love with her since they were children and he thinks that at last it will be all right for them. What do you think, David?'

Her breasts hung pendulously before him. He cupped them with protective hands and said quietly, 'Darling. Everything has always been all right for us.'

'Of course. I didn't mean—'

'And you don't have to dance for me. You never have to prove anything for me, Primrose. I love you, just as you are.'

'Oh David . . . perhaps it's because of that – because it's always been all right for us, that I wanted to dance. To celebrate.'

'Do you mean that? Do you mean you are no longer worried or frightened for me?' He held her off, looking into her eager face. 'Can our love-making be a celebration each time? Whatever happens?'

He used the word in its religious sense and it stilled her too. She stared back at him, savouring the sound of it.

'Celebration . . . celebration. Oh David. That's what it is, isn't it?'

He saw that she was recognizing her own fear over the past few years and he pulled her to him quickly and kissed her face.

'It has nothing to do with dancing, Primrose,' he warned.

'Oh I'm glad . . . glad . . . because it can still happen when I'm an old, old lady and can no longer dance a step.'

He laughed against her mouth and felt her laughter bubble inside him. And for a long time into that hot summer night, they celebrated their marriage.

March went to turn down Albie's bed at nine o'clock that night and the first thing that met her eyes were the engine bits on his clean quilt. She was hot and tired, and though the tennis party had been a success the anti-climax of her aloneness was there as always after a social occasion.

She met Albie ambling along the landing in one of his dreams.

353

'*What is* all that stuff on your bed?' she demanded.

He blenched. He had forgotten the motor cycle parts in the joy of showing off his train set to April's small daughter.

'A boy gave them to me,' he prevaricated.

'A boy? What boy? Someone from Marley of course. Someone your precious Arnold Baxter encourages—'

Albie interrupted, hoping to divert her wrath. 'Mother, Arnold says I could easily be a first-rate mechanic. He lets me help him fix his car and—'

It nearly drove March mad. 'Do I pay those fees so that you can be the odd job man at that place?' She pointed a trembling finger. 'And I'm warning you, Albert, if Aunty May sends Victor back there next term, you'll leave. I mean it. I'm not having you two boys giggling and tittering over your silly jokes like you were before. At least *that* little partnership seems to have died a death, and I intend to keep it that way!'

'Mother please—'

'Don't argue. Get a box and clear that stuff off your bed and then get into it.'

Albie tried to win her round. 'Into the box?' he enquired.

'How dare you come the smart-alick with me Albert! Just do what you are told.' She followed him into the garage for the box, then back to the stairs. 'Just because you haven't got a father doesn't mean you can walk over me as if I'm a door mat! Just you remember that. And tomorrow you will put on your best suit and you'll take me to church and—' The bathroom door closed on her words. Not too noisily, but not softly either.

She gave up thoughts of a bath herself and decided to drag the tennis court. It was eleven o'clock by then but she knew she wouldn't sleep. She scraped some potatoes for tomorrow's dinner, then strung some kidney beans and cut her finger. It was almost the last straw. She stood in the kitchen, sucking the blood, wishing she could weep and feeling the pressure boil up inside her. And at last she went to bed.

Fred lay very still where he was. The big house had been wired for electric light the year before, but March did not switch on the light. She went to the open sash and stared out at the summer night. He could hear her breathing. After a while she began to undress where she was, letting her tennis dress fall to the floor and stepping out of it unheedingly.

Fred had of course heard everything and had been sorely tempted to intervene on behalf of Albert. But that would have meant a three-cornered row, and he wanted this settled between March and himself alone. Nevertheless his determination to change things increased as he lay motionless listening to her harangue. As a child Fred had had plenty of physical chastisement, but he had never been nagged. Hettie's favourite maxim was 'easy come, easy go' and this attitude had extended to every part of her family life. He had fallen asleep most nights to the sound of bouncing bed springs from his parents' room next door, and before he had realized exactly what they were doing, he had still smiled, knowing they were happy.

355

He wanted to marry March for all kinds of reasons, all selfish. Now he saw that apart from them he was actually needed here.

March's slip joined her tennis dress. She had already discarded pumps and stockings. She stood now in some sort of cotton chemise thing and knickers that looked like a tiny skirt. Leonie never bothered with underclothes, so Fred was not as familiar as he might have been with modern lingerie. March was still adequately covered; but it seemed that was as far as she was going. She stretched with a brittleness that was very far from relaxation, then forced a yawn. Then she turned.

Her eyes were accustomed to the darkness by now and she saw Fred immediately, though she did not recognize him. Her gasp held the seeds of a scream and he spoke to her conversationally.

'It's only me. Hope you don't mind, March. I called and you were busy and I thought I'd wait—'

She let fly. 'You blithering *idiot*! My heart nearly stopped!' She grabbed at a satin dressing-gown thing over a screen and held it against her. 'What did you think you were doing – and how dare you – on my bed – as if it were your own house or something – how long have you – get out before I call Albie!'

Fred swung his legs off the bed and replaced his braces. He went towards the door.

'Well at least tell me what you came for!' March expostulated contrarily. 'You can't just walk out without an explanation of any kind!'

Calmly Fred turned the key in the lock, removed it and put it in the pocket of his trousers.

'I don't intend to. In fact I don't intend to walk out of here until the morning.'

'You . . . what?'

'I think you heard me, Marcie. ' He snapped on the light and grinned as she dropped the covering gown and turned frantically to pull the curtains across the windows. He remembered Leonie's exhibitionism. From one extreme to the other. He pulled forward a basket chair and sat down in it. She surveyed him, incredulous, aghast, but at least blessedly silent.

He said, 'Sit down, Marcie. Pull up that other chair and sit down and let's talk like old friends. That's what we are, my dear. Old friends.'

She said, 'Don't be a fool, Fred. We've never been friends—'

'Lovers then. Lie on the bed and let's be old lovers.'

'Fred, if you've come here to insult—'

'Oh shut up Marcie. For God's sake shut up and sit down. I'm the father of that boy in there.' He jerked his head. 'Have you forgotten?'

'How could I?' She spoke from a deep well of bitterness. But she sat down all the same, though a long way from him.

He smiled at her. 'I told Edwin Tomms once that I'd raped you. But I never had to, did I Marcie? I never had to force you.'

'You told Edwin that? Why?'

'It made our . . . arrangement . . . more acceptable to him.' He stared at her. She was beginning to look old, but she would age well, like her mother. Dammit all he would be so proud of her, standing by his side when he . . . when he became mayor of Gloucester!

357

Yes, with March by his side he could do anything. He leaned forward and said softly, 'He didn't like the thought of you being in love with me, Marcie. So I told him I raped you.'

She looked startled. 'That's why he . . . perhaps that was why he left the will as it was.' She thought about it and shook her head. 'No. He would have changed it before then anyway. But . . . I'm glad you told him that.' She looked away. 'I didn't mean to hurt him.'

He said quickly, 'I didn't mean to hurt you, Marcie. I swear that. Can't you forgive me like Edwin Tomms evidently forgave you?'

She shook her head dismissively, 'The two cases are completely different, Fred. You can't get round me like that. I had Albie to think of.'

'The first time, yes. But when you went back to Bath five years ago, March . . . it was yourself you were considering then.'

She was furious again. 'You've got a short memory, Fred Luker! Have you forgotten already what drove me back to Bath just then? Wasn't it something connected with you?'

'You mean Leonie. All right, there was Leonie then. I needed her husband and the only way I could keep him was through her. It was a business arrangement, March—' she made an explosive sound of outraged disbelief and he shrugged, partly acknowledging that ' – anyway it's over now. Surely your sources of information have apprised you of that?'

'Don't lie any more, Fred. Please.'

'I'm not lying, Marcie. The day after your father's funeral I saw Marcus Porterman and told him to keep her off my neck. I believe they're going on a cruise this autumn.'

She stared at him. 'Then . . . you've lost Captain Porterman from the firm?'

'Of course.'

Her throat moved on a swallow. 'You – you took your time about it.'

'Yes. I'm sorry, Marcie. I had to establish myself.'

'And you've done that? You can still run the firm? Alone?'

'Yes.'

'It's just coincidental that you're here – just a few weeks later – asking me to marry you?'

He stood up, suddenly enraged with her. 'Good God, woman! Whatever I say – whatever I do – it's wrong with you! What do you want, March – just tell me that? Go on, tell me what you want me to do?'

She didn't move. She didn't even look at him any more. Her eyes stayed where they had been, wide and gazing into the past.

She said, 'It's all too late, Fred. Can't you see that? It's like trying to stir up a dead fire. I suppose I must have loved you to let you . . . yes, I must have loved you then. But I can't even remember. I'm sorry Fred, but I think I'd like you to go away and never try to see me again. You . . . all your family . . . you're an embarrassment to us.'

'Well you can forget that. I'm never going to leave Gloucester. It's my town more than it's yours. My business is here—'

'Then move to the outskirts. Buy a house at Churchdown, or – or Painswick, or somewhere. Take

Hettie and your father and – *all* of you! Just go! You've done enough damage—'

He took her arms and lifted her to her feet.

'Your father could have done much worse than Sibbie! He'd have had to have *someone*, March! Don't you see that? He was married to a nun and no man can take that!'

March's wide stare came back to the present and to Fred. Her face was paper-white.

'My mother is a saint! You know that as well as I do.'

'She is. Exactly. A saint.'

'Let me go, Fred. I can't bear this! You and I are poles apart now and it's hopeless to pretend otherwise. Just let me go.'

He held her closer still and spoke grimly into her ear.

'Listen Marcie. I said I'd never had to rape you. But I will now if there's no other way. I'm going to marry you, March Rising. One way or the other I'm going to marry you. There's always going to be something between us . . . first there was your brother, then Edwin Tomms. Then Leonie Porterman. Now you say my sister Sibbie is coming between us. I won't *let* anything else separate us, March. The only obstacle I can see at the moment, is you. So—'

He felt the panic tighten all her muscles and the next instant she had twisted free and was grabbing at the curtains to pull them back and shout for help. He caught her to him, swung her round and clamped his hand across her mouth. The curtain fitment came down with a clatter and pulled with them as he dragged her to the bed. He fell on top of her and held her down with the weight of his body.

A voice said, 'Mother? Are you all right? What was that noise?'

Fred pressed his hand so tight across March's mouth, he wondered whether her teeth could take the strain. He put his lips to her ear again.

'It's up to you. I can tell him the truth if you like. And I mean the whole truth. Or you can send him away. The choice is yours.' Breath whistled in her nostrils and her body heaved against his. He did not remove his hand but shifted his body slightly. He whispered, 'D'you remember when I took you away from Edwin at the end of the war? D'you remember we spent the night at the George at Almondsbury on the way home? Albie cried and cried that night, but we took no notice.'

The door handle rattled. 'Mother – have you fallen down? Please say something! What has happened?'

Fred raised himself and looked into her eyes. She closed them in surrender. He lifted his hand from her mouth.

She said tremulously, 'It's all right, Albie. I turned over in bed and knocked the table lamp flying. I'll leave it till the morning now. So tired. Good night darling.'

'Oh . . .' The boy sounded surprised at her tone. 'Oh, good night Mother.' There was a pause, then he said, 'I love you, Mamma.' A moment later his door closed.

Fred said, 'We both love you, Marcie.'

She was weeping. 'Oh Freddie . . . Freddie. I can't. You don't understand. I just *can't*.'

'Darling Marcie. You can't do anything else. Neither of us can. Not now. There's only one way we can go on. And that's together.'

She let him kiss her tear-streaked face and her throat. She made no attempt to stop him when he pulled off the brassière.

'So many wicked things we've done, Freddie. Is this one more?'

'You've never done anything wicked, Marcie. Whatever has happened is my fault. And now . . . this . . . I will look after you.'

She remembered that once before he had taken her guilt and made it his. Was it possible he could do it again, and for always?

She held his head in her hands and let memory sweep her away on its tide. The fire was not dead after all. She could feel its warmth thawing the cold sterility of her being. And it was different this time; perhaps not so fierce. A forgiving warmth. Forgiving Fred. And herself.

Everyone was delighted at the news that Fred Luker and March Tomms were going to be married. At one time the match would have been so unsuitable as to be doomed from the start; now, because Florence was so obviously pleased, it was seen as part of a healing process. What Sibbie Luker and Will Rising might have destroyed for ever, was being mended by Fred Luker and March Rising. April, not needing to hug the secret any longer, pondered its advantages a little more objectively with her husband.

'It's so *good* that he's successful,' she said as she sat

one evening pleating a new fan of crêpe paper to fill the blank white radiants of the gas fire. 'I mean, if he'd still been struggling along with the taxi . . . or even just the coal business . . . she'd have been certain he was after Uncle Edwin's money. She doesn't trust anyone. Least of all Fred.'

'Doesn't sound a very good basis for a marriage, Primrose.' David shoved his spectacles to the end of his nose in order to survey his wife properly. He was marking essays on the Pragmatic Economics of Soviet Russia and Tollie had insisted on contributing what amounted to a thesis on the subject. It would take David all week just to read it. He said, 'Surely trust is essential in marriage.'

The paper fan trembled slightly, then April shook it out to a full arc and said decidedly, 'There are certain things in marriage that are better . . . left unspoken. Perhaps.'

'Secrets, you mean.'

'They need not be secrets. They can be common knowledge.' She knelt by the fender and arranged the fan.

'Fred's business methods are suspect, I suppose. But we mustn't make any judgements there, Primrose. He was a prisoner in Silesia, remember. That sort of hell breeds its own morals.'

She glanced at him quickly and sat back in her chair. 'You're right darling, of course. But I think Fred would have done whatever he has done, war or no war.'

David looked at her face and cast off his spectacles, shoved the pile of essays on the floor and got up to take her in his arms.

'You're thinking of other things. Not business methods.'

'Yes,' she said in a low voice.

'Like the name Leonie Porterman? And the old, established firm of Three in a Bed?'

'Yes,' she murmured.

He was silent, looking at her down bent head. Then he lifted her up and tilted her chin so that she had to look at him.

He said, 'Darling April. Has it ever occurred to you that morals were made to suit man. Man was not made to suit morals.'

She stared at him, searching for a hidden meaning. 'What do you mean, David?'

'I mean that Fred might have done things that would make half the citizens of Gloucester throw up their hands and faint.'

'What about the other half?'

'They might say he's a good bloke.'

'Oh David . . .' Her voice shook. 'I hope you're right.'

He grinned at her. 'Perhaps I was over-estimating. I'm not entirely certain about half. Certainly Jack and Austen think he's a good chap. Hettie and Alf . . . Gladys and Henry . . . there's six to start with!'

She laughed along with him a little anxiously. He kissed her. 'March will be a match for Fred, my darling. Don't worry.'

'I'm not worried, David, I'm absolutely delighted. I've always thought, in spite of the gossip, that Fred is . . . all right. I'm glad you think so too.' She looked across the room to where Davina sat on the floor playing with some pieces of meccano that Albert had given her. She murmured, 'Morals were made to suit man. How wise you are sometimes, David.'

He nodded owlishly, 'Sometimes.' Then he laughed like a boy – as he often did lately – and kissed her. 'Not *too* often though, eh Primrose? That wouldn't do at all.'

March told Albert the news at breakfast a week after she and Fred had come together at last. He was anxious and apprehensive.

'Uncle *Fred*? I thought you hated him?'

March, surprised at her son's perspicacity, smiled wryly and in a new, relaxed way that Albert also noticed.

'I thought I did too. I often have in the past, Albie. But we were very good friends once. Before you were born. I think we might have got married then, but Uncle Fred was taken prisoner by the Germans and everyone thought he was dead. And I married Uncle Edwin.'

'You mean Papa?'

'Yes. Yes of course. Then I wasn't very well after you were born, and Uncle Fred came to Bath in his car and took us home to Grandma and Grampa and we were friends again.'

'But after that . . . I mean, when Uncle Fred mended my engine and brought me the meccano and things like that, you would hardly look at him, Mother! You never thanked him once.'

'No. Well, darling, there are things you don't understand—'

He said stoutly, 'I know Uncle Fred isn't a *good* man, if that's what you mean.'

March said quickly, 'He started you off at Marley. He paid your fees for that first term. Before we had money of our own.'

'I thought he might have done. ' Albert saw her surprise and looked away embarrassed. 'Well, he got me out of something rather nasty at school. Saw Miss Pettinger . . . well, it doesn't matter now.'

'I know.' March poured him more tea before he had finished and the cup overflowed. 'Oh dear . . . Then you like some things about him?'

It was his turn to be surprised. 'I like him. I've always liked him. But I thought you disapproved of him so much that you couldn't possibly *marry* him.'

'I don't exactly approve . . . but business is different, Albie. Sometimes – to get a business deal *through* – one has to tell a lie perhaps. A small one. A white lie.'

He looked at her silently and for the first time she saw that his mouth was exactly like Florence's.

She said, 'Albie darling, he has promised me that things will be different. I'm not sure how much you know . . . you and Victor talk about things . . . but Uncle Fred has promised that he will be . . . good.' They exchanged glances. The word 'good' did not fit Fred at all.

'He will reform, you mean,' Albert suggested.

'Yes. Quite. And you see darling, you need a – a man behind you. When you leave school and start out . . . in life . . . Fred will be very useful. Helpful. I mean, he can do things that you and I simply could not. And

then, when you are grown-up, I shall need someone –
I shall be lonely—'

Albert said suddenly, 'It won't make any difference
to us will it, Mother? You and me?'

She scrambled up from the table in a rare display of
emotion and took his head on the front of her apron.
'None at all, Albie. We've always been together. No-
one could come between us now.'

With his face hidden he said, 'Will you have more
children? Like Aunt Bridie and Uncle Tollie?'

She said immediately, 'No. No, we shall have no
more children. In any case, we're too old now.'

He waited a while, wondering if he felt a slight
tremor in the hands on his head. Then he said politely,
'Well . . . I hope you'll be happy, Mother.'

May's reaction was also ambivalent. 'Fred used to
follow our March around like a spaniel,' she confided
to Monty. 'It was pathetic. He could hardly string two
words together and she used to make him sit up and
beg almost. I don't think she'll have things all her own
way now.'

Monty, fairly happy at Williams' as Tollie Hall's
assistant, but already anticipating the boredom of the
continuous routine, was optimistic. 'It'll be something
different anyway. And there'll be pots of money there.
March is so damned mean with her windfall. Fred
might let us have enough cash to buy a decent house.'

'We've got a house now darling,' May said edgily.
'Now that poor Pa has gone, this is our home.'

Monty did not reply and May followed up querulously. 'Don't you dare try to borrow money off Fred

Luker, Monty. Just because he'll be our brother-in-law doesn't make any difference. If you put yourself in Fred's power, he'll use you.'

Monty laughed uneasily. 'How could he do that, May?'

'I don't know. But he'd find a way.' She went to the window of the big front bedroom and looked out. Beneath her, Hettie Luker was talking to Florence through the window of the old workroom. May thought she must go down and break it up, it was too much for her mother.

She sighed. 'That's why it's such a good thing for March. Fred will look after her. She won't have to worry about a thing. He'll see to it all.'

Florence, who had looked on Fred as another son ever since he drove Teddy, April and herself back from the infirmary after the children's tonsil operations, felt the same way.

'I know you worried about March, Will,' she said silently as she climbed into her husband's narrow bed that night. 'I think you'd be very pleased about this. It means all the girls are provided for. And soon . . . very soon, dear Will, they will be happy. I know it. I feel it.'

Chapter Fourteen

They were married at Gloucester Registry Office at the end of September. April and David were the only witnesses, but there was a big breakfast at the Cadena afterwards where Davina presented a horseshoe and Bridget's girls a silver rolling pin. Albie was to stay with April while March and Fred went to Paris; at last March was to sample foreign travel. Albie was more than happy to share a roof with April and Davie. To everyone's delight he took his small cousin on his knee for the meal and fed her scraps from his own plate. April snapped them with her Brownie Box camera and promised copies of the print to half a dozen eager requesters.

March surprised herself by actually enjoying the occasion. The Luker family were there in force and should have reminded her of the downward step she was taking, but somehow they no longer irritated her. Gladys had spent years in the office now and had stiffened into a typical, but acceptable, professional spinster. Henry, loose and loud-mouthed, was certainly no worse than Jack or Austen. And Sibbie of course had not been invited. March told herself she would soon forget Sibbie's existence, let alone any connection the girl had had with Will. Hettie and Alf would always be the old neighbours from number seventeen across the road: slightly comical figures acceptable to Florence, therefore bearable, but never mother and father-in-law.

March could hardly believe her own creeping conviction that everything was going to be all right. By marrying Fred she was going to be able to forget the degradation of Edwin; her whole life was going to be legalized at last. And it was more than that. She looked at Fred as he shook hands with Tollie Hall. She hardly knew whether she actually loved him; she had loved her brother Albert and she did not feel the same towards Fred. But there *was* something there: the old link that had been born with his dumb worship when they were children; the passion that had sprung from her terrible grief at Albert's death; and now this new feeling that was so nearly friendship . . . it added up to a lot. And Fred knew about her, he knew . . . what she had done. He was father of her sins as well as her son. March had always wanted to be 'good'. Her brother's love had made her 'good'; so far Fred's love had made her 'bad', but now that they were married it would be different. A husband, after all, was responsible for his wife. She met his eyes unexpectedly and knew he was thinking of that night. They were to spend it in London before catching the boat train. She felt colour rise into her cheeks.

Gran and Aunt Sylv sat next to Hettie and talked of past events as they always did.

'I well remember last time I was here,' Gran said lugubriously. ''Twere at our April's do. Will looked lovely 'e did. One of 'is own tailor-mades 'e wore and a rose as big as a cabbage in his lapel.'

'April looked lovelier,' Aunt Sylv said with unnoticed humour. 'And she still do.' She looked sharply at her youngest niece. ''Fact she looks lovelier than usual I reckon.'

Aunty Vi chipped in. 'I sat nex' March and your Fred.' She nodded at Hettie. 'There was summat goin' on between 'em even then. Bit o' footsie under the table if I recall right.'

Gran shook her head definitely. 'Not our March. She en't like that.' She twisted her head with unexpected speed and surveyed Sylv. 'What you grinnin' at, our Sylv? '

Sylv went on grinning. 'Nothing, our mother. Nothin' at all.'

Gran continued gloomily, ''Twere our May and 'er Monty what was up to Gawd-knows-what that day. May was the side of a 'ouse with Victor and there 'e was a-pattin' of 'er stomach as if they was in their own private quarters 'stead of—'

'They was all right Mother,' interrupted Sylv with finality.

Hettie got her oar in. 'I remember your wedding Sylv. It was in January—'

'Nineteen nought seven,' inserted Sylv.

'It was snowing and after the registry office you came up 'ere, didn't you?'

'Ah. Nothing fancy. Cup o' tea and a cake.' Sylv beamed with remembered pride. 'Yes. Mrs Dick Turpin I was. He made it legal for me. Just like our March and Fred.'

No-one thought anything of this except Gran, who administered another darting look from her lizard eyes.

May said, 'I feel like a lump of suet pudding in this chiffon. It's the same sort of outfit as March's but she gets away with it.'

'She's as thin as a rail,' Monty pointed out tactlessly.

'I'm not *fat*. My muscles were never the same after Victor. You've forgotten what I went through then.'

'No I haven't.' Monty recollected Manchester through rose-coloured spectacles. 'Golly May, d'you remember going to Scarborough that first time with the Mincing? We were theatricals then, people of importance. Top drawer.'

'All I remember is that wretchedly useless Mrs Turner and all her dreadful children and you fainting after Victor.'

It was the first time she had mentioned his faint. He said nothing. But he looked at her as she sat there eating her way through everything in sight and suddenly felt it was her fault he had landed up in this dead hole with all his in-laws. He didn't like Gloucester and he didn't like clerking and Tollie Hall was a solemn sort of a chap. Now, if Will was still alive with his male heartiness and his rabbit shoot and his – his – understanding – it might have been different. Poor old Will. How on earth had he stuck it without a future. That's what Gloucester lacked: a future.

April took some more photographs, put her camera away and went over to Florence.

'Mother, are you all right? Would you like David to take you back home now and lie down?'

'Of course I'm all right, April.' Florence did indeed look better than she had looked since Will's death. 'I'm happier sitting here on my own though darling, so don't bring anyone over. The talking tires me. I like to look . . . quietly.'

'Dearest Mother. You've got us all under one roof for once.'

'Yes. And it happened just as I hoped it would.'

'What? March and Fred getting married?'

'That too. But your father's happiness. It's his legacy to us, dearest. Do you see? He's left it for all of us. I can see it covering March now. Like a shawl.'

April looked across at her sister indulgently, then widened her eyes.

'I do believe you're right. She's different. She looks so – so – young!'

Florence said quietly, 'She looks as she used to look when Albert was alive.' She smiled up at April quickly in case she was suspected of sentiment, then said, 'And you . . . you're bubbling, April! You look like you used to look when you were a little girl and had a secret.'

April nodded. 'Yes. I'm positively fizzing with happiness like Mr Goodrich's ginger beer. As soon as I get Albie and Davie off to sleep tonight I'll come round and tell you why.'

Fred moved up behind them. 'Let me give you some champagne, Mrs Rising. And April too.'

Florence said, 'Oh Fred, no thank you. And couldn't you call me Mother? It would give me such pleasure.'

The way she said that made Fred blush with a kind of schoolboy pride. He said, 'Then . . . thank you, Mother.'

April gave him an open dazzling smile and stood up. 'Fred, Mother wants to be left to look at everyone. Will you come and help me find some anchovies? I've got a craze on anchovies at the moment.'

She linked her arm in his, all very sisterly, and led him out on to the verandah. The Saturday shoppers in the main streets of the Cross could not be seen; the cathedral rose out of a browsing huddle of roofs.

April stood still, looking at it, then she turned to Fred and her eyes were intensely blue.

'Fred, I want to say something.'

He did not meet her gaze. More than anything he wanted to belong to the family of Risings, Florence's request just now had confirmed that for him. If April was about to warn him that she must ostracize him again because of her peculiar conscience, he could not look at her and tell her it did not matter.

She put a hand on his arm. 'I've thought a lot about . . . what you said in Albie's room last month. I mean – I was so pleased about you marrying March that I didn't consider then the other things you had said.' She looked anxious as he still stared above her head towards the cathedral. 'I realize how much my – my attitude – must have offended you, Fred. I realize that you can't just – well, brush the last five years off as if they hadn't happened.'

He said woodenly, 'What you really mean is that *you* can't brush them off – isn't that it, April? Aren't you going to tell me you can't imagine me as a brother-in-law and I had better keep away from you and David and Davina?'

Her hand gripped harder. 'Oh Fred – no! As far as I'm concerned . . . I told you that day how pleased I was. I meant it, Fred. If you can forgive – and forget – then . . . then it will be perfect. Perfect.'

At last he tore his eyes away from the view and looked at her. Her face was so alive, so open, he had to believe that somehow she had squared the whole thing about Davie . . . maybe she had even told Daker?

She said breathlessly, 'Fred, it's only right you should know. Next to David, you've a right to know. I'm pregnant, Fred. David and I . . . we're going to have a baby.'

Her fingers were digging into his arm and her eager face was asking him for something. Approval? Approval from a man she had feared and mistrusted?

She said, 'You've been so good, Fred. So loyal. A lot of people might think . . . your feelings are finer than anyone knows.' She smiled at him. 'But I know, Fred. That's why I wanted to tell you before Mother or anyone else. I've wronged you for a long time, Fred. I can't do anything about it. Ever. But . . . I told David that you must be the first to know about the baby.'

He said, 'That was all you told him, April?'

'Yes. If only he could know, Fred, he would understand. He would understand more than anyone else. He admires you very much. But . . . he can't know.'

He removed her hand from his arm and sandwiched it between his. He returned her smile with great warmth.

'Well then. If I am the first to know about this baby,

I can be the first to congratulate you. You and David are very lucky. A second child. A brother or sister for Davie. A new cousin for Albie and Victor. David must be very proud.'

He had said the right thing. This was what she had wanted. The smile widened to near-tears and he could see the likeness between her and her daughter.

She swallowed and acknowledged his implication. 'He is, very proud. Almost as proud as he was the first time.'

He carried her hand to his lips, a courtly, uncharacteristic gesture for Fred Luker. Well, he was changing. He watched April's cheeks colour faintly with surprised pleasure and determined not to fight the change. He might actually become as honest and upright as April imagined. One day.

They went back into the restaurant and he looked around him for his wife. His eyes met hers and he realized that she too was looking for him. He lifted a hand and walked towards her. This was his family and he was going to make the most of them, as he had made the most of everything that came his way.

It was David who found some anchovies for April and forced her to sit and eat them.

'You've been dashing around all day,' he grumbled proudly. 'You weren't like this with Davie. I hope it doesn't mean we're about to have twins.'

The idea of twins put April into a fresh spiral of joy.

'David. Wouldn't that be just about perfect? If they were girls we could call them Florence and Felicity. And if they were boys—'

'Primrose . . . please don't get so excited. You forget

I'm an old man now and I can't stand too much of it.'

She stared at him to check whether he was serious. Then, once again, they were caught in each other's aura more tightly than in a physical embrace. It happened a lot lately; it was as if a bubble of special atmosphere enclosed them from the rest of the world.

David took a quick breath that was almost a sob. 'Oh my God . . . I do love you.'

And April, gazing into the dark eyes that no longer held secrets, saw mirrored there her own special images: her father and Sibbie, Sibbie and David, David and April, April and Fred. She no longer felt pain. Morals were made for men.

'Yes,' she said. 'I know. Thank God, David, we both know.'

March had started to glance at the new gold watch Fred had given her, when two unexpected guests arrived. The door opened on Edward Williams who ushered ahead of him Sibbie Luker.

For a moment there was an appalled silence. Alf Luker bristled visibly and Hettie looked to right and left with widening eyes. Sibbie had not received an invitation, but then, neither had many of the guests here today. Hettie had been as thankful as March that Sibbie had decided to stay away. But to turn up late like this, certain of catching everyone's attention, and to bring with her her latest what-d'you-call-it . . . Hettie wished herself invisible.

Bridget broke the silence with a sort of whimper. 'Daddy!' closely followed by shouts of recognition from Olga and Natasha. Then Edward himself held up his hand and made his announcement.

'We thought we would call in and wish Fred and March all the best for the future. And to tell you that as soon as my divorce comes through, Sibbie and I will also be married.' He drew Sibbie's hand through his arm and patted it. 'This is unorthodox, we know that, but we're tired of the whispers and the gossip. Those are our plans and this is a good time and place for them to be made public.'

Hettie said audibly, 'Oh my gawd.'

Fred shrugged, 'Sounds all right to me.'

Florence, at the back of the room, stood up and walked towards the door. She looked very old and her straight back was at last bent. She reached Sibbie and without hesitation put her arms around the slender neck.

'I'm so pleased, Sibbie. It will mean – eventually – that you can be friends with May again.'

Such frankness might have been insulting from anyone else. From Florence it was like a benediction. Sibbie, tight as a spring, hanging on to Edward, enjoying the fact that she was stealing the limelight yet frightened in spite of herself, put her arms around the tiny waist and felt unaccustomed tears behind her eyes.

'Thank you . . . thank you, Mrs Rising.' She thought how pleased Will would be. How very pleased. His two worlds coming together at last.

Chatter broke out on all sides. Gran and Aunt Sylv were rigid with disapproval, Hettie fluttered like a nervous hen, Alf cleared his throat and shuffled his feet, Aunty Vi repeated, 'What's to do then, what's to do?' Bridget said, 'I'm going to give birth now, right now, d'you hear me Tollie? I cannot accept that woman – I simply cannot—' and Tollie said, 'Then I think we'd better take this opportunity to feed Beatrice, my dear.' April, feeling she might have conjured Sibbie up out of her own thoughts, said fearfully to David, 'Skeleton at the feast?' And David replied, 'Obviously not for your mother, darling. She probably needed to see Sibbie. She needed to settle that side of your father in her mind.' April still looked at him. 'And for you, David?' He returned her look steadily. 'How can you ask, Primrose? When we've got Davie, Florence and Felicity?'

March said tightly to her new husband, 'Time we went, Fred. The train leaves in an hour.' Fred held her hand. 'March, I want you to do something for me. Go and thank Sibbie for coming, then shake Edward Williams' hand and offer our good wishes.'

'I will do no such thing, Fred.'

He tightened his hold. 'Yes you will. You've just promised to obey me, for one thing. And for another, you want to get rid of Sibbie and that's the way to do it. And for yet another, everyone will think you're just like your mother if you do it. Sweet and forgiving.'

She hesitated, hating having to knuckle under to him, yet seeing exactly what he meant. She shrugged. 'If you think it's best, Fred—' and went forward. It was Fred's decision, not hers.

'. . . good of you to drop in . . .' Edward Williams' handshake was warm. She remembered working for him and finding him kind and just.

He said, as Fred had predicted, 'Thank you, March. We didn't want to steal your thunder. We'll go now.'

Better still, Florence then took her arm and smiled all her love and warmth at her. 'Take me back to my seat darling, will you?' and then very quietly, 'I'm proud of you, March, proud of you.'

March covered the thin, veined hand with her own and stood very straight. Everyone said how like her mother she was. She would make that true in every way.

Sibbie said, 'Goodbye May. Perhaps later – like your mother said – when the talk dies down, we could—?'

May stood up gladly. 'Oh Sibbie, I'm so pleased about you and – oh Sibbie.' The two women, who were no longer girls, looked at each other and smiled. May felt a small spurt of joy somewhere inside her, just as she'd felt on Christmas morning years ago when she first spied the lumpy stocking at the end of her bed.

She drew Monty forward. 'Darling, I know you met Sibbie once – unofficially—' She laughed gaily. 'But let me introduce you properly. Sibbie. Monty. I'd like you to be friends.'

And Monty took the hand that was so frighteningly familiar into his and looked into the bold blue eyes that glinted at him secretly. And he too saw the lumpy stocking of Christmas morning.

'I'm delighted to meet you, Sibbie,' he said and smiled back at her.

March retired into a small room behind the

restaurant to powder her nose and slip into the fox cape Fred had bought her. May and April went with her.

May said, 'March, you look marvellous.' There wasn't a trace of envy in her voice. 'It's so very nice that at last you'll be settled.'

It was a strange way to describe the sort of life that March might be embarking on. She had been settled before, settled into the kind of rut she had known so often, in which she hardly seemed to be alive. Now she was certain of one thing, she would be alive. Fred would see to that.

She smiled, 'Dear May.' Why did she feel no irritation at May's silly, typical remark. 'Dear May. Thank you.'

April said, 'Oh my God. I think I'm going to cry.'

May hugged her. 'Why, little sis? We're going to be together from now on. Doesn't that make you happy? What did that newspaper article call us years ago? Daffodils . . . we're going to blossom together.' And she thought of Sibbie who was so like a Rising – another daffodil.

April smiled. 'I want to cry because I'm so happy. That's all.' She couldn't tell them yet. Florence must be the first to know after David. 'I'm so very happy, girls. I can't explain.'

March said, 'I didn't think I'd get over Father betraying all of us. But after Mother . . . just now . . .'

'Quite.' May nodded eagerly.

April said, 'Let's go back inside and be with her. Come on.'

They went back to Florence and grouped

themselves around her in an unconsciously protective pose. And their husbands, looking at them, were, for a moment, over-awed by their combined beauty and strength.

THE END